The air seemed to thicken. Elizabeth tasted dust, and her hands closed over the arms of her chair, as though that solid touch would be as much protection as the Ring of Solomon that enclosed her. Doctor Dee turned to face the south.

"Michael, angel of fire, we beseech thy aid in thy master's name."

A light glowed in the depths of the stone, as though a ray of sunlight had somehow struck it. Patches and sparks of color danced across the paneled walls, like the reflection of the sun on water. Dee turned to the west.

"Gabriel, angel of water, we beseech thy aid in thy master's name."

Instantly, the sense of oppression vanished, and the air lightened fractionally. The patches of light continued to dance across the walls and floor, but the light at the heart of the stone cooled, became somehow mild. Dee turned back to the north, lowering the stone so that he held it at waist height. It cast strange reflections back at him, silvering his long beard.

"Spirits, in the names of him who creates you and in the presence of his anointed, show us the fate of this kingdom of England."

There was a rushing sound, and light fountained up from the stone, rising like Accession-Day fireworks. The sparks did not fall, however, but rose until they reached a point perhaps a foot above Dee's head, and vanished again into nothing. Against that curtain of silver fire, a face began to take shape. It was a man's face, long and lined with care, framed by flowing brown hair, the eyes mild and sorrowful above a tiny pointed beard. A voice, giddy as a girl's and sweet as a choirboy's, said, "This is the king who will be."

"Name him," Dee commanded.

"Charles Stuart," the voice chanted, "King of England and King of Scots. And this is his fate!"

With whirlwind suddenness, the mild face vanished, and was replaced with a tiny picture, perfect as a painting. Elizabeth frowned, recognizing the platform and what stood at its center. A hooded man stood beside the block, his hands folded on the haft of his axe. A second man came forward, instantly recognizable as the king the voice had named in its first vision. He knelt in prayer, then bent his head to the block. The executioner lifted his axe, and then, at the king's signal, brought the axe crashing down. The picture vanished.

Melissa Scott and
Lisa A. Barnett

THE ARMOR of LIGHT

BAEN

FANTASY

THE ARMOR OF LIGHT

Copyright © 1988 by Melissa Scott and Lisa A. Barnett

A Baen Books Original

Baen Publishing Enterprises
260 Fifth Avenue
New York, N.Y. 10001

First printing, October 1988

ISBN: 0-671-69783-8

Cover art by Alan Gutierrez

Printed in the United States of America

Distributed by
SIMON & SCHUSTER
1230 Avenue of the Americas
New York, N.Y. 10020

DRAMATIS PERSONAE
IN ORDER OF APPEARANCE

Elizabeth Tudor, Queen of England

William Cecil, Lord Burleigh, chief minister to the queen

John Dee, astronomer, mathematician, scholar, tutor to Sir Philip Sidney

Robert Cecil, a secretary of state, son of Lord Burleigh

Sir Philip Sidney, Queen's Champion

Sir Robert Sidney, governor of Flushing, Holland; brother to Sir Philp Sidney

*Robert Dudley, Earl of Leicester, deceased, favorite of Elizabeth, uncle of Sir Philip Sidney

*Hubert Languet, deceased; scholar, logician, philosopher, tutor to Sir Philip Sidney

Francis Hepburn, Earl of Bothwell, also known as The Wizard Earl

Jane Dee, wife to John Dee

*Sir Henry Lee, formerly Queen's Champion and instigator of the Accession of Day Tilts

*Edward Kelly, deceased; secretary to and medium for John Dee

Fynes Morrison, gentleman-traveller and writer, friend of Sir Philip Sidney

George Chapman, poet, member of the School of Night

William Shakespeare, player, playwright, and sometime poet

Richard Burbage, player and chief sharer of the Lord Chamberlain's Men

Christopher Marlowe, poet, scholar, playwright, and sometime government agent

Sir Walter Raleigh, explorer, scholar, founder of the School of Night

Henry Percy, Earl of Northumberland, co-founder of the School of Night, also known as the Wizard Earl

Walter Warner, mathematician, member of the School of Night

Nathanial Hawker, boy

Tomas Harriot, astronomer, member of the School of Night

Robert Poley, government agent

Mary-Martha, landlady to Christopher Marlowe

Bess, her maid-of-all-work

Edward Alleyn, player and chief sharer of the Lord Admiral's Men

Stephen Massey, known as Ganymede, player

Philip Henslowe, manager and producer of the Lord Admiral's Men, Edward Alleyn's father-in-law

Elizabeth Sidney, daughter of Sir Philip Sidney

Mary Herbert, Countess of Pembroke, sister of Sir Philip Sidney

*Thomas Kyd, playwright and former roommate of Christopher Marlowe

*Thomas Watson, deceased, poet, playwright, astrologer, friend of Christopher Marlowe

Grifin Madox, steward of Sir Philip Sidney

Goody Bourman, nurse to Elizabeth Sidney

Frances Sidney, wife to Sir Philip Sidney, daughter of Sir Francis Walsingham

*Sir Francis Walsingham, deceased, minister to Queen Elizabeth and head of her secret service

Henry Herbert, Earl of Pembroke, patron of players, husband of Mary Herbert

Fulke Greville, secretary of the principality of Wales, friend to Sir Philip Sidney

Sir Edmund Tilney, Master of the Revels

*Thomas Walsingham, nephew of Sir Francis Walsingham, ex-patron of Christopher Marlowe

*Ingram Frizer, steward to Thomas Walsingham

Barbara Sidney, wife of Sir Robert Sidney

Jan-Maarten van der Droeghe, head groom to Sir Philip Sidney

Peter Covell, a groom

Peterkin, his son

Ralph Heywood, valet to Fulke Greville

Sir Edward, a recusant

Robert Devereux, Earl of Essex, present favorite of Queen Elizabeth

Fischer, a groom

John Pyk, also known as Pig, apprentice to Edward Alleyn

Joan Alleyn, also known as Mouse, wife to Edward Alleyn

Thomas Downton, player, member of the Lord Admiral's Men

William Bird, player, member of the Lord Admiral's Men

Thomas Towne, player, member of the Lord Admiral's Men

Humphry Jeffes, player, member of the Lord Admiral's Men

Martin Slater, player, member of the Lord Admiral's Men

Richard Jones, also known as Black Dick, player, member of the Lord Admiral's Men

Augustine Phillips, player, member of the Lord Chamberlain's Men

Will Kempe, player and comedian, member of the Lord Chamberlain's Men

John Erskine, Earl of Mar, member of the court of James VI, of the king's party

Lord John Hamilton, also of the king's party

Barton, Sir Philip Sidney's valet

James VI Stuart, King of Scots

Anne of Denmark, his wife

*Prince Henry of Scotland, their son

Alexander Master of Ruthven, of the king's bedchamber

Nicholas Skeres, English agent

John Gordon, of Clan Gordon

Andrew Melville, Presbyter and preacher

Lord Malcolm Seton, of the king's party

Colin Nuscatt, preacher

Lillias Gordon, accused witch

Patrick Kennedy, Earl of Cassilis, of the king's party

Lord Linton, of the king's party

Andrew, page to James VI

John Graham, Earl of Montrose, lord treasurer of Scotland

John Lowin, player, member of the Lord Chamberlain's Men

John Heminges, player, member of the Lord Chamberlain's Men

Henry Condell, player, member of the Lord Chamberlain's Men

Patrick Adamson, Archbishop of St. Andrew's

William Forbes, of the Ultra-Protestant party

Lady Katherine Gordon, agent of the Earl of Huntley, of the Catholic party

Mephistophilis

Henry Fletcher, Englishman, Catholic, former member of the Pleiade

Henriette, his wife

Besje, her sister

Nicholas, player's apprentice, member of the Lord Chamberlain's Men

John Lord Graham, son of the Earl of Montrose, of the Ultra-Protestant party

Rollo of Duncruib, member of the court of James VI

Matthias Campbell of Crinan, member of the court of James VI

John Ruthven, Earl of Gowrie, older brother of the Master of Ruthven, of the Ultra-Protestant party

Master Ballie, consort-master

*Persons who do not appear in the book.

PART ONE

Chapter One

The trivial prophecy, which I heard when I was a child and Queen Elizabeth was in the flower of her years, was

When hempe is sponne

England's donne:

whereby it was generally conceived that after the princes had reigned which had the principal letters of that word hempe (which were Henry, Edward, Mary, Philip, and Elizabeth) England should come to utter confusion....

Francis Bacon, Of Prophecies

She had put away mirrors some years before, preferring to see herself reflected in the words of the young men who still thronged her court. Even now, she paused in the doorway, giving the two old men who waited for her time to see and admire and frame their compliments. The cool morning light that streamed through the diamond-paned windows would not flatter, and a part of her knew it and rejected it, even as she sailed forward to accept their homage.

"Spirit," she said, with real fondness, and one old man— he was seventy-five this spring, had seen three quarters of a century—bowed stiffly back. He was bundled in his robes of office, fur-lined gown pulled close about his throat beneath the narrow ruff, long jerkin buttoned close, the flaps of his wool coif pulled over his ears even in spring-time. The woman, resplendent in white figured satin that showed a vast expanse of white-powdered bosom, rejoiced that she had not succumbed to that frailty of old age. "Dr. Dee." Despite herself, her voice sharpened on the name, as she stared at the second old man in his scholar's black. There was something of the crow about him, something of the ravens that haunted the Tower, despite his protesta-tions that he used only white magic, and never more so than today. Perhaps he sensed her unease, for his bow was very deep, and he blinked weak eyes nervously at her as he straightened.

"Your Majesty." It was Burleigh who spoke first, secure in his monarch's favor—the only man now living who could make that boast. "I am very grateful that your grace has agreed to this interview."

That was more of a barb than most men were allowed, considering how strenuously the queen had resisted seeing her court wizard of late. Elizabeth's thin lips tightened further, wrinkles showing momentarily in the thick paint, and then she had smoothed her expression, seating herself carefully in her chair of state. The immense white skirt, sewn with silver and pearls and scattered with blood-red roses, pooled around her ankles, hiding her embroidered slippers; she rested her beautiful long hands on the arms of the chair, displaying them in a pose so practiced it had become natural. The rising sun shone through the upper coils of her immense red wig, glinted from the crown set precariously atop that pearl-strewn edifice. Her face, as she had intended, was in shadow.

"Well, Doctor Dee," she said, and heard herself sharp and shrewish, "what news have you brought me?" The old scholar—he was only six years older than she, though she chose to forget it—blinked rheumy eyes at her again, and she frowned. "Does the daylight trouble you, master wiz-ard? We will have the shutters closed."

Burleigh frowned, the thickets of his eyebrows drawing down toward his beard. Dee said, stammering slightly, "I beg your Majesty's pardon. It's not the light but your Majesty's presence that dazzles me."

"We could withdraw that as well," Elizabeth said, but her expression softened slightly. It was a feeble compliment, and delivered without courtly graces, but, she thought, sincere enough. She leaned back in the high chair, easing bones that woke tired now after a night's dancing. "Come, sir, my dear Spirit says your news is both urgent and alarming. Let's hear it—it may not be so fearsome in the sunlight."

The wizard bowed again, and thrust his gnarled hands into the furred sleeves of his gown to hide their shaking. The room was chill, one of the long windows opened to let in the cool spring air, but it was not only the cold that made him tremble. "As your Majesty—and his lordship—know," he began, "at the new year I cast your Majesty's horoscope for England, and share those tidings with your Majesty alone."

The queen's eyes slid toward Burleigh, and were answered by an infinitesimal nod: a royal horoscope was more than a matter for private concern; could become, in the wrong hands, a matter of state. Dee was well guarded while he served the queen, in part to protect him from the mob who feared him and had once burned his library, but those guards were also there to assure that no state secrets, however obtained, made their way into the hands of Elizabeth's enemies. If Dee saw the movements, he gave no sign of it, but continued in his soft, stammering voice, "At this new year, as my lord Burleigh has doubtless told you, the heavens were troubled, the portents strange, and I could read no certainty of anything in stars or glass. In such a case, the best remedy is delay, and I did delay, until the—storm—seemed past." He glanced up, anxiously, but could read nothing in the queen's shadowed face. Burleigh stroked his beard, weighing every word.

Dee bowed his head again. "Then, at your Majesty's express command, I cast the horoscope. The portents were —well, ominous, your Majesty."

There was a long silence, and then Elizabeth said, "Ominous, Doctor Dee? Could you perhaps be more specific in your terms?"

Recognizing the tone, Dee gave Burleigh a swift glance of appeal. The secretary of state said, slowly, "Yes, your Majesty. The signs concern what will befall England after your death."

The words seemed to hang in the air. Elizabeth's frown deepened. "Have you seen my death, then, Doctor Dee?"

"Oh, no, your Majesty." Dee's hands fluttered in the sunlight, shaped vaguely placating gestures. "I cast my horoscope for one year only, and no longer. I did not see your death in it, I swear it." He took a deep breath, calming himself. "But this year is a time of—of decision, your Majesty. And what happens now will shape what is to come for England a hundred years from now."

Elizabeth did not move. "What is this decision?"

"Your Majesty, I do not know." Dee spread his hands. "I cast your horoscope, and the stars told me of a coming conflict between the powers of light and the powers of darkness. It will occur elsewhere and concern others, but your Majesty is its center, about whom all revolve. More than that—the powers of darkness are already on the move, and the rest of the meaning was obscured." The wizard took another deep breath. "Which is why, your Majesty, I begged Lord Burleigh to secure me an audience. Your Majesty is a prince, anointed by God with the power of your office. And the matter concerns both yourself and your kingdom most nearly. If your Majesty will permit it, I wish to perform a ritual in your presence, which will allow me to see more clearly the nature of this decision."

There was another, longer silence. Burleigh frowned even more deeply than before, looking from Dee to the queen and back again. Elizabeth sat unmoving, staring blindly into space. She had faced threats—and threats of witchcraft—before, but no one had ever offered to invoke such powers in her presence, nor had anyone had the effrontery to claim that her presence was in fact necessary to such an operation. She said at last, "When did you cast this horoscope, Doctor Dee?"

"Fourteen days after the new year, your Majesty," the wizard answered.

"And today is the third day of April," the queen said,

almost to herself. "That was a fortnight ago, master wizard. Why such a delay?"

Dee bowed again. "I sought to find out more, your Majesty, and failed."

Elizabeth nodded. "Very well," she began, and Burleigh lifted his head sharply.

"Your Majesty must not consent to this until and unless Doctor Dee gives guarantees of your safety!"

The queen lifted a painted eyebrow at him, and turned to the wizard. "Well, Doctor Dee?"

Dee's hands fluttered again. "Your Majesty, my lord, I assure you, there is not the slightest danger to her Majesty, I swear it on my soul's salvation. The powers I invoke are white, beneficent, harmless to godly men. And I will seal her Majesty within a ring of Solomon, which no spirit whatsoever may cross."

"Then you'd best stand within it, too, Burleigh," the queen said, and smiled tartly. "I would not want my Spirit cut off from me."

"As your Majesty commands," Dee said, and Burleigh interjected, "Your Majesty doesn't mean to do this, surely?"

"Be quiet, Burleigh," Elizabeth said. "My England is threatened, or so this wizard says. I will know more." She nodded to Dee. "You may begin."

"If the shutters could be closed?" the wizard asked in return, his voice gaining confidence as he returned to things he knew.

Elizabeth reached for the bell that would summon her servants, but Burleigh cleared his throat first. "If your Majesty would allow me," he said, and moved to close the first shutter himself, latching it securely. "The fewer who know of this the better."

Elizabeth allowed herself a smile at that, thinking of the Puritans and their preachers, but Dee said, distressed, "My lord, my power is white—"

"Which is not the point at issue," Burleigh said. He closed the final shutter with a snap, and came to stand beside the queen's chair. Elizabeth glanced up at him through the sudden gloom, smiling slightly, then turned her attention to the wizard, kneeling now beside his satchel in the center of the room. Dee fumbled in the depths of the worn leather bag until he found a lump of chalk, then straightened awkwardly.

"It is my custom, your Majesty, to begin each such operation with a prayer," he said.

"A wise and Christian precaution," the queen answered, dryly.

Dee bobbed his head, then crossed himself and sank slowly onto his knees. The queen lowered her head slightly, folding her hands on her lap. After a moment, Burleigh removed his fur-trimmed hat.

"Oh God, from whom all knowledge and all holy desire, all wisdom and all true counsels do proceed, grant that our honest intentions may be answered honestly, and defend us thy humble servants from the assaults of thy great Adversary, that we, trusting in thy defense, may not fear his power, through the might of Jesus Christ our Lord." Dee crossed himself again. "Amen."

"Amen," the queen murmured, and crossed herself as well. She rested her hands again on the arms of her chair. "And now what, Doctor Dee?"

"First, your Majesty, as I promised my lord Burleigh, I will draw the ring of Solomon, which no spirit may cross." Dee stooped, holding back his trailing sleeve with his left hand, and began slowly to trace a circle around the royal chair. His lips moved, shaping words the others could not hear. Elizabeth did not turn as he passed out of her sight behind her, but she was very aware of his presence, and of Burleigh's disapproving frown that masked his fear. Then the wizard had reappeared, bringing the chalked line curving forward until he had closed the circle.

"Amen," he murmured, crossing himself, then stooped to sketch a strange sign just outside the circle itself. He moved more quickly now, drawing similar signs at each of the remaining compass points, then walked the circle a final time, scribbling Greek and Hebrew letters along its edge. The words were not Greek, the queen knew, but she could not place the language.

"The ring of Solomon is complete, your Majesty," Dee said. "Remain within it, and no spirit whatsoever will harm you."

Elizabeth inclined her head graciously, unable to think

of another response that would not betray her uneasiness. Dee stooped again, pushing a stool out of the way, and drew a second, smaller circle that enclosed himself and his satchel. He knelt again, sketching signs at each of the compass points, murmuring to himself as he did so. This time, the symbols were drawn on the inside of the line, as though to contain some power, rather than to ward it off. Finally, he set the chalk aside, and reached into his bag to produce a silk-wrapped bundle the size of a man's fist. He stared at it for a long moment, holding it in his cupped hands, then crossed himself and loosened the cords that held the crimson silk in place. The folds fell away, revealing a clear crystal the size of an egg. The queen drew a sharp breath, barely restraining herself from speaking. For an instant, the stone had seemed to glow with a moon-cold light of its own.

"Father Almighty," Dee said, "very God of very God, grant that we thy servants may make true use of the powers thou hast granted us." He lifted the stone above his head as though serving in the church, and his voice took on a new fullness. "And seeing that by thy grace good angels were sent to Abraham, Isaac and Jacob, to Joshua, Gideon and Esdras, to Daniel, Tobias and to many others, to instruct them, to inform them, and to help them; and seeing that this wisdom cannot be obtained in any other way than by thy great grace and comfort, either mediately or immediately granted, we beseech you, o Lord, to allow thy spirits to appear to us, that we may know thy will." He turned to the north, the crystal still held above his head. "Raphael, angel of the air, we beseech thy aid in thy master's name."

The dim air seemed to shiver, the shadows taking on palpable substance. The chalked lines and symbols seemed suddenly brighter, as though all the light in the room had become concentrated on those pale markings. Burleigh shifted uneasily, one hand tugging gently at his beard. The wizard did not seem to see, turning now to the east.

"Uriel, angel of the earth, we beseech thy aid in thy master's name."

The air seemed to thicken. Elizabeth tasted dust, and her hands closed over the arms of her chair, as though that solid touch would be as much protection as the white ring that enclosed her. Dee turned to face the south.

"Michael, angel of fire, we beseech thy aid in thy master's name."

A light glowed in the depths of the stone, as though a ray of sunlight had somehow struck it. Patches and sparks of color danced across the paneled walls, like the reflection of the sun on water. Dee turned to the west.

"Gabriel, angel of water, we beseech thy aid in thy master's name."

Instantly, the sense of oppression vanished, and the air lightened fractionally. The patches of light continued to dance across the walls and floor, but the light at the heart of the stone cooled, became somehow mild. Dee turned back to the north, lowering the stone so that he held it at waist height. It cast strange reflections back at him, silvering his long beard.

"Spirits, in the names of him who created you and in the presence of his anointed, show us the fate of this kingdom of England."

There was a rushing sound, and light fountained up from the stone, rising like an Accession fireworks. The sparks did not fall, however, but rose until they reached a point perhaps a foot above Dee's head, and vanished again into nothing. Against that curtain of silver fire, a face began to take shape. It was a man's face, long and lined with care, framed by flowing brown hair, the eyes mild and sorrowful above a tiny pointed beard. A voice, giddy as a girl's and sweet as a choirboy's, said, "This is the king who will be."

"Name him, " Dee commanded.

"Charles Stuart," the voice chanted, "King of England and King of Scots. And this is his fate!"

With whirlwind suddenness, the mild face vanished, and was replaced with a tiny picture, perfect as a painting. Elizabeth frowned, recognizing the platform and what stood at its center. A hooded man stood beside the block, his hands folded on the haft of his axe. A second man came forward, instantly recognizable as the king the voice had named in its first vision. He knelt in prayer, then bent his head to the block. The executioner lifted his axe, and then, at the king's signal, brought the axe crashing down. The picture vanished.

"No!" Elizabeth did not realize that she had spoken aloud until Dee's eyes flickered toward her.

"Please, your Majesty, you must keep silent." He returned his attention to the stone. "Answer, spirit. Who will do this thing?"

A swirl of shapes fluttered through the fire. The voice said, "The masters of England, the Parliament. And the powers of God shall be cast down."

In the fountain, a bonfire rose, fueled by books and strange instruments of brass and leather. Men in the robes of the universities watched and approved, some even going so far as to toss objects into the flames with their own hands. A spasm of pain crossed Dee's face, but he said strongly, "Answer, spirit. How may this be prevented?"

The vision of the bonfire whirled away into sparks that vanished before they reached the ceiling. Nothing appeared to take its place, and the wizard frowned. "Spirit, by the sacred names of God thy master, I command you. Answer!"

"The Queen of England is but barren stock," the voice chanted, more slowly, its pitch dropping from treble to counter. "The King of Scots shall be her heir."

Elizabeth, who had not admitted her decision even to her intimates, frowned terribly to hide the shiver of fear.

"Continue," Dee said.

"The powers of darkness are arrayed against him," the voice answered. "They seek to drive him from the middle way, to either side of which lies hell and the abyss. Send forth the Queen's champion, let him go north to aid the heir of England. His fate is England's, his fall England's bane." The fountain roared upward, almost to the ceiling, and disappeared. "This seeing is ended," the voice said, in the sudden dark, and then the power that had sustained the visions had withdrawn.

"Amen," Dee said, his own voice drained and hoarse, and folded the crimson silk back over his crystal. Even more awkwardly than before, he stooped to rub away each of the cardinal signs, then straightened slowly. "Your Majesty may leave the circle now, if you wish. The spirits have departed."

Burleigh cleared his throat. "And how may her Majesty know that this was a beneficent spirit?"

Dee did not answer for a long moment, moving instead to reopen the shutters. The cool spring air streamed into the room, washing away the last taint of the wizard's power. "You heard the names by which I conjured the spirit, my lord. Holy names and holy symbols, every one. An evil spirit cannot answer such a summons, nor, even if it could, could it remain once I had called upon the holy names."

"Even if I accept this, just what does it mean?" Burleigh glared at the wizard, who stooped again to erase the last traces of the chalked circles.

"Oh, be quiet, Burleigh," Elizabeth said. "You know as well as I what has been happening in Scotland. Perhaps better."

Burleigh grimaced, acknowledging the hit. The queen pursued her advantage. "Our own agents hint that witches conspire against him, as they did five years ago. We have discussed already what we might do to aid him—or not, as the case may be—and now these spirits tell me that the rights of kings, of the kings of England, hang in the balance. Very well." She glanced at Dee, her face softening slightly. "I think you know my champion, Doctor Dee. I believe Sir Philip Sidney was your student once."

Dee bowed. "Yes, your Majesty, I had that privilege."

"Your Majesty," Burleigh exclaimed. "He's your champion in the Tilts—it's purely ceremonial."

"Yes." Elizabeth nodded, smiling slightly. "Sir Philip is the one the spirit meant."

"How can you be sure?" Burleigh asked, and with an effort managed to keep his tone reasonable. "Doctor Dee will surely tell you—"

He broke off as the wizard shook his head. "Her Majesty is God's anointed, and so has powers not granted to others. If her Majesty declares Sir Philip her champion, it is done. And I believe it is well done."

Burleigh's lips tightened, but he said nothing. Elizabeth pushed herself to her feet. "Doctor Dee, I thank you for your services. And I know I do not need to tell you that nothing you have heard or said must ever be revealed to anyone."

"My lips are sealed, your Majesty," the wizard answered promptly. "I swear it."

Elizabeth favored him with a smile, then turned to Burleigh. "Robert Sidney is at court, is he not? We'll send him with the message."

"As your Majesty commands," Burleigh said, and bowed as she swept from the room.

When the queen had left, and Dee had been sent back to his house at Mortlake with a suitable present and a repeated warning, Burleigh moved slowly through the long gallery, pondering his next move. He was aware of servants and courtiers watching, and kept his face impassive, a corner of his mind rather enjoying the stir his very lack of expression would produce. It would do some of those who haunted the court good to search their consciences; equally, it would do him no harm to reinforce their fears. Still, he reminded himself, all that was, at the moment, distinctly secondary to the threat Dee had foreseen. Quite suddenly, for all that he had already committed himself to following the queen's orders precisely, he felt the need to discuss the situation with someone who thought as he did. He gestured to the nearest servant, and the young man came forward, bowing.

"Have my coach sent for," Burleigh said. "I will go into London."

Robert Cecil welcomed his father most effusively, bustling about his cluttered study to put aside his work, and shouting for wine at the same time. When the maidservant brought the silver tray, Cecil dismissed both her and the black-gowned secretary, begged his father to be seated, and poured the wine with his own hands. Burleigh accepted the fragile crystal glass cautiously, watching his son over its rim. As always when he did business with his son, the old minister was filled with a strange mix of pride and a sort of regretful pity. Cecil was an excellent politician, his native flair for intrigue balanced by the hard-headed practicality he had learned from his father; it was a shame,

Burleigh thought, taking a sip of the sweet wine, that his son had allowed the cares of office to age him so prematurely.

"How may I serve you, Father?" The amenities concluded, Robert Cecil reseated himself behind his long table, leaning forward to plant both elbows firmly on the scattered papers. It was a pose that had always served him well, suggesting a blunt honesty that was in fact foreign to his nature. Burleigh recognized the pose, but chose to ignore it.

"There is a matter at hand," he said, and sighed deeply. "It seems things in Scotland will be coming to a head soon, and the outcome concerns us more nearly than we thought." Quickly, he outlined what Dee had seen, but did not bother to expound on the political consequences. Cecil would see them soon enough, or should—and if he does not, the old man thought, he's not worthy to be my successor.

When he had finished, Cecil nodded thoughtfully, stroking his beard in unconscious imitation of his father's gesture. "Things aren't easy in Scotland now," he agreed. "James is still juggling his various factions—and doing a good job of it, I must say—but witchcraft's the one thing that could drive him over the edge. What does Dr. Dee think we should do about it?"

There was a faint note of contempt in the young man's voice, and Burleigh frowned. "Her Majesty intends," he said, with deliberate emphasis, "to send her champion north to deal with the matter."

"Her champion?"

"Her champion of the Tilts," Burleigh elaborated. "Sir Philip Sidney."

Cecil's lips tightened, and there was a momentary silence. At last, the younger man said, "I assume this is in honor of his arcane studies."

"I hoped you could explain it," Burleigh answered. "I respect the capabilities of your agents."

Cecil blinked, then smiled, seemingly surprised and pleased by the compliment. "I'm afraid I don't know much more than you do, Father," he said, and couldn't resist adding, "I've never been instructed to keep watch on Sir Philip's activities—quite the opposite, in fact."

"That has rarely made much difference to you," Burleigh said dryly. "I know you have at least one man in his household."

"If you are referring to the playwright Marlowe, I fear I can't at the moment call him mine."

"Yes." Burleigh's face grew thoughtful. "I can't say I approve of murder, Robert, unless it's absolutely necessary."

Cecil bowed his head, in apparent acceptance of the rebuke. "At the time, it seemed necessary—I felt there were those whose safety was far more important than an atheist poet. There was no reason to think that Sir Philip would—or could—guarantee his silence."

"True," Burleigh said, "very true. It's beside the point, anyway. I want to know, Robert, why Dee's chosen Sidney."

Cecil blinked again. "As I told you, Father, I know very little." He paused, and seemed to gather his thoughts. "Rumor has it that he has been more and more involved in his occult studies since his return from Holland—he visits often with Dr. Dee, though that may simply be out of old friendship—Dr. Dee was his tutor before he went abroad. Certainly it's general knowledge that he has taken Sir Henry Lee's place at the center of the Tilts, and we all know the significance of that."

Burleigh nodded, a little impatiently. The Accession Day Tilts, the centerpiece of the week of celebration surrounding the anniversary of the queen's succession, were filled with curious symbolism, a symbolism designed to reinforce the special aura of good fortune that seemed to surround Elizabeth. The minister's mouth twitched unhappily. Sir Henry Lee, who had initiated the Tilts in their present form, had once admitted that the theories behind it all were French, and Burleigh had never been comfortable with the idea of surrounding an English monarch with French ceremonial. Still, no harm had ever come of the elaborate productions, and it gave the younger, vainer members of the court something on which they could waste their time and money. Burleigh's mouth twitched again. If Dee were to be believed, the effects had been far greater—and Burleigh had always had a great deal of respect for the elderly wizard.

"There is one other thing," Cecil continued, more slowly.

"I have heard a whisper—servants' talk, and maybe something more—that Sidney acquired something, perhaps a book, while he was in Europe, and that he guards it most jealously."

Burleigh eyed his son dubiously, and the younger man shrugged.

"It is, as I say, little more than a whisper."

"But you believe he does practice the arcane arts."

"Yes. At least, he has a thorough knowledge of them."

Burleigh nodded slowly. "That will have to be enough," he said, and pulled himself upright. "There are two other things you can do for me, Robert. First, I want you to double the watch on Dr. Dee—not because I mistrust him," he added hastily, "but because I want to be sure he's protected. Second, I want you to forward to me every scrap of information you receive from Scotland, no matter how old or how trivial. Her Majesty will want to be informed."

"Of course, Father," Cecil said, but there was a note in his voice that made Burleigh look sharply at him.

"I mean it, Robert. This is no time for lesser intrigues."

Cecil bowed again. "I'll do as you ask, Father."

Chapter Two

They say miracles are past; and we have our phil-
osophical persons to make modern and familiar,
things supernatural and causeless.
William Shakespeare, All's Well That Ends Well

It hung in the air like thunder in winter, something
utterly out of place and time. As with the weather, too,
the animals felt it; the mare Sidney was riding was sullen
and skittish, completely out of her usual sweet temper.
She curvetted and shied at a low jump, nearly knocking
her rider into a low hanging bough. Frowning, Sidney
steadied her with a hand on her damp neck. The hounds
were snappish, too, the game poor—though none of the
other human beings in the hunt party seemed affected. He
held the mare in her place and sat still for a moment, head
raised and tilted, vaguely irritated with himself, certainly
exasperated that he was feeling as restless as his animals,
when no one else seemed troubled.

It was nothing local. He knew that, intuitively, but
something hung over Penshurst, Kent, England—Europe?
He was filled with a sudden compulsion to flee the dim
forest. He shook his head angrily. It was merely the undi-
rected night fear of a child. Yet—there was something, in

17

the verdant, overly green smell of the air. There was something . . .

"Philip!"

The sound of his name broke through his imposed stillness and suddenly the sounds of the forest resumed, normal and unthreatening. He turned; his brother Robert waved and urged his horse on to meet Sidney.

"What were you listening for?" Robert asked, as the two riders drew abreast. "You were as still as a poacher."

"Something—in the air," Sidney replied with a shake of his head. Robert looked quizzically at him, but did not pursue the point. Unlike Sidney, and like their sister Mary, Robert lacked the arcane brilliance that was part of the Dudley legacy to the Sidney line. He was more than content to leave such affairs to his elder brother, and he did not sneer. As far as the high sciences were concerned, Robert was a stone wall—but he was happy in politics, as Sidney had never managed to be. For a second son, Robert had done well for himself in the service of his queen, having succeeded Sidney as governor of Flushing, and he stood high in the queen's favor as one of her more reliable servants. He must have just ridden down from Westminster, Sidney realized, and smiled. Court life and royal favor suited his more robust younger brother. Robert had a nice sense of fashion, though the falling collar he wore in place of even the smallest ruff was definitely something of an innovation. The doublet, dark red leather slashed and guarded with gold braid, suited Robert's high coloring, and his dark slops were of the first quality. Looking at him, Sidney felt a rueful smile tugging at his lips. Compared with Robert, he was some small, drab songbird . . . Philip Sparrow, indeed.

"She wants you at Westminster, Philip," Robert was saying.

Sidney dragged himself back to the matter at hand, and looked up in some surprise. "Why?"

Robert grinned. Only his brother, of all her majesty's courtiers, would make that his first question—and expect the poor courier to know the answer. "Lord, Philip, am I you, to question her majesty when she doesn't choose to tell me?"

Sidney looked at him, one eyebrow rising in mild rebuke, and Robert held up his hands in surrender. "Before you accuse me of being craven, I can tell you it has something to do with Scotland."

Sidney's eyes darted upward, and then back to meet Robert's. He smiled, and it was the kind of smile that Robert had learned to fear in his brother, if only for some other person's sake. "When I wanted to go to Scotland, her majesty sent me to the Netherlands. And that remains the greater part of my experience—with a set of people as unlike the Scots as God could have framed."

"I rather think," Robert said slowly, "your library may have something to do with it."

"What about my library?" Sidney asked, and once again there was a hint of steel in his voice.

"I'm sure I don't know. While I was with her majesty, Burleigh broached the subject of a book you might possess. . . ." Robert let the sentence trail off, looking expectantly at his brother. Sidney looked thoughtfully amused.

"That's Cecil's doing, I'm bound. But how? Not Fulke, surely. Nor does Dr. Dee have any great love for Cecil. I wonder—Kit?"

Robert's lips thinned. "That one would be capable of anything, as he never fails to delight in saying."

"Oh, he's hardly betrayed anything. He couldn't be sure himself. I daresay—" The smile touched Sidney's eyes. "I daresay Kit was just protecting himself."

"Philip—what book is this?" Robert demanded.

Sidney shook his head, the smile fading from his face. Robert's presence had momentarily dispelled the leaden feeling of the day, but now it was back, full force, like a weight oppressing heavens and earth alike. The day was cloyingly warm, but Sidney shivered. "Not just now, Robert. Come back to the house with me, then we can talk."

Robert frowned at his brother, knowing in full frustration that there was something he was missing. Involuntarily, he glanced up and around him, as he had seen Sidney do. The sky was hazy, the air limp with springtime damp, nothing more—but when Sidney turned the dun mare back towards Penshurst house, Robert followed quickly, and kept close at his brother's heels.

The air was cooler in Sidney's library, and the heat of the sun had stirred up the warm, woody scents of the herbs mixed into the straw that covered the floor. Robert settled himself in a chair and stretched his long legs out in front of him, watching as his brother accepted a tray from one of the maidservants and politely dismissed her. Sidney poured the cool ale for both of them. Robert accepted his mug with a nod of thanks, but repeated, "What book, Philip?"

Sidney grimaced, and walked over to the window, staring out at the sunny day as if it surprised him. Watching, Robert shrugged, vaguely hurt. "Well, certainly, if you don't want to tell me. . . ."

"No, it's not that, Robert. I—" Sidney broke off and, with an apologetic smile, turned back to him. He settled himself in the window seat, stretching one booted leg out along the curtains. It was simply that it was all, still, so fantastic, and he did not know where to begin. In his youth, like so many aspiring courtiers, he had spent several years in Europe, travelling through France and on into Germany. There he had met and had earned the privilege of studying under Hubert Languet, unquestionably the most brilliant man he had ever known—but there had been a price. Once again, even after all the intervening years, Sidney felt an echo of the writhing embarrassment mixed with the gratification of which only youth is capable. Languet had conceived a doting fondness for him, and had appointed himself Sidney's guardian as well as his teacher. How the old scholar had cossetted and chided, fretted over and berated his young pupil in the letters that had pursued Sidney across Europe—Italy, especially, was not a proper place for someone of Sidney's delicate constitution, or for any devoted Protestant; the Papists would surely be the death of him if disease weren't, and he was only going there to see Don John of Austria, so like a young man.

Sidney smiled sadly at the memory. It had been a passage in one of Languet's own texts that had sent him into Italy, though he had not dared to tell the old man that, first for fear that he was wrong in his deductions, but also because he dreaded the reproaches Languet would have heaped upon himself for keeping such a dangerous book in his library. Sidney had even half hoped that, once Languet discovered his pupil's real intentions, that the discovery might dampen the old man's enthusiasm a little. Unfortunately, the tale that reached Germany some months ahead of Sidney's return had only added to Languet's version of the Sidney hagiography.

Scholars and wizards, true men and charlatans, had been scouring the countryside around Naples for over a thousand years, seeking the great Virgil's secret resting place. Naturally interested in such matters, Languet's imagination had been caught by the story that had spread through the scholarly circles of Europe like wildfire, the tale of a wizard from some ungodly, distant land who had come down out of the north and discovered Virgil's tomb, the location of which had been forgotten even by the local people who were called its guardians. This person—creature, some said, for it seemed very young and very fair, and only something diabolic could seem so and still possess the necessary knowledge—had caused the tomb to open to him, and had made his way past its wards and spells, until the very bones of the great wizard were his, and at his command. The so-called guardians had been terrified, for not only had they failed, but now their protecting spirit would be taken from them.

So the stranger had bargained, and Sidney had come away with Virgil's books, beautifully preserved scrolls that held all the learning of the greatest of wizards. He had returned to Germany on the heels of the wild story, and offered at least a copy of the scrolls to Languet, as a sort of apology for the worry he'd caused the old scholar. He could still remember the mingled shame and pride he'd felt when Languet refused. He himself, Languet had said, was not the man for them, was too old to use them wisely, or to guarantee that he could protect them. Better Sidney, who was, after all, what he was, a scholar, a soldier, a courtier destined for greatness, should keep and protect the only copy from those who were unworthy of it. Unfortunately, Sidney thought, I've fulfilled only one of Languet's predictions in all the years since then. I'm at best a

middling soldier, and I've never learned the discretion
that makes a courtier.

Robert cleared his throat, and Sidney shook himself
back to the present. He opened his mouth to speak, but
the words would not come. Finally, with a self-mocking
sigh, he gestured toward a small chest that stood on the
corner of his desk. Raising his eyebrows, Robert still obeyed
the movement and crossed to the desk. He set his mug
down and examined the plain box, then tried to lift the lid.
"All right, Philip, it's another of your sage tricks. There's
no lock—why can't I open it?"

"The box that is locked may—can—always be unlocked.
Only the box that is not locked cannot be."

"Very pretty. Sophist," Robert replied sourly. "Enlighten
me, if you will."

Sidney shifted on the window bench, dug into the pouch
at his belt. From it he withdrew a small golden triangle,
enameled in blue and green. He held it tightly for a
moment, then tossed it to Robert, who caught it with a
whispered curse. "Fit it into the back of the box," Sidney
ordered.

With a wary glance, Robert did as he was told, then
stared as a thin line became visible around three sides of
the box. He looked over at Sidney, who nodded.

"Go ahead. Open it."

Robert did so, leaning back slightly as if he expected it
to be none other than Pandora's box. When nothing
swarmed out, he leaned forward and looked in. There
were several scrolls lying in the bottom of the box, which
smelled faintly of spice, like incense. "They're very old,
Philip," he said.

"But quite sturdy, I assure you," Sidney said, unable to
resist any longer. He got up and crossed to Robert, then
reached into the box and withdrew one of the scrolls. He
unrolled it carefully, though not gingerly, and held it out
for Robert to take and read.

For a long moment, Robert was silent as he read the
elegant Latin phrases, words he did not fully comprehend,
but of which he knew at least surface meanings. Then he
looked up at his brother. "Philip—what are these?"

Sidney's eyes were dancing with an innocence that would

be ludicrous in any other man of forty years. "Virgil's texts, of course."

It was said with the cherubic smile that Sidney performed so well. Robert restrained a brief, murderous impulse and turned his attention back to the scroll he held. "And Cecil knows you have this," he said slowly.

"Cecil suspects I have something of value. Arcane value. And Fulke knows, of course," Sidney said.

"Of course," Robert echoed, trying not to feel a little hurt. Of course Fulke Greville knew. Besides being Sidney's oldest and dearest friend, he was also a scholar to whom this discovery would mean more than it would to either Robert or Mary. "Is he here?"

"Oh, yes. He's been here for a fortnight now. He's doing more work on that house of his in Warwickshire. Mary's here, too, though I daresay you know that. So you see, it's open house here at Penshurst."

"Poor Frances. A houseful of Sidneys. What a plague." Robert shook himself, recalling the matter at hand. "You said—does your playwright know about this?"

Sidney frowned. "I don't believe so. Of course, Kit has free run of my library—but he couldn't get into the box, and I doubt he'd try. He has his own sense of honor, you know. Any betrayals on his part would be on a grand scale, nothing so petty as snooping in locked boxes."

"But if he knew, somehow? Don't you think he's more than capable of giving the information to Cecil?"

"But why?" Sidney asked.

"To protect himself?" Robert answered, and when Sidney frowned, added, "Well, you said earlier—"

"I know," Sidney said. "On consideration, though, I don't see how it could protect him. And I don't think he even knows of its existence. Kit's talents are along an altogether different line. You said it was Burleigh who mentioned a book?"

Robert nodded.

"Dr. Dee knows I have a book I treasure, and he would tell Burleigh, not Cecil. I suppose it's possible that's how they knew." He rubbed his chin, then shrugged. "I don't think it really matters. Still—a book in my possession, and Scotland. That's interesting."

"I've told you all I know," Robert said warily.

"No, I'm sure. But Scotland, and my book—are James's witches stirring again, I wonder?"

"Would her Majesty trouble herself and you over another outbreak of hedgerow wizardry?" Robert asked.

Sidney glanced up at him. "You've been talking to Dr. Dee again, haven't you? That sounds like his turn of phrase." Robert smiled, nodding, but Sidney's mind was already elsewhere. "Her Majesty shouldn't need me for something like this, God knows—but I can't think why else I'd be chosen."

"Send a wizard to cure a fear of witchcraft?" Robert said, dubiously.

"Ah, but so very unprepossessing a wizard could not possibly strike fear into anyone's soul."

"You terrify me, Philip, let me tell you that."

"You flatter me, I fear."

"Hardly." Robert gently let the scroll roll up, and set it reverently into its box. Sidney closed the top and retrieved the enamelled wedge. Once again, the box was a sphinx, its lips closed on its secrets.

It took the better part of a day to ride from Penshurst to London, for all that the Sidneys could travel light when they chose. The abbreviated train, mostly grooms of Robert's household, reached Robert's London house in the early afternoon. It was too late to make the trip upriver to Westminster, a fact for which Sidney was distinctly grateful. The ride had tired him more than he liked to admit, and the wound he had gotten at Zutphen ached dully. All in all, he was not in a suitable condition to face her Majesty. He would be better for a good night's sleep, and knew it.

The next morning dawned cloudy. Sidney, dressing quickly but carefully, could hear the watermen cursing the last of the fog, and knew that Robert's bargemaster would be furious that there was no sun to gild the fantastic carvings decorating the long barge. The oarsmen, on the other hand, would be grateful.

As he had more than half expected, the barge drawn up at the watergate was the one which had belonged to his late uncle. Nothing but the best had served for Leicester;

every conceivable surface had been gilded, and anything
that did not glitter gold had been painted in colors as
bright as Florentine enamel. Even the seat cushions were
covered in tapestry rather than the more serviceable leather.
On the other hand, Sidney thought, allowing the bargemaster to hand him down into the canopied seats, Leicester
had also had a sense of humor. The beasts that formed the
gilded bosses were porcupines, Leicester's chosen crest,
and despite the carver's best efforts to instill ferocity the
animals still looked merely plump and content. Sidney
settled himself against the embroidered cushions, smiling
slightly. He had adopted the porcupine himself after his
uncle's death: it seemed an appropriate symbol of his
occasionally difficult relationship with the queen.

It was a slow journey upstream, the heavy barge awkward against the current, leaving too much time for fruit-
less speculation. Sidney was very glad when the barge
finally drew up at the dock that served Westminster. One
of the royal pages came forward, bowing deeply; beyond
the dock, a knot of ladies-in-waiting sat sewing, listening
to a singer on the lawn beside the banqueting house.
Their gowns were blindingly white against the red stone
and the vivid green of the lawn.

"Her Majesty will see you at once, Sir Philip," the page
announced, in a voice that would carry to the distant
watchers, and Sidney carefully hid a smile. He followed
the boy across the lawn, bowing politely to the murmuring
women, and then through a maze of corridors smelling of
roses and musty straw.

The boy stopped at a painted door. Sidney saw him take
a deep breath, bracing himself, then threw open the door.
"Sir Philip Sidney," he announced, and Sidney stepped
past him into the royal presence.

Elizabeth regarded her reluctant courtier approvingly.
He did not possess the gaudy maleness of his uncle, her
dear Robin, or of any number of her favorites. Clean-
shaven as always, his face was considered by some to be of
too feminine a cast for any real beauty, though the chestnut hair, cut short in a soldier's fashion, was the envy of
many of both sexes. He dressed in darker tones than his
brother, but it was not sobriety. The black doublet, trimmed

with rows of pearl clusters, flattered his fair coloring. And if he walked with a distinct limp, it only added to his glamour. Sidney was her court's parfit, gentil knight, her chosen champion. She found herself smiling as she had not since her Robin had died—and at the wary light that flared in Sidney's eyes, nearly laughed aloud.

"No fear, Sir Philip, you never yet danced to my tune. I'm not about to embarrass myself by trying now." She waved a heavily ringed hand. "Sit, Philip. You're looking well."

Sidney bowed before taking his seat. "I thank you, madam, but you've had my brother to gaze upon. I scarce dare hope to measure up."

Penciled eyebrows rose. "Stuff. Young Robert dresses quite brilliantly, but sometimes even a woman of my peacock tastes will prefer diamonds to rubies. There. I've paid you two compliments, and you've paid me precisely none—indeed, your comment on Robert might be seen as a slap, so I can safely say you've won this set. We can get down to business."

Having said this, she seemed disinclined to proceed, only sat staring into the brilliant sunshine that flooded the gallery. Like an eagle on its aerie, Sidney thought. Was it true that the eagle that blinked was thrown from the nest—and had Elizabeth learned that lesson from her mother? Had Anne Boleyn blinked? An interesting thought, and it teased him on. Semele, perhaps? Lightning was light. Had she been able to face Zeus in his epiphany, might she have survived—and their son not demonstrated so many traits undesirable in an Olympian? It was an idea that might be worth tracking down on paper. Seeking the light, being destroyed by it—he was beginning to think like Marlowe. He put the idea aside, turning his attention back to the queen.

"Philip, you're my champion—and Dr. Dee agrees with me that you're the only man for me to consult in this matter." She brought her hands up, fingers steepled just below her lips. "He has seen terrible things, Philip. A cloud hangs over England, a dark, malevolent angel, envious of our prosperity, perhaps wanting to humble our pride."

"It sounds remarkably like Señor Mendoza; is he at court these days?" Sidney asked lightly, despite a sudden tightening of his heart. The queen saw—felt this presence in much the same shape he did, and she had called Dee in to explicate.

She smiled, thin-lipped. "It does, rather, but I fear this is a bit more—potent—than the ambassador. Tell me, Philip, what do you think of the people of England executing their prince?"

"Your Majesty—" Sidney's memory of that brooding presence stopped his inarticulate protest before it began.

Elizabeth held up a hand. "A gratifying response; no, Dee assured me I'm in no danger, but our England is." She paused, hawk's eyes momentarily hooded. And why is it, Sidney wondered, we think always—when we're honest —of birds of prey?

"Executed," Elizabeth repeated. "Kings have died from time to time, and not always at God's will, or if so through the agency of some most zealous servants. But executed, by law or rather a mockery of law . . .

"Listen, Philip. I needs must make you my confidant in matters that would shock Burleigh. Yet I know my man. I can trust you because you've never sought my confidence. You don't flatter, Philip—I wonder where you unlearned that? No matter." She raised her head and looked through Sidney. "Many lay it to my charge as a grievous fault that I have no heirs of my body—yet it was because I would not give England into the hands of one not born by God's grace to rule. So, instead of pressuring me to marry, for the past ten years, Philip, my trusty councillors have been pressuring me to designate an heir. Well, I have done. I have chosen my cousin, James Stuart, as my heir. He's young enough, he has the blood, and I understand he's canny enough—when he can keep his mind above his points and off his handsome bedfellows." She looked hard at Sidney, the look daring him to contradict or to condemn. He returned the look mildly.

"Ought I to blush, madam?" he asked. "Don't forget, I have been Kit Marlowe's patron for the last two years. I have been rendered impervious to shock."

Elizabeth laughed, a short, harsh bark that some said

was very like her father's. "What in God's name caused our gentle Sidney to rescue the likes of Marlowe from the rope of his own making?"

"If it had been a rope, there would have been precious little I could have done. I've learned the effectiveness of arguing with your Majesty."

"He's a dark one, Philip. *Doctor Faustus* was written by a man aware of his own power, scornful of others who reject those powers."

"It's not, I think, an evil power, madam. Undisciplined. Fond of chaos. But, in its own way, working toward the light."

"He'll never be the wizard you are."

"No. In some respects, I rather think he is my master. Certainly so as far as practical application is concerned. I'm very much a theoretician, an historian."

For a long while, she just regarded Sidney. An historian, certainly. A book, Burleigh had mentioned—yet not even Burleigh knew what it was. Well, it was not for the resources of his library that she had summoned him, though doubtless they would be more than useful. It was for the resources of his mind. And other resources—this Marlowe, for one. His power was dark, disruptive, like the man himself, yet, if joined with someone like Philip—might one not get a picture of as complete a power as dwelt on the earth? Dionysius and Apollo. Shade and light, unreason and order. Was this crisis, then, ultimately the reason for Sidney's unlikely rescue of a troublesome playwright from that tavern in Deptford? She lifted her head; the sun struck the rubies in her hair, and sent shards of light flashing about the room.

"Philip, I want you to go to Scotland, as my ambassador. You will go—" Her eyes narrowed and she smiled. "Bearing gifts. Ostensibly for the child. Also for James—who is in terror of his life and soul. Again. He is being assailed by witches. Again. Normally I would shrug it off, but not after what Dee has seen, and told me. James is in danger of being driven off the middle way. Either the damned witches or the damned Spanish will win. We will not let that happen. I shall be long dead, but I cannot shuffle aside my obligations to England because of extreme disinterest. A king executed by Parliament? It must never be. You must put an end to this threat to James. And only you can do it without driving him to a Popish extreme."

Sidney sat quietly for a moment, assimilating all she had told him. James was fascinated by the arcane, but experiences in his life had caused him, not unreasonably, to fear it in all its forms. There was the danger. James had to be taught moderation—but in a presbyter court, Sidney was not sure an Englishman was the man to do it. Still, he could not refuse, nor did he feel inclined to. He'd felt the challenge in the miasma that had hung over Penshurst. He nodded slowly. "I am at your command, Majesty."

She looked as close to relieved as Sidney had ever seen her. "Alas, Philip, why have we wasted so many years wrangling?"

"Because no one else dared to."

"True. Thank you, Philip. Burleigh will provide you with everything you will need. Money, of course—James always needs money. You will travel post—if that is agreeable to you?"

Sidney answered the question that was actually being asked. "I can manage, madam, quite easily, and with my own horses."

Satisfied, Elizabeth nodded. She rose, and held out her hand. Sidney went to one knee before her, as gracefully as he had done even before Zutphen, and kissed the proffered hand.

"Your sworn champion, your Majesty."

"God bless you, Philip—and go with you. When do you think you'll be ready?"

"A month at the most. I should return to Penshurst, set things in order there."

"You must bring your daughter to court soon, Philip. I heard from Master Greville that she's quite a charming little lass now."

"I thank you, madam. Lady Sidney will be grateful for your offer, as well."

Elizabeth shut her mouth against the response that rose to her lips, and she saw that Sidney saw it as well. "As you say, Philip," she said, lifting her hands. He was no fool, even if Frances Sidney chose to play him for one; if

Elizabeth chose the Earl of Essex as a favorite, she was certainly aware of his faults. Was Frances Sidney? She hoped so; she was beyond her old jealousies at sharing a favorite, and she did not want to think that Sidney had married a witless female.

"So, then. Perhaps you will stop at Mortlake, and see Dr. Dee. It would please him to see you. What is this power you have over your elders, Philip? First Languet, then Dee—and me. Languet taught you logic, Dee philosophy—and what have I taught you?"

"Tact—and when not to use it. And the value of surprise, madam."

Elizabeth threw back her head and laughed aloud. "Hurry up this business, Philip. Our last argument kept you away from court too long."

Sidney bowed. "As your Majesty commands."

He made his way out into the long hallway lost in thought, only a part of his mind responding to the salutations of the servants and lesser courtiers who filled the entranceway. This mission—this trust—that had been placed on him was rather frightening, even overwhelming; it would take some soul-searching to come to comfortable terms with it. Sidney smiled slightly, aware of his own contrariness. Ten years ago, he would have leaped at such a commission from the queen, and now, when he finally had the responsibility he'd so desired, he was prey to doubt. A familiar voice spoke from the shadows to his left.

"Welcome back to London, Philip. You're very prompt, as always."

Burleigh sat in a window embrasure, the furred collar of his old-fashioned gown drawn up against the chill. He smiled as Sidney turned to face him, and rose stiffly to his feet. "Not here, Philip, but I would like to speak with you. Walk with me in the gardens."

"Of course, sir," Sidney murmured, falling into step at the old man's elbow. They made their way slowly through the dim hallway, crossing from light into shadow and into light again. Motes of dust danced in the blocks of sunlight; the shadows seemed doubly black by comparison. Sidney was suddenly, acutely aware of people watching from those shadows, the greater men eyeing them surreptitiously, the lesser—or those with less to lose—frankly staring. It had been many months since Sidney had been in London; his sudden return, without the excuse of the Tilts or of any state occasion, was cause for speculation. He frowned, annoyed by the feeling that he could drown in this sea of whispers, but then they had reached the doorway, and stepped out into the quiet of the gardens. The air was still cool, but the sun had warmed the perennial herbs, and the scent was heady.

They paced the circular paths for a few minutes in silence, Sidney glancing warily at the other out of the corner of his eye. He could see the tension in the set of Burleigh's shoulders, and the knowledge did nothing to calm him. He had a great deal of regard and even affection for the old man, perhaps more than he had ever felt for his patron and father-in-law Walsingham; but Burleigh was as shrewd a politician as Walsingham had ever been, and did nothing without motive. Sidney waited for the other to speak first: a small victory, he thought, but my own.

Finally, Burleigh stopped by a stone bench that was hidden from the palace windows by a well-grown hedge, and sat down, motioning for Sidney to join him. "Congratulations," the minister said, drily. Sidney cocked an eyebrow at him.

"My lord?"

"Very pretty, Philip, and you do it better than any man half your age, but please don't play the innocent with me."

Sidney smiled. "All I meant, my lord, was that I was not aware of having done anything that called for congratulations. I certainly did not ask for this assignment."

"No." Burleigh stared at him for a long moment, dark eyes slitted against the sun, nearly lost in the lines of his face. He had known Sidney for all of the younger man's life. He had seen him grow from a young, rather impetuous idealist into something approaching a realist. Approaching, he added, with an inward smile, and said aloud, "What do you think of it, Philip?"

"What do you mean? What do I think of the circumstances, or how do I feel at being trusted with it?"

Sighing, Burleigh shook his head. "Lawyer. Both, then." He held up his hand, cutting off the younger man's response. "I was there when Dee produced his vision. I accept that the situation is indeed dire. I accept their judgement of you as the best man to deal with it. I am aware of your reputation in arcane matters. But there's a political side to this, there always is. Are you equipped to handle that as well?"

"Well, I am her majesty's champion," Sidney said, silken-voiced. "I am also reputed to be capable of diplomacy on occasion."

"I do hope so, Philip. I've been watching you for over twenty years now. You're an ornament at this court, and more. You're more useful than certain other decorations I could mention. . . ."

"Nor yet as decorative," Sidney murmured.

"And you learned a number of lessons well, both when you were a mere boy in Europe, and over the past few years when you've turned into someone her majesty can fight with. But you're still an idealist, Philip, and one of strong feelings. I don't blame you, I wouldn't be fond of the Spanish after what nearly happened to you in Holland, but if you will remember, I was opposed to intervention then, and it was you and your uncle who favored it."

"It worked."

Burleigh regarded the younger man with something approaching exasperation. "Damn it boy, any normal man would have added an acid comment about having nobly resisted the temptation to marry the Nassau."

"Perhaps I don't like being so transparent."

"Stop fencing, Philip," Burleigh snapped, but a smile was tugging at the corners of his mouth. "But no, not you. You didn't even give the matter a second thought. You could have been Duke of Nassau, boy, and I would have been a deal easier with you if you had tried to accept it."

"I was also offered the kingdom of Poland," Sidney said blandly. "But his majesty of France convinced me it was a bad bargain."

"That was quite different," Burleigh said, and the younger man hid a sigh. It had been very different, and he would admit it to himself, if not to Burleigh. No one, not even the Poles, had really expected him to accept that crown; the Dutch marriage—marriage to the daughter-

heiress of the uncrowned king of the low countries—was
another matter altogether. Sidney had considered it: he
liked the United Provinces, felt at home there with their
practical Protestantism, and believed implicitly in the justice of their struggle against their Spanish masters. Elizabeth
had taken the offer seriously enough to forbid the young
man to accept it.

"For Scotland, however—" Burleigh broke off, frowning, then tried a new tack. "I grant you're a master of the
arcane, Dee tells me you are." He paused, and studied
the younger man shrewdly for a moment. Sidney shrugged
slightly.

"Dr. Dee has been a great teacher. But I am still
primarily a theoretician."

"Damn it, Philip, that's a large part of what I mean."
Burleigh held up his hand, cutting off Sidney's mocking
answer. "Stop putting up your quills, there's no time or
cause for that now."

Sidney bowed fractionally, accepting the rebuke—but
he'd never been able to resist any opportunity to fence
with the wily old statesman.

Burleigh continued, "Theoretician you undoubtedly are,
outstanding you may well be—I accept Dee's word on it.
But the Scots are past masters of the practical. Crude and
unsophisticated their methods may be, by comparison to
the fine words and theoricks you've learned, but they've
long known how to apply it. I need only remind you of the
North Berwick trials four years ago."

Sidney frowned. "Half-mad old women tortured into
accusing themselves and each other—" He broke off
abruptly. Burleigh was shaking his head.

"It wasn't that simple, Philip, though I grant you that
the king's men probably caught more witches than were
actively involved in the plot. But a plot there was, a truly
diabolical plot." Burleigh paused, staring unseeing across
the sunlit hedges, remembering the coded dispatches, and
his own fear as each arrived, that this one would betray
some new conspiracy against Elizabeth, a conspiracy that
could not be answered by the means at his disposal. Dee
was only just returned to England then, and still devastated by the loss of his scryer: there had been no one

reliable to stand between the queen and the forces of darkness, had they chosen to turn their attention southward. He shook away that memory with an effort.

"Hedge-witchery still," Sidney said, "and defeated by quite ordinary means." He made a wry face, hearing the pride in his own words, but made himself continue. "Forgive me, my lord, I don't mean to deny that this was serious, or diabolical—but if diabolical, surely it's as much or more a matter for the men of God as for the scholars. And, as I said before, the plot was defeated by the ordinary mechanisms of the law."

Burleigh sighed. "True enough, Philip, but you miss my point by indulging your taste for contradiction."

Sidney flushed, but accepted the rebuke unflinching. "I beg your pardon, my lord."

"What I am trying to say is that the Scots turn to this hedge-witchery, as you call it, as naturally as Italians turn to poisons." Burleigh fixed the younger man with a sudden fierce glare. "It is, has become, a part of their politics—and politics, Philip, is what I know best."

Sidney bowed again, this time in genuine apology. "True, my lord. I'd be grateful for your advice." His smile was rueful, and filled with very real regret. Can I help it, my lord, if your candor makes me uneasy? his eyes asked.

Despite his mild annoyance, Burleigh found himself smiling back at the younger man, once again charmed by the graceful flattery. And Sidney was a master of the apt gesture, the minister added silently, there was no mistaking that. He cleared his throat, putting aside such considerations. "In 1590 and in 1591, a coven of hedge-witches, as you call them, attempted first to drown the Scots king's bride as she sailed back from Norway, and then, more directly, attempted to destroy the king himself by means of their witchcraft. That is undisputed. What is less clear is precisely how the factions at the court were using these witches, or their supposed master, the Earl of Bothwell."

Sidney frowned—the name was familiar. Burleigh shook his head.

"A distant cousin of the one Queen Mary married, but no less troublesome." He paused, ordering his thoughts. "There are three great parties at the Scottish court—or perhaps I should say that there are two factions, and the king's party. First, and still most powerful, are the Ultra-Protestants—lowland gentry, most of them, with the preachers and the presbyters and, of course, most of the king's own kinsmen, who would like to see his powers restricted."

Burleigh broke off, to eye Sidney warily. He knew perfectly well that the younger man's puritan views were in large part based on the logic of a scholar, and shared none of the excesses of Geneva, but in Sidney's present mood, the younger man might well choose to champion his supposed co-religionists. "Bothwell—and his kin—have always sided with that faction, or so it's rumored."

To the minister's pleased surprise, however, Sidney nodded thoughtfully. "Odd bedfellows—but that's what they say of politics, isn't it? Still, I'm surprised the preachers—presbyters, you called them?—would countenance traffic with the dark powers."

"They don't," Burleigh answered, ignoring the question. He felt certain Sidney, of all men, understood the theological distinction between the preachers, who would accept Luther's view of the church as subordinate to the secular authority, and the presbyters, who sought to make the church's council of the elect the supreme political authority as well. "They merely share the same ends: to wit, the destruction of the royal authority. Should they win, of course, there would be quite a falling-out, what with the nobles wishing to use the presbyters, and the presbyters wishing to tame the nobles." He smiled dryly. "It would be something of a revelation to all concerned."

Sidney snorted. "So there we have the ultra-Protestants," he said, after a moment. "You spoke of other factions—the Papists?"

Burleigh nodded. "They have a finger in most things. There's the Spanish, of course—still looking to make trouble here—and then the French have always had strong ties with Scotland." He frowned thoughtfully, tugging at his beard. "Of the two, I've always thought we stood in more danger from the French, what with Queen Mary's pretended claim to the English throne, but the French are still weak, thank God, and they still hate the Spanish.

James will not risk an open alliance there, for fear of losing
his French support, or his English gold."

"English gold?" Sidney asked.

"Oh, yes." Burleigh tugged at his beard again, smiling
now. "We've given young James four thousand pounds a
year for nine years now, and it's proved a worthwhile
investment." He seemed to become aware for the first
time of Sidney's slightly shocked expression, and shrugged
slightly. "It's kept him out of the Spanish king's pay,
certainly, and was cheaper than maintaining an army on
the northern borders when we needed all our men at
home. In any case, as I said, it's not the foreign Catholics
that worry me. A goodly number of the northern earldoms
are Catholic still—and that's mountain land, hard to sub-
due even if James dared move against them openly. They'd
like to manage the king, too, just like their Protestant
cousins."

"I see," Sidney said, "or at least I'm beginning to."
Catholic against Protestant, king against noble, faction against
faction: he had seen that sort of civil warfare before, had
seen its ugliest manifestation one August night in Paris,
when the streets had literally run with blood, and any
man's life was forfeit at the cry of "Huguenot." The English ambassador and his household had barred their doors
and knelt in helpless, angry prayer, unable to do anything
to help their murdered brethren. In the morning, the
Seine had been over its banks, the bridges choked with
corpses. Sidney shivered at the memory.

Burleigh smiled thinly. "Nothing so subtle, Philip—and
I use the word advisedly—or so all-encompassing. The
commonalty are hardly involved at all; this is a matter
between the king and his nobles, nothing more."

"Except faith," Sidney said.

"Which is entangled with a much older quarrel," Burleigh
answered. Sidney nodded slowly, accepting the other's
judgment, and Burleigh went on, "Since the king has
come of age, there's been a third party in the realm,
though it's by far the weakest because James is weak."

"His favorites," Sidney said.

Burleigh smiled thinly. "Quite. Though it's been ten

years since James picked his councillors solely for their beauty."

That did not fit all the stories Sidney had heard of the Scottish court, but he said nothing, and waited for the minister to continue.

After a moment, Burleigh sighed. "It's a pity," he said, "that they drove Maitland out of office. He was a man we could rely on—and he would have helped you, it would have paid him to help you. Why in God's name did he have to meddle with that Moray nonsense?"

A snatch of music sounded in Sidney's mind, a ballad he had heard from a wandering musician whom Fulke Greville had briefly housed the last time Sidney had visited Warwickshire.

> Ye highlands and ye lowlands
> Oh where hae ye been?
> They have slain the Earl of Moray
> And have laid him on the green

"The Earl of Moray was murdered," he said aloud, frowning slightly. "Wasn't he? And by treachery."

"Yes." Burleigh fixed the younger man with another of his sudden glares. "It's a good object lesson in the manner in which things are done in Scotland, Philip. The earl of Bothwell attacked the royal palace of Holyrood, attempting to break through to the king's apartments. He was driven off, but the first nobleman whom James commissioned to capture him—such commissions are called letters of fire and sword, by the way—promptly joined the rebels. As this seemed to be a typical move on the part of the Ultra-Protestants, James made his usual response. He turned to the Catholics, to the earl of Huntly, to be precise, and gave him letters of fire and sword against Bothwell. Huntly promptly used those letters to murder his old enemy Moray."

"Good God," Sidney said. It was beginning to be borne in on him that court life in Scotland was nothing like the courts of the rest of Europe. Perhaps only in Poland were the nobles still so disrespectful of a monarch's rights—and I, he thought, with an inward smile, turned down my opportunity to learn from them. "And was this Maitland involved?"

Burleigh shrugged. "Possibly. Had I been in his shoes, I would have wanted Moray dead. But, more to the point, the removal of the most competent of James's councillors was the price the Scottish Parliament asked for acting against the Catholic earls."

"I see."

"I hope so," Burleigh said. Startlingly, his acid tone shifted, modulating into something more kindly—and that, Sidney thought, worries me the most of all. The sordid story of Moray's death is bad enough, but I think what led up to it bothers me more. Bothwell—who may or may not be a witch himself, but who certainly employs witches— storming a royal palace and getting away with it. . . .

"Philip, I don't deny that you know far more than I'll ever learn about matters arcane. However, the court of Scotland is another thing entirely—nothing like England, thank God, or France even at its worst, or even Germany. I couldn't let you go without trying to make you understand that difference."

Sidney nodded slowly. "I am grateful to you, my lord, I promise you. I'll try to bear it all in mind while I thread my way through the swamps of Scottish politics. There is one thing I'd like to know, however."

Burleigh spread his hands. "Whatever I can tell you, my boy."

"Bothwell. Is he a wizard?"

Burleigh's answer came very slowly. "I don't know. It is whispered that he is, of course, but he may merely employ them, the way he employed the witches. My guess would be that he is not—what Scot of noble birth would take the trouble to learn something that a hireling could do as well?—but I don't really know. I'm afraid I'll have to leave you to answer that question, Philip."

Sidney made a face, but nodded. He had not really expected Burleigh to be able to give him a definite answer. For a moment, the memory of the presence he had felt at Penshurst swam in his mind. It could have been Bothwell, he supposed, but the malevolence had felt wider, concerned with more than politics. "I'll do my best," he said. "And again, thank you, my lord, for your advice."

"I could hardly let you go north in your present state of ignorance," Burleigh said tartly. His voice softened again. "But God go with you, Philip. You'll be in my prayers."

"Thank you," Sidney said again, and added silently, I may need them.

The minister pushed himself to his feet, wincing a little as the movement jarred old bones. Sidney rose with him, wishing he dared offer a supporting hand. "Will you be returning to your brother's house?"

Sidney shook his head. "Not just yet. I thought—or, to be more precise, her Majesty strongly suggested—that I visit Dr. Dee."

Burleigh nodded. "A wise decision. You will forgive me, Philip, if I don't walk with you to the dock."

It was dismissal, though a polite one. Sidney bowed. "Of course, my lord."

Another page was waiting at the entrance to the garden. He bowed as Sidney approached, then led the older man back toward the long dock, his brocaded back stiff with self-importance. Sidney managed to suppress the desire to slap him into a more modest carriage, but handed him the shilling tip with the acid comment, "Good manners are cheap enough, boy. Should suffice."

Chapter Three

*Charming is in as great request as physic, and
charmers more sought unto than physicians in time
of need.*
William Perkins, A Discourse of the Damned
Art of Witchcraft

The bargemaster made no comment on the long pull
upriver to Mortlake, and even the oarsmen seemed surprisingly content. Sidney leaned back against the fancy
cushions, trying to make sense of everything he had been
told. Scottish politics. . . . They were in essence depress-
ingly familiar, revolving around issues that he knew only
too well, though their manifestations seemed cruder than
the methods to which he was used. He tried briefly to
imagine a courtier breaking into the queen's chambers
with sword drawn, and failed completely. Elizabeth
would—no, the idea was too absurd to be contemplated
for more than a moment. And yet such incidents seemed
to be a normal part of Scottish politics, he thought, and
our next king will be used to that. On the other hand,
James has survived it. I trust that's some indication of his
abilities.

Scottish witchcraft, though . . . Sidney sighed deeply.
That was another matter entirely, and one that made him

thoroughly uneasy. After all, he was primarily a theoretician—the practice of the art had always seemed of less importance than an understanding of the laws that constrained and compelled its workings. If he was to be of any use to James—and to Elizabeth, and England—he would have to overcome that handicap very quickly. At least Dee will be able to advise me there, he thought, and found the idea newly comforting.

Dee's house lay along the river bend, with a long tree-lined park that stretched down to the river's edge. The bargemaster brought the unwieldy boat up against the little dock—the barge, court length, was too long for it by almost a yard—and the forward oarsman leaped out to secure the mooring ropes. Sidney disembarked more slowly, grateful for the bargemaster's support.

The barge's arrival had been observed from the house —probably, Sidney thought, Dee's family had been watching its stately progress from the moment it came around the gentle curve—and a little procession was already coming across the park to meet him, led by Dee's wife. She moved slowly now, supported by her stepdaughter, the child of Dee's first wife, and Sidney hurried forward to meet her, taking both her hands in an impulsive greeting.

"Madam, it's a pleasure to see you again."

Jane Dee smiled, dropping an awkward curtsey. She had never quite recovered from the poverty-stricken years in which she had followed her husband across Europe, seeking the philosopher's stone. "We're always glad to see you, Sir Philip." Her son, Arthur, murmured a shy greeting from his mother's side. "John wishes you to go in to him at once, and not stand on ceremony."

"Of course, ma'am," Sidney answered, but matched his pace to her own. They made polite conversation as they crossed the lawn: there were new grandchildren to be mentioned; Arthur had begun his studies at the university, and there was a suitor for the youngest of the daughters, a respectable young man with a decent living. Then they had reached the doorway, and Dee himself came forward, smiling.

He welcomed his guest eagerly; with the long grey gown hanging loose on his thin body, he reminded Sidney incongruously of a nervous ferret—harmless looking, easy to underestimate. Certainly he was undervalued, Sidney thought, but gave no sign of that ancient discontent.

"Forgive this intrusion, Doctor," he began, and followed Dee down the paneled hallway toward the library at the back of the house.

"Intrusion? I won't have you use that word, Sir Philip, not in my house."

Sidney reached out and plucked at the old man's sleeve. Dee stopped obediently, turning a blandly curious face to his former student.

"I fear I've displeased you, doctor," Sidney said. "Why else this sudden formality?"

"You come from her majesty, my son," Dee answered. "I feared it might be Sir Philip who came to me."

Sidney's mouth twisted. As a rebuke, it was the gentlest imaginable, and more than a little deserved. Twenty years ago, he had pursued success at court much as Apollo had pursued Daphne. Then he had learned that both he and the queen found it more amusing, every now and then, not to run with or even against the popular currents, but across them. From that time, he had achieved success, but not precisely in the form he had once sought it. He shook his head. "I wouldn't presume so far—particularly when I need your help."

"You're her champion." It was not clear whether Dee intended that as dismissal or reassurance.

Sidney bent his head. "A great honor that intrigues and terrifies me, doctor. I am her champion in the Accession Day lists. This is something more. She told me somewhat—but I would like to hear from you precisely what you saw, and what you think of this assignment."

Dee sighed, and opened the door to his study. "Incredible, Philip. Burleigh thought so, completely incredible, but, God be thanked, her majesty believes, and recognized in you the man to deal with this horror."

Sidney felt a chill touch him, and sank gratefully into the waiting chair at Dee's absent invitation. Everything he had sensed so far had been vague, disturbing, but not actively threatening. Horror was not a word he had yet applied to it—but then, he was not John Dee. "She said something about a king of England slain by the people of England. Is this so?"

"It may be so. It is what the spirits showed me. A king of England, a Stuart king, executed in a mockery of law, and by Parliament."

Sidney shook his head, massaging the residual stiffness from his leg. The dull pain was almost comfortable, compared with the images both Dee and Elizabeth had conjured for him. "And I?" he asked carefully.

Dee smiled across at his former pupil. "The ceremonies commemorating Gloriana's accession are no mere pomp, Philip, as you well know. Therefore the champion of those lists must be no mere knight, but a knight versed in ceremonies and actions, symbols and realities. Such a one as yourself, in fact—why else would Sir Henry have chosen you to follow him as Champion? When he asked my advice, I told him so, speaking of course as your teacher." His smile grew rather wistful. "Though you had long passed that point. Nor would I trust even the dearest of my pupils with this."

He rose, and moved along the rows of books until he found the one he wanted, then drew it from its place. He turned to Sidney, holding out the squat volume. "Take it, Philip," he said. "Scotland is a land in the grip of a dark hand. Great though Virgil was, he was not completely brought into the light. And even though this is not so great a text as that—you may use it in complete peace of your soul."

Sidney, wondering, took the book offered him. It was only a few hundred years old, but far more fragile that the exquisitely preserved scrolls at Penshurst; the foxed pages still carried the faint pen-lines of some scribe's exuberant embellishments, scrolls and flowers and tiny creatures decorating the faded margins. "The *Book of Saint Dunstan*," he said softly. He looked up at Dee. "It's a gift I'm unworthy of, doctor."

Dee's long face twisted. "Don't do me that injustice, Philip. I know I'm still appallingly naive in many matters dealing with mankind. But in you, I'm not mistaken. I know what I do. Take it with my blessings, and carry them with you to Scotland."

Sidney looked down at the book, his fingers gently stroking the worn wooden cover. It was almost indelicate, the feeling within him at holding this almost legendary book. It was primarily an alchemical treatise, though it contained far more; Sidney had thought it among the many books that had been lost, or had never existed. All talent is a form of alchemy, he thought. Lord, how much more I can learn. . . . He looked up, controlling his pleasure. "I shall bring it back to you, doctor."

Dee smiled. "If it brings you back to me, Philip, well and good. But it is a gift, understand that." His smile widened. "And, of course, I have a copy."

Sidney laughed. "I should know better than to underestimate you, sir. How did you come by it?"

Dee looked away, the smile vanishing. "From one now dead," he said flatly, and Sidney understood. Edward Kelly had been a talented scryer. He had also been a most tempestuous, unstable personality. . . . The thought made Sidney smile a little: the description sounded not unlike Master Marlowe. Kelly had sought to reach beyond the bounds God had set on his power. It had driven him quite beyond himself, and beyond the help of any man. Dee's association with Kelly had caused many to damn the older magician as a necromancer—and was also the source of Dee's wry certainty that he was naive in the matters of men. *Scientia gratis scientiae* was not a code by which many men lived, and those who did not could hardly be expected to comprehend those who did. Sidney's face hardened. Kelly was well lost, may God forgive me for thinking so. Like Nimue, he had used his teacher, and then had done his best to destroy him with what he had learned. I can only hope, Sidney thought, that I've done something to even the balance so far as Ned Kelly is concerned.

"Forgive me, Doctor. It was none of my affair."

"Nonsense, Philip," Dee said. He spoke briskly now, shaking off memory. "You confided to me your acquisition of Virgil's texts, even let me see them. I did not, by the way, give Lord Burleigh any notion of their existence, let alone that you possessed them."

For a moment, Sidney stared at his old teacher, then

relaxed with a small laugh. "Why do you still have the power to surprise me? I should know you well enough by now to know I oughtn't be surprised by anything."

"I'm gratified. It makes me think I'm not yet quite ready for the grave, if I can still elicit that wary expression of yours. It's rather delightful for an old man. Tell me," Dee said, and seated himself again behind his desk, regretful memories banished, "you will be bringing the Virgil with you?"

"I had thought of leaving it with you, doctor," Sidney began, but Dee leaned back, shaking his head.

"Very flattering, Philip, but you may dispense with that, it's pure nonsense. Ever since my neighbors burned my laboratory, I've known better than to leave anything of such value here. No, you'll take it with you, along with the St. Dunstan. You'll need them both, I fear."

Sidney nodded, and the two men sat in silence for a while, listening to the spring wind in the trees outside, and the distant rush of the river. Occasionally, there was the sound of a child's laughter—one of Dee's grandchildren, Sidney thought. The whole day was peaceful, calm, utterly and perfectly natural, in the most arcane senses of the word. And utterly unlike the day at Penshurst when he had first become alerted to the trouble in the air. This was a day when one could relax and breathe, and thank God for such moments, and for His gifts, for the friendship of good men, learned men, whose own love and zeal for the knowledge God hid in His earth was not deterred by the intolerant.

He closed his eyes for a moment. I have three homes, he thought. Penshurst, Wilton, and here at Mortlake. Again, he heard the sound of distant laughter. He smiled slightly, and then he heard it more clearly. His eyes snapped open, his heart racing. It was no child's laughter he heard this time, nor was it audible to human ears. He had heard it, as talent heard, within, with an acuity of the soul. Fear God and fear knowledge, a voice whispered. *I* am ill-opposed by such as you. Rest easy, then. Little as you disturb my sleeps, shall I disturb your meager life. Rest easy, slave of the Four, poor chattel of the Pale One. Rest easy, rest, and you shall surrender.

Dee frowned, recognizing that there was something there, but the words were for Sidney's ears alone. Sidney shook his head slightly in negation. "Man is born to trouble as the sparks fly upward," he murmured, and the presence was gone, withdrawing before it could be banished, and laughing as it went.

"Human," Dee said sourly. "Powerful, talented, perverted—but human. Hubris, I've found—and remember this, Philip—tends to be a particularly human failing. Demons and fiends are proud, but rarely hubristic."

"I can see that," Sidney said. He raised a hand: it was trembling. Somehow, knowing that whatever it was he would face was human comforted him not a whit. It staggered him that any mortal man could command the power he had felt behind this intrusion.

Dee saw the pale, strained look on the younger man's face, and shook his head. "Philip, nonsense. I know of a dozen men with such capability—but they are good men who would not employ it wantonly. And among that number, Philip, you are one of the greatest. Always let your enemy underestimate you. Therein lies your strength. That was how that charge of yours succeeded at Zutphen, wasn't it? Four hundred men against six thousand? David against Goliath is still David."

Silently, Sidney nodded, but his heart wasn't in it. How could he explain to Dee that what gripped him now was not fear, precisely—or rather that it was not fear of the power facing him, but fear of the exultation that sang within him at the thought of the confrontation? This strange presence had touched a chord with him, and his power had answered—still in opposition, true, but Sidney knew that the potential for a fall as brilliant as Lucifer's lay within him, as great as the talent Dee said was his. For a grim moment, Sidney envied the papists, with their comfortable rite of laying the burdens of one's soul on another. He sighed, shaking the thought away, and lifted the St. Dunstan.

Dee frowned slightly. "You're welcome to stay here, Philip."

"Actually, I'm staying with Robert, in the city. And besides, I have this mad impulse to keep moving. I don't know. It may not be sound strategy, but it's how I felt in Holland, and it's how I feel now. Just keep moving and don't look to either side." Sidney smiled suddenly, almost impishly. "Panic, I think it's called."

Dee studied him suspiciously for an instant, and then his face eased into a rather sheepish grin. He picked up the bell that stood on his desk and rang it. A few moments later, the eldest grandson entered. "Tell your mother she's to see that Sir Philip's boat is ready."

The boy, a sturdy child of eight or nine, bobbed an ungraceful bow and vanished. Dee held out his hands to Sidney.

"Do give my regards to your family, and to Lady Sidney, of course. God go with you, Philip. He is not unknown in Scotland, though to judge from recent events, one might wonder."

Sidney raised an eyebrow. "You reassure me no end," he said drily. He bowed over the old man's hands, but Dee forestalled him, and kissed him on the forehead.

"My blessings as well, my son. Come back safely."

Sidney nodded mutely, and tucked the St. Dunstan carefully under his arm. The door opened again, and the child appeared, nervously clearing his throat.

"Excuse me, Grandfather, but Mother says Sir Philip's boat is waiting."

"Thank you," Dee said, austerely, but there was a twinkle in his eye. "Make your bow to Sir Philip. You may show him the way to the dock, if you like."

"Oh, yes!" The boy—Sidney could not remember his name, though he knew he had been told it more than once—controlled himself instantly, and managed a hasty reverence.

Dee lifted an eyebrow, and Sidney said hastily, "Thank you, that would be very kind." He was very aware, as he followed the boy through the halls and across the beautifully kept lawn toward the dock, of the child's awed, sidelong glances, and did all he could to keep from laughing. Such hero-worship was almost silly, when the child had Dee for a grandsire.

Sidney left Mortlake in a thoughtful mood, and strangely exhilarated. It was the same kind of madness that had seized him at Zutphen, and which was channeled and transmuted into something more decorous for the Accession Day Tilts. It was something to have seen that his enemy was also human. It troubled him not at all that his opponent seemed scornful of his abilities. Sidney smiled wryly then. Well, perhaps it did trouble him somewhat, but he would be damned if he would admit it.

He leaned back against the cushions of the barge, listening to the call of the stroke oarsman, and the birdlike cries of the other boats making their way along the busy Thames. It was a warm afternoon, unusually so for April, and he lifted his face to the sunlight, of a color and intensity in and about London that was unlike anywhere else in the world. It had been too long since he had last visited London, not since the most recent Tilts last November. The winter had been a busy one at Penshurst; but now he had the excuse, and if he was shortly to be banished to Scotland, albeit on the Queen's business, Sidney had every intention of enjoying the city while he had the chance. Robert, bless him, shared his love for the city; not for him the suburbs of Mortlake or Chelsea. Robert lived as close to the heart of the city as one could and still maintain a household suitable to a gentleman.

The barge slowed, creeping through the heavy traffic of the city proper, then angled across the current toward the dock below Robert's town house. Sidney sighed, and then his eye caught sight of the flag, snapping in the freshening afternoon breeze along the bankside. It stirred a feeling of defiance within Sidney, and he leaned forward to direct the bargemaster to dock there, rather than at the house. The man gave a long-suffering sigh—he had to work the barge back across the current and through the swarms of lesser craft—but was too well trained to protest. Sidney leaned back again. If he returned to the house now, he would likely run into Robert, and he owed Robert, as next senior member of the family, a complete explanation of what was happening. . . . He deliberately pushed all thoughts of the matter in hand from his mind, and grinned. *If I don't disturb your sleeps, see how little you trouble my days. Such a cheap activity, play-going. Yet I rank it rather above troubling about you.*

There was a goodly crowd at the theater when he arrived. In one of the galleries, he saw a knot of acquaintances, Fynes Morrison among them. Morrison saw him, and beckoned him over to join them. It had been some time since Sidney had seen the inveterate traveller, so he slid into the seat cleared for him.

"Philip, my sparrow, you've been disputing with her majesty again," were Morrison's first words as Sidney sat down.

"I'm in London still, so I fail to follow your reasoning," Sidney replied.

"Scotland, Philip. She'd hardly have sent you unless you'd irked her again. Will you never grow out of this precocious idealism of yours?"

Sidney hid a sigh. Court gossip had always travelled fast, but this seemed almost indecently rapid. "Not so long as it serves a purpose," he said. "And her majesty seems to be under the impression that she's doing me an honor by giving me this embassage. So I believe her."

"You would, Philisides. Well, I suppose it's better than London in the summer. Oh, good Lord, another history. First Marlowe and his *Edward*—can't keep his personal life off the stage, can that one? —and now this. *Richard II*. Not much blood and thunder there."

"Fynes, why don't you go down and stand with the groundlings so you can throw apples at the players? You'd be much more in your element."

George Chapman wedged his solid bulk in between Morrison and a support beam, and grinned across at Sidney. For all that the poet was a member of Raleigh's School of Night, and thus an advocate of a magic darker than any Sidney trusted, Sidney found himself smiling back at him. "G'den, Philip. What make you with this lackwit who can write about only what he sees?"

"Oh, old affections die slowly," Sidney said, and allowed his smile to become virtuous. Morrison drew an indignant breath, and Sidney sat back to enjoy the sparks.

"The words are at least my own, George. I don't need to steal from the ancients. Besides, if people can't read Homer in the original, they don't deserve to."

"Like an English prayerbook?" Sidney asked innocently,

then sat back with his hands clasped around his good knee
as the players' boy appeared with the placard that announced the start of the play.

For the next three hours, Sidney did not have to make
any effort to put the Scottish question from his mind, and
he ignored both the occasional comments of his friends
and the mercifully infrequent interpolations from the crowd
below. He watched and listened, sometimes closing his
eyes the better to hear the flow of words, and fought to kill
a canker of envy that had started to gnaw within him.
There was no doubt that the man was a poet. The language was exquisite, as worthy of print as of the stage;
still, Shakespeare was no slave to his words, as Marlowe
could be, but made them instead the finest of tools.

I will have to revise my own printed opinion of the
theater, Sidney thought, remotely, watching Richard's child-
queen move delicately across the stage, the boy maneu-
vering the old-fashioned Spanish farthingale with practiced
skill. *The Defense of Poesie* did not go far enough—these
new conventions are as worthy as any of the Greeks'. My
defense lacked scope. . . . He sighed. He doubted that
Stephen Gossen—and Thomas Greene; it really was amazing that the most vocal critics of plays and playwrights
tended to be lesser specimens of the breed—had grown
any less reactionary over the years. Besides, he added,
with a faint, devilish grin, it was always pleasant to fly in
the face of those who expected him to disapprove. Especially those so-called puritans who, unlike Sidney, who
styled himself one, forgot the joy of grace, the inherent joy
of the Lord and His gifts.

He stared at the bare stage, the flow of language, the
actors' gestures, transforming it into the final terrible cell
beneath Pontefract Castle, then to Windsor and the final
scene, so bitingly accurate, of the gratitude of princes and
Bolingbroke's secure remorse, his enemy dead. Shakespeare's was indeed a divine gift. The play ended, and the
company's oldest member stepped forward in his proper
person to speak the brief tag. Sidney joined in the enthusiastic applause, but shook his head in response to Chapman's invitation to join him at the Anchor, the most
expensive of the theater taverns. Instead, he sat for a long

moment, letting the brightly dressed gentryfolk who could afford the expense of a gallery seat push out past him, considering what he had just seen. It was an oddly disturbing play—fully satisfying, he amended immediately, but still disturbing, and not merely because Shakespeare's Richard was, despite his faults, an attractive man. A weak king was a liability and a danger to the land, but usurpation was an uneasy matter. Had Marlowe, perhaps, feared the inherent uncertainty of the subject? Sidney wondered suddenly. His *Edward II,* for all it dealt with rebellion against and the unsavory murder of a weak king, had concluded with the true king firmly on his father's throne. Had he felt a need for the proprieties after all?

Sidney shook himself almost angrily, hating what he had to do. Usurpation was, simply speaking, dangerous ground, especially this usurpation, and especially now. England rejoiced in the reign of her Gloriana. It was a period of wealth, an achievement unseen before in England, the great dangers that had threatened at the beginning of the realm had been resoundingly defeated—yet there were always worms in the bud. Caterpillars of the commonwealth, Sidney thought, rolling the player's phrase in his mind, and then remembered that Gossen had used the phrase before that, though to far different intent. He pushed himself to his feet, sighing a little as he realized how his leg had stiffened up again, and made his way through the jostling crowd to the tiring house.

Even those in the company who did not know him recognized quality, as who would not, when these companies lived in the hopes of a great man's patronage and commissions, or in fear of an attack. Most did remember him, of course—Sidney had always taken an interest in the players, and had stood godfather to the son of the great comedian Richard Tarleton some years before—and broke off their own busy conversations to offer carefully polite greetings. Sidney had a reputation as a tolerant patron, but he was also the first gentleman of Europe, and no one would willingly offend so open-handed a man.

Sidney made his way slowly through the tiring house, his progress impeded by the hampers of costume and the stacked props, and by the need to respond to each man who spoke to him. At last he found Shakespeare, sitting on a battered-looking hamper at the back of the room, helping the young boy who'd played Richard's queen free himself from the awkward farthingale. The boy wrestled himself out of the wired underskirt, leaving himself naked except for drawers and a pair of patched and none too clean stockings, then stood staring open-mouthed at the newcomer.

Sidney hid his grin, and said, "Good evening, Willem."

Shakespeare looked up, and smiled in pleasure. He tossed the boy's shirt to him, and rose to his feet. "Sir Philip, this is an honor. Welcome. Would you care for some ale, sir?"

"In a bit, Willem. I'd like to talk to you, if I might. Will you walk with me?"

The playwright looked shrewdly at Sidney, who continued to smile pleasantly, and sighed almost imperceptibly, reaching down to do up the last buttons of his sober doublet. "Of course, sir. Dickon!" There was no answer to the randomly directed shout, and he looked quickly around the crowded room. "Dickon?"

An arm waved above the heads, and then Burbage waded through the chaos to join them, silver-laced ruff discarded, shirt undone, and bare-legged, a sweating pitcher in his right hand and a sheaf of papers in his left. He wiped his mouth on his shirtsleeve as he approached, but Sidney politely ignored the gesture.

"Sir Philip." The player's nod was more than half a bow, and he glared at Shakespeare, who seemed unaware of it, or of any reason for it.

"Master Burbage," Sidney acknowledged. "A beautiful performance."

"Thank you, Sir Philip. It's a beautiful piece, of course. Nothing without Will."

"Richard," Shakespeare cut in quietly. "Sir Philip has invited me to go with him. See to things here, would you?"

There was the same wary glint in Burbage's eyes as had been in Shakespeare's. It would have been open suspicion had it been anyone but Sidney. Sidney, however, had a reputation for fair and honest dealing that few patrons could match. . . . The player shook himself subtly. " 'Right. Good evening, Sir Philip. Come along, brat," he added, dragging away the apprentice. The boy was staring—though he had remembered to close his mouth so he could not be accused of gaping.

Shakespeare managed a not-quite-mocking bow. "I'm at your disposal, Sir Philip."

It was cooler out in the streets now, and most of the afternoon's crowd had thinned away to their homes. On the thin, cool air, the sound of a bell pealing for evening prayer was almost unnaturally clear. The air carried a hint of salt, and nothing at all of the filthy river so close at hand. The sky was a pale, darkening blue of a knife's-edge clarity. Sidney lifted his head to the evening, and drew in a deep breath, for a brief moment utterly content. Shakespeare glanced sideways, watching the older man surreptitiously, and smiled. You could write him in a play, he thought, but no one would credit it. Still, there had to be a way: scholar, soldier, statesman . . .

Sidney sighed, shaking himself back to his unpleasant duty. He glanced at Shakespeare, but the player, engaged with his own thoughts, was staring intently at the rutted street. "It's a beautiful play, Willem," he said softly. "Your finest to date. Of course, that's the way it should be, each one finer than the last. But this . . . This is exquisite."

"And even the groundlings liked it," Shakespeare replied, coming out of his reverie with a quick grin. "Terribly difficult to do, please both groups. But thank you, Sir Philip. It's high praise, from you. I know your standards are quite different from ours."

Sidney laughed. "Two years with Master Marlowe as my very own protege, and two years of watching you grow and develop—something Kit has yet to do, though I have hopes—well, I trust you don't believe me hidebound, Willem. The poetry was very fine, as fine as any I've heard, and you laid out your story well. I have never spent a more pleasurable day at the theater."

Shakespeare was quiet for a moment, digesting the unexpected praise. It was like a fine wine coursing through him. Sidney was a poet himself. Sidney had always maintained the perfection of the Aristotelean unities, but now, he was won over to something freer in style—and by a man who was neither of court nor university. It was an achievement to be proud of. "But?" he asked.

Sidney looked surprised for a moment, then smiled in surrender. "Was it that obvious? Do I never praise without caveat?"

"No. It's not that. But there's something about you. You're troubled. And if you wanted to tell me what a genius I undoubtedly am, you would have stayed at the theater. So, but?"

Sidney stopped in the middle of the street and to the playwright. "I would very seriously consider pulling it from repertory," he said.

"Good God. Why?"

Sidney shrugged and started walking again. "It's not very—tactful. The death of kings. For all our prosperity, these are far from certain times." The vision of an anointed king executed at the will of Parliament swam up in his mind. No, it seemed unlikely her Majesty would appreciate even so stunning a creation as Shakespeare's Richard, not now—but how was he to explain that to the player?

"What about *Edward II*?" Shakespeare asked, trying to keep a note of desperation from his voice. "This is a history, Sir Philip, that's all it is. I leave the allegories to you and to Master Spenser."

"It's less that her Majesty is likely to see herself as Richard so much as she might see—some others—as aspiring to be new Bolingbrokes," Sidney answered, feeling his way. "An anointed prince is a valuable thing these days, especially such a one as ours. We don't squander, and we don't offend."

"The Master of the Revels passed it, though."

"I doubt her majesty would feel herself bound by the judgment of her master of the revels," Sidney said, dryly. "I'm sorry, Willem—it's only my opinion, but I don't want to see this play banned. And I think the only way to prevent it is for you to pull it before ideas are put into some very receptive minds. Believe me, I think it's a beautiful work, the finest I've seen and enjoyed. But the time calls for tact. Your pulling it now may speak volumes with her majesty later. It can only help you. I don't think it could hurt you."

"Whereas if we left it in, we could be accused of treason?" Shakespeare asked. Put in such bald terms, the thought sounded ridiculous, but to his dismay Sidney did not seem amused.

"If there are those who dislike you, Willem, who dislike players and playwright? Well, perhaps not treason, but without noble sanction, without being attached to a household . . . ?"

"Enough. No, I see it, Sir Philip, though I don't pretend to understand what's going on these days in the halls of the mighty." Shakespeare sighed, a profound sadness in his face. "And I hadn't even had my day at it."

Sidney nodded, sympathizing with the loss he would incur—the customary arrangement was for a playwright to receive the full receipts of the second day's performance.

"Well, you're a good judge of these things. If pulling it now means we can play it later, then so be it. I'll get my day then." Shakespeare shrugged convincingly, trying to hide his regret. "You're for Scotland, I understand, Sir Philip."

"Is it the favorite topic of conversation in the city?" Sidney asked with a sigh. "Yes, her majesty has done me the honor of appointing me her ambassador to James's court. To offer her thanksgiving for the child's recovery."

"That's 'wee bairn,' Sir Philip, you know."

Sidney just looked at the younger man. "So I understand. As I said, the child lives and flourishes, and we go to offer our respects."

"It's a rare place for witchcraft, I hear," Shakespeare added, as though it had been the topic under consideration.

Sidney did not flinch. "Could be. But considering that Queen Anne did make it safely to Scotland, that James lives and reigns, that the child did recover . . . I would have to say they're damned inefficient ones, if they've been causing all the trouble."

"Never tempt the fates, Sir Philip."

"I never do," Sidney assured him, with more confidence than he felt. After all, what else had he been doing at the theater? They were outside the Anchor now, he saw, with some surprise, and he nodded toward its open doors. "Would you join me?"

Shakespeare hesitated, then shook his head. "Thank you, no, Sir Philip. I think I need to talk to Richard about what you've just said. He won't thank me if I keep it from him 'til tomorrow. He's nervous enough about such things. And I need to do some thinking about it myself."

Sidney shook his head, feeling obscurely guilty. Even though he knew he was giving the playwright the safest possible advice, he felt rather like a murderer. "I understand, and I'm sorry, Willem, to blight your pleasure. But do think about what I've said. The time is out of joint. Hold your Richard in reserve."

Shakespeare nodded quickly, his expression abstracted. "Thank you. From anyone else, I could shrug this off. I could even suspect that you somehow had Kit's interests at heart—we are rivals, after all. But I know you mean us well. I'll think about it." Then he was gone, his head bowed as he pondered the unpalatable words. Sidney watched him go and sighed. It was not pleasant advice to give, either, and he found himself resenting the fact that this mysterious presence could so affect men whom he respected, but with whom he had no further connection. But what affected princes eventually affected everyone else. And players stood in such ambiguous relation to princes. He shook his head, and turned back along the rutted street, heading toward the river and his waiting barge.

Chapter Four

Beneath the stars, upon yon meteor
Ever hung my fate, 'mongst things corruptible.
        Thomas Middleton, The Changeling

It was cold in the narrow room, despite the twin candelabra and the fire in the great stone fireplace that filled
one entire wall. Christopher Marlowe curled his toes uncomfortably inside his boots, wishing he had worn a thicker
pair of hose, and wrapped his hands around the bowl of his
silver goblet. The hot metal had cooled a little, was pleasant to the touch. He sipped cautiously at the spicy liquor—a
mixture of ale and hippocras, what his family's Canterbury
neighbors, and probably Raleigh's Devon kin as well, would
call a gossip's cup, good but common—and glanced under
his lashes at the rest of the party. Sir Walter Raleigh,
seated in the host's chair closest to the fire, saw the look,
and lifted his own cup in mocking salute. Marlowe smiled
back—one had to admire a man who had the gall to serve
precisely what he liked, no matter how common it was—
but his eyes slid sideways toward the Earl of Northumberland, who sat deep in argument with Raleigh's astronomer. *A gossip cup for a belted earl?* the gesture asked, as
plainly as if he'd spoken aloud. Sir Walter's lips tightened
fractionally, but he refused to be drawn, turning instead to

57

answer some comment of George Chapman's. Marlowe leaned back against the paneled wall, still smiling.

"My lord." That was Walter Warner, another of Raleigh's mathematicians, his voice less point-precise than usual. "My lord, when will you show us this game you promised?"

"It's not a game." Henry Percy lifted his head slowly, a faint smile just curving his lips. He was not a big man, even in the new-fashioned heeled shoes he affected, but there was something about him that made the others give way a little. Marlowe felt the hairs rise on the nape of his neck. He had not been paying attention earlier, when the earl first mentioned the gift he'd brought; now, hearing the odd, gloating note in Northumberland's voice, he wished he'd listened more closely.

"If you would, Sir Walter?" the earl continued, still with that faint smile playing on his lips.

"Of course," Raleigh answered, and reached for the bell that stood on the table beside his chair. He shook it, twice; when the steward appeared, bowing, he said, "Bring his lordship's boy."

"At once, Sir Walter," the man answered, and vanished.

"His lordship's boy?" Marlowe pushed himself up off the bench where he had been sitting and moved to stand by the fire.

"Not in your sense, Kit," Northumberland answered. "In fact, quite the opposite. His virginity is to be preserved, not squandered."

"You did bring your scryer, then," the astronomer Harriot exclaimed. "I'm very glad, my lord, I've been wanting to see a demonstration of his powers."

"And so you shall," Northumberland said. "With Sir Walter's permission, of course."

Raleigh gestured his acquiescence, a superbly theatrical movement that showed off his long-fingered hands. Marlowe, watching him, knew suddenly where Ned Alleyn had stolen some of Tamburlaine's flamboyant graces.

"The—seeing boy, Sir Walter," the steward announced from the doorway, his superior, upper servant's voice tinged with an indefinable disapproval.

"Thank you, Blake, that will be all." Raleigh spoke

without moving from his chair. "Come into the light, boy, we won't eat you."

There was a sort of squeak from the doorway, and Northumberland said, "Come here, Nathanial."

The boy edged nervously into the globe of candlelight, bobbing a sort of bow, his cap clutched in front of him with both hands. He was younger than the men had expected, no more than nine or ten, and plainly terrified: for all that Northumberland had had him bathed and decently clothed, he was obviously no more than some illiterate laborer's son, ill-suited for a gentleman's study. Or for a gentleman's bed, Marlowe thought, even if he were old enough. Still leaning against the mantel, the fire warm on his booted legs, he studied the boy. It was a meager little thing, skinny and small, with straw-colored hair cut very close above a thin, big-eyed face and unfortunate ears. His dark blue jerkin was worn, and hose and shirt both had been mended, though neatly enough. Northumberland's parsimony was galling, and Marlowe smiled down at the boy, hoping to win some response. The boy's brown eyes moved warily, but he gave no other sign.

"Sit down," Northumberland said, and shoved his footstool away so that it stood in the center of the circle of men. "These gentlemen wish to see you practice your talent."

The boy edged forward a few steps, then, with a sudden burst of movement, scuttled across the floor to the footstool. He seated himself, hunched forward, hands clasped tight in his lap, and looked up at Northumberland.

"He'll need something to look into," Northumberland said, glancing around the circle. "A mirror, perhaps, or a glass of wine?"

Chapman fumbled in the purse at his belt. "Here," he said, and held out an oval mirror framed in silver gilt. The whole thing was no larger than a man's palm, and Warner whistled thickly.

"Very pretty, George."

"Thank you," the poet said, and looked at Northumberland. "Will it do, my lord?"

"Admirably," the earl answered, and gave the glass to

the boy, who took it carefully, holding it in both hands. "Are you ready, Nathanial?"

"Yes, my lord." At the sound of the boy's voice, Marlowe looked up sharply. Despite the ugly northern vowels, the tone was rather beautiful, a pure, silvery treble completely unexpected from so unprepossessing a child.

"Quite lovely," Chapman said quietly, and leaned against the mantel beside his fellow playwright. "What a pity he's so plain. And the accent's impossible, of course."

"He could be taught to speak," Marlowe said, and Chapman smiled rather maliciously.

"I thought you disliked boy-actors, Master Marlowe."

Marlowe scowled, but managed a shrug. "Only in my bed, Master Chapman. I've learned better. In any case, I doubt his lordship would let him go."

"Gentlemen, if you please." Northumberland frowned reprovingly at them, and Chapman swallowed his next retort. Marlowe rolled his eyes, but said nothing.

"Now, Nathanial," the earl continued. "Say the prayer I taught you."

"Yes, my lord." The boy pulled himself up straight on the little stool, and rested the mirror on his bony knees, steadying it still with both hands. "*In nomine patri, filii, et spiritu, sancti, amen. Dum medium silentium tenerent omnia, et nox in suo cursu medium iter haberet, auctores et servi potentissimi tuus, Domine, de caelis et realibus sedibus misisti.*"

The boy was obviously speaking by rote, garbling what were to him merely meaningless sounds. Marlowe shivered, translating the altered verses and fragments of prayers hastily and literally. *While all was in silence and the night was in the middle of its course, you sent your agents and most powerful servants, Lord, out of heaven. And as this was done in the past, so let it be done again. Let all your angels from the most high to the most low listen and obey, according to the names of power which you have revealed to us. When I call them, let them come to me in this glass.*

"*—audite me, amen. Venite, venite, omnes spiriti.*" The boy ended his recitation on a high, scared note, and glanced quickly at Northumberland. The earl nodded, and made a complex gesture over the boy's head.

"Christ, Harry," Raleigh said, softly, and crossed himself.

Northumberland held up his hand for silence, saying rapidly, "*Scapulis suis odumbrabit tibi Dominus, et sub pennis ejus sperabis, amen.*"

The Lord will overshadow you with His shoulders, and under His wings shall you trust. Marlowe wondered briefly if that promise would have much effect, coming from the earl.

Northumberland sketched another sign, and looked up with a smile. "Don't worry, Walter, the boy's protected by his own innocence, and my power. The spirits can only enter the mirror, not the room." He looked back at the boy. "What do you see, Nathanial?"

The boy did not answer, staring huge-eyed into the mirror. Raleigh said, still softly, "Those were dark names you had him call."

"Merely powerful ones," Northumberland answered, and Raleigh looked away, frowning unhappily.

"And a half-papist ritual," Marlowe muttered. He could feel a cold draft on his shoulders, despite the fire, and looked round with a start. There was nothing in the corner but shadow and a shuttered window.

Northumberland said, "I thought you were the man who claimed that the papists had the better rites, Master Marlowe." The mockery in his voice, too lazy to be contempt, stung. The playwright straightened.

"Only to hold common men in awe, my lord, which is the purpose of all religion. Ceremonial toys always fascinate little minds."

Northumberland frowned, and for an instant Marlowe was afraid he'd gone too far again. Harriot said, "For God's sake, look to the boy."

Nathanial swayed suddenly on his stool, the mirror sliding in his hands. He caught at it, gasping, his eyes seemingly even wider than before. Northumberland said sharply, "What do you see, boy? Answer me!"

"I see—" The skinny body went rigid, and the sweet voice broke in a squeak of pure terror.

"A fit?" Warner started to reach for him, and Harriot tugged him back.

Northumberland murmured something under his breath,

his hands moving rapidly, and then said, more loudly, "Malcochias, release him. Answer me, what do you see?"

The boy licked his lips, shivering. "Demons, my lord, demons dressed like the priest in the church."

"Go on." Northumberland leaned forward as though he would drag the answer out of him bodily. "What are they doing?"

"They—they're talking to folk, preaching to them," the boy answered. "There's a great gate behind them, I don't know it but it's very fine—" He screamed then, a cry of fear and horror like a bird's voice, and pushed himself blindly away, flinging himself off the stool. The mirror fell and shattered on the wooden floor. Marlowe caught him before he stumbled into the fire itself, and gathered the shaking body against his own, muffling the boy's sobs against his chest.

"Easy, Nate," he murmured, hardly aware that he spoke. "Easy, little love." The boy's hands tightened convulsively on the front of the playwright's doublet, but the racking, silent sobs did not slow.

Northumberland was frowning terribly, glaring at the sobbing boy. After a moment, he mastered himself, and bent to pick up the broken mirror. He handed it to Chapman, saying, "I'm sorry, Master Chapman. I certainly owe you a replacement."

Chapman took the mirror reluctantly, holding it by the very edge of the frame, and set it quickly on the mantel. "Thank you, my lord, but that's not necessary. One must expect—accidents—in the pursuit of knowledge."

"Nevertheless, I must insist," Northumberland said, and Chapman bowed. The earl turned his gaze on the boy again. "Nathanial, I am most displeased with you. You will come to my study tomorrow morning after prayers."

Marlowe made a face, feeling an obscure sympathy—like any schoolboy, he remembered the beatings that followed such a summons—and eased Nathanial's hands away from his doublet. The boy struggled briefly, then let go, hunching his shoulders miserably.

"Come here, Nate," Harriot said softly, and beckoned. The boy crept to him, and, after a moment, buried his face in the mathematician's hanging sleeve. Harriot stroked his hair absently, as he would pet a dog.

Marlowe picked up the broken mirror, studied it idly. The glass had broken in a strange, star-shaped pattern, but none of the pieces had fallen from the ornate frame. He stared into the crazed reflection, wondering what the boy had seen to frighten him so dreadfully.

"What, Master Marlowe," Northumberland exclaimed. "Are you reconciled to ceremonies?"

"I confess, I'm curious," Marlowe answered. In spite of everything, he grinned. "I'm almost sorry I'm not—qualified —to see for you, my lord."

Northumberland smiled. "There are rituals that we could use, if you were willing."

"Harry, no," Raleigh said. "No more, not tonight."

The earl shrugged. "He did express a cautious interest, after all. But as you wish."

"By God, I'll do it," Marlowe said. "I'll look in mirrors for you, my lord, or anywhere else you like."

"You see?" Northumberland said. "It's his own wish, Sir Walter."

Raleigh hesitated. "On one condition," he said at last. "You'll send the boy to bed—he's had enough to bear tonight, Harry—and you'll take precautions, this time. Christ's blood, I can still feel whatever it was you called."

Northumberland nodded. "Very well. Are you still willing, Master Marlowe?"

The playwright nodded quickly, before he could change his mind. "Tell me what to do."

"Sit there," Northumberland answered, nodding to the footstool. Marlowe did as he was told, watching the earl from under his lashes. Behind him, Raleigh sounded his bell again. The steward appeared after an interval that was barely decent; Marlowe grinned at the newcomer, and had the pleasure of seeing him blush.

Raleigh saw the byplay, but ignored it. "See his lordship's boy to bed, Blake," he said, coldly. "Then you may retire yourself."

The servant drew himself up to his full height. "You'll wait on yourself, then, Sir Walter?" Voice and posture both expressed his disapproval.

"Yes," Raleigh answered. The steward opened his mouth to protest further, and Raleigh frowned him down. "Do as you're told, Blake. I've no more need of your services tonight."

The steward bowed. "As you wish, Sir Walter," he said, and beckoned to the crouching boy. "Come along, boy."

The child hesitated, and Harriot gave him a gentle pat on the shoulder. "Run along, Nate," he said, "it's past your bedtime."

Thus urged, the boy went, eyes on the floor. The steward grasped the nearest wrist, and hauled him toward the door. Harriot blinked mildly at Sir Walter.

"Perhaps someone—one of the women, perhaps—should stay with him? He was very frightened."

"Nonsense," Northumberland said, but Raleigh nodded. "See to it, Blake, if you please."

"Very good, Sir Walter," the steward answered. Marlowe, glancing sideways, saw the man's bland expression change to a scowl as soon as Raleigh looked away, but then man and boy had gone.

"You wished me to take precautions, Walter?" the earl asked, lazily still leaning back in his chair with his feet stretched out to the fire.

"Yes," Raleigh said, in a voice that brooked no argument. Northumberland shrugged elaborately, not moving, and Harriot cleared his throat.

"If you wish, my lord, I'll set the circle."

"Thank you, Doctor Harriot," Northumberland murmured.

Harriot fumbled beneath his gown for his purse, and, finding it, emptied its contents into his hand. Marlowe watched with undisguised curiosity. Some coins, a shilling and a few pennies, a twist of paper that might hold tobacco, a pewter disk chased with peculiar symbols, a seal, a pair of bone dice—the last in particular seemed an odd thing to find in a scholar's pouch—and finally the object of the mathematician's search, a roundish piece of chalk. Harriot scooped the rest of his belongings back into the purse, and knelt on the rough floor to trace the first lines of the circle of Solomon. Marlowe was suddenly aware that Northumberland was staring at him, and made himself meet the earl's gaze squarely. Northumberland was not a handsome man—he had the Percy sandiness, and the sallow skin—but his eyes were as coldly grey as a winter sky, and as compelling. The poet looked away, but found himself drawn again to the icy stare.

Around him, the room seemed to fade, yet at the same time his perception felt somehow heightened, so that he was peculiarly aware of every slightest movement, every whisper of sound, and at the same time pleasantly distanced from it. It was a warm, half-drunken feeling; Marlowe gave himself up to the sensation, and caught himself smiling into Northumberland's cold eyes. The fire was very warm on his side, the hiss and crackle of the embers providing a counterpoint to the murmur of conversation. He could hear the voices, recognized them as belonging to Raleigh and to Chapman and Harriot, but he could not seem to make out the words, blurred as they were by the snap of the fire and the distant rushing of the wind. Someone—Chapman, he thought—tossed a log onto the fire, and Marlowe watched the sparks swirl up, to vanish before they reached the chimney-mouth.

"Kit." Northumberland's voice broke the spell. Marlowe blinked hard, and pulled himself upright. Chapman's mirror tilted in his hand, and he caught it quickly before it fell again. "There is a spell you must say, repeat it after me."

Marlowe glanced down quickly, saw the familiar lines and symbols of Solomon's circle, and looked up again to meet the earl's stare. "All right, my lord."

"Then we'll begin." Northumberland sketched another symbol in the air—definitely not a blessing, Marlowe thought—and intoned a string of nonsense syllables. The poet repeated it carefully, and thought he heard the wind shift outside, skirling viciously around the chimney pots. Northumberland repeated a second set of words, and this time, repeating them, Marlowe thought he recognized Greek and Latin words among the meaningless babble. He puzzled over them even as he repeated a third nonsense-phrase, but could come up with no coherent meaning. Northumberland spoke a fourth phrase and Marlowe parroted it.

"Do not repeat this," the earl said, and sketched a series

of symbols in the air between them. His voice rose almost
to a priest's chant as he intoned a final series of syllables,
changing at last to something recognizable. "—*audi et
pare, Malcochias. Sic fiat, amen.*"

The air inside the circle grew chill, as though the fire
had dwindled suddenly. Marlowe shivered, and thought
he saw shadows move between the line of the circle and
his own shoulder, whisking out of sight behind him. It
took all his strength to keep from looking round convulsively.

"Look in the mirror, Christopher," Northumberland said.

Marlowe lifted the cracked mirror a few inches, then
bent his head reluctantly, looking into the broken glass.
For a long moment, all he saw was his own reflection,
bizarrely distorted by the cracks, and behind that the
distant image of the painted and paneled ceiling. Then,
almost imperceptibly, the glass began to darken, shadow
seeping out of the cracks to cloud the bright images.
Something hovered behind him, something as black and
solid as the night itself, and more tangible. Marlowe held
himself rigid, knowing that something was there, and knowing with equal certainty that if he turned, there would be
nothing there. Or, worse, he would see the demons Faustus conjured, and there would be no familiar faces behind
the masks and the hellfire. Still, there was something
there. . . . He closed his eyes, fighting back a strange,
sick fear, but opened them again as the thing stooped
closer. Not knowing was worse; better to do and be damned.

He raised the mirror before he could think better of it,
lifting it to shoulder height so that it showed his own face
and the room behind him. A darkness swam between him
and the lines of the circle, so thin that he could see
Raleigh's worried face through the veil, and yet solid
enough that he could make out the shape of it, cruelly
male, great wings half raised to shadow the circle. It
smiled, and it was beautiful, fearsomely so, one taloned
hand rising to beckon. *Turn, surrender*, the gesture seemed
to say, *turn and I will make you mine.* Marlowe trembled,
his lips parting almost against his will, feeling the heat of
its power on his back. In self-defense, he summoned up
the classical images he had learned at university: Medusa
could only be viewed in the mirror of Perseus's shield,

Psyche had lost Cupid by looking on his face. To turn was death and worse than death, and he clung to that thought, his hands white-knuckled on the edges of the mirror.

The thing smiled still, and reached for him, hand cupped to touch his cheek. Marlowe shuddered, imagining he could feel the claws' caress, but did not turn. Instead, he flung the mirror sideways, toward the fireplace. Metal and glass shattered against the bricks, and the broken fragments rained into the fire. Faintly, Marlowe thought he heard a cry of anger and frustration, and then the thing had vanished utterly.

"Christ, Kit," someone said, in a shaken voice.

Marlowe did not answer, still crouched, trembling, on the footstool. Gradually, his heartbeat slowed, the ordinary warmth of the fire penetrating the chill of fear. If there were a man who could touch me like that, he thought, when he could think again, I would follow him to the ends of the earth. Then, impossibly, a sort of smile tugged at the corners of his mouth, and he added silently, and I would hate him for it.

"Kit?" Marlowe was suddenly aware that Chapman was kneeling beside him, bearded face drawn into a worried frown. "Are you all right?"

The poet shook himself, fending off a final shiver. "Yes," he said slowly. "Yes, I am."

"What did you see?" Harriot demanded, and Northumberland added, "Why did you break the spell?"

Marlowe looked from one to the other, from Harriot's worn, scholar's face to Northumberland's angry frown, and said, the words still coming slowly, "I saw—demons, my lord, as did your boy."

Harriot crossed himself, and, a moment later, the earl did the same. Raleigh said strongly, "Then there will be no more scrying tonight, gentlemen, nor any other night until you, Harry, can tell me why you only seem able to summon such unholy creatures. George, fetch Kit some drink. God knows, he's likely to need it."

Marlowe accepted the cup from Chapman and drank deeply. The hot liquor scalded away the last uncanniness, and he was able to look around again with something like his usual enjoyment.

"Now, gentlemen," Raleigh said, "I confess, I'm loath to send you each to bed, since my house seems haunted by demons. I suggest we watch the night out—perhaps with dice, and certainly with wine?"

There was a general murmur of agreement, more polite than eager, and Warner rose to fetch the dice board. Marlowe took another long swallow of the hot liquor, and did his best to ignore Northumberland's measuring glance. *Raleigh was right,* he thought, *though I doubt he knows entirely why. But dice and wine—good common fellowship —will do more to keep away that demon than any priestly exorcism.*

It was almost dawn when Marlowe left Durham House, a cold, grey dawn heavy with the promise of river-fog. Already, the first tendrils were coiling up the rutted street, and Marlowe drew his cloak close around his shoulders. He was not—quite—drunk, but the drink he had taken was souring in him. At the first opportunity, he stepped into an alley-mouth; as he finished tying his points, he heard a movement in the street, and turned quickly, reaching for his dagger. The street was empty, no one moving among the strands of fog. He stood very still, listening both for an attacker and for the people of the neighborhood, who had to be stirring now, and might come to his aid if there were a fight. Into the silence, a small voice said, "Sir?"

The silvery tone was unmistakable. Marlowe's hand slid from his dagger-hilt. "Boy—Nathanial?"

"Yes, sir." A skinny figure edged out of the shadow of a doorway. When he came no closer, Marlowe beckoned impatiently, and the child scuttled forward to the corner of the house. The poet started to ask what the boy was doing, in the streets at this hour, or where he was going, then thought better of it, reading the fear in the boy's eyes. Nathanial took a deep breath, visibly marshalling all his resources for some final effort.

"Sir," he began again, and stopped as abruptly as he'd started. Marlowe bit his tongue to keep from speaking, afraid of frightening him away.

"Well?" he said at last, softly, when the boy seemed unable to continue.

Nathanial took another deep breath, spoke in a sudden rush. "Sir, will you take me with you? I'd be grateful—I'd do anything for you, anything at all."

Marlowe blinked, somewhat taken aback—it was not usual, even in his experience, for boys to make that offer unprovoked, and with no coin in sight—and stared down at the slight figure. "Do you have any idea of what you're saying?" he said, after a moment.

"Yes, sir." Nathanial nodded bravely. "I'd like you to sleep with me." When the poet made no answer, he added, "To—to bugger me, sir, if you please."

Marlowe bit back a laugh. "Do you know what that means, boy?"

Nathanial nodded again. "Yes—" He faltered as the man raised an eyebrow. "Well, no, sir, not entirely. But if you did it, I'd no longer be suited for his lordship's work, and I'd like that very much, please, sir."

This time, the poet did laugh. "And why have you picked me for this—service?"

The boy frowned, vaguely affronted. "His lordship said I should be careful of you, that you liked to do—that—to boys, so I thought you'd help me."

"Oh, he did, did he?" Marlowe hesitated, torn between anger and amusement, then, slowly, began to grin. It was his own fault, for circulating the manuscript of his *Ganymede* the previous winter; even if the poem stated—among its other truths—that the satire's subject was too old still to be called a boy, it was unlikely Northumberland had ever read beyond the title, or listened to more than the scandalized whispers.

"Will you, sir?"

Nathanial's voice broke the poet's reverie. Marlowe stared at the boy, the grin fading from his face. He owed Northumberland a bad turn or two, after the—thing—that had haunted him—the same demon, presumably, that had appeared to the boy—and this was as good a revenge as any he could have devised on his own. In the rising light, he could see the worn elbows of the boy's jerkin, the ugly, serviceably patched hose and battered, boxy shoes. Beyond anything else, a man as rich as Northumberland shouldn't grudge what it costs to keep his servants decently clothed,

Marlowe thought. "All right," he said. The boy's face
tensed, bracing himself for some imperfectly imagined
assault, and Marlowe added hastily, "I'll take you in for
now, and we'll decide what's to be done with you."

"But, sir, if you don't," Nathanial began, and the poet
held up his hand.

"If his lordship finds you, which I don't intend him to,
you can tell him I've had you—which will save you some
misery. You're too young for me, Nate."

Nathanial considered this for a moment, then nodded,
satisfied. "All right—and thank you, sir."

"Come along, then," Marlowe said. "You don't want his
lordship to find you."

It took almost three hours, counting the time spent
buying breakfast—small beer and day-old bread, the best
Marlowe could afford on such short notice—at a newly-
opened cookshop, to make the walk from Durham House
to Marlowe's lodgings in Norton Folgate. Nathanial did
not seem inclined to talk, clinging close to Marlowe's side,
and as the wine he'd drunk wore off, the poet found
himself grateful for the time to think. He himself could not
keep the boy, even if he'd desired to do so; however, it
was not easy to find willing sponsors for a boy with no
particular talents. As they passed St. Giles Cripplegate, he
began to ask the boy a few questions; by the time they'd
reached the edge of Moorfields and turned onto Bishopsgate
Street, his worst fears had been realized. Well, not quite
the worst, Marlowe amended, as they turned into the
sudden shadow of his own street. At least the boy could
read a little, and he did have that beautiful voice to buy
his way—as long as he could unlearn his northern speech.
Perhaps Alleyn would take him on as an apprentice, assuming Marlowe could raise some sort of payment for his
keep. If not, perhaps Sir Philip or his sister would take the
boy as a page.

The door of the house where he lodged stood on the
latch, as always. Marlowe pushed it open, and stopped in
the doorway as Nathanial hesitated on the worn step.

"This is where I live," the poet said, a little impatiently.
The sleepless night was beginning to affect him at last; he
could almost feel the warmth of his bed. "You'll stay with

me for now—you weren't afraid to offer your virtue before, and it's still not in danger. Come along." He turned
away before he saw the boy's sudden flush, shouting,
"Martha! Mary-Martha!"

There was an answering shout from the back of the
house, too distant for him to make out the words. "Wake
me at noon!" he shouted, and started up the narrow stairs
without waiting for her indignant answer. Nathanial followed at his heels, balancing himself with one hand flattened against the rough plaster wall. Marlowe paused at
the top of the stairs for him, stretching, and felt the
muscles of his shoulder crack painfully. It had been much
too long a night.

"My room's in the front," he said, pushing away the
memory of the looming demon, and beckoned for the boy to
follow. The door was unlocked, as always, and swung open
to his touch. "You can—" His voice died as he realized
what was waiting for him.

A man was sitting in the room's only chair, a trim,
unobtrusive man, very neat in a suit of oxblood wool
trimmed with gilt, his sandy beard just touching the edge
of his discreet ruff. "Good morning, Kit," he said, and
smiled cherubically. "Your charming landlady let me wait."

Marlowe froze. The honeyed voice brought back a memory he'd worked hard to forget, Mistress Bull's tavern and
the scattered dishes, the musty curtains and Frizer's weight
against him, the bearded face grinning at him, while the
hands tightened inexorably on his throat, and Poley drawled
at his partner to finish it, in God's name. . . .

"I seem to have interrupted something," Robin Poley
continued, still smiling. "I do apologize."

The malice in his voice stung, driving back remembered
terror. Marlowe took Nathanial's shoulder, turning him
back toward the door. His fingers brushed the boy's cheek
in passing, and he knew from Nathanial's shiver and questioning glance that they were as cold as ice. "Go back
downstairs to the kitchen," he said, in a strange, dry voice
he barely recognized as his own. "Tell Mary-Martha or
Bess that you're to be an apprentice, and you'll be staying
here a few days." He gave the boy a gentle push, propel-
ling him through the doorway. "Go on, now." This was not

the way he would have chosen to introduce Nathanial to his formidable landlady, but he had been given no choice in the matter. He tilted his head to one side, listening as Nathanial's hesitating footsteps made their way down the stairs, but did not take his eyes off Poley.

"Good God, Kit," the sandy-haired man said. "You're taking them young these days."

"What in hell's name do you want?" Marlowe asked.

"No hard feelings, surely," Poley answered, with just enough arch surprise to add a sting to the words.

Marlowe scowled, only too aware of his own fear. He could feel his hands shaking, and made himself cross the room to his writing table. The papers, the draft of one act of one of Munday's plots, had been shifted. He fought back another surge of panic and anger—there was nothing there that could hurt him—and reached for his pipe. He filled it, deliberately turning his back on the other man, and fumbled with his tinderbox. "You were doing what you're best at," he said, around the stem of the pipe. "Following someone's orders."

Poley's mild expression froze for an instant, but then the moment passed. "Is that a way to greet me? And I've brought you good news, too."

"What's that?" Marlowe asked, suspiciously. The tobacco had caught; he set the tinderbox aside, glancing at his hands. They were steady now, but the knot of fear refused to vanish from his chest.

Poley lowered his voice discreetly. "Our—mutual employer is willing to overlook your having been so careless as to come to the Privy Council's notice the year before last. In fact, he has a job for you."

"Oh?" Marlowe drew deeply on his pipe, pleased at having achieved the proper note of independence, as though he might actually refuse to do whatever Cecil had in mind. In bitter fact, of course, he didn't dare—neither of his patrons was so powerfully placed as to be able to shield him from the secretary of state a second time—but it was impossible for him not to make the gesture. "I'm in the middle of a play, Poley—"

"One act, which you have finished," the other man interrupted. "No, no one's watching you, Kit—would it be worth our while? But you hardly make a secret of your affairs." He nodded toward the table with its litter of papers.

Marlowe's mouth tightened, but he managed to ignore both the jibe and the veiled threat. "Why don't you tell me what you want?"

Poley smiled, very sweetly. "Her majesty is sending your present patron to Scotland, to carry gifts to the young prince, who, we understand, is newly recovered from the smallpox. You will accompany him."

Marlowe raised an eyebrow. That might be the official explanation for a Scottish journey, but he was quite certain there was more involved than a matter of the prince's illness. Elizabeth was notoriously unenthusiastic about her distant cousin's heirs. But at least it had nothing to do with him, personally. Slowly, the poet began to relax a little, and enjoy the irony of the situation.

"Actually—" Poley lowered his voice again, until Marlowe had to strain to hear him over the noise in the street below. "Actually, Sir Philip's presence has been ordered by her majesty herself." He lowered his voice still further, almost to a whisper. "It's a matter of witchcraft."

"In which case," Marlowe said, in his normal voice, "I should've thought you'd want to send Raleigh. Or Dr. Dee." He took a malicious pleasure in the expression of fear that flickered across Poley's face.

"Dr. Dee is too old for such a journey," Poley answered, and added primly, "and her majesty doesn't wish Sir Walter to be absent from court just now."

Or the Cecils don't, Marlowe thought. I wonder what Raleigh's done now—have they got wind of Northumberland's latest tricks? The thought chilled him, and he pushed it away, saying, "And why am I supposed to accompany this embassy?"

"Sir Robert wishes to be sure Sir Philip has someone with him on whom he can rely," Poley said, his confidence returning. His smile vanished as abruptly as it had appeared. "And he wishes you, Kit, to keep him informed of events in Scotland."

"In other words," Marlowe said, "you want me to spy on Sir Philip. I assume you've brought some warrant?"

Poley nodded, and slipped a much-folded piece of paper out of the cuff of his glove. "Sir Philip has been too much inclined to act without consulting the secretary, lately," he said.

Which, translated, means he's been thinking for himself, Marlowe thought. The corners of his mouth twitched upward briefly. One of those acts undertaken without the secretary's approval—in fact, against Sir Robert's expressed wishes—had been the saving of his own life. There was a certain rather theatrical irony in being ordered to spy on his rescuer for the very man who'd ordered his murder—and in having the message carried by one of the three would-be murderers. There was an even nastier irony in the assumption that he'd do it. Sighing, he unfolded the slip of paper Poley had given him, and scanned the familiar spiky handwriting. It was no more than a letter of credence, a curt order to treat Poley's words as Sir Robert's own, and Marlowe refolded it thoughtfully. It was a little unsettling that Cecil had seen fit to add nothing more, either threat or promise—as though Sir Robert's hold was so complete that there was no need for either one. But of course there wasn't, Marlowe thought, bitterly. Even after Deptford—perhaps because of Deptford—he didn't really have any choice. Still, the idea of meek acquiescence choked him; he said instead, "Where's Sir Philip staying these days, at Penshurst?"

Poley nodded, a superior smile on his lips. "Yes. But Sir Robert wishes to see you first. Tonight, after evensong, at Paul's."

"Does he," Marlowe said, sourly. "All right, I'll be there."

Poley's smile widened. "Of course." He gestured imperiously toward the cluttered table. "The letter, burn it."

Marlowe bit back an automatic refusal. After a moment's search, he found an earthenware dish, then held the twisted letter to the smouldering tobacco until it caught, laying it in the dish as the flame grew. It burned quickly, shrivelling into a fragile shell of ash; almost before it cooled, Marlowe crumbled it between his thumb and forefinger.

"I'll inform Sir Robert," Poley said, briskly, and held out his hand. That was what Marlowe had been waiting for: as they joined hands, he managed to drag his sooty fingers across the other man's clean, embroidered cuff. Poley jerked his hand free with a curse.

"So clumsy of me," Marlowe jeered.

Poley gave him a murderous glance, but said only, "At Paul's, for evensong, Marlowe. You'd best be there."

"I will be," the poet said, but he was talking to the other man's back. Poley stalked from the room, and slammed the door behind him.

Left alone, Marlowe leaned back against the table, mechanically wiping the rest of the ash from his fingers with a scrap of rag. It had been a petty revenge, unsatisfying, ultimately unworthy of the situation. Almost in spite of himself, he began reworking the scene, reshaping it into something dramatically useful. The basic situation was good, filled with perverse ironies; he would keep that, but raise the stakes—perhaps the patron should be in danger himself, accused of witchcraft or of treason? The dialogue, too, would have to be rewritten. . . . Experimentally, he murmured a line, and then another, the blank verse coming almost as easily as prose, the characters tossing the thread of the scene back and forth as if it were a child's ball. Double meanings and a veiled insult capped with a classical tag, a not-so-veiled remark breaking suddenly into violence, a drawn dagger and a marked face. . . . He stopped abruptly, the images vanishing. If the spy were the aggressor, it would spoil the vague plot taking place to hold the scene—there was no room in it for the inevitable, necessary retribution. It would work better if the Poley-character were the attacker, but he couldn't see how to get to that point.

He shook himself, frowning, and put aside the now-dead pipe. There was no time for this sort of day-dreaming—already Mary-Martha was probably preparing his eviction, unless he could convince her that Nathanial was only a temporary visitor and no bedmate of his. In spite of his better judgment, his mouth curved into a reminiscent grin. She had raised enough objections when his Ganymede had come to stay, and he had been a man of nineteen. He pushed himself off the edge of the table, and started back down the stairs toward the kitchen.

To his surprise, Mary-Martha was nowhere among the pots and crockery. Bess, the maid-of-all-work, glanced up from the great cauldron simmering on the hearth, and favored him with her cheerful, gap-toothed smile. "That was a kind thing you did, Master Kit."

Marlowe raised a sardonic eyebrow, but the young woman continued unheeding, "Poor lamb, he's in the garden with the mistress."

"Thank you," Marlowe said, and started for the garden door. Mary-Martha had only a small walled plot, but it was enough to keep her provided with at least some of her vegetables and herbs, and she was duly proud of it. Already, Marlowe saw, she had put the boy to work digging in one of the end beds; as he stepped onto the flagged path, she rose hastily to her feet, brushing the dirt and the winter's dead leaves from her skirts.

"No, Nate, you go on with that, I only have a few words to say to Master Marlowe." Unobtrusively, she motioned for the poet to stay where he was, and came to join him, tucking a few loosened strands of hair back under her embroidered coif. "Well, Master Marlowe, it was a kindness to the boy, taking him away from there, but what am I to say if his old master comes looking?"

"I trust it won't come to that," Marlowe temporized.

"And I trust you'll give me a better explanation." The woman lifted an eyebrow at him.

Marlowe sighed. It was beginning to be borne in on him that apprenticing the boy with the Admiral's Men would not be as easy a solution as he'd hoped. "*If* anyone comes looking, tell them the truth. I brought the boy here, and you don't know anything more than that."

Mary-Martha's foot tapped impatiently on the flagstones; she stilled it instantly, frowning. "If you were my husband, Marlowe. . . ."

"God forbid," Marlowe muttered, only half in jest, and the woman smiled. She had buried one husband already, owned her house and its land and a part-interest in her late husband's business: she was in no need of something so unchancy as a poet for anything except a lodger.

"And maybe not even for that," she murmured, and shook herself. "He can sleep in the storeroom next to

Bess's room," she said aloud. "Two shillings to house and feed him 'til the end of the month, and two more shillings for the bed and sheets—which I will launder. And sixpence to take care of his clothes."

Marlowe nodded, too tired to haggle. "Agreed."

"In advance," Mary-Martha stipulated.

Marlowe sighed. "I'll give it to you this evening," he said, and held up his hand to stop her automatic protest. "I have to meet some people this afternoon, Mary-Martha, and I had no sleep last night. Will you wake me at three?"

"A filthy habit, sleeping out the day," the woman said, but nodded. "I'll wake you. Have the money for me this evening, mind."

"I will," Marlowe said, and stepped back into the house before she could answer. Sighing again, he made his way back up the stairs to his room and, after a moment's thought, bolted the door behind him. Mechanically, he began to undress, loosening the strings of his wilted ruff, then kicking off the long boots. He left them where they fell, taking care only with his doublet—his second-best, peach satin trimmed with flax-blue braid—and the paned slops. He laid them carefully on the clothes-chest, and stretched out on the bed still wearing hose and shirt. He closed his eyes, savoring the mattress's comfort, then turned onto his side, drawing the blankets over himself still half-clad. In the dimness, the demon's memory waited; he walled it out with the tricks he'd learned to cheat all bad memories, barring it from everything but the worst dreams, and, slowly, slept.

Chapter Five

*You have heard of Mother Nottingham, who for
her time was pretty well skilled in casting of waters, and after her, Mother Bomby; and then there
is one Hatfield in Pepper Ally, he doth pretty well
for a thing that's lost.*
Thomas Heywood, The Wise-woman of Hogsdon

The promised knock at the door roused him from a fitful
dream. "I'm awake, Mary-Martha," he called, and sat up
against the pillows, trying to recapture the fading image.
It was somehow important, he thought, something I need
to know. . . . But he could remember only standing in a
London street and looking up between the houses, to see
a great dark wing obscuring half the sky. He shivered,
digging his hands into his thick, close-cut hair, and pushed
the image away again. "What's the time?"

"Just past three." It was Bess who answered, still standing at the door. "Are you awake, Master Marlowe? Unbolt
the door, I've brought your hot water."

Groaning, Marlowe pushed himself out of bed, and
padded across the warped floor to slip the bolt. Bess gave
him an appraising glance, and a quick grin, and slipped
past him to set her tray on the nearest cleared surface.
The poet, who had forgotten until that moment that he

78

had gone to bed in shirt and hose instead of the longer, concealing nightshirt, rubbed his chin and tried to appear unconcerned.

"And I've brought your dinner," Bess continued, "if you want it." Her smile widened. "Will there be anything else?"

Marlowe shook his head. "How's the boy settling in?"

Bess's grin vanished, and she said quite seriously, "Well enough, I think. Witches ought to be burned, if that's what they do to people. The mistress has him helping in the garden still—she thinks he ought to be kept busy, and I think she's right about it. And he'll be next to me, if he has nightmares."

"Thank you, Bessy," Marlowe said, and the woman nodded, accepting her dismissal. She paused in the doorway.

"The mistress says, don't forget you owe her five shillings."

"Four and sixpence," Marlowe said, but Bess was gone. Sighing, he turned his attention to the tray she'd brought. A tankard of beer and a generous wedge of pie, besides the hot water . . . not a bad dinner, considering that Mary-Martha so disapproved of his habits. He took a long swallow of beer, then pushed back his sleeves to wash hands and face. His hands rasped against his stubbled cheeks, but after a moment's hesitation he shook his head. He was still too tired to risk shaving himself, and there was no time to visit a barber—and in any case he'd been shaved the day before.

The hot water revived him somewhat, and he dragged off shirt and hose before he could change his mind. He dressed quickly then, between bites of the pie, pulling on clean shirt and not too much mended hose, then the tawny slops and his everyday judas-color doublet, and finally fastening the long boots to the slops-leg. He finished the pie and washed his hands again before taking his smallest ruff, no deeper than a finger-joint and starched to expensive perfection, from the bandbox and tying it carefully around his neck. He reached for his mirror, lying buried in the litter of papers on the writing table, and stopped at the sudden memory. It took an effort of will to pick up the little glass and look into it; he gave a sigh of relief when no dark figure loomed behind him. Instead, there was just his own long, hollow-cheeked face, unshaven and still puffy-eyed, and the whitewashed wall for a background. He grimaced at the image—there was no time for vanity—and swept up his flat cap, adjusting it one-handed to just the proper rake. His reflection stared back at him, an emblem of dissipation; he frowned, and put the mirror away. At the door, he paused, and turned back to pick up his rapier on its worn belt, at the same time sliding his dagger onto his right hip. It was never wise to meet unarmed with princes: he stored the phrase for possible future use, and started down the stairs.

The Admiral's Men did most of their business at the Bell in Southwark behind Winchester House. Marlowe felt his purse for the tenth time since crossing the river, feeling for the rolled manuscript. Philip Henslowe, who financed the Admiral's Men, liked to cut his costs by parcelling out a single plot among three or four men, each one writing a single act, and his son-in-law Edward Alleyn, who was also the company's leading man, raised no objection to the practice. The writers themselves would rather die than admit they liked the work, but it did mean an easy fee, and that was something to be coveted. If I hadn't needed a few pounds, with Sir Philip on progress with the court, Marlowe conceded, I'd never have done it—but it was a good thing they needed plays.

Bell Road was wider than most, running almost at once into the open land of St. George's Field, so wide in fact that the jutting second stories barely shadowed the sides of the street, and the ditch in the center of the roadway ran almost clear. The sun had burned away the morning's fog long before; now, setting, it bathed the open yard in front of the Bell, and the knot of day-laborers drinking on the benches outside the door. The two men standing at the doorway itself cast long shadows back along the street. Marlowe recognized them both, but it was the slighter of the two that made his breath catch in his throat. Ganymede himself, perfect from his tarnished-gold curls to his trim, unpadded calf, very neat in a suit of the shade of scarlet known as kiss-me-darling: very appropriate, Marlowe thought, sourly, and did his best to ignore the knife-thrust of longing in his belly.

The other man saw him then, and touched the blond man's shoulder. The latter glanced back—he's grown a beard since he left me, Marlowe thought, startled—then said something to his friend, and vanished into the Bell. Marlowe kept on, uncertain whether he was glad or sorry his Ganymede had chosen to avoid what could only be an unpleasant encounter, and nodded to the man remaining in the doorway.

"Good evening, Kit." Edward Alleyn's knobby, short-bearded face was faintly wary. "Bringing Henslowe the second act?"

Marlowe nodded. "It's in my purse."

"And when will you be offering us a play of your own?" Alleyn continued. "It's been almost two years since *The Massacre at Paris.*"

He's had time to get away, Ned, Marlowe thought. He bit back his annoyance, saying, vaguely, "I've some things in mind. Wait for me, Ned? I want to talk to you."

Alleyn nodded. "Henslowe's within."

"I know." The poet brushed past the actor into the Bell's cool dimness, drawing the rolled manuscript from his pouch. He glanced quickly around the main room, but Ganymede had vanished; the long tables held only a scattering of actors from the Admiral's Men, and the tight knot of writers clustered about Henslowe at one end of the smallest table. Marlowe moved to join them, skirting the murmuring actors.

"Ah, Master Marlowe." Henslowe looked up, a polite smile on his face. He was a small, round-faced man, with a streak of white in a beard that was trimmed to be fearsome to his enemies, rather than mild to his friends.

Marlowe, who had seen that serene look before, held out the manuscript at once. "Master Henslowe. The second act's complete."

Henslowe sighed. "Master Haughton is ill, and asks to bring his share tomorrow." His tone suggested he'd heard the excuse before. "Will you come back for the reading?"

Marlowe spread his hands, a calculated gesture of regret. "I'm sorry, Master Henslowe, but I'm going out of town. You have my part, surely one of the others can read it with theirs."

"And I suppose you expect to be paid on that basis?" Henslowe asked.

"I do."

One of the playwrights made a choked noise that might have been laughter, which was quickly stifled as Henslowe sighed a second time. He loosened the ribbon that fastened the manuscript, and glanced quickly through the close-written pages. "Oh, very well," he said at last, and fumbled in his purse.

Marlowe accepted the proffered coins—the remainder of the two-pound fee—and tucked them into his own pouch. "Good evening, then, Master Henslowe," he said, and could not resist adding ironically, nodding to the other playwrights sitting silent beside the manager, "Gentlemen."

One of them mouthed a curse, but Henslowe chuckled. "And a good evening to you, Master Marlowe."

Marlowe turned, fully aware of the other playwrights' jealousy, and made his way to the door. Alleyn, still leaning in the doorway, shook his head.

"You are a troublemaker, Kit." He tucked his arm through Marlowe's and urged him toward the bench vacated by the knot of day-laborers, gesturing with his free hand for the innkeeper's boy. "Ale?"

Marlowe nodded, and settled himself on the bench. Judging by the length of the shadows in the dusty street, it was still some time before he had to start toward St. Paul's to keep his other appointment. He accepted a pint mug from the boy when he brought them, and made no argument when Alleyn offered to pay.

"Now, what are these things you have in mind?" Alleyn leaned back against the wall of the tavern, one knee drawn up like a schoolboy's, and regarded the other over the rim of his mug.

Marlowe took a long swallow of his ale, buying time. In point of fact, he had no subjects in mind—*Hero and Leander*, the *Ganymede* satire, and then the single act he'd worked on for Henslowe, had taken up a good deal of his thought, and he'd read nothing recently that had inspired him. With a fleeting pang, he remembered the excitement of reading the *Faustbook*, but thrust the thought aside as unprofitable. "It's very vague yet, Ned, and I don't want to talk too much about it." Alleyn's eyes narrowed—the poet was not noted for his modesty, or his reticence—and Marlowe added quickly, "I'm thinking of a classical subject."

Alleyn nodded, but there was a note of disappointment in his voice. "Histories have been doing well. And comedies."

"Comedies, Christ." Marlowe took another drink of ale as though he'd wash the taste from his mouth. The play he had been working on for Henslowe was a comedy of sorts, and he had not cared for it. "Think of it as a classical history."

Alleyn made an appraising face. "That's possible. Who's—"

Marlowe spoke quickly over the question. "I need a favor, Ned."

The wariness returned to the actor's mobile face. "What sort of favor?"

Marlowe grinned, and said deliberately, "No, it has nothing to do with my sweet Ganymede." He took a deep breath, the smile fading. "It's about a boy."

"Isn't it always?" Alleyn growled. "For Christ's sake, Kit, can't you manage your own affairs?"

"It's not like that," Marlowe protested. "What I wanted to know was, do you have room for another apprentice—you or any of the others?"

Alleyn's eyes were still wary, but some of the disapproval had faded from his expression. "Not easily," he said. "What's he like, this boy of yours?"

Marlowe answered carefully, feeling his way, "Clever, but biddable. And he has a truly lovely voice."

"Does he sing?"

"He's not trained," Marlowe said.

Alleyn grunted. "And his looks?"

"Ordinary enough," the poet answered. "He'd pass quite easily, under paint."

Alleyn stared into his ale, then made an undecided gesture. "What is he, a London boy?"

Marlowe hesitated, and the actor looked up quickly.

"Out with it, Kit, what's the catch?"

"He was born in Yorkshire," the poet admitted.

"Oh, no." Alleyn shook his head decisively. "And he talks like a Yorkshireman, I'm bound. No, Kit, there's no room with us for a boy who'll have to be taught to speak before we can use him."

"He's young," Marlowe said. "He could learn. And the voice, Ned, is beautiful."

Alleyn shook his head again. "I'll listen to him, Kit, but I'll tell you now, there's not much hope."

There was a note of finality in his voice that stopped the poet's insistence. "All right," he said. "But I will bring him to you, Ned."

"Where did you acquire this boy?" Alleyn began, and the poet set his emptied mug aside.

"I found him," he said, and grinned.

"If there's trouble connected with him," Alleyn said, "I doubly don't want him."

"There isn't," Marlowe said blithely, and pushed himself to his feet. "I'm sorry, Ned, I've another appointment tonight."

Alleyn nodded. "Don't forget the play," he said. "Henslowe's willing to offer eight pounds—two in advance."

Marlowe's eyebrows rose in spite of himself—he had expected to earn an eight-pound fee, but he had not expected to see any of it before the manuscript lay in Henslowe's pudgy paws—and he whistled softly. "I will keep that in mind."

The offer remained in his thoughts as he made his way to Bankside and hailed a waterman to carry him back across the river. He lay back against the boat's greasy cushions, shivering a little in the chill river air, trying to think of some suitable subject. The easy subjects, the ones that sprang first to mind, were stale, unprofitable, holding none of the special magic that had carried him through the first plays. So let the offer sit, he told himself, as the boatman swore cheerfully behind him, cursing the river and the heavy traffic. You are going to Scotland first, whatever happens.

That thought was enough to drive away the last of his mild contentment; he scowled unseeing at the army of little boats to either side of him, and wondered if there

were any way to evade Cecil's commission. Not likely, he
thought. The man who'd ordered his murder once already
would hardly be likely to scruple at trying it again—and
there was no counting on Sidney's rescuing him a second
time.

He paid off the waterman at the docks below Baynard's
Castle, automatically adding a generous tip from the money
Henslowe had given him, and started through the crooked
streets toward St. Paul's. The sun was setting now: already
rushlights were lit in the taverns and behind a few house-
windows, and here and there apprentices were busy folding away the day's stock and preparing to shutter the open
storefronts. Marlowe moved through the homing crowd
without really seeing it, his mind on the meeting ahead of
him. Witchcraft—Scottish witchcraft—and spying on Sidney . . . His mouth curved upwards into a humorless
smile. It had the makings of an unholy mess.

St. Paul's was quiet, the bustle of the day's commerce
fading into the twilit peace of evening. The booksellers'
stalls were boarded up for the night, their contents spirited away, back to the printers' shops. The congregation,
gathering slowly in the side chapel, was mostly of the
merchant class, men and women in good, sober stuffs,
with a sprinkling of those apprentices pious enough to put
off their dinner for an hour or so. Marlowe let himself
merge with the crowd, following a middle-aged woman
whose bottle-green skirts and stiffly boned bodice were
trimmed with canary-colored ribbons, scanning the figures
around him for any sign of Cecil or Cecil's agents. He
recognized no one, but he had not really expected to see
them yet—Cecil, certainly, would not make himself conspicuous by attending such a middleclass service. He
found himself a place in the shadows at the side of the
chapel where he could put his back against a pillar, and
composed himself for the service, pulling off his hat.

The sound of boys' voices broke his reverie. He straightened reluctantly, glancing toward the priest's entrance. A
small choir, he thought, three boys and as many men—
what most would consider suitable for a weekday service.
The priest who accompanied them was also of the sort
suitable for a weekday service: a youngish, balding man,

whose face bore the indrawn lines of a man greatly concerned with others' opinions. A typical junior minister of
the cathedral, Marlowe thought. And, God help me, that
could've been me.

The processional ended, and the priest turned to face
the congregation, somehow contriving to look disapprov-
ingly down his nose at them all. "The sacrifices of God are
a broken spirit," he intoned, "a broken and contrite heart,
o God, thou wilt not despise."

Marlowe sighed, his intentions of getting easily through
the service, of conforming without annoyance if not with
belief, vanishing utterly. He withdrew his thoughts from
the service then, using the too-familiar words and phrases
to build a barricade against the reiteration of certain sin
and necessary damnation, of absolute submission, keeping
a tight rein on an old resentment. If nothing else, he
would need all his wits about him when he met with
Cecil—and it would not be unlike Sir Robert to have
planned the meeting for this time and place in order to
disconcert his agent.

The words of the first lesson broke through the fragile
barrier. "And Joshua said unto the people," the priest
recited, "Ye cannot serve the Lord: for he is an holy God;
he is a jealous God; he will not forgive your transgressions
nor your sins."

Marlowe smiled. Yea, even from the walls of Jericho,
yea from the height of victory—Joshua knew, he thought.
This was the God he scorned—the God that had driven
Faustus from theology, and then made repentance useless
even if it had been possible. . . . The voices of the choir
rose abruptly into the psalm that followed the second
lesson, a boy's soaring mean and then, nearly an octave
above that, the pure, piercing treble, rising and re-echoing
even in the confines of the chapel.

He forced his thoughts away from the service, made
himself concentrate instead on the meeting with Cecil,
mouthing the creed and the final prayers by rote. At last
the service ended, and the congregation made its way out
of the chapel, sharp London voices rising to resume conversations begun before the service. Marlowe hung back,
at the side of the crowd, scanning the faces for Cecil or his

agents. Despite his care, he recognized no one until a hand caught his elbow. The poet started, cursing, and Poley said softly, "This way, Kit. In the side chapel."

Marlowe bit back an automatic protest, heart racing. Poley had him by the right arm, neatly preventing him from drawing his rapier—if there was murder planned, he was already half disarmed. But why should Cecil be planning a death? the poet demanded silently. There was no need for it. . . . Even so, it took all his will not to reach left-handed for the dagger at his right hip.

"This way," Poley said again. Marlowe let himself be urged toward the archway of the smallest chapel, his body tensed either to fight or to run.

Half a dozen candles were burning before the altar, casting a wavering light in the confined space. A papist touch, Marlowe thought, but for once said nothing, his eyes on the man who waited just inside the globe of light. The stooped figure stared back at him for a long moment, then nodded.

"Well, Marlowe," he said aloud. "That will be all for now, Robin."

"Yes, Sir Robert." Poley released the poet's arm, and slipped away into the shadows. He had not gone far, Marlowe guessed, just out of earshot of a quiet conversation, but within range of a shout. The poet's mouth twisted wryly. He wasn't likely to try anything—if he had been, he would not have waited until two years after the attempt at Deptford—but it was typical of Cecil to take precautions. That was one thing to be said for Walsingham, Marlowe thought, as he stepped forward into the light. The old man had never been afraid, either of his agents or of the information they brought him.

"Well, Marlowe," Cecil said again. "Poley told you why I've sent for you."

It was not entirely a question, but Marlowe answered anyway. "He told me some things, not much."

When Cecil did not answer immediately, the poet tilted his head slightly, studying the other man. Robert Cecil was not an old man by any reckoning—a year older than Marlowe himself—but his neatly trimmed hair and beard were already sprinkled with grey, and his clothes, the long-skirted, fur-lined gown worn over a suit of soberest black and white, were the wear of a man twenty years his elder. Some of that sobriety was to help disguise the stooped back—Thomas Walsingham had whispered once, not without considerable malice, that the younger Cecil was actually crook-backed—but much of it was policy, the policy of the ambitious son of a renowned father.

The silence stretched between them. Marlowe recognized the tactic and set his teeth, refusing to speak until the other did. Cecil smiled austerely.

"You'll go to Scotland, then," he said, as though they had been discussing the topic for some time already.

Marlowe nodded, grudgingly. "Yes."

"And you'll keep me informed of Sir Philip's actions," Cecil continued.

"And how am I to do that?" Marlowe asked, and kept his tone coldly academic. "It'd be hard enough, and expensive enough, to arrange for couriers—not to mention that Sir Philip might grow suspicious."

Cecil made a face as though he'd bitten into something unexpectedly bitter. "You will use cipher," he said at last. "Walsingham's cipher. Once you reach Scotland, you may give your messages to the ambassador, he will see that I receive them. You will have a letter to that effect. Before then, I—trust your ingenuity, Marlowe."

"Very well," Marlowe said. So far, the secretary had told him nothing new, nothing that could not have been relayed through Poley; the poet shivered suddenly, wishing Cecil would come to his real business.

"There is a further commission," Cecil said at last, and gave the younger man a sudden fierce look. "And if you betray this by so much as a breath or a glance, you will wish you had died in Deptford. Inquire of your friend Kyd as to the least I can have done to you. . . ."

Kyd had been arrested two years earlier on suspicion of publishing a seditious libel, and the Privy Council had used the rack to aid their inquiries. Marlowe pushed away the memory of his last, unpleasant meeting with his fellow playwright—Kyd had been limping still, a year and a half later, and not without some reason blamed the younger man for his arrest—and managed a curt nod.

Cecil lowered his voice still further, until he was speaking at a pitch just above a whisper. "Your task is officially to aid King James. Insofar as this means preserving his life and his throne from this threat of witchcraft Dr. Dee has seen, you will do it. However—" The fierce eyes flashed again. "You will not do anything more than what you must to keep him alive and king."

Marlowe frowned, and said in spite of himself, "Not do more than—?"

"He must not be made strong or secure," Cecil hissed. "If he were to become either, he would not need England— English money, English help in other ways—and if he no longer needed England—" The secretary of state broke off abruptly. "But that does not concern you, Marlowe."

The poet bowed his head, aware that he had accidentally been granted a glimpse of very dangerous ground. It was not so much that James might no longer need England, he guessed, but that James might no longer need Cecil, and God only knew how many years of scheming such a rejection would ruin. "No," he said obediently, and added hastily, "but these witches, Sir Robert. Their destruction—"

"They are not to be destroyed," Cecil said, flatly. "Driven back, driven off—bought off, for all I care!—but not destroyed."

It was a voice that brooked no argument. Marlowe opened his mouth anyway, intending to urge the very real dangers of such a policy, then closed it again, recognizing the futility of his appeal. "I'll need money, then," he said instead. "And you spoke of a letter."

Cecil nodded, and reached for an oddly shaped packet lying on the altar. As the light hit it, it became identifiably a bulging purse. Marlowe held out his hand automatically, and the secretary tossed it to him, saying, "The letter's within."

The poet caught the pouch one-handed, and whistled at its weight before knotting it to his belt, half hidden under the skirt of his doublet.

"That will be all," Cecil said. "Don't fail me."

Marlowe nodded—he would not bow to this man, except in mockery—and turned away. He had taken perhaps five steps before the secretary called his name.

"The Earl of Northumberland has lost a boy—a page in his household, I believe. Would you know anything about it?"

Marlowe froze for an instant, then, with exquisite care, made himself glance casually over his shoulder. "Not about any pages—and unless it's older than the usual run of pages, I wouldn't want it." He saw the shadow of disgust in Cecil's eyes, and pressed his advantage. "I've rather lost my taste for boys."

"One would hope so," the secretary murmured. "Very well, Marlowe."

This time, the poet did bow, a fraction too deeply, and had the satisfaction of seeing Cecil frown. Then he was outside the chapel, past the niche where Poley waited patiently for his master's call, and into the nave itself. The deeply shadowed space was almost empty, except for a single disapproving deacon trimming the few lamps, and it was all Marlowe could do to keep from running. He reached the twilit street with a gasp of relief, and stood for a long moment in the arch of the main doorway, his back to the still-warm stones, his attention divided between the street and the cathedral behind him. Cecil had given him an almost impossible task and, in the process, had let slip two very dangerous pieces of information. One, perhaps, was less dangerous than the other—it was easy enough to guess that the queen's ambassador to Scotland was also Cecil's agent—but the other . . . Marlowe shook his head, appalled by the double-edged power he suddenly possessed. That Cecil aspired to manipulate the king of Scots was information of an entirely different class. Sir Philip would not be easy to deceive about this mission, either, nor was he likely to approve of letting some, or any, of the witches escape—the hero of the Low Countries was, among other things, a very thorough man. And there was still the boy to be dealt with. If Northumberland's gone so far as to inquire of Cecil, Marlowe thought, I can't apprentice the brat to Ned—I can't do that to either of them—and I daren't leave him with Mary-Martha. I'll have to bring him with me, throw him on Sir Philip's mercy. . . . Which might not be a bad thing on its own, he added, after a moment's consideration. Having the boy to deal with might help distract Sir Philip from exactly why I'm here, and exactly what Cecil wants of me. I'll have to tell him some of it, of course—but never all. He loosened his rapier in its scabbard, feeling the awkward weight of Cecil's fee at his belt, and stepped into the darkening streets, bracing himself for the long walk home.

Chapter Six

Though dusty wits dare scorn astrology,
And fools can think those lamps of purest light
—Whose numbers, ways, greatness, eternity,
Promising wonders, wonder do invite—
To have for no cause birthright in the sky
But for to spangle the black weeds of night;
Or for some brawl which in that chamber high
They should still dance to please a gazer's sight.
For me, I do Nature unidle know,
And know great causes great effects procure;
And know those bodies high reign on the low.
And if these rules did fail, proof makes me sure,
 Who oft for judge my after-following race
 By only those two stars in Stella's face.
  Sir Philip Sidney, Sonnet XXVI

Sidney leaned against the sun-scarred paneling, staring out into the long garden. The ground had dried out somewhat since his return from London: the gardener's boy was lazily spading one of the beds bordering the main approach, now and then glancing up at the scudding clouds that threatened to cut off the thin sunlight altogether. Sidney smiled ruefully, one hand stealing to the knotted bone just above his left knee. I fear you're to be disappointed, Tom, he thought. I don't feel any signs of rain.

92

He sighed then, only too aware of the rent rolls and account books lying in an untidy heap on his broad desk, and of Dr. Dee's book, now locked with his own most treasured text in the brass-bound box in the cupboard beneath the window-seat, but did not turn away from the long window. For all that Madox expected—needed—his master to look over the books and certify the understewards' accounts as correct before issuing the instructions for maintaining the estate during this Scottish journey, and for all that it needed to be done very soon, Sidney could not quite bring himself to settle down to work again. I worked most of the morning, he told himself, attempting to salve his conscience. I only rode for an hour, or a little less, and then sat down to the accounts. Surely I'm entitled to a few moments' daydreaming. He smiled again, less comfortably than before. His wife would insist that he'd already done enough, that there was more than enough money in their coffers, so that he could afford to let Madox manage things as he pleased. Even though he knew it to be true, and knew even better that Madox could be trusted with his life as well as with his income, he found it impossible to rid himself of the habits formed in his youth, when his entire family had lived more or less hand to mouth, and he himself had lived in constant expectation of having to sell his land—sell his capital—in order to meet his mounting debts. Though the campaign in the Low Countries, and the governorships that had followed it—and his marriage to Sir Francis Walsingham's only child—had changed all that, he could not seem to change himself.

A movement in the yard below drew his attention, and he leaned forward slightly, his mild curiosity changing to alarm as he caught sight of the little procession. His daughter Elizabeth was at its head, her willow-green skirts draggled with mud; behind her came her nurse, her apple-cheeked face pink with angry concern, and the head groom, grey hair ruffled and on end, cap clutched nervously in both hands. She's had a fall, Sidney thought, and held his breath. He knew perfectly well that Rivers would never have allowed her to do anything dangerous—and, more important, that the groom was equally capable of stopping a sometimes willful child—and he could see that the girl wasn't seriously hurt . . . but she was still his only child, and likely to remain so. Sometime during the terrible days in Holland following her husband's near-fatal wound, Frances Sidney had miscarried of a seven-months' son, and had not conceived again.

Then Elizabeth looked up toward the study windows, losing her already battered hat in the process, and Sidney felt himself breathe again. The girl's face, flushed as much with embarrassment as with anger, broke into a sudden smile, and she dropped her father a quick curtsey before stooping to recover the hat. Its plume was sadly bent, and the nurse rushed forward, scolding, to sweep the girl indoors again. Left standing in the yard, the groom glanced up to the windows himself, touching his forehead respectfully as he saw Sidney standing there. His whole posture conveyed a sort of respectful reassurance; Sidney nodded, smiling, and waved in response. The groom bowed again, and backed away.

Sidney shook his head, wishing that Elizabeth would be more careful, then turned back toward his writing table. Before he could seat himself, however, there was a knock at the door. "Yes?" he began, but the door had already opened, and his sister sailed into the room.

"Good God, Philip, what are you wearing?" Mary Herbert, Countess of Pembroke, lifted both thin eyebrows in laughing disbelief.

Sidney glanced down at himself—he wore a long, fur-lined gown, common wear for scholars who sat unmoving at their books for long periods—and looked up guilelessly. "A gown."

"No, I meant those." Mary pointed an imperious finger at the boots that showed beneath the gown's hem. Obligingly, Sidney let the gown fall open further, extending his crooked leg to show the thigh-length boot. "Yes, very nice," the countess continued, "but do you know what they call that color?"

"Brown, I think," Sidney said. "Or perhaps tan? Greyish tan?"

"It's called 'dead Spaniard,' Philip. Is that tactful?"

Sidney laughed, unable to continue his pretense. "I know, I couldn't resist it." His laughter faded quickly, remembering Holland. "Though I can't say it's that good a match for the real thing."

"Which is probably just as well," Mary began, and stopped at the sound of hoofbeats on the road outside. "Were you expecting visitors?"

"I can't say I was. Henry is here . . . I think," Sidney answered, and stepped to the window. A single horseman was making his way up the long approach, a dark man in a short dark cloak, a man who handled his horse competently but not skillfully. In the same instant, Sidney recognized Christopher Marlowe, and realized that the playwright was carrying someone pillion. Sidney raised an eyebrow at that, but dismissed the thought almost at once. The strawhaired boy seemed no older than Elizabeth; whatever had possessed Marlowe to bring him here, it wasn't lust.

"Who is it?" Mary demanded.

"Master Marlowe," Sidney said, frowning slightly. And what, I wonder brings Marlowe to me? he wondered silently. I daresay Cecil has a hand in it, and I don't deny an experienced agent could be useful—but what could a boy have to do with anything?

Mary, who had been watching her brother's reactions closely, hid a frown of her own. Though she had asked no questions, she had friends enough at court to guess at many of the reasons behind Sidney's Scottish embassy, and could not feel entirely comfortable with the idea. Still, she knew better than to ask directly, and said only, "I should like to meet him, Philip. I've heard a great deal about him."

"I daresay." Sidney grinned. "I wouldn't believe all that Master Kyd says, either—I understand you're his patron now?"

"Henry is," Mary answered. "And I don't. I've also read his work—Master Marlowe's, I mean—and he once wrote a very pretty dedication to me." Her expressive face clouded briefly. "For Thomas Watson's last book, the one published just after he died." She shook herself. "Still, it was a very pretty piece of flattery."

"I'm sure." Sidney studied his sister for a moment longer. Mary Herbert was one of the handsomest women in England, he thought—even if ill-disposed persons described

her hair as copper gilt—as well as one of the most learned.
It would do Marlowe good to have to deal with such a
formidable lady. "If you wish it, I'd be glad to present him
to you."

"Thank you." Mary seated herself in the windowseat,
settling her wine-colored skirts with a practiced twist. The
pearls dangling from her cap bounced as she looked cheerfully up at her brother. "I'm doubly grateful you didn't
feel it necessary to warn me about him."

"I know better," Sidney answered, and smiled. "And
didn't I send you a copy of the *Ganymede* as soon as I'd
read it?"

The Countess of Pembroke lifted the painted fan she
carried at her girdle, modestly veiling her face, if not the
breasts half-revealed by her low-cut bodice, and winked at
him over the pearl-trimmed edge. Sidney managed to
smile in return, but could not help wondering if some of
the gossip he heard about his sister could be true. Surely
Pembroke would not be so complacent, he thought, and
surely Mary would think better of herself than to consort
with grooms—and surely I am only wondering this because I suspect my wife.

A discreet knock at the study door interrupted those
thoughts. "Yes?" Sidney called.

The door opened slowly. "I beg your pardon, Sir Philip,"
Grifin Madox said, with chilly disapproval, "but Master
Marlowe has arrived."

"Show him in, please, Madox," Sidney answered.

The disapproval in the steward's voice became glacial.
"Very well, Sir Philip." The door closed behind him with
pointed courtesy.

Mary laughed behind her fan. "I take it Madox doesn't
like your protegé."

"Not particularly." In spite of himself, Sidney's lips
twitched into a quick grin. "Marlowe can—does go out of
his way to shock the unwary."

Madox knocked again at the door, then opened it, saying
grimly, "Master Marlowe."

The playwright entered warily, still in his riding clothes,
though he'd discarded his cloak somewhere below. "Sir
Philip," he said, with a passable bow, and a wary glance

toward the windowseat. "Ma'am." The boy at his heels did his best to copy the man's gestures, his eyes huge and frightened.

Sidney's eyes narrowed—what was this boy, that Marlowe should bring him in here?—but he said, with perfect courtesy, "Mary, may I present Master Christopher Marlowe, sometime of Cambridge University, and now one of our more accomplished poets." He glanced at Marlowe. "My sister, the Countess of Pembroke."

Marlowe bowed again, more deeply. "My lady." He straightened, fixing his eyes on Sidney. "I beg your pardon, Sir Philip. If I'd realized you were engaged, I wouldn't've brought the boy."

"You surprise me, Master Marlowe," Mary said, and lifted her fan again. "I hadn't heard you were the man to conceal any of your affairs."

"I don't see any reason to conceal anything, my lady," Marlowe answered promptly. "Especially since I see my lady is a kindred spirit."

Two of a kind indeed, Sidney thought, and I think they should be separated. A thoughtful smile tugged at his lips. If only for Marlowe's virtue. He cleared his throat. "Mary, will you excuse us? I hadn't realized Master Marlowe's business was urgent."

The countess sobered at once, responding not so much to the words as to the note of appeal in her brother's voice. "Of course, Philip." She rose with a stirring of satin. "I trust we'll meet again, Master Marlowe."

The playwright bowed as she swept from the room, drawing the child out of her way. Straightening, he gave Sidney a truculent glance. "It's about the boy, Nathanial—" He stopped abruptly. "I don't even know your family name."

"Hawker." The boy's voice was faint with fear.

"Hawker," Marlowe repeated. He looked back at Sidney. "He's run away from Northumberland's household—he used to be his seeing boy. I found out the earl was still looking for him, so I couldn't apprentice him with Alleyn after all, and I brought him here. Will you help him?"

Sidney sighed. He was certain there was a good deal more to the story than the bald outline Marlowe had given him—and he meant to hear the full version before he committed himself irrevocably to anything—but there was no resisting the child's mute appeal. Or, he admitted, the opportunity of doing Northumberland a disservice. He distrusted the earl's supposedly classical magic, could have sworn, the one time he had attended a demonstration of the Percy's talent, that he had smelled sulphur. "Of course you may stay, Nathanial," he said aloud. "What do they call you—Nate?"

The boy nodded.

"Well, then, Nate. I'm Sir Philip Sidney, as Master Marlowe no doubt told you. As I said, you're welcome to stay here for as long as necessary—and you need not worry about his lordship." Sidney allowed his voice to drop slightly, having learned with his daughter that a touch of theatricality did no harm. "Northumberland is not welcome on my estates." That was a slight exaggeration, but Nathanial brightened.

"No, my lord?" he said eagerly, then, remembering his place, ducked his head in a sort of bow. "Thank you very much, my lord."

"You're most welcome," Sidney said. "Are you hungry?"

Nathanial hesitated. "We ate on the road, my lord."

Sidney smiled. "But are you hungry?" After a moment, the boy nodded silently. Sidney politely hid his grin, and reached for the bell standing on his table. When Madox appeared in answer to its summons, Sidney said, "Send for Nurse, please, Madox."

"At once, Sir Philip." The steward vanished, but reappeared so quickly that it was clear the nurse had been close at hand. "Goody Bourman," Madox announced, and closed the door behind the woman.

She darted a single curious glance at the boy, then curtsied briskly, fixing her eyes on her employer. "You sent for me, Sir Philip?"

"Yes, Nurse." Sidney nodded to the boy, who had crept close to Marlowe's side again. "This is Nathanial—Nate Hawker, who will be staying with us for a while." He saw the frown forming on the nurse's otherwise cheerful face, and added quickly, "Nate was in service with his lordship of Northumberland, and was badly treated there."

The frown had vanished from the woman's face as Sidney spoke, to be replaced by an expression of genuine concern. Northumberland's reputation had penetrated even into Kent. "Of course, Sir Philip," she said, and curtsied again. "Poor lamb." She turned to the boy. "Come with me, Nate?"

Nathanial nodded again, shyly. "Yes, ma'am."

"Nurse," the woman corrected firmly. "Just Nurse. Now, come along, I'm sure you're hungry, riding all the way from London—riding pillion," she added, with a disapproving glance at Marlowe. "I'll see you fed, and then we'll see what we can do about some clean clothes." She held out her hand, and the boy came to her willingly. They paused in the doorway, the nurse glancing over her shoulder. "I beg your pardon, Sir Philip, but I thought you should be told. Mistress Elizabeth took a fall today, riding with Rivers, but she's not hurt, more than a bruise or two."

"I saw," Sidney said, nodding. "But thank you."

The nurse curtsied again, and left the study, drawing Nathanial after her.

Sidney looked back at the younger man, waiting. After a moment, Marlowe's full mouth curved briefly into a humorless smile, but he said nothing. Sidney's answering smile was equally cold.

"You didn't come here only on the boy's account."

"No."

Marlowe's expression hardened for a fleeting instant, and Sidney felt a moment's bitter pleasure. So I was right, he thought, and said aloud, "Sir Robert sent you."

Marlowe looked up quickly, eyes widening a little as though the words had startled him. Sidney's smile twisted. You were never an actor, Christopher, he thought, but kept silent.

"He did," the poet said at last, and spread his hands as though abandoning a position. "He told me her majesty was sending you to Scotland, and suggested—" He gave the simple word a savage turn. "—you might find some use for me." He paused, and, when Sidney did not reply, added, "As I am an experienced agent."

There was a note of bravado in his voice, but Sidney

ignored it, staring past the younger man toward the books that lined the study's interior walls. There was more to Cecil's orders than Marlowe had said, of that he felt certain. The question is, he thought, whether it's worth forcing him to admit it. He turned his gaze back to the poet, studying the other man dispassionately. Marlowe's face was set, closed, thoughts veiled behind his truculent stare. I expect, Sidney thought, he's been told to spy on me—to keep Cecil informed. That would be Robert Cecil's style, even if it wasn't Marlowe's. Or is it? he wondered. There was a cold anger rising in him, and he disciplined it with the control born of long practice. Marlowe had spied on friends before: his first work for the government had been at Rheims, spying on the English Catholics there. Some of those would-be priests would have been classmates of his from the university; all would have been men he'd come to know well during his months of supposed study. Sidney's mouth tightened fractionally. Walsingham had let slip once that Marlowe had done good work at Rheims.

But that was neither here nor there. Sidney smiled inwardly, still watching the poet. I told Robert that any of your betrayals will be grand ones, he thought. I fear this may be your chance. He allowed the smile to touch his lips, rather enjoying the new wariness in Marlowe's eyes. "I'm sure you'll execute your various commissions satisfactorily," he said, and saw the poet's mask slip for an instant. I knew I was right, Sidney thought again, but before he could pursue the matter, there was a knock at the door, and one of the maidservants entered.

"I beg your pardon, Sir Philip, but Lady Sidney would like to see you as soon as she may."

Sidney sighed. It was either Elizabeth's fall or the boy Nathanial; he had rather hoped that both could be put off until the evening, but one look at the maid's mild determined face told him otherwise. "Tell Lady Sidney I'll come to her," he said. "Is she in her rooms?"

"Yes, Sir Philip." The maid bobbed a quick curtsey. "I'll tell her."

Sidney nodded, dismissing her, and the woman backed hastily from the room. Sidney glanced again at the poet, considering just what he should say. His anger had cooled slightly, enough so that he could recognize and even sympathize with the awkwardness of Marlowe's position—Robert Cecil was not a man whom one could refuse with impunity—but things had to be clear between them. "Cecil set you to spy on me," he said flatly. Marlowe blinked, began to stammer some answer or denial, but Sidney held up his hand. "Don't bother, I know him—and you—better than that. I'm simply asking you if I can rely on you."

There was a long silence, and then, quite slowly, Marlowe nodded. "Yes," he said, "you can."

And I even think I believe you, Sidney thought, with another inward smile, though God alone knows why I should. "You'll excuse me, then," he said aloud, and gestured to the books shelved along the walls. "Make free of my library, if you wish. Madox will show you to your room when it's ready."

Marlowe bowed to his patron's departing back, and did not straighten fully until the door had closed behind him. Only then did he allow himself an almost soundless sigh of relief. At least Sidney had not questioned him further about Cecil's orders—though he might still, and this had been unpleasant enough. The poet grimaced at the memory, angry at the taint of fear and humiliation it had left behind. He did not like this feeling of being a helpless pawn between two greater forces; he would have to find some way of asserting his own real power. After all, he told himself, he knew enough about Cecil's ambitions, and Sidney had said enough, about Cecil and about others, the trusting man, to let him make his own terms with either side. . . . For some reason, though, the idea of carrying tales to Robert Cecil made him feel like a schoolboy again, caught playing questionable games with the other boys. He shied away from the doubled image, and was angry at himself for flinching. Almost in defiance, he turned to the shelves of books, reaching for the oldest binding.

To his annoyance, it was an edition of Hesiod; he started to return it to its place, but the title page caught his eye. It was an Italian edition—Venetian—and old, but it had been rebound at least once since its printing some fifty years earlier. He turned the pages with automatic caution, grateful at first for the distraction, and then with the scholar's genuine curiosity. He knew the *Works and Days*, and the *Theogony*, but bound with those familiar pieces were a collection of hymns praising the ancients' gods. He turned through those more slowly, wincing at the condition of the pages—they looked as though the book had been carried in a leaking saddlebag—and pausing now and then to murmur a line or two aloud. Several were, on a hasty reading, quite lovely, deft recountings of familiar myths, and he wondered briefly if it would be worth his while to make a proper translation. He reached for the next page, and it stuck. He swore mildly, prying cautiously at the fragile paper, but it refused to come loose. The next twenty pages seemed to be glued together into a solid mass, as though something viscous had set there. He glanced toward Sidney's desk, looking for a penknife with which to slit the obstruction, but hesitated. There was too much chance of damaging the pages; he would wait until he could treat it properly. Instead, he turned over the stuck pages together, frowning.

He was no longer in the hymns, that much was obvious at once. Instead, a marginal note in Roman characters identified the writer as Proclus and the work as the *Chrestomathy*. However, it was the note beneath it that caught his eye. He squinted at the crabbed lettering, a clear if elderly hand, automatically translating the Greek: *Then came the Amazon, the daughter of great-souled Ares, the slayer of men.*

He tilted his head to one side, studying the words. The text to the right was a summary of a tale about the Amazon —Penthesileia—who fought at Troy and was killed there by Achilles, who was then mocked by the bitter Thersites for supposedly loving her. Achilles kills Thersites and, after some dispute, was purified of the killing by Odysseus. There was more to the story, but Marlowe did not turn the page, staring unseeing at the faded print. The simple plot had potential—the conflict between passion and duty or, better still, between the passion of love and the passion to kill, twin passions shared by twinned enemies. . . . It would play. He spoke the Greek line aloud, enjoying the stark power it conjured for him: "Then came the Amazon, the slayer of men."

The sound of footsteps outside the door roused him from his reverie and, almost instinctively, he tucked the battered little volume into his purse and turned to face the door. There was a knock, and it opened, to reveal Sidney's grim-faced steward.

"Your room is ready," he said. "If you'll come with me."

Marlowe nodded, and followed the older man from the library. Madox led the way through the main hall, toward the main staircase, and the poet's mouth twisted into a quick grin. Clearly Sidney had left orders that he was to be treated as a guest rather than a client; Madox would obey, but his very obedience would be a reminder of the other's real place. Marlowe glanced around the hall with the deliberate appreciation of an equal, and saw Madox's lips tighten, biting back an angry comment. The poet hid his smile, and looked up toward the gallery at the far end of the hall.

Two figures stood there, framed by the carved posts like figures on the upper stage. Sidney and his lady wife, Marlowe thought, and slowed his steps slightly, watching with disguised curiosity. Like every man in London, he had heard the rumors that said there was no love lost between the two. He had read Sidney's sonnets, too, and knew—along with all of England—that the Stella of the poems was not Frances Sidney. He had also heard, though this was less common knowledge, a matter more to be whispered than to be trumpeted abroad, that the Earl of Essex wasn't content with the Queen's somewhat dusty favors, and sought his real amusement elsewhere. Marlowe's eyes narrowed, staring at the stiff figures above him. He had never quite believed that talk, though he'd never expected to see much evidence of passion in what was, after all, a merely advantageous marriage. Now, however . . . There was something in the very stillness of the pair, and the set quiet of Sidney's face, like a man contemplating amputation, that proved it all to be true. I wonder why? Marlowe thought. She's fourteen years his junior, true, but it's nothing out of the ordinary—and he seems vigorous enough. The stillborn son? God knows, there was talk enough about it at the time—I still remember the intercessions, and the thanksgiving pamphlets—and there were one or two who criticized her for taking too little care of the Sidney line. Still, Sidney himself would never have blamed her . . . and maybe that in itself was the problem. How can you be forgiven your guilt, if the other won't accuse you? His lip curled slightly. If it was forgiveness she wanted, she need only ask.

He glanced again toward the gallery. There was something disconcertingly familiar in the carriage of Frances Sidney's head and shoulders, something about the quiet, waiting hands that reminded him of someone. . . . Walsingham, of course, and she was Walsingham's daughter, his namesake. She would respond in bitter kind to what she could only see as silent charity, and Sidney's courtesy would fail against Walsingham pride. Marlowe shrugged the thought away. Let Sidney sort out his own troubles, he told himself, and followed Madox from the hall.

"So there is a chance that the Earl of Northumberland—the Wizard Earl of Northumberland—will be looking for his boy?" Frances Sidney placed one thin hand on the carved rail that edged the gallery, the gesture a mute declaration of war.

Sidney shook his head, willing himself to ignore the signal. "A remote one, if any at all, and I doubt he'd expect Marlowe would have the sheer nerve to bring him to me. I can't think that Northumberland would have placed too much value on young Nate. He was a tool, nothing more, and when you're the Earl of Northumberland, you can always buy another tool."

"If it means spending, he won't be happy."

She looked like a small, fragile doll, Sidney thought, but was not deceived. Fashion dictated the milky skin, half veiled by the sheer lawn partlet, the fine white hand displayed so carefully against the rich garnet-red velvet of her skirt, the heavy jewels studding her cap and woven through her dusty-brown hair. Her true self showed only in the hand she had laid against the railing, flattening it until the veins showed stark against the pale skin, and in her heavy-lidded eyes.

Frances sighed, aware of his scrutiny, and even more aware of his standards of comparison. Mary Herbert was a much-admired beauty, whatever else she might be. . . .

She pushed the thought aside before it was fully formed, turning her mind to the matter at hand. "I trust you when you say he won't be looking. But what do you intend the boy should do here? You certainly don't need a scrying boy." She spoke the last words with a touch of the dry humor that always caught her husband by surprise, making him catch his breath and look again. He started to smile, but she hurried on, oblivious to his sudden pleasure, prodding at her ancient, unhealed wound. "Or do you simply need a boy around, in general?"

Sidney bit back his first, instinctive answer. Never, by word or thought, had he blamed her for their son's death. How dare she now take his act of simple charity as a rebuke? "I had thought," he said, slowly, keeping his voice even with an effort, "that he might provide a companion for Elizabeth. They're of an age. And he's clever. He might as well have the benefit of some learning—he could be schooled into a suitable secretary."

Frances fixed him with a hawk's stare, the heavy lids lifting slightly. "Elizabeth is young. She's at a very impressionable age. I'm not at all sure that some farmer's son from Northumberland—"

"Yorkshire, actually," Sidney corrected, in his most precise tone.

Frances nodded with deceptive meekness. "Yorkshire, then—is a fit companion. We don't want to risk a mesalliance."

"The girl is ten. She may be impressionable, but she's still very young, and she isn't ignorant of her station. Besides, a girl is older than a boy of that age. If anything, she'll twist Nate around her finger, and turn him into her faithful esquire. She has a gift for it."

Frances shook her head, rejecting the tentative olive branch. "I cannot like it, Philip. Doesn't this boy have parents he can be returned to? Perhaps he'd even be happier with his own family. Most children would be."

"Happier on some miserable farm in Yorkshire, in such proximity to his grace of Northumberland?" Sidney's voice was sharper than he had intended. "I wouldn't return him to the family that could sell him into such service."

Frances studied her husband's face for a long moment,

then, with a movement that was not in the least submissive, bowed her head. "Very well, my lord."

Sidney took a deep breath, his anger frustrated by her outward docility. "Very well, then." He paused, wanting to stalk away, but forced himself to stop, to continue the conversation. "You will mind Penshurst in my absence? You know where all the papers are." He smiled faintly, unable to keep a hint of malice from his next words. "Madox is usually much happier with you in charge. I wish you the joy of him."

For a brief second, Frances's eyes betrayed her anger, but then the heavy lids veiled their gleam. She dropped a shallow curtsey. "As ever, the soul of consideration, my lord."

Sidney winced at the twist she gave the simple words, though he kept his face impassive. Surely she was just referring to the occasionally heavy household responsibilities he placed on her, not taunting him outright with giving Essex the entry to her company while he was away. For a brief, murderous moment, the words he'd never yet spoken, blame and bitter accusation, trembled on his lips, but he bit them back. He would not brawl with her: they both deserved better.

"For dinner this evening," Frances said, "your Master Marlowe, Sir Robert, and Lady Mary?"

"You're forgetting Henry again," Sidney said.

Frances looked honestly startled. "My lord of Pembroke? Did he accompany your sister this time?"

The words were meant to sting—though how she dared to hint at Mary's unchastity was beyond his comprehension—but there was so much truth in Frances's surprise that Sidney could not stop himself from smiling. It was Pembroke's own fault that he was so often overlooked. A scholarly, bookish man, he was like some kind of nocturnal animal, rarely viewed outside his native habitat of the library—until he returned to London and his beloved theaters. "Yes, he did."

Frances nodded, sighing softly. "My lord of Pembroke, then, and, of course, Fulke Greville. I don't suppose you can promise that your playwright and your sister won't be too outrageous?"

"I'll do my best," Sidney said, and knew he would do nothing of the kind. Frances dropped him another curtsey, this one so deep he could not help but suspect her of irony, and swept away down the gallery, her skirts hissing behind her. Sidney stared after her, and swallowed a curse. He would not allow himself to be provoked, not now, when there was so much still to be done. He took a deep breath, running a hand through his close-cropped hair. At the moment, his chief responsibility was to his guests, and to Pembroke in particular; he straightened his back, wincing at the dull ache that had settled again in his scarred thigh, and went in search of his brother-in-law.

To his surprise, Pembroke had not hidden himself in the library, but instead had been persuaded to join his wife and Fulke Greville in the bowling alley that ran alongside the formal garden. Mary's laughter echoed clearly along the shady walk, and Sidney paused just outside the trellised entrance to the alley, suddenly uncertain of himself. He could see Mary quite clearly from where he stood, the sunlight spangling her coppery hair with lights like jewels. She was laughing still, her overskirt caught up in one beringed hand, her half-bared breasts heaving against the stiff edge of her bodice. Pembroke watched her with something like adoration, a faint, sweet smile touching his lips; Greville was smiling, too, though his gaze was less besotted. Even Sidney's own Elizabeth, her riding clothes exchanged for a more decorous dress of sanguine wool, was looking at her aunt with an expression of worship. And that, Sidney thought, I must put a stop to. If my sister—and perhaps my wife—are wantons, I can't let my only daughter follow their example. Oh, Mary, why must you do this to me?

Still, he did not move from beneath the archway, unwilling to spoil their pleasure in the foolish game. Mary stooped then, controlling her laughter, and made her cast. The heavy ball trundled across the smoothed lawn, urged on by her excited cries, but stopped short of its target.

"I have you now, my dear," Pembroke said, and Elizabeth gave a little cry of disappointment.

"Uncle Pembroke, it's not fair. You have all the luck today."

"You may play my bowl, Mistress Elizabeth," Greville interposed smoothly, glancing toward the trellised arch. "I want a word with your father. If you'll excuse me, my lord?"

Pembroke nodded, already studying the pattern of the scattered balls with the same concentration he would give a line of verse, or a newly printed manuscript.

"Hurry back, and bring Philip with you," Mary said cheerfully, but her attention was also obviously on the game.

"Philip? What's wrong?"

Sidney managed a smile, knowing already that he could not deceive his closest friend. "Waiting. Wanting to be started, I think."

"I see." Greville smoothed his moustache, absently twisting it to the proper upward curve, studying Sidney out of the corner of his eye. "Shall we walk?" He took Sidney's arm firmly without waiting for a reply, turning him down the shadowed tunnel. Sidney resisted for an instant, then relaxed with a rueful smile, and let the other man lead him back into the arbor's green light.

Greville watched him sidelong as they walked, gauging his moment. "Have you spoken with Frances?" he asked at last.

Sidney shook his head. Greville could seem so guileless, so utterly innocent in his questions, when in truth he was perhaps the most crafty man at court—and that very innocence kept one from resistance. After a moment, Sidney laughed. "You're worse than Marlowe, you know. I think the reason the two of you don't get along is that you're cut from the same cloth. Yes, I spoke with her." The smile died from his face. "And I think I've driven her into Essex's arms at last. God, what am I to do?"

Greville kept his hand on the other man's arm. "What happened?"

Sidney stopped, staring blindly at a vine twining its way through the hedge. It bore a delicate flower, pale yellow, the petals already fraying from the stem. "She wanted to know what I intended to do about Nathanial—the boy Marlowe brought with him."

Greville nodded.

"I didn't think it needed to be explained. The boy needs a home, and I will be damned if I'll send him back to Northumberland. It's the only thing to be done. But she doesn't want him here."

Greville smiled sadly. Of course she doesn't, he thought, and of course there's nothing else you could do to protect the boy—what a tangle. He hesitated, searching for just the right words, and Sidney rushed on, unheeding.

"I told her I thought it would be good for Elizabeth to have a companion of her own age, that, if the boy proved clever, he could be trained as a clerk or a secretary . . . She did not agree." In spite of himself, there was a world of bitterness in the words. "She fears Elizabeth—a child of ten, mind you—might form an affection for him, that we should fear a mesalliance. Good God, I intended to send him away to school in a few years anyway—" He broke off abruptly, glaring at the flower.

Greville waited, uneasily twisting the end of his moustache, but Sidney seemed to have made an end. Greville sighed. "There is a thing you can do, Philip. To make things easier for her, I mean. She's a proud woman—name of God, she's a Walsingham—and she blames herself for losing your son."

Sidney turned on him, his eyes hot and hard. "Damn it, I've never—"

"Never uttered a word of blame," Greville agreed. "No. Nor blamed her by your manner. Don't you think that makes it worse? She does blame herself, and others have blamed her—"

Sidney looked away, his face set. "She has no need—it would be foolish to feel guilty for it, and I never thought my wife was a fool."

Greville made a face, but accepted his defeat. "Be that as it may, Philip, there is something you can do that will make it better."

"Oh?" Sidney's tone was not encouraging.

"Take the boy with you. You don't have a page at the moment, do you? He's been in a noble household, he should be able to learn his duties quickly enough."

Sidney paused, turning the suggestion over in his mind, searching for flaws. Greville was right, unfortunately, and

Sidney sighed. "That would be kinder, wouldn't it? God, Fulke, I didn't mean to hurt her. I thought she'd see that. Damn Marlowe anyway for bringing him here." Greville grinned at that, and Sidney managed a rather rueful smile. It faded quickly. "Fulke, all I've done is clear the way for Essex."

Greville snorted, feeling himself on somewhat firmer ground. "I told you, she's a Walsingham, and therefore a woman of discernment." Sidney lifted an eyebrow in pointed question, and Greville sighed. "Of course, I don't understand what her majesty sees in him, either. He seems to have the most astonishing effect on women of sense."

"I've never been able to see it, either. Not after Robin," Sidney agreed softly.

"No. Leicester was a man."

"Take him for all in all, I shall not look upon his like again." Sidney took a deep breath. "God help me, I'll do as you suggest. You're right again."

Greville smiled. "There's a price, Philip."

Sidney looked up, startled, but answered instantly, "Name it."

"Let me come with you."

"My God, Fulke, there's nothing I'd like better, but this isn't an ordinary embassy—"

Greville held up his hand. "I guessed as much, and Robert's told me some of what he knows. And, to be perfectly blunt, her majesty's still as stingy as ever. I can help with the immediate expenses."

Sidney shook his head. "My affairs are better than they used to be, I promise. But I would welcome your company." He grinned suddenly. "If only to lend presence to the delegation."

Greville smiled back. "That's settled, then. Shall we join the others?"

Sidney hesitated for a moment. He knew he should probably go to Frances, inform her of his decision regarding the boy, but he could not bring himself to force a second confrontation in a single day. He nodded, and let himself be drawn back toward the bowling alley.

PART TWO

PART TWO

Chapter Seven

Anger makes dull men witty, but it keeps them poor.
  Francis Bacon, Apothegms attr. to Elizabeth I

The court had removed to Richmond. The air was sweeter there, the park wider and wilder, and, though the young men who danced attendance on her might pine for the excitements of London, the queen of England felt herself renewed. Come the height of summer, she would go farther afield: to Hampton Court, or, better still, to her beloved Nonesuch. It was too early in the year, and there was too much business still to be attended to, to think of that, but Elizabeth sighed a little, and did not heed the pretty youth who sang for her in her privy chamber. The boy—he wore the livery of the choir school—faltered, aware of her inattention, and his exquisite voice cracked. Elizabeth recalled herself enough to smile at him, and the boy sang on. His cheeks were red with shame, but the blush faded as he gained confidence again. The queen's smile grew almost wistful as she listened. Her Robin, her own Leicester, had sung that song for her many a time, though his voice had never been as pure as this. Sitting here, with the windows opened to the breeze from the immaculate gardens, heavy with the scent of sunlight and

113

early flowers, her ladies in white and silver murmuring over their embroidery, she could imagine that he might still come riding up to her, across the magnificent park, to sweep her away with his compliments.

She laughed a little as the song ended, and beckoned to the boy, who came up to her with a pretty bow, blushing again. "Well sung, lad, you have a lovely voice. And you may tell your teachers, too, you've been well trained." She gestured to Lady Rich, who sat nearest the royal chair, and that lady rose quickly. She curtsied, and presented the queen's purse; Elizabeth took it, and, without examining the contents, handed it to the boy.

"Take this," she said, "and see that you and your fellows dine well."

The boy bowed again, and stammered shy thanks, clutching the purse. Elizabeth could see one wondering finger tracing the monogram embroidered on the heavy canvas, and was absurdly flattered by the naive admiration. A steward came forward at Lady Rich's discreet signal, and drew the boy and the young music-master who'd accompanied him away toward the kitchens. They would be fed there, and sent home in one of the royal barges, a treat that would feed their conceit for weeks. Elizabeth leaned back in her chair, still smiling. After a moment, one of the younger ladies-in-waiting took up the discarded lute, and began idly to pick out a tune, the instrument golden against her snowy silks.

"Your Majesty."

Elizabeth looked up at the steward's apologetic voice.

"I beg your pardon, but my lord Burleigh craves a word with your majesty."

Elizabeth lifted an eyebrow in surprise. "Admit him. And you, my ladies, be so good as to withdraw."

The ladies-in-waiting were far too well trained to resent such an order, but rose hastily, silks rustling, filing out through the door at the far end of the apartment. Only Lady Rich hesitated and, when the queen did not order her to follow the rest, seated herself on a cushion by the door, just out of earshot.

"My Lord Burleigh," the steward announced gravely, "and the Master of the Revels."

Elizabeth's eyebrows rose further, even as she extended her hand for their salutations. "Well, Spirit, I hadn't expected to see you again today. Sit down, sir, by all means."

"Thank you, your Majesty." Burleigh lowered himself stiffly onto the stool that stood by the queen's feet, and folded his hands over the head of his ebony cane. Sir Edmund Tilney hovered unhappily at his shoulder, and Elizabeth shot him a wary look.

"What brings you here?"

It was Burleigh who answered. "It's a matter of a play, your Majesty."

"A play?" Elizabeth frowned.

"Yes, your Majesty," Burleigh said. "It was brought before Sir Edmund in the usual way, and he judged its contents to be of interest to me. I recommended that the license be refused, and thought, further, that the matter should be brought before your majesty."

"What is this—play?" Elizabeth asked, and glared at the Master of the Revels.

"It's entitled *The Astronomers*, your Majesty," Tilney answered. He was sweating freely beneath his heavy gown, though the privy chamber was not particularly warm. "Written for the Lord Pembroke's Men, by one Benjamin Jonson—a new playwright, your Majesty, but of unsavory reputation."

"That matters less than the matter of the play," Elizabeth said tartly. "Which was?"

The Master of the Revels so far forgot himself as to wipe his brow. Burleigh said, with deliberation, "It concerns a lady of title and fortune, a very great lady indeed, who is gulled of that same fortune by a pair of astronomers. One of them is a fool who believes he speaks with angels, and the other—the younger—is a lascivious rogue who seduces the lady, persuades her to marry a man much inferior to herself when it is clear he has gotten her with child, and then persuades the cuckold that the child is an angelic changeling."

There was a dangerous silence. The queen's mouth contracted into a thin line, and the jewels at her throat winked suddenly, as though she breathed more quickly. Burleigh continued, with even greater deference, "I could not think, your Majesty, that this was a fitting time to mock so excellent a servant of your Majesty's as Doctor Dee."

Elizabeth drew a deep breath, and looked at the master of the revels. "You did right to refuse the license, and did well to bring it to my lord Burleigh's attention. I compliment you on your acuteness." She looked back at Burleigh, her painted brows drawing together into an angry frown. "Spirit, where is the Earl of Pembroke?"

Burleigh bowed his head in thought, outwardly unmoved by his mistress's awful tones. "I believe he is either at Penshurst or at Wilton, your Majesty. I do not think he is in London."

"Fetch him," Elizabeth said, and rose from her chair. Burleigh rose with her, hastily, and the Master of the Revels bowed very low. "I wish to speak with him. As soon as possible."

Burleigh bowed profoundly. "It shall be done, your Majesty."

It took two days for Burleigh's messengers to find the earl, and another day for Pembroke to post hurriedly up to Richmond. Elizabeth received him in her presence chamber, a sure sign of her displeasure, and Pembroke's nervousness was very evident in his voice.

"I am here at your command, your majesty," he said, with his most deferential bow. "How may I serve you?"

Elizabeth eyed him judicially. "I understand you lend your name and countenance to a company of actors, my lord."

"I have done so, an it please your Majesty," Pembroke answered.

"It does not please me," Elizabeth snapped, but she had heard honest confusion in Pembroke's voice, and her temper eased a little. "They do not please me."

"Indeed, your Majesty, I am most heartily sorry, and will do whatever I may to make amends," Pembroke answered. "Say but the word, and they shall be chastised even as I chastise myself."

"Have you read a new play—your company's new play, my lord—entitled *The Astronomers?*"

Pembroke shook his head. "No, your Majesty, I have

not, nor was it offered to me for my opinion, though it seems I was remiss in not demanding it. But, sooth to say, your Majesty, I didn't know they were planning to offer a new work."

"I do believe you, my lord," Elizabeth said. She fixed Pembroke with another long stare, the deepest lines easing from her face. "Were you at Penshurst when my Spirit's men found you?"

"No, your Majesty," Pembroke answered, warily, "but I'd just returned from there."

"Then you're aware that Philip Sidney rides to Scotland as my ambassador?" Elizabeth waited until Pembroke had bowed his head in acknowledgement before she continued. "I speak in confidence, my lord, when I say I fear that this—satire, I suppose one must call it—has something to do with his mission there. It is a matter of some arcane concern, foreseen by Doctor Dee, and I find it troubling that this play seems intended to undermine confidence in my astronomer."

"I can't say, your Majesty," Pembroke stammered, "not having seen the manuscript."

"It portrays an old astronomer who is the foolish dupe of a younger man, a rogue and criminal," Burleigh interjected quietly, "who tricks his master into believing he speaks with angels."

Pembroke's eyes widened in sudden understanding. "Ned Kelly," he said softly.

"Just so," Elizabeth said. "I'll be plain with you, my lord. The mob has attacked Doctor Dee before, and I'll not have that again, not now. Tilney has refused to license this—play—which should be enough for any band of common players. Nonetheless, my lord, I wish you to convey my personal displeasure."

"I will certainly do so, your majesty," Pembroke answered. He hesitated, but then, encouraged by the queen's moderating tone, said cautiously, "Is it only coincidence, your Majesty, that this happens now?"

Elizabeth smiled without humor. "If it is not, my lord, I trust you to find it out."

Pembroke made his deepest bow. "I shall, your Majesty, I swear it."

Elizabeth's expression softened then. "I know you will, my lord, for I've ever counted on your good service. But the time's too dangerous for such a play."

"And so I will tell them," Pembroke answered fervently, and kissed the hand extended to him. "So I'll tell them indeed."

Chapter Eight

We must make philosophy wait and submit to divinity. Every science must keep its proper bounds.
Thomas Hall, Vindiciae Literarum

It took several days for Sidney, occupied as he was with the complex business of his departure, to find a moment's private conversation with his wife. Even then, hesitating at the door of her withdrawing room, he could hear Madox's respectful tones and her own low-voiced replies, and knew he could find reason to delay another hour or more. He shook away the craven thought, and tapped lightly on the door, then pushed it open before he could change his mind. Madox looked up at his entry, and made a respectful bow. Frances glanced toward him, but said nothing.

"I trust everything's arranged to your liking, madam?" Sidney asked, and knew he sounded hostile.

"Admirably so, sir," Frances answered, quite calmly.

"You may go, then, Madox," Sidney said. "I wish to speak to Lady Sidney alone."

Madox blinked, looking as close to discomfited as Sidney had ever seen him. The steward bowed again, and moved with stately dignity toward the door. As he pushed it open, Mary swept in, past Madox's polite reverence.

"Good day, Frances, Philip. Do either of you ride to-

119

day?" Mary herself was dressed for riding, her mannish doublet only emphasizing the magnificent femininity of the body beneath, a man's tall hat perched precariously atop her artfully untidy curls. Frances's mouth tightened almost imperceptibly, well aware of the contrast between her own sad-hued gown, the partlet pinned close to hide her slenderness, and Mary's abundant beauty. Penelope Rich was just another such, she thought. But . . . *the brown girl, she has house and land; Fair Stella, she had none.* Or not enough of either, to recoup the Sidney fortune. She pushed aside the thought, and managed to respond with a sort of off-hand grace.

"I thank you, no. I still have a great deal of business to attend to."

"Philip?" Mary glanced at her brother, apparently unaware of the barb hidden in the other woman's words.

"Not at the moment, Mary," Sidney answered.

Mary gave an impish grin, but mercifully did not speak her thought. "I'll wish you both a good morning, then," she said, and withdrew, closing the door behind her.

Sidney stood for a long moment, only too well aware of the shuttered tension in his wife's face. It's not true, he wanted to say, it's just a nasty, scurrillous tale, this whisper that Mary and I are more devoted than is proper for brother and sister. I don't know where the rumor sprang from, fully grown and fully armed, but it's there, and as false as any other myth. There was something in Frances's eyes that silenced his outcry, rendering protest both useless and vaguely undignified. He said instead, "There were some things I felt we needed to discuss, before I left."

"Of course, sir." Frances turned away, to seat herself on a low footstool. Her dark grey skirts pooled around her, the gold chatelaine a bright fall across her lap, but the picture was unconscious, unstudied. She gestured to the room's single chair. "Please, be comfortable."

I haven't been comfortable here in years, Sidney thought, but seated himself, stretching the scarred leg out to its fullest length in hopes of easing the nagging pain. As usual, he wore high boots below the loose slops, hiding the twisted bone that was revealed by even the thickest stockings, but today he fancied he could see the deformity outlined by the soft leather. He thrust the thought aside, and said, "I hope you're satisfied with the arrangements I've made with Madox?"

It was, he had thought, an unobjectionable opening, but Frances hesitated anyway, weighing the words. "Yes, I believe so," she said at last. "I appreciate your leaving me such authority."

"To whom else would I leave it?" Sidney asked, with some asperity. He curbed his temper with an effort, and hurried on before she could respond. "There were two other things which I needed to discuss with you. First, I must tell you that Master Marlowe will be returning to London tomorrow."

"Good." A fleeting smile crossed Frances's lips. "He does distress the household."

Sidney's mouth twitched in spite of himself. That was a mild term for the reaction of some of the older and more conservative servants—men and women who had been members of his father's household, and remembered with brutal clarity the reversals of religion under Edward and under Mary—to the atheist poet's presence. "He won't be back here before we leave," Sidney continued aloud. "We'll meet him in London—he says he has business there."

"I daresay," Frances murmured. She nodded briskly, visibly reshuffling her table and her menus. "I can't say it's bad news. And the other matter, sir?"

Sidney hesitated, uncomfortably uncertain of how to begin. "It's about Nate Hawker," he said at last, and winced as Frances's face closed against him. "I—wish to apologize for having seemed unfeeling. I had no intention of injuring you in any way." He paused, but she said nothing, and he continued, more slowly, "I thought— It seemed the best thing I could do was to bring the boy with me to Scotland, to act as my page. When I return, we can make proper provision for his future. He has served in a noble household, after all; I've spoke to Madox about training him—"

Frances nodded. "So Madox said."

"Burn him," Sidney exclaimed. "I wanted to tell you—" He broke off, flushing in embarrassment.

Unaccountably, Frances smiled. "And so you have." Her face softened slightly. "I am exceedingly grateful for this, Philip."

Sidney managed a rather shamefaced smile. "I'm afraid I was thick-headed, my dear. It was Fulke who suggested it."

"That was kind of him," Frances answered. "But I am grateful." Her face changed subtly, as though a shadow had passed across the sun. Sidney, recognizing the fleeting pain, bit back an exclamation of dismay. He wanted to reach out to her, to catch her hands in his and tell her that it was all right, not to mind, that there would be other sons—but that last, at least, did not seem to be true, and nothing he had ever said had served to convince her that in the end it did not matter. She had been herself an heiress; she understood even better than most women the value of a son and heir. That bitter knowledge made her untouchable, and killed his words of reassurance. Sidney stared at his wife, wishing he could find some way to ease her pain, and saw her shoulders stiffen. The moment had passed, and she was businesslike again.

"There are just a few things I would like to go over with you," she said, and rose gracefully to her feet. Sidney rose with her.

"Of course," he said.

"Young Madox will go with you, in charge of the baggage?"

Sidney nodded.

"Then we'll need to consider who takes his place as understeward," Frances said. "Old Madox has suggested Paul Atwood, but I'm not certain he has the experience for the post."

"He is young," Sidney agreed. "Still, Madox is no fool. . . . Perhaps we should have him in, and discuss this more fully?"

It was a sort of peace offering, and Frances nodded her agreement. "I think that would be good, Philip. Thank you."

Marlowe knelt by his open clothes chest, sorting through a heap of sleeves and shirts and stockings, one ear cocked to the noises from the street. He had ridden up from Penshurst only the day before, pleading business of his own that must be settled before leaving for Scotland, and Sidney had insisted that he take one of the horses from the Penshurst stables, rather than continuing to pay for the rented hack. Marlowe had not protested too much—it was a pleasure to ride a steady, sweet-tempered animal instead of the bony nags most of the hire-stables supplied, and a double pleasure to do so at another's expense—but now that he was in London, he could not help feeling a little nervous. Mary-Martha had no stable to her house, of course. The poet had been forced to rent a stall from squint-eyed Michael Gorges, who owned the ale-house at the end of Hog Lane, and a part interest in a bawdy-house across the river, if neighborhood gossip spoke truth, and was beginning to regret the bargain. Not that the borrowed horse was any great steed, just a placid, somewhat elderly animal that would get its rider to his destination in one unbruised piece, but he had no desire to lose something belonging to Sidney.

Marlowe shook himself, annoyed with his preoccupation, and turned back to the chest. His two best suits, the sheep's-color doublet slashed and lined with watchet blue satin and trimmed with blackwork and fish scale pearls and the peach-colored satin with the flax-blue braid on doublet and breeches, were already packed away, folded expertly into the battered saddlebags. He hesitated for a moment over his heavy winter doublet, two layers of thick gingerline wool, but settled instead for unlacing the matching sleeves from the armscye. They would go equally well with the judas-color doublet, or with his other everyday suit of pansy-colored linsey-woolsey. He added a second pair of sleeves, his best, rich black wool thickly banded with gilt braid, to the lefthand saddlebag and sat back on his heels to contemplate the rest of his belongings. It irked him that there was no time to have a new suit made—certainly Sidney would have paid, and paid well, to have his protegé decently clad—and it was even more annoying to know that he would have to spend God only knew how many months in Scotland with only one good suit to his name. Two good suits, he amended, rather sourly, counting the change of sleeves, but the peach-colored satin had definitely seen better days, and would no longer do for courtly dressing.

He grimaced, and began sorting through the heap of shirts. Most were limp with much washing, and showed fresh patches at elbows and yoke, but he crammed them into the bag anyway, determined to have as much clean linen as he could carry. The fancy shirt that matched his best doublet he folded more carefully, turning the embroidered sleeves to the inside and tucking the entire package into the breast of the pansy-color doublet. Clean drawers, patched cloth stockings for riding and every day, knitted stockings for court wear— He stopped abruptly, fingering a hole that had suddenly appeared in the foot of one of his second-best stockings. It was a moth-hole, too, despite the herbs strewn throughout the chest. He swore irritably, bundling both legs together into a ball, and flung open the door of his room.

"Bess! Hey, Bess!" He reached into the purse at his belt, pulling out a sixpence, and wadded the coin into the knitted fabric.

The maidservant answered from the bottom of the stairs. "Coming, Master Marlowe. You've a visitor, too."

Marlowe stiffened, one hand going to the dagger at his belt as he recognized the neat figure that followed Bess up the narrow stairway. Poley smiled, seeing the movement, and Marlowe took his hand away. "Here, Bess," he said, and held out the bundled stockings. "There's a hole in the left foot. Can you darn it for me? And did you take my ruffs to the starcher?"

Bess's thin lips tightened, but she answered cheerfully enough, "I took the ruffs to Goody Andries, and they'll be done tomorrow, as you asked. It's a shilling each, with eightpence more for the big one, and as much again for having it done so soon when there're others waiting."

Marlowe winced, though the price was not unreasonable, and nodded. The maidservant held out her hand. "I'll take the stockings now, and see what can be done."

Marlowe nodded again, and gave her the bundle. Bess felt the coin through the wadded fabric, and dropped a careless curtsey, smiling. "I'll see what I can do," she said again, and hurried down the stairs.

"Thank you, Bess," the poet said, and waited until she had vanished into the back rooms before added, "Well, Poley?"

Cecil's agent smiled even more sweetly. "I want to talk to you, Kit. May I come up?"

Marlowe hesitated, tempted to say no, but such a refusal would serve no purpose and anger the secretary. "If you must," he said, and made himself turn his back on the other man. He was very aware of Poley's footsteps on the unsteady stairs, but made himself wait until the other had reached the landing before turning to face him. "What is it you want this time?"

"News." Poley pushed past him into the room, pulling off his scented gloves. He glanced around, lifting an eyebrow at the clothes littering the floor, then seated himself in the single chair.

The poet's lips thinned, but he forced himself to give no other sign of anger. "Sir Philip is going to Scotland," he said, "and I am going with him. What other news can there be?" He leaned against his writing table, carefully not touching his dagger.

"What preparations is Sir Philip making?" Poley asked. Marlowe shrugged, and the other man held up his hand. "Specifically, I'm sent to ask if you think he will—if he can succeed in his mission." Poley smiled with deliberate malice. "After all, he's only a paper knight—this Queen's Champion nonsense means nothing, really."

Marlowe bit back his first response, well aware that he was being provoked, and annoyed that he had almost taken the bait. He looked away, and said, "I don't know his plans. Sir Philip seems to feel they're adequate, certainly."

Poley frowned. "And are they?"

Marlowe hesitated. If he said yes, not only was he admitting that he was privy to Sidney's plans—which could be a liability later on, if he had any intention of protecting Sidney from Cecil's malice—but he was also saying that Sir Philip was capable of upsetting the secretary's plots, and that was asking for Cecil to set up obstacles in their

path. On the other hand, if he said no, he was risking
Cecil's deciding that his own services were no longer
worth purchasing. Before he could answer, there was a
shout from the street.

"Kit! Hey, there, Christopher!"

Marlowe hid his sigh of relief, and crossed the room to
throw open the shutters. He leaned out into the weak
sunlight, one hand holding tight to the windowframe just
in case. "Will?"

The tall man below stepped back into the rutted street
to peer up at the opened window, and lifted a hand in
greeting. He pointed to the door then—Marlowe could
hear the scissors and needlecase at Bess's girdle jingling as
she unhooked the latch—and said, "I'm coming up."

"And very welcome," Marlowe said, to his departing
back. He turned away from the window, to find Poley
already on his feet, drawing his gloves back over his hands.

"What shall I tell Sir Robert?" the agent asked.

"Tell him I don't yet know Sir Philip's plans." Marlowe
paused, but could not resist adding, "He may not fully
trust me—the secretary was hardly subtle in ordering me
down to Penshurst."

Poley's eyes narrowed, but he shrugged elaborately.
"Sir Robert will expect to hear from you often."

"I'll do my best," Marlowe answered.

Poley turned away, and slipped from the room, letting
the door close gently behind him. Marlowe counted to
ten, listening to the footsteps on the stairs, and then
opened the door himself.

"What in God's name was that, Kit?"

"An old acquaintance," Marlowe answered, a trifle grimly.

The newcomer grinned, but let the opening pass. "So
you're going travelling, too?" He nodded to the open
saddlebags and the looted chest. "Accompanying your distinguished patron?"

"Yes." Marlowe gestured for the other man to seat himself, and turned back to the chest. "You'll forgive me if I
go on."

"Of course." The newcomer's eyes were bright with a
sort of mischievous curiosity. "But tell me, why is Sir
Philip bringing you along?"

Magpie, Marlowe thought, snapper-up of unconsidered trifles—and considered ones, for that matter. Someday, Shakespeare, you will ask one question too many, and get an answer you can neither use nor forget. He said aloud, "I offered to go, and he agreed to take me. They say James is fond of theater, and it's good odds he'll be the next king. I've a fancy to come to his notice."

"Are you to his taste, I wonder?" Shakespeare's tone was bland, pointing up the double meaning. Marlowe grunted, acknowledging the hit, and the player continued, "After all, the man who wrote *Doctor Faustus*—and displayed such a wealth of uncomfortable knowledge in the process—isn't likely to be too popular in a witch-ridden court."

Marlowe's hands tightened on the shoe he was packing, distorting the painted leather. He made himself relax, and took his time fitting it and its mate into a corner of the saddlebag. Once again, Shakespeare's guess was too close for comfort—but then, there had been enough pamphlets on the Scottish witch-scares of the previous two years to make it unlikely that it was more than a guess. Still, Marlowe thought, someone went to a deal of trouble in those little books to make James seem a fool and a coward, and I wonder why? *Cui bono?* Too many people, and that was the trouble, but players and poets came into contact with them all. He swung round, still on his knees, but the sight of Shakespeare's familiar open face drove away his suspicions before they were even fully articulated. The man who lounged there, tall hat pushed back to show his high forehead, decent long-skirted jerkin belted over tobacco-colored doublet and breeches, was no one's dupe or agent. "We'll see," Marlowe said, deliberately vague. "At least I have Sir Philip's name behind me." One saddlebag was full; he strapped it closed, and pushed himself to his feet, stretching. "But I doubt you came here to ask my travel plans."

"No." Shakespeare shook his head. "Congratulate me, Kit, I've bought my share. I'm a full holder now."

"I do congratulate you," Marlowe said, and meant it. Still, he could not resist adding, "Now you can bear your part in every lawsuit—and the Burbages such a peaceable lot, too."

Shakespeare gave a rueful smile, but did not take the bait. "I'll buy you a drink on the strength of it," he said. "Dinner, too."

Marlowe's eyes narrowed. "Just what are you up to, Will?"

The player laughed. "Nothing ill, I promise." He sobered quickly, however, and Marlowe hid a frown. Shakespeare was a rival, both with the players' companies and for the favors of at least one noble patron, but the man himself was so unassuming—so engaging—that Marlowe sometimes found it hard to remember the fact.

"It's this, Kit," Shakespeare said. "Our new play—have you seen it?"

"I've heard of it," the poet said, sourly. "I hear it owes a lot to my own *Edward.*"

The player shrugged, not the least disturbed by the accusation. "It plays well," he said obscurely, and returned to his original tack. "Your Sir Philip's seen it, at any rate, and came backstage afterward to tell me it should be pulled from the repertory. The sharers have voted on it, and we intend to do it—but I'm still uneasy. After all, when Sir Philip Sidney says a play's tactless . . ." He let his voice trail off invitingly. When Marlowe did not take up the lure, the other sighed, and finished, "What in God's name is going on that makes a mere history—one passed by the Master of Revels, mind you—such a danger?"

Marlowe hesitated. This was the sort of appeal, from one professional playwright to another, that was very hard to resist. Not hard enough, however, he added, with an inward smile. To explain the situation—the vision Dee had seen, the specter that haunted his own nightmares still, the Scottish situation—would be to betray entirely too much of his own precious store of information. He shrugged. "I wish I knew," he said, with all the false candor he could muster. "What's been happening among the players, to make the city fathers so uneasy? I saw half a dozen placards against the theaters, as I rode into town."

Shakespeare grinned, though the other man could not be certain if the player had truly been diverted, or just accepted the change of subject with his usual grace. "Nothing more than the usual," he said. "Nashe took all too accurate an aim at a pair of citizen-gentlemen last month, and then there's that song that's been making the rounds of late. Have you heard it?"

Marlowe shook his head. "What song?"

The player's smile widened. "They call it 'The Precisian's Text.' " He drew breath, and launched abruptly into song.

> "You friends to reformation
>   Give ear to my relation
> For I shall now declare, Sir
>   Before you are aware, Sir
> The matter very plain.
> A Gospel Cushion Thumper
>   Who dearly loved a bumper
> And something else beside, Sir,
>   If he is not belied, Sir,
> He was a holy Guide, Sir,
>   For those of canting name."

The tune was familiar, the old one Marlowe knew as "A Soldier and a Sailor," but the words were new, and unquestionably incendiary. The poet grinned, beating time with his fingers, as Shakespeare continued.

> "And for to tell you truly,
>   His flesh was so unruly,
> He could not for his life, Sir,
>   Pass by another's wife, Sir
> The spirit was so faint.
> And then he spied Jack's sister
>   He could not well have missed her
> She made his mouth to water,
>   And thought long to be at her,
> Such Sir is no great matter
>   Accounted by a Saint."

Marlowe gave a crow of laughter, and Shakespeare said, "Oh, that's just the first shot, my boy. Listen to the rest of it." He took another breath, and went on.

"Says he, 'My pretty Creature
    Your charming handsome Feature
Has set me all on fire
    You know what I desire
There is no harm in love.'
Quoth she, 'If that's your notion
    To preach up such Devotion
Such hopeful Guides as you, Sir,
    Will half the world undo, Sir
A halter is your due, Sir
    If you such tricks approve.'

"Says he, 'My charming daughter,
    'Tis evil, true, to barter,
Or sell what should be cherished,
    But still, it should not perish:
That too is counted sin.
As a man of God I offer
    To fill up your Soul's coffer
Your conscience I will salve, dear,
    And know that I'll absolve, dear,
For I'm fast in my resolve, dear,
    To plant the light within.'

"You can't get much plainer than that," Marlowe said.
"God's blood, no wonder the Precisians are up in arms."
    Shakespeare held up his hand for silence, still smiling,
and sang, "But still our good Jack's sister,

His blandishments resisted,
So he took up her garment,
    And she saw there was no harm in't
Or i'the text that he did preach.
And so he did persuade her
    'Til nothing could dissuade her
And then they went full at it,
    According to his habit,
Until the parson had it:
    Her conversion was complete.

"So take warning all you brothers

> And husbands, too, who'd rather
> Your girls had no such teaching
> Beware of all such preaching
> That caused the lass to fall.
> For women sure are weaker,
> And many love a preacher
> And preachers love the women
> For tempting them to sinning
> And then their lives amending
> Makes rich men of them all."

Marlowe, who had been humming an improvised harmony, choked on sudden laughter. "Christ's nails, who wrote that?"

"If I didn't know better," Shakespeare answered, "I'd suspect yourself."

Marlowe shook his head, and the player continued, more soberly, "Be that as it may, I can tell you who swears he'll use it in his next piece—which is planned to be a 'merry jest against the over-reformers.'" He gave a bitter twist to the last words. "Just the sort of impiety they can use to close us down."

Marlowe grunted agreement. "Jonson?"

Shakespeare nodded. "The same."

"You'd think his last brush with the law would've taught the bricklayer the advantages of policy."

"From you, Kit, that's remarkably unconvincing."

Marlowe opened his eyes wide in an elaborate show of innocence. "It wasn't my play that the great Sir Philip Sidney called tactless. It wasn't I who had to leave my native town for poaching a gentleman's deer. It wasn't I—"

"Oh, hold your peace," Shakespeare said, without heat. "Will you dine with me?"

Marlowe paused, tempted, but shook his head. "Another time, Will, thank you." He gestured vaguely to the clothes still scattered across the floorboards. "I leave tomorrow, early."

"I understand," the player answered. He pushed himself lazily to his feet. "God send we don't meet on the road—it's too early in the year to go touring." His voice dropped suddenly. "And God go with you, Kit, whether you want Him or not."

Marlowe grimaced, but let the blessing pass without comment. "Send Dickon round to kick some sense into Jonson," he suggested, and unlatched the door.

"It's been tried," Shakespeare answered, "and with a singular lack of success." He started down the stairs, but paused just before the bottom step. "Do you want to see me named in a suit so soon after buying my share?"

The poet grinned. Shakespeare laughed, and pushed through the front door. A few moment's later, Marlowe could hear his voice raised in cheerful song.

"You friends to reformation, Take heed to my relation—"

The words stopped abruptly, as though the player had suddenly realized what he was doing. Marlowe laughed, and returned to his work.

It did not take him long to fill the second saddlebag. When he had shoved the last shoe into place, he sat back on his heels for a moment, contemplating his handiwork. There was not much more he would want, just the silver chain Southampton had given him, and the book he'd taken from Sidney's library . . . And one thing more. He sighed, his expression hardening, and reached into the clotheschest. The long, well-polished case was buried at the very bottom, beneath a doublet too badly worn to be mended. He lifted the box out carefully, and laid it across his knees. Thoughtfully, he rubbed a finger across the maker's mark carved into the lid, the wood as smooth and warm as a man's skin. The set had been a gift—the last gift—from Thomas Walsingham, received not three months before Walsingham's steward Ingram Frizer had done his best to strangle the poet. There were more ironies there, Marlowe thought, and lifted the lid.

The twin pistols gleamed dully in their velvet nest, the late-afternoon sunlight glinting from the metal fittings. The poet lifted one at random, sighting cautiously down the long, plain barrel. They were Dutch guns, Walsingham had said. They were plainly made, without the fancy engraving that seemed to characterize German or Italian work, but fitted with the new snaphance lock in place of the older wheel-lock. Experimentally, Marlowe pulled back the flint—the mechanism was more like a musket's than the older pistols with which he was most familiar—and heard it click into place. He pointed the muzzle at random toward the bed, and touched the unprotected firing stud. The flint snicked forward, striking sparks from the battery plate. Marlowe nodded to himself, but nevertheless flicked open the metal ball that weighted the butt. There were three more flints, already chipped to shape, stored inside.

He returned the pistol to its place and lifted the other, working the mechanism and checking the flints hidden in the butt. He put it aside as well, and went methodically through the rest of the objects in the case. Powderflask, bullet-mold and the scant supply of bullets he'd made the night Walsingham had given him the pistols were all in their place. He would need fresh powder, he decided, and it could not hurt to mold a few more bullets, but both could wait until morning. He closed the case, and wedged it into the second saddlebag, drawing the taut leather closed over it. It felt strange to be carrying pistols again, and doubly so to be carrying those pistols. He sighed again, and pushed himself to his feet. He knew that neither pistols nor swords would be much use against the sort of demon Northumberland had conjured, but such dark powers often employed human agents, too. He would at least be ready for those.

Chapter Nine

Black spirits and white, red spirits and gray,
Mingle, mingle, mingle, you that mingle may.
Thomas Middleton, The Witch

Frances Sidney glanced down the length of the long table, gauging the food and the wine and the candles with the eyes of an experienced hostess. The second-course dishes were almost empty, the kid carved to the bone, the remaining slivers of meat congealing with the fat, the tart reduced to a broken wedge of pastry, the last stuffed pigeon cooling on its platter, and she nodded to the servant waiting silently at the sideboard. The man bowed and slipped away; a moment later, a pair of maidservants appeared and began to clear away the dishes.

"Another bottle?" Sidney asked. There was a general murmur of agreement, and Frances hid a smile of satisfaction. It had taken her several years to persuade her husband to abandon the old-fashioned practice of passing a single greatcup among his guests, and adopt the French service that gave each guest his own goblet—crystal now, a gift from the queen—but he seemed pleased with the new custom now. She had won the battle over the candles, too, insisting that they could at last afford to light the dining parlor properly.

She leaned back in her chair as the maidservants returned, bringing in the final course. The silver dish of preserved oranges stuffed with marmalade was nothing out of the ordinary, but the main sweet, a finely molded marchpane porcupine, quilled with cinnamon and surrounded with candied roses, was a special treat, a kind of peace offering. She glanced discreetly at her husband, and saw that he was smiling.

"Beautiful work," Greville said, and the others echoed him.

Frances nodded her thanks, letting her gaze sweep the table again. The warm candlelight worked a sort of magic, enriching the silks and velvets, and waking tiny flames in the hearts of the heavy jewels. It worked the same alchemy with the faces, transforming her sister-in-law Barbara's rather ordinary prettiness into something exotic, adding distinguishing shadows to the smooth, faintly foolish mask Greville presented even to his friends. It erased the hints of grey from Pembroke's tidy beard, and redrew the rather heavy line of Robert's chin and jaw. But we are growing older, all of us, Frances thought—except for Philip. The candlelight made no change in him; there was nothing to take away. His long face, with its high forehead and pointed chin, seemed ageless, eternal, infuriatingly untouchable. And I wish, Frances thought, that this were the only kind of magic confronting him.

"How long do you expect this Scottish affair to last?" Mary Herbert's clear voice, magnificent in its implicit condemnation of the "Scottish matter" as unspeakably frivolous, cut through the younger woman's musing, and Frances sighed. Mary, too, was unchanging.

Sidney looked up warily. "I don't know, really. I trust no more than a month or three. Why?"

His sister raised an eyebrow. "During which time you will accomplish nothing."

"Nothing?" Sidney smiled, deliberately misunderstanding. "My dear Mary, I had better, or my political life at least will be over."

Frances darted a quick, troubled glance at her husband, but said nothing. Greville sighed, looking toward Pembroke, but the earl was busy with an orange, seemingly oblivious to the conversation.

"Which would probably be just as well," Mary retorted. From any other woman, Frances thought, that tone would be described as "tart." "Philip, you were never a fit player for this game. That's why we let Robert handle all these sordid political demands."

"Thank you," that gentleman murmured, and eyed his empty glass. Greville handed the bottle across to him. "Do I understand you're bound back to Holland, Robert?"

Robert nodded grin thanks. "Flushing, in fact. It's becoming an hereditary governorship in our family—first Philip, now me."

"Where her majesty commands, I'm not about to say no," Sidney commented mildly.

"No, of course not," Mary answered. "You refuse to admit that your true talents lie elsewhere. You still want to be some knight errant in the political arena as well as in the lists."

Sidney blinked. Was the metaphor actually mixed, or merely hopeless? he wondered, then spread his hands in a gesture of innocent helplessness. "What would you have me do?"

Mary's eyes glittered dangerously, and Greville hid a sigh. This script was ten years old now, but Mary would not relinquish the argument. And, so long as she chose to attack, Sidney would defend his position—and as long as he defended, she would infallibly attack.

"Leave the field to Robert," Mary said. "He's a much more suitable knight and no mean politician." She let her voice plummet, making full use of its throaty lower register. "You have other responsibilities."

Sidney lifted his wine cup. "Which are?"

"Your writing, Philip, pray don't be a fool. God's nails, how long has it been since you even looked at your *Arcadia*?"

"I finished the *Arcadia*, Mary."

"My *Arcadia*," Mary answered. Her voice took on a new sincerity. "It's a masterpiece, and it's sitting in some odd corner, gathering dust, and will be lost to the ages if you don't do something about it."

"It very nearly was, my dear," Sidney answered. "I left instructions that it was to be burned if anything befell me in Holland."

Mary turned to stare at Greville. "I trust you would have disobeyed."

"Not I," Greville answered promptly, but Mary had already turned back to confront her older brother.

"You're capable of anything." Her accusation was that of a Roman matron confronting a Visigoth. "You have a gift, a talent, and it's a sin to let it go to waste as you've been doing. The *Arcadia* needs to be finished, Philip, I want to read it. I want to know what happens."

"All ends happily and justly," Sidney said, and drained his glass of wine. Pembroke instantly handed him the bottle, and Sidney refilled the goblet, the crystal glittering in the light.

Mary's thin brows contracted dangerously. "Philip, one day someone is going to murder you."

"No use, Mary, I've tried telling him that," Robert interjected, in a vain attempt to turn the conversation. He was ignored.

Sidney sighed. "Mary, I have no immediate plans for going back to work on the *Arcadia*. I have more important matters to engage my mind."

"Your *book*," Mary said, with exquisite contempt. "Your studies. And what good are they, may I ask?"

"Yes, my studies," Sidney answered, goaded at last into perfect seriousness. "Because you see no visible results, you disdain them as worthless? Merely because you see no immediate utility in them? I assure you, they are far more important—and they engage my interest more—than does a pastoral romance." He took a deep breath, realizing he had gone too far, and said, more calmly, "If you so greatly desire to see *Arcadia* completed, you have my full permission to do it yourself."

There was a moment's silence, and then Mary leaned forward, accepting the olive branch. "Then I must see your notes. I wouldn't want to disturb your intentions."

Sidney shrugged, unable to resist one final provocation. "I'm sure they're around here somewhere. When I return from Scotland, I'll look for them."

Mary lifted an eyebrow. "Your studies have rendered you quite insensitive to more important matters, I hope you know."

"Nonsense, Mary," Robert interjected firmly, with a sidelong glance at his sister-in-law. "You like a good fight as much as any of us."

Frances pushed herself to her feet, and the others rose with her. "This discussion usually goes on for some hours. Fulke, Barbara, my lord, would you care to join me in the gallery? Robert, I wish you would stay and arbitrate. Philip might like to live long enough to start out for Scotland." She made a shallow curtsey toward her husband, and took the arm Greville extended for her, acutely aware of having managed the Walsingham trick of getting the last word. Pembroke and Barbara Sidney meekly followed her from the room.

One of Madox's understewards had obviously run before; the candelabra at each end of the gallery were already lighted, and a maidservant with a lighted spill was busy with the smaller tapers that stood on the table beneath the long window.

"A game of backgammon, Lady Barbara?" Pembroke asked, and the woman nodded. Frances watched from the railing as the two settled themselves and began to set up the game, laying out counters and shaking dice for the first move. She was aware of Greville's presence, calm and undemanding, but did not turn to him. It was no wonder Philip was so fond of him, she thought, idly, and sighed.

"I owe you thanks, I believe, Fulke. Philip tells me you suggested bringing the boy with you to Scotland. I'm grateful."

Greville managed a wry smile. "I'm glad to have been of service, Lady Frances."

You understand too much, Frances thought suddenly, and I find that—unnerving. She looked at him as though seeing him for the first time, a tall, lean man dressed in the height of French fashion, the tight cannions and doublet, the tall hat, and even the short puffed trunk hose only serving to emphasize the long line of his body. Greville touched his moustache nervously, well aware of her scrutiny. To her own surprise, Frances laughed, and tucked her hand into the curve of his elbow, turning him toward the far end of the gallery. Greville moved easily with her, saying nothing until they reached the staircase. Then at last he said, almost tentatively, "Things seem better now?"

Frances sighed, considering the question. They had spoken, fought, perhaps cleared away some of the misunderstandings—but, more than that, more disturbing than that, it had made her remember why she had ridden to Arnhem all those years ago. . . . No, she corrected herself with an inward frown, it made you realize that you still care, that you still would make that ride, and pay that price again, no matter how many times you've damned yourself for it. Oh, Philip, was that kind in you, when I thought I'd settled with my heart? She blinked away the too-easy tears, and said, "I have few illusions about this embassy, Fulke. Or, rather, I have a good idea of what's being asked of him. It would be kind of you to give me something real to chew on."

Greville hesitated, but then nodded slowly. The question itself was answer enough, from the Frances Sidney who had so assiduously ignored her husband's business for the past nine years. Still . . . He glanced toward the long windows, weighing his words. What could he tell her? Most of his own knowledge had been gathered from hints and by guess, from the piecing together of things heard and overheard—but then, the woman was a Walsingham, with politics bred into her very bones. Like her father, she was an utter realist—and perhaps for that very reason not the right wife for Sidney. Someone like Mary, Greville thought, fire to Philip's air, not good, solid earth, however lovely the earth might be. All man is clay, he thought, irrelevantly. Where did that leave the Sidneys and the Dudleys, if the Cecils and the Walsinghams marked the true type of man?

He shook his head, annoyed with his own hesitation. "I don't know that I can judge the danger, Frances. I don't know the Scottish court very well. Philip—Philip is a master, whether he'll admit it or not, and he usually doesn't. He has an almost Greek fear of hubris."

"Oh, Roman, surely," Frances murmured, with a slight smile. Her question answered, though perhaps not in the

way Greville had intended, she was willing to help him
turn the subject. "Doesn't Philip strike you as the very
embodiment of *gravitas*? Not some prosing old stodgy fool
of a Roman senator, but someone who lives his life by his
code of honor, without making a martyrdom of it? And
Horace says that the upright man need fear no arrow, nor
venom."

Greville blinked, and did his best to hide his surprise. The
Walsinghams were an educated family; there was no reason
that any of them should not quote the *Odes*. Still, it seemed
oddly out of joint, to hear the realists speak of honor.

Frances went on unheeding. "The Romans were devoted to the finer concepts of the Greeks, so doubtless
they too knew the dangers of hubris. You're right about
Philip, though. He has his self-esteem—but I can't help
thinking that just a little pride might go a long way here."
She shook her head. "Do go on, Fulke. I apologize."

"No need," Greville said, wondering at the exactitude
with which she had crystallized his own image of Sidney.
Maybe a woman of Mary's nature wasn't what Philip needed,
he thought—if only Philip could see it. If only Frances
could be brought to show him. Frances smiled up at him,
the slightly blank smile of the well-bred lady.

"Let's join the others."

Sidney paused outside the door to his study, then turned
the handle, and went in. The room was very dark, the
shutters closed and barred against the night; the candle in
his hand flickered and burned low, barely making head-
way against the darkness. The night itself seemed almost
palpable, pushing against the shutters, seeping in through
the cracks and fissures, rousing a host of half-forgotten
ghosts. The smell of books commingled with the odor of
damp, of flowers long since dried or gone to seed, of ink,
papers. They hung in the still air, drifting turgidly at the
edge of Sidney's awareness. And in the absolute and strong
dark silence, it all mocked at him, spoke of idleness,
uselessness, futile and prideful probings into the wells of
knowledge, not for the glory of God, or for any use of a
God-given talent, but for the sake of the well itself, for
knowledge alone, for the greedy pride of possession.

The silence hammered at the night. With a small, strangled noise, Sidney crossed the room and wrenched open two of the shutters. A cricket, startled, fell silent, but others still sang, and there was a high-pitched peeping of tree frogs beyond that—all real sounds of the night that scorned the products of a febrile imagination. Sidney rested his hands on the sill and leaned out, drawing in deep breaths of the night air. It was clear, cool, damp, the stars half veiled by a mist of clouds. With a sigh, he turned and dropped onto the windowseat, the same one from which he had watched Robert puzzle over his unlocked box. It was well past midnight; he and Fulke and the rest of his modest train would be leaving in only a few hours, but he was unable to rest.

He stared out into the darkness instead, looking away from the candle, until the darkness receded into shades of grey. Did witches have night sight? he wondered idly. It was said they did, laid to their charge, but what was the harm in it? Night wasn't darkness. It was created as day was, by God, for rest from labor. Therefore, what was so wrong about seeing in the night? He shook his head, shaking away the pretty argument. There were other kinds of night, and Sidney feared that a very dark one lay ahead of him in Scotland. Perhaps I should've taken Poland's offer, he thought, with a quick, inward smile. If not to have gained the experience of a nobility as troublesome as James's, than because if I had, I wouldn't be in this position now.

Stop that, he told himself, sharply. This was a challenge, a challenge to his talents and to powers that remained, as yet, untested—or at least not seriously tested. This is the challenge you've been longing for, what you've watched and waited and studied for, for even longer than these last ten years, and yet you've tried to deny it. Afraid of pride, you desperately tried to rekindle a cooling love of the political; failing there, you turned to writing. You knew when you started revising the *Arcadia*, you would never finish. Your heart was never in it, you were only trying to deny your very essence. This is your gift, your talent, this power that lives within you. Once you put aside your fear and opened that book, you knew. And

that's why the *Arcadia* grew, became more lovingly—
desperately—involved and convoluted, a game of chambers within chambers. It was something to hide in, a
reason for denial.

Sidney caught his breath. It was true, all of it—but not
like this, not this pelting of images and thoughts like
stones, like accusations. He reached up and dug his hands
into his eyes until the darkness reeled. He lifted his head,
leaning back against the frame, and waited until the candle-
blindness had receded.

It was there again. The night had gone silent, the insect
noises stifled by the louring presence. Sidney rose to his
feet, feeling a cold hand on his heart. This was far more
ominous than the malicious taunting he and Dee had
sensed at Mortlake, more threatening than the presence
that had first caught Sidney's attention. He lifted his hand,
began the first gesture of a spell that would repel it and
with it his own sudden fear, but stopped in mid-movement.
Something within him whispered that this was not the way
or the time to face it; if it wished to hold him in contempt,
to taunt him so, let it. He would take its measure, and it
would still know nothing of his own abilities. He managed
a taut smile. Caution was a politician's attribute; at least he
had learned that painful lesson well.

Slowly, deliberately, he turned away from the window
and the night, hardening his mind. He'd done a similar
thing only once before, in Italy, after he had found Virgil's
tomb. That had been a physical threat, though. Turning
his back on armed men had been frightening; the space
between his shoulder blades had cringed, but he had
known, in some quiet corner of his mind, that he could do
it, that the custodians of Virgil's tomb could not strike
down the man who had actually located it, and caused it to
respond to his will. This was only more of the same.

Behind him, the presence seemed to roll forward like a
wave, as though only his blind stare had kept it in check,
and he knew with sudden fear that this was very different.
The darkness swelled in the windowframe, odd tendrils of
itself creeping across the sill, touching him. It was a gentle
pressure, subtle, probing, inquisitive, frightening in its
very lack of force. Sidney shuddered, but did not turn. He

had made his stand: he would maintain it. In the darkness, things crept and whispered, odd shapes whisking out of sight at the corner of his eyes. Minor demons, Beelzebub's flies, petty uncleaness muttering its spite against the world, daring him now to turn and defy them, while beyond that something else waited, pulling their puppet-strings. . . .

He stood still, denying the presence, its power. After an interminable time, the soft touch receded, falling away like the ebbing tide. The shadow-demons slithered back across the windowsill, drawing back into nothing. As they faded, the night became normal again, cool, clear, filled with the sharp noises of the insects and the frogs. A wind stirred and died. Then the presence was gone, its promise never fulfilled, like a distant storm that threatens and troubles, but never strikes.

Sidney shuddered, and was suddenly aware that his hand was shaking, spilling wax from the candle. He steadied himself carefully, and as carefully made himself consider the presence he had faced. It had not reached him—it could not, not so long as his stance was merely defensive—but the sheer power leashed within it was terrifying. God help me when I have to face it, he thought, when I have to attack.

"Philip? It's late."

Sidney shook his head to clear it; the voice had been distant, heard as though through water. Frances stood in the doorway, her brown hair spread across her shoulders. It fell almost to her waist, fine and straight, taking odd lights from the chamberstick she carried in her right hand. The same candlelight made ivory the plain white linen of her shift, and darkened the tawny satin of the Spanish surcoat she wore open over it. She was frowning lightly, but with worry, not anger. Sidney felt his heart lift slightly, but could not find the words. "I didn't think I could sleep," he said instead. "Not until now."

Frances came further into the room, lifting the candle slightly to look at her husband. There was something in his voice, in the odd expression in his eyes, that made her voice sharpen slightly. "Are you all right?"

Sidney shook his head again, and raised a hand to rub at

his eyes. The candlelight trembled on the gold threads in his ice-green doublet. "Yes. Yes, I think so."

"What was it?" she asked.

"A . . . power. Wanting to test me, I think, for all it's scornful of my abilities—which I made sure it did not."

"So soon?"

Her voice sounded odd, and Sidney took a step toward her, frowning now with concern. She turned away from the conjoined light of the two candles, but he caught her arm gently, turning her back to face him. Frances looked up at him, her own face set with an unfamiliar concern. "If it's started now, Philip . . . what will you be facing in Scotland?"

"I wish I knew what it was I faced just now," Sidney answered, with a rueful laugh. "Or who."

Frances touched his cheek lightly. "Philip—oh, it sounds so lame." She shook her head, her mouth twisting, but did not look away.

Sidney, greatly daring, reached out to smooth her long hair, then let his hand rest on her shoulder. He could feel the sharp bones through the cloth, as uncompromising as everything about her. She was thin, too thin, or so Mary said, but dangerously strong. "I give you my word, I will be careful—if you will, too."

"I?"

Sidney could feel that he was on thin ice; the wrong word, and everything the two of them had accomplished would be shattered beyond repair. He spoke slowly, choosing his words with almost painful care. "Together, perhaps, Essex and I would make an ideal man, the gallant as well as the scholar. But we both have our faults."

There was a momentary hesitation, and then Frances met his gaze frankly. "He's very . . . facile, Philip. Very gallant." She studied her husband's face for a long moment, then, very slowly, nodded. "Very well. I promise to—be careful."

And that was all she promised, Sidney thought. He did not dare press for more. Still, if anyone could see past that facility, she could. He glanced toward the darkness beyond the windows. "What's the time?"

"Gone three," Frances answered.

"And I intend to be on the road to London early," Sidney said wryly. "Poor Fulke. I'm going to be foul company."

"Not you, Philip," Frances said, with a sudden, almost startling warmth. "Come to bed."

Sidney looked at her, one eyebrow lifting, and she laughed softly, the color starting to her cheeks. "I'm not here to tempt you," she said, "you'd be in even worse shape tomorrow morning. But . . ." Her chin lifted slightly. "I thought you might want company."

Sidney looked into her eyes for a long moment, then nodded. "I might, at that." He turned away, crossed to the opened windows. He stood before them for a moment, afraid somehow that if he relaxed his vigilance the presence would return, but the night was empty and free. He pulled the shutters closed again, fastening latch and bar, and, after a moment's hesitation, blew out his own candle. Frances slipped her free hand into his and drew him away.

Chapter Ten

*Methinks there be not impossibilities enough in re-
ligion for an honest faith.*
> Sir Thomas Browne, Religio Medici

The party set out from Penshurst on a foggy morning, a
modest cortege, a dozen servants, all mounted, and a
single baggage cart. It was an easy day's ride to London,
but young Madox, who would have overall charge of the
servants' train, fretted over the preparations as though
they would have to cross fifty miles of trackless waste. It
was the first time the steward's son had had the sole
responsibility for managing his employer's travels, and the
strain showed. Sidney charitably turned a blind eye to the
young man's drawn face as they set out, concentrating
instead on the pleasures of the ride. He was tired after the
previous night's exertions, but not as much as he had
feared he might be. It was more lack of sleep than any
great effort on his part, he reflected ruefully. He lifted his
face to the fog, and let its cool damp touch sharpen his
senses.

The weather had been unseasonably dry for the first
months of the year, worrying the farmers, but hardening
the roads. As long as it stayed dry, Sidney thought, even
the cart would give them no trouble. He turned in his

saddle, glancing back along the line of riders. Of the dozen servants, all but two were well known to him—three of the four undergrooms had been born on the Sidney estates, and the fourth came from no further away than Sevenoaks, while the head groom, Jan-Maarten van der Droeghe, had been sergeant-major in Sidney's Holland company and gone willingly from the Dutch armies to the more congenial household post. Even the boy who tended the cart was the son of the oldest undergroom, and Frances Sidney had stood godmother to him. Sidney smiled, looking at the pair of boys perched atop the bundled baggage. Peter Covell's Peterkin was just shy of fourteen, a good age—just old enough to handle his duties, but not so old that he would not make a friend for Nate Hawker. Sidney's smile faded a little, watching the smaller boy. Perhaps it wasn't wise of him to bring the boy along, when their road led through Northumberland's holdings, but he did need a page. Besides . . . Sidney's expression hardened. He would not mind the opportunity to tell Northumberland just what he thought of using boys for man's work.

"Worrying about your Yorkshire lad?" Greville reined in gently, matching his horse's gait to the pace of Sidney's mare.

Sidney smiled. "Yes, in part, though how you know . . . I'm not sure it's fair to ask him to start his duties as my page at the royal court of Scotland."

"Lord, Philip, how royal can it be? I wouldn't fear," Greville said. He lounged comfortably in his saddle, the practiced slouch of a man who could—and did—ride for days on end. "My Ralph says young Madox says he's shaping up nicely."

And if young Madox said it, as panicked as he was about every aspect of the journey, Sidney thought, Nate would do. He nodded. "Thank you, Fulke. I'm relieved to hear it."

"Poor Madox," Greville said, and grinned. "Between his father and his own pride, the man's run ragged."

"He'd better not be, so early in the journey," Sidney answered. His voice was oddly grim, and Greville lifted an eyebrow.

"And what's amiss with you, Philip?"

Sidney made a face, unable to put words to the sudden feeling that had grown on him as the fog burned off. It was not as frightening, as oppressive as it had been three weeks ago, when Robert first brought the Queen's message to Penshurst . . . or as malicious as that which he'd felt the night before . . . but it was definitely there, a strange, circling presence. He shrugged, unhappily aware of his own edginess, and Greville stiffened.

"Is it trouble?" He reached for the pistol cased at his saddlebow, laying his hand gently on its butt. The movement, shockingly reminiscent of Holland for such a quiet English lane, brought Sidney back to himself.

"No—no real trouble, at any rate, just . . ." He shrugged again, still unable to find the words he wanted. "Shadows, Fulke, a touch of . . . something. Nothing for arms, yet."

Greville nodded, and let the pistol slide back into its case. Sidney glanced over his shoulder, hoping none of the others had noticed. The boys were still on the top of the cart, heads together; Covell slouched on the tongue, hands loose on the traces, letting the draft horse pick its own way. The grooms followed in a laughing knot. Greville's Ralph rode a little behind them, holding himself aloof as befitted a gentleman's valet. Only van der Droeghe seemed to have seen the movement, but he had also seen its sequel, and rode easy in the saddle, eyes flicking only occasionally toward the hedgerows. Even young Madox seemed to have relaxed a little, was smiling in the sunshine.

Sidney turned back to the road, shaking his head at his own foolishness. The probing touch of the night before was causing him to over-react, of that he was certain. The presence hovered, watched, but did not threaten; it kept its distance, for now. *When we get a little further north, though . . .* His mouth tightened. There were arms in the baggage, more heavy pistols and heavy falchions for each man, and van der Droeghe had drilled the undergrooms, at least, in the rudiments of their use. Once the party reached York, he would distribute them, and make sure the men rode armed.

They reached London toward the end of the afternoon, clattering through the gates of Robert Sidney's townhouse into the cheerful bedlam of the courtyard. Sir Philip allowed himself to be spirited indoors, and submitted to the combined ministrations of his valet and Robert's chief steward, but, once he'd bathed and rejoined the others, he could feel the cold nervousness on him again. He frowned, withdrawing himself deftly from the conversation, and leaned against the long window, staring out across the city. The spire of St. Mary's rose sharply above the householders' roofs, turning his unease to sudden resolve. At the first break in the talk, he touched Robert's beribboned sleeve, drawing him gently aside.

"I've a fancy to hear evensong, Robert. Make my excuses to your lady?"

Robert frowned. "The chaplain will be holding our service within the hour, Philip, if you need—"

Sidney shook his head, smiling a little at his own foolishness. "Thank you, Robert, but—" He shrugged helplessly, and Robert managed a rueful grin.

"Shall I make up a party, then, or would you rather go alone?" His voice made clear which he would prefer, and Sidney's smile widened. Robert was very much a Dudley, with a Dudley's preference for observing no more than then necessary proprieties.

"Alone, you needn't trouble your people."

Robert's eyebrows rose, but then he shrugged. "I trust your judgment, Philip," he said, in a voice that made the opposite quite clear, but did not make any further attempt to dissuade his brother.

The bells were sounding for the evening service by the time Sidney reached the churchyard. St. Mary's was a rather ordinary city church, once monastic, now remade by the twin forces of the reformation and the city's growth. The glass in the long windows was old, and here and there panels that did not meet the tastes of the reformers had been replaced by plain glass, but the parson's chair was newly gilded, and there were good silver candlesticks on the altar. The congregation, though small, seemed both prosperous and devout, and there were a few better-dressed groups, men and women both, who might be minor gentry, or upper servants of wealthy households. That explained the candlesticks, Sidney thought, and the others

explain the missing windows. This was primarily a citizens'
church, despite having households like his brother's or
Walter Raleigh's in the neighborhood, and the citizens
were more zealous than most in pulling down the remind-
ers of the old ways. Marlowe would claim it was because
they disliked encouraging anyone to spend money, even
on the glory of God, Sidney thought, with an inward
smile, or because they somehow profited from the removal. I think it's only because they're zealous, and still
touchy of their faith's honor.

It was the feast of St. Philip and St. James. A good
omen, Sidney thought, as he stood and knelt patiently
through the long service, and an all too pertinent text. The
lines from the psalm, in particular, seemed apposite: *My
help cometh of God, who preserveth them that are true of
heart.*

*God is a righteous Judge, strong, and patient; and God
is provoked every day.*

*If a man will not turn, he will whet his sword; he hath
bent his bow, and made it ready.*

*He hath prepared for him the instruments of death; he
ordaineth his arrows against the persecutors.*

*Behold, he travaileth with mischief; he hath conceived
sorrow, and brought forth ungodliness.*

*He hath graven and digged up a pit, and is fallen
himself into the destruction that he made for other.*

*For his travail shall come upon his own head, and his
wickedness shall fall on his own pate.*

Sidney murmured the last lines aloud, praying that this
would be a true indication of his opponent's ultimate end.
"I will give thanks unto the Lord, according to his righteousness; and I will praise the Name of the Lord most
high."

The elderly priest seemed to fix his eyes on him, beginning the final psalm, and Sidney wondered uncomfortably
if he had somehow been overheard.

"What is man, that thou are mindful of him?" the priest
intoned firmly, "and the son of man, that thou visitest
him? Thou madest him lower than the angels, to crown
him with glory and worship. Thou makest him to have
dominion of the works of thy hands; and thou hast put all

things in subjection under his feet . . . O Lord our Governor, how excellent is thy name in all the world!"

It was a comforting sentiment, a necessary reminder of the liberality of God's gifts, to balance against the stern injunctions of the lessons, with their insistence on complete faith and on belief. Sidney shook his head slightly. It could not be idle coincidence that the day's reading was what it was. *Yet hast thou not known me, Philip?* Sobering words—but perhaps I'm in need of sobering. A word of caution, of counsel, a reminder—*for he that wavereth is like a wave of the sea driven with the wind and tossed.* Waver I will not—but, dear Lord, give me strength, guide my hand, let me not be driven by anger, or hatred. Let the deed stand on its own, exist because it must. Not my will, but Thine, o Lord.

He moved mechanically through the rest of the service, murmuring the responses by rote, the words of the gospel lingering in his thoughts. He knelt for the blessing, then stood for a few moments in the nave's dwindling light, the congregation ebbing around him, guiltily aware that he'd hardly heard the last half of the service. Then he shook himself. He had been preoccupied with God's Word, with the truly important part of worship; if there were sin in that, it was a lesser one. Drawing his cloak about his shoulders, he trailed after the rest of the worshippers into the street.

As he started back toward Robert's house, a hand touched his elbow. He turned, slowly, his hand on the pommel of his rapier. Then his eyebrows rose in surprise.

"I didn't mean to startle you, Sir Philip. But I would like to have a word with you."

Raleigh's darkly handsome face was grave, almost troubled. In the dusky, twilight air, the single pearl that dangled from his left ear was startlingly clear. Sidney nodded slowly. "If you wish."

Raleigh gestured toward the nearest alehouse, perhaps a dozen doors from the churchyard. The sign of an anchor swung above its open door, and there were rushlights in its low windows. "It's a good house," the explorer said, his hand still on the other man's elbow, urging him on. "A merchant's place, but good."

Sidney hid a smile—he was as aware as anyone of Raleigh's comparatively lowly origins—and let himself be led. Inside, the air was heavy, sweet and warm from cooking fires and from the number of people within. Raleigh surveyed the room, and swore under his breath. "This won't do," he muttered, and directed Sidney back towards one of the private rooms. Involuntarily, Sidney thought of Marlowe in Eleanor Bull's tavern, and he drew back slightly. Raleigh didn't seem to catch the hesitation, and, annoyed with himself, Sidney followed. His hand stayed on the hilt of his sword, however, and he shifted the heavy black cloak back off his shoulder.

"Frank! A pitcher of your best, in here!" Raleigh shouted to the tavern keeper, and Sidney sighed in relief. Of course, he had no real reason to suspect Raleigh of double-dealing, but if he were shouting his presence to the world, he could hardly hope to carry out some dark scheme. The keeper bowed the two gentlemen into the stuffy inner room, and bustled about with a large pitcher of ruddy ale and two tankards, adjusting the cracking shutters and brushing off the tabletop. Then he bustled out again, and closed the door behind him.

Sidney unfastened his cloak and draped it carelessly on a bench. Then he sat down and waited, looking patiently up at Raleigh in what he knew was a deliberately provoking manner. Raleigh looked a trifle thunderous, and then he grinned.

"Damn it, Philip, I don't know if you look more like a schoolboy or a schoolmaster when you do that, but it's damned disconcerting."

"It was meant to be," Sidney replied mildly, and waited.

"Well, it works." Raleigh dropped into a leather-backed chair. He filled the two tankards, sliding one across the table toward the younger man, then took a long draught of his own. He set down the mug with a thump, and set his hands on his thighs, leaning forward. "Right, then. You're bound for Scotland, I hear."

"You and half of London, I think. Yes."

"And it has something to do with the fact that you're Her Majesty's champion in the lists. Which means it has something to do with . . . power. Wizardry."

"Really?" Sidney asked. "I thought it was to bear gifts to the young prince." He picked up his own tankard, and regarded Raleigh guilelessly over the rim.

"Well, then, you thought wrong," Raleigh said, with a dry laugh. "I don't blame you for not trusting me. Our systems are completely antithetical."

"Yes," Sidney murmured, only just refraining from adding, "mine works."

It seemed Raleigh sensed the unsaid words. "Believe me, Sidney, if my system were a fraud, I wouldn't be talking with you now. But I need—I don't know. Your advice. Your suggestions. Knowledge, perhaps, to damn us both as spoilers of Eden. There's something odd about this, Sidney. Something rotten."

The explorer's eyes were hard as flints, and stared past Sidney at some unknown, unpleasant memory. "Your protegé knows about it, too. I don't know what he's told you. . . ." Raleigh raised an eyebrow at Sidney, who shook his head.

"I haven't seen Kit in some days. And he's not a confiding man."

"About a fortnight ago, we met. We weren't looking for anything in particular. . . ."

"You never are," Sidney said wearily. "Just good games and fellowship and a scrying glass to see what demons are receiving tonight?"

Raleigh flushed, but he managed a grim smile. "Something of the sort, yes," he answered evenly. "Anyway—Northumberland brought his boy—but whatever it was, it terrified the child." He glanced sharply at Sidney, expecting him to comment. Sidney kept silent, though his lips were a thin line. "So . . . Kit offered to have a look. I think he was just trying to prove that virginity is overrated, it's one of his favorite catechisms. So, we repeated the ritual." He took another long swallow of ale, the movement not quite hiding remembered fear. "I don't know what it was. But I have never sensed anything so rotten, evil if you like, in my days of such matters. It—overarched everything. It wasn't small. Malice is small. This seemed to taint the entire room. Only the earl seemed untroubled, but I think that was more of a good act than anything. It frightened the hell out of me. And I know it frightened Kit. Now I hear the Queen has dispatched you to Scotland—ostensibly as her ambassador. But if what I felt is as encompassing as it seemed, it's likely Dr. Dee has sensed something, too. Or yourself, perhaps?"

Raleigh tilted his head and looked at Sidney, who studied the scarred tabletop for a long moment. So the School of Night was frightened, too. At least it meant that Sidney wouldn't have to contend with them as well, unless this were some extremely elaborate trap. He shook his head. Not only would the power he had sensed not bother with such a device, Raleigh was too honorable a man knowingly to be used by it. They had been closer associates once; now his way and Sidney's had diverged, and each viewed the other with suspicion and disdain. But in the end, Sidney had to admit he trusted Raleigh, and, for all he could not countenance the systems employed by the Ludus Noctis, he had to admit that they did seem to produce some results. Raleigh could be an invaluable ally. Certainly he could be a good friend. Sidney looked up slowly.

"Yes," he said, "there is—something. I wish to God I knew just what."

Raleigh nodded once, bracing his hands against the table's edge. "Is there anything—anything at all—that I can do to help?"

Sidney hesitated only for an instant. "Keep—listening, watching, whatever it is you do. And if you do encounter this thing, this person, again, write to me. Tell me every little detail, everything you saw or felt or thought you heard. That would be a very great help, Walter, I promise."

Raleigh nodded again, his handsome face taking on a new determination. "By God, I will. You have my word on it, Philip. And God go with you."

Remembering the day's lessons, Sidney said wryly, "I trust He will."

The cortege left London with the sunrise, and made its way by easy stages north and west. The weather was still good, dry and clear, and they made good time, arriving at Greville's Warwickshire house early in the afternoon of the second day. It was a magnificent building, though the impressive facade was marred by the builders' scaffolding that still mantled the northern wing. Greville apologized profusely for the inconvenience of the accommodations, but, as he escorted Sidney through the newly-completed gallery and out into the long sweet-scented gardens, his pride was very plain. Sidney hid his smile, and displayed only genuine admiration for Greville's dominion.

The next day was Sunday, and, as was the custom, they did not travel. Instead, the entire household set off across the fields toward the parish church. It was a little more than a mile away, an easy walk, but Marlowe found himself resenting it fiercely—resenting even the fact that Sidney and Greville rode, though he knew perfectly well that it was only Sidney's old wound that made the older man resort to the horse to carry him across the distance. The poet scowled, glancing up at the sky. A thin wash of clouds veiled the sun, but the air was warm and dry, and there was a stiff breeze blowing. It was a perfect day for travelling, the sort of day in which they could have covered thirty miles or more, but instead here they were, held fast by nothing better than superstition. He frowned more deeply, and was suddenly aware of the way young Madox edged away from him. Marlowe's expression did not alter, but he managed a rather nasty inward smile. His reputation as atheist and blasphemer had preceded him; young Madox and the rest were staying out of the way of any lightnings he might attract.

The parish church was small, by the standards of London or Marlowe's Canterbury, but still too large for the congregation meeting in it. Marlowe glanced over his shoulder at the common folk making their way along the dusty road from the village that must lie beyond the gentle curve of the hill. Most looked prosperous enough, for countrymen, but there seemed to be few freeholders among them; the majority were dressed like day-laborers rather than craftsmen, and there were quite a few livery-coats and maidservants' caps among the younger people. The nearest of the girls, demure in her starched linen cap and spotless apron, met his glance briefly, her eyes bright with curiosity about the London visitors, but then a fair girl spoke to her, and both looked away, giggling.

The sound of hoofbeats on the hard-packed surface of

the road made the common folk scatter quickly, clearing a path for the approaching rider. Marlowe stepped back, too, less willingly, and stumbled on the uneven ground. He caught himself awkwardly, staring at the rider. It was a big man, red of face and black of eye and beard, his short bright cloak snapping behind him like a banner. He pulled up abruptly at the churchyard gate, the horse snorting and protesting, and flung himself from his saddle, his face set in a portentous frown. He led the horse through the gate, and then knotted the reins to the nearest tree limb.

"I'm here, Frank Warden, I'm here," he shouted. "And you, Giles Overton, note me down."

One of the churchwardens, standing in the main doorway, made a curious half-bow, and the other said, in his rich country accent, "I see you, Sir Edward."

"Note it down, then, note it down," the gentleman answered, and stormed past them into the church.

Marlowe hid a grin—he himself had been fined for non-attendance before this—and made his way sedately into the church. The older warden gave him a sharp, suspicious glance, but the younger man murmured something deferential, and the older man said nothing. The disapproving look sharpened the poet's earlier ill temper, and he said bitterly, to no one in particular, "In St. Helen's parish, each Thursday the wardens give out brass tokens to all the taxpayers, to be handed in at the communion table on Sunday." He smiled, aware that van der Droeghe at least was listening, and added, "You give the warden your token and you get your bread and wine—it's rather like an alehouse. Though if Christ had instituted the sacrament with a pot of beer and a pipe of tobacco, there'd be no trouble getting men to church."

Van der Droeghe glanced down at him with a sort of weary distaste. "You have an idle, vicious tongue, Marlowe."

"And what are you doing here?" the poet retorted. "You're no member of the English church."

"It's the law," the Dutchman answered, shrugging. "And it pleases Sir Philip."

And you would do whatever was needed to please Sir Philip, Marlowe thought, but did not pursue the conceit aloud. He had made his point—the undergrooms and some of the local congregation were eyeing him with something approaching horror—and there was nothing to be gained by saying more. He took his place with the rest of the household, eyes downcast demurely. Covell, his nearest neighbor, edged away from him, and Marlowe smiled sweetly, his temper somewhat restored.

Sidney, seated with Greville in the latter's pew, shifted uncomfortably, trying to ease his stiffened leg. It would get better the further they rode, he knew from experience, as the sinews stretched and loosened, but for now he could only endure the sullen aching.

Greville glanced sideways at him, and said softly, "I'll have Ralph prepare a hot bath for you tonight, and see that Goody Watson sends up one of her herb brews."

Sidney gave his friend a wary look. "Herb brews?"

"Oh, yes. She learned the recipe from her grandmother, who was accounted a very wise woman."

Sidney gave him a twisted smile, and shrugged. "Why not? But no witchery, I trust, Fulke."

Greville looked surprised and a little hurt. "Not at all. Her sister nursed me, they're both very wise women. They know their limits."

"Wisdom indeed," Sidney murmured, thinking of his own case.

The service was very plain, with none of the flourishes expected in a London church, or even at Penshurst, where the new young chaplain was very conscious of the reputation of his more notable parishioners. Sidney smiled gently, made aware by the very simplicity of the priest's delivery both of the vital words and of the ritual, and of the transcendent meaning behind both. The priest's voice wavered slightly, but it was from age rather than from ignorance, and Sidney found himself eagerly waiting for the sermon. As the priest stepped up into the lectern, however, there was a sudden disturbance across the main aisle. Sidney turned, startled and rather shocked by such disrespect, and saw a ruddy, black-bearded man pushing his way out of his pew.

"Now, Sir Edward," the priest began, and the black-bearded man held up his hand.

"No, no more," he said, and pushed himself out into the

aisle. He pointed his finger at the priest. "Say what you have got to say, and then—come and dine with me." He turned his back on the pulpit and stalked toward the door, the church wardens giving way before him.

Sidney's eyebrows rose—there was a practiced air to all this that suggested it had happened more than once—and he turned to follow the bearded man's departure. In spite of himself, he glanced toward his own household, standing together toward the back of the nave. Young Madox was crossing himself, his thin face shocked and appalled, but Marlowe's head was down as if in prayer. That I doubt, Sidney thought, and was not surprised to see that the poet's shoulders were shaking with suppressed laughter.

Greville said, almost apologetically, "Sir Edward is a recusant, but he doesn't like to pay the fines."

Sidney nodded. Twelve pence for every missed Sunday mounted up very quickly, had ruined richer men than a mere Warwickshire knight.

"Dearly beloved." The priest's voice was resigned, but also faintly, tolerantly amused, and there was a faint smile on his face. "Our text today is taken from the twelfth chapter of the Gospel according to St. John."

It was a good sermon, Sidney thought, expounding intelligently on the mystery of faith without taking the discussion out of the reach of the common folk who were the majority of the congregation. The plain metaphors brought home the essential points in a new and heartfelt way, and he approached the communion table with a renewed sense of gratitude.

When the service had ended, Greville led the way back down the long aisle, pausing only to exchange greetings with a few of his neighbors. The priest, standing in the doorway to cast a watchful eye over his congregation, smiled benevolently as the two men approached.

"It's good to see you home again, Master Fulke. And an honor to have you in my church, Sir Philip."

"My very great privilege," Sidney replied sincerely.

"Will you dine with us, Father?" Greville asked. There was a schoolboy nervousness about him suddenly, and Sidney gave him a rather startled look.

"Now, Fulke, you know I'm already invited elsewhere,"

the priest answered. "But I thank you nonetheless. It was a kind thought."

"So you do dine with this Sir Edward, Father?" Sidney asked, and the priest studied him curiously, but with a light of humor in his eyes. Sidney spread his hands. "It was not the most gracious invitation I've heard."

"More like an order, yes," the priest answered. "But say it masks a true desire to learn, to be taught. Then surely there can be no refusing. If I'd thought you were objecting to my dining with a Catholic, I would be forced to reprove a lack of charity."

It was a deft rebuke, and Sidney grinned, feeling suddenly like a boy again. "And I think I shall be rebuked for saying I was more concerned with his manners than his religion."

"As you see the fault, my son, I see no need to chide. And after all, I have hopes I may amend both some day."

"I trust you shall, Father," Sidney said, with unexpected feeling in his voice.

"God bless you, my son," the priest said, and the younger men backed away.

Marlowe made his way back through the fields to Greville's house in a better frame of mind than he'd left it, cheered by the recusant Sir Edward's flamboyant gesture. It was the sort of thing he would have liked to do himself, if he had the position and the influential friends that would let him get away with it, and he enjoyed seeing it in other men. A calculated, glorious rudeness, he thought, and a magnificent statement of unbelief. I wonder which bothered Sir Philip more?

Greville and his better-born guests dined apart from the household in a new fashioned dining parlor, attended only by a few servants. Marlowe, whose university degree was considered to make him a gentleman of sorts, sat quietly through most of the meal, watching Sidney. To his annoyance, however, the older man made no mention of the disturbance—he seemed, in fact, strangely tranquil—and Greville deftly steered the conversation onto other matters. Mildly disappointed, Marlowe excused himself as soon as it was decent, pausing only in the outer hall to steal half a partridge and a nearly-full pitcher of ale from among the broken meats set there for the kitchen servants.

The room he had been given was recently remade, the smell of paint and new wood lingering in the air beneath the scent of the herbs mixed into the straw spread across the floorboards. Marlowe set the dented plate on the table, and took a long swallow of the ale before putting it aside as well. He loosened the strings of his ruff, and set it on the end of the bed, then undid the first eight buttons of his doublet, wrenching open the neck of his shirt as well. His saddlebags lay on the floor just inside the door, and he crossed to them, rummaging in the first until he'd found his writing case. He pulled it out, frowning at the cracked leather. Shrugging a little—he would buy a new one when he could afford it—he carried it across to the table, and opened it, shoving the half-eaten partridge out of the way. He settled himself on the low stool and took out paper and quill and the tightly stoppered inkwell, then sat for a moment, smiling thoughtfully at the painted figures of Susanna and the Elders capering on the plastered wall.

He had intended to draft the first of his required letters to Robert Cecil, but instead he found his mind turning to other things. The line from the *Chrestomathy* echoed in his thoughts: *Then came the Amazon, slayer of men.* It would make a magnificent play, he thought, brushing the tip of his quill back and forth across his lips. And what a marvelous pair of matched entrances it could be: first Penthesilea enters with her train of Amazons, and is greeted by the Trojan court mourning for Hector. Priam explains what has happened—that should set things up for the groundlings—and then end with a dignified set piece for Penthesilea, telling of her grief, and promising revenge on the Greek who so mutilated noble Hector. And then . . . Marlowe's smile widened. Then we shift to the Greek camp. Enter Achilles carrying a pair of severed heads, which he adds to the great heap of skulls filling Patroclus's shrine. That would be within, of course—perhaps a pair of pages to discover it formally, to add that touch of perversity to the scene?

Almost without volition, his pen began to move across the paper, sketching the opening. Priam and Hecuba, strophe and antistrophe, remembering their lost son—and then trumpets above, and the Amazon enters. He paused then, looking for the right words, the tip of the quill tapping nervously against his lips. Grief and venegeance and a sort of doomed boyish brilliance, that was what was needed here—but the voice he heard was the voice of his Ganymede, polite and deliberately uninvolved. He cursed, scratching out the last few lines, and shoved the paper aside.

He did owe Cecil some notice of their progress, if only to keep his own skin whole, and there was a certain perverse pleasure in dating the note from Greville's house. He paused for a moment, considering, then quickly scribbled a few lines in his own abbreviated Latin. He had little to say, after all, just that they had reached Warwickshire successfully, and that Sidney had not yet taken him into his confidence regarding his plans for Scotland. He compressed the first note into two epigrammatic sentences, then sat for a moment, studying the scrawled words. Can I abbreviate it any further? he wondered, then shook his head. No, that would look as though I were trying to confuse him, while this is just ambiguous enough.

Smiling to himself, he reached for the thin chain he wore beneath his clothes, drawing out the two objects that dangled from it. His fingers touched first the thin lead disk, marked with the signs and sigils of Scorpio, sovereign against vermin and good as a protection against attack. For no good reason, the familiar touch evoked the memory of the man who'd made it for him: Thomas Watson, poet, sometime playwright, dabbler in magic. . . . Marlowe's mouth twisted. My good friend Tom, dead of the plague these past two years. At least my medal seems to have done more good than all your spells and potions. He ran his thumb lightly across the engraved surfaces, remembering the night it was made. Watson's little chamber had been filled with the choking reek of the twin braziers, incense and the smell of sulpher mixing with melted metal and the stink of the cheap candles, all the shutters latched tight to keep out the noxious night air, and to keep in their secrets. Watson's wife had cowered abovestairs, hiding the children's heads in her skirts and praying for an end to her husband's unhallowed rituals. Well, Marlowe thought, she had gotten her wish, though, like all the devil's gifts, it had not taken quite the form she'd intended. . . .

He pulled his mind away from that despairing theme, running his fingers again across the crudely engraved scorpion in its circle of symbols. *Kit's holy medal*, Watson had called it, laughing. Marlowe sighed, remembering his own answer. *I expect it to be more use than most of that kind*. At least it had kept him freer of vermin than most men, and he'd not died yet in any fight, fair or otherwise— though the latter, he had to admit, was due more to Sidney's intervention than to the powers of the sigil. Unless, of course, the seal had somehow caused that rescue? Even as the thought took shape, Marlowe rejected it. The powers Watson had wielded had no dominion over Sir Philip.

The admission annoyed him, and he released the leaden circle as though it had burned him, fumbling instead for the thin metal cylinder that hung next to it. Anyone seeing it would have assumed that it was some other charm of dubious origin, and let it alone—or so the poet intended. Still frowning to himself, he unscrewed the main cylinder, leaving the cap attached by its ring to the chain itself, and pulled out the tightly rolled slip of paper that held the key to his cipher. He unrolled the stained and fraying paper, flattening it with his left hand, then quickly and carefully copied out his message a final time, switching letters according to the key. When he had finished, he returned the key to its case, tucking it and the sigil back into the front of his shirt, then crossed to the fireplace to uncover the last embers of the morning's fire. As he'd hoped, a few coals still glowed red. He filled his pipe, then twisted the sheet of paper that held the rough draft of his letter into a spill and used it to light the tobacco. Even after the pipe had caught, he did not shake out the fire, but let the paper burn until the flames had almost reached his fingers. Then he set it gently on the hearth, and, when it was ash, crumbled it into nothing. He glanced around automatically, making sure he had left nothing else incriminating, then folded the coded letter into a tiny packet, sealed it,

and tucked that into his purse. He would find someone—a
carter, or any likely traveller—in the next day or so to
take it into London.

That business finished, he leaned thoughtfully against
the windowframe, pushing open the shutter to let in the
cooling air. The breeze had died down as the sun crept
toward the horizon, but there was a distinct scent of rain,
and Marlowe made an angry face. That's what comes of
piety, he thought, a day's ride in the rain. We'll cover half
the ground we could've made today—if we're lucky. He
scowled out into the evening, unmoved by Greville's carefully arranged lawns, thinking of the heavy cart. A muddy
road would slow it unbearably; better in some ways to
have left it behind.

He sighed then, putting the thought aside. It was amazing enough that a gentleman of Sidney's status was travelling with only the one cart, and no coach; that as much as
anything pointed up the importance of the mission. Whatever that mission may be, he added to himself. Or, rather,
whichever mission we end up fulfilling. Sidney has his
commission from the Queen, and I have mine from Cecil—
and God only knows who else among us is committed to
some other plan. For a moment, he toyed with the fantastic thought that every member of the party might be an
agent of some party—van der Droeghe, of course, would
serve the United Provinces; Greville perhaps could be the
French king's man; young Madox was fastidious enough to
be a Spanish agent, while Ralph Haywood would make an
excellent Italian—but rejected it almost at once as unbearably frivolous.

I wish to hell I did know precisely what Sidney intends,
he thought, and pushed himself away from the window.
However, I doubt he'd tell me for just the asking. Of
course—his eyes strayed to the sheets of paper left on the
table—there was another way of finding out.

He hesitated for a moment, remembering the creature
that had lurked in Chapman's mirror, then reached for the
pen before he could change his mind. The ritual Watson
had taught him was of an entirely different nature, its
power far more restricted, than the one Northumberland
had invoked. Slowly, he inscribed the question, *What is*

the intended mission of Sir Philip Sidney in Scotland?, keeping it to a single line, then drew a box around the words. Focussing all his will on the question, he inscribed the paired symbols that compelled an answer, first above and below, and then to either side, reinforcing them with a circle made of the signs of Solomon. When he had finished it, he sat for a moment, studying what he had written, then crossed to the fireplace, bringing the paper with him.

The coal that he had used to light his pipe still glowed faintly. He blew on it, and the glow pulsed gently, like a heartbeat. Quickly, he laid the sheet of paper across it, murmuring the words Watson had made him memorize. A thin curl of smoke rose from beneath the paper, and then, with startling suddenness, the entire sheet blazed into flame, and was completely consumed. Although he had been expecting it, Marlowe flinched back, suppressing a curse. The flame died as quickly as it had bloomed, leaving behind a fragile skin of ash. An instant later, a sudden breeze whirled through the open window, breaking that skin into fragments and scattering them across the hearth. Marlowe sat back on his heels chewing on the stem of his pipe, to study the pattern of fallen ash.

At first, the scraps and smears made little sense, but then, slowly, he began to pick out letters, first an 'm,' and then an 'e,' until he could just make out the shadow of the words *to meet*. To meet what? he thought. At the right side of the hearth, the fall of ash had been much lighter, as though the power that had directed the formation of the letters had weakened before it could finish. He frowned at the faint marks, first leaning closer, then pushing himself away again, but could not make the shapes take on a coherent form.

Behind him, a floorboard creaked. Greville, come to spy on me, he thought, and in the same moment could feel the other man's presence in the doorway. The poet swung round, his brief panic changing to anger, but there was nothing there. He froze, the anger curdling within him, and felt the same presence watching from the curtained bed. He thought he heard the ropes that held the mattress sigh softly against the wood of the frame, and made himself turn again. The curtains were open, the bed apparently empty—but he knew with a sudden sick certainty that something was there. He pushed himself to his feet, a curse dying on his tongue, and tried to control his fear. He didn't have many options—the door was a good four paces away, even if he chose to flee, and, in any case, either flight or a shout for help would only bring Greville's household down on him. That was still something to be avoided, if possible.

"Who are you?" he said aloud, and was surprised at how calm he sounded.

There was no answer from the presence, though he somehow knew that it was aware of him, watching him. Experimentally, he lifted his hand, began one of the testing gestures every university student knew. Nothing seemed to happen at first, but then the room's air thickened. A wave of negation, colder than the air, washed over the poet, implacable in its austere hostility. Marlowe lifted his hands quickly, spreading them wide in a gesture of surrender and apology. After a moment, the pressure lessened, and the room returned to normal. Now what? Marlowe thought, and, after an instant's struggle, managed to speak the words aloud.

The presence did not answer, but slowly, almost imperceptibly, it began to change. The hostility seeped away, draining out of the little room, and in its place came a strange sense of almost dignified appeal. It was almost as if the presence were beckoning to him, Marlowe thought, and knew that the simile was completely inadequate. By degrees, the presence became an invitation. An awareness of its own power, its own immense wealth of knowledge, radiated from it, but beneath that serene surface the poet could feel a sort of passion, a dark intensity that matched and could master his own deepest desires. He shivered, repelled and fascinated, but did not look away. Very slowly, the presence began to take shape before him, a man fair and long-limbed as Ganymede.

Marlowe wrenched his eyes away, remembering the demon he had seen before, but knew the shape was still there. He could almost hear its gentle laughter, not yet—not quite—mocking, could too easily imagine its caress.

He choked on a despairing curse, and made himself lift a nerveless hand to sketch the sign of the cross between the shape and his averted eyes.

"*In nomine patri, filii, et spiritu sancti,*" he whispered, the familiar, hated words bitter on his tongue. "*Abiri!*" The last word was almost a sob, but he could feel the presence lessening, dissolving into nothingness. Even after he was certain it was gone, he stood waiting, afraid either of its return, or that it had vanished forever. At last, he forced himself to move, to cross to the window and close and latch the shutter as though it were the end of any normal day. Then he leaned against the wall, his cheek against the ordinary rough plaster as though that were somehow a link with everyday things. *At least today I've proved the papist doctrine that the virtue is in the words rather than in the speaker,* he thought, but the words rang hollow. Unaccountably, his eyes filled with tears.

The next day dawned cloudy, and before the party had been on the road for an hour, the rains closed in. Sidney watched the clouds approach across the rolling land, curtains of mist falling to hide the low hills, draping themselves across the narrow road. He shivered, and drew up his cloak, pulling the hood well forward to protect his face. All along the line of riders, men muttered curses, adjusting cloaks and hats against the damp. Marlowe's voice rose above the rest, blasphemously ingenious, but Sidney did not look back.

As they rode further, the mist thickened, became a steady, soaking rain. By noontime, the hard ground of the road had softened into a quagmire. Covell nursed the horses, easing them over the worst ground, but by midafternoon it was clear that they would not make more than twenty miles that day.

"At this rate," Greville said, "we'll be lucky to make Nunseaton."

"How you do it . . ." Sidney darted an amused glance at his friend. Greville shrugged almost apologetically, and Sidney shook his head. "I'd counted on getting further. Well, you know the country around here. What's to be done?"

"There's an inn in Nunseaton, a good one," Greville answered.

Sidney grimaced. "Will it be large enough? I don't like inconveniencing our people."

"It has a good reputation, though I've never stayed there," Greville said. "Myself, I'd call it a worse inconvenience to try to push on to Leicester, on a day like this."

Sidney nodded. "If it clears tomorrow, we can make up time then."

Somewhat to Sidney's surprise, however, the inn proved to be both large and prosperous, managed by a bustling apple-cheeked woman who was the widow of a local merchant. She sized up young Madox's inexperience at a glance, and promptly raised her prices. Young Madox, on the other hand, clung stubbornly to his notions of what was suitable for his master, and succeeded in hiring the last of the inn's private dining rooms away from a party led by a stout preacher and his rail-thin wife. Both dining room and bedroom were spotless, with fresh linen on the table and the bed, and the meal, when it arrived at young Madox's orders, was lavish enough to make Sidney raise an eyebrow.

Summoned to explain himself, the steward's son answered that, though the ordinary was quite good, Mistress Massie's talents appeared extensive enough to allow him to order a better meal for the gentlemen, such as would serve to restore them after the unpleasant ride.

"The rest of us are quite comfortably placed," he added guilelessly, forestalling Sidney's next question, "and if you'll excuse me, sir, I'll join them and make sure all's well." Sidney nodded dismissal, and young Madox backed away, pausing in the doorway only long enough to add, "Oh, and by the way, sir. Mistress Massie says it should be clear tomorrow."

"Thank you," Sidney said, and the steward vanished.

"Not that the roads will have dried by then," Marlowe said, quite audibly, from his place by the fire.

For a moment, Sidney toyed with the idea of telling the poet precisely how tiresome he was being, but put the thought aside with some regret. Instead, he nodded to Nathanial, waiting nervously at the sideboard. "You may carve now, Nate. And fill a plate for yourself when you're done."

The boy managed the service deftly enough, carving the mutton and the rabbit without much grace but without waste, and hesitated only over the birds stuffed with fruit.

"One for each of us," Greville prompted softly, "and leave the other for later."

Nathanial blushed, and finished filling the plates. When he had presented them, and poured wine for Greville and Sidney—Marlowe waved the bottle away, calling instead for a mug of beer—Sidney smiled, and dismissed him to join the others. The boy bowed solemnly, but did not forget his promised plateful.

"He'll share that with the other one—Peterkin, is it?" Greville said idly.

Marlowe's mouth curved into an unpleasant, knowing smile, and Sidney lifted an eyebrow at him, daring him to speak. After a moment, the poet looked away, turning his attention to his plate. Sidney listened with half an ear to Greville's rambling flow of conversation, wondering what precisely had troubled the younger man. Marlowe sat silent through the rest of the meal, and excused himself as soon as it was decent, saying he wanted to buy a pipe of tobacco. Sidney hid a sigh of relief as the door closed behind him.

"Perhaps he doesn't like getting wet," Greville suggested.

Sidney said thoughtfully, "I wish I didn't find his silences more disturbing than his conversation."

Greville laughed, but Sidney's smile was rather rueful. I suspect I know where Kit's gone, he thought, but it's not something I want to share with you, my Fulke. I'd almost lay wager that he's gone to find a London carrier, and that there's a letter somewhere about him addressed to Robert Cecil. . . . He pulled away from that train of thought, forcing himself to pay attention to the other man.

"—hand of primero? I'm sure we could borrow a deck from our hostess."

Sidney considered the offer for a moment, tempted, but shook his head. "I'd be no match for you, I'm afraid. I'm more tired than I knew."

Greville nodded. "If I thought I could keep track of the cards, I'd've suggested maw."

"Oh, very well, then," Sidney said, smiling. "But for gleeman's stakes, no more."

"Agreed," Greville answered, and shouted out the door for the potboy. The man appeared promptly, bowed in response to Greville's order, and vanished, to reappear a few moments later with an almost new deck.

"French suits," Greville observed, and dealt the cards.

They played perhaps half a dozen hands before Sidney put aside his cards. "No more, Fulke, I'm playing like a child."

"You, Philip, were never a child." Greville collected the cards expertly, and pushed himself away from the table. "To bed, then?"

Sidney nodded. "Yes. We've a lot of ground to make up in the morning."

Marlowe lay awake in the darkness of the hayloft listening to the noises of the animals in the stalls below. Their shifting and thick breath mingled with the faint snores of the man beside him, and he stretched out a stockinged foot to stroke the stranger's bare ankle. The man shifted, edging closer, but did not wake. Marlowe sighed, grateful for the other's warmth, but could not rid himself of a vague dissatisfaction. He had gotten what he wanted, both the carter's promise to deliver his letter to a certain address in London and momentary oblivion in the other man's arms, but somehow neither success seemed entirely worth the effort. Safe in the familiar stable-dark, barricaded within the ordinary sound and the smells of hay and dung and man-sweat, he let himself remember the tantalizing presence, conjuring the fear and the promise and desire. Mephostophilis should have looked so, been so, he thought. Who then wouldn't've been Faustus?

The wind shifted suddenly, rattling the loose boards of the stable wall, and sending a cold draft under the piled cloaks. The spell was broken. Marlowe cursed softly, and burrowed closer to the oblivious carter, composing himself to sleep.

The next day dawned cloudy, too, but the wind was

already warm, promising a steamy ride. The carters and other professional travellers who had to be on the road at first light, to make up for time lost in the rain, rose cursing, and grumbled their way through hasty breakfasts, hoping to be well along before the heat set in. The change in the weather woke Sidney, too; he slid from the inn-keeper's best bed, and crossed to the window, easing the shutters open as quietly as he could. Greville shifted at the faint noise, but did not wake.

The sun was not yet up, but the stableyard was busy. Sidney frowned as the damp air touched his face, and let the shutters close again. He dressed quickly, not bother-ing to wake Nathanial, asleep on his pallet by the door, and made his way downstairs to the inn's main room. The dampness had left him stiff; he leaned heavily against the stairwell, wishing he had thought to bring his cane.

Most of his household was already awake, gathered around one of the long tables, a platter of salt herring and a wheel of cheese already set out before them. Even as Sidney watched, one of the maidservants, her cap askew and the laces of her bodice hastily done up, appeared, balancing a basket of bread and a jack of ale. She slid them carelessly onto the table, dodging a groom's perfunctory caress, and turned back toward the kitchen, rubbing her eyes as though she were not yet awake. Another woman brought bowls of pottage, dealing them out as though she were dealing a game of cards.

Van der Droeghe, turning to ask for a second pitcher of beer, was the first to see his master, and pushed himself instantly to his feet. The others started to copy him, but Sidney waved them back to their places, saying, "Don't disturb yourselves, please. Jan-Maarten, I just want a brief word with you."

"Of course, Sir Philip." Van der Droeghe came forward quickly to join Sidney, bowing.

"And what do you think of this weather, Jan-Maarten?" Sidney asked quietly.

Van der Droeghe grimaced. "Not a good day for travel-ling, sir. The roads will not dry, I think. And it will be hot. Best we get an early start."

Sidney nodded, his own expectations confirmed. "Young Madox?"

"In the stables, I think, sir, talking to Covell." Van der Droeghe carefully did not smile. "We have spoken, too."

Sidney nodded again. "I'll speak with him myself. Thank you, Jan-Maarten."

Van der Droeghe touched his forehead and backed away. Sighing, Sidney started for the stableyard. A knot of carters made way for him, and he acknowledged the courtesy with a nod and a smile. The tightness in his leg was easing as he walked; he hardly noticed the dull pain. Young Madox was nowhere to be seen in the busy yard. Sidney paused for a moment, but, when the steward did not appear, started for the stable itself.

The dim barn was startlingly quiet. Most of the carters had already harnessed their animals and were on their way; the other animals, belonging to less hurried travellers, still stood placidly in their stalls. Sidney stopped just inside the door, one hand resting on the worn frame, letting his eyes adjust to the dim light. He drew breath to call for young Madox, and heard boards creak in the loft overhead. He looked up, and saw a familiar figure stooping at the head of the ladder, one hand braced against an overhead beam. The light of the new sun fell through the tiny window below the rooftree, striking directly in his eyes; Marlowe lifted his hand against it, wincing. He was disheveled, Sidney saw without particular surprise, doublet half buttoned, stockings sagging, long face set in a curiously blank expression. Then he saw Sidney, and his expression changed, flickering from surprise to something like fear to deliberate, provocative satisfaction. He came down the ladder with a tomcat swagger, grinning. Sidney nodded blandly, ignoring the unspoken challenge, and had the satisfaction of seeing the younger man's mask slip slightly, the wariness returning to his eyes.

"Good morning, Sir Philip."

"Good morning, Marlowe," Sidney answered, and made the words a dismissal. "Madox! Are you here?"

Marlowe slipped past him into the stableyard, seemingly glad of the reprieve. Sidney glanced over his shoulder, and saw the poet wave to a burly man who was tightening the harness of a sturdy-looking cob. The carter paused in his work long enough to grin and nod, and Sidney's eyes narrowed.

"Madox?" There was no answer from the depths of the barn, and Sidney stepped back into the yard. The carter was still struggling with his harness. Sidney hesitated for an instant—do I really want to know that Marlowe's betraying me? he wondered—then started toward the carter. The man looked up at his approach, visibly wary, and Sidney put on his most affable smile.

"London bound?"

"Ay." The carter's eyes were still wary, his face set mulishly against any self-betrayal. Sodomy was a crime against the church as well as against the state, could bring a man to the stake; Sidney kept his expression as open and innocent as possible.

"Then Marlowe found someone to take his letter. Good."

"Oh, ay." The carter straightened, his relief plain. "I said I'd take his letter, no trouble. I'm London bound, should be there in less than a week, if the roads hold."

"That's good time," Sidney said. "I wish you luck."

The carter ducked his head, visibly remembering he was speaking to a gentleman. "Thank you, sir."

Sidney nodded a vague acknowledgement, and started back into the inn after Marlowe. The sight of the crowded main room brought him up short, and he paused just inside the doorway, considering. At the moment, he wanted nothing better than to go in search of the poet, to force a confession and demand to know the contents of the letter, but he knew that to do so would only worsen an already difficult situation. He had guessed from Marlowe's arrival at Penshurst that the poet had been sent to spy on him, had told Greville as much before the journey had even begun. Why then, he demanded silently, should mere confirmation of my suspicions anger me? I knew what Marlowe was—I know the position he is in, and the kind of man he is. More than that, I know that company he kept, those years in London before I became his patron, and, much as it shames me to admit it, I may well need that kind of knowledge before we finish this Scottish business. He sighed deeply, then forced a smile as he saw young Madox approaching across the crowded room. At the moment, he had no choice but to trust Marlowe, and pray that that trust would not be misplaced; should the situation change, however. . . . He put the thought aside unfinished to concentrate on what the steward was saying about the road ahead. Should the situation change, Marlowe might find that he had finally gone too far.

Chapter Eleven

Thrice toss these oaken ashes in the air.
Thrice sit thou mute in this enchanted chair.
Then thrice three times tie up this true love's knot,
And murmur soft: She will, or she will not.
    Thomas Campion,
    "Thrice toss these oaken ashes in the air"

Frances Sidney rested her needlework in her lap, staring at the intricate geometry, black silk on white linen, without really seeing the pattern that was emerging under her hand. The windows were open, to let in the unusually warm air, and with the faint breeze came the sound of a rider, hooves and furniture jingling as he made his way along the approach road. She cocked her head to listen, but the sound faded without bringing a call from the stables. Not a visitor for us, then, she thought, but did not resume her stitching. A bird was singing somewhere nearby—perhaps in the elaborate, untenanted gardens— each heavy note piercing the quiet. The air smelled sweet and soft, soft as the ground washed by the May rains. There was a trill of laughter from the hall below the gallery, and she frowned, recognizing the voice. The youngest of the housemaids, who was maid no longer, but who would be a wife before the babe was born, if Frances had anything to say in the matter, was at her tricks again. . . . Frances shook away the uncharitable thought, and reached for the bell that would summon the housekeeper. Before she could ring it, however, there was a knock at the gallery door, and Madox himself appeared.

"I beg your pardon, my lady," he said, and Frances saw with a little thrill of fear that he was looking unusually grave. Not Philip, she thought, not again, and Madox continued, "The Earl of Essex is below, and craves a moment's private speech with you."

The man's mad, Frances thought, but knew her face did not betray her anger. How dare he even offer to compromise me so? She could read the veiled disapproval in Madox's face, and her lips thinned. "Tell his lordship," she said, steadily, "that I will see him here. Bring refreshments, please, Madox. I believe his lordship is partial to Philip's Rhenish wine."

Madox bowed unspeaking. At her back, Frances heard the rustling of skirts, and knew that her women were gathering themselves to depart. She turned then, allowing herself a small, malicious smile only when her back was to the steward. "No, ladies, you must stay. We'll talk at this end, if his lordship really must be private."

Madox bowed again, more deeply, and Frances felt a momentary pang of guilt. She should not tease him, merely because she was out of temper. . . . She said, with more grace, "Show his lordship here, please, Madox."

"Yes, my lady," the steward said, and disappeared down the stair that led to the hall.

Frances cast a quick eye over the room and her women, dispassionately assessing the picture they presented. The two housemaids in their neat blue dresses, busy at the household's constant mending, her own maid deftly stitching new gilt braid onto an old gown, her own embroidery, all were emblematic of the virtuous household. That should put him in mind of who I am, she thought, and bent her head to her stitching. A part of her wished she had chosen to wear a more becoming gown, but she killed the thought, stabbing her needle into the inoffensive linen. Sad colors became her, and it was just as well for her reputation that she was wearing a closed bodice.

She could hear footsteps on the stairs now, Madox's heavy tread and a lighter, younger step, and in spite of herself her heart gave a little skip of pleasure. She could feel the hot blood rising in her cheeks and bent her head even lower over the embroidery until she had mastered her face.

"The Earl of Essex, my lady," Madox announced from the doorway, and Frances made herself look up slowly.

Robert Devereux bowed gracefully, flourishing his plumed hat, and came forward, a warm smile—the smile of a man quite certain of his welcome—curving his full lips. Frances rose to meet him, holding out her hands in greeting. Essex, covering, folded them into his larger palms and bowed again, reverently, bestowing a light kiss on each set of fingers. Frances shivered at the touch, even as she wished he would not be so obvious in his attentions in front of her household.

"Welcome, my lord," she said, and was pleased that her voice sounded as cool and remote as she had intended, betraying nothing of her inward excitement. "Madox, if you'd fetch wine for his lordship?" That was a mistake, she knew—she had already ordered that—but Madox did not betray his thoughts by even the flicker of an eyelash. He bowed profoundly, saying, "Very good, my lady," and disappeared again.

"My dearest lady," Essex said. He had a marvellous voice, husky yet oddly musical, and he pitched it now to a confiding murmur. An insinuating voice, Frances thought, and became aware that he was still holding her hands. She drew back slightly, and he released her at once, with only a wistful smile. He was all in black velvet, save for falling collar and silk-embroidered cuffs, the sobriety of the doublet relieved only by huge arabesques of pearls. Black and white were the queen's colors, she remembered, and was annoyed by her own momentary jealousy.

"My very dearest lady," Essex said again.

"My lord," Frances said. "What brings you to Penshurst?"

A frown flickered across Essex's pale face, was gone almost before Frances was sure she had seen it. "Matters of some importance, my lady, if I might prevail on you to hear me privately."

Frances hid her own frown at that, and was saved from having to make an immediate reply by Madox's reappearance. The steward set his tray on a carved sideboard, and poured two glasses of the amber wine. Frances let him serve them in silence, and rewarded him with a smile as he backed away. She said, smiling at Essex, "The world being what it is, my lord, let's walk apart. We can be private enough here."

"My lady's wish is a command," Essex answered promptly, and offered her his arm. Frances slipped her free hand into the curve of his elbow, and Essex tucked it close against his body, trapping her hand gently against his ribs. She could imagine with startling clarity the body beneath the layers of cloth, and glanced away too late to hide her faint blush. Essex smiled slightly, but did not press his advantage.

They walked the length of the gallery in silence. Only when they had reached the end, and were out of earshot of the busy women, did Essex pause at last. "My lady," he said, and pitched his voice to the very bottom of its register. They're the same tricks that Mary Herbert uses, Frances thought, but could not break the spell.

"I realized that it is somewhat—awkward—for me to visit here in the absence of your husband," Essex continued, with another of his little smiles, "but I plead an excuse—besides my passion—that must satisfy even the most precise moralists." He paused, as though expecting a cue, but Frances did not respond. "You are doubtless aware of the circumstances surrounding your husband's mission."

This time, his hesitation was long enough to force some answer. "I know something of it," Frances said, and took refuge in the wifely, downward glance. "But certainly not all the particulars."

Under her hand, she felt Essex take a deep breath, but she could read nothing of his emotions in his gentle smile. "You, of all women, would be aware of the larger consequences of helping the king of Scots," he said at last, and Frances did not hide her own lightning smile. That, at least, was something that could be said in Essex's favor:

while none of Elizabeth's courtiers could fail to acknowledge the queen's political wisdom, he at least recognized
that other women might well share her interest and ability.

Essex went on as though he had not noticed her change
of expression. "Sir Philip—forgive me, my lady, but I'm
not certain he is fully aware of what may come of his
actions in the north."

"Indeed?" Frances murmured, and was surprised at her
own sudden indignation.

Essex ducked his head in apology. "I can only ask you to
forgive me, sweet lady, for mentioning what can only be
an unpleasant truth. But Philip has never been the wisest
of politicians, or the coolest of courtiers."

That was true enough, and Frances nodded, offering a
rueful smile of her own. "Still, her majesty has always
valued his freedom. . . ."

"The king of Scots may find that less—endearing," Essex answered, with another smile, this one filled with
tolerance for an older man's folly. "More than that—it's a
delicate game her majesty is playing, and Philip's unswerving
championship of what he sees as the right may well upset
the balance."

He paused again, waiting for some cue, and Frances
responded with a soft, interrogative murmur that hid her
own racing thoughts. It was true that Philip had never
hesitated to speak out even at the cost of banishment from
the court, as his opposition to the queen's proposed French
marriage—a *crowning piece of folly, had she meant it*, had
been his final, bitter verdict—had amply demonstrated.
But it was equally true that Elizabeth valued his candor
even as she punished him for it, and had never allowed his
rivals to take advantage of her moments of pique. So if it's
English matters you're concerned about, she thought, I
think you're worrying over nothing. She smiled inwardly,
rather touched by Essex's feeling for his old rival. Well,
perhaps not rival, truly, she amended, not in politics or—I
trust—in love. Essex was speaking again, and she dragged
her attention hastily back to him.

"I must speak to you on a matter of some delicacy, my
dearest lady, for I know I can trust you with my life as well

as with England's future." Essex lowered his voice almost
to a whisper, though there was no likelihood that the
women, still sewing at the far end of the gallery, could
overhear even an ordinary conversation. "My sweet, it is
decided—it is quite certain—that James will be her majesty's heir, and it's equally certain that he will come into
that inheritance in not very many years. Her majesty, God
keep and protect her, is an old woman; it would be of
immeasurable advantage to the country if she would admit
that fact, and name her heir openly. Scotland is a dangerous neighbor, with its French connections and its troublesome nobles. Until her majesty names her heir, it is to our
advantage to keep the king of Scots dependent on England
in other ways. And that, dearest lady, is where Philip may
destroy years of policy."

But not necessarily wise policy, Frances thought. Gratitude might well count for little with princes, even the
gratitude for so great a favor as freeing James from the
persecution of Satan's agents, but it was a safer force than
threats. Even a man as precariously poised as James would
have to take risks to free himself from what he could only
view as English tutelage, some day, and that would not
bode well for England.

"If he sets James securely on his throne," Essex continued, "what reason will James have to listen to England's
advice?"

More rhetoric, Frances thought, and I'll have an end to
it. Whose voice are you aping, I wonder? She found
herself looking at Essex as though she had never seen him
before—which perhaps I never have, she thought, or never
hard enough to glimpse what lies behind the handsome
mask. Even did I love you—and the thought was shocking
now, that she might have done so—I could not love this
backhanded dealing, nor countenance it for the sake of my
own good name. "It's good of you to tell me all this, my
lord," she said, and marvelled that she was able to keep
up the brittle courtly tone. "But I cannot see what help it
does me now. Had you told me a month ago, perhaps
. . ." She let her voice trail off, watching Essex from under
her lashes.

"My lady—my very dearest lady." Essex caught both her bands in his again, pulling her around to face him squarely. "I thank you for your kindness, too great to be deserved. There is one thing you can do for me—not that for which I have so ardently striven all the years, but something which I may ask and you may grant, in all honor and indeed in service both to Philip and to England."

Frances did not answer, schooling herself to utter immobility, and Essex hurried on. "My lady, Philip has sent no word to the court of his plans. Not even the queen knows precisely what he intends once he reaches James's court."

Another lie, Frances thought. I know Philip's sense of duty too well to believe that—and this tells me, too, that you are not so far in her majesty's confidence as you would have me believe. There was a growing coldness in the pit of her stomach, half anger and half the pain of a lost dream. She swallowed it, tasting bile and managed to say with false concern, "Indeed, my lord?"

"I fear so, my lady. And yet rumor speaks of unimaginable things."

"Rumor often does," Frances said. "And rarely speaks true."

"So we pray, and most devoutly," Essex answered.

It's time we drew unbated blades, Frances thought, dispassionately, and high time I struck first. "My lord, I understand your worries—" *All too well*, she added silently, and was shocked again by the depth of her anger. "—but I cannot understand why you've come to me. While Philip was at home, perhaps I could have helped you, but not now."

"There is one thing, madam," Essex answered. He was watching her very closely now, though he did his best to hide it. "It is said that Sir Philip can promise—and boasts he can fulfill that promise—the king of Scots many things— that he will offer to protect him against these dark powers, that he can even offer to rid the kingdom of Satan's minions forever. A dangerous boast, my lady, if it's true, but there is one thing more. Rumor whispers that Sir Philip Sidney owns a great and powerful book that will allow him to do these things—though rumor cannot name the author, nor the provenance of this mysterious text."

Frances made herself meet Essex's stare with wide and innocent eyes. Behind that mask, her thoughts were racing. She knew of Virgil's book, and Philip knew she knew of it, though he had never spoken of it to her; she could only guess, though she was no such scholar as the Sidneys, at the powers it commanded. The mention of Virgil's name would certify the magic to be of the whitest, that she knew, and put an end to some of the whispering—but setting any parameters to the powers Philip wielded might well endanger him, give his unknown Scottish enemy some advantage. Better in the end to risk the accusation of black magic, than to betray anything to Essex. "I fear, my lord," she said slowly, "I know nothing of such matters. I am not learned in the arts, though I have ever believed—and do still believe—Philip's magic to be of the purest."

"I have no doubt of that, my lady," Essex said, with a quick and private smile. "It is this rumored book that concerns us all."

"Us, my lord?" Frances asked, and winced as Essex gave her a rather sharp look in return.

"Why, the court, my lady, and the queen."

"Indeed," Frances murmured, and did her best to sound impressed by his superior knowledge. Apparently, the pretense satisfied him, and he returned to his primary interest.

"Has Philip never said anything to indicate that he might own such a fabulous thing? Is there nothing he treasures so highly, or has forbidden to you? Anything at all that you can tell me, dearest lady, would serve not only me but Philip, too."

Frances fought down her surging anger, and shook her head. "I regret, my lord, I know nothing that would help you—nothing that would indicate either that he has or does not have such a thing—should such a marvellous book exist at all. I cannot help wondering if common folk have been deceived, or have perhaps tangled Philip's library—which is a marvel in and of itself—with his more arcane studies."

That was a bow drawn at a venture, but she was pleased to see a flicker of consternation cross Essex's face. It might not discomfit a more knowledgeable man, but any doubts she could sow would only help Philip.

Essex bowed again. "That might in truth be so," he conceded, and straightened. "My lady, I am most grateful to you for receiving me, all unannounced, and with only your women to accompany you."

What, will you leave me already? Frances thought. A most ungallant gallant! She suppressed the temptation to continue with the game, to force Essex to play out his lover's hand, and schooled her expression to a wistful smile. She allowed Essex to extricate himself from the situation with only the minimum of protest required to keep the earl from suspecting her revulsion of feeling—a surprisingly small amount, she thought, but then, he's always had a great conceit of himself. She walked with him to the main door, calling for Madox to have the earl's horse brought, and stood for a long moment in the open doorway, watching her would-be lover ride away. When at last the little cavalcade disappeared around the distant curve of the approach, she turned away, and sought refuge in Sidney's study, ignoring Madox's wary, scrupulously unquestioning presence.

Once inside, the door firmly latched behind her, she leaned against the edge of the massive table, staring blindly at the shuttered windows, closed to keep the room safe against Sidney's return. Oh, fool, fool, she repeated silently, though of herself, Essex, or her husband, she was uncertain. There was cause enough on all three parts, that she knew, and writhed inwardly at her own guilt, but of the three, Philip's was the most minor folly. It was a folly of honor and loyalty that had brought Essex into her company in the first place, and a further folly that allowed him to remain there, to court her still. And how could Philip, of all men, have ever so adored that foppish fool? she railed, but knew the answer even before the question was fully formed. Essex had seemed to be everything Sidney was and all he had never been as well, the successful courtier and favorite as well as the poet and patron and soldier. I felt that too, she thought, I was drawn to that—that pliant charm that Essex has and that Philip never could possess. But beneath that pretty surface, there's none of Philip's steel.

She trailed her hand along the edge of the table, aware of the birdsong outside, so different from the uncanny silence of his last night at Penshurst. They had been so close then; everything could have been made new again, with just a little time. Essex's plan threatened that, too—and God help me, she thought, with a ghostly smile, I'm woman enough to count that the greatest of his sins.

She looked down at the table. On it—it was as though he had just left—a quill lay across a blotted page, and near it lay the simple ring Philip always slipped from his hand when he was working. Frances picked it up, closed her fingers over it, fancying it still warm from his hand. There was much to consider now, plans to make, but she needed knowledge before she could act to any purpose.

"Madox!"

The steward appeared so quickly that she knew he had been hovering in the hallway, but in her present mood she could forgive him much for his loyalty to Philip. "My lady?"

"Tomorrow I will travel to Mortlake, to Doctor Dee. My errand should not take more than the day, but in the event that I must remain overnight you must see to matters here. If my lord of Essex should return, tell him—" She paused, trying to think of a lie that could not be disproved too quickly. "Tell him that I have gone to Wilton—no, better still, tell him I've ridden out to oversee some little matters concerning the estate. On no account must he know I've gone to Mortlake."

More than surprised, but trying not to let it show, Madox bowed. "Very good, my lady. Will you take Fischer with you?"

"Yes. And I want to travel quickly. Tell the grooms."

"I shall, my lady."

Frances watched him go, smiling faintly in the shadowed light. Both Philip and Essex thought they knew her well. They were both about to find out how wrong they were.

The ride to London had never seemed to take so long. The household was up before dawn, and Frances herself was dressed and ready well before Fischer brought the horses around to the main door. She checked briefly, seeing that the groom had a pillow prepared for her so that she might ride pillion like a great lady, but allowed Madox to throw her up behind Fischer without open protest. When the cortege—Fischer and four grooms, each with a cased pistol at his saddlebow—reached Sevenoaks, however, and Fischer called a halt to breathe the horses and feed the men, Frances slid from her seat with an impatient frown. She glanced around the busy innyard, gauging the place's resources, and her frown eased a little.

"Fischer, I told you I was in haste. Hire me a woman's saddle and put it on the bay gelding. I'll ride the rest of the way myself."

"But, my lady—" the groom began, and stuttered to a stop as Frances turned on him.

"It's a matter of importance, man. Do as I tell you."

"Yes, my lady." Fischer swallowed hard. "And Hugh, my lady?"

Hugh was the groom who had been riding the gelding. Frances controlled her annoyance with an effort. "Let him stay here—or hire a hack for him, if your sense of propriety's too nice to let me travel with only four to my escort. We've money enough. But I will ride." She paused, and managed what she hoped was a winning smile. "Let's spare the horses, Fischer, as much as we may."

The groom's expression softened a little. "Very well, my lady," he said. "If your ladyship would accept a glass of ale, we'll be about it."

"Thank you, Fischer," Frances answered, and bunched her skirts together to slip into the inn's main room. The innkeeper and his wife bustled about her, neglecting their lesser patrons, but she declined more than the pot of ale and a single savory tart. By the time she had finished it, and shaken off their further courtesies, Fischer had negotiated the hire of a woman's saddle. He had also, she saw with some amusement, hired a piebald hack for the extra groom.

"Well done, Fischer," she said again, and was gratified by his sudden blush. "Are the men seen to?"

"Yes, your ladyship, thank you."

"Then we ride," Frances said, with decision, and swung herself up into the new saddle, arranging her skirts deftly as she settled herself.

It took them much of the daylight to come within sight of London. Fischer led them by the best roads, hardened now by a few weeks of summer warmth. The rolling land was planted now, the fields ripening toward the promised harvest, the hedgerows already bright with early flowers. The youngest of the grooms sang cheerfully to himself, his voice rivaling the birds that answered him from the clustered trees; twice a peasant girl straightened from her labor to stare after him, and, glancing back, Frances saw one pause and pluck a hedge-rose, setting it defiantly between her breasts.

"Pity you won't have the picking," an older groom said, and the singer blushed and fell silent.

Frances lifted an eyebrow, but could not bring herself to reprove either man. There were too many things at stake now, too many uncertainties, to waste time on such trivial matters. Her mouth tightening again to a grim line, she set spurs to her horse, urging it to a faster trot. The grooms exchanged nervous glances, their teasing forgotten, and followed her.

As they passed through the hamlets surrounding London, they began to meet more travellers on the road, farm-folk, mostly, bearing empty baskets away from the city's daily markets, and their pace slowed perceptibly. Frances swore softly, but made herself accept the pace Fischer set them. She could not ride down the dull-eyed folk, whose only concern was to reach their homes before the sunset, and who could only be cursing the lady whose horses forced them from the roadway. . . . She swore again, this time at a swaying wain, and reined the gelding to a walk.

Then at last the spires of London were visible in the distance, and Frances named them with a sort of idle impatience, St. Paul's and St. Mary-le-Bow, St. Laurence fading behind them, and St. Bride's to the west, marking time until they reached Walworth, and could turn southwest along the river toward Mortlake. The distinctive shapes of the playhouses showed now among the dirty chimneypots of Southwark, but no flags flaunted above the thatched circles. Frances frowned, glad to forget her own troubles for a moment. This was the height of the players' season, warm enough to attract proper crowds, but too early in the year for plague to have set in. It was more than strange that at least one playhouse was not open—or was there plague after all? she wondered suddenly, and dismissed the thought. That sort of news travelled like the wind. There were other reasons in plenty for London's aldermen to close the theaters, and she put the question from her mind. That was more her brother-in-law Pembroke's affair, or Philip's, were he here; she had no choice but to busy herself with politics.

Fischer led them southwest now, roughly paralleling the river, but avoiding the worst of the city traffic. He chose the route well, Frances admitted: they met only the occasional dray or heavy cart to slow their passage. It was a pity she could not go by water, she thought, not for the first time, but her presence in London would have been noted, and the visit would eventually have come to Essex's ears. Better to travel quietly by road, and hope to meet no one who would recognize her on the way. And there was not much danger of that, she thought, with a quick and private smile, unless the queen was hunting from Richmond today.

They reached Dee's house as evensong was sounding, the bell's strokes heavy in air that thickened toward an amber sunset. Frances, dismounting in the pleasant courtyard, tilted her head at the first stroke, breathing a silent prayer. She shook herself briskly then, straightening her crumpled skirts, and stepped forward to meet the woman who came slowly to greet her. She was an older woman, grey hair tucked neatly beneath an embroidered cap, and, by the quality of her plain gown and equally plain apron, no servant.

"Mistress Dee?" Frances hazarded, and was answered with a shaky curtsey.

"I am she, my lady." The woman's eyes were wary, and Frances could see a younger woman hovering in the doorway, ready to offer whatever support was needed in the face of this invasion.

"I am Frances Sidney, madam. I've come to speak with your husband on a matter of some urgency, if you would tell him that I'm here."

The woman hesitated, her eyes darting almost involuntarily toward the bay at the end of the house where Dee's library lay, and Frances bit back her own impatience. "Madam, I beg you, this concerns my own husband. If he's with another, I will wait, I ask only that you tell him that I'm here, and what my business is."

Dee's wife made an odd face, the expression so fleeting that Frances could not be sure what it meant, but nodded. "Of course, my lady. Won't you come in? Margaret will see your people housed."

The woman in the doorway came forward then, beckoning to Fischer, and Frances followed Mistress Dee through the carved doorway.

"The boy will tell him you're here, my lady," she said, and nodded to a round-eyed boy who was hovering just inside the hall. The boy skittered away down the long hall, but reappeared almost at once.

"Grandfather says you're to come in, please, ma'am—my lady, I mean."

"Thank you," Frances said, with a smile for both of them, and followed the boy back down the panelled hall. The old scholar was waiting in the open door of the study, and bowed to her as she approached. He was very fine today, Frances noted, a fine velvet gown over his sad-colored suit, and Venetian lace edging his small ruff. He welcomed her with ill-concealed nervousness, and when he at last bowed her into the room, she saw why. Sir Walter Raleigh stood near a long window, open now to the evening breeze. He had a book opened in his hand—a very handsome study in the pursuit of knowledge, Frances thought, but not convincing. He must have heard the announcement of my arrival.

Frances managed a brilliant smile, and held out her hands. "Sir Walter, we've been strangers far too long.

How pleasant to see you again—and in such circumstances, too."

Raleigh's eyes flickered over her head to Dee, but the look in them was almost of supplication. It was not the look of a conspirator, and that, Frances thought, had always been Raleigh's difficulty. He lacked a certain quality of calculation—unlike Essex, who rarely acted without artifice. It was hard to believe, today, that she had once been flattered by those studied attentions. . . . She shook the thought away, and let Dee lead her to a chair by the unlit fire. She smiled up at him as she seated herself, spreading her marigold skirts carefully about her. "Forgive me, Doctor Dee, I had no idea you already had a guest, but I hope you will both forgive me. The matter is urgent."

Dee looked down at her gravely, recognizing the steel in her voice. "I feared it might be, Lady Sidney. I wonder if it has aught to do with what has brought Sir Walter here."

"As I did not expect to see Sir Walter here, I can hardly answer that," Frances said. "But if it has anything to do with Philip, I would appreciate learning of it."

Raleigh squared his broad shoulders. "As a matter of fact, Lady Sidney, it has."

"Please," Dee interrupted, "sit down, Sir Walter, let us all be comfortable."

Raleigh hesitated, but did as he was told, settling himself sideways into the window seat. It was a boy's position he'd chosen, one silk-stockinged knee cocked up, beringed hands clasped around it, and Frances did not hide her smile. So refreshingly unlike Essex, whose boyishness was as calculated as any other gesture. . . . Dee lowered himself slowly into the tall chair behind his working table, and she turned her attention back to him, fixing him with an unwavering stare.

"Lady Sidney." Dee acknowledged her look with a rather sad brief smile. "It's indeed fortunate that you're here—indeed, it gives me to wonder if perhaps the angels are not guiding us today. I do not believe in coincidence, only in the co-incidence of events—and your and Sir Walter's both arriving here, this same day . . ." He shook that thought away, and continued, "May I be so bold as to ask the reason for your visit?"

"Only if I may first be told Sir Walter's," Frances answered, and her tone, though polite, was utterly implacable. "He has said it has something to do with Philip. He and Philip have cordially disagreed, in matters both arcane and political, for some time now. In the face of this, I feel he must speak first."

Dee nodded gravely, and glanced toward the man in the window seat. Raleigh bowed as best he could in his seated posture, reflecting bitterly that he'd always hated dealing with the Walsinghams. Frances was unlike her father in her frankness, but that very frankness was almost more devastating than all Sir Francis's wiles. It was rather like riding point-blank into cannon fire, and while that might suit Sir Philip Sidney, Raleigh thought, it does not suit me. What can one do? The Walsinghams are masters of lies and, being so, they know one almost before it leaves one's lips. Uncanny, inhuman creatures from whom the human soul can have no secrets . . . A dry voice in his head told him that he was overstating the case: that, though this was born a Walsingham, it was also a woman, a wife who had been less than faithful to her husband for the better part of a decade, and whose questions, therefore, could not be motivated by concern for him. But that voice sounded too much like Northumberland, an antiquated voice, dusty from too long seclusion from the things of this world—and if Frances Sidney was fool enough to be seduced by Robert Devereux, Raleigh thought, looking at the stiff figure in her marigold gown, the skirts still a little dusty from her long ride, I would be very much surprised. Philip, now, that's another matter—but that was ten, no, twelve years ago, and who would not have been flattered by Essex's obvious adoration, each gesture made with the cheerful sincerity of a puppy? No man could resist that slavish imitation—though women, Raleigh thought suddenly, more often than not see through that sort of man. And yet her majesty has not—which I do believe as an article of faith means only that Essex is that rare soul who can change his ways from that which will deceive a man to those that will win a woman. But if that's so, why is

Frances here? He took a deep breath then, pulling himself back to the present with an effort.

"Lady Sidney. I've come to Doctor Dee because he is one of your husband's oldest friends, his teacher and wise councillor, and I believe Philip to be in some danger. A danger not wholly to do with this Scottish business."

"Indeed?" Frances said, with a lift of her eyebrows. "I should have thought that to be peril enough."

Raleigh drew breath again, unable to free himself from her quelling stare, and tried once again to collect his thoughts. "Philip and I have never agreed about arcane matters, nor, therefore, have Doctor Dee and I. But it seems that Philip is moving—beyond—both what Doctor Dee and I know, to something else entirely. Certainly Doctor Dee has told me so much today. And it's that—new art—which has brought me here, which I have reason to suspect is a cause of danger to him."

Frances directed a quick glance toward Dee, surprised that the old man should have revealed so much, but could read nothing in Dee's still face. The news was nothing new to her: at odds though she had been with Sidney for some years, she had not failed to take note of what he did and who he was. He had changed since Holland—as witness our estrangement, she thought, which nevertheless had nothing to do with some new school of magic, comforting though it might be to think it. That had more to do with youthful folly, a vast embarrassment, even perhaps a love too complicated to be easily articulated. But, more even than the wound that had been the physical cause of so many different troubles, Holland had made Sidney a soldier—and that, she thought, with sudden triumph, that was the real root of this new magic. As he learned that art, he had grown less enchanted with Dee's rigorous, calculated, deliberate forms of magic. Perhaps there was less need for that discipline, or there was some new discipline, which, she knew, would have to be a more demanding one if Philip were to embrace it. It had always been so, or so even Greville said: each challenge met and mastered meant that Sidney must seek out one newer and more difficult. Having mastered the conventional magic of the angels that

Dee taught, Philip had invented one still more rigorous—or had he? she wondered suddenly. Essex had spoken of an ancient book: though he had not fully grasped the significance of what he asked, had sought a purely political advantage. Virgil's book then was the source of Philip's new knowledge. How did this trouble Raleigh?

She smiled slightly. "I do not share in my husband's studies, Sir Walter. My family have never possessed the Dudley brilliance, in those areas, at least. However, I shall be candid with you. Philip possesses something that the earl of Essex wishes to acquire."

"I daresay he does," Raleigh said grimly. "And he's not alone. Madam, permit me to ask—does Philip possess a special text of some kind, some ancient book?"

Frances lifted an eyebrow, buying time, and Dee said softly, "Why do you ask, Sir Walter?"

Raleigh turned as though goaded. "So that I know exactly what it is his grace—" He gave the words a savage twist. "—of Northumberland wants, and how not to give it to him."

"I thought you and the earl were in agreement in arcane matters," Frances said.

"So generally we are, but I can't like the extremes to which Henry's willing to go," Raleigh spread his hands like a man abandoning a position. "It's no longer seeking knowledge for its own sake, for the glorification of God and his gifts or even of England, my lady. It's all pure greed and jealousy, a kind of madness. After all, he's known as the Wizard Earl, while Philip's never had a name in that direction—at least not commonly, though anyone who's ever participated in the Tilts, or knows him as a scholar, knows better than that. But those are precisely the men who make or break a scholar's reputation, and Henry's jealous of them, of the way they regard Philip. And now he's hinting Philip has some near-mythical text." He paused, and managed a wry smile. "And I grant you, if anyone could find Virgil's long-lost book of power, it would be Philip Sidney. And he's done it, hasn't he?"

Frances did not answer for a long moment, weighing her choices. On the one hand, Raleigh had always been

Northumberland's staunch friend and ally, and even if he meant what he said now, she doubted it would take any great use of power on Northumberland's part to find out anything she revealed. On the other hand, she did not think Raleigh was lying when he said he did not wish the Wizard Earl to take the book—and, more important still, Raleigh had never been a friend to Essex. "Yes," she said, "he has."

Raleigh groaned. "I was afraid of it. Henry will stop at nothing to possess such a thing."

"I do wonder," Frances said, "how Northumberland came to hear of it."

Raleigh spun to face her, his eyes widening. "Not through me, ma,am, I swear to it. It was only when Henry started hinting, questioning, that I suspected—guessed, more like. But I didn't know."

Frances smiled up at him. "No, I didn't think you'd told him, Sir Walter, truly. But someone must have, and I would say I knew just who it was—if only I knew how he'd come to know. . . ."

"Not Marlowe," Raleigh said, and Frances laughed aloud.

"No, not Philip's poet. Essex, sir, Essex who's come to me already to hint that there's a book of doubtful provenance in Philip's hands, a book he might not be able to control."

Raleigh nodded slowly. "That's the story Henry whispers, too. You may well be right, my lady, and as to how he knows . . . Philip may well have told him something of it years ago, when they were still friends. Philip used to tell him everything."

"He didn't tell Fulke Greville about it," Frances said. "Why tell Essex?"

Raleigh shrugged. "Why not? The boy was plausible enough. And Philip, God bless him, is as susceptible to flattery as the rest of us poor mortals." He glanced to Dee then, who had listened unmoving to the exchange. "And Essex wants it, too?"

"He wants to make political use of it, at any rate," Frances snapped, and with an effort banished the anger from her voice. "I came to you, Doctor Dee, because I know very little of the arcane, nor have I any way of judging how I may help Philip here in England until I know what this book means, and what besides the human threats I understand he may face in Scotland. From you, Sir Walter, I must ask both your silence, and your knowledge of how things stand at court. I have not been there for any length of time, the past three years, and I am out of touch."

"However I may serve you, lady, I'm yours to command," Raleigh answered instantly, and the fervor in his voice was unmistakable.

Dee cleared his throat gently. "I think Sir Walter's silence will not serve us at all, Lady Sidney." Frances frowned, and Dee gave her a rather embarrassed smile. "Though I doubt Sir Walter intended any duplicity. But I think his coming here was not entirely at his own behest. Before Philip left for Scotland, he came to me, and we discussed the safety of his text—including the possibility of leaving it here, in my care. Northumberland is a talented man, if misguided. He may have become aware of our discussion." He turned his smile on Raleigh, who sat open-mouthed. "Though not of our ultimate decision, which was simply that Mortlake is no safe place for a book of that power."

Raleigh closed his mouth with a snap of teeth. "I did not—I had no intention of bearing tales to Henry, Doctor Dee, so help me Almighty God! I simply wished to know what it was he wanted, to keep it from him—"

"I believe you." Dee held up his hand, and added gently, "But you must not blame Lady Sidney if she does not."

Frances smiled, forestalling the explorer's protest. "No, Sir Walter, I do believe you. I'm well enough acquainted with you to know that such treachery isn't within your nature."

"Thank you, Lady Sidney," Raleigh said, and Dee cleared his throat again.

"Nonetheless, we may turn this to our advantage, I believe. I do not wish to spend my old age fending off attacks. You must tell Northumberland, Sir Walter, in whatever roundabout way you wish, that I do not have the text. And if you must tell him what text it is, well, I don't think that will harm Philip either." Dee turned troubled eyes on Frances then. "Your mission, my lady, is the more important, and I confess I do not know quite where to begin to aid you. If you could stay with me for some few days? We're no great distance from London, or from the court; perhaps from here you could more easily juggle both politics and magic."

"If I can help you, Lady Sidney," Raleigh began, and Frances smiled at him.

"I will call on you, Sir Walter, never fear." She looked back at Dee, her expression hardening. "And I will also accept your offer, Doctor Dee, I assure you. I'd hardly dared hope for so much."

Chapter Twelve

I pray you, good man Fakques, let me have my
money, for ye have my money, the which I lost,
and that was taken from and conveyed out of my
bowchett [purse], for ye have it as it is shewed
me by a soothsayer.
London Diocesian Records, 1510, quoted in Keith
Thomas, **Religion and the Decline of Magic,**
p. 256

The clouds pressed low over the city. Edward Alleyn,
crossing London Bridge toward home, glanced up as he
felt the first cold drops on the back of his neck, and
grimaced at the ragged clouds drooping down between the
housetops. He turned up the collar of his good wool cloak
and quickened his pace a little, but as he reached the end
of the bridge, the rain poured down as though a giant
knife had slashed the sagging clouds. St. Saviour's offered
the closest shelter. Hunching himself into the suddenly
inadequate cloak, Alleyn ducked into the churchyard and
dashed between the tombs until he reached the door. It
was propped open, and he slipped into the nave, to stand
dripping on some worthy's marking stone.

It lacked some hours yet to evensong, and the church
was hardly crowded. The drunken beggar-woman who

cried flowers and curses at the end of the bridge span crouched by the nearest pillar, wringing out her filthy skirts. She darted a malevolent glance at Alleyn, but, to his intense relief, did not break out into one of her tirades. Nevertheless, he gave her a wide berth as he strolled up the main aisle.

Beyond her—well beyond her reach, the actor noted, with sympathetic amusement—two more women, each with a shopping basket on her arm, stood chatting, clearly glad of the rain as an excuse to prolong their conversation. Alleyn recognized the stouter of the two as a near neighbor, and bowed to her. She rewarded him with a simper and a gap-toothed smile; her friend, however, sniffed ostentatiously, and looked away. The stout woman nudged her hard, expostulating with her, but Alleyn turned away before he could see the outcome. That was what came of troublemakers like Jonson, he thought, and directed his steps into the side aisle. Honest actors are tarred with his brush, and we've difficulties enough these days.

At the far end of the nave, the verger was lighting one of the hanging lamps, stretching awkwardly up with a piece of slow match hooked on his long pole. The flames spluttered in the damp air, but drove away some of the gloom. Sighing, Alleyn seated himself on the edge of St. Saviour's oldest tomb, running a hand idly across the deep-carved letters. Usually this link with past centuries was reassuring, but today it only reminded him of the security he could no longer provide his family. The London theaters were closed, and no one seemed willing even to consider setting a day on which they might reopen; that was beginning to sound like a summer's tour, with all the hazards and slim profits travelling always implied. Damn Benjamin Jonson, Alleyn thought. I hope to God he hangs for this. It was an unworthy thought, particularly in this setting, but his fingers itched to strike the man.

There was a movement in the shadows, up by the side chapel. Alleyn glanced toward it, and saw a liver-colored mongrel, its jaunty tail as tightly curled as a pig's, making its way down the side aisle and sniffing at the tombs as it went. It was followed by a boy in a flat cap and a long-skirted coat—a familiar boy, Alleyn thought, his face easing into a smile, and an all too familiar hound. He lifted his hand to beckon to the boy, but even as he gestured, the boy looked up. He lifted his own hand in eager response, whistling the dog to heel, and came to meet the actor, his scarred and homely face breaking into a grin.

"Hello, master, I was sent to look for you."

"And was it clairvoyance, Pig, that had you looking in the apse?"

The boy's grin didn't waver, unperturbed by the mock reproof in Alleyn's voice. "Well, it came on to rain, master, and I knew you wouldn't walk in such a downpour. So Bartholomew and I came in here to wait."

"I'm glad you credit me with the sense to come out of the rain," Alleyn murmured. John Pyk was his own apprentice, and the best, in Alleyn's not always private opinion, of the half-dozen boys presently attached to the company. "Who sent you, Pig? Or who wants me?"

Pig made a little shrugging motion. "Mistress Alleyn sent me, master, but it was Master Henslowe who sent to her. Master Henslowe says, master, that the Chamberlain's Men have gone all together to the Recorder, and would you meet him at the Anchor to wait for their return?"

Alleyn sighed, all his worries returning in a rush. Two days before, on a fine day that should have filled the Rose, he and his father-in-law had spent five hours in the mayor's antechamber, waiting to deliver a petition begging his worship to reopen the theaters. They had been fobbed off in the end onto a junior clerk—and what reason, Alleyn thought indignantly, does Burbage have to think he'll do any better? The jealousy passed in an instant: if he can get the playhouses reopened, Alleyn promised silently, I'll thank him myself, and publicly.

Pig was looking at him nervously, all the good humor gone from his expressive face. "Master," he said, "will we go on tour this summer?"

Alleyn sighed again, but forced a smile. "It's early days, Pig, I don't know. If the mayor won't let us reopen—yes, I'm afraid we may. But there's no need for your tragedy-voice yet. Maybe Burbage will have better fortune than we did."

"Maybe," Pig agreed, but he did not sound very confident.

Nor, to tell the truth, am I, Alleyn thought, shrugging his damp cloak more comfortably around his shoulders. He had been on tour two years before, during the plague summer of '93, and still could taste the fears of it. *Robert Browne's wife in Shoreditch and all her children and household be dead, and her doors shut up*: his own wife Joan had written that to him toward the end of the long summer, when they were all numb with grief and the protracted fear, and ever since, that had formed the core of his private nightmare. *Edward Alleyn's wife on Bankside and all her children. . . .*

"God forbid," he whispered, and crossed himself. A papist gesture it might be, but it did give God some evidence of one's sincerity, and gave a man something to hold up against the dark. The verger was scowling at him, and Pig imperfectly hid his smirk. Alleyn ignored them both, bowing his head. "Sweet Lord Jesus, if we must go on tour, protect my family while I'm gone, amen." The muttered prayer did little to reassure him: they lived through the great plague, a small voice seemed to whisper, why should they have such fortune twice?

He shook the thought away, and glanced down at the still-smirking Pig. "Mind your manners, imp, and show some respect," he said, and cuffed the boy lightly on the back of the head. "At the Anchor, you said?"

Pig straightened his expression and his cap, cheerfully impenitent. "Yes, master, that's what Master Henslowe said."

Alleyn nodded. "We'd best be off, then."

Pig seemed to droop visibly. "In this rain?"

"You're not made of sugar-candy," Alleyn answered. He glanced up at the nearest window, its colors dulled by the cloudy day. "Besides, I think it's stopped."

Pig gave him a rather doubtful look, but whistled shrilly. Bartholomew came loping up out of the shadows, and the apprentice scolded him to heel.

The rain had not quite ended, but it had eased considerably. Alleyn loosened his cloak a little, letting the folds fall free, curtaining him from the rain. Pig pulled his cap down over his ears, then jammed his hands into his breeches' pockets, hunching his shoulders against the damp. The dog Bartholomew frisked at his heels, darting from the house walls to the ditch at the center of the street in an ecstasy of investigation.

Their way took them past Winchester House, its courtyard empty and rather forlorn now that the bishop was out of town, and then curved around under the shadow of the Clink prison. As always, there were a few ragged women, dirty children at their skirts, huddled in the meager shelter of the main gate, hoping to catch a glimpse of or even speak a word with some imprisoned kinsman. A stick-thin boy, perhaps twelve years old, perhaps older, waited with them, sitting in the mud with his back against the prison wall and his head bowed on his drawn-up knees. One of the women, baby in dirty clouts at her breast, called hopelessly after them.

"Alms, sir, alms for a poor prisoner's babe who's never done no harm. . . ."

Alleyn's mouth tightened painfully, but there was nothing to spare if they were to tour this summer. He walked on, the woman's plea turning to a spiritless curse, and was aware that Pig had drawn closer to his side. *The poor you will have always with you*, the actor thought, but the biblical saw brought no real comfort. Someday, if ever I make my fortune . . . He put the thought aside as unprofitable. "Run ahead, Pig," he said aloud, "and tell your mistress you've done your errand."

Pig hesitated. "I thought you might let me come with you, master," he said, with unwonted meekness.

Alleyn sighed. "You may join me at the Anchor, if you hurry. Run, now."

Pig grinned, his always buoyant spirits fully restored, and darted off. Bartholomew bounded after him, the absurd curled tail beating madly. Alleyn felt his own spirits lift a little. There was always Pig, and the other boys of the company, too, to be cared for, and that was something.

By the time he reached his own doorstep, Pig was waiting for him, and Joan Alleyn peeped out the door behind him, one rusty curl escaping from under her plain cap. Alleyn paused, knowing that his smile was foolishly fond, and was rewarded by her quicksilver smile of welcome.

"Since you're going to the Anchor, Ned, will you bring back a pottle of clary? Margery wants it for the kitchen."

Alleyn nodded. "Gladly, Mouse. I'll send Pig back if it seems like to go on late."

"I'd be grateful," Joan answered, and vanished back into the house.

"Well, come along, Pig," Alleyn said, and started down the side street that led to the Anchor. Pig gave a little skip and followed, the dog still prancing at his heels.

The Anchor was a prosperous tavern, with a well-kept main room and a garden that backed on the river, and prices high enough to keep away the rabble. When the playhouses were open, it was invariably crowded, yard, garden, and main room all filled with men of fashion and their companions, but today the yard stood empty except for a brewer's cart, and the brewer's boy asleep under it. Bartholomew showed a distinct desire to sniff at the creature, but Pig whistled him back, and took a firm hold of the leather strap that served as a collar. Alleyn nodded his approval, and ducked under the low doorway.

The main room was surprisingly crowded, given the deserted yard, most of the long tables filled, but it was a very sober gathering. Alleyn paused for a moment, searching the crowd, and picked out any number of familiar faces both from his own company and from the Chamberlain's Men. One or two of Pembroke's Men were present, too, but they had withdrawn themselves into a corner and were making very little of their presence. As well they ought, Alleyn thought, with some bitterness. Had they used the intellect God presumably gave them, we wouldn't be in this predicament.

"Ned!" The voice and the waving hand were Henslowe's. Alleyn lifted his own hand in acknowledgement, and threaded his way through the tables to join his father-in-law. Several of his fellow-sharers were seated with Henslowe, Thomas Downton very sober in his long-skirted rat's-colored doublet, William Bird only a little brighter in a workaday suit trimmed with bean-blue ribbons, and Alleyn included them in his murmured greeting. The long

faces matched the sad clothes, and he felt almost indecently cheerful to be wearing plain tawny wool.

"Pull up a stool," Henslowe said, with an awful glance at
the hovering Pig.

Alleyn, unmoved, did as he was bid, and gestured for
the boy to sit beside him. "Pig said you sent for me, sir?"

"I sent for you," Henslowe answered grimly, but declined to press the issue further. "Young Burbage has gone
to the Recorder to see what—if anything—can be done.
They've agreed to come back here, so that we can share
the news, and make some decision."

Alleyn nodded. Rivals though they might be in almost
everything else, the closing of the playhouses was too
great a strain on everyone's purses to permit anything less
than cooperation. Touring companies were smaller than
the companies employed in London; he and his fellow
sharers—and the sharers of all the other companies as
well—owed it to each other to make sure that the sharers,
at least, would have work on the road.

A potboy edged up to the table, his red livery badged
with tarnished braid. "What will you have, my masters?"
He spoke the standard appeal with a marked lack of interest.

"Ale for myself, and small beer for the boy," Alleyn
answered. He glanced toward Pig then, and, reading the
appeal in the apprentice's face, added, "and a plate of
bread and cheese." Pig grinned, but the expression was
banished by Henslowe's quelling stare. The apprentice
meekly gathered his dog between his legs, and sat very
still. The potboy returned a few moments later with the
tankards and a cracked wooden platter; Alleyn eyed the
aged cheese rather dubiously, but Pig fell to with a will.
Downton shuddered visibly.

"What's to be done?" Bird asked mournfully. "We'll be
touring again, you mark my words."

"Damn the bricklayer," Henslowe said, between clenched
teeth. "As for what's to be done, that's what we're here to
decide—when the rest of your fellows condescend to
appear."

"Here's Tom now," Downton said, soothingly, "and
Humphry Jeffes."

Alleyn smiled his greeting as the other sharers made

their way to the table. Thomas Towne seemed to share the
gloom that enfolded most of the company—not without
cause, either, Alleyn thought, and took a pull of the thick
ale—but Jeffes still managed an air.

"Did you know, my masters, that there's been a sermon
preached about us?" he asked, pulling up his stool.

Bird groaned.

"That was all we needed," Downton said.

"Oh, it was most edifying," Jeffes protested, fiddling
with the none-too-clean ruffs at his wrists. When the potboy appeared, he called for a glass of genever, ignoring
Henslowe's snort of disgust, and continued, "I give you
my word, it was."

"Did you attend?" Alleyn asked, and felt suddenly very
old. He was not more than three or four years older than
the other man, but somehow Jeffes's cheerful irresponsi-
bility made him feel ancient—rather the way Marlowe
does, he thought, and bit back a grimace.

"Most certainly I did," Jeffes answered, his pale eyes
sparkling. "Nay, Tom, it was indeed a valuable experience."

"God save us, has he become a precisian?" Downton
muttered to his tankard.

"What happened, Humphry?" Alleyn asked, and was
not entirely sure he wanted to hear the answer.

"Well, my masters, the parson preached on the wickedness of the actors, and told how all such were surely in the
service of Satan and wore his livery, no matter what great
ones' names might be on their patents—"

"That might land him in prison for a month or three,"
Bird interjected, brightening a little.

"—and sure, it must be so, for even as he said it, and
called on all his hearers to tear out Satan from their hearts
and cease spending their pennies on his wiles and ways,
when crack! there came flames and smoke and the smell of
sulphur, and one cried out that the devil himself had come
to hear the sermon. The crowd fled, and the parson was
knocked in the mud and trodden on, which greatly freed
his tongue." Jeffes grinned. "So in truth it ended as a
filthy sermon, no matter how it began."

"The squibs from *Faustus*," Towne said, into the preg-
nant silence.

"Christ's balls—" Downton began, and bit off the rest of his words, remembering that there was an apprentice present.

Alleyn drew a deep breath, let it out slowly. "Did it never occur to you, Jeffes, that this sort of—further scandal—could only strengthen the Lord Mayor in his determination to keep the playhouses closed?"

"Does he think at all?" Towne growled.

"Did I say it was my doing?" Jeffes protested, unconvincingly.

Downton snorted. "If that's the best you can do, it was a mistake to let you buy your share."

Jeffes grinned.

"Here's Martin, and Black Dick," Bird said hastily.

"We'll talk later, Jeffes," Alleyn said, and turned his attention to the newcomers. Martin Slater, who had been his closest friend at the founding of the company the year before, was wearing his most sober face, and Alleyn felt his heart sink. "What's the news, Martin?" he asked, but it was Richard Jones who answered.

"Bad news, Ned, did you expect otherwise?" As always when he was angered, the Welsh lilt was back in the dark man's voice. He had dressed with defiant pride, Alleyn noted, a gaudy Spanish cloak—and the braid was gilt if not true gold—worn at the correctly careless angle over his best scarlet doublet and black-paned hose.

"We met Richard Burbage on the London side of the river, and shared his boats across," Slater said. "The Recorder can hold out no hope of the playhouses reopening this summer."

"Christ, have mercy," Bird murmured, and seemed startled to hear his own voice.

"He hasn't so far," Jeffes said, and the others turned on him.

"Did you help the matter with your little games?" Downton demanded, and Towne snarled, riding over the other man's words, "Kit Marlowe had more sense than you."

"You should be fined for a troublemaker," Henslowe declared, and that awful pronouncement, coming from the man who financed them, silenced the company.

Alleyn cleared his throat. "We can debate that later, sir,
if you please. Where's Richard, Martin?"

"Coming up the garden," Slater answered. Even as he
spoke, the rear door opened, and a little knot of men
pushed into the room, Burbage in the lead. They were all
dressed in their best suits—or their second-best, Alleyn
thought, treading the fine line between a proper conceit of
themselves and their supplicant's role. He nudged Pig
gently, and, when the boy glanced at him, fished a sixpence from his purse. "Off with you now, and get the clary
for your mistress. Tell her I shouldn't be too late."

Pig pouted slightly, but did as he was told, starting for
the serving hatch at a snail's pace.

"A bad business, this," Burbage said, and leaned heavily
on the table. Henslowe waved him to a seat, and the actor
took the stool Towne slid toward him. The rest of the
Chamberlain's Men edged themselves into the table, too.
The Admiral's Men shifted to make room. Alleyn was
suddenly aware of the hush that had fallen, of the way that
the scraping of the stools against the rushes was the only
noise in the tavern, and bit back a bitter sigh. How can
they do this to us? he thought, and knew how empty that
protest was.

"Martin's told you what happened?" Burbage went on,
and waved away the potboy. A few of the others among
the Chamberlain's Men gave their orders in low voices,
but most refused.

"The end of the matter, no more," Henslowe said, and
Burbage sighed.

"There's not much more to tell. We presented our
petition, and were granted speech with the Recorder—
and he was most courteous, I promise you—but it came to
naught. Jonson's offended too many people, both in the
city and at court. There's no hope of the playhouses opening before the end of the summer, if then."

There was a murmur, half of denial and half of appeal, at
the unvarnished statement. Alleyn shook his head, suddenly aware of how the actors who had been sitting at the
other tables had gathered in around them.

"What were Pembroke's Men thinking of, to play it

without a license?" It was Augustine Phillip's voice, but he spoke the thoughts of all of them.

Alleyn glanced toward the corner where he'd seen the two men from Pembroke's company, but they had vanished —and wisely, too, he thought. There're plenty here who'd happily pay them a broken head for all the trouble they've caused.

"Yes, why did you play it, Nathan?" Jeffes demanded.

A thin-faced man in his mid-twenties ducked his head in answer. "They said the Earl of Essex proposed it," he said, "and when it was rejected, said he'd protect us, if we'd play it."

"And I see him protecting you now," Jones jeered. "Tell us another, boyo."

Phillips sneered visibly. "Next he'll say her Majesty appeared to him in a dream, and licensed the play."

The thin-faced man winced again. "I'm only a hired man," he protested. "I do what I'm paid for, that's all—"

"You must know something more," Downton said, and Shakespeare looked up from his ale.

"No, how would he? Let him be, Thomas, what do our hired men have to say to anything?"

"Nothing, and that's as it should be," Will Kempe muttered audibly. "And I don't care who knows it." The comedian's wrinkled face was unspeakably weary: here's a man, Alleyn thought, struck with an unexpected pity, who should be comfortably by his own hearth, not strolling up and down the length of England this summer.

"That's what the Lord Mayor's man said to us," Henslowe said, to Burbage. He glanced around the table. "This means touring, my masters."

There was another murmur, this time of protest. Only the man who's staying home could say that so blithely, Alleyn thought, but knew the matter had to be discussed. "I'm afraid you have the right of it, sir." He looked at Burbage. "Which brings us to a tricky matter, Dickon."

Burbage nodded. "In 'ninety-three, we broke up the companies, toured catch-as-catch-can. I won't deny I'm loath to do that this time, Ned."

"As am I," Alleyn agreed. "And the rest of the compa-nies, too, I don't doubt. But that still doesn't answer. The

companies will have to be reduced, and there will be
those who can't go as far afield as others. I'll make the
offer first, if you'll reciprocate: what extra places I have,
for whatever reason, will go to sharers first, before I take
on hired men." He could feel a chill settle over the actors
as he spoke, and felt an irrational spasm of guilt.

Burbage nodded again, more slowly, and Alleyn heard
the same regret in the other man's voice. "I'll agree to
that."

"One moment, if you please," Richard Jones said. "Is
this between our two companies, or is it in general?"

Alleyn and Burbage exchanged a wary glance, and Alleyn said, "I'd intended it to be among all the companies."
Burbage nodded his agreement.

"Well, there's one company shouldn't benefit from it,
and that's a fact," Jones said.

Towne nodded. "Pembroke's Men are the cause of all
this, and I don't see that their men should profit, to the
hurt even of our hired men."

"He has the right of it," Phillips agreed. "I say the
agreement should exclude Pembroke's Men, even the
sharers."

"Especially the sharers," Kempe muttered, and drained
his wine at a swallow.

Shakespeare leaned forward a little, frowning. "It's too
easy to misjudge court politics," he protested, mild eyes
sweeping the length of the table. "And what of the sharers
who voted against the play? I've never yet known any
decision to be unanimous."

That brought some wry grins, and Henslowe uttered a
barking laugh, quickly choked off. Shakespeare quirked an
eyebrow at him. "Any one of us could be in their position
one day, and they've wives and children, too, like any of
us. I say we count them as part of the agreement—so long
as they hold to the same, of course—and do as much for as
many hired men as we may."

"Shakespeare has the right of it," Bird said softly, and
most of the others nodded. Jones grimaced.

"Very well, I won't stand against the majority. But
you're too Christian-kind, Shakespeare."

"Sweet William," a voice mocked from the back of the crowd, and Shakespeare winced.

"Towne?" Alleyn asked.

The actor shrugged. "I see the justice of the argument. I'll hold with the rest."

"August?" Burbage tilted his head, and Phillips managed a reluctant smile.

"I'm outnumbered. So be it." He sighed. "Where will we go?"

"That's for later, I think," Burbage said warily, and Alleyn smiled in wry agreement. Rival companies could cooperate only so far, even in these straits.

"Thank you, Dickon, for bringing us the word," he said aloud.

Burbage shrugged. "I could only wish it had been a better." He gathered his fellows with a glance, and Alleyn pushed himself to his feet as well.

"God go with you, then," he said.

"And with you," Burbage answered.

And I believe he means it, Alleyn thought, with a faint smile, and glanced at Slater. The other actor rose in obedience to his cue, and at Alleyn's nod the two men let themselves out into the muddy garden. The privies behind the wall were full, as usual; Alleyn turned into the corner of the waterstairs with some relief.

"We stand to lose money on this, Ned," Slater said.

"I know it. But what can we do?" Alleyn knotted his points hastily. "Actors, too, I'm afraid."

"Yes. Ledbetter, Thomas Hunt, Sam Rowley, Stephen Massey—those are the ones I'm worried about. And I wish to God Marlowe weren't in Scotland. We could use a new play to take on the road."

"I don't want to play *Faustus*, not this year," Alleyn said. They turned back toward the tavern, but at that, Slater stopped dead in the middle of the garden.

"And why not, in God's name? It's the best money-maker we've ever had, including the Jew, and less trouble to carry the props."

Alleyn shook his head slowly, unable to explain. It's been a chancy year, he wanted to say, an uncanny time, and I don't want to antagonize whatever dark powers are abroad. . . . But none of that was an answer that could not be overturned, and he said only, "I won't do it, Martin, and that's final. And before you even think it, there's not a man in the company who could take the part."

Slater sighed. "As you wish, I made no such suggestion. But I think you're being a fool about it."

"It's my chosen folly," Alleyn said, and Slater sighed again.

"Shall the company meet tomorrow, at the Rose?"

Alleyn nodded. "Tell them so, Martin. I'm for home." *I won't have much more time there*, he added silently, and Slater managed a sympathetic nod.

"I'll do it. And we'll come to some decisions then?"

"God willing," Alleyn answered, and let himself out through the garden gate.

Chapter Thirteen

Sorcerors are too common; cunning men, wizards, and white witches, as they call them in every village, which, if they be sought unto, will help almost all infirmities of body and mind.
  Robert Burton, The Anatomy of Melancholy

North of Leicester, the roads grew steadily worse, forcing them to travel extra miles in order to find tracks wide enough for the cart and to hire local guides from the towns they passed. While the weather held good, the delays were not too great, but, as they drew closer to York, the spring rains returned, drenching the roads. They spent the next Sunday at the episcopal palace—even Marlowe did not complain of the delay—and were forced to remain with the bishop two days longer, until the worst of the storms were over and the roads were passable again. The delay did allow van der Droeghe time to continue drilling the undergrooms in the use of both the falchions and the pistols, and from York north the men rode armed. Almost as soon as the cortege had left the city walls, however, the rains closed in again, a thin drizzle punctuated now and again by downpours. Riding was a misery but the roads remained just hard enough to bear the cart's weight. In such weather, it was hard to find reliable guides willing to ride with them between hamlets; Madox was hard put to bribe or cajole even the poorest farmers to send their sons or day-laborers along. The further north they rode, the more difficult it became, until at last Madox stopped asking for guides, and requested only the next set of landmarks. That slowed their progress even further. Even Sidney grew silent, counting wasted hours.

A heavy, soaking mist had been falling for three days; now as they approached Alnwick it once again became a downpour, stinging like needles. Sidney sighed, turning in his saddle to gauge how the cart was handling the mud. Marlowe glanced across at him, and winced as the movement dislodged his carefully arranged cloak, sending rivulets of water down his back. Sidney looked toward Alnwick then, frowning.

"A cheap effect," the poet ventured, with a sidelong glance back toward Nate, riding on the cart. "His grace's nipfarthing ways rob it of any real intimidation."

"Yet for nothing in the world would I lodge there tonight," Sidney answered, almost absently, as though he had spoken some private thought. His eyes were still fixed on the mist-draped hills that hid the town and castle.

Marlowe followed his gaze, wondering what the other saw. There was nothing there, of course, except the low-hanging clouds, but for a moment the poet felt the touch of some distant presence. The feeling vanished in an instant—probably nothing more than the castle's outward reflection of the sour soul that governed it, Marlowe told himself lamely. Northumberland's nature and Sidney's could never dwell easily with one another. That was all, most likely.

"Nor I, especially," he agreed. Something withering, then, to follow that up, something Juvenalian, epigrammatical—but the heavy weather doused the venomous spark, and rather than make a lame remark, he said nothing.

There was a shout from the riders behind, and then a volley of Dutch curses. Marlowe took his hand from the hilt of his rapier—the pistols were useless in this weather—and read the same abrupt fear and release in the others' eyes. Sidney reined in sharply, swinging the horse around to face back the way they'd come. The rest of the train was stumbling to a halt, too, the horses sliding in the muddy track, and van der Droeghe urged his animal back down the long slope. The cart was stuck again.

Marlowe cursed and kicked his horse into unwilling motion. The grooms were already dismounting, faces set and angry beneath their dripping hat brims; the two boys slid down from their place atop the baggage and ran to hold the men's horses. Covell and van der Droeghe were at the horses' heads, alternately cursing and cajoling. The animals strained forward, heads and hooves plunging, but the cart was thoroughly mired.

"Come on, lads," someone called, his voice hoarse and tired despite the encouraging words. "Put your backs into it. Soonest begun, soonest ended."

Someone else groaned at that, but then the men moved forward, throwing off their cloaks, to position themselves around the cart's sides.

"Ready, boys?" van der Droeghe called. "And, now!" He and Covell tugged at the horses' harness, urging them forward, while the grooms threw their weight against the stubborn cart. They heaved it forward a few inches, but the mud sucked it back again, the grooms slipping and cursing beside it.

"Whoa, easy," Covell shouted, calming the struggling horses.

"We need more men here," van der Droeghe said. He was staring at the two valets, who as gentlemen's body servants were not generally expected to demean themselves with such physical labor, but Marlowe cursed again, and flung himself from his horse. He handed the reins to Nate, who was shivering visibly, and, after a moment's hesitation, shrugged off his cloak and draped it around the boy's slight shoulders. Nate huddled gratefully inside it, teeth chattering, his eyes fixed in fear on the distant castle. Marlowe turned away, to set his shoulder against the cart's tail. After a moment, Ralph Haywood joined him, round face screwed up against the lash of the rain, and then Sidney's Barton was there as well.

"Now, boys," van der Droeghe called, and Marlowe

threw his weight against the wood. His feet slipped in the mud; he clung to the cart, steadied himself, and pushed again. He was vaguely aware of Haywood's heavy breathing, and the gasps and curses of the undergrooms. Covell called to his horses, urging them on, rousing them to one last effort. The cart lurched forward, and stuck again.

"Once more," van der Droeghe shouted. "Once more."

Marlowe took a deep breath, and shoved with all his strength. The cart resisted a moment longer, and then, quite suddenly, rolled free, the horses heaving it up onto more solid ground. The poet stumbled after it, slipping, and sprawled full length in the churned mud. He pushed himself up, cursing, the muck cold between his fingers. Doublet and hose were plastered with the stuff, and he could feel a thin trail of ooze working its way down the length of one boot. He had lost his hat, too, and his hair was already plastered to his head. Faintly, he heard a strange familiar laughter, as high-pitched as a child's. It had seemed to come from a very great distance, but he rejected that as impossible, and rounded on the two boys, ready to backhand the one who'd giggled. The scared pale faces shocked him back to his senses; he flung his head back, letting the rain sluice down his face.

"A pox on the whoreson spider who sent us here, if he could find woman or boy to bear him. Did the devil himself send these jades to plague us?"

Covell bristled at that, but van der Droeghe nodded solemnly, and offered a scrap of dirty cloth. There was a twinkle in the Dutchman's eye; Marlowe scowled, ready to lash out at him as well, but accepted the proffered rag. When he had finished cleaning his face and hands, and scraped the worst of the mud from his clothes, van der Droeghe offered his hat. Marlowe took it without thanks and swung himself back onto his horse. Slowly, the cortege began to move again.

Greville glanced back at the bedraggled line of riders, and nudged his horse forward, drawing alongside Sidney. "So what's to do, then, Philip? It's God-forsaken country . . ."

Marlowe, riding a little to their left, remembered the spirits Northumberland had invoked and the ghostly laughter that had mocked him, and wrapped the wet reins tightly about his hand to keep from crossing himself.

". . . and little likely we'll find a decent place to lodge."

"Skirt the town. We'll find a place," Sidney said.

"*Before* we reach Edinburgh?" Marlowe asked. Sidney just smiled, and shrugged apologetically. Greville didn't much like the idea, either.

"Philip, we don't know how far we'll have to go. Your leg must be tired already . . ." Greville broke off, aware too late of a tactical error.

Sidney turned in the saddle, and turned a dangerously sweet face to his friend. He kept his voice deliberately light, striving to control a temper already frayed by the week's delays.

"Fulke, dearly I love you, but if you continue in that vein, I have but one word to say to you. Languet."

"Oh." Crestfallen—blushing a little, Marlowe thought, with an inward crow of delight—Greville subsided. Sidney was instantly remorseful. Fulke was privileged, his oldest and closest friend, and one of the few who knew precisely what Sidney's physical limits were. Nor was it gracious to use Languet's name so. Nor, Sidney thought suddenly, is it like any of us to let such trivial things—ordinary hazards of travelling, for God's sake—disturb us.

The rain fell even harder, and the wind rose to drive it against them; it seemed to blow from all directions, as though actively seeking weakness. It *was* a cheap effect, Sidney realized, but was it the same spirit that had oppressed him and dismissed him back at Penshurst? It felt smaller, and his eyes turned again toward Alnwick. He had half expected some action from Northumberland—little though the man had valued Nate, he doubtless smarted at the defection, and now sought his revenge in petty terrors. The realization angered him, but he forced the anger down. It was not blood yet, mere bile.

The presence scorned them, exulting in its influence over weaker minds; the rain fell unnaturally cold, and the wind was ever in their faces. Very well, then, Sidney thought, and called up words he had almost forgotten, words from Virgil's book. Simple words, stark and pure—a

simple spell, the master had called it, the proper answer
to malice and to *maleficia*: a charm to restore balance. His
face grew still, and the effect spread outward from his
center. Marlowe felt its touch first, and glanced toward
the older man, wondering what the hell he was up to.
Then the serenity touched him fully, making ridiculous his
anger, and he recognized the intent of the conjuration.
Marlowe shook his head in honest wonder. Sidney would
never impose his will on nature to shape it away from
itself. All he had done was restore the balance, shut out
the imposed shape of the storm, and release the natural
one. Further outward it spread, until it encompassed the
whole cortege. It still rained, and the wind blew, but the
louring presence, the malicious intent behind the stinging
wind, was banished. It was May, after all; it rained.

They spent that night at an inn just south of the Scottish
border. It was a small place, not much frequented except
by drovers and their animals, but after some discussion
the innkeeper agreed to supply clean linen for at least the
best bed, and a few dishes beyond the ordinary. Both bed
and extraordinary dinner were, of course, reserved for the
two great gentlemen; Marlowe, reduced to a supper of
mutton and sharing a lesser bed with a wary young Madox,
found himself grateful for Watson's sigil. The steward rose
cursing, scratching at the bites on his wrists and ankles.
Marlowe, untouched, allowed himself a sardonic grin, and
a few pointed remarks. The grooms, grumbling as they
saddled the hacks and backed the carthorses into their
traces, concluded bitterly that the devil looked after his
own.

The storm had blown itself out overnight and the morning sky was streaked with ragged clouds. For all that the
road was still muddy, Sidney felt his spirits lift in the
watery sunshine. The oppression that had haunted them
since leaving York seemed to have lifted at last; at the back
of the train, a pair of grooms raised their voices in cheerful, bawdy song. Greville grinned, whistling a counterpoint, but after a few verses Peter Covell's voice reminded
the singers that there were children listening. The grooms
rode in silence for a few moments, and then one took up

the old song of Dives and Lazarus. Despite the quick-moving tune, that was unobjectionable, and Covell signaled his approval by providing a rumbling bass. The innkeeper's boy, hired to guide them across the border, already excited by the prospect of a day freed from his usual work, bounced happily in the saddle of his employer's dun gelding. When the singers had finished, he overcame his shyness to suggest The Maid Freed from the Gallows. His tune was unfamiliar to the others, but easily learned. Sidney found himself humming along with the rather ragged chorus, and heard Marlowe's voice soaring in improvised harmony.

They sang tavern rounds for a few miles—only the polite ones, in deference to Covell—and then the innkeeper's boy suggested another song.

"It's about the Scottish king's marriage, how he sent his captains to fetch his bride, and how the witches drowned them all."

Sidney started at that, but with an effort kept himself from swinging around in the saddle to confront the boy. At his side, Greville gave him an expressive glance.

Sidney shrugged. "It's only to be expected," he said softly, so as not to disturb the boy's wavering treble, and looked away from Greville's lifted eyebrow. Anne of Denmark had not been drowned, but the attempt had been made. Stories of the sensational revelations of the witchtrials had reached London early; it was not so surprising to find songs made of them, so close to the border. I wonder, he thought suddenly, did I make a mistake, using my powers to banish this—thing? Was there something beneath it, more than just Northumberland's malice, something I failed to see? He had acted almost without thought, worn down by the miseries of the journey. Did I just play into its hands? If that were so, then the change in the weather took on a rather sinister cast, as though he had been considered and, at last, dismissed.

In spite of himself, Sidney stood in his stirrups, turning to look back at the line of riders, half expecting to see some monstrous ambush rising from behind the low hills. Instead, the ordinary sights—the grooms in cheap russet

and serviceable indigo, singing or idly talking as they rode;
Marlowe for once honestly animated, one hand beating
time against the saddlebow; the two boys clinging to the
piled baggage, still undaunted by the days on the road—
made him feel suddenly ashamed. He had been wise not
to challenge the presence at Penshurst; now, however, he
had acted, and would have to bear the consequences. He
frowned thoughtfully. It did not seem likely that this presence, if indeed it had been there at all, could read too
much from the spell he had used against it—but even if it
could, he told himself firmly, it was done. There was no
good to be gained from fretting over it.

The boy led them easily across the border, leaving them
a little after noon on a well-marked track that, he swore
with encouraging sincerity, would take them into Roxburgh,
where the gentlemen would find an inn much finer than
his master's.

"I should hope so," Greville murmured, but waited
until the boy was out of earshot.

Somewhat to everyone's surprise, the inn proved to be
exactly what the boy had said it would be: a clean, well-
appointed house in a prosperous town, where young Madox
was able to hire the best rooms without fear of disappointment. The innkeeper agreed to send his eldest son, a
youth just turned twenty, as a guide not merely for the
next day, but for the two days it would take to reach
Edinburgh, and for good measure recommended them to
his cousin's inn in Sotray. It was as decent a place as the
first, though somewhat sobered by its proximity to the
town church, a foreboding structure of grey stone unre-
lieved by any bright paint or colored glass.

"As coldly chaste as a presbyter's boy," Marlowe said,
and was ignored.

The next morning, since the road to Edinburgh was well
marked, young Madox sent one of the grooms ahead on
the best hack to inform the Scottish king's household of
their imminent arrival. The rest of the cortege, travelling
at a more sober pace, would reach the city around sunset.

By mid-afternoon they could see the grey spires and
slate roofs of the town from the top of each low hill. The

road wound in a leisurely fashion down through the broken country, and Sidney sighed, calculating the time it would take to reach the city walls. At least another hour, on these roads, and perhaps longer, if they had to slow for the cart.

"Not too much further," Greville said, deliberately misunderstanding the look, and Sidney gave a reluctant smile. He had been on edge since they left York, partly because of the weather and the uncanny force he had sensed behind it, but also because of the more mundane dangers travellers so often faced in the wild northern lands. He swung in the saddle, reassuring himself for the hundredth time that day. The grooms rode armed, each with a brace of heavy pistols cased at the saddlebow and a falchion at the belt; Covell carried a musket as well, tucked in among the baggage at the front of the cart, easily reached from his place on the tongue. Glancing at the cart, Sidney's smile became an open grin. The two boys had been bitterly disappointed when van der Droeghe decreed that they could not have pistols of their own, and had only been appeased when the Dutchman explained that they were to be in charge of reloading, should the travellers be attacked. Van der Droeghe had drilled them busily, and the two now swaggered about with shot cases dangling awkwardly from their belts.

"Sir Philip!" Benjamin Niles, the youngest of the grooms, stood in his stirrups, pointing along the road ahead. "There's a party coming out from the town!"

Sidney swore, swinging around in the saddle, and swore again as the hasty movement jarred his aching leg. As Niles had said, a group of riders was clearly visible on the road just outside the main gate. Sidney eased his horse to a walk, trying to make out the details. There were at least a dozen men, he thought, perhaps more, and he thought he saw livery coats among the riders at the back of the procession.

"A welcoming party, I hope," Marlowe said, reining in alongside. He slipped his long-barreled pistol back into its case as he spoke.

"So do I," Sidney answered, still studying the approaching riders. There was nothing to do but go on, of course, and no real reason to think that the strangers would be hostile, but . . . "Jan-Maarten!"

"Sir Philip?" Van der Droeghe eased his horse between Marlowe's and his master; the poet wrenched his snorting animal away.

Sidney ignored the byplay. "What do you make of it?"

Van der Droeghe took his time answering, staring across the low hills toward the city. At last, he shrugged, and said, "I don't see any muskets, Sir Philip. And the leaders are very well dressed."

Sidney frowned, shading his eyes against the sunlight that seeped through the thin clouds, but could make out no details. "All right, Jan-Maarten, thank you. We'll assume it's a welcome party—"

"Wouldn't it be wiser to assume the opposite, and be surprised later?" Greville muttered. Sidney pretended he had not heard.

"—but have the men be wary."

Van der Droeghe touched his forehead. "I'll see to it, Sir Philip."

As the riders drew closer, however, it became obvious that Sidney's worries were unfounded. The man at the head of the little column was brilliantly dressed, short scarlet-and-gold cloak flying back over a popinjay blue doublet and grotesquely padded breeches, and the man at his left was almost as decorative. The riders behind them were resplendent in dark red livery, badged with the royal lion. Definitely a welcoming party, Sidney thought, and saw Greville surreptitiously adjusting his somewhat battered hat.

The man in the scarlet cloak brought his party to a halt perhaps twenty yards from the approaching Englishmen, and rode forward alone, doffing his hat and bowing. "Do I have the honor of addressing Sir Philip Sidney?"

His voice was lightly, almost pleasantly accented. Sidney bowed in return. "I am Sir Philip Sidney."

"Welcome to Scotland, Sir Philip." The Scotsman straightened gracefully. "I am John Erskine, Earl of Mar. His Majesty sent myself and Lord John Hamilton—" he gestured to the bravely dressed man behind him, "—to escort you to Holyrood, knowing you would be tired after such a long time on the road. His majesty sends his apologies for not meeting you himself, but the affairs of state press on him."

"I'm grateful to his majesty for sending us so exalted an escort," Sidney answered, wondering how long the exchange of courtesies would continue. "May I present to you Fulke Greville, a close friend of mine and of her majesty's?"

"Honored, sir." Mar bowed again, and gestured to his escort. The train of liveried riders divided, backing their horses off the narrow track, and turning them to form a double line along the edges of the road. "If you would do me the honor of riding with me, Sir Philip," the earl continued.

Flashy, Sidney thought, but kept his face impassive. "I thank you, my lord."

Mar wheeled his horse—another parade-ground movement—and took his place at Sidney's right hand. Greville, hiding his grin, held back, and waited for Lord John to take the place beside him. The gentlemen rode forward, and, after a moment's hesitation, the rest of the train followed them. The liveried servants waited impassively for them to pass, and then fell in at the end of the line of riders.

Holyrood was a pretty, surprisingly modern palace, with long windows set into the sides of the hall, and into the walls of the multiple towers. The pale stone seemed almost to glow in the evening light. Sidney stared up at the buildings, smiling in honest pleasure, and Mar cleared his throat nervously.

"His majesty suggested that, since he himself is unable to welcome you at the moment, you and your party might wish to refresh yourselves first."

Sidney nodded. "That's very kind of his majesty. I'd be glad of a chance to rest—perhaps to bathe? —before dinner." He touched the aching, knotted bone above his right knee, and Mar nodded.

"Of course, Sir Philip, everything can be arranged as you wish. In fact—" He hesitated, glancing at Hamilton, then hurried on. "In fact, his majesty suggested that, since it is already so late, he would hold you excused if you wished to go directly to your rooms. He would be willing to see you in the morning, if you chose."

"I would prefer that," Sidney said frankly. "It's extremely gracious of his majesty."

And it was gracious, he thought, as he dismounted and followed a bowing servant into the palace. More gracious than I would have expected, in fact. I can only hope this bodes well for our mission.

PART THREE

Chapter Fourteen

Dreams out of the ivory gate, and visions before midnight ...
        Sir Thomas Browne, On Dreams

The queen of England walked in her garden at Richmond, ignoring the murmuring knot of courtiers clustered at the far end of the flower-bordered path. Her oyster-colored skirts, embroidered in black and silver, brushed the close-cropped herbs to either side of the flagstones, but she was hardly aware of the heady fragrance thus released. She toyed with the great rope of pearls around her neck—pearls that had once belonged to the queen of Scots, though that reflection brought little comfort this day, made her think instead of her own inevitable mortality. She frowned, but could not banish the thought, or the memory of the dream that had brought her bolt upright in her bed, hands pressed to her mouth to keep from screaming.

In that dream she had lain dead, flesh, coffin, winding sheet all decayed, so that she was a tangle of bones and earth, and the roots of trees that twisted through the remains of her shroud. She had been surprisingly content to be dead, to be so peaceful, but then, quite slowly, she'd become aware of the voices that whispered around her, sifting through the earth and sliding along the tendrils of the roots. They whispered first of disloyalty, a parliament in defiance against its anointed king, then, laughing, of civil war, Englishman against Englishman until the land ran with blood and the countrymen in desperation turned against all strangers, striking down any who ventured near, robbing and killing without hope or purpose. *I will not have it*, she had cried, though the dirt filled the mouth of her bare skull, *how dare you treat my England so?*, and she had struggled to rise, to throw off the earth that bound her, so that she might whip the rebels back to their kennels—she had done that once in her girlhood; she could answer the threat again—and heal her kingdom's wounds. But the grave had held her fast, the roots become little sharp devils'-hands that clutched and kept her, so that she could only weep and rage, pebbles rolling soft against her skull like tears.

She frowned again, new tears stinging her eyes, and swore bitterly. This would never do, this moping; a prince must act. But act how? she demanded. Who is the enemy, and where do I strike? Doctor Dee would know, of that she was certain, or he could find out, but she disliked his methods. She swore again, and turned back toward the waiting courtiers, well aware that one or two cringed at her approach. The Earl of Essex was not among those, at least, and her spirits lifted a little. Foolishly proud he might be—though I will break him of that fault before I make more use of him, she vowed—but that pride made him brave, and he was a vastly handsome man, and the black and silver that he affected for her sake flattered his fairness enormously.

"Well, my lords," she said, lifting her voice so that it carried to the most distant courtier. "What can you propose for our entertainment this day?"

One or two of the younger men exchanged glances, and the Earl of Pembroke bowed low. Elizabeth held up her hand. "Don't waste your breath, my lord," she said, and was meanly glad of an excuse to vent her temper. "I'll restore no players, nor no playwrights, neither."

Pembroke bowed again, and effaced himself. Elizabeth glared at her courtiers. "Well, my lords?"

"Perhaps her majesty would care to ride." That was a voice the queen had not heard in some weeks, and she looked up in some surprise.

"I was not aware you had returned to court, Sir Walter."

Raleigh bowed very low indeed. "Only just returned, your Majesty, and beg your leave to present my most humble respects."

Elizabeth eyed him thoughtfully. He was dressed in white and black, impudently reversing Essex's preferred colors, and she was conscious of an old pleasure at this sign of rivalry. Not yet dead and buried, my lords, she thought, and said, "Your return is opportune, Sir Walter, since you alone seem to have some desire to please your queen."

There was an outcry at that, the other young men protesting their willingness to serve her even unto death, and Raleigh bowed again. "Nay, your Majesty, I must confess an other motive."

"Indeed, sir?" Elizabeth's voice was cool, but inwardly she was not displeased.

"I almost fear to acknowledge it, your Majesty, but I hoped you might, an you liked my proposal, allow me the privilege of riding with you." Raleigh saw the queen's smile and allowed himself a roguish glance in Essex's direction.

"Well, Sir Walter, that seems small enough reward." Essex was scowling, Elizabeth saw, and lifted an eyebrow at him. He did not take the hint, and both eyebrows rose. She smiled deliberately at Raleigh. "Too small, in truth, when no one else seems willing to do me service. You shall certainly ride with me, and you alone."

"Your Majesty does me too great honor," Raleigh answered. "I am overcome."

"Not too overcome to ride, I trust," Elizabeth said.

"Your Majesty's grace revives me." Raleigh bowed again, and offered her his arm. At Elizabeth's nod, one of the white-clad pages darted off to warn the stables; by the time queen and courtier reached the palace's main courtyard, the horses were saddled and waiting, several grooms and two of the queen's ladies already mounted to ride with them. Elizabeth allowed Raleigh to lift her into the saddle, and gathered the horse easily beneath her. Raleigh swung himself neatly into the saddle of his own glossy chestnut, and turned to face the queen.

"And where did you intend us to ride?" Elizabeth asked, forestalling the courtly deference. "For I'm quite sure you had a place in mind."

"Your Majesty is far too wise for me to deceive her," Raleigh answered. "I did think—I had thought we might ride along the river."

Elizabeth's eyes narrowed. "With what destination in mind?"

"Mortlake, your Majesty, and Doctor Dee." The courtly flattery had vanished from Raleigh's face and voice. "It seems—I greatly fear that there's an English dimension to this Scottish trouble."

I more than half expected that, Elizabeth thought, but she said nothing. There were men in plenty intriguing to have her name her successor—Parliament itself had committed the major blunder of making that demand its last session—and she was aware that not a few of those not privy to her intentions were nonetheless backing James's chances. Raleigh, however, was not one of them—to the best of her knowledge, he preferred his own cousin Arabella Stuart. Which is not surprising, she thought, if somewhat less than politic. She frowned slightly. There had been no word from Sidney since his departure, of course, though Cecil had relayed the report of one of his agents saying that the party was well advanced on its way. . . . By the mass, she thought, Philip can barely have reached Edinburgh yet, and already the dogs are yapping at his heels. She controlled her temper with an effort, remembering her dream. Perhaps it would be better to hear Dee's explanation of it, she thought, and nodded. "Very well, Sir Walter, Mortlake it is."

It was a pleasant ride to Mortlake, across Richmond park and then along the river, but Elizabeth barely saw the countryside, her mind instead leaping ahead to picture the meeting with Doctor Dee. As the procession turned onto Mortlake's main street, she roused herself to answer the cheers of a horde of villagers, and to accept a speech—a very pretty speech—and a posy from the aldermen. She dismounted then, and thanked each one, reducing even the most severe precisian among them to the blushing stammer of a schoolboy, before she allowed Raleigh to turn their path toward Dee's house.

The astronomer had been privy to Raleigh's plan, and his family had had ample warning of the queen's approach. The entire household was drawn up in respectful rank before the main door, Dee and his wife and children in the center, the servants, from the patient steward down to the kitchenmaid and the boy who turned the spit, arranged to either side. They made their deepest curtsies as the queen made her way up the narrow track, and did not lift their heads until Raleigh had handed her down out of her saddle.

"Doctor Dee, I thank you for this welcome," Elizabeth said, and pitched her voice to carry. It would do no harm to Dee's reputation for the neighborhood to hear her speak his praise. "You've ever been my good and faithful servant."

"Your Majesty, I'm deeply honored that you should condescend to visit me," Dee answered. "May it please your Majesty, my wife has prepared a small repast within, if you would honor us by partaking of it."

"It would be my pleasure, Doctor Dee," Elizabeth answered. "Once we've attended to my business." She swept her gaze along the waiting figures, and her eyes narrowed. The slight, dolllike figure in the brocade gown stiff with golden braid was none of Dee's kin. "Lady Sidney," she said aloud, "I did not expect to find you here."

Frances Sidney curtsied to the ground. "I came here out of concern for my husband, your Majesty."

Elizabeth's painted eyebrows rose, but she contented herself with a sardonic smile. "We will go within, Doctor Dee."

Dee bowed her into the house, and then into his study, where the best chair had been hastily covered with an expensive turkey carpet. Elizabeth sank into it with some relief—it had been a jolting ride—and accepted a goblet of chilled wine from Dee's wide-eyed grandson. The boy seemed inclined to linger, but Dee hurried him off as soon as his errand was complete, and closed the study door behind him.

"How may I serve your Majesty?" he asked, with another deep bow.

Elizabeth took her time answering, looking deliberately from the astronomer to Lady Sidney to Raleigh, and back to Dee again. "I believe," she said at last, "that the question is rather what you want of me?"

Raleigh and Frances exchanged quick glances, and then Frances curtsied again. "Indeed, your Majesty, there was a favor I wished to beg of you, for Philip's sake as well as my own, but you spoke of business. That must take precedence."

"I think it falls to me to decide such questions," Elizabeth said sharply. "This favor, Lady Sidney?"

"Your Majesty." With a movement as abrupt as it was unplanned and unpracticed, Frances dropped to her knees at the queen's feet, her skirts billowing about her unheeded. "I knew when Philip left for Scotland that he was going into danger. Now—"

She hesitated for an instant, seeking the safest words. Essex was still high in the queen's favor; she did not dare go too far. "I have reason to fear that he has enemies at court as well. It's being whispered that he uses illicit magics; ill-intentioned persons hint that he trafficks with demons himself. Your Majesty knows as well as I this is untrue."

Elizabeth stared for a moment at the younger woman. *Just like your father,* she thought. *He always had that trick to presenting me with facts, indisputable but unpalatable, and waiting to see what I would do with them. Will a point-blank question confound you, too, I wonder?* "What do you expect me to do about it, Lady Sidney? It is often wisest to ignore rumor."

Frances blinked, momentarily disconcerted, but rallied. "I ask only that your Majesty promise to withhold judgement on any such—perverse accusations—until Philip can return to defend himself. Even your Majesty's champion cannot fight in two lists at once."

Elizabeth threw back her head and laughed shortly. "By the mass, you are your father's daughter. Very well, Lady

Sidney, you'll have my word on it—if Doctor Dee can give me his assessment of these tales." She saw a look of injury flicker across Dee's face, and added hastily, "I don't truly doubt him, or you, doctor, but there are certain circumstances. . . ." She let her voice trail off, then continued, more slowly, "I dreamed last night that I was dead, and that England had come to that pass of which your spirit, Doctor Dee, warned us. A dreadful dream. . . . But is it true, or is it some lying vision of these same demons, and what's to be done to prevent more of the same?"

Dee bowed his head, either in thought or in prayer, before answering. "As to whether the dream was true or false, your Majesty, I cannot say with any certainty. It could indeed be another warning, benevolently meant, or alternatively it could be the sending of some hostile creature, seeking to create fear from a godly vision. Or in truth it could be nothing at all, I cannot say for certain. But, for the other . . ."

His voice trailed off as he turned toward the high cabinet that stood against the wall between the long shelves of books. He rummaged in its depths until he found a green glass jar as tall as a man's forearm. He drew that out and set it on his table, tugging at the stopper that sealed its wide mouth. The cork came away slowly, and released a wonderful fragrance, musk and roses and other, softer herbs. Elizabeth smiled involuntarily, and Dee looked almost shy. "If your Majesty would accept an ounce or two of this, and place it in a linen purse beneath your pillow, I think you will no longer be troubled by such dreams." Even as he spoke, he ladled a careful measure of the dried mixture onto the pan of the balance that stood beside his German clock, and set two small weights in the opposite pan. When the two lay equal, he poured the herbs onto a square of paper, and closed it with an apothecary's twist. Elizabeth accepted it with a smile.

"Thank you, doctor, I believe I shall sleep well tonight."

"For absolute efficacy," Dee said, almost as though he had forgotten to whom he was speaking, "it should be placed in a purse prepared for it, with certain signs embroidered on it." He seemed to recall himself, and bobbed a sort of bow. "With your Majesty's permission, one of my daughters will make that, and I will send it to the palace—your Majesty's at Richmond?"

"Yes. That would be most kind," Elizabeth answered.

"Your Majesty." Frances, kneeling still at the queen's feet, could hear the urgency in her own voice. "I must beg another, and a greater, favor."

Elizabeth looked down at her in some surprise. "Say on, Lady Sidney."

"That Philip has enemies at court I knew, that they move against him now does not surprise me." Frances looked up, her delicate face hardening abruptly. "But that they have chosen to turn arcane weapons against him—and against your Majesty—changes matters. I wish your Majesty's permission to travel to Scotland, to warn him."

"What, not a messenger?" Raleigh exclaimed, and Elizabeth said, "There's no proof that this dream of mine was an attack, Lady Sidney."

"Do you dare assume it was not?" Frances responded.

A true Walsingham, Elizabeth thought, and smiled. "I concede I cannot."

"Your Majesty is always honest." Frances looked to Raleigh. "I dare not send a messenger, Sir Walter, not now. None of them could stand against a wizard's attack."

"And you consider yourself to be invulnerable?" Raleigh exclaimed.

"I intend to ask Doctor Dee for some protection," Frances answered steadily, and lifted her chin. "Moreover, not even N—" She stopped, abruptly aware that pride had almost betrayed her, and Elizabeth's eyes narrowed.

"Not even who?" she demanded. "Speak, girl, in this matter your husband's enemies are mine."

Frances hesitated, uncertain of her ground, and Raleigh cleared his throat. "Your Majesty, what I suspect is very far from a certainty, and concerns a man I had counted my dear friend."

Elizabeth said curtly, "Explain yourself, Sir Walter."

"These rumors that Lady Sidney spoke of," Raleigh said. "I have some reason to fear that Northumberland is somehow involved."

"Indeed," Elizabeth said softly. "Indeed." She looked

down at Frances again. "Very well, Lady Sidney, you have my permission, and my blessing."

"I have one further request, your Majesty," Frances said, "and I fear you'll think this the greatest impertinence yet."

Will I? Elizabeth thought, and kept her face still with an effort. The only thing I'm like to think an impertinence is if you ask me to send Essex with you. That I will not tolerate.

"Send Sir Walter as my escort." If Frances had sensed the disapproval in the queen's bearing, she gave no sign of it. "He knows Northumberland's magics, he may be able to help Philip once we reach the north."

By the mass, the queen thought, and could not hide her dawning smile, by the mass and the host and the wine, too, you do love him, even if you haven't quite noticed it yourself. "You choose wisely, Lady Sidney," she said aloud. "Sir Walter, you'll oblige me by accepting."

"It would give me the greatest pleasure," Raleigh answered instantly. "I thank your Majesty."

Elizabeth pushed herself slowly to her feet, feeling her years catch in her joints, and nodded to the astronomer, still standing by his table. "I leave you to your plans, Lady Sidney, Sir Walter. Doctor Dee, you spoke of a small meal? I would not like to disappoint your wife."

"Your Majesty honors our house," Dee answered, and hastened to throw open the door.

Elizabeth paused in the open doorway, looking back at the two who remained behind. "Is there anyone else of whom I should be wary? Be plain, I command you."

Frances hesitated, well aware of Raleigh's anguished glance of appeal. Essex was the royal favorite, could do no wrong in Elizabeth's eyes, and she knew she should say nothing—and yet, he moved against her husband, and therefore, by the queen's own logic, against England itself. She said, choosing her words with exquisite care, "Your Majesty. I can only urge you to have a care of those who would drive where they should follow."

Elizabeth frowned. That had an echo of an unpleasant remark Essex had made some months before, when she had banished him from court as a curb to his pride—and, knowing the Walsinghams, the girl had meant precisely that. "Sir Philip should be pleased he's not married to a coward," she said, but the words lacked the usual bite of a royal rebuke. "I will bear your words in mind."

She swept from the room, without waiting for an answer. Frances gave a sigh of relief, and rose stiffly from her knees.

"You're a lucky woman, Lady Sidney," Raleigh said.

Frances darted a glance at him, an almost impish smile hovering on her lips. "I trust I'll remain so," she said. "I hope you don't regret your decision, Sir Walter?"

"Not yet, Lady Sidney," Raleigh answered. "Not yet."

Chapter Fifteen

In the earth God hath assigned princes with other
governors under them, all in good and necessary
order. The water above is kept and raineth down
in due time and season. The sun moon stars rain-
bow thunder lightning clouds and all birds of the
air do keep their order.
Homily of Obedience

The rooms assigned to the Englishmen were surprisingly comfortable, well furnished, well aired, and warmed
by huge fireplaces set beneath mantels carved in the new
English style. Sidney sighed with pleasure when servants
brought a tub and steaming buckets, and allowed his valet
to ease him out of his riding clothes. The same servants
bore away his shirt and stockings, while young Madox, his
face set into an expression of grudging approval, super-
vised the unpacking, arguing in a low voice with the valet
Barton over the proper clothes for the next day.

Sidney ignored them all, crouching beneath the bath
curtains. The hot water had helped ease the worst of the
pain in his leg. Still, it ached fiercely, and he ladled
another handful of water over the twisted scar. It was an
ugly thing even now, nearly nine years after he had fallen.
He ran his fingers absently across the seamed white flesh,

tracing each wound. This, the central knot as big as his palm that was the source of the throbbing pain, was where the musket ball had hit; the long, thin cut slicing diagonally down toward his knee was the mark of the first, unsuccessful probe. This and this—he traced two more short scars radiating out from the central wound—were two more probes, one for the flattened ball and the other for bits and pieces of the thighbone. He shivered, remembering the weeks of agony in Holland, and snatched his hand away.

"Barton!"

"Sir." The valet appeared instantly, Sidney's nightgown and nightshirt draped across his arm. Nathanial hovered at his side, holding a heavy towel. Sidney freed himself from the clinging curtains, and levered himself, wincing, out of the bath. Nathanial stepped forward as he'd been taught, eyes widening at the sight of the knotted scar. Sidney's mouth twitched in reluctant amusement, but he controlled the urge to laugh, and took the proffered towel. The air was chill, despite the generous fire. He shivered, and was very glad to wrap the heavy gown around his shoulders. Nathanial brought his nightcap, and Sidney settled it on his damp hair, grateful for the additional warmth.

"Sir Philip?"

Sidney turned. "Yes, Madox?"

The young steward bowed. "I beg your pardon for disturbing you, but his majesty of Scotland's sent a message."

"Show the man in, by all means," Sidney said, sighing.

"The gentleman's left already," young Madox answered, stammering in sudden confusion. "I thought—"

"What was the message?" Sidney asked, well aware of Barton's smirk of pleasure at the younger man's discomfiture.

"His majesty welcomes you to Scotland," young Madox parroted, "and would be pleased to receive you tomorrow morning. He invites you also to a banquet in your honor tomorrow night."

Sidney nodded thoughtfully. He had really expected nothing less. "Very well. I'll wear the black tomorrow, Barton. And the green and gold for the banquet."

It was the valet's turn to be discomfited—he had wished his master to wear the green and gold for the royal reception—but he bowed obediently, hiding his chagrin.

"Is everything else in order, Madox?" Sidney continued.

"Yes, Sir Philip. The household is very comfortably lodged, and the other gentlemen's rooms are as they should be."

"Excellent." Sidney hid a yawn, suddenly aware of his own exhaustion. "Then you may go."

The steward bowed himself out. Sidney, stretching, allowed Barton to turn down the sheets, and settled himself against the cool linen. The valet drew the heavy bedcurtains. Sidney lay in the sudden dark, listening with half an ear to the trained quiet movements of his household as they finished unpacking the baggage, until, at last, he slept.

Marlowe leaned against the window frame, staring out into the twilit courtyard. It was late, but the sky still held a violet glow, as though this northern sun had withdrawn only a little distance from the horizon. It was a strange, eerie light, oddly beautiful; he turned words over and over in his mind, looking for some image that would capture the faerie colors. *Faerie* . . . Yes, that was part of it, but not Spenser's kingdom. This was an older, darker world, before the poets had reclaimed and reshaped it—as Scotland was an older, darker kingdom than Elizabeth's England, he realized suddenly. What a play I could write here, with these colors, these hills and shadows, to inspire me. I could almost think my namesake Merlin lived beneath those hills. . . . Unbidden, an image rose in his mind, drawn from a scrap of university reading: the boy-wizard, child of no human father, standing fearless before the wicked king Vortigern, prophesying the king's death. There was a play in that, certainly. He could almost hear his Ganymede declaiming the prophesy, the cool ironic voice pointing up the rich images. . . .

"Master Marlowe?" The voice of the servant who had unpacked the baggage shattered the forming speech.

Marlowe swallowed a curse, and forced himself to answer reasonably. "Are you done?"

"Yes, sir." The servant was Scots, but understandable. "I was told to tell you, the king will receive Sir Philip and his party tomorrow morning, and there will be a banquet of welcome tomorrow night."

Wonderful, Marlowe thought sourly, but said only, "Thank you, that will be all."

The servant bowed himself out, leaving the poet standing by the window. A lighted candelabra stood on the larger of the two tables, and, after a moment, Marlowe crossed to it, catching up his writing case in passing. Merlin was a subject for another time; for now, he had his Penthesilea to consider. He pulled out paper and stoppered inkwell, then hastily trimmed his pen, his mind already busy with the lines that would prepare Achilles' entrance. Henslowe would complain about the expense of two severed heads on top of so many skulls, but what an entrance it would be. He took a deep breath, and began to write.

He worked until well past midnight, but despite that, he woke long before the servant appeared to bring his breakfast, and sat for a while in shirt and tattered stockings, contemplating his meager wardrobe. With the reception and the banquet taking place the same day, he could not wear his best doublet for both: even with the change of sleeves, it would be only too obvious that he had only the one good suit. The peach satin would have to suffice for the reception—and it was Sidney's own fault if it made him look pinch-penny. In spite of that resolve, however, he spent some time smoothing the crumpled flax-blue braid that trimmed the body and the padded shoulder rolls, and sent the servant who appeared with the breakfast of small beer and bread for a barber.

When the man had finished and bowed himself out, Marlowe contemplated his reflection in the small hand mirror, stooping and twisting slightly to see as much of his body as possible. Clean-shaven, and with his hair trimmed back to something approaching neatness, he looked less like a London bravo; the wide John-the-Baptist ruff helped hide the way the braid had begun to come unstitched below the collar, and the broken button at the neck. The slightly darker trunk hose were the short French style, going out of fashion now, but they set off the line of his leg well. All in all, he thought, with some satisfaction, it was a creditable picture. He adjusted his tall hat to the proper angle, and then, after a moment's hesitation, put aside the mirror to unknot the black silk cord he wore in lieu of an earring. Smiling slightly to himself, he felt through the pouch that held his few pieces of jewelry until he found the garnet studded cross, and worked the loop of wire through his earlobe. Another ironic gift from Thomas Walsingham, he thought, and his smile widened, remembering precisely where it had been given. He could still smell the cloying sweetness of the plague-herbs hung at the four corners of the bed, and the stink of tallow candles.

Wages of sin, a mocking voice whispered from the hearth. In the same moment, Marlowe caught a glimpse of a small black shape, and heard the scraping of claws on stone as it scuttled out of sight. He swung around, heart in his throat, but the hearth was empty. Instinctively he lifted a hand to cross himself, but stopped, the gesture unfinished, and let his hand fall to his side. What the—whatever it was—had said was true enough: the pretty earring and the silver chain and half his possessions were just such gifts, and the wages of that sin and a dozen others he cheerfully practiced were eternal death. . . .

As I should know, he added, reaching for the defiant detachment he had cultivated for years, who was a divinity student six years. And what is that thing to remind me of it? He shivered then, imagination supplying details of the imperfectly glimpsed shape. As soon as he could, he would enclose the room in a circle of Solomon, to prevent any more visitations of this sort. Until then . . . His hand went to the breast of his doublet, feeling for the sigil beneath the layers of cloth. Until then, he would have to trust that Watson had known how to use his talents. He sighed, and lifted the mirror for the last time, giving his hat a final rakish tilt. His face was very pale, and he rubbed at his cheeks like a woman until some color returned. Only then did he move to join the rest of Sidney's party.

As always, Marlowe was the last to arrive, but this time, at least, he was not actually late. Sidney gave his entourage a final measuring glance, taking in the poet's rather battered finery, Greville's dove-grey magnificence, the boy Nathanial dwarfed by his plumed cap and braided doublet, listening huge-eyed to Barton's last-minute instructions, and nodded to himself. "Is the escort here, Madox?"

"Just arrived, Sir Philip." The steward bowed, his hand on the door.

"Then let's go," Sidney said.

The escort, a pair of liveried servants and a very superior-seeming secretary in a soberly expensive brown velvet suit, led them through the long halls, past knots of courtiers who bowed with practiced insouciance and then whispered together eagerly as soon as the group had passed. Sidney was very aware of the chorus of voices, but did not dignify it with his notice.

The royal reception room was crowded, sunlight streaming in through the long windows to make the courtiers' satins and velvets jewel-bright, and striking cold sparks from gold braid and precious stones. The secretary paused just inside the doorway, and announced, "Sir Philip Sidney!"

There was a moment of silence, and then a quick murmur of interest. Sidney took a deep breath, and started toward the paired thrones that stood at the far end of the room. Nate Hawker kept pace at his side, carrying the elaborately sealed letters of introduction. Among the groups of brightly-dressed courtiers, Sidney could see a few men all in black, some with Geneva bands, some without, and then still others in drab academic gowns. Protestant divines, he guessed, and possibly scholars from St. Andrews, but pride forbade him to be seen to look more closely. At the base of the low dais, he paused, bowing deeply.

"Welcome to Scotland, Sir Philip," James said, and pushed himself to his feet. James's queen followed suit, her heavy gown rustling loudly.

Sidney blinked at the unexpected honor, but said, with tolerable aplomb, "May I present my credentials, your Majesty?"

As he had been taught, Nathanial came forward to kneel at the king's feet, offering the sealed letters. James took them with a nod of thanks, and a flickering glance toward someone standing in the crowd behind Sidney, and broke the first seal. Sidney allowed himself an almost noiseless sigh, and glanced toward the king, studying him curiously.

James of Scotland was a man of middling height some twelve years Sidney's junior, but he seemed shorter than he was because of bowed legs and a tendency to stoop. To make himself a smaller target, Sidney guessed, with a quick rush of sympathy. His face was long, saturnine, and made even longer by a pointed sandy beard. His dark, heavy-lidded eyes were oddly restless. Even while he read, they darted about almost of their own volition. Anne of Denmark waited patiently at her husband's shoulder, her good-natured mouth curving into a faint calm smile. Her brown eyes were her best feature, letting a man overlook the aggressive nose. Ox-eyed, Sidney thought, ox-eyed Hera, and somehow it was a flattering epithet for the woman James had called his "earthly Juno." Her gown was cut scandalously low, her breasts only partially veiled by a lace kerchief tucked into the front of her bodice. For an appalled instant, Sidney thought he saw not merely the lace edge of her chemise, but the coral edge of a nipple, and looked away in haste.

James finished looking through the documents—more thoroughly than was strictly polite, but Sidney felt no offense had been meant. James was simply determined to prove to all and himself that he had no further need of guardians or regents or protectors. He looked up and smiled at the English ambassador, and the movement completely transformed his face, so singularly sweet was the smile.

"Well, Sir Philip. It's honor enough to welcome the first gentleman of Europe, but now I may greet you as England's ambassador. And 'tis a fair honor our cousin Elizabeth does us. Pray make your companions known to me."

Sidney bowed again. "With pleasure, your Majesty. I present to you Fulke Greville, secretary of the principality of Wales, gentleman of her majesty's court, poet, scholar, and historian."

Greville made his best bow—a gesture Elizabeth had often commended—and James nodded his appreciation. "Master Greville, aye, sir, we have heard your name spoken here, and always with respect and affection. England flatters our appetite for learning mightily, I fear— and yet, it's most kindly thought on, Sir Philip."

"I thank your Majesty," Sidney murmured. "Knowing of your Majesty's love for the theater, I took the liberty of bringing along my protege, Master Christopher Marlowe."

An almost frightened light flared in James's eyes, but it was immediately suppressed, as though from long practice, and replaced by a look of wary interest and frank assessment. Sidney restrained a sigh, and then a grin. James might well prove to be Marlowe's match, sharing his taste in bedmates, and likely to be more interested in Kit than the poet would be comfortable with. And Marlowe was looking rather handsome, in a particularly raffish way. . . . Marlowe discomfited: it was an interesting thought.

James's dark eyes flickered back to Sidney. "A formidable array of talent you've brought with you, Sir Philip. It does our court honor." The eyes slid sideways again, glancing from Marlowe to the person in the crowd, and back to Sidney. "And yet from what our cousin of England says, you are the most talented of the lot, Sir Philip. A gentleman well versed in arcane matters, she says."

Sidney bowed again, hiding his surprise as best he could. He had expected James to conceal that part of the queen's letter, or at least to gloss over it as quickly as possible—and if he didn't, Sidney thought, with a sudden chill, it can only mean that things have gotten worse since I left London. "I have made some study of such things, your Majesty," he temporized. "It is kind of you to mention them." The exchange of compliments past, he returned to his original script. "Her majesty has entrusted me with a gift for Prince Henry, to commemorate his safe recovery, and sends with it her prayers for his continued good health."

At Sidney's discreet gesture, Nathanial held out a red velvet purse embroidered in gold with the Scottish lion. Inside were five hundred pounds in gold, and a gilt-silver plate: more contributions to the king's economy, under the fiction of a present for the year-old prince. James took the purse, whistled softly at its weight, and beckoned to a grey-bearded man in a long gown.

"I'll give this into your charge, my lord Treasurer, for it seems to belong to your department. You may tell her Majesty that I—and my son, of course—are very grateful for her generosity." Sidney bowed in answer, and the king continued quickly, "But for now, Sir Philip, I'd be grateful if you would give me the benefit of your learning, in private. Johnnie—" He nodded toward the Earl of Mar, in the front rank of the courtiers. "—I trust you'll see our guests are properly entertained."

Mar bowed deeply in acknowledgement, murmuring some deferential response.

"Your Majesty honors me," Sidney murmured, and was aware of Greville's whispered exclamation at his back. So you've come to the same conclusion, Fulke, he thought. I just wish the matter were in your hands, and not mine.

"Then let's withdraw." James turned without waiting for an answer, and started toward a painted door set into the wall beside the dais. His bowed legs made his walk ungainly. We must make quite a pair, Sidney thought, with an inward smile, my limp and his stagger. He could hear the rising noise of the courtiers behind him, but did not turn. Greville would have no difficulty dealing with Mar, or with keeping Marlowe in line—though from all accounts, the poet's behavior was no worse than the king's.

The withdrawing-room was hung with tapestries, some panels slightly faded from the sun that streamed in the single long window. French work, Sidney thought, and wondered if they had belonged to James's unfortunate mother. Then the king had seated himself with a grunt in the room's single chair, and waved for Sidney to take one of the padded stools. Sidney did so, and a spotty page brought wine and comfits. Sidney refused the latter—he disliked sweets at such an early hour—but the wine at least was good. He sipped cautiously at it, regarding James over the rim of the silver goblet. The king picked nervously at the tray of sweets, then, sighing visibly, dismissed the page and leaned forward slightly.

"Our cousin of England has offered me your services in our troubles," he said abruptly. "Are you willing?"

Sidney blinked, somewhat taken aback by the abruptness of the request. "I will of course do all I can to aid your Majesty," he temporized, "but I must confess, I'm not sure what it is you're asking of me."

James smiled briefly, but his eyes slid away toward the tapestries as though he expected to see something lurking in their folds. "You will have heard that we have been plagued by witchcraft here in Scotland."

The statement seemed rhetorical, but the king paused as though he expected some answer. After a moment, Sidney said, "Her majesty did tell me that much, sire, yes. But she didn't tell me anything of its—manifestations."

"Oh, we've had enough of those." James bit back some further comment, his hands closing into fists. "Things that creep about the corridors at night, things that whisper in corners, things that laugh and make mock—" He broke off then, and managed to continue more calmly. "That is bad enough, and dangerous enough. But at least they've done no overt harm, though they've frightened the women at the court half to death—you may have noticed, Sir Philip, that there's a shortage of wives and daughters here at Holyrood? It's because they're afraid to stay, and I cannot blame them for it. And there's no telling what harm these things might encourage in persons who are—shall we say, weak-minded? Perhaps already have done . . ." He took a deep breath. "More important than these—hauntings—is this: there was a poppet found, in the rooms of a noble whom I had cause to suspect of treachery. He was a friend of Lord Home, who in turn is an ally of my great enemy Bothwell. Sir Philip, that poppet was meant for me, and only God's providence allowed us to find it before it was used against me." James shuddered visibly. "We sought to arrest and question him, of course, but he evaded us. We found him two days later, dead—strangled—at the bottom of the deepest oubliette in Edinburgh Castle, with marks on his neck made by no human hands."

"God have mercy on him," Sidney murmured automatically, then wondered if James would consider the reaction entirely appropriate. He said, more loudly, "And from that time forward, you've had no clues as to who might be behind this?"

James shook his head, and managed a bitter grin. "Suspicions I have in plenty, Sir Philip—I can name you three men who consider themselves to have more right to the throne than I, and if I'm killed there's only baby Henry between themselves and rule—and then there's Bothwell, who's played these little games before—but no, I have no real proof of anything."

"Bothwell? Secretary Burleigh mentioned the name to me."

James took the bait without looking twice at it. "And well he might. Five years ago—he was behind that plot, playing master to that coven of witches." He leaned forward even further, his voice dropping conspiratorially. "And I tell you, Sir Philip, I've made a study of such matters, and I know. These were real witches, pledged to the devil himself. Why, one of them told me exactly what I'd said to Anne on our wedding night—" He broke off, flushing. "But no matter. It was Bothwell who egged them on, who paid for the materials they needed for their noxious rites. Still, I banished him last year, and as best my spies can determine, he's still in France. Surely no witch has that much power, to torment me from across the seas."

"It seems unlikely," Sidney agreed. Privately, he was not so sure. Certainly the presence he had experienced was that powerful—but there was still no reason to think it was the Scottish earl. "Did Bothwell ever show any signs of possessing so much power?"

James snorted. "A good deal of impudence, yes, but not so much power. Had he been so strong five years ago, I wouldn't still be living."

It was a good point, but not decisive, Sidney thought. Men could learn much in five years. Still, the point remained unsettled, and he put it aside. "How may I serve your Majesty?"

James shuddered again, his eyes roving nervously around the room. "Last night," he said softly, "last night as I lay abed, I felt a chill. I looked up, and saw the bedcurtains opened, and a—a demon peering through them. It had eyes like hot coals, and teeth like a wild boar's, and it stank of carrion. It laughed at me, Sir Philip, laughed at my fears and laughed when I called on God to protect me. It could have killed me then, and I don't know why it didn't." He looked directly at Sidney then, his dark eyes haunted. "Protect me, Sir Philip. And find out who is behind this—this plague of demons."

Sidney sighed, unable to refuse the appeal, but equally uncertain of how he should begin to deal with the threat.

"I'll do my best, your Majesty," he said, and tried to keep his voice as ordinary as possible, after James's heightened tones. "As her majesty no doubt told you, however, I have been primarily a scholar all these years." He saw the disappointment in the king's eyes, and added, with a smile, "Still, I think I can contrive something."

James sighed, only somewhat appeased. "I have told the court what you are and why you've come here because I think at least some of them are involved, or at best would not be sorry to see me weakened." He grinned suddenly. "And I would like them to think you can protect yourself."

What you want is a stalking-horse, Sidney thought, but James's manner was so unapologetic that he found himself smiling back. After all, it was a king's prerogative to have others face danger for him . . . but one could wish that James were a little less cavalier about it. He bowed politely. "I'm happy to be of service to your Majesty."

"I trust you and your people will enjoy the banquet tonight," the king said, and levered himself to his feet. "Shall we rejoin the others?"

Sidney rose, bowing again. "As your Majesty wishes."

Once the formalities of the reception were ended, Marlowe managed to slip away from the rest of Sidney's party. The English ambassador had not been present at the reception—an oddity in and of itself—and the poet's second report to Cecil was beginning to be something of a weight on his purse, if not his conscience. He turned into a long empty hallway, dimly lit by windows at each of the ends, and paused in confusion. Obviously, he thought, I misunderstood the damned directions—and where the hell is a servant when you need one? He turned back toward what he hoped was the main body of the palace, swearing under his breath.

"Master Marlowe."

The voice came from the far end of the hall. The poet swung around, reaching instinctively for the dagger he hadn't worn.

"I believe you're looking for the English ambassador." The tall figure moved toward him, passing through the faint bar of light. Marlowe recognized the Earl of Mar, and breathed a sigh of relief.

"Indeed, my lord, I was."

"I'm afraid you'll look in vain, his lordship's ill." Mar kept walking unhurriedly toward the other man. "Perhaps I can help you."

Marlowe schooled his face to an innocence he did not feel. "Thank you, my lord, but I don't know how you can." He watched the Scotsman's approach with some nervousness. Mar was about his own height, dark haired and dark eyed, and moved with the unconscious arrogance of a strong man who had never yet been defeated.

"Oh, I think I can." Mar smiled lazily. He was no longer the flashy gallant who had greeted the riders the day before, but something considerably more dangerous. Marlowe kept his face expressionless with an effort.

"You should have a message for a friend of mine," Mar continued, lowering his voice slightly. "And if you do not, I think Sir Robert Cecil will be most displeased with you."

Marlowe's shoulders twitched, and the poet damned himself for that self-betrayal. He hesitated for a moment longer, but there was something in the earl's expression that made him shrug, and reach into his purse for the sealed packet. The letter was in cipher, after all; it was also true that he needed to send word to Cecil, if only to save his own neck. "I would be grateful, my lord, if you would see that Sir Robert receives this."

Mar smiled. "Of course. Then I will see you at the banquet tonight, Marlowe?"

It was a rude dismissal, and the poet's eyes narrowed. "Until tonight," he said, deliberately raising his voice a little, and drew a startled glance from a passing servant. Mar flushed, but said nothing, and turned on his heel to stalk away. Marlowe grinned, and started back to his room in a somewhat better frame of mind.

Chapter Sixteen

*For my part, I have ever believed, and do now
know, that there are witches.*
   Sir Thomas Browne, Religio Medici

The great hall was very noisy, men and women alike
shouting to be heard over the skirl of the musicians in the
galleries at the end of the hall and the laughter and shriek-
ing conversations of their neighbors. Marlowe edged back
in his place, subtly disassociating himself from his companions, and thought he saw, at the table opposite, Greville's
acid smile. The poet smiled sweetly back, tilting his head
gently toward the buxom young woman at his left, who
was leaning away to press her almost naked shoulder against
the fair man beside her. An enameled ship was poised in
the valley between her breasts, very bright against the
powdered skin, and there were more jewels scattered
across her bodice and her voluminous skirts: whatever else
she might be, she was one of Queen Anne's ladies-in-
waiting, and seated accordingly.

Marlowe sighed, the smile fading a little. He had been
seated at the least of the three high tables more as a
courtesy to Sidney than through his own merit or his
university degree; the knowledge galled him, even though
he was grateful to be seated no lower. He glanced down

the length of the hall, toward the hard-worked musicians. There were bodies in the shadowed corners beneath the galleries, men—and perhaps even a woman or two—too drunk to stay on their stools, and dragged aside so as not to impede the servants. He looked toward the king's table, wondering what Sidney thought of the Scottish court. Sidney's face, exquisitely framed by a wired whitework collar, was quite impassive, and Marlowe grinned. That was comment enough, from the man whom all Europe acknowledged to be the pattern of a gentleman.

His right-hand neighbor swayed heavily against him, and Marlowe caught him with shoulder and elbow, automatically fending him away from his own purse and knife. It was a movement learned in Southwark taverns, and the poet winced inwardly, hoping the Scotsman didn't recognize its significance. To his surprise, however, the Scot leaned closer still, blowing stale wine fumes in the younger man's face. Marlowe swallowed hard, pushing away the memory of Deptford. He had not drunk wine since that day—the taste and the smell still sickened him.

"Look there," the Scotsman said, in thickly accented but comprehensible English, and nodded toward the king's table. "Will you look who's to serve the toast?"

Marlowe looked where the Scot was pointing, glad of the excuse to turn away from the other's reeking breath. The remains of the last entry had been cleared from the king's table; now a little procession was winding its way between the tables, led by a dark-haired young man carrying a huge enamelled cup. The poet whistled soundlessly, and the Scotsman laughed.

"The Master of Ruthven," he said. "And a few things else besides." Ostentatiously he turned, and spat on the rushes behind his bench.

Marlowe lifted an eyebrow, wondering if the dark boy had seen. Ruthven's attractive, insolent face did not seem to change, but the poet thought he saw the very red lips thin briefly. Not an easy position, in more ways than one, to be the king's favorite, Marlowe thought, and ventured a small, approving smile. Ruthven gave no indication that he had seen, stepping up onto the dais to kneel before the king. The movement showed his long-limbed body to advantage, and the poet's eyebrows rose even higher. Ruthven was dressed in the height of French fashion, short, heavily padded and bejeweled round hose worn over skintight canions. Canions and garters and hose were all the same jet black, emphasizing—advertising—the perfect leg and the not-quite-hidden roundness of the buttocks.

"Shameless," the Scotsman said, and, strangely, laughed again.

Drunk, Marlowe decided, and kept watching the king. Another young man, this one fair, and almost as well-dressed as Ruthven, poured wine from a Venetian-glass pitcher that glittered in the shifting torchlight. His job done, the fair youth backed away, and Ruthven, still kneeling, leaned forward to offer the cup to the king. James took it, smiling slightly, and then, with a theatrical gesture, drained the cup. He returned it to Ruthven, saying, "Carry the cup to our most honored guest."

Ruthven bowed, and turned to the fair youth, who refilled the cup to the brim. Ruthven knelt then before Sidney, who rose to his feet, bowing gravely to the king.

"Your Majesty honors me," he said, and the hall quieted suddenly, listening for the foreign wizard's response. Sidney gestured gracefully to the kneeling youth, somehow managing, with the simple movement, to reduce him to a mere court functionary. "Not merely by this great compliment, but with the freedom of your court. In return, I can only ask God to grant your Majesty long life, a peaceful and prosperous realm, and all the pleasures that should attend upon a king." On the last words, he bowed slightly toward the queen, whose bovine face colored beneath the layers of paint. With a faint smile, Sidney took the cup from Ruthven, and drank. He returned it—empty, Marlowe saw, for all his vaunted temperance, and knew the others saw it, too—and bowed to the king a final time before taking his seat again.

Ruthven recovered himself gracefully, and knelt again before the king. James smiled down on him benevolently, and accepted the filled cup. He drained it—in two swallows, Marlowe noted, and grinned to himself—and handed the cup back to Ruthven. "To Master Marlowe, with our compliments." The fair boy moved instantly to refill it.

Marlowe sat very still, the grin frozen on his face. He had not anticipated—had not desired—any such show of royal favor, but knew only too well what was expected of him. Some pretty compliment—preferably in verse, Master Marlowe, are you not a poet?—and then to swill down that grotesque cupful of wine. . . . He shook himself hard, forcing his mind to work. Already Ruthven was advancing on him, the cup balanced easily in his hands. He was smiling slightly, almost contemptuously, and Marlowe's lip curled in answer. I know your kind, the poet thought, and I've already written lines for you. Hastily, he recalled them, recast them slightly to turn the lines on Jove into an at least superficially flattering reference to James. He rose as Ruthven bowed—he did not kneel, not to a mere university gentleman—and took the cup in both hands. Ruthven's hands were unexpectedly ugly, broad of palm and short of finger; the incongruity of the defect was strangely reassuring. Marlowe took a deep breath, trying to ignore the thick smell of the wine rising between his hands, and bowed to the throne.

> "Sweet Jupiter, if e'er he pleased thine eye,
> Or seemed fair, wall'd in with eagle's wings,
> Assure his immortal beauty by this boon:
> Hold poets in thy heart, and in our turn
> We'll add his name when we thy conquests sing."

There was a moment's silence when he had done, as though the entire court was holding its breath, and then, quite loudly, James began to laugh. "Well put, Master Marlowe, neatly said." He gestured to the cup. "Drink up, man. You've earned it."

"Yes, drink up, Master Marlowe," Ruthven hissed, under the relieved laughter of the courtiers.

Marlowe lifted the cup, first to James, and then, ironically, to Ruthven. Then he could delay no longer, and put the cup to his lips. It was the same French claret. That was his first thought, even though he knew it could not be true, the same thin, blood-warm claret Frizer had ordered for them that day in Deptford. He gagged on the first mouthful, tasting remembered terror, forced himself to swallow, to drain the cup to its last sickening drop. Smiling slightly, Ruthven took the cup from the poet's nerveless fingers. Marlowe made himself bow again toward the king, and sank back into his place.

"That's plain speaking," the Scotsman said, with new approval. His voice changed. "Are you all right, master poet?"

"Yes," Marlowe said, through clenched teeth, and willed it to be true. The wine lay heavy in his stomach, the stale, sour taste of it filling his mouth. The emptied dishes and broken meats spread out across the table seemed to swim before him, became the luncheon dishes piled to one end of the short table in Eleanor Bull's private room. . . .

"You're drunk, Kit," Frizer said, his own voice slurred from the wine they'd been drinking since mid-morning. "Why don't you lie down for a while?"

The voice was not unkindly, but Marlowe hesitated, feeling the wine wash over him like a wave. "Baines—?"

Little Skeres shrugged. Poley looked up from the counters he was rearranging on the trick-track board, a thin smile on his bearded face. Of all of them, he seemed the least affected by the amount of liquor he'd drunk. "He'll be here. Have patience."

Marlowe grimaced, but did not answer, toying with the buckle of his sword belt. He could not lie down comfortably with the heavy rapier at his side—and there was nothing in his purse to steal, since Frizer was paying his share of the bill. He unfastened the buckle and slid the belt out from under the skirts of the doublet, leaning the rapier in its case against the post of the bed. He loosened the strings of his ruff as well—it was a hot day, the first really hot day of June—and tossed it aside, then unbuttoned his doublet and stretched out on the musty coverlet. The bed curtains were threadbare, hastily darned in places: Mistress Bull had not done more than was absolutely necessary to repair them. A thrifty housewife, Marlowe thought, his lip curling slightly. The room swam, sunlight and shadow shifting in his sight. He closed his eyes, throwing an arm across his face to shut out light and the click of Poley's counters.

How long he had lain there he was never sure, nor did

he know precisely what woke him. He thought, when he was able to think soberly about it months later, that perhaps it was the touch of Frizer's knee against the mattress that jarred him out of sleep. He opened one eye, the movement hidden in the curve of his elbow, and saw Frizer looming above him, cheap dagger already drawn. Had it been Poley, or even Skeres, he might have hesitated, but he had never liked or trusted Frizer. Almost without thinking, he rolled off the bed, landing on his hands and knees at Frizer's feet. The steward swore, falling forward himself, the knife slicing into the mattress to release a shower of dirty feathers. Marlowe swung round, still on his knees, scrabbling for the weapons he'd left at the foot of the bed. Skeres, thin face suddenly pale, snatched them up, backing away toward the wall. Poley, his own blades drawn, set his back against the door that led into the main part of the tavern. Marlowe froze for an instant, then lunged for one of the eating knives discarded on the table. The dishes fell, clattering, but the horn-handled knife eluded him.

Then Frizer caught him by the collar of the doublet and threw him bodily onto the bed. Marlowe tried to roll away, but Frizer hauled him back, planting his knee in the poet's belly. Marlowe retched, body trying to double up in pain, but Frizer leaned his full weight against the younger man, flattening him into the mattress. Then the steward's big hands closed around Marlowe's throat. Marlowe fought back in panic, breath gone, reaching first for Frizer's throat and face. The steward leaned back a little, but did not relax his hold, smiling down at him like a lover. Marlowe clawed at the other man's wrists, fighting for air, wondering vaguely which of his sins had come home to roost. He felt Frizer's thumbs caress his throat, feeling for the bone. Frizer's smile widened, savoring the moment; Marlowe could feel his own hands loosening, struggles slackening. Over the roaring in his ears, he heard Poley say, in his honey drawl, "Finish it, in God's name."

Frizer's hands tightened further. Marlowe closed his eyes, surrendering to the darkness that scalded him, swept away on a wave of pain and terror and strange black ecstasy.

Then, miraculously, the pressure vanished. He drew an agonizing breath, both hands going to his bruised and burning throat, and heard a cold voice—a schoolmaster's voice, thin and chill and painfully precise—from the doorway leading into the garden.

"I believe your instructions were to finish him discreetly. I suggest that this is no longer possible."

Frizer was no longer holding him, Marlowe realized belatedly. He rolled away, sliding off the bed, Frizer's dagger falling with him. He reached for it instinctively, and no one tried to stop him. He hauled himself to his feet, clinging to the rotten curtains, the knife wavering in his hand. He set his back to the bedpost, not daring to look round, and saw the other three staring toward the garden door. Frizer's bearded face was set in a snarl of frustration, and Skeres was pale as chalk, still clutching Marlowe's weapons. Only Poley seemed unmoved, standing against the other door, face impassive behind the neat beard.

"Sir Robert will hear of this," he said, with silky menace.

"I have spoken to him myself," the schoolmaster's voice said. There was a note of contempt in his tone that made even Poley flush. "Master Marlowe, if you would come with me?"

Marlowe managed to nod, but pointed toward Skeres. His hand was shaking badly, and there was blood on his cuff, and more on his hand. Somehow in the struggle, he had cut himself, could feel the smarting gouge across the base of his palm. On the table's corner, perhaps, he thought, or when I was struggling with Frizer, but he could not bring himself to care. "Skeres—" he began, but the word tore his aching throat, and he stopped, wincing.

"Give him back his things," the schoolmaster ordered.

After an infinitesimal pause, Poley nodded. Skeres moved forward warily, holding out the belt with its dangling weapons. Marlowe took it from him, and slung it across his shoulder, unable to do more.

"Now, Master Marlowe," the schoolmaster's voice continued, and for an instant, Marlowe could have sworn there was a note of laughter in it. "I think we should be leaving."

Marlowe backed toward the garden door, knowing with a sick certainty that he moved like a beaten dog, and knowing equally well that he would not dare turn his back on those men again. At the door, a firm hand caught his arm just above the elbow. The poet flinched in spite of himself, and knew that Poley saw.

"Come along," the schoolmaster said. "My people are waiting at the gate."

Marlowe managed a nod, though he knew those words were as much for Poley as for himself, and lurched through the door out into the blinding afternoon sun. The thick scent of the herbs, coupled with all the wine he'd drunk, sickened him further; he stumbled somehow along the garden path, to vomit his heart out at the base of the garden wall. When he had finished, his throat hurt even worse than before, but he felt perversely better. He looked up then, into the face of the man who'd rescued him. There wasn't a man in England who wouldn't recognize that long-chinned face, not after all the thanksgiving sermons, printed with their matching portraits of the recovered hero and the preacher who praised him, but Marlowe stared blearily at him, unable to believe his eyes. Why in God's name would Sir Philip Sidney, of all men, bother to save him? He knew he shouldn't care, should simply be glad to have his life, but the mystery nagged at him.

"Why—?" he began, his voice a ragged croak, and Sidney held up his hand, wincing in sympathy.

"Don't talk," he said, and pushed open the garden gate. As he had promised, there were men in the lane beyond, big, competent countrymen mounted on expensive horses. "Can you ride?"

Marlowe nodded, not quite certain if he could, and Sidney smiled at him. In that moment, the poet thought, he would have done anything for the older man. A groom stepped forward, offering a hand, and Marlowe pulled himself awkwardly into the saddle, fumbling for the reins. The same groom gave Sidney a leg up—an awkward movement, the stiffened leg dragging, but Sir Philip hardly seemed conscious of it—and turned away to his own horse. Sidney collected his reins, and glanced back at the poet, still smiling.

"I dislike wasted talent, Master Marlowe," he said. "That's all."

Marlowe shook his head, staring at the emptied dishes. He still did not fully believe in Sidney's explanation—the older man's views on the theater, his preference for the classical forms, was only too well known, and most of the published poetry was hardly to his taste, either—but in the two years since, Marlowe had discovered no other motives, no possible self-interest that could be served. He disliked—distrusted—that sort of benevolence, even while he knew he should simply be grateful to be alive. And I am, he thought, with another, inward shiver, feeling ghostly hands on his throat again. But I don't understand.

The sweat was still cold on his forehead, but the worst of the sickness had passed. He glanced down, slowly relaxing his hold on the table-edge, and saw the red stain spreading across his cuff. He knew it was only wine, not blood, but this second malignant echo was too much. He pushed himself blindly away from the table, conscious only of the need to escape the stinking, overheated hall, and stumbled toward the door. Enough others had left in the same condition for his departure to rouse only a little laughter, but he barely noticed. He blundered through the archway, almost colliding with a pair of heavily-laden servers, and emerged into the darkness of the outer hall. A second door stood open to the courtyard, spilling pale moonlight onto the rushes. Marlowe lurched out into that eerie light, drawing deep, grateful breaths of the chill air.

He leaned heavily against the curve of the tower that flanked the door, suddenly aware of the pair of soldiers that eyed him from their post at the far side of the court. They were big, fairish men, with hard Scots faces, short cloaks drawn close against the night air. The lantern above the gate cast their nightmarish shadows across the yard. They eyed the poet for a moment longer, leaning, careless and professional, on their short pikes, and then one of them said something in a voice that was meant to carry. He spoke in his native Scots—it was doubtful he had much English—but the intent was clear. The other soldier laughed harshly, and turned back to the gate.

Marlowe's mouth twisted, but he knew better than to

argue with their sort. Instead, he pushed himself away from the wall and moved on around the tower, until he was hidden in the shadow of the doorway itself. He paused there, resting his shoulders against the rough stones, and rubbed his hand across his mouth as though that would take away the taste of bile. It was cold. The night wind swept into the hanging sleeves of his doublet, cutting through the fine Holland of his shirt. He shivered convulsively, but did not go in. After his abrupt departure, there would be too many curious eyes looking for his return; he could not bear, yet, to face that mockery. He looked up, toward the empty sky. The setting moon drowned much of the stars' brilliance, and a thin veil of cloud had crept across the zenith; there was a strange, brief flicker of light to the north, like lightning, no sooner seen than it had vanished utterly.

"So. There you are."

Marlowe started, even though he recognized the voice of the man who had been sitting to his right at dinner.

"And it was a good French wine, too," the man continued, his English suddenly all but free of the Scots burr. "None of your Italian horse-piss."

"It wasn't to my taste." Marlowe eyed him warily, uncertain of the stranger's motives. Certainly he was grinning, the broken line of his teeth visible in the moonlight. Strangely, though, the right side of his face was blotched with shadow, despite the light full on it—or, no, Marlowe realized almost in the same instant, the dark stain that covered most of the Scotsman's cheek and jaw was a birthmark, or possibly a powder burn. The moonlight leeched all color from the world, making such identification uncertain.

The Scot's smile widened further, but before he could speak, there was a movement in the shadowed doorway. Greville stepped out into the courtyard, his amiable face hardening at the sight of the stranger. "Master Marlowe," he said. "You're looked for."

"And by whom, I wonder?" the Scotsman murmured.

Greville lifted an eyebrow at him, but the Scot seemed unabashed.

"He has a fine man to run his errands, at any rate," he continued.

"Might I ask how this is your concern?" Greville said, in his most remote voice.

The Scot bowed deeply. "I am Ian—John Gordon, and very much at your service, gentlemen." He glanced toward the doorway. "But I think I hear the dancing, so I'll take my leave." With a second, deeper bow, he vanished into the darkness.

Greville stared after him, frowning, then turned back to the poet. "Are you all right, Marlowe?"

The poet nodded, his words bitter in spite of himself. "I am now."

"Philip sent me," Greville continued, as if he hadn't heard the self-disgust in the younger man's voice. "The dancing has begun."

Marlowe looked up, startled both by the note of compassion—of understanding—in Greville's tone, and by the tact of the message. Now that the tables had been cleared away and the revels had truly started, almost no one would notice one more arrival in the crowded hall. He nodded his thanks, and said, "Then let's go in."

The servants had cleared away the tables in record time, stacking the trestles against one wall and the tops against the one opposite. The remains of the food had vanished—presumably to the kitchens, to be consumed by the people who had cooked and served it—but there was still wine and beer and the fiery whiskey the Scots seemed to favor in plenty. The sweating musicians struck up a lively tune, and James led his wife onto the cleared floor. He danced only the one dance, Sidney saw, though he was not as ungainly as might have been expected, and then left Anne to the attentions of a host of young courtiers, returning to his place on the dais. The Master of Ruthven came to stand beside him; as they talked, James rested one arm comfortably about the younger man's waist. After a few moments James lifted the other's hand, kissed it lightly, then pushed him gently away. Ruthven bowed, not at all discomfited by his dismissal, and moved to join the dancers forming for a round-dance.

Sidney raised an eyebrow. Even Marlowe was rarely so ostentatious, he thought—but then, Marlowe was not a king. He glanced curiously down the hall, wondering what the poet made of this, but the younger man's expression was unreadable, watching the dancers and listening with half an ear to a fair-haired young woman in an old-fashioned gown of scarlet brocade.

Somewhere, circles were described, and incantations shaped, spirits summoned and sent forth. Sidney lifted his head at the first whisper of power, faint as the first light breeze that prefaced a storm. Almost without thinking, he moved to put himself between the door—the source of that too-gentle touch—and the king. The musicians faltered, their instruments loud and off-key in the suddenly heavy air. The dancers stumbled to a halt. Most of them were more than half drunk, but even a drunken man could feel that sudden power. A scent of mildew, of cellars and forgotten caverns, floated into the hall. There was a shout from the courtyard, and then, from the antechamber, a woman's shrill scream. James rose to his feet as his nobles scattered before him, seeking the dubious protection of the dismantled tables. He was on the edge of blind panic, Sidney knew.

"If your Majesty will pardon me for a moment," he said, pitching his voice to cut through the king's fear, "there's a thing that needs dealing with."

James sank back into his seat, hands white-knuckled on the arms of his chair. The air had thickened at the end of the hall, and tendrils of oily black fog seemed to eddy in the doorway. Even as Sidney watched, the tendrils coalesced, weaving together into a shape like a taloned paw. He lifted his hands, marshaling all his strength. This was the time for Virgil's magic, not Dee's: the Roman art was immediate, a matter of the indomitable Roman will. Not for Virgil the drawing of circles, the casting of seals and sigils: the act itself was everything. One acted when one was acted upon—and readiness was all.

Sidney acted. Theory became practice in a splintering second, his will freezing the very air itself to stop the oncoming shape. The roiling mass of spirit energy recoiled, the air around it rolling with thunder. It recovered in an instant, rearing back like some great animal to throw itself against the barrier Sidney had so hastily erected. Sidney smiled grimly, and drove his will hard against it, holding the barrier in place. The amorphous mass hurled itself again at the barrier but could not pass it. Sidney's smile widened, and in the same instant he felt the familiar touch of the presence he had first encountered in England. Then that was gone, and Sidney spoke a final command. The oily black cloud burst apart into a blinding shower of blue light. There was a final mutter of thunder, and then all was silent in the hall.

James rose slowly to his feet, and bowed deeply to the Englishman. "Our cousin has done us greater honor than we had suspected, Sir Philip," he said, with only the slightest tremor in his voice. "She has indeed sent us a formidable champion. Scotland rests in your debt."

Sidney returned the bow. "Not yet, your Majesty. Matters are not yet concluded, I fear."

"Yet can we doubt the outcome?" James surveyed the hall sternly, unable to resist indulging his fondness for rhetoric. "We stand in your debt."

At the far end of the hall, Marlowe shook himself convulsively, one hand still clutching Watson's sigil through the cloth of his doublet. There had been nothing he could do to help—and in any case, Sidney had used a magic like no other he had ever seen before. This instantaneous spell-casting was almost unheard of; there were always parameters, guards and guides to be set and to be ignored at your peril. These things did not vary, whether the magic was black or white. Only the words of the invocations changed, or so Watson had said. . . .

The poet shook himself again, forcing a sort of calm. He would find out, would make Sidney teach him, but not just now. He glanced around the hall, grinning at the sight of a pair of noblemen crawling out from under one of the trestle tables, their finery sadly spotted. And what good did they think a wooden table would do them? he wondered, and looked away. The man who had sat next to him at dinner—the mark on his face was an old powder burn, as though a pistol had missed fire right beside him—was brushing straw from the voluminous skirts of an older woman, who was busily adjusting the upper hoop of her drum farthingale. No, Marlowe realized abruptly, not adjusting the hoop, but tucking a heavy pistol back into concealment through a slit in the skirt seam. She saw his glance, and winked; the poet looked away, not knowing what to think.

Sidney was standing at the far end of the hall, the courtiers—even those who opposed the king—crowding around to congratulate his skill. His face was very pale, paler than the bleached collar, and oddly rueful. Marlowe frowned. When the apparition had been destroyed, vanishing into that cloud of sparks, an expression almost of surprise had flickered across Sidney's face. So it didn't work quite as he intended, Marlowe thought, and grinned almost without malice. It was still an effective display. There was one broached hogshead of whiskey that had not been overturned in the confusion. The poet glanced around until he found a dented silver cup that someone had dropped, dusted it perfunctorily against his stockinged leg, and ladled it full of the harsh liquor. Then he worked his way through the crowd to Sidney's side.

"An impressive display, Sir Philip," he murmured into the older man's ear. Sidney turned to him, and realized that Marlowe had seen—and recognized—his own surprise. The rueful smile widened into true self-mockery.

"It was, wasn't it?" he said.

"Rather," Marlowe agreed, and handed Sidney the cup. "You need it."

Sidney recognized the stinging smell of it, but drained the cup in one quick swallow. The Scotsmen around him applauded cheerfully, giddy with the release from fear—but to Sidney, the liquor might as well have been water. It could not compete with the thrill of power within him, was drowned by the power that he had commanded, directed, and released. And that, he realized, was where the true danger lay. *Yet hast thou not known me, Philip?* The words of the lesson swam in his brain, rebuking his pride. He closed his eyes for a moment. This power is a gift, he told himself. A gift to be used, yes, but not to be taken pridefully. Pride is something my opposite could use against me, I daresay.

He opened his eyes, smiling a little. The whiskey was working, relaxing him. He felt calmer now, more secure and less frightened of what he had released. If he had not

expected the outward manifestations of his power, he had
successfully controlled its direction and intent, and that
was what mattered. He was suddenly aware that the young
Master of Ruthven was staring at him from his place
beside the king—but the black eyes were void of all expression, that very lack of emotion made the gaze malevolent. A man who doesn't want to reveal his animosity in his
eyes, Sidney thought, and by hiding it, he reveals it all the
more obviously. A dangerous boy . . . But there was something else there, deep in those shadowed eyes, the look of
a man let down rather abruptly from some expected pleasure. The eyes slid away, the emotion vanishing so quickly
that Sidney could not be sure he had not imagined it.
Later, he told himself, later he would inquire about this
Master of Ruthven, but for now he was too tired, too
elated by his unexpected victory. He smiled wearily at the
thronging courtiers, giving himself up to their adulation.

The repercussions followed almost at once. The French
party, which prefered James to align himself with the
Most Christian King, offered their congratulations to the
English wizard, but mixed their gratitude with a delicately-
worded caveat. After all, their sidelong looks implied, the
mysterious demon had not attacked in such force until
Sidney arrived to draw its danger down on them all. . . .
The Ultra-Protestants, who disapproved of all wizardry on
scriptural authority, found themselves briefly in agreement with their archrivals, and the more political recoiled
in confusion. The true dogmatists, however, accepted the
unfortunate coincidence of Catholic/Presbyter agreement
as simply that, and were loud in their condemnation of the
Englishman's efforts. The Sunday sermon, preached in
turn by members of the various Protestant factions, was
slated this week to be given by Andrew Melville, the most
vociferous of the Presbyterians, and Sidney braced himself
to face the inevitable tongue-lashing. That freedom of
speech was, after all, a preacher's privilege; besides, Melville's lack of moderation in the face of such an obvious
danger might well sway the more sensible of the Ultra-
Protestant nobles toward a decent neutrality.

"Will you attend?" Greville asked, and glanced at his
friend across the rim of his glass.

Sidney grimaced, turning away from the window and the fading purple of the hills. "I don't know. It's the ambassador's custom to bring his household, especially when the Archbishop or any of the bishops is preaching, and I don't like to flout that. But . . ." He let his voice trail off, and Greville nodded.

"But Melville's another matter. God's death, Philip, isn't it enough to say we're not of his church?"

"But can we?" Sidney said, and reached for his own wine. "I broached the subject to the ambassador, and his advice was for us to attend." He shrugged. "We will look Christian and forgiving—and properly Protestant—while Melville—"

"—has any number of shots at a standing target," Greville said sharply. "I don't think it's wise."

"Sweet Christ, do you think I'm looking forward to this?" Sidney snapped. He controlled himself instantly. "I'm sorry, Fulke, that was uncalled for. I think we have to trust the ambassador—after all, he's been here longer than we have, he should know these people better than we do. It's just unlucky that Melville is the preacher, that's all."

Greville grimaced, but nodded. "Most unlucky."

The Sunday dawned clear and warm, a few high clouds riding the gentle wind. It was the sort of day that invited hunting, a day's escape into the countryside. Sidney himself gave the distant hills a wistful glance, before turning away to dress himself in his most sober black. Neither he nor any of his people could afford to give the dominies anything to reproach just now. Young Madox had recognized the situation without prompting, too: the entire entourage was waiting to follow him to church, each man dressed in his best plain blue-coat livery, the two boys scrubbed to an unnatural godliness. Greville had abandoned the most startling eccentricities of French fashion, was sober and comfortable in a suit of argentine grey, embellished only with collar and cuffs of the finest lace. Even Marlowe had made an effort to be conciliatory, Sidney saw with an inward smile. The poet's rich purple doublet was hidden beneath a borrowed academic gown, and ruff and biretta were decently fastened rather than fashionably askew.

Somewhat to Sidney's surprise, given the seductive summer weather, the church was quite crowded, most of James's court in dutiful attendance. The sunlight streamed in through the plain glass of the windows, falling in broad bands of light and shadow across the congregation. *And with His stripes,* Sidney thought, *we are healed.* He hid a smile. Not quite what had been meant, perhaps, but the metaphor pleased him, allowed him to postpone for a few moments longer any contemplation of the service to come. He made his way up the side aisle, Greville at his elbow, responding with grave courtesy to the greetings of various members of the court, and made his bow to the ambassador, seated with his household at the head of the aisle. The ambassador, still pale and drawn from his illness, inclined his head in polite response. In the same moment, a young man in a plain suit rose quickly from his low stool, offering it to Sidney with a mute bow. Sidney thanked him, and seated himself; a moment later, the ambassador's son rose at his father's discreet nod, offering his place to Greville. Greville accepted it with thanks, and only the faintest hint of an ironic smile. Sidney saw, but contrived to ignore it, turning his attention instead to the ambassador's platitudes.

Marlowe, standing at the back of the church with the rest of the lesser members of the court, saw the way the bars of sunlight slanted across the nave, and smiled sourly to himself. God's grace, poured out at random across the crowd, separating the elect from the damned in no uncertain terms. . . . How appropriate for this dour place, he thought, and stepped back out of a band of sunlight. No doubt someone will point up the lesson. He fixed his eyes on the king and queen, sitting together in plain, high-backed chairs just below and to the right of the dais that held the communion table. The chairs were in shadow: *oh, see, see, my brethren, how neither rank nor royalty hath merit in the kingdom of heaven.* Marlowe's mouth twisted again, this time with mischief. Beyond James, in the press of courtiers who chose to stay with their master, he could just see the sun gleaming off Ruthven's raven-black hair. If the sun touched him, perhaps this was a devil's baptism, an anti-grace dispensed in an antichurch. . . . The smile vanished as he realized just how true that might be, and he shook the thought away.

The service was spartan even by strict Protestant standards, a few hymns sung standing and in Scots, and then the preacher rose to his feet and crossed with deliberate steps to the pulpit. Melville was wearing a black academic gown, but that was his only concession to the traditional cassock. Geneva bands showed at his throat, the starched white linen stark against his severe black doublet. He climbed slowly up to the raised lectern—relishing every step, Marlowe thought—and stood there for a moment, his hands resting on the polished wood to either side of the great Bible.

"Brothers and sisters in the Lord," he said at last, and lifted the cover of the massive book. "I take for our text today these words from Joel: *Hear this, ye old men, and give ear, all ye inhabitants of this land. Hath this been in your days, or even in the days of your fathers? Rend your heart, and not your garments, and turn unto the Lord your God.*"

Melville closed the Bible gently, but in the waiting silence that had descended on the church, the sound was clearly audible. At the front of the church, Sidney schooled himself to bear the attack he could guess was coming, and was aware of Greville's quick glance, at once angry and sympathetic.

"*Hath this been in your days, or even in the days of your fathers?*" Melville repeated. He turned slowly in his place, so that his stare seemed to sweep across the congregation. "The question is a pertinent one even for you this day, for which of us has seen such license given to the Devil for our chastisement? Demons stalk the very halls of royalty, yea, even into the bedchambers of kings, but what is our response? Do you search your hearts for sin, and root out iniquity from your thoughts? Do you do as the prophets bade, and fast, and weep your prayers? Do you bear your afflictions humbly, in the knowledge that your chastisement is just, a just recompense for your sins?" He paused again, then turned to stare directly at the king. "No, that is not what you have done, James Stuart. You have turned to foreign prophets—foreign wizards—and to wordly scholars, to the whisperings of women, and not to the Lord. *Rend your heart and not your garments:* that is meant for you, and all those who would turn to such mummery, and attempt—in vain!—to deflect the chastisement of the Lord."

Sidney took a deep breath, biting back his anger. How dared the man speak so to his king? And how could James permit such insolence to continue? Even as the thought took shape in his mind, he saw James rise slowly to his feet.

"Andrew Melville, come down out of there." James's voice echoed in the bated silence, unexpectedly imperious.

The preacher stopped, throwing back his head like a nervous horse. "You interfere with the work of the Lord," he began, and James interrupted.

"I've heard a great deal from you these past weeks, Andrew Melville, and I'm still waiting to hear sense. Answer me this, here in plain words: when I'm confronted with one of these demons, what am I to do, by your advice?"

"You must endure the Lord's chastisement, and search your heart for sin," Melville answered.

"Come down out of there," James repeated, and, very slowly, Melville obeyed. The two men stood facing each other for perhaps a dozen heartbeats, the preacher in his black against a king magnificent in pale blue satin, and then, quite abruptly, James slapped his thigh.

"Endure, is it? Contemplate my sins, is it? By God, we'll see how you like that remedy, sir preacher." Before Melville could move, James had caught the sallow preacher by the collar of his gown and propelled him stumbling down the aisle toward the door. The court made way for them, too shocked for an instant to speak. Melville twisted once against the inexorable grip, then submitted with what little dignity he could muster.

"Good God," Greville said blankly, and his words were drowned in the rising hum of consternation.

Sidney laughed aloud, but quickly swallowed his mirth. Deserved chastisement or not, this would be no laughing matter, if the majority of the Kirk chose to take this as an attack on their power. He pushed himself hastily up off his stool, and followed the king toward the door. The rest of the congregation was moving, too, some smirking openly, some honestly shocked and angry, most caught between laughter and offense. James paused just inside the door, his hand still on Melville's collar.

"Follow me, my lords—all of you," he shouted. "It's a fair test I'm offering." With an effort, he propelled the preacher ahead of him out into the courtyard.

Marlowe elbowed his way through the crowd, heedless of rank and station, and managed to reach the courtyard only a little behind the king. James strode ahead of them all, shoving Melville before him, heedless of the Archbishop bobbing at his elbow, of the Treasurer's gasping protest, of the queen, skirts hoisted ungracefully above her ankles, stumbling after him, ox eyes wide with protest. Her women hastened after her, calling disjointedly, and were swallowed in the crowd of courtiers. James was heading for Queen Mary's closet, Marlowe realized suddenly, and did not bother to hide his grin. If even half the rumors about that place were true, Melville would get what he deserved.

The crowd fell back a little as its leaders realized where James was going, the courtiers eddying at the bottom of the crooked stairs that led up to the closet. Marlowe used that confusion to edge past his betters, slipping up the stairway before anyone could see and protest. The upper hall was crowded, too, the guards at either end of the corridor standing slack-jawed, halberds half lowered in uncertainty. Cursing under his breath, Marlowe shoved his way along the outer wall, no longer caring who he offended, and at last came out almost at the front of the crowd. The nobles stood well back from the door, its painted cupids sadly still visible beneath the layers of whitewash, feet braced to keep from being pushed any closer by the press of men in the corridor behind.

"Let me by," a woman's voice demanded breathlessly, and a greybeard turned sideways to let the queen into the first rank. She put her hands to her mouth, stifling any pleas she might have made, and waited.

"Out of my way, poet," a soft familiar voice said, and in the same moment a slight figure brushed past, pushing into the front row. Marlowe caught his breath, scalded by the casual, knowing contact of body and body, and saw the Master of Ruthven glance back at him, beautiful face alive with malicious mischief.

"Your majesty," the archbishop began, sounding harassed and shaken—as well he might, Marlowe thought, having to defend a man who hates him and will never be grateful—and James shook his head.

"I will hear you later, your Grace, but not now." He was pale now, standing so close to the place that had been the center of all the manifestations, and sweat stood out on his forehead, but he did not step away. He glanced around as though assessing the crowd's reaction, and lifted his voice so his words would carry even to the men still on the steps. "You've heard the sermon that was preached today. Well, I've an answer to it now, and I say you all will bear witness. Tell me, Master Melville, can you endure this?"

Without waiting for an answer, he yanked open the door to the room, and shoved Melville inside, slamming the door closed behind him. Sidney, standing with Greville perhaps three men behind the queen, could see that the king was shaking, and a detached part of his mind wondered if it were anger or fear that caused it.

"Contemplate your sins," James said again, but his voice cracked on the last word, and he cleared his throat unhappily. Easy, now, Sidney thought. His hands closed into fists at his side. You've made a good beginning; you mustn't show fear now.

There was a long silence in the hall, stretching for a dozen, two dozen quick heartbeats. Marlowe found himself holding his breath, waiting for something, anything, from inside the room. Then at last the silence was shattered by a shriek, a cry of pure horror, and the door was flung open from the inside. For a moment, they all saw it, the cloud of fat droning flies, corpse-flies, that swarmed around Melville, fastening on his gown, settling in his eyes and hair, and darting effortlessly away from his frantically batting hands. And then the flies were gone, and the minister stumbled out into the hallway, still waving insanely at the empty air, throat filled with little choking cries. An older woman in the second row crossed herself hastily, and a dozen others forgot themselves and did the same. Melville continued to beat the air, his eyes bulging madly, striking at things only he could see. The sight was suddenly ridiculous. Someone at the back of the crowd laughed weakly, and a few others picked up the sound, then more, until the entire crowd was chuckling. Melville stopped abruptly, as though the noise had broken some spell, and flushed to the roots of his hair. James forced a smile, though the sight had shaken him more than he dared admit.

"Well, Master Melville? Do you—endure?"

Melville's flush deepened to the hot red of pure fury. "The Lord's purpose is inscrutable," he ground out between clenched teeth.

"And even godly men may be chastised, like Job, for no fault?" James pursued, still smiling.

"God's will be done," Melville spat, as though the words choked him. "Your Majesty—"

"And I believe there is another word that applies here," James continued mercilessly. *"Judge not*, the gospel says, *that ye be not judged*—how does the rest of it go, Master Melville?"

Melville's mouth tightened. James's eyes narrowed, and the preacher said reluctantly, *"For with what judgment ye judge, ye shall be judged: and with what measure ye mete, it shall be measured to you again."* He managed a stiff, uncompromising bow, his face still set and furious.

James nodded in response. "You have leave, Master Melville."

For an instant, it seemed as though Melville would protest further, but then he turned on his heel and stalked away. The courtiers made way for him with ill-concealed laughter. A voice floated after him from the front of the crowd—Marlowe's voice, Sidney realized, without surprise.

"Thus endeth the lesson."

Chapter Seventeen

*I sold apples, and the child took an apple from me,
and the mother took the apple from the child;
for the which I was very angry. But the child died
of the smallpox.*
> Statement made by Temperance Lloyd be-
> fore her execution for witchcraft, 1682;
> quoted in *A True and Impartial Relation of
> the Informations against Three Witches*

In the weeks following Sidney's dramatic defense of the king, and despite James's spirited defiance of Melville and all who condemned the presence of the English wizard, the king grew warier. No great rituals, especially of a public or semi-public nature, could be tolerated; Sidney could only do that which was absolutely necessary for the king's safety.

"The man's a fool," Sidney exclaimed, but even here in the privacy of his own rooms, he did not name the man, or raise his voice beyond the conversational. Madox, standing by the door in case of visitors, beckoned discreetly to the page, drawing him out of earshot.

"He's no soldier, he hasn't the least understanding of simple strategy," Sidney continued, and pushed himself to his feet to pace the length of the chamber. Marlowe,

268

lounging in the window seat, started and looked up as he passed, then turned his head away, to stare out across the dry parkland, his mind very obviously elsewhere. Greville grinned.

"Sit down, Philip," he said.

"God's blood," Sidney continued, as though he hadn't heard, "he fears my powers—any display of magic, no matter how well intentioned, no matter how necessary for his own survival, by God!—and I'll swear he fears the magic at hand even more than whatever it is that's abroad."

"You're not doing him justice," Greville said.

Sidney grimaced, but came back up the length of the room, to seat himself in the carved chair that stood beside the unlit fire. "Am I not?"

"No." Greville was still smiling, regarding his friend with unconcealed amusement.

"It's a waste," Sidney said, "a waste of my time and energies to follow him around like—like some black hound, when I could as easily set wards around his chambers, let him sleep without fear. God's name, I'm not some sort of talisman!"

"Obviously his majesty thinks you are," Greville answered, and darted a sly glance at the poet oblivious in the window seat. "He's had plenty of hangers on, and a good many favorites, but I don't think he's ever had a talisman before."

"You're very merry." Sidney gave his friend a sour glance.

Greville shrugged, his smile fading. "And I say again, with no jesting, you do him less than justice, Philip."

Sidney grimaced. "Fulke, he won't let me defend him fully. What am I to think?"

"That he has good reason for his decision," Greville answered. "Think on it. With the papists on one side, offering him their rites to use as he'd use magic, and the presbyters on the other, damning him to hell for so much as uttering a prayer for help instead of repentance, how can he blithely take what you're offering? To do so would be to alienate the presbyters—who don't like you much anyway, my Philip—and drive him into the arms of the

Gordons or some other Catholic family. And that would serve no one."

"You sound like Burleigh," Sidney said. "I'm not completely ignorant of politics, Fulke. I would simply wish his majesty of Scotland could understand that if I don't set wards, he's not likely to live long enough to juggle his factions again."

"Is it that bad, Philip?" Greville pushed himself to his feet, frowning slightly.

"Not yet," Sidney answered, with a reluctant smile. "But it could be. And, God help me, I think it will be, if I'm not allowed to set the wards I want. I can't be everywhere, Fulke; I need a line of defense I can fall back on when I'm hard pressed. It's a matter of sound tactics, if nothing else."

Greville nodded, almost to himself. "Have you tried that argument on him?"

Sidney looked away, shamefaced. "I've been afraid of losing my temper with him. Much good that would do."

"With your permission, then, I'd like to try what I may do?" Greville asked.

"Always the courtier," Sidney muttered.

Greville shrugged. "There's less at stake for me."

Sidney grimaced. "I beg your pardon, Fulke, I'm not fit company for the beasts today, and you're too good to bear it. Please, go to the king, and God send you can persuade him. I'm even further in your debt for the attempt."

Greville smiled, but shook his head, his hand already on the latch. "No talk of debts between us, Philip. This— we'll see what a change of tactics can do."

Sidney swore half-heartedly at him, but Greville was gone. He stood up abruptly. The day was overcast, with high, scudding clouds. A good hunting day, he thought, longing for Penshurst and the familiar land around it. No man, no man is so bound and driven, coddled and used, as I am at this court. Feared, too—but clutched at. He sighed, staring out the open window without seeing the rough hills that sloped down to the firth, a long finger of the sea. It was all so unnecessary, and dangerous, too, for until he had the leisure to discover who or what was behind James's torment, he could do very little more than

what he had been doing. And he would not have that
leisure until the king relented, and allowed him to set the
wards he so desperately wanted.

Sidney smiled rather bitterly at that. Doctor Dee would
approve, he thought. Dee's magic had in fact answered
admirably the situations he had faced so far, indeed was
the only kind of magic that could ward off these attacks, if
only he were allowed to apply it—except for that first
night, at the banquet, when there had been no time for
anything but action. And it had been glorious. He remembered it with a shudder in his soul, and turned his thoughts
away from the tantalizing memory. A dangerous memory,
certainly—everything here was dangerous to man, in one
way or another. Body and soul were in peril here, and
there was a very fine line between saving the body and
damning the soul. He did not care to think whose either
body or soul might be.

"I need air," he said aloud, and pushed himself away
from the window. "Accompany me, Marlowe?"

Beware, Marlowe thought, still unmoving in the window seat, though of what he was uncertain. He understood enough of the cast of Sidney's soul to guess that the
powers he had mastered troubled him, and did not understand his own forbearance. He had never had patience for
men who were frightened of their own talents—and yet
Sidney was not of the common sort, recoiling from talents
and responsibilities almost wholly imaginary. Where the
fear was real, Marlowe thought, and the ability as well,
there are no words to express either.

"Well?" Sidney said, impatiently, and the poet dragged
himself back to the present.

"As you wish, Sir Philip."

Sidney was uncharacteristically curt with his grooms,
who came very near to tripping themselves in their anxi-
ety to please. Only when he had dragged himself grace-
lessly into the saddle, hauling the stiffened leg into its
stirrup by main force, did his expression ease. Then his
face hardened again, and Marlowe, wrestling with the
spirited hack his patron had provided for him, glanced
over his shoulder to see Lord Malcolm Seton, the Earl of
Dunfermline's eldest son, striding across the stableyard

toward them. Sidney could not repress a forbidding frown, but Seton did not seem to notice it, smiling knowingly up at the Englishmen.

"You've chosen a fine afternoon for a ride, Sir Philip," he said, in lilting English. "Or could one say it was forced upon you?"

"Hardly that, my lord," Sidney demurred, and forced a small, stiff smile. "Every man needs to recoup himself whenever he can. This seemed like an ideal opportunity."

"I had much the same thought myself," Seton answered. "May I ride with you and Master Marlowe, then?"

"I'd be honored," Sidney lied. Seton was something of an unknown quantity, much in evidence about the court but allied with no particular faction. Still, Sidney thought, how freely can I talk with any of James's nobles?

They rode west through Holyrood's park, and past its boundaries into the farmland beyond. The low hills were just greening now, the narrow fields new-sewn, when England had been in the grip of summer for some weeks. Sidney sighed for Kent, his eyes fixed on the distant hills. The summer was even later coming in those highlands, the planting hurried and the harvest correspondingly hard-won; it was no wonder, he thought, that only the dourest Calvinism had served to wean these people from popery. He shook his head, and felt most of his ill temper drain away in the sharp-edged air. He glanced sideways at Seton, who rode at a discreet distance, and said with a half smile, "Was this a commission from the king, my lord, to make sure I didn't hare off back to England?"

"It was intended as support, Sir Philip, back-handed though it might seem," Seton answered. "I've heard what you say to the king, and I've never thought it wise to patch holes in rotten cloth." He shrugged. "As you've said yourself, it's best to have more than one line of defense. A lesson from Holland, sir?"

"The Dutch have more lines of defense than you can imagine," Sidney answered with a wry grin, "and I've always admired their tactics. As for the matter at hand, certainly, I have defended the king in close engagement before, but I would prefer not to do it again. It's not my life, to take such risks with it."

"Little enough risk if what we saw at the banquet was fair measure of your art," Seton said. "That was a display of power such as I doubt any of us have ever seen."

Sidney did not answer, seemed fully occupied in managing his horse. Seton glanced toward Marlowe, one eyebrow lifting in question. The poet shrugged, and improvised. "Would you, my lord, finding yourself, a foreign stranger in a court known for its—admittedly understandable— aversion to witchcraft, be happy to find your function as ambassador usurped by the need to play court wizard? An Englishman protecting the king of Scots, since the Scots have proved singularly incapable of doing so?"

Seton grinned. "Ah, well, there is a little ill feeling, of course."

"But not on your part," Marlowe said, lifting the end of the phrase into a question, and in the same moment slowed his hack discreetly.

Seton shrugged. "I'm his majesty's man, Master Marlowe. He's no Alexander, and God knows his life's been hard from before he was born. . . ."

Marlowe raised an eyebrow at that, and Seton's lips curled bitterly. "You've seen the black seraph who's his majesty's favorite? The master of Ruthven, brother to the Earl of Gowrie? Well, their father, the old earl, kidnapped the king in the faction fights thirteen years ago, and was executed for it; their grandfather was the man who held his knife to the late queen's belly, she being then with child with the king, when the earls murdered David Rizzio."

For a moment, the Scots pronunciation made the name unfamiliar, but then Marlowe's eyebrows rose even higher. No one in London had missed a single scandalous detail of the stories surrounding Queen Mary of Scotland, and her execution eight years before had been the occasion for the reissue of the more lurid pamphlets. Rizzio had been the queen's Italian secretary—her lover, or so her own husband had claimed, when he masterminded the Italian's death. The king-consort had been murdered himself a year or so later, quite possibly with Mary's consent if not actually at her orders. . . . This was not England, and Marlowe hastily pulled away from that train of thought. *Where kings and princes die so easily, who would miss a mere poet?* He said aloud, "His majesty would seem to have little cause to love the Ruthvens, then. . . ." He let his voice trail off invitingly, and Seton snorted.

"You've seen the lad, and can say that? A gesture of defiance, maybe, but the boy is a Ganymede."

A Ganymede, Marlowe thought, but next to mine. . . . Next to him, Ruthven would have to shrivel up into the creature he actually was. It was an odd image, and the poet tilted his head to one side, assessing its worth. Certainly he did not trust the lynx-eyed master of Ruthven, but there was no cause to call the boy a changeling, or place him any lower in the great chain of being. The metaphor was getting out of hand. He lifted his head, letting the wind clear his brain.

"A fine animal," Seton said, and nodded to Sidney. Marlowe, for whom a horse was a mode of transportation or a set-piece subject for his characters, looked away. The fitful wind strengthened then, bringing with it a faint familiar noise.

Sidney looked up sharply, his mouth setting into a thin line, and turned to Seton. "Where?"

"There's a village on the far side of the hill," Seton answered, his own face suddenly grim.

"Follow me," Sidney said, and set spurs to his horse without waiting for an answer. Seton obeyed without question. Marlowe swore softly, glancing over his shoulder at the trailing grooms. He had heard the sound of a mob before now, and dreaded what they'd find.

"Come on," he said aloud, and kicked the horse into a reluctant canter. The grooms followed more slowly, muttering to each other.

The village was a tiny place, half a dozen thatch-roofed hovels clustered in the lee of the hill, a few fields and a muddy common pasture visible beyond the last house. Fifteen or twenty people, men and woman about evenly mixed—the entire population, probably, Marlowe thought—milled in front of the largest house, where two men of middling age pinned a struggling woman. A few of the crowd were shouting at a greybeard who stood in the door of the house, their words overlapping and mingling until the broad Scots was incomprehensible to the Englishmen, but most stood silent, watching the struggling woman.

"Witch hunt," Seton said. "Such loyalty to the king . . . very touching."

"I'm sure that here on this lonely heath we've found the king's great enemy," Sidney snapped, and spurred his horse forward again.

Seton managed a brief grin. "Was this what he was like in Holland?"

"Don't ask me," Marlowe said, with acid resignation. He jerked one of Walsingham's pistols from its case at his saddlebow and cocked it, glad he had thought to carry them today. "I wasn't with him." He was speaking to empty air. Seton was already at the older Englishman's side, braced and ready. Marlowe snarled a curse, but brought his horse up beside them, the pistol resting across his thigh. At least Sidney has the sense to stay horsed, he thought, though if the damned peasants knew how to use those pikerels they're carrying, it won't do him much good. Not that he'd ask his horse to commit suicide, of course; that honor's reserved for those unfortunates under his protection. . . .

"Let her be," Sidney said, his voice cutting through the noise of the crowd.

The greybeard turned to him eagerly, welcoming an authority greater than his own, but someone in the crowd hooted angrily.

"We don't need a foreigner to deal with a witch," a woman shrilled.

"Hang her, the bitch of Satan!" another voice cried. "One less to trouble our king's sleeps."

Marlowe lifted his head sharply at that. That wasn't the usual cry of a country witch hunt; those were usually local matters, local grievances, not something political—particularly when a monarch was as little known as James. "'Ware, Sir Philip," he said aloud, and Sidney nodded, not taking his eyes from the woman.

"Who's in authority here?" he said, and charged his voice with the landowner's rich contempt. "What's this woman done?"

"No concern of yours, Englishman," one of the men

who held the accused witch snapped. He wore a better suit than most of his fellows, and there was a silver hilt to the dagger at his belt. "Be gone, before you have serving the devil's minion on your soul."

"I'm as good a Scot as you, Colin Nuscatt," Seton called. "Oh, ay, I know you, and your preaching. Come along, what's the woman done?"

There was a confused outcry, not all of it accusatory, and the woman lifted her head. "I've done no harm, my lords, no harm."

"It says in scripture, *Thou shalt not suffer a witch to live*," Nuscatt retorted, and shoved her to her knees. "You pollute the kingdom by your presence, and endanger the king."

"If she's done no wrong, how can you accuse her?" Sidney said, with deceptive mildness.

"He has the right of it," Seton agreed. "Go home, good people, this isn't a business for honest folk. Man, it's Sir Philip Sidney, the king's own defender, who says to let her go."

"And why does the king's defender protect the witches who daily threaten him, aye, and have since he was a babe?" Nuscatt glared at the villagers; but there was no answering murmur from them.

"It wasn't witches who threatened his mother," someone called from the back of the crowd, and effaced himself as Nuscatt turned on them in fury.

"So one of you knows truth when he hears it," Seton said, and pointed to the accused witch. "What can she have to do with his majesty?"

"It's all part of the same evil," Nuscatt retorted, "of which Scotland will be purged."

Seton glanced toward Sidney. "The kirk speaks at last. It's well for you you're such a brave defender of the faith."

Sidney's mouth twisted. "Not your faith."

"It'll do."

Nuscatt sneered openly, and turned to the villagers. "He's a witch himself, and proud of it. We'll rid Scotland of him first, and then the witch."

There was a noise from the crowd, more uncertain than eager. Marlowe grinned, but kept a tight grip on his pistol nonetheless. How like countryfolk, to be ready to hang the common woman, but balk at facing down a lord.

"Colin Nuscatt," Sidney said slowly. "Let's put an end to this. I'll fight you, for the woman's life, and let God judge the right."

"Lord Jesus, it's the thrice-damned Tilts," Marlowe said, and did not care who heard.

The crowd murmured again, the sound approving now, and the greybeard in the doorway called, "Ay, let God judge."

"Your answer?" Sidney's face was remotely amused, looking down at the preacher. Nuscatt's face contorted.

"Be damned to you!"

Seton swore softly, and said, almost to himself, "She's not worth his death. . . ."

Sidney heard nonetheless, and glanced back over his shoulder, one eyebrow quirking upward. "I doubt God would see it that way, my lord."

"God might not, but I know the king would," Seton muttered, but flushed to the roots of his pale hair. He cast an imploring glance at Marlowe, but the poet looked away, shrugging. There was nothing anyone could do to stop Sidney now; the wise man realized it, and made ready for the consequences. Marlowe shifted the pistol against his thigh, making certain the villagers had seen it. And what will London say when it hears of this? he wondered. Sir Philip Sidney, the queen's champion, defender of the king of Scots, stood champion again for the life of a woman falsely—and of course the accusation would have to be false; it would be utterly unworthy of Sidney's legend if it were not—accused of witchcraft and— He shook the thought away. Time enough for that when we've survived.

Sidney slid from his horse, and took a lurching step toward the Scot. Nuscatt's eyes widened, and Marlowe restrained a rather hysterical laugh. That the great Sir Philip Sidney should stoop to such deception—a fencing-master's trick, to bait a country coney into a fight he could not win. . . . No one, no one in London would ever believe it. Nuscatt grinned tightly, and released his hold on the witch. He stepped forward, drawing sword and dagger in a single movement. Sidney did not quite smile, and drew his own weapon. For a moment, no one in the watching crowd realized what he held, and then, with a sudden twist, he separated the long blade from the slim dagger that fitted flush against it, twin blades in the same sheath. An Italian toy, Greville had called it once, but only in jest.

Nuscatt came forward in a rush, trying to overrun the other, to make him move on the stiffened leg. Sidney stepped back, moving more easily now, and parried neatly, the light Italian dagger turning the Scotsman's rapier easily. He lunged in the same instant, and Nuscatt's blade just turned the thrust. There was a quick exchange of blows, shortened thrusts made at close quarters, turned aside by the left-hand daggers, and then suddenly Sidney was inside the other man's guard. Nuscatt stepped back instinctively, seeking room, and Sidney's foot shot out, tripping him. Nuscatt went sprawling, the rapier flying from his hand; Sidney staggered—it had been a risk, throwing his weight onto the bad leg, but a calculated one—but recovered, and set his shortened sword to the Scotsman's throat. Nuscatt froze, the dagger forgotten in his hand. The villagers were very silent.

Sidney stood utterly still, looking down at the man almost without seeing him, a voice whispering in his mind. *Not pride, not pride, to force you to this demeaning battle, nor even common sense, but fear. You know you cannot win, even against such as these. What hope, then, against the Enemy of the king?* Sidney's face hardened. He knew what the voice wanted, what it proposed without words: a death for a threatened death, Nuscatt's blood for the blood he had intended to shed, and the part of him that was still a soldier could not but agree with that prompting. If Nuscatt lived, he would preach again, and some other woman would die; better that Nuscatt die, to save the innocent unknown.

"No," Sidney said aloud, and drove his sword into the ground just above the preacher's shoulder. The man flinched, then opened startled eyes, as though he could not believe he had been spared. *I am not God, Sidney thought, I cannot, will not play His part.* "Colin Nuscatt," he said slowly, fumbling for the words that might reach the man, that might convince him of the truth of Sidney's own conviction. "You spoke from the old dispensation; we are of the new. Did our savior not speak of mercy, save the woman—a guilty woman—from stoning. . . . ?" There was no answering understanding in Nuscatt's eyes, and Sidney turned away, sickened by his own failure.

"Get the woman," Marlowe said softly, to Seton, and spurred forward, lifting his pistol. To his surprise, Nuscatt did not move, though he stared after the Englishman with hatred. Sidney looked up then, and Marlowe was appalled by the bitterness in his face.

"You did what you must," the poet said, not knowing certainly why he spoke, or if the older man would be willing to listen. It was as if the words were forced from him by the near-despair in Sidney's eyes. "I know what you were thinking, I saw it gathering in you, and there's not a man alive would have blamed you for it. And I saw you banish it. Pride it may have been, but a wiser pride, a braver pride, I've never seen."

Sidney raised an eyebrow and resheathed his Italian blades, the hilts snapping home to betray his anger. He took the reins from the ashen-faced groom, and pulled himself up in the saddle. His eyes swept the crowd. Sidney's lips curled, and Marlowe remembered that this shepherd knight had never seen any necessary virtue in poverty and ignorance, not even in Arcadia. Then Sidney's eyes widened, and the poet saw a knot of horsemen, badged in royal red and gold, coming over the hill from Holyrood. He breathed a curse, and Sidney's mouth twisted. He looked over his shoulder at Seton, and the accused witch riding pillion behind him.

"And what good have I done here today?"

"She lives, doesn't she?" Marlowe answered, almost roughly. "And so does he. You've not done so ill."

Sidney lifted a skeptical eyebrow at that, but turned toward Seton again, studying the woman who clung to the saddle behind him. She seemed ordinary enough, her skirts bunched up to show much mended stockings and bare knees, her coif pushed askew to release a loop of mouse-brown braid, a young-old woman with sturdy, short-fingered hands, and dirt on her weathered face. "I trust

you're unharmed, mistress?" he said aloud, and was rewarded by a fleeting, urchin's grin.

"I am so, my lord," she said, and the lilt of her voice
was very different from the accents of her neighbors. "I
only hope, my lord, you don't find yourself misguided in
this act of charity. I am what they say I am, though I
would never stoop to what they accuse me of."

Sidney drew back slightly, instinctively, but managed a
smile. "I must confess, it never occured to me to wonder if
you were. I saw a woman mistreated, and I could only
act."

"Even a witch-woman?" she asked, eyes wary.

"Even a witch," Sidney answered, wryly. "Perhaps I do
you an even greater injustice when I say I don't believe
you to be the king's dire enemy, or to be in league with
him. I don't doubt your powers, but I've become familiar
with his—scent, these past few weeks."

"Have you, then?" The witch darted a glance at the
approaching horsemen, and slid suddenly to the ground,
shaking out her tattered skirts. "No, I'm not offended, for
I've felt these things too—who could not, and be alive in
these times? But a word for you, in thanks and common
courtesy, and your king may live to see another day, and
you too, my lord. Watch carefully tonight. *He's* abroad,
and the air stinks of blood. Watch the king—and watch
yourself, if you be the knight of the south."

The horsemen were within earshot now, the crowd of
peasants scattering before them, and the witch lifted both
arms. "Iain Min!" she cried, and then something more in
an unfamiliar, liquid tongue. It sounded very like the Irish
spoken in Galway, Sidney thought, and saw the leading
rider pull up abruptly. He was a thin-faced man with the
dark scar of a powder burn across his cheek, and Sidney's
eyes narrowed.

"John Gordon," Marlowe murmured, and smiled. Seton's eyebrows rose.

"And what's he doing here?"

The scar-faced man ignored them both, holding up his
hand to stop the soldiers who rode with him, and stared
down at the witch. He spoke to her in the same strange
language, voice rising in question, and she answered volu-

bly, broad hands gesturing. After a moment, Gordon nodded, and spoke again, cutting off her spate of words. He looked then at Sidney. "Sir Philip, it seems I owe you thanks on my mistress's behalf. This woman's of our kin, and we wouldn't willingly have seen her killed—whatever she may be. I will take her now." As he spoke, he held out a hand, and the woman scrambled up behind him.

"What will become of her?" Sidney asked, and was surprised to feel so little apprehension for her. He had no reason either to trust or to distrust Gordon—or to feel such concern for an admitted witch, he added silently, but could not retrieve the question.

Gordon looked puzzled. "She's of my kin," he said again, as if that answered all questions. And perhaps it did, Sidney thought. It had done so in Ireland, certainly.

"My lord," the witch said, and leaned forward against Gordon's shoulder. "My lord, remember what I said. Watch well."

Sidney straightened in the saddle, a deep pulse of apprehension throbbing through him. Danger assumed was one thing, every soldier knew both the feeling and its proper value, but viewed so clearly . . . God shield me from that talent, he prayed silently, and said aloud, "I'll heed your words, mistress."

Seton edged his horse forward. "Sir Philip, if this is true . . ."

"It is," Sidney said.

"Then we'd be returning without delay," Seton continued. "Perhaps now you can convince the king your method is the best."

Sidney glanced at him, one corner of his mouth lifting into a wry smile. "And how am I to do that? Inform his majesty that a witch encountered on the borders of Holyrood park, about to be hanged for her witchcraft, gave me the information in payment for her life?"

"The source seems unimpeachable," Marlowe murmured.

Seton said, "Need you tell him that at all? Tell him it's your own sense of foreboding—"

"God's blood, don't you think I've tried?" Sidney bit back his anger. "You're right, though, we should be getting back." He glanced at the witch again. "I thank you for your warning, mistress, and will refrain from asking precisely how you know—what you know."

She smiled, an ancient, faerie smile, and in that instant Sidney knew quite certainly that she was what she claimed to be. Not evil, precisely, but other, outside the bounds of even Catholic law. God send I've done right in saving her, he prayed. She pointed to Marlowe. "Ask him, perhaps. If I could be as intimate with the great ones as that one is, then I should be feared indeed. . . . But he's too much a part of this world—of you, perhaps?"

"Only insofar as I'm his patron," Sidney answered. He glanced at Marlowe, wondering just what the woman had meant, but the poet's face betrayed nothing, except, perhaps, a certain wistfulness about the eyes. Sidney started to pursue the question, then thought better of it. He said instead, "Is there anything that we may do, as well as your kinsmen?"

"Only what you've done already, my lord," the witch said, "For which I thank you, and for which even the great ones may hold their hands until you're ready."

"Hold your tongue, Lilias," Gordon said. He bowed to Sidney. "Sir Philip, pardon me, but we must be gone." He wheeled his horse without waiting for an answer, the soldiers clustering at his heels, and rode away, the witch clinging to him.

Sidney watched them go, his mind on the woman's final words. They were troubling, but more disturbing still was the look in Marlowe's eyes, an expression almost of loss, that haunted Sidney all the way back to Holyrood.

The sun was low on the horizon by the time they reached Holyrood, though it lacked some hours yet to sunset. Sidney's absence had been noted, and much commented upon: the air was thick with sidelong glances, accusations unvoiced as yet but nonetheless palpable. Sidney felt himself growing tense, and had to force himself to relax, to keep himself from exploding at the wrong time or the wrong man—like an overwound pistol, he thought suddenly, and the homely metaphor eased a little of the tension.

"Shall I say something that I think would perversely please you?" he said, to Marlowe, and did not bother to lower his voice. Campbell of Ardchatten, passing down the hallway from the king's chamber, winced noticeably, but young Seton gave a reluctant grin.

"Only if you promise I can write it down—and if my lord will bear me witness—" Marlowe added, with a glance between mischief and malice at Seton, "—so that all the world may know that Sir Philip Sidney has uttered something scandalous."

Seton shied back a little, but Sidney smiled tightly. "If you insist."

It was a soldier's smile, Marlowe thought, who had known many a common soldier, and I don't envy his enemies. "Say on, Sir Philip, the world is waiting," he said.

"I think I envy the papists."

Marlowe glanced warily at him, waiting for the rest, then opened his eyes in mock incredulity. "You surprise me."

"The scandal or the sentiment?" Sidney retorted.

Marlowe opened his mouth to continue the game, saw the look in Sidney's eyes, and answered honestly, "Your reasons would interest me, sir."

Sidney, too, looked momentarily startled, then laughed softly. "Witchcraft, wizardry, what you will . . . the Catholics could—can—deal with it. They have always—accepted, if that's quite the word, met it on its own terms, at least—while we condemn. In gaining the greater truth, I think we've lost the trick of, well, some earthly things. I swear that if this were a Catholic kingdom still we could lock James within the confines of a church, and he would be perfectly safe there. But we have decreed that a church is a building still and only—and haven't we robbed it of its benign influence?"

Marlowe lifted an eyebrow. "I think that's heresy, Sir Philip."

"Hypothetical, certainly. I can't stop thinking." Sidney smiled again, with more true humor. "You must be sure to credit me with that opinion, Marlowe, and not steal it for yourself."

"Thank you, no, I won't claim it, nor will I father it on you," the poet answered promptly. "My reputation is bad enough, and I need a patron. If you go down, I won't stay afloat." He drew breath, aware of Seton open-mouthed at his elbow, and of half a dozen others within earshot, and prepared to expound on the theme, but something in Sidney's expression checked him. "Then you believe what the woman said."

"Don't you?" Sidney answered, and Marlowe grimaced.

"I do." He took a deep breath. "What may I do to help you?"

Sidney turned to him with a gently mocking smile. "A great sacrifice, Kit."

The poet shrugged. "As I said, I need my patron. You brought me along because of my peculiar knowledge of devils. Perhaps if one shows itself tonight, I'll be able to name him, and so dispel him."

"Oh, if only it were that easy," Sidney murmured, still with that mocking smile playing about his lips.

"People do tend to be a bit more stubborn," Marlowe agreed, and hid the sudden flash of anger. "Demons and devils know and play by the rules. Which is why I think we're facing a someone, rather than just something."

"And somehow, the thought comforts me not at all," Sidney said grimly.

They had reached the door of the royal bedchamber now, and Marlowe swallowed his quick retort. As always, a group of petty nobles had gathered, jostling each other in their attempts to have the last word with the king before he retired. Sidney set his jaw, knowing he would have to offer some apology for his earlier disappearance, but before he could give his name to the chamberlain waiting beside the door, the man had bowed profoundly.

"Sir Philip. His majesty would like a word with you."

I do daresay, Sidney thought wearily, but said, "I am at his majesty's command."

The chamberlain tapped on the door, said something in a voice too low to be heard. The door opened more fully, and the Master of Ruthven bowed deeply. "Sir Philip Sidney, sire," he said, and fixed Marlowe with a dismissing stare. The poet restrained a sudden desire to slap the pretty moll, and in a splintered second knew that Ruthven had seen his anger, and himself saw Ruthven's response.

Arrogance, certainly, but also contentment: Marlowe had conceived an intense dislike for the pretty creature the night of the banquet; he wondered now if he should also fear him.

Sidney had caught a glimpse of the exchange, but knew he could not spare the time to deal with it now. He put it from his mind, bowing deeply to the king, who was sitting in a carved chair, his nightgown thrown loosely over shirt and hose.

"Good evening, Sir Philip," the king said. "We missed your presence today."

Sidney straightened carefully, allowing himself one quick glance around the room. The few privileged tonight were mostly young men, James's friends rather than his political allies. The Earl of Mar was absent, for once, but his crony Lord Hamilton was there, leaning against the wardrobe to the carefully concealed annoyance of the royal valet, and so was the young earl of Cassilis. Lord Linton leaned against a bedpost, Stewart of Grandtully at his side: none of them open enemies, but neither had any shown themselves to be friendly to the English wizard. He said, cautiously, "I hope your Majesty will excuse my absence, in that I have been able to put it to some use."

"How so?" James's voice was relaxed. Here, at ease among his friends, one could almost see the man he might have been, had he not been a pawn from such an early age. Sidney hesitated, startled and distracted by the vision, and James frowned slightly.

"How is that?" he said again, though without anger, and Sidney shook himself back to the present.

"I have had a warning," he said slowly. "From an unexpected source, but one that I nonetheless believe to be a reliable one. I fear, your Majesty, that you will be in grave danger tonight."

In an instant, James's ease vanished, dissolving into fear. Sidney watched the transition sadly, but pressed his advantage. "I am told that there will be an attack on your life tonight, an arcane attack. I beg you once again, your Majesty, allow me to ward your bedchamber."

James had himself under control again, though the fear still lurked in the depths of his eyes. Before he could speak, however, Cassilis said, "Sir Philip, is this not the chance you've been waiting for? After all, you know this attack will come, you are prepared—and then you could defeat it, perhaps find out precisely who is behind this, perhaps even, with God's aid, destroy it utterly."

Sidney breathed a silent oath, but said, "Perhaps, my lord. But it's too great a risk to the king."

"Risk?" Cassilis looked suddenly very young, blue eyes shining. "Oh, yes, but still . . . Isn't it worth it, if you might destroy—" He became aware suddenly of James's indignant glare, and faltered to a stop.

Damn the boy, Sidney thought. He said aloud, as firmly as he dared, "Your Majesty, I cannot advise it. The risk is too great."

James fixed the young earl with a malevolent stare. He said, as though the words choked him, "Patrick has the right of it, I think. To trap this thing—it's worth a certain risk."

"Your Majesty," Sidney began, then stopped, recognizing the futility of any protest. James was doing his best to act the king, misguided though his attempts might be—though why in God's name he must choose to be fearless just when fear is justified . . . Sidney killed the thought, and said slowly, "Your Majesty, if you must do this, it is over my abject plea that you reconsider. . . ."

James waved a hand dismissingly, and Sidney sighed. "As your Majesty commands. But I will—I ask you to let me sleep here, in your bedchamber, tonight."

"I would have it no other way, Sir Philip," James answered, and somehow managed a wry smile. Incredibly, Sidney felt the sting of a reluctant admiration. Afraid though he was, at least he was facing this immediate danger with a certain bitter humor. Sometimes I think I've fulfilled my commission too easily, Sidney thought, as James gave low-voiced orders to his stewards. Not that it's been easy defending him, but I know I haven't faced the worst that this—enemy—can do. He shook the thought away. I have studied, even if James will not allow me to ward the room, and I will be prepared. With that, and prayer—no man can do more.

Chapter Eighteen

There's no hate lost between us.
Thomas Middleton, The Witch

Sidney woke reluctantly, his tongue thick with the remembered taste of poppies. For an evil moment, he thought
himself back in Holland, chained to his bed by the weakness and the terrible pain that not even the physicians'
decoctions could extinguish. There was the same drugged
heaviness of body, the same light languor of mind, and he
pushed himself up on his elbows half expecting to see
Frances there beside him, and to feel her hands on his
shoulders, easing him down again.

Certainly there were hands on his shoulder, but they
were pulling, not pushing. In the same instant, he remembered where he was, and why, and heard, over a babble of
Scots voices, the harsh noises of a choking man. He shook
his head, trying to drive away the strange inertia, and felt
himself roughly shaken.

"Sir Philip, in God's name, the king—"

The words were Scots, but the sense penetrated the fog
surrounding him. Sidney pushed himself up off his pallet,
and staggered toward James's bed. The curtains were drawn,
and one of the pages had had the sense to bring a lantern,
but its shaky light showed a scene weirdly unreal. The

king sat bolt upright among his pillows, his hands at his throat as though to ward off some attacker. His fingers tore at empty air, but still his face darkened, and the dreadful strangled noises came from his gaping mouth. The oldest of the pages lay sprawled at the foot of the bed, a pulsing gash across his face and neck, blood staining his night-gown; the other boys huddled whimpering beside him.

The sight was enough to drive away the lingering drowsi-ness from Sidney's brain. This was the sort of thing for which Dee had trained him, the demon—or at least its mode of attack—familiar from half a dozen crabbed texts. Sidney smiled tightly, and lifted his hands in a complex gesture.

"Rabdos! Strangler, leave him!" He could feel the invisi-ble creature shifting, turning its attention away from its victim toward the new attack, and a part of him relished that challenge.

Begone, mortal, a husky voice said, out of nothingness, a deep, dry voice that was the sound of sand speaking, whispering out of some distant desert tomb. *Do not inter-fere, or I will consume you also.*

"But I know you, Rabdos," Sidney said. It was a matter of time, he knew, of holding the demon off from James and from himself until he could remember the proper forms, the correct names and formulae, for calling up the power that was the antithesis of this particular demon. "I know you well."

No mortal knows me, no wizard, the voice answered. Almost imperceptibly, James's breathing eased, then hoars-ened again.

"No?" Sidney asked, hastily. "What of the mere mortal who commanded you here? He knows you, even as I do, you lesser creature, accursed of God."

There was a hissing sound, as though the words had struck home. *Presumptuous mortal—*

"I do not fear you," Sidney cut in. "In the name of the Father and of the Son and of the Holy Ghost, I exorcise you. By the holy names of God, by the powers granted to the angels and to the archangels, by the power granted unto the apostles and prophets, I exorcise you. Begone, accursed spirit; return to him who sent you, unclean one."

Rabdos hissed again, this time angrily, and Sidney could feel its attention fully on him. James sagged against his pillows, hands still at his throat, but his breathing had eased perceptibly. I've bought a little time, Sidney thought, but nothing more—until I remember. He closed his eyes, conjuring the memory of Dee's study. He had been very young, then, first embarked on his course of study, and still filled with a sort of proud amazement that John Dee would choose him as a pupil. They had been discussing black wizards, Sidney with indignation, Dee with a sort of resigned regret that made him seem to be a fount of worldly wisdom. *For each specific demon, there is an angel set against its power, on whom one may call without fear of harm, to counter such attack,* Dee had said. *If you will learn their names, my boy, none will be able to harm you by that method.*

"Brieus," Sidney said, and opened his eyes. "Very God of very God, who has granted extraordinary powers unto certain of thy servants, send unto us thy servant Brieus, whom thou hast given power over this demon Rabdos, that the lives and souls of thy faithful servants may be preserved. Smite this demon through the arm of thy servant Brieus, banish him from our presence as he was long past banished from thy sight. In the name of our lord Jesus Christ, amen."

The room was suddenly filled with a presence like a rushing wind. Sidney lifted his head, as always awed and astonished by the power that he called upon, and thought he caught a glimpse of peacock wings in the uncertain air. Rabdos shrieked, a sound to tear the ears, and fled. The rushing presence—*Brieus,* Sidney thought—followed, its passage scouring the room of the demon's lingering taint and leaving in its place a faint and vanishing perfume.

James pulled himself upright, his breath coming now in crowing gasps. One hand was still at his bruised throat, but he groped with the other for the bell on its stand beside the bed. "The boy—" he began, his voice a broken whisper painful to hear, and Sidney nodded. He dropped to his knees beside the sprawled body, catching the nearest page by the shoulder. The boy—he could not have been much older than Sidney's own Elizabeth—started back, eyes as wide and rolling as a fire-stricken horse. There was no time for sympathy, or for hysterics; Sidney shook him, saying, "Fetch a surgeon, boy."

The page quivered, but did not move, brown eyes rolling in a chalky face. Sidney shook him again, harder this time. "Do you hear me, villain? Bring a surgeon, for him and for the king."

The page started again, and pulled himself away. He ducked his head once, convulsively, and ran. Sidney swore under his breath.

"One of you, go after him, see he does it. You—" He nodded to the red-haired boy who crouched beside the injured page, holding a blood-soaked cloth to the ugly gashes, and made himself moderate his impatient tone. "—you've done well, but let me have him now."

The red-head nodded slowly, but did not move his hands. Sidney gave him what he hoped was an encouraging smile, and ripped at the royal sheets. Hastily, he folded the torn bit of cloth into a rough pad, and slid across the floor until he was beside the red-haired boy. "You've done well," he said again, and meant it. The injured page was still breathing, though the movement of his chest was too quick and shallow for comfort, and the bleeding seemed to have slowed a little. He placed the crumpled pad over the red-haired boy's hand, and pressed down hard. The boy eyed him warily for an instant, then edged his own hand away. Sidney nodded, and eased the limp body into his own lap. He felt suddenly helpless, crouching there: the only remedies he knew were battle-field medicine; neither Languet nor Dee had ever seen much cause to teach him medicinal magic. The only spell he knew that was remotely relevant was to prevent the festering of wounds—useful, certainly, but not what was needed at the moment. And I should have known I'd need that knowledge, he thought, studying the waxy face. A soldier's life—

He shook the doubts away, frowning a little. Medical magic, even more than other aspects of the arcane arts, was a matter of preparation, of sigils and seals and long-brewed ointments; even if he had studied all the texts, they would avail him nothing unless he had already prepared the proper materials. The boy would be helped more by what he had learned in Holland than by all the medical books ever written.

He looked down again, staring as though he were seeing the thin youth for the first time. The boy's hair was the color of dirty straw, and there were freckles strewn across a face unscarred by smallpox, but in no other way remarkable. The eyes, he hazarded, would probably be grey, if the boy ran true to his race, but would bring no particular distinction. Just a very ordinary boy—not so ordinary, he corrected himself, not if he were willing to brave a demon in defense of his king.

As if he had read the older man's thought, the red-haired boy said, "He won't die, will he? Not after what he did."

"He tried to fight it," a plump, dark-eyed boy agreed. "He fought for the king."

"It's in God's hands, boy," Sidney said, as gently as he could. "But we'll do all we can." It was not enough—it was never enough, not for the young—and then he was aware of James kneeling at his side, holding the boy's limp hand in his.

"In God's hands, ay," the king whispered, and shook his head. "Ah, Robbie."

Sidney, suddenly, felt very old. Surrounded by children, he thought—and James was young, too, and seemed younger— He felt every hour of his forty-one years, each one a palpable weight on his shoulders. *Too old,* a dry, distant voice seemed to whisper, *too old, and crippled besides.* . . . Sidney shook himself then, recognizing almost too late an attack more subtle than most of those to which he had been subjected. *Let us trust that old age and wisdom are allies*: after only a moment's hesitation, he let that thought wing free into the void, and turned his eyes again to the injured page. The boy was breathing still, but only barely, his skin turned cold and waxen. Sidney bowed his head, framing a weary prayer. As in Holland, form and propriety eluded him, leaving only naked appeal: *Lord Jesus, don't let him die.*

The door crashed open then, and the bedchamber was suddenly filled with a confusion of men, the royal guard

clashing their pikes against the legs of night-gowned nobles, who cursed them and demanded some explanation in
the same breath. A black-robed doctor, hair and beard in
disarray beneath his forgotten nightcap, knelt hastily beside the king, but James waved him angrily away, gesturing to the injured page. To give the doctor his due, he
took in the situation at a glance, and moved quickly and
competently about his business. Sidney relinquished his
hold on the boy, and pushed himself to his feet. The
drugged heaviness he had felt before returned in full
force, and he had to catch at the bedpost to steady himself. And was I drugged indeed? he wondered suddenly. It
would not be difficult, at this disordered court, to slip
something into a man's drink. Almost against his wishes,
his eyes swept the crowding courtiers as though he hoped
to startle the guilt in some man's face. He had enemies
enough already at James's court, and knew and named
them, one by one, but none seemed more than honestly
alarmed.

"Be silent!" That was the king's voice, rasping and painful, but indisputable proof that he was still alive. James
winced as he spoke, his hand going again to his bruised
throat, but the nobles quieted obediently. The king nodded to the red-haired boy. "Speak up, Andrew," he said in
an aching whisper. "Say what happened."

Oh, wise man, Sidney thought, and did not allow a
single muscle to move in his face. If I were to tell, there
would be endless debate, but Andrew's loyalties should be
beyond question for most of them.

"Sirs—my lords, the king—"

His voice was thin, and shook a little with remembered
fear. "Speak up, boy," the Earl of Montrose said, not
unkindly. The boy shivered, but nodded. This time, when
he spoke, his voice was steadier, and in the profound
silence that had settled over the king's bedchamber, it
carried clearly. He told the story matter-of-factly, not dwell-
ing on the horror of the invisible attack, but in a strange
way his determined calm made the tale even more dreadful. At the end of it, Sidney was not surprised to see one
or two old men cross themselves unashamedly.

"As you see, my lords," James rasped, "I'm well enough—

thanks to Sir Philip." He glared at his courtiers as though daring them to challenge him. When no one spoke, he nodded, and went on, whispering now, "You may return to your beds, though I thank you for your concern. Sir Philip—"

"If your Majesty will permit," Sidney said quickly, "I'll watch the night out here."

James nodded, but his eyes were questioning. "You said before, you wished to create some protection?"

Sidney sighed, and looked for a tactful way to say what must be said. "Before, your Majesty, it was daylight, and all the signs were favorable for the project. It would be better to wait for dawn."

James nodded again, his mouth curling into a self-mocking smile, but he said nothing until the last of the courtiers had filed from the room. "And if I had listened to you, this would not have happened, ay, I know."

"You should spare your throat, your Majesty," Sidney said, but could not dislike the proffered apology.

James ignored him. "I couldn't do it then, don't you see? Not for me. But now the boy's hurt, I can protect us all. God forgive me." The last was said in a dying whisper, almost too soft for Sidney to hear. He did hear, nonetheless, and felt himself strangely touched by the admission. It was not easy for a king to protect himself, especially a king who had lived all his life in fear, and had let himself be seen to be afraid.

"Go to bed, sire," he said, gently, and beckoned to the red-haired page. "Help me build up the fire—Andrew, is it? We'll watch the night out together."

The dawn came slowly, the sky fading reluctantly to grey. Sidney watched the fire die, and the strands of cloud along the eastern horizon turn first pale and then flush pink with the dawn. As the light strengthened, James rose from his bed, drawing his nightgown more closely around his shoulders, and came to stand beside the window. The sun rose, a disk so nearly white as to be blinding, and Sidney heard the king's sigh of relief.

"Well, Sir Philip," he whispered, "your witch was right— but I've survived it, thanks to you."

Sidney bowed. "I'll ask again only what I asked before. Allow me to ward these rooms."

James looked away, his sallow cheeks coloring. "I had no choice," he said. "Yes, do it now."

Sidney bowed again. "Thank you, your Majesty." He beckoned to the page. "Go to my rooms, and ask Madox to give you my ephemeris. And have someone wake Master Marlowe."

The boy bowed and vanished. James raised an eyebrow. "You need Marlowe's help?"

Sidney bit back a tired anger. "Marlowe is as familiar with such matters as I—and I am tired. Yes, I need his help."

James's color deepened, but he made no answer. They waited in silence until the page returned. To Sidney's surprise, Marlowe was with him, the collar of his doublet open as though he'd dressed in haste. There was something harried about his eyes, and Sidney gave him a questioning look, which was met by a stare so forbidding that the older man recoiled instinctively. Very well, he thought, not now—but later, Marlowe, I'll know what this is about.

"I want your help, Marlowe," he said aloud. "His majesty has given us permission to ward these chambers."

For a moment, he thought the poet would say something unseemly, but then Marlowe nodded. "As his majesty wishes," he said, almost demurely, and held out the ephemeris.

"Then let's begin." Sidney turned away without waiting for an answer, nodded to James. "If your Majesty would be seated . . . ?"

"And stay out of the way?" James murmured, with a crooked grin, but did as he was told. He settled himself in the carved chair and drew one leg under him like a schoolboy, watching avidly as the wizards began their work.

The ritual was a simple one, based on the same principles that created the smaller circle of Solomon, but strengthened by siting the symbols according to the positions of the planets in their ruling houses. The symbols would have to be changed as the year waxed and waned again, but there was no stronger method of creating such protection. At Sidney's low-voiced direction, Marlowe sketched the outline of the circle in chalk, adding the lesser symbols, while Sidney himself consulted the ephemeris and

made his calculations. The poet finished first, and stood
waiting; Sidney looked up after a moment.

"We will pray first," he said, in a tone that brooked no
argument. Marlowe looked aside, but, reluctantly, bowed
his head.

"Almighty God, who art a strong tower against the face
of our enemies, we yield thee praise and thanksgiving for
our deliverance from the great dangers of this night past.
We beg your mercy and your grace for the boy Robbie,
wounded in the service of his king, in the performance of
his duty, and beg also your strength and protection in this
which we now attempt." Sidney looked up abruptly, fixing
his eyes on Marlowe. "Amen."

"Amen," James echoed, and, a heartbeat later, Marlowe
said, "Amen."

The rest of the ritual proceeded quickly enough. Sidney
directed the placement of each symbol, and himself closed
the ring. When they had finished, he closed his eyes,
feeling a new resonance, a new harmony within the royal
chambers, and knew he had succeeded. He smiled, allowing himself a moment's pleasure in a job well done, and
the king cleared his throat.

"Thank you, Sir Philip," he said.

Sidney bowed, suddenly feeling the effects of the long
night. "With your Majesty's permission?"

"Of course," James nodded his dismissal. "I am grateful."

In the hallway outside the royal chambers, Sidney
stretched luxuriously, not caring who saw. "God, I'm exhausted," he murmured. "I'm for my bed."

Marlowe made a rather odd noise, and Sidney turned
on him, every sense suddenly alerted.

"Well?"

"Sir Philip, there's a matter you should know of first. . . ."

"God's nails," Sidney said. "I should have known." He
took a deep breath, controlling his temper. "Well, what is
it?"

"I'd rather you saw it first," Marlowe answered. "Or—
felt it, rather." He smiled crookedly. "It's nothing of immediate danger, but I think it might be of some interest."

Sidney stopped in the doorway that led to his rooms, his
eyes sweeping over the scene. Greville sat in the window

seat, his expression unusually grave; Nate Hawker crouched at his feet, his eyes huge and frightened. Madox had bullied the rest of the household into continuing with their duties, but their eyes roved nervously toward the corners, looking for something. There was a sour taint in the room, hanging high in the corners like smoke; even as Sidney became aware of it, it faded and was gone.

"Something—" he began, and stopped.

"Something wanted very badly to be in this room, last night," Marlowe said. "I stopped it."

Sidney nodded. He could almost smell the last ghost of it, frustrated rage as pungent as musk. "How could it attack two places at once?" he murmured, and swept his eyes across the room. The scent, sense, a sensation indescribable except by inadequate metaphor, seemed strongest by the door to the bedroom. He moved toward it warily.

Marlowe shrugged, his dark eyes ablaze. He's enjoying this, Sidney thought, with some envy. Frightened he may have been, but he liked the testing. He stopped beside the door and glanced back at the poet. Marlowe bared good teeth in a grimace that might have been intended for a smile. "That's the question I would've asked you, sir. If it's the same. Because, by God, we—" he pointed to Nate, "—we know who's behind this sending."

Sidney paused, testing the taint in the air, seeking the fading hand behind it. I've felt this workmanship before, he thought, felt this craft, this malice. . . . "Alnwick," he said at last, and looked at Marlowe.

The poet nodded. "Oh, yes, it's Harry Percy's hand that raised this." *And mine that stopped it*, an inward voice exulted. He controlled that sternly, watching the older man.

Sidney glanced at Greville. "Fulke, are you all right? And is Nate? What happened?"

Nate managed a white-lipped smile, but Sidney could see the fear still lurking in him. Greville nodded, and laid a hand on the boy's shoulder. "We're—unhurt," he said. "As for what happened . . ." He glanced helplessly at Marlowe, who said nothing. "Some thing tried to enter your bedroom, Philip. We could hear it—and smell it, by

God—scratching at the windows, and crawling along the walls. Beyond that, I don't know." *But I wouldn't like to hear that sound again, not if I live to Methuselah's age,* he added silently. It was not a thought to be spoken before the servants.

Sidney sighed. He knew, or could guess with a certainty that approximated knowledge, what the sending had sought: Virgil's book lay safely sealed in its casket beside the head of his bed. He could see it from where he stood, could feel that its seals were intact; though he still longed to be absolutely certain, to see the scrolls for himself, and so verify their continued existence, he made himself stay where he was.

"Was it the same?" Marlowe said again, more insistently this time.

Sidney paused, considering, matching the memory of the night's battle to the thing that had been in his rooms. "No," he said at last, "no, I don't think so. "This is—" He stopped abruptly. He had been going to say *more recognizably a man*, but perhaps that was not the thing to say now, with so many people listening. "This is somewhat different," he said instead, and Marlowe grimaced.

"Northumberland has an interest in Scottish politics, and in the succession," he said.

Sidney shook his head, more certainly now. "No. Or, not enough of one, even—maybe even because of—Raleigh's interests in that regard. It's not Northumberland who threatens the king."

"Who, then?" Greville asked, and Sidney shook his head.

"I wish I knew."

Chapter Nineteen

There never was a merry world since the fairies
left off dancing and the parson left conjuring.
John Selden, Table Talk, XCIX

The heat was prodigious for so far north. Stephen Massey winced, wiping sweat and dust from his face, and loosened two more buttons of his doublet, so that only the collar was closed beneath the falling band. The sleeves hung open too from wrist to shoulder, but there was no wind to provide even the slightest relief. He was lucky, he knew, in his more rational moments—after sunset, usually, when the air had cooled and it was possible to lie in shirt and drawers and let an evening breeze stir sweat-matted hair. He was only a hired man, and there were sharers in London companies who lacked positions; he should be grateful to have work—but why, he thought, what devil prompted me to the Chamberlain's Men, and the north?

"I could've been in Cornwall with Master Alleyn," he muttered, and was instantly ashamed. If nothing else, there were fewer men in this company who thought of him only as Kit Marlowe's Ganymede. He glanced hastily over his shoulder, but no one seemed to have heard. Augustine Phillips and George Bryan walked to one side of the cart's track, just out of its dust, heads together and gesturing in some one of their interminable arguments. The youngest of the apprentices, his face unhealthily flushed, crouched whimpering in the back of the cart among the property-hampers; Robert Goughe—like Massey, a refugee from the Admiral's Men—walked beside him, his expression torn between sympathy and envy. Massey sighed, wishing he could ride, and could not refrain from an envious glance at Richard Burbage. The leading actor bestrode his tired bay hack like a conquering king. More important than that, Massey thought, he's not walking, and he's out of the dust.

He was being unfair, and knew it, and John Lowin's rich chuckle did nothing to restore his good humor. "When you're his equal, lad, then you can think of riding."

Massey turned on him, a blistering retort trembling on his lips, but the sight of the older man made him bite back the angry words. Lowin was as red-faced as the apprentice, though he had long since discarded his doublet, and wore only shirt and open jerkin over his loose slops. He had sweated off some pounds since Newcastle, when the heat set in, but his belly was still the size of a small ale-barrel: no easy burden, in this weather.

"And will you mock at me for saying I envy our Dickon?" Shakespeare asked mildly. He pushed the sweat-damp hair off his high forehead and set his battered hat back in place, grimacing at the hazy sun. "I'd as soon ride, and so would you, Johnny."

"It's a bad business," Lowin said. "A damn bad business."

"What possessed Pembroke's Men?" John Heminges asked, not for the first time. His bristol-red doublet was stained in back from shoulders to waist, and there were dark circles under each arm, staining the cane-color ribbons.

"The Earl of Essex, or so I hear," Lowin answered, and managed a fleering grin.

"Damn the Earl of Essex," Heminges retorted, and then glanced quickly over his shoulder.

"There's no one to hear," Shakespeare said soothingly, and Heminges grimaced.

"You're too easy, Will, that's your trouble."

"Do you think we'll get a license to play in York, Master Shakespeare?" Massey asked.

Lowin shrugged. "That's in God's hands, boy, if I don't voice a blasphemy to say it."

Shakespeare shook his head, his mild eyes troubled. "I don't know. Dickon had friends on the council there, two years ago; we can only hope they're still in office."

"His friends were in office at Newcastle," Heminges said darkly, "and you saw what happened there."

"York's further from London, and the city's always had a mind of its own," Shakespeare began, and Lowin laughed again.

"But they've a name for strictness in religion, William, don't forget it."

"Why borrow trouble?" Shakespeare answered. "Time enough for that when they refuse."

"Yes, but if they don't grant the license—" Heminges began, and broke off abruptly, glancing at Massey.

The hired man looked away, only too aware of the awkwardness of his position, but Lowin managed a reluctant laugh.

"If and when," he said. "Will has the right of it, John, we've troubles enough without borrowing more."

Heminges grunted, plainly unconvinced, but did not speak again. Massey lengthened his stride, leaving the sharers to debate the matter among themselves if they wished, but it was too great an effort to sustain for very long. His pace slackened, and he licked his dry lips, tasting dust. Heminges was right to be afraid, he knew; they had not earned a decent fee in two weeks, and there was already talk of sleeping wild a few nights, while the weather was warm, to save the innkeepers' fees. Not a pleasant prospect, he thought, nor was the specter that lay behind those economies: if they could not earn some money soon, they might have to sell the costumes to pay their way back to London, and that loss would certainly destroy the company. He glanced at Shakespeare, who walked whistling faintly to himself, and wondered how the man could seem so unconcerned. After all, he'd just paid thirty pounds, more money than Massey had earned in his entire life, to buy his share of the company; how could he not worry about losing the investment, and before he'd played a single season?

Shakespeare looked up then, as if he'd suddenly become aware of the younger man's regard, and managed a smile. "You were on tour in 'ninety-three, weren't you, Stephen?"

Massey nodded. "Yes, with the Lord Admiral's Men." Shakespeare looked slightly puzzled, and the younger actor sighed. "My cousin's a sharer with them—Charles Massey. I was his apprentice." He saw the smile that touched Shakespeare's eyes and scowled. "No, not Marlowe's."

"I never thought it," Shakespeare answered mildly. "I asked because I knew your voice had broken then, that's all."

Massey nodded again, somewhat appeased. "There's always room for messengers and such, and I still played old women. Zabina, for one."

"Of course." Shakespeare removed his tall hat again, scrubbed at his sweaty face with a patched shirtsleeve. His expression was suddenly remote, and very tired.

Massey's eyes widened. "You are worried," he exclaimed.

"Of course I'm worried, I've a wife and three children to feed," Shakespeare answered, and instantly made a gesture of apology. "I'm sorry, Stephen, it's not you I'm angry with."

Massey knew he'd reddened painfully, and was saved from some stammering answer by a shout from the apprentice riding in the cart.

"Look what's coming, masters!"

Massey glanced over his shoulder, and heard Shakespeare curse softly. A heavy coach, its curtains drawn against the dust of the road, was following them—and rapidly overtaking us, too, Massey thought. There was a baggage cart as well, and a train of a dozen or more outriders. Burbage swore, and waved to the actor driving the cart.

"Pull up, Henry, if you can, and let them pass. The rest of you, out of the road, quick as you can."

The orders were greeted with a storm of oaths, but Burbage was obeyed. The cart slowed, and drew toward the side of the hard-beaten track, until its outer wheels were perilously close to the ditch that ran beside the road. Massey vaulted across the little stream, and turned to stare at the oncoming riders.

"I'll be damned," Augustine Phillips said, and darted a malicious glance at Massey. "It's the wife of your Jove's patron, Stephen. Quick, make your bow."

"Pox take you," Massey said, his temper snapping at last, all thought of the respect due a senior member of the company vanishing from his mind, and Shakespeare caught his arm.

"They're pulling up," he said.

Frances Sidney, riding with Raleigh at the head of the little column, saw the cart and the straggling party that followed it, and swore softly. Raleigh gave her a wary glance, but lifted his hand, signalling the coachman and the head groom to slack their speed. Frances saw his eyes on her, and nodded, forcing a smile. I must not lose my temper now, she thought, God knows, I've grown as bad as Philip, these past days.

"Poor bastards," Raleigh said. "It's a hard day to be walking."

"A hard month," Frances said. She and all her people could ride, even if they had to travel more slowly than she liked, to spare the horses; if she could no longer bear to ride inside the stifling coach, how much worse must it be for a man afoot in this weather? She shuddered a little, in spite of the heat that left her chemise soaked with sweat almost before they'd left their previous night's lodgings, and was suddenly aware of a new heat, a pinpoint source of warmth between her breasts. She started, her horse sidling in response to the involuntary movement, and realized abruptly what it must be. The token she had begged from Doctor Dee, which had hung unnoticed about her neck since leaving London, had chosen this moment to spring to life. She fumbled with the buttons of her bodice, heedless of Raleigh's sudden shocked stare, laying it open almost to her waist, and tugged at the strings of the chemise until she could grasp the thin silk cord. She drew the sigil out from beneath her corset, and cupped it in both hands, letting the reins hang slack along the mare's neck. The stone at its center burned steadily blue, the color of certain icy stars. Not the red of danger, she thought, but what precisely does it mean?

"Lady Sidney?" Raleigh reined to a halt beside her, bearded face wary.

"The sigil," Frances answered, and was surprised to find her voice so steady. "It gives us a sign."

Raleigh whistled sharply, and his hand went to the pistols cased at his saddlebow. "But I know these men," he said. "They're actors, the Lord Chamberlain's company."

"Oh?" Frances stared at the sigil, growing brighter and hotter with each step the reluctant mare took toward the strangers. Blue was a holy color, she knew that much, and racked her memory for more. It was the color of truth as well, and of hope. . . . Are we meant to meet these men? she wondered suddenly, meet them and bring them with us? The thought had the blinding certainty of revelation. She dropped the sigil and spurred forward, lifted one hand in greeting.

"Well met, masters. Master Burbage, I did not expect to see you so far from London, even this summer."

Burbage made his most courtly bow, somewhat hampered by the hack's sudden skittishness. "Lady Sidney, I'm most honored that you should remember me. Sir Walter, I'm honored."

Raleigh nodded politely enough, but his attention was on Frances. She smiled, included all the actors in her gaze. "Permit me to extend my sympathy, that you should have to tour this summer, and in this weather."

"I thank you, Lady Sidney," Burbage answered, and could not conceal a nervous glance toward his fellows. Heminges, who with the leading actor served as the company's paymaster, edged close beside him.

"I hope your travels have been as profitable as I'm sure they have been onerous," Frances continued, still smiling.

"Alas, my lady, we've had some misfortunes," Burbage said warily. "To be frank, we've had trouble getting licenses."

I knew it, Frances exulted silently, I knew it before you spoke. God bless you, Doctor Dee, you've served us well. She had to swallow hard before she could say, with appropriate sympathy, "It pains me to hear it, Master Burbage, I do assure you. Are you bound for York?"

Burbage bowed. "We are, my lady."

"Perhaps Sir Walter and I can be of assistance there," Frances said, and paused thoughtfully. She's up to something, Massey thought, watching silently from the ditch. God, save us from politics.

"The aldermen have been much opposed to players, I fear," Frances continued, and heard the little moan run like a wind through the company. "Or, say, I've a better thought." She smiled again. "We are bound for Scotland, as I daresay you've guessed, to join my husband there. Why don't you travel with us, not just to York, but all the way to Holyrood? I expect you would find good employment there."

Burbage and Heminges exchanged glances. Shakespeare's eyes widened. An odd assembly that would be, he thought. An extravagant bravo—a hero, certainly, genuinely, but a bravo nonetheless—the wife, loving or not, of England's most beloved champion, and a band of players . . . and something else, a thrill of power riding with them, not black magic, certainly, but unquestionably magic. He shivered in spite of the heat, and cast a sidelong glance toward Massey. The younger actor had felt it, too, and his eyes roved nervously, as though seeking the source of the contagion. Shakespeare suppressed a fleeting grin. It was amazing how perceptive so many actors had become since that performance of *Doctor Faustus*, when there had been one demon too many on the stage. . . . More important, though, what could bring Frances Sidney north in her husband's wake, and in such gallant and unexpected company?

"There's safety in numbers," Frances said, "and, to be blunt, Master Burbage, there's safety in the company of such as us. And surely a royal engagement in Scotland is better than begging the aldermen of York for the right to play?"

"A royal engagement, Lady Sidney?" Burbage repeated. Walsinghams did not promise lightly, he knew that, nor did they promise cheaply.

Frances smiled gently. "His majesty of Scotland is fond of theater, and has precious little chance to indulge that love. Philip is fond of you—has stood good patron to you before now, I believe. I think it would please him to see you again, and I am certain it would please King James to have such a diversion from his troubles. And it could only profit you."

Burbage returned the smile and added a flourishing bow. "My lady, what can we say to express our gratitude for such an offer, not only of protection but of employment? May we ride with you as far as your halting place tonight, and give you our answer in the morning?"

Frances's smile did not waver. "Of course, Master Burbage, I perfectly understand the workings of your company."

And I suspect she does, Shakespeare thought. What a terrifying idea.

The White Hart grudged them lodging, but the Sidney purse—or more precisely, money and Walsingham determination—won out. The actors clustered together around the largest table in the taproom, their low, southern voices contrasting sharply with the louder Yorkshire voices surrounding them.

"I say we do it," Henry Condell said. It was the first time he'd joined the discussion, and the others jumped. Condell shrugged, embarrassed. "It's clear great events are toward. I'd rather like to be a part of them."

"Great events," Heminges muttered, and Phillips said, "Great events are death to players, Henry, remember that."

"So is lack of funds," Burbage said. "If Lady Sidney says we can play in Scotland, I believe her—and if she's wrong, which I doubt, Sir Philip's an honest man enough to pay us for our pains. Money in hand, against an uncertainty: there's no choice, to my mind."

He glanced around the table, and saw the agreement in their eyes, the agreement he had intended to win before putting the matter to anything so divisive as a vote. He nodded, to himself, and said, "Well, my masters? Are we for Scotland?"

"It's better than Denmark," Phillips muttered, but joined then in the general murmur of acceptance.

"Scotland, then," Burbage said, and pushed himself to his feet. "We'll inform her ladyship in the morning."

Chapter Twenty

*First he must know your name then your age, which
in a little paper he sets down. On the top are
these words, in verbis et in herbis, et in lapidus
sunt virtutes. Underneath he writes in capital letters, AAB ILLA, HYRS GIBELLA, which he
swears is pure Chaldee, and the names of the
three spirits that enter into the blood and cause
rheums, and so consequently the toothache. This
paper must be likewise burned, which being thrice
used is of power to expel the spirits, purify the
blood, and ease the pain.*
H. Chettle, Kind-Heart's Dream

The king of Scots was now like a sick man, grasping at
any regimen, however unpleasant or foolish, that held out
the hope of a cure. If Sidney's wards offered him comfort,
was there not safety in numbers, in a variety of practices?
Did the spaewives mutter of oak and ash and rowanberries?
Then the king's bedchamber would be festooned with
prophylactic garlands. The masters of art pulled their beards
and offered leaden seals carved with curious figures. The
king demanded them as a greedy child begs for candy, and
strung one after another on the chain beneath his shirt,
until he clicked gently inside his quilted doublet. The

dominies, Ultra-Protestants all, murmured darkly of endurance and submission to God's will, but after James's handling of Melville, did not speak aloud. The Archbishop of St. Andrews, consulted on the matter, brooded for some days, and then suggested diffidently that frequent communication, if it did not drive away the demons, might at least ameliorate their effects. James accepted the suggestion as he accepted all the others, and it became an almost nightly ritual for the king's household to gather in the chapel for evening prayer.

The chapel had not seen such regular use since the late Queen Mary's day, when it had served for her private, papist prayers. It had long since been reconsecrated to the reformed faith, the stained glass smashed and the carved saints chipped from their places, but nothing could desecrate the pure, severe lines of the little room. Sidney, though he suspected that James's application of the archbishop's suggestion bordered on the papist, found that the spare ritual brought him peace, and helped strengthen him for whatever alarms lay ahead. Adamson was a good man, a kind and well-meaning man, who tried to offer the service himself whenever he could; for all that James might use the offering as a papist used his rote prayers and indulgences, the intention, at least, was holy. And perhaps that would be enough, Sidney thought, if what I fear happens tonight.

Marlowe, kneeling dutifully with the rest, was less sure of the propriety of the service, but he had, after the months at Rheims, hopes for its efficacy. Catholic wizardry taught that unclean things could not enter the presence of the Host: proper Protestant or not, he thought, that's what we're attempting. I just hope it works.

"Oh merciful God and heavenly Father," Adamson intoned, "who has taught in thy holy Word that thou dost not willingly afflict or grieve the children of men, look with pity, we beseech thee, on the sorrows of thy servant James Stuart, king of Scots, for whom our prayers are offered. In thy wisdom, thou has seen fit to allow thine Enemy to visit him with troubles, and to bring distress upon him. Remember thy servant, o Lord, in mercy; endue his soul with patience, and his heart with strength against this affliction; comfort him with a sense of thy goodness; lift up thy countenance upon him, and give him peace. Amen."

The congregation murmured its response, and Adamson turned to the table that was placed where the carved and glorious altar had once stood. Plain cup and dish stood ready on the simple white cloth, and the archbishop glanced toward them once, and then away.

"Hear now what comfortable words our Savior Christ saith to all who truly turn to Him."

And should I cringe in terror, hold my hand, merely because of a Name?

They all heard it, harsh and clangorous as thunder in the little room. Sidney rose slowly from his knees as though lifted by an invisible hand, his eyes fixed on the blankness behind the table. Adamson reached protectively for cup and paten, fumbled them—he was an old man, an old man's palsy trembling in his hands—and the unconsecrated wafers fell, shattering like glass on the stones before the table. The wine spilled, too, a great gout of red like the blood it symbolized staining the white cloth. The archbishop sank slowly to his knees, reaching futilely for the broken wafers. The light of the candelabra to either side of the table sparked from a single tear caught on a wrinkled cheek, the brilliance perfect as a diamond.

Sidney spoke then, a single word as solemn as a prayer, and James, caught still on his knees before the table, felt the air thicken around him. He had felt that stillness before, knew it for security, but reached out anyway, across the shattered wafers, to touch the stained hem of the tablecloth. Sidney saw the movement, and a strange, distant part of him laughed softly. So like James, to hedge his bets . . .

Marlowe flattened himself against the chapel door, dagger naked in his hand. He had moved instinctively, both to cut off any panicked escape and to prevent the well-meaning, disastrous, intrusion of the royal guard. The fair page crouched beside him, hands folded at his lips in fear and prayer; Ruthven knelt a little farther off, eyes roving nervously. Mar had risen to one knee, but froze there, his eyes fixed on the table.

Then a hand, more terrible than the hand that had written on the wall behind Belshazzar, reached out of nothingness, and tore the air apart. The figure of a man stood there, idealized, immense, terribly beautiful, awful to look upon. The candles flickered once, then roared almost to the ceiling, smoky and unnatural, their baleful light feeding the dreadful vision. Marlowe caught his breath, and choked down the prayer that rose unbidden to his lips. He recognized the demon that had haunted him, and would not give it the satisfaction of his fear; more than that, he would not interfere with Sidney's planning.

"You claim to be prepared for me, knight." The demonic shape spoke with the voice of a whirlwind, of hellfire itself, a hissing shapelessness that somehow formed words. "Pray your God you are."

Marlowe flinched. It was a cunning attack, one calculated to make Sidney hesitate, and in that moment, he would be lost. Pride was damnable, after all; how could Sidney chose damnation, for any necessity, when his whole cause was salvation?

Sidney did not move, or show any sign that the figure's words had affected him. "In this place, you can only skirmish," he said, almost softly. "I am ready for that."

"Oh, so-wise knight," the figure jeered. "Are you?" Even as it spoke it lifted a hand, and the candles roared again, their flames bending toward Sidney and the kneeling king.

Sidney smiled, lifted one hand, and the flames curled back as though they had struck an invisible wall. He spoke, quietly, and the flames turned and twisted, darting back on their creator. The figure lifted its hands, but the flames sprang past its defenses, winding it in cords of flame. The figure writhed, but could not free itself. Then, with a crack of thunder, the figure shattered, gobbets of fire scattering through the chapel. For one brief instant, as the vision shattered, the figure diminished, and became merely a man, unknown to Sidney, but recognizable to the Scots present.

"God in Heaven, it's Bothwell," Mar murmured, and others echoed him.

And then it was gone completely, figure, man, and

power, the unnatural fire become merely candle-flames flickering demurely in their places. The silence thundered. Slowly, very slowly, James pushed himself to his feet, feeling the protecting spell dissolve around him. Something was expected of him, he knew, and turned to face his people.

"The Earl of Bothwell," he said aloud, experimentally, and was surprised that his voice was no more unsteady than it was. He cleared his throat, and tried again. "He was a great master of witches, but never did I know him for such himself . . . but England's champion seems greater still."

"We don't know that yet, your Majesty," Sidney demurred, no longer smiling, and James darted a wary glance at him.

"Who else could have done what Sir Philip has done today?" That was the Master of Ruthven, a boyish quaver in his voice—charming, Marlowe thought sourly, but not quite sincere. The words were perilously close to the kind of blasphemy Marlowe wanted no part of now, the kind that would tempt fate to destroy them all. *For if Sidney be for us, who can . . .* Marlowe shook the thought angrily from his mind. Leave the spell uncompleted, he told himself, it cannot harm you. He stepped forward, to stand beside the Earl of Mar. "I thought the earl of Bothwell was dead."

"So did we," Mar muttered bitterly, and James managed a white smile.

"Even then his power was to be reckoned with—and we knew it not." He glanced around his little court, somehow summoning up the presence of a king. "I trust we will not make that mistake again."

Sidney remained behind as the others filed from the chapel behind the king. Greville, walking beside young Seton, saw his friend's hesitation, and came to join him. Seton followed the court, but looked back curiously.

"It seems we can pray for a quiet night now with some confidence," Greville said, with a quirky smile.

"I believe it will be so," Sidney answered.

Greville saw the sourness in the other Englishman's face and sighed. Oh, yes, he thought, you've given Bothwell something to think about. Oh, Philip, if you give yourself up to recriminations now, when all you've done is for the good . . . He hesitated, and Sidney gave him a fleeting smile.

"I'm not fit company for you tonight, Fulke."

"Nevertheless, I don't know if I should let you stay here by yourself," Greville answered.

Sidney deliberately misunderstood. "It's safe enough now, it—*Bothwell*, damn the man—he has been driven back, and I doubt he'd try anything again tonight."

"I don't know if I should let you stay alone anywhere," Greville said, with outward patience. "I know you, Philip. You can't hide that you've been shaken by what's happened—by your own strength, I daresay. Perhaps a little frightened. God knows, you may even have enjoyed what happened today—and what of it? It's no different from riding in tournament on the queen's behalf. You're her champion, and she has sent you to defend James—"

"Damn that," Sidney broke in. "A good sound defense, a job well done? I should be a fool not to take pleasure in those, but that's not what troubles me, Fulke, and you know me better than that. I don't fret over trifles—if it were only that I took joy in my duty, I'd stand head high and dare damnation, if my motives were pure. And that is what I begin to doubt."

Greville glanced sideways, startled, but kept his silence.

"Pox take him, it was too easy," Sidney went on, speaking now as though to himself. "It makes me wary—as well it ought. I *know* that it—he, Bothwell, wasn't throwing his full might against me. But there's a part of me that wonders, what if that was all? I broke him, Fulke, I held him and I beat him back—almost easily, even. I hold him, and James, God help me, in the palm of my hand. I could be master here." He drew a deep breath. "That pride is sin, and deadly." He paused for a long moment, then shook his head. "I need to be by myself, Fulke."

Greville paused, then nodded reluctantly. "Good night, then, Philip—and God bless you."

"Good night," Sidney said, and even managed a smile, but his mind was elsewhere. The chapel seemed very quiet now, utterly removed from its papist origins. There was no smell of incense, or even the faint stench of still-warm candles; only the air itself, chill and quiet—unsanctified, comfortless in its simplicity. There was no comfort to be had here, in this house of God, Sidney thought suddenly; not for one who had lost his way. All his learning, all his much-praised intellect, meant little when weighed against the teachings of childhood: this power—all power, perhaps—was vanity, the devil's gaudiest bait to catch men's souls. Even rejecting that—as reject it he must; Languet, and then Doctor Dee, were too honest, too good to be damned by that too-simple formula—he could not deny that he had gone beyond Dee's lessons, had made use of knowledge of which even Dee had been, perhaps rightly, sceptical. Virgil's book, shaped and honed by his time in Holland, given form and context by the studies with Dee, was still something new and therefore dangerous, unprecedented. He had used it to defend the king of Scots, certainly, but Dee's magic would have served for that. Virgil's magic . . . The power it summoned was sheer pleasure, unbridled, outside law and structure. By using it, Sidney thought bleakly, I set myself up as equal to God. That, unquestionably, is mortal sin—but if I do not use it, I cannot save the king, and thus I cannot save James without damning myself. An all too simple equation.

He knelt then, seeking the comfort of prayer, but the words would not come. A coldness was welling in him, a desolate pride of despair. He raised his head and stared like Oedipus into the gathering dark, and smiled bleakly. Despair was like amputation: the pain was gone; what remained—the emptiness, the body's knowledge of a thing-that-had-been—was perhaps as bad, but it could be borne.

Then he heard it, the soft whispers, scuttling sounds, that warned of sprites, imps, unholy spirits, heard too a small sigh of laughter, a sound of sated lust. He lifted his head sharply, the spell broken. Not in you, he told himself, not in you, but without. Damnation's not within you; God does not create man with poison in his soul, but man takes it into himself willingly, and thereby kills himself to God's grace. Where no man can be worthy, the gift can only be accepted. I bear this power. I know I trafficked with no demons to secure it. What I am, God Himself has created, and what I do with myself, though known to Him, is my responsibility. I may not refuse that choice— and I will not turn aside like a craven from the duty my queen, God's own anointed, has laid on me. He laughed softly, and felt the demons retreat further. *More than accept, I embrace it. I am her majesty's true knight, and my duty to her can never be damnation. I follow my God and my queen, and serve both to the height of my abilities, whatever they may be. And if you fear me so much that you try to weaken me with this oldest of threats, then when we meet again, I shall fear you the less.*

It was gone, completely now. Sidney drew a shuddering breath, and pushed himself to his feet. He felt almost as tired as if he had ridden in the Tilts, and smiled at the simile. This time, too, he'd been the victor.

Marlowe leaned against one of the slender columns that marched the length of the great hall, letting the crowd of petitioners ebb and flow around him. There were more than usual, he noted, and hid a grin. The Scots nobility seemed willing to risk themselves—and even a few of their women—in James's presence now that Sidney had proved that he could drive off the worst of the manifestations surrounding the king. Even the Ultra-Protestant notables had returned: the alliance between the dominies and the nobles was always uneasy, and James's handling of Melville, though it might be publicly deplored, did not entirely displease certain gentlemen of Melville's own party. Certainly the Earl of Mar was far from displeased.

Mar was very much in evidence, too, the poet thought. His smile twisted, watching the sunlight glitter on the earl's cloth-of-gold doublet as he maneuvered his clients into the king's notice. Mar was Cecil's man, there was no question about it, and he had the king's ear. Sidney should be warned—though explaining the source of that knowledge could be more than a little awkward. I can put it off, he thought, maybe drop a hint or so, prepare the ground. Cecil's and Sidney's interests should run together a little longer: long enough, I hope, to find a safe way to break the news to Sidney.

There was a stir by the door then, and the poet craned his head to see, glad of the interruption. A tall man,

tawny-haired and tawny-bearded, pushed his way awkwardly through the crowd toward the king. He stumbled a
little as he came: drunk already, Marlowe thought, and
allowed his lip to curl. He had seen the man around the
court before, and it seemed a piece with his other follies,
to go to the trouble of donning his best black suit and then
spoil the effect by one too many drinks to keep up his
courage. Then the man stumbled again, rebounding from
an ancient gentleman without so much as a hint of an
apology, and Marlowe's attention sharpened. That, surely,
was wrong; not drunk, perhaps, but sick, or injured.

"My lord?" someone called. "My lord, are you all right?"

The man still did not turn his head, or give any sign of
having heard. Almost without knowing why he did it,
Marlowe pushed through the crowd after him, caught at
the hanging sleeve of the doublet.

"My lord—"

The man twitched himself free without a backward glance,
but in that brief moment of contact, Marlowe felt the
strangeness about him, sharp as the scent of brimstone.
"Sire— My lords, look to the king," he shouted.

The tawny man lunged forward, upper lip lifting in an
unnatural, animal snarl. Marlowe reached desperately for
the trailing sleeve, but missed, cannoning into a stocky
man in a long scarlet gown. The stocky man cursed him
dispassionately, shaking dust from the velvet folds, but
Marlowe barely heard him, his attention fixed on the knot
of men around the king. They were turning, but slowly,
too slowly, their faces still puzzled rather than alarmed.
Then the treasurer Montrose saw the tawny man and cried
out, "Get the king away, protect the king!"

The tawny man had produced a knife from somewhere,
the long blade glittering briefly in the sun. There was a
confusion of movement around the king, some nobles trying
to hustle James away, others—fewer of them—doing their
best to place their bodies between the king and danger.
The treasurer's son John Graham flung himself at the
tawny man, but the man flourished his knife, and Graham
fell back, wincing, a bloody rip across the breast of his
doublet. They were unarmed, of course, all the men around
the king, and Marlowe groaned aloud. James's well-founded

terrors were being turned against him. Mar moved then, rapier and dagger drawn—Mar, of all of them, was privileged, Mar had the royal favor—flinging himself into the tawny man's path even as the soldiers who had been on duty outside thrust themselves into the hall. They were too far away, Marlowe knew, even as he himself was too far from the king to do anything to help, but he kept pushing ahead as though there were something he could do.

"William Forbes, have you gone mad?" That was Mar, old Montrose now ranged at his right, the powder-scarred man to his left.

The tawny man snarled again, and lunged. Mar gave ground, batting the shorter blade aside, but made no riposte. "William—"

Forbes reached for the earl's sword hand, and Mar twitched the blade away, his face contorting. "William," he began again, but the word died of its own futility, fading into a curse.

"The king, my lord," Montrose cried.

Mar struck, flicking his blade past Forbes's clumsy parry. The rapier sank home, and Marlowe clearly saw the blade bend against bone before it was withdrawn. Forbes kept coming, his eyes fixed on the king. Someone screamed, the voice as high as a boy's or a woman's; Mar fell back, paling, recovered himself enough to lunge again. This time Forbes was ready. He caught the blade with his left hand—Marlowe winced in spite of himself, imagining the edged blade slashing to the bone—and wrenched it from Mar's slackening grip. He flung the bloodied sword aside and lunged for Mar. The scar-faced man dove for his knees, trying to bring him down, but Forbes seemed to sense his movements, and dodged away. The voice screamed a second time, the sound abruptly cut off. Then there was a pistol shot, the noise almost deafening even over the noise of the hall. Forbes staggered and went down, to lie in a boneless heap. The scar-faced man pushed himself to his knees, crossing himself without shame. Marlowe glanced over his shoulder, almost unable to believe what had happened, and saw the older woman he had seen the night of the welcoming banquet, her pistol held loosely now at her side. Her wrinkled face showed no particular emotion, but the gilt buttons of her bodices winked in the sun, as though she were breathing very fast. The poet turned away then, pushing through the crowding nobles to kneel beside Forbes's body.

The man was dead, there was no doubt about it this time. Marlowe bit back a laugh he knew to be compounded too much of hysteria, and rolled the body onto its back, carefully avoiding the ragged hole where the ball had struck. *Right through the spine too, a sure shot one way or another.* . . . He shook that thought away, staring at the twin sword thrusts, two neat—and now just slightly bloody—slits in the man's doublet. Either one of them should have been mortal, but it had definitely been the bullet that brought him down. He looked up at the rustle of satin, to see the older woman standing beside him, her pistol tucked decorously into the folds of her skirt.

"A fine shot, madam," he said, and kept his voice low. "Do you always charge your pistols with silver?"

It was a bow drawn at a venture, but the woman drew breath sharply. Then she smiled. "Only in these—most uncanny times, sir poet."

"Lady Gordon." That was the king, putting his nobles aside now that the danger was over. "I owe you thanks, ma'am."

"Thank my father, sire, who taught me to shoot," the woman answered, and handed her weapon to the scarfaced man. Now that the crisis was over, Marlowe thought, she was showing a womanly distaste for her handiwork—or was that directed at the men who had stood by, or acted so ineffectually? "The rest was no more than duty."

"Indeed, madam, it was all our duty," Mar snapped. He was red with anger—with jealousy, Marlowe realized, jealousy of his position as royal protector. "Perhaps Master Marlowe could explain how these—" He gestured to the wounds in Forbes's chest. "—struck home, and didn't kill."

"It would be useful knowledge," James agreed. There was a strange expression lurking in his eyes, fear giving way to sadness as he looked at Mar. And no one in all this assembly, Marlowe saw with sudden understanding, no one at all had feared for James, or would have mourned for him. For the king, yes, and a round dozen would have died for the king, but none for James. Perhaps even the queen would not have wept for the man alone. He crouched beside the body, struck silent, the poet's demon within him already looking for a way to use that knowledge, a part of him uncomfortable with the pity he could not help but feel for a man of twenty-seven who was so unloved. *I myself am hated, and well hated, too, but I'm also loved.* That thought was even more uncomfortable, and he pushed it angrily away.

"Well, Master Marlowe?" the king said.

"I beg your pardon, your Majesty, I was—ordering my thoughts." Marlowe drew a deep breath, looking down again at the body. "Bothwell's work, I'm sure of that—"

"As are we all," Mar snarled.

Marlowe managed a shrug. There were spells . . . Watson had at least known of them, spoken of them once as things too black even for him to soil his fingers with, but that was not something James needed to hear. *Well, your Majesty, what we have here is a thing called possession, which proves that Bothwell not only traffics with minor demons but can control one or two of the major ones. And the only cure for this that I know of is a mass exorcism . . . which is politically inexpedient even if I really thought it would work.* He said, choosing his words with care, "I've heard of such tricks before. They can be dealt with, your Majesty."

"Do so," James said, and gave the body one shuddering glance. "Lady Forbes must be told, poor woman. He was your friend, Johnnie, I'll not ask you to handle it—"

Montrose cleared his throat, and the king looked at him. "Your Majesty, my wife was cousin to Forbes's kin. If you'll allow, I'll speak to the wife."

"Thank you, my lord," James said, with genuine gratitude. He looked back at Marlowe, the hooded eyes sharpening suddenly. "As for you, Master Marlowe, I'll thank you to tell me how Bothwell corrupted a man I would have called my friend."

Marlowe hesitated again. "Your Majesty, I'm a stranger to the court, I didn't know the gentleman. How can I

know what Bothwell might have offered him?" He saw the
beginning of a disapproving frown on the king's face, and
added hastily, "Or how he might have trapped him?" But
I'd lay wager it was temptation, not force, he continued
silently, and kept his face expressionless only with an
effort. Bothwell had a gift for finding men's weaknesses. . . .
For a moment, the vision of his private demon swam in his
mind, but he put the thought hastily aside.

"Should you find out how, or by whose agency," James
said, "you will tell me." There was an unexpected note in
his voice, one that promised a grim revenge.

Marlowe glanced up, startled, but James had already
turned away. The Earl of Mar extended a hand, and the
poet took it warily, allowing the Scot to draw him to his
feet.

"You'll tell me as well, Marlowe," the earl said softly.

"I'll do that," Marlowe answered. Mar's momentary jealousy seemed to have vanished; the poet said cautiously,
"The lady—who is she?"

"Lady Katherine Gordon," Mar answered, frowning again.
"A word in your ear, Marlowe: she's Huntley's agent at
the court." He saw the poet's look of confusion, and sighed.
"She speaks for him as leader of the papists, she and
Maxwell."

"A woman?" Marlowe asked, in spite of himself.

Mar's frown deepened, the brooding jealousy returning.
"You saw what she did. She's as clever as any man—and
more use to Huntley than most of his kin." The earl
turned away then, easing himself through the crowd that
surrounded the king until he stood at James's elbow. Marlowe stared after him, but the king's attention was fixed on
Lady Gordon, and Mar's presence remained unacknowledged. Sweet Jesus, more trouble, the poet thought, and
edged toward the door. The papists had the credit for this
rescue, and Mar—never the most certain of allies—seemed
inclined to take this latest attack, and Sidney's failure to
prevent it, as a personal insult. Marlowe sighed as he
slipped out into the empty hallway. More trouble, indeed.

The bad news had travelled fast, Marlowe saw without
surprise, as young Madox swung back the door of Sidney's
rooms. Greville was there before him, and Sidney himself

was seated by the window, the crooked leg stretched out in front of him. His face was thunderous, and Marlowe made a hasty bow.

"I beg your pardon, Sir Philip, but I'm afraid there's been another—incident."

"We heard," Greville muttered.

Sidney gave him a quick, reproving glance, but said only, "We were told that someone tried to kill the king, someone under Bothwell's control. Is that true?"

Marlowe nodded, and couldn't help feeling a sort of perverse pleasure in being the bearer of bad news. "Certainly the man was possessed by something. Two good sword thrusts didn't even prick him; it took a silver bullet through the spine to bring him down."

Sidney muttered a startling oath, then looked rather embarrassed.

Greville said, "You've been expecting this, haven't you?"

Sidney gave a twisted smile. "Say rather I've feared it." He became aware of the fact that Marlowe was still standing, and waved the poet to a chair. "Sit down, Marlowe, in God's name. I'll need your help in this."

After that beginning, however, he showed no inclination to continue, staring instead at the unlit logs in the fireplace. Marlowe seated himself on the stool brought by a disapproving young Madox, and waited. The silence lengthened.

"What are the alternatives, Philip?" Greville said at last, and Sidney started.

"I'm not entirely sure," he admitted, with another rueful smile, and looked at the poet. "Marlowe?"

Marlowe lifted both eyebrows, unreasonably annoyed by the question. *How in hell's name would I know?* he wanted to ask. *I'm not the great wizard trained by Doctor Dee.* He recognized the reaction from fear, and controlled his temper. "I suppose somehow the entire palace has to be protected, so that Bothwell can't come at any of the court—that's the key, isn't it, to keep him from approaching them as well as James?—but I don't know how you'd go about sealing off a palace. I've never heard of a ritual so large."

Sidney was nodding even before he'd finished. "I agree.

But I have heard of rituals—protective rituals—performed on such a scale—in France."

"God's nails, of course," Greville said, and Marlowe lifted his head. He had heard of such a thing, when he was at Rheims, and then vaguely afterward: of a circle of French scholars who had attempted—in vain—to protect their king from the horrors of the civil wars.

"By the Pleiade?" he said, and was unduly pleased when Sidney nodded again.

"That's right. I've corresponded with them, I know something of their methods. But not enough to perform such a rite myself." He shook his head. "And correspondence is impossible—there simply isn't enough time." He looked up sharply, fixing his eyes on Marlowe. "I need their help, and I need it as soon as possible, Marlowe. I'll give you the letters you'll need. I want you to go into France as my courier, and bring back any of the school who'll come with you."

Greville stirred uneasily. "You can't ask him to do that, Philip, not after—"

Sidney lifted an eyebrow at him, and Greville fell silent, grimacing a little. Marlowe's head lifted. "I'll go," he said, and there was more than a touch of belligerence in his voice. "I'm willing. All I ask is that you pay my passage."

"That, I think, I can manage," Sidney said, a little dryly. "But thank you, Marlowe."

The poet nodded, already wondering precisely why he had allowed himself to be persuaded so easily. After all, Greville had offered him, if not the perfect excuse, then the perfect bargaining point: the year he had spent spying at Rheims and then at Douai had marked him—at least in certain circles—as an English agent. But he wouldn't play the coward, not before Greville, and especially not in front of Sidney—and in any case, he realized belatedly, the danger was only an added spice. He was aware that the older men were looking at him curiously, and cleared his throat. "If it suits you, Sir Philip, I'll land in Holland, go overland into France."

Sidney nodded. "I leave that to your discretion. But what about landing at Flushing? Robert might prove helpful to you."

Marlowe hid a grimace. He had once, under freakish circumstances, been arrested by Robert Sidney in Holland—Flushing, in fact—for the crime of counterfeiting, and he was quite certain that the elder Sidney knew all about it. He glanced sidelong at the older man, expecting to see laughter, but Sidney's face was unobjectionably grave. It was a sensible idea, after all, and the poet sighed. "I shall. With your permission, then?"

"Of course," Sidney answered, almost absently, and the poet backed from the room. Sidney glanced sideways then, and saw Greville smiling.

"You're a wicked man, Fulke," Sidney said, but a smile was tugging at the corners of his own mouth.

Greville shrugged, unsuccessfully attempting to ease his face into a more sober expression. "He wouldn't've gone so willingly, if I hadn't hinted it was dangerous. You know that. He'd've bargained just to spite you."

"Do you really think so?" Sidney asked, and there was a note of rather wistful disappointment in his voice that made Greville look sharply at him. "Well, be that as it may, he is going. And I'll get the help I need."

Greville accepted the change of subject with equanimity. "You need more support than I can give you, or even than Marlowe can. But wouldn't it have been wiser to send to England? After all, the French—"

"There are Huguenots among the Pleiade, Fulke, have no fear of that," Sidney said. He sighed then. "As for England . . . There's no one in England who knows as much as the Pleiade about this sort of magic, not even Doctor Dee."

He fell silent then, staring at the unburned logs in the grate. Greville sat still, waiting, said at last, "This magic—these French rituals, are they like the Tilts?"

Sidney shook himself. "Something like, I believe. The purpose was the same at any rate. But I don't know any more."

Well, Greville thought, if you won't talk, you won't. So be it. He said again, "At least you'll have some help," and did not add, *once Marlowe returns.*

Chapter Twenty-one

*From all inordinate and sinful affections; and from
all the deceits of the world, the flesh, and the
devil, Good Lord, deliver us.*
                                        The Litany

That night, it was as if William Forbes had never been.
His own kin, certainly, were absent, but the rest of the
court dined in state in the great hall. The last dishes had
been carried in and broken open, the courtiers toying with
the heavy sweets, and the wine flowed freely. The candles
were low in their sockets when the word was mentioned.
James lifted his head sharply, glad of the diversion. "What's
that, Alex?"

The Master of Ruthven turned to him, an eager light in
his dark eyes. "It has occurred to me, Sire, that in Sir
Philip Sidney you have at court one of the finest knights in
Europe—not merely a poet and a scholar, but a master of
arms, as well. Wouldn't it be a shame not to take the
chance to do him honor?"

James sat up straighter and considered. Tilts, such as
those that annually celebrated his English cousin's accession to her throne, were popular everywhere; James himself was fond of them, though he was well aware that
malicious tongues said it was only because the rebated

weapons were kept well away from the royal person. It was true that Sidney was redoubtable in the lists, and equally true that it would honor both Sidney and Scotland if the Englishman would fight. But had he ridden much, since his near death in Holland? The title of Queen's Champion could be merely honorific. James glanced down the length of the hall, to see Sidney deep in conversation with the Earl of Mar. I think he has, James thought, I'm almost certain . . . but it wouldn't do to embarrass either Sir Philip or myself. The poet Marlowe stood nearby, his back against a pillar, a slight, sardonic smile on his face. It was a disquieting expression, scorned itself as much as the world around it. . . . James pushed the thought away. Sidney thought much of the man, and that must be enough. He nodded to Ruthven. "Fetch Master Marlowe."

Ruthven bowed and moved away, his walk an impertinence. James watched him approach Marlowe, and saw the poet's reaction to Ruthven, a sort of withdrawing in spite of himself. It was a reaction the king understood, better than many men. Marlowe found Ruthven attractive —as who would not, did they dare to admit it, James added silently. But the poet would not tamper. *Touch me not, for Caesar's I am,* James quoted to himself, pleased with himself, with Ruthven, and even with Marlowe, for his compunction. The rest of the couplet floated through his mind then, less comforting—*And wild for to hold, though I seem tame*—and he was glad when Marlowe made his bow before the dais.

He was a fine-looking man, in a dark way—not as Ruthven was, all milk and ebony, but as though his own black nature was prefigured in his face and body. A dangerous man, Master Marlowe, James thought, if even half the things Mar said about him were true, and he looked it. His face was long, with high, narrow cheekbones and dark shadows hollowing cheeks and temples. The dark brows were almost straight and very thin, the eyes beneath them bright, with cynical lines at the corners. He was long-bodied, a lean man, with a good leg even in patched stockings; his dark brown hair curled over his narrow ruff, long and thick with a stubborn wave that must cause him much repinning. James was aware of the desire to tangle his fingers in that hair, and recalled himself sternly to the matter at hand. He beckoned the poet onto the dais, saying, "You'll be able to answer a question for me, Master Marlowe, one I'm almost embarrassed to admit to."

"It would be an honor, your Majesty." Marlowe spoke with perfect deference, but there was a lilt in his low voice that bordered on mockery. James caught his breath.

"It has been suggested that we honor our guest by holding a joust—except I know not whether Sir Philip does indeed still enter the lists."

Does he not, Marlowe thought. He could still remember, with almost violent clarity, the first Accession Day he'd witnessed. That had been nine years before, in November of 1587; he himself had only just come to London, a new-minted Master of Arts fresh from his triumph over Cambridge University in the matter of his degree. Sidney had just returned to England the wounded hero, and the echoes of the thanksgiving sermons had not yet died from the London churches. He was not yet Champion then, and no one had expected more than a ceremonial appearance, if that, perhaps with some suitably apologetic *impressa*, linked emblem and motto, on his pasteboard shield. Instead . . . Sidney had appeared all in white and silver, riding a white horse, accompanied by pages in long white robes. His *impressa*, borne before him by the smallest of the pages, had showed as its emblem a new-born child, a falling star, and a rising sun, and the motto beneath had been *Reborn to her service*. Marlowe had listened with increasing disbelief as a second page recited the usual verses. In the usual idiom of the Tilts, the new-born knight declared that, while lying wounded and near death, a hermit—it was always a hermit, Marlowe had sneered at the time—had spoken to him of a greater lady than the star he had once worshipped, and the new-born knight had made a vow to see that lady for himself, should he recover. Recover he had, and now that he had seen her, he freely admitted the superiority of the hermit's lady; he begged only that he be allowed to do her service by breaking a lance or two that day.

There had been a murmur almost of awe from the crowd then: Sidney sat his horse stiffly, and his face was very pale beneath the silvered helmet; the white plumes trembled a little, and not with wind. The queen herself had risen to her feet to accept the *impressa*, as was the custom; now, uncustomarily, she beckoned Sidney closer. They had spoken, and then Sidney withdrew, shaking his head. By the laws of chivalry, having accepted the service, Elizabeth could not forbid the fight. She sat slowly, her frown visible even from the spectators' runs along the sides of the tiltyard. All of that, Marlowe thought, had been comprehensible, graceful, courtly, but not exceptional. It had been what followed that had shaken him. One by one, the other knights had ridden forward, touched Sidney's *impressa*-shield in token of their acceptance of his challenge, and then, one by one, driven lances into the ground in front of Sidney. There would be no fight; they conceded their defeat before a single course could be run. Sidney's face . . . Marlowe shook his head. The man had been honestly angry, even to the point of spoiling the presentation by arguing with Greville and with Sir Henry Lee as they made their submissions. The crowd at Whitehall had nearly deafened the knights with their applause. *No man*, Marlowe had said then, speaking to Watson, but not caring who overheard, *no man who's neither fool nor Machievil can be what Sidney seems.* That thought had sustained him until the day Sidney stepped into Eleanor Bull's Deptford tavern, and saved one poet's life. He shook his mind away from that still almost inconceivable act, and looked up at the king.

"Oh, yes, your Majesty. Sir Philip still jousts." The word was inadequate, but, knowing none better, he let it stand.

"Splendid," James said, and nodded to Ruthven. "An excellent notion, Alex."

Marlowe's eyes widened. If this was Ruthven's idea, he thought, I want no part of it. "Forgive me, your Majesty," he said aloud, "but is this a wise time for such things, when your Majesty is so threatened? To risk your best defender?"

James smiled. "It's known even in Scotland that the Tilts are more than mere entertainment, Master Marlowe. It seems worth the danger—and I have every faith in Sir Philip."

Marlowe mimicked the words savagely in his head, but bowed as James rose to his feet.

"My lords," the king said strongly, and a slow silence descended in the hall. "My lords, we have long sought and are most pleased to declare that we have found some means to do honor to our guest, England's champion and our own most gallant defender. We will hold a joust, to celebrate the presence of so notable a knight."

At least he's left Sidney a loophole, Marlowe thought. If it's just to celebrate his presence, he doesn't have to joust. But that was a forlorn hope, and even the poet knew it. The man who had tried to fight in '87 was not the man to refuse a challenge here, even under these peculiar circumstances.

Sidney rose slowly to his feet, and bowed profoundly. "Your Majesty does me too much honor," he said. "Nonetheless, I would be pleased to run a course or two, for my own queen's sake."

Marlowe bit his lip to control the desire to grin. Sidney's voice was entirely too sweet, too reasonable. *'Ware fireworks,* he thought, *but Christ's nails! did you have to accept? Is this the time for such trivialities? Oh, no, you wouldn't think of that, just of your own damned honor. . . .*

"You must forgive our importuning you," James said, "but the chance to see you in the lists must tempt any prince who has the means to provide you with a fitting arena."

"I should be delighted, your Majesty," Sidney said again. "And to joust against whomever your Majesty names as his challengers."

And that puts this squarely into the realm of the political, Marlowe thought, even more than before. At least James doesn't quite seem to realize all the implications.

"Excellent, Sir Philip," James said. "If you will acquaint our chamberlains with anything you require, it shall be done."

Sidney lifted a hand in appeal. His first, almost instinctive acceptance had faded; he spoke more cautiously now. "If I might beg a favor, your Majesty."

"Sir Philip, you have but to name it," James answered instantly.

Good, Sidney thought. "Your Majesty is gracious," he said aloud. "You do me a great honor—will you permit me, and Fulke Greville, of course, as her majesty of England's sworn knights, to return the honor? Permit us, through your chamberlains and household, of course, to have the ordering of the joust, so that we may honor you as we would honor our prince."

Dangerous, very dangerous, Marlowe thought. Or does Sidney know more than he's letting on? Does this—*could* it mean that Elizabeth has finally made up her mind, that James will be her heir? He eyed the king of Scots with some misgivings. I cannot picture it, somehow. Thank God I'm for Holland, and will avoid this lunacy.

"Sir Philip, I thank you and Master Greville," James answered. "I leave the ordering of this matter to you—and my household will second you to the best of their abilities." That, at least, was unmistakably an order. Sidney bowed again, in thanks this time, and almost at once was surrounded by younger nobles, eager either to offer their challenges or simply to find out more about the English way of managing a Tilt. Marlowe slipped away from the dais, wondering how he could warn Sidney of precisely who was behind the idea. Sidney was still surrounded, and it appeared he would be busy for some time, but Greville was free. The poet edged up to him, touched the padded sleeve.

"Master Greville. You'd do wise to be very careful. The Master of Ruthven's the only begetter of this—very great honor the king wants to do Sir Philip."

Greville glanced involuntarily toward the dais. "That young man troubles me."

"You're not alone in that," Marlowe answered, and gave the older man an impudent smile. "Does Sir Philip see it, or is it only those of—my taste?"

Greville sighed. "I dislike an obvious slattern," he said flatly. "And you?"

"A touch, sir," Marlowe answered, but sobered quickly. "Can this be made safe? For the king, and for Sir Philip."

If I can get Philip to keep his temper in check, Greville

thought. Though Philip's answer was remarkably controlled, considering. And God knows James may be right, hoping for some parallel with the Accession Day ceremonies; I'm no wizard, I simply don't know. He smiled grimly. "Oh, don't worry. If Philip and I are making all the preparations, nothing, I assure you, will be left to chance."

And scour the Trojan plain with Greekish blood. Marlowe scribbled the final word of Penthesilea's speech and shivered, suddenly aware of the chill that had settled with the night. The fire had burned low, the logs crumbled into glowing fragments; the twin candles—not his, and tallow besides; he was not paying for the extravagance—were low in their sockets, the wax grown thick on the side away from the window. He shivered again, pushing himself up from the table, and stooped to toss the final log into the grate. The coals shattered further, throwing sprays of sparks, but a few feeble flames began to lick at the dry bark. Shivering still, the poet reached for his jerkin, shrugged it on, then pulled the borrowed academic gown on top of that. The stone jug on the hearth was almost empty, the liquored posset cold, but he upended it anyway, draining the last thick sweetness, and glanced at the sheets of paper piled on the table. The first act was finished, the second act well begun, with only the final two scenes to be written. Those were the confrontation scenes, and the first of Achilles' great courtship speeches. Marlowe hesitated, the first lines of promise and persuasion forming in his mind, but put the temptation firmly aside. He had done enough for one night, especially if he were to sail for Holland on the morning.

He reached for a sheet almost at random, scanning his spiky hand. Kyd had laughed, and flaunted his own ornate Italianate penmanship—but I got my own back, Marlowe thought, and grinned. He copied *Doctor Faustus* for me, and *Edward II*, too, and I paid him for it, every farthing of the copyest's fee. Which he could not afford to refuse, not even from his rivals. The grin faded as he remembered where his own carelessness had so very nearly landed Kyd—*six feet under, in a pauper's grave*, as Kyd himself had shouted at their last meeting—but he thrust the thought aside. Kyd's innocence was admitted even by the Privy Council, and Pembroke was a better patron than that damned lawyer had ever been. It had ended better than Kyd had any right to expect, better than he deserved.

He glanced again at the paper, but the pleasure of the words, of Achilles' challenge and Penthesilea's furious response, had dimmed a little, and he put it aside. Still, even on sober reflection it had been a good evening's work. It was almost a pity, with things beginning to work so well, that he had to go to Holland. His mouth twisted then, into an expression not quite a smile. If one other's work were not being even more successful, he would not be sailing on the noonday tide. . . .

Something rustled in the corner of the room, well outside the circle of candlelight and the lesser glow of the fire. He spun round with a gasp, snatching up the candlestick as though it were a weapon. Tiny lights sparked like eyes, and a finger-long shape scuttled hastily along the boards into shelter. A mouse, he thought, I'm cowering like a woman at the sight of a mouse, and set the candlestick back on the table. His heart was racing; faintly, very faintly, he felt a thrill of something, the breath of a dark wind against his neck. It was gone in an instant, but he recognized the touch: Bothwell's demons were in the castle.

He shivered, once, but stood very still, straining every sense to follow that black progress. Wood creaked somewhere, the great beams settling into their places; there was a ghost of laughter—a woman's laughter, a servant's laughter, imperfectly hushed—and then silence again. The poet hesitated. Sidney would deal with this, as he'd dealt with every other attack, petty or great, that threatened the king. Except that Sidney had not dealt with the last attack because no one had known of that temptation, that seduction—or conquest, to give the devil his due—until the man had drawn steel on the king. He hesitated for an instant longer, trying to ignore the dangers, then reached for the satchel lying open beside the table. Sidney might have his precious book, he thought, but so do I—even if I strongly suspect mine to be less powerful. Still, they say you fight fire with fire, and this magic, I know, is kin to Bothwell's.

He shook the thought away, and flipped through the worn pages until he found the design for which he had been looking. Two pentagrams, each circumscribed with names and symbols of power, bound to each other by the double twist of the lemniscate, its curves also chalked with names and symbols. A note in Watson's sprawling hand filled the page's outer margin: *To bind any spirit sent for mischief, and to compel its answers; very sure.* Very sure indeed, Marlowe thought. I recognize those names.

He reached into the bag again before he could change his mind, and drew out the lump of chalk. He kicked aside the rushes until he had cleared a length of dirty floorboard perhaps six feet in length, then brought the candlestick from the table and set it down in the center of the space. He knelt beside it, head cocked to one side, studying the book for a final time. Then, very carefully, he drew the first lines of the first pentagram, copying each of the controlling signs in its proper place, and surrounded that with the familiar protective circle. He pushed himself to his feet and measured off three paces from the edge of the first circle, then knelt again to draw the second pentagram. This would confine Bothwell's demon once he had called it; the symbols at each point of the star would compel it to give truthful answers to his questions. He drew the lines with finicking care, and brought the candlestick closer to be certain everything was correct, before he finally closed the circle.

Only the lemniscate remained to be drawn. He rubbed damp palms along his thighs and made himself stoop, muttering the protective prayer Watson had taught him. He drew the double circle, a numeral eight, the number of eternity and immortality, the meeting of heaven and hell, marking each sign in its proper place. He took a deep breath, closed the final circle, and stepped back into the protection of the first pentagram. Nothing happened, and he allowed himself a sigh of relief. Nothing should have happened at that point, but it was as well to be prepared.

He opened Watson's book again, turned the page to the invocation that accompanied the double symbol. It was hard to read in the fading candlelight, the thick letters running into each other, but the words were clear enough.

"In the name of our Lord Jesus Christ," he began, not quite self-consciously, his voice small in the chill air. "Who delegated His power unto his disciples and apostles, that they might bind and loose the powers of darkness, I, Christopher Marlowe, scholar, command the unclean spirit that has entered this place to appear before me in the circle of binding prepared for it. I command it by the holy names, Adonay, Amay, Horta, Vegedora, Mirai, Hel, Suranat, Ysion, Ysey, by all the holy names of God and by all he-saints and she-saints, by all the angels and archangels, by the powers, denominations, and virtues, by the name that Salomon did use to bind the devils and shut them up, Elrach, Ebanher, Agle, Goth, Ioth, Othie, Venoch, Nabrat, I command that unclean spirit to appear as I have ordered, and to give me a true answer of all my demands, without the hurt of my body or soul or anything that is mine, through the humanity, mercy and grace of Our Lord Jesus Christ, which liveth and reigneth with the Father in the unity of the Holy Ghost, one God, world without end."

He had been so intent on the book between his hands that he had not noticed the candlelight fading further, the flame diminishing to an ember cupped in the hot wax. The fire had burned down, too, its flames strangely lightless. Even as he looked up, sparks flickered along the lines of the lemniscate, the fugitive blue light that scattered from a cat's fur on a cold night. He held his breath, willing the conjuration to have been complete and accurate, and a shadow thickened to something inky and solid in the center of the second pentagram. Marlowe blinked, fear and triumph shooting through him, and said, "Spirit, by the holy names with which I summoned you: what is your name?"

The shadow shifted its position, became momentarily less black, taking on the shape of a toad the size of a lapdog, squatting on its swollen haunches. The broad mouth opened, grinning, and the tip of its tongue lolled briefly over the pendulous lip. The room stank of the jakes.

"Spirit, by the names which compel you, answer!"

The tongue flicked upward once, insolently, and vanished. A moment later, a voice like a creaking hinge said softly, "I am Sonneillon the bellringer, that waits at doors and hangs in corners, to fetch my masters when their names are called."

A true infernal courtier, Marlowe thought, but managed to keep the edge of hysteria from his voice. "I command you then, Sonneillon the bellringer, tell me true. Who sent you here?"

The toad-shape shifted uneasily, lowering its ugly head. "I beg you, do not force me, master."

"The names I have spoken bind you," Marlowe said. "Answer me."

The heavy head drooped further, the tongue appearing at its lips. "Francis Hepburn," it answered at last, "Earl of Bothwell."

That was hardly unexpected, Marlowe thought. "What other spirits does he command?"

Sonneillon shifted again, twisting its head sideways to dart an almost coy glance along the glittering lines of the lemniscate. "My master commands many spirits; many powerful spirits and demons obey his will."

"Number them, by their ranks and powers," Marlowe said. He held his breath. Of all the knowledge Sonneillon could give him, that might be the most useful.

The demon lowered its head again, hunching its misshapen shoulders. "I may not answer."

"You are compelled to answer, by the names I've spoken," Marlowe snapped. "Speak, Sonneillon—" He glanced hastily at his book, almost forgotten in his hand. "—in the name of the angel Innon who drove you once from heaven."

Sonneillon made an odd whimpering noise, as though the uttering of the name had caused it actual pain. "I will speak," it said, "but under duress."

"You will do nothing of the kind."

The voice came from the shadows beside the fireplace, a cool, rather dry voice that was at once strange and oddly familiar. Marlowe froze, but kept himself from turning. He said, "Answer, Sonneillon, as you were bid."

"Oh, begone." The voice sounded more amused than annoyed, but the toad-shape vanished instantly, collapsing in on itself until nothing remained but its stench. Marlowe turned slowly, dreading what he would find.

The shape leaning by the fireplace was still mostly in shadow, but enough light leached from the embers to outline a tall, slender man in red, and to carve one half of his face from old ivory. It was a wonderful face, too, to match the shapely body: darkly handsome but marked with strong lines of knowledge and willful experience. Marlowe caught his breath, and then, almost too late, recognized both face and clothes. It was Humphry Jeffes's face, just as the costume was the same red suit—blood scarlet, mortal sin—he had worn to play Mephistophilis, but both were subtly transformed, as though the demon had, for a jest, for a compliment, put on the mask of the actor who had portrayed him, and by doing so revealed both his own true nature and the actor's inevitable failure.

"I see you know me, Master Marlowe." The red-clad shape pushed himself lazily away from the wall and came forward like a newly awakened cat. Light—not firelight, or candlelight—shone from the jewels at his belt and purse, and glittered on the pins in his hat and the rings on his fingers and in his ear.

"I would as soon hear your name," Marlowe answered, and was amazed that he could speak at all.

The full mouth curved upward into a peculiarly knowing smile. "Why, I am Mephistophilis—though I could not think you'd like me best in the habit of a friar."

Marlowe tightened his jaw to keep his teeth from rattling. It was bad enough to have an arch-demon here, in his room, kept from him only by the frail wards of his chalked circle, but it was infinitely worse to have that same arch-demon quoting one's own play. Ned didn't know how bad it could have been—what was one pitiful extra demon, to this visitation?

"Why are you here?" he said aloud.

The demon smiled again. "Curiosity," it said. "My besetting sin—and one we share, I think."

"Surely not a sin," Marlowe murmured.

"Surely so—and I speak with some authority, do I not?" Mephistophilis countered. "I have a few more years' experience of damnation even than you, Marlowe."

Marlowe nodded slowly. "Yes: *Think'st thou that I, that saw the face of God And tasted the eternal joys of Heaven,*

Am not tormented with ten thousand hells In being depriv'd of everlasting bliss?"

"And they say the devil may quote scripture," Mephistophilis jeered. His slanted eyes narrowed slightly, as though it took an effort to remember. *"What, is kind Kit so passionate for being deprived of the joys of heaven? Learn thou of demons manly fortitude, And scorn those joys thou never shalt possess."*

The poet shivered. Faustus's words to Mephistophilis were entirely too easy to turn against their author. The demon's eyes narrowed further, this time with laughter.

"Joys you certainly won't possess, as well you know, my Christopher, late student of divinity."

"Not your Christopher," Marlowe said, and the old bitter pride prompted him to add, "nor any man's."

"Not Sir Philip's? Or Sir Robert's? Or even Ned Alleyn's or his fat father-in-law's? Or Thomas Walsingham's, for that matter, or Southampton's?" Mephistophilis's smile was cruel. "I suppose one might say you'd sold yourself often enough that you're no one man's—servant."

That stung, but Marlowe kept his face impassive. Watson's book still dangled in his nerveless fingers. He lifted it, made himself turn the pages, though he was not certain that even Watson had known any conjurations powerful enough to deal with the being standing here before him.

"Stay your hand a moment, Christopher." Mephistophilis's voice changed, became cajoling. And that, Marlowe thought, *tells me something I didn't know before. There is something here that can banish him, if only I can find it. I'm not defenseless—and even he cannot cross the circle.*

"Why do you persist in this foolishness? You, you of all men know that these—good deeds—" Mephistophilis gave the words an ironic twist, and the poet winced. "—will avail you nothing. You are damned, my Christopher—and mine you are—doomed and damned, and repentance—were you capable of it, did you truly repent—would avail you nothing. Why grovel before the good? Damned you are, and you would be welcome—honored—among the damned." Mephistophilis smiled slowly, and this time the expression was almost human, oddly wistful. "You have a certain understanding, which is part of what has damned you; even when you try your hardest to convince yourself otherwise, as in your *Doctor Faustus,* that knowledge— Eve's sin, not Adam's—still peeps through." He held out his hand, very white and shapely in the ruddy light. "Come, my dear, you know me better than any mortal in many a long year, better than anyone not already sealed to me by bloody contract. I could teach you so much more— you were wrong, you know, to make what I showed Faustus naught but tricks." His eyes slitted, cat-like, and his voice took on a dreaming note. "To show you the secret in the heart of every man, the flaw in the diamond, the canker at the core of the rose—to give you that deepest knowledge of others would be the first of my gifts. Riches, gold for your purse, silks and satins and velvets to delight your body—" He waved a dismissing hand. "I will give you those, of course, it's no more than your due, but that is nothing to the rest of what I offer. I'll let you know myself, you're halfway there already. I'll teach you all the secrets known in hell." He extended both hands now, in appeal and offering. "I will give you power, Christopher, the knowledge of secrets that is true power. And no man will resist your will."

Had I as many souls as there be stars, I'd give them all for Mephistophilis. The lines, unspoken, seemed to hover in the air between them. Mephistophilis did not move, his hands still outstretched, far more beautiful in his lined, imperfect, almost-humanity than the shape that had appeared in Greville's house in Warwickshire. Marlowe seemed to feel the floorboards shift beneath his feet. Oh, God, he thought, to have so much . . . He wrenched his eyes away, felt tears torn from them at the deprivation.

"No," he said aloud, and fumbled at the pages of his book. "I will not. . . ."

Mephistophilis smiled sadly. "You will not refuse me always, Christopher."

Marlowe ignored him, his fingers unbearably clumsy on the frayed paper. Through the film of tears, he found the words he wanted, began to read in a shaking voice. "By the living God, by the holy and all-ruling God who created from nothingness the heaven, the earth, and the sea, and all the things therein, I exorcise thee. By the ineffable names of God, which I am unworthy to pronounce, I exorcise thee. By the virtue of the most holy sacrament of the Eucharist, and in the name of Jesus Christ, and by the power of this same Almighty Son of God, I exorcise thee. *Sic fiat, amen.*"

Even before he had finished reading the third command, he knew that the presence had vanished. The candles, flaring a final time before the last of the wax was consumed, cast monstrous shadows. Marlowe studied them warily, and realized he was half hoping for Mephistophilis's return. *And if you want him back, fool, why did you not say yes when he was here?* he berated himself, and stooped to rub away the ring of symbols. *Fool, damned fool, inconstant as a woman, he was right, and you could have had all that for the taking—for the price of a thing already lost.* He straightened slowly. *Yet if it's such a little thing, why do I hesitate to name the true price? It's my soul he wants. . . . Had I as many souls as there be stars, I'd give them all for Mephistophilis.*

"I am not Faustus," he said aloud, angrily, and scraped his foot across the last symbols, blurring them out of recognition. *But, oh, my God, how I do wish I were.*

PART FOUR

PART FOUR

Chapter Twenty-two

Now does my project gather to a head:
My charms crack not; my spirits obey; and time
Goes upright with his carriage
      William Shakespeare, The Tempest

The remove to Whitehall did nothing for Elizabeth's temper, already tried by the evil genius that seemed to hover over her England. Her sleeps were undisturbed, thanks to Doctor Dee's herbal, couched now in a sack embroidered by his granddaughter with powerful and propitious signs. Her days, however, seemed longer than ever, longer even than an old woman's days, which lasted well into the night, and began again before those of sweet-sleeping youth.

Nor was her mood improved by Essex's sweet cajolery. She knew, as did all London, that he had paid a sort of court to Frances Sidney, and chose to ignore it, believing—as London seemed incapable of doing—that Essex would always choose power over beauty—though there was a time, she added silently, when there would have been no choice there, either. The boy was a bit of a fool, she admitted, considering the matter, but he had always seemed a likely one, one she could instruct and shape, and presently cure of his folly. Frances Sidney, it seemed, had already dismissed him as incurable. Unwillingly, Elizabeth's thoughts turned to the day she had ridden with Raleigh to Mortlake, the day that Frances had betrayed her love not for Essex, but for her husband. Not so much a fool as I thought you, girl, Elizabeth decided grimly. She had always suspected that the girl was too young, too untried—and certainly too much a Walsingham, of that cold humor—to be any suitable wife to Philip Sidney. But there was fire there, banked until now, but ready now to be fanned into a glorious blaze. Will Philip see it? she wondered, and irritably dismissed a distant pain that might have been envy. I could hold them all, she told herself, if I chose, but I prefer to hold them all at arm's length. Caesar's I am not—that was Wyatt's poem, written for her long-dead mother—Caesar's I am not, but Caesar. *Non Caesaris, sed Caesar.* That was a conceit worthy of her own tilts, and for a moment, she played with the idea. My champion is absent—what a wonder it would be, to enter the lists in my own person, with the crowned phoenix for my emblem, and that for the inscription. I have ridden in armor before now.

That was seven years before, in the miracle of the Armada year. She sighed, and put the thought aside, to be used in her next argument with Burleigh. *Non Caesaris* indeed—I can ill afford that foolery, for England's sake, but if I could . . . But my sweet Robin is dead, and the Robin left to me is scarcely half the man. She glanced at the young man who hovered at her side, dressed as always in black and silver—black velvet this time, doublet and hose both slashed with figured cloth-of-silver, with a handful of pretty chains wound around his arm. In captivity to me, my lord? she wondered dryly. Or holding them in readiness against the unlikely day I honor you beyond your desert?

Suddenly aware of her regard, Essex smiled, and stooped to kiss her hand. "My lady queen looks upon me, and bestows a light more radiant than the sun's on my life."

"On a day such as this, my lord, that is no great hardship." Elizabeth stared pointedly at the cloudy sky visible through the long windows of her privy chamber. "I did not smile."

"Perchance I can persuade you?"

Elizabeth took a deep breath, her thin mouth turning down in annoyance. She knew what this was prologue to, and had refused it once already. No one, not even you, shall brave my refusal twice, she thought. "And what do you seek to persuade me to do, my lord? Grant you my smiles—or Philip Sidney's place as my only champion?"

Essex drew back slightly, and bowed his head. "Your Majesty knows which I value more highly—"

"I do indeed," Elizabeth interrupted. "Pray be silent." She lifted the letter that lay unregarded in her lap, unfolded the stiff sheets.

There was a brief silence, and then Essex ventured, "It is September already—the end of the month, indeed. The news from Scotland does not seem encouraging. The preparations for your Majesty's tournament take some weeks. And never was there a prince in Christendom who more richly deserved to be championed."

Elizabeth's head rose. "I am championed, and well championed, too, my lord." She only just kept her anger in check, though she knew Essex heard the fire and ice in her tone, and a part of her rejoiced to see him quail. "Sir Philip's absence from court on my business does not mean that I would welcome substitutes or successors. An Philip does not return in time for the Tilts, my lord, we shall regret his absence, and appoint no one to ride in his place. I suggest, Robin, that you do as I do, mourn his absence, made necessary by that very office of my champion." She saw the surprise on Essex's fair face, and went on, relishing the words, "And do not be so patently foolish as to think you can replace him." That was stronger even than she had intended, but as she listened to her speech, repeated it in her mind, she was not displeased. Still, it would not be the same without Sidney in the lists, her Philisides, her good shepherd knight. *Non Caesaris*, she thought again. If Caesar's knight could not be present, perhaps Caesar should ride.

More moping, she thought, and stood abruptly, her stiffly jeweled skirts rattling. The sound startled her women, busy at their sewing in the distant corner; she smiled thinly at them, and they returned to their work. Outside the windows, rain had begun to fall. She sighed again. She would not have thought summer so truly gone, in September, but it felt so, in her bones. *From winter, plague, and pestilence, good Lord, deliver us:* for a moment, she could not remember where she had heard those words, but then the image came to her. Croydon, the Archbishop's house, and that strange masque—*Summer's Last Will and Testament*, that was the name—that for all its jesting could never be free of the plague that drove them all from London. Summer gone, and winter to come, winter brightened usually by the Accession Day celebrations in November, and the coronation anniversary in February. Accession Day was less than two months away, and the most recent letter from Sidney was not precisely encouraging. Which means, she thought, with a growing, petty displeasure, that it's unlikely that my champion will be back in time for my tournament.

She shook the thought away, and turned her attention to the papers in her hand, newly arrived that morning. Sidney's tone was confident, certainly, as coolly confident as Sidney usually was, but the careful descriptions of events in Scotland chilled her blood. And not just for the politics either, my lords, she thought, though they were bad enough. This witchcraft . . . She frowned again over the brief paragraph in which Sidney described his encounter with—more precisely, his rescue of—a witch on the very edges of Holyrood park itself. You waste your time saving witches, Sir Philip, she thought, when your energies must bent on the king. Then she smiled. Little thanks you must have earned for that piece of gallantry, though I warrant it was prettily done. Nor would you boast of it, either; I read between the lines as well as the next. Her expression softened as she reread the letter. No, truly, did I expect aught else of you? More fool me, then. But tread warily, Philip, for save you I cannot, nor will not, if you fall.

There was a discreet shuffling behind her, and Elizabeth turned. The chamberlain bowed profoundly. "Your Majesty, Lord Burleigh and Sir Robert Cecil crave private speech with your Majesty."

So, Elizabeth thought, with a thin smile that did not touch her eyes. Cecil too has had word, and from whom, I

wonder? His poet, or his Scots—observer? And what do
the Scots make of what goes on? "My ladies will pardon
us," she said.

The knot of women, their gowns welcome spots of color
in the rainy light, gathered themselves and sank into low
curtsies before disappearing into the room beyond. Essex
seemed inclined to linger, dallying beside the queen's
chair as though he had some right to be there, and Elizabeth turned on him. "And you, my lord. If you will."

Essex looked startled, contrived to look hurt, but then
bowed low, a graceful, sweeping movement that showed
an exquisitely shaped leg.

"Very pretty, Robin," the queen said. "Now go."

Burleigh and his son entered behind the chamberlain
and bowed very low. Elizabeth gave her hand to Burleigh
as the chamberlain bowed himself out, and said, "You
come most carefully upon your hour, my Spirit. Sir Robert."

"Your Majesty," Burleigh answered. "I trust I will be at
hand whenever my prince has need of me."

"Oh, not need, my lord," Elizabeth answered, with a
sly smile and a quick glance at Cecil. "Rather you were
expected. I have this day received messages from Scotland
and Sir Philip; I rather expected you might have, too, if
not by the same messenger or from the same source."

Cecil had served the queen too long to let his slight
discomfiture show. Burleigh smiled behind his beard. "Your
Majesty's prescience watches over England."

"Oh, I hardly think that's necessary," Elizabeth said,
more tartly. "Come, my lord, share your news with me."
She made no promise of what she would or would not
share with him, and Burleigh expected none. He nodded
to his son.

"Little that is actually of import, your Majesty," Cecil
said. "Matters do not seem to have progressed—or re-
gressed, either, for which we must be grateful. Sir Philip
seems to have maintained the balance. A very keen talent
that can do so, I must say. And as balances are so tenuous,
I can only hope he does nothing to upset it."

"You may hope what you wish, Sir Robert," Elizabeth
said. "I want that balance upset, if maintaining it means
that the situation remains as it is. I sent Philip as my

ambassador and my champion, to free James of this plague
of witches. I trust he will see fit to do as I have instructed
him, not as you deem politic."

Cecil bowed again, his face grave. "Forgive me, your
Majesty. I do understand the threat under which his majesty of Scotland lives and labors. It was, therefore, distressing to me to learn that, rather than purging the kingdom
of witches, Sir Philip has, in fact, come to the rescue of
one such, commonly known to be a witch, and given her
out of the reach of God's justice."

"I have heard it said that the voice of the people is the
voice of God, and have had cause to believe it," Elizabeth
said, "but I have yet to hear that their justice is God's."

Burleigh stirred then, but received a hard look from his
mistress, and fell silent. Don't fence with her in this
mood, boy, she's too dangerous, the old man thought.
Cecil saw the thin line between the queen's painted brows,
and swallowed hard.

"I spoke without consideration, your Majesty. Yet, how
must King James view this act? He expects Sir Philip to
protect him from such as these, and has welcomed him as
his protector. And in return for this welcome, Sir Philip
aids one who can only be thought to be an enemy of the
king."

"Because a woman practices the arts, she must needs be
a black witch?" Elizabeth retorted her voice rising. "By
the Mass, Sir Robert, it was this—witch—who gave warning that James was in grave danger that very night, and
that warning saved his life. Perhaps you're of the same
mind as my lord of Essex, and think ill even of so noted a
scholar as Doctor Dee!" She took a deep breath. "By
Christ's holy wounds, you tread bravely close to treason.
Doctor Dee has ever served me well, as has Sir Philip,
and yet now you see them both as servants of an Enemy
far greater than a mere witch."

"I dare to protest, your Majesty." Cecil took a deep
breath, waiting for the explosion. When it did not come,
he rushed on, "That Doctor Dee is a good and devout
man, I have never had any doubt. Nor have I ever doubted
Sir Philip's loyalty to your Majesty. Yet he has never been
overly wise in matters of politics—"

"Sir Robert." Elizabeth did not raise her voice further, but there was that in her tone which struck the younger man silent. "I appreciate that it might well be difficult for one who holds high office at my hands to betake himself to some distant place until you have come to see that wisdom of my views. However, difficult as it may be, would you be so kind as to go efface yourself for some short time?"

For an instant, time slid away, and Burleigh saw her again the canny red-haired girl-queen, Henry VIII's true daughter, but subtler, wiser, than he had ever been. Even through his pain for his son, Burleigh was hard put to restrain a smile of pure pleasure. This was the queen he loved and served, true prince, true English, even in her rages. Besides, he knew he need have no fear for Cecil. Elizabeth knew his value perfectly well, and would not waste him. She would not hold his single-mindedness against him, just as she had always forgiven Sidney's free-speaking ways. Appallingly similar, the two men, Burleigh thought. Sidney the idealist, speaking for what his heart dictated was right, and what, in a perfect society, must certainly be. Cecil the pragmatist, weighing politics in finely calibrated scales, so determining the right course, the safest course, for the England of his vision. He spoke for that with the same candor as Sidney, and received much the same treatment for his pains.

Paler even than was his wont, Cecil bowed painfully low, murmuring his apology. Elizabeth's tone softened. He spoke for England, she knew, and from heart and mind together.

"You have leave, Sir Robert," she said. "But be at hand, should I need your counsel."

It was a reprieve of sorts, and Cecil bowed even more profoundly. "Thank you, your Majesty," he said, and backed from the room.

Elizabeth looked up at Burleigh with an almost impish expression on her thickly painted face. "Sit down, Spirit. You know everything, of course."

Burleigh did as he was told, settling himself awkwardly onto a low stool. "Everything that came from Robert's sources. I would be interested in what Philip has to say for himself."

"Oh, Philip does not stoop to defend himself. He states, as calmly as you please, that, having witnessed an attempt to hang an accused witch without benefit of law, he decided that the lack of law might as well excuse her as condemn. It's very prettily phrased—almost lawyerly. I think he's laughing."

"Your Majesty!"

"Oh, not at me, Spirit, Philip's too devoted for that. It's devotion that prompts his openness, we've both known that from his youth." Elizabeth smiled, leaning back in her chair. "I think I did right in not permitting him to marry your Anne, fond as I know you are of the boy . . . listen to me, of the boy he was then. It's taken some years, but I think Frances Walsingham is proving to be the match for him—and more than a match, too, if I am not mistaken."

"And yet, it was a match your Majesty liked very little, if at all."

"That is ungenerous to an old woman, Spirit, and ungallant in a gentleman. If I choose to misremember, or to adjust matters to be as they should have been, you should not correct me."

Burleigh smiled. "Your Majesty is far from old, and I stand well corrected. But Scotland?"

Elizabeth's face twisted. "Always a hard taskmaster, my lord. For Scotland, Philip seems to be preceding with a becoming caution. I don't say I wouldn't wish the matter well settled already, but it would be a dream to think so. Dee, Sidney, even Sir Walter spoke of a very great power; we'd be fools to think it could be defeated so quickly." She sighed. "I sent my champion in the tilts to James, but I think I was wise in sending Holland's favorite soldier, too. How fortunate for me that they are one and the same man."

"And for James," Burleigh said.

The queen smiled thinly. "My dear Spirit, if it's fortunate for James, it must be fortunate for me. I will not see my England torn on the rack of dissension and treason—and don't dare say to me that I'll be dead, and will know nothing of it. I have seen already. James must stand free of faction, free of both extremes, or we have lost already."

Chapter Twenty-three

Present fears are less than horrible imaginings.
William Shakespeare, Macbeth

It was not a good crossing. The stiff winds, too favorable to waste, whipped up heavy seas that tossed the little cog unpredictably as it beat across the North Sea, then turned contrary as soon as the ship reached the relatively sheltered waters of the Dutch coast. Captain and crew cursed its perversity as they struggled to tack southwest toward Flushing, eyes constantly scanning the horizon for Spanish ships or renegade Dutchmen. One or two, the bravest among them, added their passengers' names to the litany of damnations, for bringing them to a crossing at this time of year, but always in an undertone. After all, the two men had paid well, and they did serve Sir Philip Sidney. Even ten years after Sidney's war had ended at Zutphen, the Dutch remembered him with respect and love.

Marlowe, lying braced against the sides of his damp and uncomfortable bunk, was only too aware of that forbearance. He had been prepared to face the discomforts of an autumn passage, an unhappy crew, the uncertain weather and the constant stink belowdecks, compounded equally of the fish that made up the cog's usual cargo and the un-

cleaned bilges, with a certain stoicism, but the sailors'
undisguised reverence for Sidney was an unanticipated annoyance. He said as much to van der Droeghe, who occupied the cabin's other bunk, and was answered by placid,
monosyllabic acknowledgement.

"I wonder you're not sick on all this sweetness," the
poet snapped, and added hastily, "but not in here."

"I am never seasick." Van der Droeghe did not move
from his position, long legs braced against the cabin's wall,
one arm thrown across his face to shade his eyes from the
swinging lantern.

"Amen, while we share a cabin," Marlowe answered.
"Or do you attribute that to Sir Philip, too?"

Van der Droeghe shifted slightly, lifting his arm to peer
under the sleeve of his doublet. "I hadn't thought of that.
It could be so." He was smiling.

"Pox take you," Marlowe said, and pushed himself up
out of the bunk. He clung for a moment to the nearest
bulkhead before he caught the movement of the ship, and
was bitterly aware of the Dutchman's grin. Marlowe cursed
again, and staggered from the cabin.

He made his way on deck and crossed to the windward
rail, clinging to the tarred rigging. The ship had rounded
the headland some hours before, was now beating its way
up the West Schelde to Flushing. The water of the inlet,
choppy from the conflict of wind and tide, had changed
from rich blue to a sort of silvered grey, touched here and
there with patches of bright foam. The setting sun, emerging briefly from the low clouds, cast fugitive shadows
across the waves. Marlowe smiled, moved in spite of himself by the sober beauty, but the smile soon faded. Flushing had never been a lucky town for him; he had done
better service at Douai, and at Rheims.

The cog turned north at last, borne by the flooding tide
toward Flushing's harbor. The coast of Zeeland rose out of
the grey waters, at first little more distinct than a cloudbank,
then slowly growing more solid, until Marlowe could pick
out the squat spires of the church and the town hall, twin
towers rising above the uneven line of the town's chimneys.

The harbor itself was busy, dozens of little boats crowding the grey-green water, the long quays bristling with

masts. Marlowe leaned back against the railing, trying to stay out of the way of the suddenly hurrying sailors, as the captain bawled the orders that reduced sail, bringing the cog decorously into her place along the longer dock. Single-sailed craft—the poet knew them only by their French name, *semaque*—careened past, one so close that he could see the shock-haired man at the tiller, and the boy crouched with his dog amid the confusion of buckets and ropes in the rounded bow. One of the sailors paused in his work long enough to shout incomprehensible curses after them; the semaque's steersman lifted one hand to gesture in languid, insulting response.

Then the cog was alongside the dock, one party of sailors tending the lines that drew her against the pilings, another group furling the last scraps of sail. Marlowe blinked, amazed as always by the purposeful chaos, and realized that van der Droeghe had come on deck. The Dutchman had their baggage slung over his shoulder, two satchels small enough to be carried easily afoot as well as on horseback. He nodded to the poet, but did not move to join him until the cog was securely at her moorings.

"Do we go directly to Sir Robert?" van der Droeghe asked at last, and handed the poet his satchel.

Marlowe took it, accepting for now that they were in a sense equals, and glanced over his shoulder, judging the hour by the fading light. "It's late," he said. "You said you knew a place where we could lodge?"

Van der Droeghe nodded.

"We'll go there, then."

The captain had been well paid before he agreed to leave Scotland. It was the work of a moment to give him insincere thanks for an easy passage, and then Marlowe scrambled down the unsteady gangplank. He hesitated for a moment on the dock, assailed by the smells and the foreign voices—he spoke French and Spanish well, could make himself understood in a sort of Flemish, but Dutch had always defeated him—and van der Droeghe touched his shoulder.

"This way."

Marlowe nodded, and followed the other man down the length of the dock. Brick warehouses indistinguishable from their London counterparts formed a wall at the end of the docks, dark and stinking alleys dividing one from another. The poet eyed them warily, and was glad when van der Droeghe turned down a broader, though still shadowed, street. The houses' upper floors overhung the roadway. The poet picked his way carefully, avoiding both the puddles beside the walls and the shallow ditch running down the center of the street. At the first crossing, van der Droeghe paused, and produced a battered lantern from his pack. He fiddled with flint and steel until the candle was lit—Marlowe leaned against the nearest wall, resting his bag on one booted foot—then reshouldered his satchel, balancing the lantern in his right hand.

Once they were away from the docks, the streets grew silent, the shops already locked behind their heavy shutters. Marlowe glanced warily from side to side, and loosened his rapier in its sheath. In his experience, empty streets were to be avoided after sunset, and the sun was almost gone. He glanced toward van der Droeghe, but the Dutchman's face was expressionless. Marlowe allowed himself a mental shrug—surely van der Droeghe wouldn't lead them through a neighborhood which he knew to be dangerous—but kept close to the other man's shoulder.

The quiet street led into a square only a little wider than the road itself. A fountain stood in the center of the cobbled space, the splash of water falling into its basin mingling with the sound of voices from the nearest side street. There was music, too, and a snatch of singing: a tavern, Marlowe thought, and slanted an envious glance toward the sound. Sure enough, lamplight spilled from an open door into the rutted street, to color the figures leaning against the doorpost. They were youngish men in slashed and tattered finery, with serviceable blades under their short cloaks and an air of watchfulness that went badly with the tankards in their hands. There were unemployed soldiers even in the Low Countries, but there was something about them that raised the hackles on the poet's neck. Instinctively, he touched the sigil hanging at the open neck of his doublet, but kept walking. As he passed the fountain, he glanced back, and saw the first of the strangers just emerging from the side street.

"Jan-Maarten."

Van der Droeghe turned, the lantern swinging in his hand. "Ah," he said softly, and let the satchel fall from his shoulder.

Marlowe lifted his voice, switching into French, the least offensive of his languages. "You're looking for something?"

The first two strangers exchanged a wary look. The third man, coming up behind them, said something in Dutch, and laughed. Van der Droeghe sighed.

"That's done it," he said, in English this time, and set his lantern carefully on the fountain's edge. Marlowe bit back a curse, and let his satchel slide from his shoulder. Another man eased into the square, his cloak wrapped around his left hand. Four of them, two to one . . . The poet swore again, and drew his own blades, glancing over his shoulder for a line of escape. Two darkened streets led out of the square, both slanting away to his left. He shifted his ground slightly to allow himself the choice of either, and waited: it wasn't much of a choice, but he preferred a fight, even at these odds, to being hunted through the unfamiliar streets.

"What do you want?" he said, still in French, and then repeated the question in his broken Flemish.

One of them, a dark man whose hair hung in greasy ringlets, laughed softly. Another, his face invisible in the shadow of his feathered hat, answered in English, "Your goods, gentlemen, nothing more."

Van der Droeghe spat onto the cobbles, and lifted his sword. Marlowe hesitated. There was something wrong here, something out of place—sober thieves, and these were sober enough, didn't work this way, they struck from behind or not at all, rather than risk spoiling the goods. Almost without thinking he stooped, lifted his stachel in his dagger hand. He held it out slowly, ignoring van der Droeghe's astonished glare, saying, in English this time, "Take it, then, and let us go."

He wasn't sure if they understood the words, but the gesture was plain enough. The soldiers exchanged uneasy glances, and then the dark man said, "Set it down. And you, also."

The poet lowered his bag toward the cobbles, not daring to take his eyes from the soldiers, and willed van der Droeghe to follow his lead. The man in the plumed hat snapped, "The fee's twice what they'd be carrying!"

One of the others made a noise that might be agreement or protest, but Marlowe did not wait for more. He swung the bag at the nearest soldier's face, and had the satisfaction of seeing the man fall staggering backward. He rushed the dark man, trying for a quick, crippling blow, and heard van der Droeghe shout something at his back. The dark man parried skillfully, trapping Marlowe's rapier momentarily in the crossguard of his dagger and drawing it up and to the side. The poet felt the blade lock, and turned with it, spinning into the dark man's lunge. The rapier's point ripped across the back of his doublet, drawing blood, but the unexpected turn had spoiled the soldier's aim. His rapier came free; in the same instant, Marlowe smashed the dagger's pommel into his opponent's teeth. The dark man staggered back, dropping his own dagger, left hand going to his bloodied mouth. Marlowe pursued his advantage, slashing backhanded for the dark man's ribs. The soldier parried awkwardly with long rapier, and dodged away. Marlowe shouted after him, hardly aware of what he said, but then a second soldier lunged at him, and he fell silent, saving his breath for the fight.

There was shouting from the side street where the tavern lay, and from the houses surrounding the square. Marlowe was vaguely aware of the noise, but did not dare take his eyes from the quick-moving blades. This soldier was good, better than the other, and this time there would be no chance of surprise. Marlowe let himself be driven back, thinking curses, looking for an escape. The soldier feinted to his right, lunged to the left. Marlowe stepped back, parrying, and knew in the same instant that it had been a double feint. He dragged his dagger back across his body, twisting away from the thrust. The blade jumped the crossguard of his dagger, skidding painfully across his knuckles, but the rapier slid harmlessly past his side. Instinctively, he shortened his own sword, stabbing blindly, and felt the blade sink home between the other's ribs. The soldier sagged forward with a breathy moan; Marlowe wrenched his sword free, and stepped away from the falling body.

"Jan-Maarten?" he called, and swung round to see the Dutchman standing over a fallen soldier. A third man, an unobtrusive man in a good, sober cloak, stood beside the fountain, cleaning his twin swords with a lace-edged handkerchief. He looked up then, his sandy beard catching the lantern-light, and Marlowe caught his breath in recognition. In the same moment, he became aware of the sound of running feet, and Dutch voices calling in confusion.

"Poley," he said aloud, and the sandy-haired man bowed.

"At your service, Marlowe."

Van der Droeghe looked up sharply. "Robert Poley?"

Marlowe nodded, but before he could say anything more, a voice said, in accented English, "Put up your swords, sirs, and come with me."

The poet started to obey, but checked, seeing the blood on his rapier. He stooped to clean the blade on the nearest body's cloak, keeping his eyes fixed on the newcomers. There were perhaps a dozen of them, a core of solid-looking burghers with well-polished partisans and watchman's cloaks, and behind them a straggle of householders in gown and nightcap carrying clubs or—one—a scythe-bladed fouchard. The chief of the watch, sword drawn in one hand, lantern in the other, peered warily past the circle of light.

"To what end?" van der Droeghe asked, and sheathed his sword with an audible click of metal.

"You disturb the peace, sir," the chief watchman answered, still warily.

"We were set upon," Marlowe protested. "Must honest travellers let themselves be murdered in the streets?" He sheathed his own rapier, and then slid his dagger into the sheath fastened above his purse. The movement drew the rough cloth of his shirt across the long cut on his back. He winced, arching his spine, and reached instinctively to probe the wound. It wasn't much, shallow and messily painful, but his hand came away bloody. He held out the reddened fingers for emphasis. "You see, sir."

The chief watchman gave him a jaundiced look, then

jerked his head at the nearest of his henchmen, murmuring something in Dutch. The man nodded, and he and two others vanished around the corner, to return a moment later with a tradesman's two-wheeled cart. One balanced it while two others heaved the soldiers' bodies onto the shallow bed. The chief watchman said, "That's as may be, sirs, but it is for the governor to decide. You'll come with me."

His tone brooked no argument. Marlowe sighed, wincing again, but rinsed his bloody hand in the fountain's basin. "As you wish." *Not that Sir Robert Sidney will be any too happy to see us,* he added silently, *at least not in this guise, or with this escort.*

"And you, too, sir," the chief watchman said. He was staring at Poley.

"I?" Poley mimed surprise and confusion. "I saw these gentlemen set upon, and came to help them, that's all."

There had been the slightest of pauses before the word *gentlemen*, and Marlowe's eyes narrowed angrily. Before he could speak, however, van der Droeghe said, "That's true enough."

"The governor will want your witness," the chief watchman answered. He nodded to his own men, the largest of whom heaved up the handles of the cart and began trundling it away down a side street. The citizens fell back, relieved that the fight was over. One grey-bearded man slipped away, clearly returning to his own fire. The chief watchman glanced around again, and lifted his lantern. "This way, sirs."

Marlowe fell in behind the chief watchman, taking good care to stay out of Poley's reach. He didn't know what Cecil's agent was doing in Holland, or how he had happened to be so close at hand when the others were attacked, but it wasn't a reassuring coincidence. He glanced warily at Poley, but could read nothing in the other man's impassive face. *Not reassuring at all,* the poet repeated silently, and looked away.

Robert Sidney had the governor's palace, of course, a set of handsome, new-fashioned brick buildings arranged around a bricked quadrangle. There were more soldiers on duty at the gates—Englishmen, this time—and one of them darted ahead to wake the household. Marlowe eyed the darkened windows, and sighed. It looked very much as though Robert's people were abed. Van der Droeghe shook his head gloomily.

"Sir Philip will not be pleased."

"I doubt Sir Robert will be, either," Marlowe snapped.

"I meant that this wasn't what he intended," van der Droeghe answered, with the first hint of temper Marlowe had heard from him. His eyes slid again toward Poley, and the poet frowned.

"You know Robin?" he asked, in an undertone.

"Sir Philip has spoken of him," the Dutchman answered, in an equally quiet voice. "He was in service in our household, once."

To spy on Sir Philip, I'd lay wager, Marlowe thought, but said nothing. He glanced instead toward Poley, and saw that the spy was frowning lightly. I hope you're worried, Marlowe added, with silent malice; you're a twisty whoreson, but Sir Robert's cleverer than he looks. With any luck, you'll underestimate him, and then we will see fireworks. He pushed aside the memory of his own first meeting with Robert Sidney, and with it the unhappy knowledge that he had failed to convince the governor of his innocence. He was still unsure if he owed his release more to Robert's dislike of the accuser, or to the governor's sense of humor.

A door opened across the courtyard, and a steward hurried out, his fingers still fumbling with the strings of his collar. He bowed jerkily to the chief watchman, and said, "Sir Robert will be down directly, since you say it's important, Master Hendrik. You may wait in the hall."

"Thank you," the chief watchman said, not without irony, and the steward bowed again.

"This way, if you please."

The great hall was still half in darkness, though a pair of servant boys in shirt and breeches were busy lighting the second great candelabrum. Marlowe glanced discreetly around, and saw a half-armored soldier waiting just inside the far door; another soldier followed them inside, and took up his position beside the courtyard door. The candles flared, sending a wave of light across the tapestries

that covered the long walls. Under the sudden play of
light and shadows, the antique figures seemed to shift
their stance above the stacked, dismounted tables, then
froze back into woven immobility as the light strengthened. The poet shivered with pleasure. One of the servants brushed past him unheeding, and knelt beside the
hearth to stir the embers back into life. Marlowe watched,
strangely fascinated, as the young man fed tinder and then
larger wood into the growing flames. The new light turned
the plain, placid face into a devil's mask of light and ruddy
shadow.

Marlowe looked away then, cursing to himself. He knew
this mood too well, the detached exhilaration that followed
a danger survived, and knew he could not afford it yet.
Van der Droeghe was looking at him with some concern.

"So, Master Hendrik, you've caught some important
malefactors?"

Robert Sidney stood at the head of the stairway that led
down from the state apartments on the second floor, his
nightcap thrust to the back of his head, a fur-lined gown
thrown hastily over shirt and hose. Somehow he looked
even bigger in this disorder, his robust health unfettered
by the modesty of doublet and hose. The chief watchman
bowed, and, after a moment's hesitation, his prisoners did
the same.

"I'm sorry to disturb you, sir, but the matter seemed
worthy."

"And quite right, too." Robert came down the stairs
with some caution—he was wearing backless slippers over
his stockinged feet, Marlowe saw—and moved to stand by
the fire. Without being told, one of the servants poured
wine for him, and retreated to the shadows. Robert lifted
the glass in half-mocking salute.

"Sergeant, I never expected to see you in such equivo-
cal company. And Master Marlowe. It's been some time
since I last saw you here." Robert's voice sharpened. "But
I don't think I know you, sir."

Poley hesitated for a fraction of a second, but answered,
"My name is Robert Poley, my lord."

"Robin Poley?" Robert's brows drew down in a rather
fearsome scowl.

Poley hurried on. "Some call me that, yes. I saw these people set upon, four against two, and came to their aid. Your watchman said I must bear witness to the fight."

"Robin Poley," Robert said again, almost to himself. He glanced sharply at van der Droeghe. "Well, Jan-Maarten, let's hear what happened."

"Certainly, Sir Robert." The Dutchman drew himself up as though a straight back would give order to his thoughts. "Master Marlowe and I arrived this evening—I believe you were expecting us, sir—but so late that we thought better to spend the night at an inn I know of, and wait on you in the morning." He shrugged, not looking at either Marlowe or Poley. "As we came through the square behind Saint Anthony's church, four men—soldiers, I think—who had been drinking in the tavern there set on us. We fought them off, two were killed, and then the watch came up."

Robert looked at the poet, his face unreadable. "Is there anything you'd add, Master Marlowe?"

Marlowe hesitated. Probably van der Droeghe hadn't heard, or hadn't considered, the leader's words—*the fee's worth more than what they're carrying*—but to the poet it could only mean a well-paid ambush. And with Poley appearing so conveniently close on their heels . . . In spite of himself, his eyes slid toward the sandy-haired man, who returned the look impassively. But if Poley had been behind the attack, why had he helped to beat them off again? And in any case, could he really afford to voice his suspicions? Marlowe's mouth twisted into a grudging smile. Poley certainly won't have any qualms about explaining just what I was doing in Scotland, might well have copies of my reports, if he's as well, as forethoughtfully prepared as usual. He said aloud, "Nothing, Sir Robert. That's what happened." He touched his back again, wincing visibly, hoping to distract the governor from this line of inquiry.

Robert lifted an eyebrow. "See to Master Marlowe, Jabez, if you'd be so good." One of the older servants came forward, bowing coldly, and Marlowe submitted to his examination. Robert turned back to the sandy-haired man. "It was fortunate you were handy, Poley."

Poley met his stare guilelessly. "I'm quite certain the gentlemen could have dealt with them without my assistance, sir."

Robert smiled slowly. "Still, having rendered my brother's friends such brave assistance—you must allow me to show his gratitude and mine. You will do me the honor of staying here in my house."

Poley opened his mouth as though to protest, but then, thinking better of it, bowed instead. "You do me too great a favor, Sir Robert."

"Not at all, Master Poley," Robert murmured, still with that slow smile. He glanced over his shoulder and beckoned to the hovering steward. "Deems, see them housed, please."

"At once, Sir Robert."

Marlowe swore as the servant pulled shirt and doublet away from the long cut. The man's hands checked, but he said nothing for a brief moment. Then he released the cloth, saying, with chill reproof, "It's no more than a scratch, sir, though it should be washed."

"Did I say it was more?" the poet muttered. He could feel blood flowing again, hot and stinging where the shirt had ripped away the scab, and cursed again.

"This way, if you please," the servant said.

The steward's men had run before. Candles were lit in the little bedroom, and a cake of chamber perfume was smoking on the new-laid fire, masking the damp smell of seldom-used hangings. A can of heated water stood on the hearth-edge, and even as Marlowe glanced longingly toward the curtained bed, another page appeared, carrying clean linen.

"Your doublet, sir," the older servant said.

Marlowe undid points and buttons, then allowed the older man to ease off the torn shirt. The page brought the hot water and a roll of lint; Marlowe stood wincing while the older servant washed away the worst of the blood, then placed a thin pad over the cut and wrapped a rough bandage around the poet's body to hold it in place.

"This shirt's beyond saving, sir," the page said shyly, and held up the torn and stained cloth to prove it. "Shall I bring you a fresh one?"

Marlowe sighed—it wasn't a new shirt, by any means, but the lawn had been expensive—and nodded. "Can the doublet be mended?"

It was the older servant who picked up the worn garment, turning it disdainfully to study the torn back. "I believe so, sir. If you wish it."

"I do," Marlowe said, and achieved a brisk condescension. "See to it, if you would."

The older servant bowed, and turned away, chivvying the page ahead of him. Marlowe watched them go, a crooked smile on his lips—clearly, his reputation had preceded him—then began painfully to divest himself of hose and stockings. The room was chill, in spite of the fire. Marlowe shivered, but made himself wash face and hands in the rapidly cooling water before shrugging himself into the nightshirt the page had brought. There was a nightgown as well, the cloth a little faded, but not yet patched. He wrapped it gratefully around his shoulders, sinking his fingers into the thick fur of the lining, and moved closer to the hearth. The cut across his back stung still, but it was a clean pain, easily dismissed.

He sighed then, and lowered himself onto the carved stool that stood beside the hearth, extending one bare foot cautiously toward the flames. The air was too cold, and the fire too distant; he grimaced, and tucked it back under the folds of the gown. The elation he had felt earlier, the unholy satisfaction of death evaded and turned back onto the attacker, was fading now to an unfamiliar longing, a hunger for something more than sex. He stared into the glowing heart of the fire, letting the light burn clouds into his vision. Out of the corner of his eye he saw flames run up a twig, consume it, saw the shell of ash hang trembling, a palpable shadow. Mesmerized, he picked up a straw from the floor and reached for it, blinking away the greenish lights that hung before his eyes. In the same instant the lowest log shifted, cracking into two chunks of glowing coals. The fragile ashes crumbled, vanishing into the fire. The poet sighed again, and tossed the bit of straw onto the glowing logs. Ganymede had seen a salamander once, or so he said, a little thing no longer than his smallest finger, with eyes as bright as the coals it sprawled on. It had lain there, he said, lazy and content as a cat, right in the heart of the fire—*right in the center of a London fire, right there on my mother's hearth*—with the flames rising around it, until he himself could bear the heat no longer, and looked away. When he looked back, the animal was gone. Dissolved into its own element, Marlowe thought. I've never seen such a wonder.

In spite of himself, he began to fit words to the memory, turning the image into a lover's pleading. *O armored heart, give o'er, cease to deny, And with that lizard, triumph now, and die.* He winced then as he recognized the metaphor, and glanced over his shoulder, but the ghostly shape that had haunted him in Scotland did not manifest itself. Perhaps it doesn't like bad poetry, Marlowe thought, and managed a crooked smile, but even as he formed the words he knew he was mistaken. Despite the conventional demand, he had not been seeking passion, but a rarer fellowship.

He shook his head, and leaned forward to stir the dying fire. There had been a time in London once, one hot and edgy summer, when he and Ganymede had been caught up in a riot of drunken apprentices spilling out of the Hope Theater. They'd fought their way free—an easy enough matter; the prentices had been intent on some quarrel between rival companies, and on stealing, not on men with neither money nor jewels—then leaned panting inside St. Saviour's wall while the blue-coated tide surged past them, and the shopkeepers along the bridge fought to close their shutters against the mob. They had made their way back to Norton Folgate in the crowd's wake, dodging it and the constables of the watch, who, if they could not control apprentices en masse, could always find time to arrest an actor. Once safely back in Marlowe's room, they had sat shoulder to shoulder to share a cold pie and a pitcher of ale, talking—boasting—to convince themselves that they had fought bravely, and done well.

The poet shivered, drawing the nightgown closer around his shoulders. That was what he wanted tonight, assurance and close company; more than that, he wanted it from his Ganymede. No one else, not Watson, not Kyd, not even Thomas Walsingham or Southampton, had given him that, or let him give much in return. His mouth twisted into a bitter grin. He himself had made any reconciliation impossible, not unless he got down on his knees and asked for pardon—and probably not even then, even if he could bring himself to act the penitent. Oh, yes, he thought bitterly, those were the last two lines of a sonnet, all right—but meant for me, not Ganymede. He pushed the thought away, angry at his own weakness, and turned away from the fire.

"I'd almost prefer your company, demon, my Mephistophilis, to being such a fool." He had spoken without true intent, but the words seemed to echo in the little room. He froze, but pride—and a species of bitter desire, barely acknowledged—kept him from uttering the denial that might drive the thing away. He shivered slightly, every muscle braced and waiting, and heard the rustle of silk taffeta in the shadows by the bed.

"Did I not tell you you would call me?" The voice was rich with laughter. "You have my company now, my Christopher, and never shall be rid of me."

I didn't mean it. . . . Marlowe killed the craven words unspoken, and lifted his head, sure that the quick pounding of his heart was audible even across the room. Mephistophilis leaned against the bedpost like a man certain of his welcome, one long leg crossed over the other to display hose and jeweled garter to their best advantage. The firelight gleamed from the silken doublet, vanished in the folds of his short cloak. Night and fire, Marlowe thought, the cloak the changeable color of the night sky wracked with cloud, diamonds like stars—or perhaps they were stars in truth; Mephistophilis, if not omnipotent, was strong enough for that—winking in the velvet while the flame-tawny doublet beneath glowed warm as an invitation. Night and fire, flame and shadow-smoke, the perfect setting for so magnificent a creature. . . . The demon smiled gently, and beckoned.

Marlowe took a step forward in spite of himself, and then, defiantly, stepped forward again, until he was so close that he could have reached out and touched the demon's sleeve. Mephistophilis's smile broadened.

"My dear Christopher." The whispered words were a caress, and the poet shivered again. "Have you reconsidered?"

"I have not."

"Yet you did call me."

That was unanswerable, and Marlowe looked away, his mouth tightening. There was a little silence, and then Mephistophilis said, cajolingly, "And behold, I am here. How may I serve you?"

You can go, and never trouble me more. The words trembled on the poet's lips, but he did not speak, for fear he would be obeyed. "You could serve me rather than Bothwell," he said instead, "and cease to persecute the king of Scots."

Mephistophilis laughed again. "For the first, my sweet, there is a price—as you well know. As for the second . . . What do you care for Scotland, or its king? Ask something for yourself."

Marlowe did not answer at once, and the demon gestured gracefully. An embroidered purse appeared in his hand, its sides swollen with gold. "Coin of your English realm," Mephistophilis murmured, tilting his head to one side. "Or of any other you desire."

The poet shook his head. "I thank you, no."

The purse vanished instantly. Mephistophilis gestured again, and this time a book, a sestimo volume bound in dark-red leather, appeared between his fingers. "This might be more to your taste, I admit. Knowledge, Kit—a complement to that which Thomas Watson left you. Neither white magic nor black, I promise you, merely useful rituals."

Marlowe shook his head mutely, and could not refrain from sighing when the book, too, disappeared.

"What else?" Mephistophilis mused, and stopped abruptly, his snake's eyes flicking sideways. "Alas, I'm summoned—to business, Kit, not to pleasure, more's the pity. But take this of me." He plucked the air again, and brought forth an oval the size of a Dutch florin or a pin for a man's hat. Marlowe received a brief impression of a brown and white stone in a gold setting, and then the demon tossed it gently onto the bedclothes. "And one thing more."

Marlowe looked up, startled and newly wary. Mephistophilis smiled again, and reached out lazily to take the poet's chin in his hand. His fingers were thin, and very cold, stinging like ice. Marlowe let himself be drawn forward, until their lips met. Mephistophilis's kiss was as cold as his touch, the brief contact deceptively chaste. Marlowe closed his eyes, all other sensation drowned by the gentle pressure against his lips. It was like a lighted match laid to a powder train; he shivered, reaching out for the other in helpless response. The tantalizing contact was withdrawn instead. He opened his eyes to find himself alone again, and did not know whether he would weep with frustration or be grateful for his narrow escape.

He shivered again, desire souring as swiftly as it had quickened, and hugged the nightgown tighter around himself. His lower lip stung, the pain increasing with each heartbeat. He put his hand to it reflexively, and brought his finger away daubed with blood. He stood for a moment staring at the dark stain, then shook himself hard, and made himself look away.

The single candle was still burning on the table beside the fireplace. He went to fetch it, shielding the flame carefully with his hand, glad of its enveloping light. As he turned back toward the bed, he caught sight of the thing Mephistophilis had thrown there, and checked abruptly. After a moment's hesitation, he picked it up, muttering a charm to cleanse it of its origins. The gold glittered a little, but did not vanish in his hand. It was a pin for a hat, as he had guessed, a carved stone like a seal set in gold. He turned it curiously in the candlelight until the shadows filled the incised design. Pan, double pipe raised, danced in the dark stone. He should throw it away, he knew, or, better still, turn it over to a priest or a wizard who could destroy its demonic taint before it harmed anyone else, but the thought of damaging the perfect gem made him wince a little. There was nothing to be done until the morning, he told himself, and set pin and candle down together on the stand beside the bed. In the morning, I'll decide.

Chapter Twenty-four

Surely, if a man will but take a view of all Popery, he shall easily see that a great part of it is mere magic.
        William Perkins, A Golden Chaine

The silvery clouds of the previous day had closed in to bring a heavy, soaking downpour. Marlowe stared past Robert Sidney's shoulder at the rain-washed tiles of Flushing's roofs, very red against the louring sky, and waited for the governor to notice him. Robert took his time—less, Marlowe admitted grudgingly, from a desire to intimidate his somewhat unwelcome visitor than because his table was heaped high with business—but finally put aside one sheaf of papers to take up a single closely covered sheet. Marlowe recognized the letter van der Droeghe had carried from Edinborough, and brought himself to inward attention.

"Well, Master Marlowe." Robert's voice was pleasant, verging on the jovial, but the poet was not deceived. "So Philip wants me to arrange a safe conduct for you into France. Why?"

What did he tell you? The words trembled on Marlowe's lips, but he was not so unsophisticated as to voice the question. Instead, he said, "He wants the advice of one of

364

the Pleiade wizards—he can't go on protecting the king piecemeal. The Pleiade invented the techniques he wants to use."

To his surprise, Robert nodded. "Still, they didn't help the late King Henri very much, did they?" He glanced again at the letter. "Were you directed to anyone in particular?"

Marlowe shrugged. "I have letters of introduction to the leaders of the academy, that's all."

Robert leaned back in his carved chair, frowning slightly. "There is a man, newly settled here under our protection, who used to be a part of the Pleiade, before the present king dismissed it. It's said he's a wizard, and I know he's a scholar—and he's English. If he'd serve your turn, you'd be back to Scotland that much faster, and you wouldn't have to risk a French journey."

"That wouldn't cause me much sorrow," Marlowe said. "But what was an Englishman doing as part of the Pleiade?"

Robert's quick, humorless smile answered the question even before he spoke. "He's a recusant, a Catholic, which caused me trouble enough when he applied to live here. Still, he's not a priest despite Rheims and Doaui, and he was a member of the Pleiade, so he can't be entirely orthodox—and he can't hate Protestants too much."

"One hopes," Marlowe murmured, remembering his own months in Rheims. The English students there, who had given up everything for their religion, were more bitter even than the Jesuits against the servants of the Antichrist. "Where can I find him?"

"He lives in the printers' district," Robert answered. "He writes almanacs."

And probably practices minor wizardry on the side, Marlowe thought. Tom Watson did, and he was just as learned as this Englishman. "What's his name?"

"Hal—Henry Fletcher."

Marlowe froze. There had been a Hal Fletcher at Douai with him, a quiet man some few years older than himself, to whom he had been inexplicably drawn. Or not so inexplicably, he thought. That Hal Fletcher, for all his devotion, had been a man who thought even while he believed, and was not afraid to probe the underpinnings of the

Jesuits' theology. His company had been a comfort in those exhilaratingly dangerous months—but his name had gone down on Walsingham's list all the same, condemning him to death as a papist agent should he ever try to return to England. Still, Marlowe thought, Hal was never a dabbler in arcane philosophy. It may not be the same man. "How old is he, this Fletcher?"

Robert lifted an eyebrow. "A little older than yourself." His tone left no doubt that he knew precisely why the poet had asked the question.

"You said I'd find him in the printers' quarter?" Marlowe's face and voice hardened, daring the governor to challenge him. Robert nodded. "Then I'll look for him. As you said, if he'll help—if he knows enough to help us—it'll save me the journey into France."

He sketched a bow and turned away. Robert nodded imperturbably, acknowledgement and dismissal in the gesture, but Marlowe barely noticed the movement. He had done his best to forget the precise details of his year at Rheims, though the danger of it, the excitement giddy as passion or wine, had stayed with him ever since, and the aftermath, the degree forced from an unwilling university by fiat of the Privy Council itself, had been a triumph particularly sweet. Nevertheless, he had bought those successes with the names of men who had been his friends, and he had no great belief in his own righteousness to remove the taste of betrayal. Still, he told himself, they chose to sacrifice themselves for something unreal—I was only the instrument of the martyrdom they wanted. The memory of the mass, the sensual splendor embellishing the cold chastity of the Latin rite, mocked the easy sneer.

"A word with you, Marlowe."

The poet spun, his hand going to the hilt of his rapier. Poley stood in the doorway of a side room, the chairs behind him covered with white drapes that glowed like ghosts in the rainy darkness.

"What do you want?" Marlowe asked, and the other man beckoned impatiently.

"In here, quickly."

Marlowe hesitated, glancing over his shoulder for any awkward witnesses, then stepped inside. He kept his hand

on the rapier's hilt as Poley shut the door gently behind
him. "What is it?" he said again.

"What is it?" Poley mimicked irritably. "What do you
think, ass? I have a word for you, from our mutual employer. I'm to remind you of your orders, and to say again
that the witches are not to be destroyed. Consider our
meeting last night a reinforcement of the reminder."

"Listen, Poley—" Marlowe bit back his first response.
Anger would do him no good here; only an explanation, a
rational submission, stood any chance of convincing Cecil's
agent. He took a deep breath, and tried again, fumbling
for the words that would carry the most weight. "Listen,
Robin, I wrote to Cecil already, I told him that things
have changed, that the enemy's too strong for that kind of
game. Either the witches—either Bothwell will be destroyed, or James will. There's no other choice. And I
don't think he wants to see James lose."

Poley's smile was contemptuous. "Sir Robert's received
your very dutiful letters. So the paper knight's converted
you, after all?"

Marlowe's hand tightened on the hilt of his rapier, but
he made himself swallow the insult. "I'm speaking from
what I've seen. God's blood, I know more about this than
either of you, and more than Sir Philip does. Cecil's asking
the impossible."

Poley grimaced, gesturing for the poet to be quiet, and
Marlowe hastily lowered his voice. "All right, I've done,
I'll remember what he wants. But tell him what I've said.
It's not possible."

Poley lifted an eyebrow. "Oh, I'll tell him. It won't do
you any good, Kit, but I'll tell him."

The threat was unmistakable. Marlowe managed a sour
smile, knowing that further protest would be useless, said
instead, "Enjoy your stay in Flushing, Robin."

Poley's mouth twisted, but Marlowe's hand was already
on the door latch. He slipped out before Cecil's agent
could find an adequate response.

The streets were quiet, the few citizens who could not
avoid a journey—mostly women and apprentices, all huddled into heavy, hooded cloaks—hurrying along the narrow passages. The women in particular moved like great

ungainly birds, skirts and cloaks bunched high to show mud-spattered ankles, hopping and dodging across the puddles. Marlowe drew his own cloak tighter around his body, hunching head and shoulders to keep the hood from blowing back in the capricious breeze. It was a long walk to the printers' district: despite his care, he could feel the damp spreading along his neck and down his spine, and rising through the worn soles of his boots.

He stopped first in a modest-looking tavern to inquire his way. The surly publican left off snarling at his wife long enough to deny any knowledge of a man called Fletcher, but the woman broke the rhythm of her scrubbing to nod toward the shop next door.

"The booksellers," she said, in accented French, and sat back on her heels to contemplate the stranger. "They might know."

"Thank you, mistress," Marlowe said, and the publican rumbled something challenging from behind his counter. The poet backed away in haste, but was uncomfortably aware of the woman's eyes watching his departure. He braced himself, stepping out into the rain, but to his surprise it was the woman's voice that rose in shrill vitupuration, and the man who offered apologies.

The bookseller's apprentice, a plump boy who blushed for his breaking voice, knew nothing of an almanac writer, but the cat-eyed journeyman left off setting type and came forward, wiping inky hands on his apron.

"Master Fletcher lives around the corner, at the sign of the black hen," he said, in good French. The slanting greenish eyes lingered speculatively on the poet's face, swept down to study the serviceable, ungentle clothes half revealed beneath the sodden cape. "Would you be a kinsman of his wife's?"

Marlowe shook his head. "No. I was at school with Master Fletcher once, that's all, and thought I'd take the chance of seeing him again."

"So." The journeyman nodded, his eyes bright and curious. "At the sign of the black hen, then, that's where you'll find him."

"I thank you," Marlowe said, and suppressed the desire

to ask the younger man's name. "Around the corner, you said?"

"Yes, to the left." The journeyman nodded again. "You can't mistake the sign."

"Thanks," Marlowe said, and made himself turn away.

The black hen wasn't hard to find, the glossy, freshly painted bird perched complacently in its painted nest above the door. Despite the rain, everything about the little house looked bright and new, from the whitewashed walls to the scrubbed doorstep. Marlowe jangled the polished brass bell that hung beside the door, and waited as the discordant music died away. Water dripped gently onto the step beside him, and he shifted away.

For a long moment, nothing happened. He lifted his hand to the bell again, but before he could touch it, the upper half of the door snapped open. A small woman—a tiny woman, Marlowe thought, startled and bemused by the faerie size and female ripeness—peered out, neat hands resting on the edge of the lower door.

"You want something?" she asked, in French-accented Flemish.

Marlowe answered in French, "I'm looking for a friend of mine, Hal Fletcher. I'm told he lives here?"

The woman took her time answering, sparrow-bright eyes darting up and down. She was a pretty thing, brown curls escaping from under her embroidered cap to frame a heart-shaped face, full breasts imperfectly confined by corset and bodice, but there was a determination in the set of her pointed chin that must, Marlowe thought, warn off her suitors.

"Gascon?" she said at last, then shook her head. "No, English."

Marlowe nodded, newly wary. "Yes, mistress. My name's Christopher Merlin. If Master Fletcher's the man I want, he'll know me." And may know me all too well, he added silently. I hope to God he'll give me a hearing.

The Frenchwoman frowned, and for an instant Marlowe thought she meant to slam the door in his face. Then, grudgingly, she said, "Wait here, English. I'll see if he knows you."

"Thanks," Marlowe said, but she had already turned

away, leaving the upper door open behind her. The poet scowled, bleakly tempted to reach inside and see if he could hook anything of value off a side table, but the little entrance hall, though neat enough, held nothing really worth stealing. *At least that explains why she was willing to leave the door ajar,* Marlowe thought wryly, *but it's not very flattering.*

After what seemed an interminable time, doors opened and closed somewhere down the dim hallway, and shapes bustled out into the rain-greyed daylight. The foremost was a man in a long gown, richly furred at neck and wrists, but neatly patched at hem and elbows: a scholar's gown, unmistakably, Marlowe thought, even if the square black cap hadn't marked him further. Two women followed at his back, the one who'd answered the door and another almost as tiny, drying her hands on a linen apron. Then the man had come fully into the light, and Marlowe recognized the once-familiar face. Fletcher hadn't changed much over the years—he trimmed his beard in the French style now, and the lines running from nose to chin were deeper—but the mild eyes and the eyebrow perpetually quirked in good-humored question remained the same.

"Christopher," he said. "Come in out of the rain." He lowered his voice as the poet stepped inside. "Are you in trouble? You needn't fear—even the servants are good Catholics here."

Marlowe froze. He had anticipated half a dozen possible receptions, but this—to be greeted as a fellow student, a fellow Catholic, had not seemed probable. "No, I'm not in trouble," he temporized. "It was a professional matter I came about—I understand you're a scholar, a maker of almanacs?" Out of the corner of his eye, he saw the taller woman give a sigh of relief. *Fletcher's wife?* he wondered. *Or did he have the bad luck to be married to the miniature virago?*

Fletcher's face took on an odd expression, a subtle wariness. "I am. But let me take your cloak, Christopher."

Marlowe shrugged himself free of the water-heavy wool, but before Fletcher could take it, the taller of the women had slipped forward, deftly intercepting the scholar.

"You must be soaked through," she said in French,

sounding glad of the merely domestic concern, and Fletcher frowned.

"Come in by the fire, then, it's a raw day." He glanced at the taller woman, a singularly sweet smile transforming his sternly bearded face. "Have Besje set another place at dinner, Henriette."

"Of course, my Hal," the woman answered, and bustled away, the sodden cloak bundled in her arms.

Marlowe followed the other man down the long hall toward the back of the house, trying not to stare too obviously at the rooms around him. The house of the black hen was small but comfortably—almost lavishly— furnished, the compulsive tidiness of the Dutch maidservants vying with the indulgent disorder that usually accompanied small and much-loved children. A toy horse on wheels, its bright paint somewhat battered, stood in a corner, and there was a small, smudged handprint on the wall below a framed engraving of a shipwreck. It was just the sort of picture that would fascinate a child, Marlowe thought, and felt a sudden brief lightening of spirit. In the background, the bowsprit of the sinking ship pointing accusingly toward heaven, while the gallent captain fought to drag one more man into the overcrowded boat, and— most conspicuous and deliciously horrible of all, filling the entire foreground—sharks devoured a screaming seaman.

"It gives my son nightmares," Fletcher said ruefully, "but he won't let us take it down." He pushed open the door to a side room. "In here's my study. There's a good fire laid, you can dry off."

"Thanks," Marlowe said, and stepped past him into the study. It was a little room, well warmed by the generous fire. The poet moved close to the tiled hearth, holding out his hands to the blaze, and glanced once around the panelled walls. It was a typical scholar's chamber, at least in that one quick look, with its cluttered table and the rack of instruments—orrery, astrolabes, a narrow brass-bound tube—balanced precariously above the precious books, and Marlowe felt his own waning confidence revive slightly. This was familiar territory, this crabbed scholarship and minor, hissed-at magic; he had been clever enough to avoid this fate for himself, but he remembered enough of it to know he could use such men.

"Sit down, please," Fletcher said, and settled himself in a worn carved chair beside the table. "How have you been—what have you been doing? We didn't hear of you, after Rheims; we thought sure the authorities had taken you." He smiled slightly. "I see your vocation was no more permanent than my own—or do I misjudge your clothes?"

Marlowe forced a smile, and sat on the settle, stretching his legs to the fire. The damp leather steamed faintly, thin streams of vapor curling up off his legs. He stared at them, willing himself to think of some innocuous reply. "No, I'm no priest," he said at last, and was violently aware of the understatement in those words. His momentary cynicism had vanished with Fletcher's first words; he was swamped instead with fragmentary memories, guilts cold and unacknowledged, that choked any further reply. How could he explain what he'd been doing in the past eight years? *Well, Hal, actually I was in Rheims just to spy on you anyway, so when I came back to England, I just gave Walsingham the names and went up to London to write plays, though I still do a little spying when I need the money. Oh, yes, and I don't spell it "Merlin" any more— never did, much, except abroad—but Marlowe.*" Oh, that would sound a truly heroic note—and ruin any chance I'd have of persuading Fletcher to help Sir Philip. I don't dare tell him the truth, but maybe somehow I can shape half-truth to a story that will bring him with me.

He realized that Fletcher was looking curiously at him, and managed another smile. Before he could speak, however, there was a knock at the door, and a maidservant appeared, carrying a tray laden with tankards and the ubiquitous Dutch cheese. She bobbed a curtsey, eyes flashing in her apple-cheeked face, and set the tray on the worktable. Fletcher thanked her in Dutch, and she curtsied a second time before disappearing. The scholar turned back to his guest with a slightly apologetic smile.

"Not the best ale, I'm afraid, but at least it isn't sauced. That's a habit I've never been able to get used to, for all we've been living here six years now."

"Not a favorite of mine, either," Marlowe lied, and accepted the proffered mug. For a wild instant, he wished it were sauced, mixed like the cheapest tobacco with blackapple and belladonna and less identifiable herbs, but shook the thought away. He would need all his wits about him now. "I see you're married," he said, and carved a sliver of the cheese.

Fletcher smiled almost shyly. "Yes. While I was in Paris, I met Henriette—she's the daughter of an old teacher of mine, who introduced me to the academy there when I decided I wouldn't enter the priesthood. He was, I think, pleased with the match." His face clouded slightly. "He died just after Julia-Marie was born, and then she died, too, of a putrid fever. She was always sickly, poor lamb, we were lucky to keep her two years. . . . But Cyprian at least is healthy, thank God."

Marlowe nodded, nibbling the strong, salty cheese. Children, including his own nieces and nephews, were little more than nuisances to be tolerated when they could not be ignored, in his view, but at least the conversation had taken a less threatening turn.

The respite did not last, however. Fletcher visibly shook away his own concerns, and said, "But what of you? What brings you to Holland?"

The question could not be evaded any longer. Marlowe said, choosing his words carefully, "Your father-in-law's Academy, it was the Pleiade, wasn't it?"

Fletcher nodded, unsurprised. "Yes. It's a bit of a come-down, I admit, to be writing almanacs, but the skills required are just as great, if not as—respectable."

There was a faint note of defensiveness in his voice, but Marlowe resisted his desire to pick at that weakness. He said instead, "It's that connection I'm interested in. I was told you had been a member—" He broke off, knowing more explanation was needed, and tried again. "You asked what I'd been doing. I went back to England; I'm—in service to Sir Philip Sidney now."

As he'd expected, the bald announcement raised Fletcher's eyebrows. He watched the scholar work through the ramifications of the lie—Sidney was a Protestant champion, though not overtly hostile to Catholics who were not

political enemies, and a scholar as well as a writer—and
bit his lip to keep from adding to the story. After a
moment, Fletcher said, "Then you converted."

Marlowe looked away. "I've made my peace," he muttered. It was a phrase he'd heard Catholic converts use,
when reproached for faithlessness. He hesitated, searching
for a convincing reason for his defection, and finally added,
"I couldn't live outside England, in the end."

"Oh, Christopher." Fletcher closed his teeth on any
further reproach, but the rueful words stung. Marlowe felt
himself flush painfully. The scholar regarded him sorrow-
fully for a moment longer, then shook himself. "You said
you were a part of Sidney's household?"

Marlowe nodded.

Fletcher managed a slightly bitter smile. "I suppose that
goes a long way toward explaining it. It's hard to believe a
man like that could be so willfully mistaken in his beliefs."

Not you, too, Marlowe thought, but managed to suppress his anger. He said instead, "He's a good man—" and
Fletcher nodded.

"I know. He used to correspond with the senior members of the Academy, before Navarre dissolved us."

"It's on his behalf that I'm here," Marlowe said baldly.

Fletcher frowned. "What would Sir Philip Sidney want
with me?"

"Nothing," Marlowe answered, honestly. "I'm not sent
to you particularly, but to any members of the Pleiade
who might be willing to help. I was to go into France, but
Sir Robert told me you were here, that you'd been a part
of the Pleiade, and I thought I would speak to you first."
He looked up at the older man, making his expression as
guileless as possible. "Time is of the essence."

"What does Sir Philip want?" Fletcher said again.

Marlowe took a deep breath, trying to guage the depth
of the other's skepticism. "Her majesty sent him to Scotland to help the king of Scots against the witches there,"
he began. "I've brought a letter." Quickly, he outlined the
situation, trying to make things clear without betraying too
much of his awkward political knowledge. When he had
finished, he handed over the letter, and there was a long
silence. Marlowe waited, counting heartbeats, not daring

to throw even words into the gap that had opened between them, for fear of what the echoes might bring.

At last Fletcher nodded, once, and looked up. "All right," he said quietly. "I'll come with you."

Marlowe looked back at him, unable to hide his sudden suspicion, and Fletcher frowned.

"What, I'm to trust you and your Sir Philip, and you don't trust me?"

"That's not it," Marlowe began, but Fletcher went on as if he hadn't heard.

"I've felt it, too, damn it, something—" He gestured almost angrily, the same gesture every other scholar had used, trying to describe the enemy they'd felt, hands cupped to shape the immense power, a frown for its indistinctness, and a shake of the head to drive away both the fear and the uncertainty. "—not a demon, I'm almost sure, but evil, quite evil. And that's not a word I use lightly." His voice changed, became almost contemplative. "It's been in the air here, sometimes, literally in the air overhead, streaming past on the wind. Like the Wild Hunt, but riding silent, just the rush of something between me and the stars."

Marlowe shivered in spite of himself, though a part of him stored the image for his Merlin play. He had never lived on the Welsh border for any length of time, was a Kentishman born and bred, but tales of the Wild Hunt had reached Cambridge, and one or two of the Welshmen there had sworn, lilting voices lowered to thrilling whispers, that they had heard the Hunters' horns in the hills, and the beat of ghostly hooves in the wind.

Fletcher shook himself then, breaking the spell. "So I will come with you, Christopher. When do you—we—sail?"

"I don't know," Marlowe said, and hated himself for the remembered fear in his tone. He continued more briskly, "As soon as I can hire a ship."

Fletcher nodded. "I hope you'll still stay to dinner?"

Marlowe shook his head, and forced a smile. "I'm afraid I can't," he lied. "I need to find out if Sir Robert's factor has found a ship yet."

"Of course," Fletcher answered, and Marlowe wondered for a bitter moment if he'd heard a note of relief in the other man's voice. "Send to me as soon as you know anything."

"I will," Marlowe said, and at last managed to take his leave.

The rain had eased considerably, but the streets were still empty. At the first corner, he paused for a moment, wondering when the bookseller's closed and if he could persuade the cat-eyed journeyman to come with him when it did, then turned away. Safer, always, to find the accepted meeting places, find someone there who could be bought for a few coins or a pretty trinket; safer still to find a tavern, and drown memory and conscience alike with gallons of beer, rather than burying them in some willing body. And all for nothing: even if he kept the truth from Fletcher long enough to bring the scholar safely to Scotland, someone there, out of malice or simple ignorance, was bound to betray him as Fletcher's betrayer. And even if some stranger didn't reveal the true story, Sidney was not the man to let another go into danger for him under false pretenses. He cringed away from the thought of Sidney explaining, in his quiet, polite voice, just what he had been doing in Rheims—apologizing, probably, for sending such a man as his agent.

With an effort, Marlowe shook the thought away. If Sidney wished to complicate his own life, that was Sidney's problem; his only commission was to bring a Pleiade wizard to Scotland, and that he would do. The rest was up to Sidney.

Chapter Twenty-five

*For if they which are troubled with the disease of
the eyes called opthalmia do infect others that
look earnestly upon them, is it any marvel that these
wicked creatures, having both bodies and minds
in a higher degree corrupted, should work both these
and greater mischiefs?*
W. Fulkbecke, A Parallele or Conference of the
Civil Law, the Canon Law, and the Common
Law.

"The Master of Ruthven will joust."

Sidney paused at Greville's words, the gold-chased manifer forgotten in his hands. There was an unholy glee in his friend's eyes that he knew must be reflected in his own. Still, inborn caution kept his voice low, so that the armorer at work on the straps of a back-and-breast did not hear. "Fulke, you are a wonder. How did you do it?"

"James really did most of it." Greville leaned against the armorer's bench, legs outstretched before him. A stream of sunlight fell from one of the high windows, pouring across his primrose stockings. His shoe-ribbons, that shade of dusted rose called love's-longings, looked almost orange in the buttery light. "I merely asked his majesty if the Master of Ruthven fought, and, Philip, I swear, for one heartbeat he looked as you did when I told you it was certain. So, he said, 'Shall we ask my Alexander, Sir Fulke?', and—summoned him, from out of thin air, for all I know, that's an uncanny one. 'Sir Philip has done you a signal honor, Alexander. He invites you to be part of the company that will joust against him in this tourney.' "

Greville paused, the glee fading from his expression. Sidney frowned, but held his tongue. Greville went on, more slowly, "For a moment, I almost think I was frightened." Then he shrugged. "But he made the best of it suggesting he wasn't worthy of such an honor at your hands, Philip—it was beginning to sound liturgical and vaguely blasphemous—but then James cut in in that brisk way he sometimes has, and suggested that Ruthven had better prove worthy of a knight's honor if he expeted to be worthy of a king's favor. Oh, Philip, it was beautifully done—but I'd be wary of him in the lists. I don't know if, after all, I've done you any favor."

Sidney shook his head, smiling faintly. "Never worry about that, Fulke. I'd rather have him on the field where I can keep an eye on him. What say you—a general challenge, skill only. You and I against all comers." His hands tightened on the manifer, betraying a brutal excitement. Greville sighed inwardly, envying that pleasure. At forty-one, still England's undisputed champion, Sidney always looked twenty years younger when there was a tourney at hand. Then Greville smiled. God help young Ruthven, facing that.

"I think there are some Scots who'd rather ride with us," he said aloud. "Young Seton, for one, perhaps Mar, probably Lord Graham, the treasurer's son, and certainly some others. You said before you didn't want this to become English against Scots."

Instantly, Sidney's smile became apologetic, almost abashed. "I did, and you're quite right. No symbolism, and, please God, no antagonism."

"Except toward the Master of Ruthven," Greville murmured.

"Oh, no, Fulke. No antagonism even there. Just—a salutory lesson."

Greville mimed a toast. "To salutory lessons, then."
And may I deliver one of them.

There was a noise from the doorway, riding over the sawing of the armorer's knife against the well-tanned cowhide. Sidney looked up, frowning, and a brown-haired youth in the royal livery bowed deeply.

"Your pardon, Sir Philip, but his majesty requests your presence."

Sidney and Greville exchanged quick glances, and Greville muttered, "God's teeth, can't the man look after himself for an hour?"

Sidney suppressed a grin. "At once?"

"If you please, Sir Philip."

Sidney set the manifer aside. "Then his Majesty will pardon me if I come to him as I am."

James had for once abandoned his privy chamber for the great hall. Sidney followed the page through the warren of corridors, and slowly became aware that they were not following the most direct route. There were more servants in evidence than usual, too, and a surprising number of men in the red sashes of the royal soldiers. Sidney lifted his head warily, wondering if there had been another attack. Surely I would have felt anything like that, he thought—wouldn't I? He shook the doubts away. If there had been an attack on the king, the page would have brought him directly to the hall, instead of by this roundabout passage.

The page paused then before one of the doors to the hall, and spoke softly to the soldier on duty there. The man stiffened to attention, and swung open the door. "Sir Philip Sidney," the page announced, and Sidney stepped into the hall.

The door through which he had entered was not commonly used; he stood for a moment in some confusion, trying to get his bearings, and then the king's voice spoke from uncomfortably near at hand.

"Sir Philip. Forgive me from taking you away from your preparations for what is, after all, my entertainment—but there are some people arrived whom I thought you'd wish to see at once."

Sidney swept automatically into his bow, his mind rac-

ing. He was not in the mood for games—but there was a
note in James's voice that reminded him of his own daughter's, the time she had presented him with a nightcap
embroidered with her own hands. He straightened, and
saw, beyond the king's shoulder, a familiar figure—two
familiar figures, he amended silently. But what in God's
name had brought either Frances or Raleigh this far north?

James smiled. "Lady Sidney is twice welcome," he said,
"as your wife and for her own fair self. And Sir Walter's
reputation precedes him." He gestured then to the knot of
men in plain, serviceable clothes who stood a little behind
the rest. "And the Lord Chamberlain's Players, as well—I
vow, my court shall shine as bright as any in Europe. How
bereft England must feel, since so many of her brightest
stars now shine in our northern firmament. Come, come,
Sir Philip, greet your lady wife. I shan't intrude any longer,
I assure you."

He turned away, drawing the laughter of the court with
him, but Sidney was still aware of their eyes on him as he
stepped forward to take Frances's hands. She smiled at
him—she must have changed clothes, he thought, bemused and delighted, that sanguine gown was never meant
for riding—and he bent to kiss her hands, not certain how
the kiss he suddenly longed to give her would be received. As he straightened, he thought for an instant he
read disappointment in her eyes, but then Raleigh had
stepped forward, and the two men embraced.

"Small wonder Essex thinks he can control that one,"
Raleigh said softly. "Faith, Philip, you're looking hearty."

"Essex?" Sidney repeated, glancing from one to the
other with new wariness.

Frances nodded with a humorless smile. "Indeed. He's
doing his level best to destroy whatever it is you're trying
to do. I doubt he really means it—he hardly thinks enough
to recognize consequences, if he thinks at all. I spoke—
very circumspectly, I assure you!—to her majesty, but you
had to be warned as well."

"I thank you," Sidney said. He did not ask why she had
not merely sent a letter: there were bound to be sane,
sober, Walsingham reasons for it, and he preferred not to
hear them just now, to cherish the thought, illusion though

it might be, that she had preferred to be with him, as she
had been with him in Holland. And yet, he thought, she
practically called Essex a fool. . . . "The danger isn't really
Essex," he said slowly. "It's those he can inspire."

"Or those he can be used by," Raleigh interjected.
"Philip, there's a demon just to the south you've not been
chary of."

"Northumberland?" Sidney shook his head. "No, I've
been ware and chary, I promise you. But I know his
power—and so do one or two others in my household,
even were I mistaken—and this—" He broke off, realizing
just how much he still had to explain to both of them, and
finished rather lamely. "The great danger here is from
someone else, the Earl of Bothwell, in fact. Northumberland's a conjurer, a middling Faustus."

Frances smiled in spite of herself at the scholarly disdain in her husband's voice, and Raleigh had the grace to
look away. "Still," he said, "join what power he has with
Essex's charm?"

Sidney winced. "Then it's a mess indeed," he said shortly.
There was a moment's silence. Then he saw the players,
still huddling together just out of earshot, waiting for
someone to notice them. He smiled, and beckoned to
them. Burbage and Heminges, the senior shareholders,
stepped forward, bowing; at Burbage's hasty gesture, Shakespeare joined them.

"Welcome, masters," Sidney said. "How is it you're
away from London at this time of year? I trust—not plague?"
His voice sharpened in spite of himself, imagining his
Elizabeth alone at Penshurst.

"No, no," Burbage answered hastily. "Or, rather, a
plague of wit, and deadly enough to our season."

Sidney's eyebrows rose in spite of himself, and he darted
a questioning glance at Shakespeare. The player gave a
rather chagrined laugh.

"No, Sir Philip, not my play. I—we—did as you suggested, and pulled it from our repertory. Little good it did
us, though, when someone else offended."

"Marlowe is with me," Sidney said, half to himself, and
frowned. "Who, then?"

"Jonson," Heminges answered, with loathing in his voice.

Sidney shook his head. "I don't know the name."

"I wish the rest of London were in that blessed state, Sir Philip," Burbage said.

"He's a new man," Heminges said, "quite young—writes comedies, mostly, full of bawdry—and a friend of Thomas Nashe."

"I take it that's where the trouble lies," Sidney said.

Burbage snorted. "Never trust a bricklayer with so delicate a thing as wit. What can be applied daintily will be taken for beauty, but applied with a trowel—it can only offend."

"What was this play?" Sidney asked, bemused. He had rarely seen the Chamberlain's Men so exercised about anything.

"It's called *The Astronomers*," Shakespeare answered. He gave a wry smile. "A satire, of sorts. The important thing is, the Master of the Revels refused to license it, but Pembroke's Men played it anyway—at the behest, they say, of the Earl of Essex."

"Indeed?" Sidney murmured. He glanced at the players, but no more information seemed to be forthcoming—and I should know better than to ask for it in the present circumstances, he thought. Later, when we can be private. He beckoned instead to the nearest page. "See that the players are well bestowed." He turned back to Burbage. "His majesty will doubtless be demanding. You may well find yourselves almost as busy as you would be at the Globe."

"The better for us, if so," Burbage answered, and bowed. "Thank you for your kind welcome, Sir Philip." He bowed then, and backed away, then followed the page from the hall.

Sidney turned back to the others, trying desperately to keep the sudden longing from his face. He could not meet Frances's eyes, looked instead at Raleigh. "I can't say I'm sorry to see you here, Walter. If only because I'd welcome another skilled knight at my back."

Raleigh frowned, puzzled. "Are things that bad?" he began, and Frances said, almost impatiently, "A tournament—isn't it, Philip?"

Sidney nodded.

Frances shook her head, frowning now in thought. "What purpose does it serve?"

"That remains to be seen," Sidney answered. He grimaced. "It's all too complicated to explain here—suffice it to say it was proposed by a man—a boy, really—who shows no signs of loving me." He nodded discreetly toward the crowd of nobles who surrounded the king at the far end of the hall. "The one all in black. The Master of Ruthven."

"A pretty bit of poppetry," Raleigh said.

"As darkly fair as Lucifer himself," Sidney said, and was surprised by his own words. He added, striving for a lighter tone, "Except that he has unfortunate hands."

"Ah, well." Frances smiled at him, matching the change of mood perfectly. "I could never be convinced by a man with ugly hands."

Raleigh sighed theatrically, and displayed his own hands, long-fingered, but square and hard, common hands. "Alas, I am already rejected. Madam, I am devastated." Frances lifted an eyebrow at him, and he went on, more seriously, "Philip, I'll ride with you, or do anything else I can to aid you. We were good friends, once, and I'm not sure but you don't have the right of our quarrel—or mostly so, at any rate. And I'll be damned if I'll be anyone's tool." He snapped his fingers for one of the hovering pages. "In the meantime, I've my household to see lodged, and I know you've things in hand." A moment later he was gone, his short cape swinging gracefully as he made his bow to the king.

Left alone with his wife, Sidney hesitated, knowing that the Scottish courtiers were watching covertly from the far end of the hall. He forced a smile, knowing the expression to be both formal and stilted, and said, "Would you care to retire to my rooms, at least until the king's chamberlains can attend to your household?" He paused again, then added recklessly, "Though I hope you'll consent to share my lodging."

Frances smiled, with sudden, almost startling warmth. "I had hoped that would be acceptable," she murmured. "I will need rooms for my women, however."

"Of course," Sidney said, at once delighted and a little

appalled, already wondering what she wanted from him. But that was an unworthy thought, and he did his best to dismiss it, bowing instead with a lover's grace. He held out his hand; she took it still smiling and they made their reverences to the king who smiled himself in naked relief. So the rumors were false, malicious, as he had known they must be, he thought, and signalled his permission for them to withdraw. And I'm foolishly glad they chose to prove it in my court.

Marlowe drained the last of the jack of cheap sauced beer, then reached, frowning, for his pipe and the twist of tobacco. He misjudged the distance slightly, and bruised his knuckles against the tabletop, but managed to fill the pipe without spilling more than a few shreds of the coarse tobacco. It was as adulterated—and therefore as illegal—as the beer, but the potent Spanish herb might create what the black henbane seeds had failed to provide. He rose carefully to his feet—his body was more fuddled than his mind, which remained painfully clear—and crossed to the fireplace. The stool was not where he'd left it: Robert Sidney's household was an efficient and tidy one. Rather than search for it, Marlowe dropped loose-jointed onto the tiles, and sat for a moment staring into the flames, before reaching for one of the spills from the metal box hanging from the bricks above him. It took a moment to light it, and several moments more to light the clay pipe. When at last the tobacco caught he drew cautiously on it, then held the pipe away, grimacing, as the acrid smoke clawed his lungs. Worse than the cheapest English stuff, he thought, and I hadn't known there was such a thing—but the tobacconist had sworn the stuff capable of working miracles. He took another lungful, inhaling and then exhaling with deliberate care, and choked on the last bit of it. The foreign herb stank; his eyes watered from the smell. He persevered, however, and as the top layer of tobacco turned to ash, felt a sort of languor finally stealing over him.

He leaned against the bricks of the fireplace, feeling the heat of the dying fire harsh on his left hand and arm, the night chill numbing his feet in their thin boots. Or perhaps that was the beer, at last; he was no longer certain, and had never really cared. He lifted the pipe to his lips again, and realized too late that he had picked it up by the bowl. The clay was painfully hot; he shook it away with an oath, and saw the pipe shatter on the tiles of the hearth, scattering glowing ash. He swore again, heart racing with the panic-fear of fire, but the embers had not reached the rushes. Even so, he leaned forward, and laboriously ground each red coal into nothing with the broken pipe-stem. It was a pity he'd broken it, he thought vaguely, but the mixed tobacco had certainly done its work.

He rested his shoulder against the fireplace, staring at the smudges on the blue-painted tiles. He knew he should get up, undress, go to bed—or at least lie on the bed, not here on the hearth like any drunkard, but he could not seem to muster the will to move. And if I do get up now, I will be sick, he thought. The room was already moving under him, rising and falling like a ship at sea every time his eyes closed. He forced his eyelids open, the aftereffects of the smoke making them sting and water, and saw, lying on the cloak he had discarded on coming in, a glitter of gold.

It was the pin Mephistophilis had given him: he recognized it instantly, though he had done his best to forget about that dubious gift since the night four days past when the demon had given it to him. He stared at it intently, the gold seeming to glow with a light of its own, as Mephistophilis's jewels had glimmered. I meant to be rid of you, he thought. I will be rid of you, now, while I have the sense to do it. He pushed himself painfully to his feet, walking his hands up the bricks behind him until he was upright. He crossed to the cloak easily enough, but stood for a moment, gathering strength, before stooping to pick up the brooch. The movement almost undid him; he swallowed hard, and waited until his stomach settled. Then he moved to the window, and flung open the shutters. The night air rushed in, smelling of rain and winter, the midden-smell of the courtyard deadened by the cold, and his head cleared a little. He had intended simply to fling the brooch away, out into the yard—but that would hardly do, would only mean that some servant of Robert's would take it and its curse. Not that that matters, he added hastily, one servant is hardly worth remorse, but the thing would surely be discovered, and its origins, and traced to me. That I cannot afford. No, I'll have to do what I'd planned from the beginning, find a wise man to take away the taint of it.

That decision made, he turned away from the window, not bothering to close the shutters, and fell sprawling across the bed, the pin still clutched in his hand. He could not find the strength to release it, or even to loosen his clothes, but sank into seasick sleep.

He woke the next morning with a hangover, and a bloody tear in the heel of his hand where the brooch-clasp had stabbed him as he slept. The news, brought by Robert's sternly disapproving steward, that Sir Robert had bought them passage on an Edinburgh-bound ship, did nothing to improve his temper. It was to sail the next day; Sir Robert trusted this would not be inconvenient. The only thing that did please him, a balm to aching head and rebellious bowels, was the news—imparted by Sir Robert himself, with one of his beaming smiles—that Robert Poley was to remain a guest in the governor's household for some unspecified length of time. Fletcher received word of their imminent departure as calmly as he had accepted the entire venture, and promised to present himself at the docks well before noon, their intended sailing time, blandly ignoring Marlowe's half-hearted attempt to pick a quarrel. The poet returned to the governor's palace in no better temper than he'd left, and retired to his bed in a vain attempt to sleep away the misery.

The return journey was not much better than the first crossing. The ship smelled, not of fish, but of some cloying spice that had been its cargo, gone rancid now, and mingling with the less-definable stench of the bilges. The seas, once they'd left the West Schelde, grew very rough, and the sailors, less enamoured of the Sidney family than the men of the first ship had been, muttered darkly about the wisdom of carrying wizards. One went so far as to suggest the wizards be dropped over the side, and Marlowe had been glad of the pistols he kept handy, powder sealed tight against the sea-damp; but cooler heads, and the promise of the remainder of the generous passage-money, prevailed. After that, however, Marlowe took care to stay belowdecks, and advised Fletcher and van der Droeghe to do the same. The Dutchman answered calmly that he was in no danger—no one suspected *him* of any dubious powers—but Fletcher quietly did as he was told, and spent most of his time in the cabin he shared with Marlowe. It was not a comfortable companionship. Fletcher spent most of his days with one devotional book or another, while Marlowe, unable to work on his Penthesilea because of the pitching of the ship, stared at the bulkheads and smoked cheap tobacco until the cabin's air was an acrid fog.

"What would they do if I were to tell them it's you who are the wizard?" Marlowe asked. "And a papist to boot?"

Fletcher gave him an odd glance, but shrugged. "Your reputation precedes you. I rather fear they wouldn't believe you—you act the part so much better than I do."

"God save me from humble scholars. Abelard was such a one as you."

Fletcher looked up again, this time with a smile at once surprised and pleased. "Why, thank you."

"Remember Abelard's—losses," Marlowe muttered, and turned his face to the bulkhead. There would be hell to pay in Scotland, one way or another. Sidney would not be pleased to have a Catholic wizard, with or without impeccable Pleiade credentials, and Fletcher . . . well, how could anyone predict his reaction when he learned Marlowe had been Walsingham's spy at Rheims? I should have gone into France, followed Sidney's plan, Marlowe thought, not for the first time. But, sweet Christ, am I supposed to hazard my neck, and possibly for nothing, when the man I was sent for is waiting in Flushing? Sir Robert understood that.

As will Sir Philip, a more reasonable part of his mind argued. You're seeking out this quarrel, and well you know it. He can only be grateful; the strongest emotion you're like to get is chagrin—for putting you into an awkward position.

Marlowe winced. Why, now, did the voice of reason have to be Ganymede's? True, the boy had always spoken with moderation, with deliberation, even at the worst of

times, but it had never been for that coolness that he had
loved him. More fool you, then, he thought, and twice a
fool to lose him. No man could be called a fool for loving
Stephen—and it had been so long since he'd used that
name it sounded foreign to him—nor any woman neither,
but only a fool would drive him away.

He grimaced then, angry with his own sentiments. Who's
taken up what I threw down? he wondered, but that held
less truth than the next question rising in his mind. *Can I
lure him back, with this play? It's the only currency that
might make his price, he's not to be bought with trinkets,
not even with pearls of great price, or diamond-like stars.
He's only to be bought—to be won with coin wrenched
from one's very soul. . . .*

It was an ill-omened thought. The poet winced, fearing
the shadow of his demon—a shadow against which even
Ganymede must look wan—but the cabin remained as it
was. Fletcher read on in the flickering lanternlight, oblivious to the other's sudden fear. Saved by his devotions,
Marlowe thought bitterly, and flung an arm across his
eyes. This was madness, this longing for a man—a boy—
who had already rejected him, and whose rejection he had
consummated with regrettably brilliant invective; worse
madness was the suspicion that it was not desire but some
more delicate emotion that spurred that longing. Not desire—no longer desire, Mephistophilis's kiss had seared
that in him; no man now would be enough, compared to
that dark magnificence, to waken even the echo of lust.
Marlowe's lip curled. *Mephistophilis is truly kind: he's left
no man the power to tempt me, and so spares me from
shame.*

No, he thought suddenly, I won't have it so. If this
demon tempts me, by God, I've tempted him. I've made a
player-demon, a stage-Mephistophilis so like the real, true
thing that I, I, Christopher Marlowe, scholar and gentleman, have fascinated him. I have charmed and intrigued
him, and he's bound me so because he wants me. Should I
give in to him, what price might I demand? I could laugh
cities to scorn, and make these petty men, these Cecils,
writhe—

He paused in mid-flight. Strange, he thought, with a

new detachment. Let Cecil rot, let Tom Walsingham hang—or burn, more like, with his tastes and graces—let all the ministers and minions who'd employed and used and finally decided to see him quietly murdered at Deptford fall into hell's lowest depths. . . . There was no hate there, for England or her queen, nor could he curse her, even now. It was an almost frightening thought, to understand her power over her state, and even over him, who had always thought himself beyond such things. I may have laughed before, as at any overblown conceit, he thought, but perhaps it's true: perhaps we do live in some time of particular glory, and if so, it springs entirely from her.

The thought was too disturbing, made him too like Spenser and all the other poets—Sidney included, by God!—who produced reams of verse glorifying the Protestant Virgin. He slanted a look at Fletcher instead, wondering how the Catholic scholar responded to the more eloquent proponents of the Marian metaphor. Calmly enough, probably, or with a pointed jest: the man was capable of that cool steel, or had been, at Rheims. Marlowe smiled slowly. Well, my lad, you'll need all of it, once we reach Scotland. You're in for a nasty surprise—and I hope your magic is more efficacious than your prayers.

Chapter Twenty-six

If this be magic, let it be an art
Lawful as eating.
    William Shakespeare, The Winter's Tale

The Scottish workshops were not as extensive as those at Greenwich—armor in Scotland tended to be a practical matter, intensely personal to each lord—but the armory was well enough supplied for the Englishmen to suit themselves out of its stock. The long-limbed Greville had more difficulty than Sidney in finding an easy fit, but with Seton to translate the head armorer's broad Scots, he, too, found pieces that met with his approval. The armorer, who obviously had strict ideas of what would appeal to an Englishman, brought forth the brightest, most heavily decorated pieces the armory possessed, and did not know quite how to take it when they were politely refused. Seton, recognizing the quality of the pieces chosen, hid his grin, and continued with his dutiful translations.

The chosen suits were laid out on the worktable for inspection, and Greville stepped back a little, eyeing Sidney's choices. "I don't know about that breastplate," he said, after a critical survey. "It looks heavy to me."

Sidney shook his head. "Not enough to matter. I can strap it tight."

"The straps can be adjusted, too," Seton offered, and Sidney nodded. The Scotsman turned his attention to the armorer, explaining what was required.

Greville stared thoughtfully at the suit his friend had chosen. It was plain, not at all like the elaborate harness usually worn in English tilts, or even as pretty as the manifer they had examined a few days before. This was plain dark steel, embellished modestly with a few chaste bits of incised scrollwork at neck and waist and shoulders. Not at all Philip's style, he thought, and said aloud, "What are you up to, Philip?"

Sidney grinned. "Merely some simple theatrics. Something I learned from Robin."

Greville snorted. "You've nothing to learn from him."

"The man knows how to use theater," Sidney said, and grimaced as he realized the double meaning of his words. Certainly Essex knew the value of a grand gesture: the white armor he had affected in 1587, to celebrate his then best friend's recovery, had made a striking show, and the all-black harness he had affected ever since had set him apart from all the others. It was the only thing that did, Sidney thought. The man did not disgrace himself, certainly, but neither could he distinguish himself against the core of riders trained by Henry Lee, for all his mock-simplicity of harness and his carefully-chosen pageants. Essex also knew how to use the professional theater, if the Chamberlain's Men were to be believed. But why, Sidney wondered, why is it important to him to disgrace Doctor Dee now? The obvious answer was that he wished to deprive the queen of her best arcane defense, to lay her open to some sorcerous influence of his own, Sidney thought, and if that's the case, I must warn Dee at once. Send Walter home? That's a possibility—

A shadow fell across the table then, and Sidney looked up quickly, train of thought broken off in mid-career. The Master of Ruthven was standing in the doorway. He saw the four men looking at him, and bowed, with flourishes.

"Your prodigal is returned, Sir Philip."

Sidney's lips tightened, as he wondered why Ruthven, of all men, should consent to act as messenger. He smiled, however, and said, "Thank you, my lord."

There was dismissal in his voice, and Seton caught his breath, almost inaudibly. Greville bit back a smile. Perhaps it wasn't wise to antagonize the king's favorite, but the impulse was completely comprehensible.

Ruthven stiffened, but forced himself to relax. Sidney had the unhappy knack of making him feel like an importunate child—but there would be a time, not too long distant, when the Englishman would not be so proud. He bowed again, with even more elaborate grace. "His majesty thought you might wish to know."

Sidney glanced up from the armor. "Does his majesty require my presence?"

"Why, no, Sir Philip," Ruthven answered. "A courtesy, that's all."

"Then, if you would be so kind, my lord, would you tell Master Marlowe that I would welcome the chance to speak with him this evening, once he's recovered from his journey?" Sidney smiled blandly, no hint of triumph in his expression. At his side, Greville smothered a chuckle. Oh, neatly done, Philip, he thought, there's no way now the boy can refuse you—and it's been some years since anyone's treated him like a page.

Ruthven bowed a final time, hiding his fury. "I'll take your message to him Sir Philip." He turned away not waiting for an answer.

"Thank you, my lord," Sidney said to his retreating back, and glanced at Seton. "I hope I haven't inconvenienced you with my unruly tongue, my lord. But I fear the Master of Ruthven is the sort to hold a grudge."

Seton shrugged. "He won't love me any better, but he couldn't love me worse. I don't suffer for this, Sir Philip."

"That's a comfort," Sidney murmured. He sighed, staring at the armor without really seeing its cold lines. "If I were James, I would indeed wish to have the son of my enemies close at hand—but perhaps not quite so close."

"Nor would I," Greville agreed. He leaned against the battered table, stretching cat-like in the sun. "The whole Ruthven family—it seems, well, unnatural, that kind of enmity. To persecute the king from when he was still in his mother's womb . . ."

Sidney shrugged, deliberately choosing a lighter tone.

"Ambition puts on odd faces. Do you know, Fulke, I wish we had Henry Lee here."

"You would," Greville said shortly. Seton caught at Sidney's words, as eager as the Englishman to draw back from the dangerous topic of the king's favorite.

"Lee? He was champion before you, wasn't he?"

"Yes. And I was only named champion because he chose to retire, not because I bested him." Sidney smiled, this time with genuine warmth, and could not resist a glance in Greville's direction. "One of the best men I know. And what he could do to one such as Ruthven . . . I sometimes wonder if Henry doesn't mourn the passing of melee."

Seton grinned. "He'd feel at ease among us, then, sir."

Sidney shook himself hard. "This isn't going to be a melee," he said firmly. "That's precisely why I asked his majesty if Fulke and I might take charge of the arrangements."

"Philip. Aren't you at all curious as to who—or what—Marlowe's brought back with him?" Greville interrupted.

"Extremely," Sidney answered, and gave a wry smile. "But I'll be damned before I'll run at the Master of Ruthven's bidding. Have we set down anything regarding the use of locking gauntlets?"

There was an implacable note in the other man's voice that told Greville there was no point in urging him further. He sighed, and accepted the change of subject without demur. "Do you think we need?" He glanced at Seton as he spoke, and the Scot shrugged again.

"They're hardly common, sir, though a few men use them."

"Then I hardly think we need worry," Greville said firmly. The noise of weapons drifted through the windows from the practice yard beyond, and Seton's head lifted eagerly.

"Would you care to view the preparations for the lists, Sir Philip? Or to take a turn in the yard?"

Sidney nodded slowly. "Yes, yes to both, my lord. I feel in need of the—exercise."

It was mid-afternoon before he returned to his rooms, pleasantly tired from the physical labor of the arms-court. Frances was waiting for him, somewhat to his surprise, sitting comfortably in the window seat, her embroidery spread across her skirts. She sat stitching until Sidney had changed his clothes, then, with a smile and a nod, dismissed the servants and poured wine for her husband with her own hands. Sidney accepted the glass with surprised gratitude, and was even more surprised when Frances settled herself onto the stool beside his chair.

"You look tired, Philip," she said.

"It's been a pelting day," he admitted. "And I've still not come to a decision about Essex—about how to warn Doctor Dee."

"There are messengers you can trust," Frances said, and sighed. "What is it he wants? Surely he has as much as any reasonable man can desire, with the queen's favor."

Sidney grimaced. "God may know, I don't." He sighed. "No, that's not fair. I think—well, what else can it be, but that he wants to influence the queen to something she does not wish to do? What that something is, however, is beyond my guessing. I'm grateful Marlowe's back from Holland; he may be able to tell me more."

"I met your Pleiade wizard today," Frances said, and turned to him a smile that more than hinted of mischief. "Your great care for the king still hasn't allowed you to do that, has it?" There was more of a bite in her voice than she had intended; she grimaced, and went on hastily. "No, I know how his majesty keeps you occupied. I must confess, I'm not easy about this joust."

"Nor am I," Sidney said, his eyes following the intricate brocade of Frances's underskirt. "And yet . . . it's necessary, more than entertainment. Call me proud but I feel a need to let these Scots know who I am, what they have to deal with." He smiled, rather wryly. "I am tired of being called the 'foreign wizard,' when it's my power that's kept their king breathing and sane these past weeks."

"Do you mean to tell me they fear you more than they fear Master Marlowe?" Frances asked, lightly.

Sidney smiled. "James does not, which speaks well for his instincts. And he's fascinated by him—went so far as to procure copies of his work, especially the *Ganymede*. It's all made for an interesting game."

"I daresay Marlowe was in part relieved when you sent him off to Holland."

"Not precisely relieved," Sidney answered. "From what I hear, though, I gather he stayed in Holland."

"In Flushing, under your brother's eye," Frances agreed, "and still found you your wizard." She looked up then, her face betraying an amused sympathy. "You didn't know, then, that Master Fletcher is a Catholic—an English Catholic, at that?"

Sidney sighed. It was just like Marlowe, he thought, and of a piece with everything else the man has ever done, that he finds—chooses—the most complicated possibility. But I required a member of the Pleiade, and a member of the Pleiade he's brought me. "It should not be a surprise," he said heavily.

"You mustn't blame Marlowe," Frances said. "It must have seemed like Providence to him—or whatever he calls Providence—to be able to locate the man you needed without venturing into France. Not a pleasant prospect, even for one of Marlowe's vaunted bravery."

"No, I don't blame him," Sidney said. An unwilling smile tugged at the corner of his mouth. "Nor do I really think he did it deliberately, to discredit me. After all, Cecil's displeasure's more like to fall on him than me." And if it does, he wondered, can I protect him once again? He pushed the thought away. English politics were only of remote concern just now; the Scots factions were far more immediate—and far less subtle. His smile widened. And that, I think, must be what prompts Robert Cecil to interfere: the expert player finds it hard to tolerate the excesses of the novice. And I'm not immune to that myself. This joust. . . . Ruthven will ride, and that will be a pleasant meeting.

Frances saw the change come over his face, and smiled. It was not difficult to follow her husband's thoughts this afternoon, and in any case she had seen that look before. Say what you will, Philip, she thought, you love these jousts, and God forgive me, it's a source of insufferable pride in me that my husband is her majesty's champion and can still unhorse men half his age. "This is not White-hall," she said aloud. "These Scots play in earnest."

Sidney shook his head. "Oh, no. I've been assured—repeatedly—there will be no melee, and I've handled the preparations myself to be certain of it. James is fond of spectacles, not battles; he very much wants an English joust. Pretty speeches, fine clothes, feats of arms, and no malice."

"And will Bothwell oblige?" Frances asked.

Sidney's face grew cold. "Let come what may," he said, with quiet satisfaction. "If there is any deviltry afoot, I'll know where to meet it."

On his return to Holyrood, Marlowe handed Fletcher over to one of James's stewards, and bullied the servants into heating bathwater for himself in his room. Once he had washed away the worst of the voyage's dirt, he pulled on clean shirt and stockings, listening to the gently accented gossip of the barber who trimmed his new-grown beard and hair. When the man had finished, Marlowe dismissed him with a tip from his dwindling store, and finished dressing, mulling over the news he had received. The Master of Ruthven had conveyed the message that Sidney would see him—and Fletcher—after the evening meal; the barber had brought word of new arrivals, and provided details of the planned tournament. That still struck him as a piece of arrant stupidity, but Sidney had had no choice. As for the new arrivals . . . Marlowe shook his head, his fingers slowing on the buttons of his peach-colored doublet. It was probably good fortune, at least for him, that the Chamberlain's Men were here, but what business could either Raleigh or Frances Sidney have in Scotland?

He fastened the last button, and reached for the good purse, now regrettably salt-stained, he had taken to Holland, sliding it onto his dagger-belt. Through the thin leather he could feel the twist of paper that held the Spanish-herb tobacco he had bought in Flushing. That gift would certainly assure his welcome among the players; it might even, if he handled things properly, buy further information, especially if the barber's tale were true and the Chamberlain's Men had travelled with the noble party. That decision made, he hastily knotted his collar-strings, adjusted his hat to a properly gallant angle, and started in search of the players.

The king's stewards had housed the actors in the lesser parts of the palace, where the middling servants slept. Still, the rooms were comfortable enough, with beds for all, so that only the apprentices were relegated to pallets on the floor. The senior sharers, Burbage and Heminges, had even been allotted a room with an antechamber and two good fireplaces, and the rest of the company had quickly made that their meetingplace. Marlowe found them there, gathered around the serviceable long table as though in the alehouse, a covered bucket filled with beer set in the room's coolest corner. The sharers had their heads together, studying a stack of battered prompt-scripts by the light of a branch of tallow candles, while apprentices and hired men threw dice at the far end of the table. Marlowe tapped on the doorframe, and grinned as the sharers' heads came up warily.

Burbage pushed himself to his feet, almost overturning his stool, and came forward to clasp the poet's hand. "Kit. We'd heard you were in Holland."

"I'm just returned today," Marlowe answered, his eyes sweeping the company. He knew them all, or all but the apprentices, but not all were regularly of the Chamberlain's Men: an enforced tour then, not chosen for some obscure promised advantage. And then he saw a more than familiar figure, tall, lightly muscled, the fine face bearded now, but still filled with the old elusive, mutable beauty. Oh, yes, he thought, the dulled emotion not entirely pleasure, nor precisely unpleasant, too old now for Penthesilea, and Alleyn must play Achilles, but Patroclus's Shade, the voice of unheeded reason, the lost, mature beauty. . . . He became aware that the rest of the players were watching eagerly, waiting to see what he would do or say, and he found himself rising helplessly to the challenge.

"What in the devil's name are you doing here, Ganymede?"

Massey managed a disdainful smile for the greeting, as aware as the poet of the curious audience. "I'm with the Chamberlain's Men."

"You've left Alleyn?" Marlowe was unable to repress the question, though he succeeded in keeping his tone almost disinterested. Inwardly, though, he could feel panic rising: Alleyn's company would play the *Penthesilea*, it was a compact between him and Alleyn, and, besides, the Chamberlain's Men had playwrights enough of their own. But Massey had to play in it, there was no other voice could do that part justice, and now the play had to be good enough, temptation and gift enough, to win him back from Burbage.

"For the moment," Massey answered, warily.

"It seems to have been a bad choice, if you've been driven up here," Marlowe observed, and made himself look away, ignoring the players' thinly veiled disappointment. "What happened, William, did your historical allegory earn her majesty's displeasure?"

Shakespeare smiled, and waved his fellow-poet to a stool. "It wasn't my doing, and it isn't just us. We're all on the road this summer, hadn't you heard? Last word we had, Ned was headed into Warwickshire, trying to stay close to the city in case of a miracle."

"Not a common occurrence, where London's concerned," Heminges muttered.

Burbage nodded. "Still, we were luckier than most to encounter Lady Sidney. It looks as though we will find employment here, as promised: their majesties seem most fond of theatre." He grinned. "Ned will be livid."

"Like enough," Marlowe agreed. "Lady Sidney and Sir Walter both made their appearance, I hear? Christ, the road north must have been more than usually crowded."

Shakespeare nodded, but did not take the proffered bait. "We're here because Ben Jonson performed as promised—you remember I warned you, Kit?—and offended the greatest number with the least possible effort, or wit. What were you doing in Holland?"

"I was sent," Marlowe said, rather shortly, and reached into his purse to produce the twist of tobacco. "I've brought a present, too."

Burbage accepted the packet, loosening the paper expertly. "Sauced tobacco," he said, and sniffed again. "I don't recognize the herb."

Marlowe shrugged. "It's a Spanish weed, I'm told, from the New World. At any rate, it produces the most miraculous effects."

Lowin grunted. "I've tasted that," he said. It was not clear from his tone whether he wished to do so again. "I'll vouch for its effectiveness."

"Help yourselves," Marlowe said, and remembered too late the pipe he had broken in Flushing.

"Won't you be joining us?" Burbage asked warily. Seemingly of their own accord, his hands stopped in mid-movement, the pipe half-filled.

Marlowe shrugged, trying to make the best of it. "Only if someone can loan me a pipe. I've been using the sea-captain's second-best one, 'til I left the ship."

"No gift from a patron?" Massey murmured, just loudly enough to be heard, his voice all mock-solicitude.

Marlowe leaned back in his place, and lifted his eyes to the younger man's. "Admit it, Stephen—the poem was brilliant."

Massey's mouth twisted into a smile that was half a grimace. "I can hardly deny it. You gave me a fame I pray acting never brings me. But I can hardly claim the dubious honor of inventing the role. More an imagined villain for an imagined slight."

"You did leave me," Marlowe said drily. "Or was that also imaginary?"

"Oh, pernicious villain," Massey retorted. "And how many have you loved and left?"

Marlowe shrugged. "If they'd had wit enough to write such a thing—"

"Perhaps they were too much the gentleman," Massey said, and smiled. "You've boasted of your well-born lovers before now."

"Oh, hold your tongues, the pair of you," Burbage said, belatedly recalling himself to his duty. "Kit, I won't have you make a mock of any of my company." He reached for the nearest candle, saying at the same time, "John, I know you have a pipe to spare."

Lowin nodded, and produced a short-stemmed clay pipe from his capacious purse. Marlowe accepted it, and filled it with the Dutch tobacco, then slid the paper down the length of the table. "Tell me about what's to do about this tournament," he said.

Burbage shrugged, lighting his pipe. "I don't know much

more than you do. It's to entertain the king of Scots." He
glanced over his shoulder before adding, in a lower voice,
"And, faith, he's a man who needs more entertaining than
any I've ever seen."

Phillips laughed softly. "He certainly doesn't lack for it."

One of the apprentices, who had been edging closer to
the sharers, cleared his throat. Burbage glanced at him,
and said, "Well, Nick?"

"I've been at the tiltyard, master, watching the practices," the boy answered, with a touch of self-importance.
"It's not at all like an English tourney."

"And what do you know of them?" Burbage asked. "Sit
down, Nicholas, and mind your manners."

"Let the boy talk," Shakespeare said, and grinned. "But
he would do well to watch his manners."

"Yes, master," Nick answered, somewhat chastened.
"But I have seen the tilts for Accession Day, and all the
others, too, when I can, and these are nothing like. There's
no theme, or, or any fiction at all, or even pageants.
They're just going to fight."

"No *impresas*?" Burbage choked on the harsh mix of
tobacco and herbs, recovered himself enough to continue,
"No stinging little one-word condemnations? No costumes
and commentary? What's the sense of a tournament, then?"

"Well, it's not an English tournament, now, is it?" Phillips snapped.

"No. Of course not." Burbage sighed, thinking of previous commissions. He had earned princely wages before
now, painting the pasteboard presentation shields for courtiers who needed a theatrical hand with their *impresas*.
"But it could have meant good money."

Marlowe shook his head. He still could not understand
why Sidney had chosen to accept this challenge—except
that Sidney never refused anything, and, in any case,
Ruthven had left him little choice. "I just hope he knows
what he's doing," he muttered.

Massey caught the soft comment, and gave the poet a
startled look. That was something new, to hear Marlowe
express concern for his patron. Burbage heard too, and
lifted a hand in protest. "Man, you are speaking of Sir
Philip Sidney. The bravest, truest knight in Christendom,

a man to strike the poets of old dumb with contemplation of his excellence. Of course he knows what he's doing."

"Soldier, scholar, courtier," Shakespeare murmured, staring at the smoke curling from his pipe. "The beauty of the world, the paragon of animals—" He stopped short, as though his own words had startled him, then smiled, a pleased, remote little smile.

"Oh, I know, I've heard it all before, more times than I like to think," Marlowe said. "He's only my patron, you should save your praises for his ears." Despite his words, he could not keep the note of worry from his voice. It was all well and good, this devotion—Sidneydolatry?—but what good did it do to believe the man invulnerable? They all sat back, rested on the man's laurels and trusted in his virtues. . . . Marlowe shook his head, a strange vision rising in his mind. There was a tourney field, like to the one at Whitehall, and Sidney fought a man afoot, but that man . . . He was an anonymity, a knight whose armor, whose very being, seemed to flicker with the wind, a knight of air, of shadows. Yet this knight of air, impervious to Sidney's master-strokes, drove Sidney back and back, and down at last, hacking at a fallen figure that struggled, then shuddered and lay still. And in the stands, the spectators—Burbage, Shakespeare, James himself, and all the rest—watched, applauding politely, so confident of their perfect knight's victory that they were blind to the horror before them. Sidney always won: there was no suspense, no fear. No one could defeat him, it was folly even to try. Yet Sidney would die. Maybe not tomorrow, or even in the lists; but the loving complacency of those who admired him would kill him.

Marlowe shook his head again, driving away the dreadful vision, made himself look slowly around the little room. The fumes of the Dutch tobacco hung heavy in the air, adding to the sense of fellowship; sharers and hired men alike murmured drowsily together, relaxing at last from the tensions of the road. And then, quite suddenly, he was aware of Massey's curious stare, the slight frown, half puzzled, half troubled, marring the perfect face. Before the poet could frame some bitter jest, Massey said, low-voiced, "Are you all right, Kit?"

Intentionally or not, he'd caught the tone of the old days. Marlowe answered honestly, as he would have then, "Visions and dreams, my dear. But not, I think, true."

Massey's eyebrows rose at the inadvertent endearment, but there was something in Marlowe's voice, an uncommon sincerity, that silenced his intended rebuke. He said instead, "An ill omen."

Marlowe grimaced, faint laughter, Mephistophilis's laughter, brushing his ears like a lover's kiss. "I can—and I will—do something against it, in any case." He frowned down at his pipe, wishing it would bring him the stupor it had given him in Holland. "Damn the man, anyway."

"Sidney?" Massey smiled. That was more the poet's normal tone. "He is a marvel of the age."

"He's not perfect," Marlowe snapped, "he's not some demigod, and certainly not God Himself, despite what some of you lot seem to think—"

"Can you list any faults?" Phillips demanded.

Marlowe scowled, and Massey cut in, not knowing quite why he deflected the quarrel, "Well, the temper's legendary. If the Earl of Oxford calls you a puppy, you say 'thank'ee, zur' and make an upstage exit. You don't challenge him."

Marlowe shook his head. "It's to the point where it's no longer considered a fault. It lends dash." He looked speculatively at Phillips. "What about his wife, then?"

"What about her?" Phillips repeated uncomfortably.

Marlowe smiled, remembering the scene he'd witnessed at Penshurst, the thin hand, laid flat, challenge naked in the small gesture.

"Vicious London gossip," Massey said, "that even you should be ashamed to be repeating."

The poet looked at him in some surprise. "You're hot in her defense."

"Maybe because I've had not to be what people have thought me, this past year," Massey answered sweetly. "I'm rather sensitive to gossip now, Kit."

Marlowe glanced down, flushing. That gentle voice still made womanhood seem exaggerated, a soft rebuke, yet utterly implacable. *And if I've lost him, if even* Penthesilea *isn't enough* . . . He pushed the thought away, unwilling to contemplate it, or to remember his demon, laughing softly now at the edge of hearing. There were too many other things to consider now—Sidney, for one, and the dangers of the tournament—to allow something so minor to gain undue importance. He looked back at his pipe, already focussing his mind on the immediate future. He had been granted this vision: God willing, a false one, but a vision nonetheless; it would be almost a sin not to act on that knowledge. He pushed himself to his feet, a ritual already shaping itself in his mind, and nodded to the company. "Gentlemen, I'll bid you farewell, at least until tomorrow."

Chapter Twenty-seven

*The Castle, or picture of policy, shewing forth
most lively, the face, body and partes of a common-
welth, the duety, quality, profession of a perfect and
absolute Souldier, the martiall feates encounters
and skirmishes lately done by our Enligh nation,
under the conduct of the most noble and famous
Gentleman M. Iohn Noris Generall of the Army
of the states in Friesland. The names of many
worthy and famous Gentlemen which live and have
this present yeare. 1580. ended theyr lives in that
Land most honorably.*
> *Title of a military handbook
> dedicated to M. Philip Sidney*

The day of the great tournament dawned cloudy, but
the clouds ran high and thin, with breaks that showed the
sky like tatters of blue silk, a lady's favor bright against
steel grey. The wind was light and steady: with luck, the
conditions would last the day—and the jousts were sched-
uled to begin at midday. By early morning, however, the
knights slated to joust were already at the tiltyard, inspect-
ing the field, their horses, and their opponents' arms.
Sidney was there with the rest of them, leather jerkin
laced hastily over his oldest doublet. Unlike the English
jousts, this was not the time to bring out his best clothes.

"No one will be riding into the sun today, if the weather holds," Greville said. "That's good."

Sidney nodded, his eyes roving again over the tiltyard, from lists to the barriers to the stands where king and court would sit. The tilt barriers each had angled ends, to help the rider, encumbered as he was with a twelve-foot lance, vision severely limited by his closed helmet, to control his horse, and keep it from running into the taller barriers that enclosed the yard and protected the common spectators—an English innovation, but no one had raised any objections to it.

Greville shook his head. "Truth, Philip, I don't know if I've done you any favor, by making sure Ruthven will joust," he began, but Sidney interrupted him.

"Fulke, you've said that a dozen times." He smiled to take any sting from the words. "Believe me when I say you've done me a very great favor—and his majesty, too, I hope."

"You are expecting—something?" Greville said.

Sidney smiled again. "I'm not yet reckoned a fool, am I? But now, I haven't seen any danger. I'm merely assuming it will be there, since the conditions are so favorable."

Greville shook his head against sudden fear. "If Bothwell enters the lists—you will be in grave danger."

"I don't think so," Sidney said. He was smiling still, his voice coolly assured, as distant from arrogance as could be. The knowing competence calmed Greville considerably. So that's what you're up to, he thought, drawing him into a trap. Lord God, that would be a coup as great as Axell—

"I'm just grateful there's to be no foot combat," he said aloud. "When I think this could have been a three-day affair . . ."

"James would never make that mistake," Sidney said. "This is very courageous of him—he could be a man, if he were permitted."

You may make a man of him, Greville thought, but Ruthven won't. He glanced involuntarily toward the favorite's black pavilion—a monstrous expense, walls and pennons all of silk brocade—but the young man was nowhere in sight. Instead, Seton rode up to them, grinning in boyish anticipation. He dismounted politely, allowing the older men plenty of time to admire his mount, and then invited them back to his pavilion for a cup of wine before they armed themselves. Sidney agreed cheerfully, and as they made their way across the yard the younger man spoke eagerly of the day's matches. As at Whitehall, each man would ride six courses, against six different opponents. This limited the number of men who could face Sidney, and there was some resentment that so untried—so youthful, the politic said—a knight as the Master of Ruthven should be one of them.

Seton grinned. "And so might I, didn't I think it would prove a lesson too long in coming to him. Faith, a part of me regrets not being one of those to face you—though there's honor enough for any man in riding at your side." He sighed, his exuberance momentarily dimmed. "I do wish there were to be a tourney as well as jousts, but I suppose present politics wouldn't allow it. Can you imagine it, Huntley's kin against Moray's friends—no mock combat there."

"No," Sidney agreed drily. "I imagine it would be rather like being in France again."

"Some day, perhaps, when his majesty's more secure," Seton said.

"Or should you travel to England, as well you might," Greville offered, but Seton's gaze barely shifted from Sidney. His adulation was becoming vaguely uncomfortable, Sidney thought. It should be reserved for—should be earned by—his king.

Resign yourself to the worship of men, whispered an inward voice. *It has won you the hearts and lives of the greatest men of Europe, Dee, Languet, Bruno, William of Nassau . . . and think how easy it would be to have this king among them. What great and good influence you would then possess . . .*

The devil tempts me to do good, Sidney thought. Truly, my lord Bothwell, a clumsy offering. I never sought nor desired the worship of men. The voice chuckled, fading, and Sidney winced. That, if not a lie, was not wholly the truth. What courtier did not want to influence his prince?

He had slowed without realizing it, and Greville turned to him, frowning. He directed a pointed glance at Sidney's crooked leg, but Sidney shook his head. "My mind was elsewhere for a moment, nothing more."

Greville snorted, but did not press the issue. Seton, ever the courtier, nodded to the piece of amber silk Sidney carried in his left hand, and said, "A favor, Sir Philip?"

"From Lady Sidney," the Englishman answered, his hand closing tight around the piece of cloth. It had been an unexpected grace, one he still half feared would vanish.

They had reached Seton's pavilion then, and pages brought wine in silver cups. The knights drank the thick, sweetened liquor without really tasting it, tension already settling in their bones, and the Englishmen excused themselves as soon as they decently could. Sidney made his way back to his own pavilion—it was actually some dead prince's campaign tent, conspicuously soldierly—and, to his surprise, found Marlowe waiting for him, an older, greying man who could only be the Pleiade wizard at his side. Sidney made himself smile, inwardly cursing the poet. Now was not the time to greet the Catholic wizard. . . . He put the thought aside, spoke as graciously as he could. "Master Fletcher, I believe?"

The greying man bowed silently.

"I beg your pardon for not having found the opportunity to thank you for agreeing to help me," Sidney went on. "I am aware, only too well, how difficult it must be for you to come to the aid of a Protestant defender of a Protestant king."

"The power abroad is a threat to us all, Sir Philip. In such perilous times for godly men, vain distinctions are best ignored," Fletcher answered.

"Nevertheless, I do thank you." The man had a good voice, Sidney thought. He would have made a fine preacher— He stopped that thought before it went too far, and turned to Marlowe. "I'll want to talk to you about Holland, Marlowe, but later. Tonight, perhaps, if the banquets don't go on too long."

"At your convenience, Sir Philip," Marlowe answered. "But, if I may—"

He sounded oddly hesitant, and Sidney looked at him curiously. The poet shrugged.

"I know this is to be a very plain joust. I know the

ceremonies implicit in the Whitehall jousts would be dangerous here. But it doesn't seem right that you should ride without . . . some ceremony, no matter how private. Sir Philip Sidney should never enter the lists without a suitable *impresa*." He held out his hand. In it was a circle of hardened wax, with some small tatters of cloth dangling from it. "I'm not an artist as Burbage is—but what I could do, I've done. May it serve."

Sidney took the sigil carefully. In the smooth central space, hard to see except when the light fell at just the proper angle, was carved the single word *Credo*. Sidney tilted his head sideways to look at Marlowe, a trifle warily, this time. Again the poet shrugged, but there was an impudent gleam in his eye. "It's a memorial of the '87 tournament, Sir Philip," he said, and would say no more.

Sidney smiled, and closed his hand over the wax seal. It was solid, but faintly warm to his touch, and on the underside he could feel graven symbols and words. Marlowe had worked long and well on this, he realized, and could not help but be moved by that care. "Thank you, Kit," he said, and wished he could say more.

"Good fortune today, Sir Philip," Marlowe answered, and slipped away, drawing the Pleiade wizard after him.

"But not 'God go with you'?" Fletcher asked quietly. "God alone knows what he'll face out there, if even half of what you told me is true."

Marlowe turned to him, mock innocence lighting his face. "Oh, no, Master Fletcher, you know I don't believe in God." The mask slipped then, and he gave a wry grin. "But I can't but believe in Sir Philip Sidney."

He walked quickly away, leaving the Catholic staring after him. Fletcher did his best to suppress a smile. I ought to disapprove of that remark, he thought, but I can't. From Marlowe, it's not even blasphemy. It's a sort of truth, and, God willing, this profane belief may be the first step to a more sacred one. He watched the poet stride away into the crowd, and could not recognize the pious scholar he had known at Rheims. And even that was a lie, he thought. He had guessed during the voyage from Holland—and a few not-quite-casual remarks since his arrival here had confirmed it—that Marlowe had been

Walsingham's spy at Rheims, had been at least indirectly responsible for arrests and deaths since then . . . but he could not seem to find it in himself to feel more than a profound sadness. The anger he should feel simply wasn't present; there was only regret, and a species of wry understanding. *There but for God's grace—and lack of opportunity—go I*, he thought, and smiled suddenly. *If nothing else, being understood will annoy Christopher more than my anger ever would—and this is a failure of charity which I'll find hard to regret. Oh, let him call Sidney his deity. He could do worse, and I for one would find it hard to stay sober-faced should that one belief lead him further than he intended. God send it does.*

Shortly before noon, the king and queen arrived at the tiltyards to great ceremony. The sky still held clouds, but there was no threat of rain, and the advantage of not riding into the sun still held. Above the stands rose flags bearing the colors and emblems of the knights who were to take part. Marlowe, glancing over them, noted with some amusement that Sidney still used the porcupine—an apt symbol of his relations with England's queen.

James himself appeared then, to enthusiastic cheers, and Marlowe sneered, wondering if the crowd had been seeded. It could merely have been the excitement of the day, a special occasion now capped by a royal appearance rare when the king went in fear of his life and almost never ventured into crowds. Indeed, James was a splendid sight in his elaborate white and gold suit, doublet and hose both slashed with peacock blue satin. He glittered even in the clouded light, gem-crusted aigrets, marked with "A" for Anne, nodding in his hat. The queen was also dressed in gold and white, the colors not the most flattering to her extreme fairness, but excitement touched her cheeks with color so that one could not call her precisely unattractive. Frances Sidney sat at Anne's left in the royal enclosure: a necessary honor, Marlowe thought, considering it was her husband who was providing the entertainment. Her rich azure gown was trimmed with silver braid and pearls, worn with a petticoat of dark amber brocade. She seemed a different person from the quietly dressed woman Marlowe had watched at Penshurst. There's no lover here, madam, to lure with fancy dress, he thought, and was startled by his own indignation. If Sidney can't keep his own house in order, it's none of my affair. He turned away, pushing through the crowd to join the Chamberlain's Men at the edge of the barriers.

In his pavilion, Sidney heard the commotion greeting the arrival of the king and queen, and turned to Greville with a quicksilver smile.

"Soon, now."

"Try not to enjoy yourself too much," Greville said, with an answering smile. "You know how the presbyters would frown." He sobered quickly, however. "Be careful today, Philip."

"And you. If anything looks amiss, cry off." Sidney did not need to name the opponent he had in mind, and Greville grimaced.

"Considering it was I convinced his majesty to let the boy joust—"

"Fulke."

"Very well. But there's no need to worry for me. They take no note of me—I'm no threat, not the way you are, and everyone knows it. It's you I'm worried for."

"I will take care," Sidney said, and pushed back the tent-flap. There were good crowds at the barriers, and the stands were filled with brilliantly dressed nobles; the Scottish knights, most of whom were already mounted, looked very fine indeed. James will be pleased, Sidney thought, and stepped out into the smaller yard.

Van der Droeghe brought his horse, and Sidney took its reins. It was an ugly thing, a large-boned, piebald gelding, but any man who knew horses would recognize the quality beneath the ugly coat. Sidney gentled it absently, feeling the tension hovering in the air, mingling with the smell of steel and men and horses. He cast a last glance over them all, then led the horse across to the mounting block. He pulled himself up into the saddle with practiced awkwardness, van der Droeghe supporting him against the weight of the armor, then reached down to take his helm from Nate. The boy stared up at him with huge eyes, half excited, half frightened, and Sidney winced at his own thoughtlessness. There had been a withdrawing in the boy ever since Northumberland had attempted to seize the book, but there had been no time to do anything about it. Now, however, was not the time to make the boy his attendant.

"Thank you, Nate," he said, and leaned down to touch the boy lightly on the bared head. "Now, go attend on Lady Sidney, and have no fear. This is a game, no more."

Nathanial nodded mutely, and took a step away. He bowed—he was growing quite courtly, Sidney thought, with a pleased smile—and scurried away, not quite running. Greville watched him go, and nodded.

"That was well done, Philip."

"A precaution, no more," Sidney answered. He lifted his hand to the amber scarf wrapped around his arm, bright as sunlight against the dull metal of his armor, then set the reins into his left hand. The manifer that protected hand and forearm—the most exposed parts of his body—rendered the limb almost immobile; he adjusted his hold with finicking care, knowing he would have no better chance later. Then the trumpets sounded, and Sidney hastily caught up his lance, lifting it to gather the other knights of his party in line behind his mount.

Marlowe, watching with the rest of the players from the barriers just beside the stands, leaned forward as the trumpets sounded. From the two ends of the tiltyard, the knights rode in, Sidney at the head of one group, the treasurer's son Lord Graham at the head of the other. That was a signal honor, certainly, but young Graham, though he would never match his father's statesmanship, had acquitted himself more than well on the field. The Earl of Mar was in that group as well, flamboyant in gold-starred armor, a white silk surcoat flaunting above it. His skirts and pennon were blazoned with a plumed A: more marks of royal favor, Marlowe thought. I wish to hell he weren't riding against Sidney. But then, Mar's crony Lord John Hamilton was part of Sidney's party, and the young Earl of Cassilis, too, another of James's personal friends, so perhaps it would not matter too much. There was some remarkably fine armor, he noted, with some surprise, especially when you consider there's no one here to match the armorers of Greenwich for providing fancies at short

notice. Gilt—and golden, and silver—chasing, bright silk
and brocade for the surcoats . . . Sidney's armor and dove-
grey surcoat looked very plain against that brilliance. A
sop to Scottish sensibilities? the poet wondered. Or simple
necessity? He could see that the extremely ornate armor
Sidney usually wore, with its learned allusions in every bit
of beaten gold, would find little favor in this presbyter-
plagued court, but surely such simplicity was sarcasm.
Greville's armor was less bald, Raleigh's almost elaborate
by comparison. . . . Then the last knight entered, and
Marlowe whispered a curse. The Master of Ruthven rode
in black armor, as ornately chased and figured as the black
velvet of his surcoat. The poet was forcibly reminded of all
the times Essex had adopted the same device. Lowin laid
a hand on his arm, spoke in the poet's ear.

"Does he wish to seem the villain of the piece?"

Marlowe shook his head. "It's a piece of his peacockery,"
he said, lip curling. "I've never seen him in anything but
black." Still he leaned forward slightly keeping his eyes on
Ruthven as the knights presented themselves to James and
tendered him their honor. There was nothing out of the
ordinary about the boy—in fact, he seemed more demure
than usual, more aware of his humble station. And that,
Marlowe thought, makes me exceedingly wary. Still, there
was nothing out of the ordinary as the parties split again,
and rode to opposite ends of the lists.

By the luck of the draw, Mar and Cassilis rode first. It
was a nicely managed bout, Cassilis acquitting himself well
despite his inexperience, but most of the spectators cheered
only listlessly, their eyes on the campaign tent that served
as Sidney's pavilion. They wanted to see the Englishman
joust. Don't disappoint them, man, Marlowe thought. Your
audience is primed and ready; all you have to do is take it.

There was a cheer from the far end of the field then,
and an instant later Sidney rode onto the field. He was
alone, without the pageant that would normally accompany him to the lists. Marlowe's eyes narrowed. There was
something odd about the armor. He had dismissed it as
dull and necessary when Sidney first appeared, but
now . . . There was something different. The steel was
still daringly plain, but somehow it had changed. Another

back-and-breast, and a quick change while the others jousted? Such a deception did not seem to be part of Sidney's nature. Then Marlowe smiled slowly. It was the same armor, of that there could no longer be any doubt, but no wash of gold or silver could lend base steel such brilliance. It should be painful to look upon, he thought, it's too bright, but then he realized that the brilliance, too, was an illusion. The light he perceived came from within, from some virtue in the steel—or with which Sidney had imbued the material. At his side, Lowin pounded the rail with his fists and cheered with the rest of the crowd. Philips stared open-mouthed, and then swore.

"I don't understand. What has he done to it?" the boy Nicholas, who had somehow edged himself into the front row with his betters, demanded.

Burbage was shaking his head. "It's beautiful, the man should have worked for the theaters."

"But what—" The apprentice broke off as Burbage's heavy hand descended on his shoulder.

"I don't know," the player said. "What is it, Kit?"

"I'm not sure," Marlowe said. "He's played up some quality of the steel itself, I think. It takes in light and only seems to give it off." *It's—beautiful*, he added silently, words failing, struggling to discover an image to preserve what he was seeing, the glossy grey suddenly more overpowering yet kinder than the veiled sun. No pageant armor, tinted and figured, could compete with that brilliance; it cast Ruthven's black glamour into its own shade.

James stared at Sidney with something perilously close to adoration. "What am I seeing?" he murmured. Anne shook her head, wondering, and did not answer. Frances said nothing, her eyes, fixed almost greedily on her husband, filling with tears. She shook them away almost angrily and settled herself to watch. Philip had never looked grander, a thought to inspire her with pride—but then, the Accession Days had never been like this. She shivered then, and breathed a silent prayer. *From all evil and mischief; from sin; from the crafts and assaults of the devil, good Lord, deliver him.*

Again by the vagaries of the draw, Mar would be Sidney's first opponent. The Englishman guided his horse into the end of the lists and settled his lance under his arm. The trumpet sounded, and he drove hard at Mar, seeing in the same instant Mar's lance-point drop and his spurs go home. Sidney lowered his own lance, crouching in the saddle. The lance's rebated end caught the Scot firmly in the shoulder; Mar's blow struck, then glanced up and off. Sidney's lance shattered, and Mar rocked backward, his own unbroken weapon swaying wildly out of control. He kept his seat, however, and the two parted to the cheers of the crowd.

"Mar didn't win much by that encounter," Nick announced. "Points only, and broken lances count for a lot more."

Burbage cuffed him for being self-important, but not too hard: one did not see Sir Philip Sidney joust every day. Marlowe allowed himself a sigh of relief. At least Mar had not been unseated; there was no need to antagonize Cecil's henchman any further.

Raleigh rode next, against Lord Linton, but the crowd's attention was not with them. Sidney would have the next course, against Rollo of Duncruib, and then he would face Lord Graham, the acknowledged Scottish master. Sidney grinned behind his helmet, well aware of their interest. He met Rollo's blow squarely, rode it and delivered a blow of his own that cleanly unseated the stocky man. Rollo picked himself up, shaking his head, but was generous enough to lift a hand in grudging salute before limping off the field. Sidney accepted a fresh lance from van der Droeghe, and turned to face his next opponent. John Graham was taller and stronger than he, but, for all he was accounted the best in Scotland, lacked experience. Sidney smiled again behind the helmet, automatically judging the weight of the twelve-foot lance. Let me show you how it's done, he thought, and was no longer aware of his own arrogance.

The trumpets sounded. Sidney spurred forward, his attention focussing on the steel-clad figure that rushed to meet him. His point shocked home; in the same instant, he felt Graham's point strike and slide and shatter. No clean hit, my lord, he exulted, and saw the younger man fall. The crowd roared. Graham might be acknowledged their best, but he was not universally loved—and Sidney's had been a master-stroke. It was easy to forget he was a foreigner, and a wizard, when he could handle horse and lance like that. So there was more to this than pleasing the king and his own private passion for the tilts, Marlowe thought. A calculated risk to win some support among James's people—and I think I like him the better for it.

Ruthven was Sidney's final opponent. His black armor was dusty now—he had been unhorsed thrice so far, and done no better than to break his lances—and there were a few catcalls from the crowd. Most of them had eyes only for Sidney, however, drunk on the romance of the occasion. Marlowe shivered, remembering his vision of the night before, but could not restrain a feeling of confident anticipation. It was like being on the rack—he was just frightened enough to fear courting disaster by envisioning it too clearly, yet he did not dare be part of a murderous conspiracy of complacency. Careful, careful, he thought, as much to himself as to Sidney. Ruthven was no soldier, and no jouster either, but he was feral, dangerous. Marlowe had done what little he could by devising the amulet Sidney bore beneath his armor; all he could do now was wait and watch.

The heralds cried the names and titles then—*Sir Philip Sidney, knight; Alexander Master of Ruthven*—and Sidney rode out into the tiltyard. He reined in slightly before he reached the end of the lists, and paused with one hand on the lifted visor, smiling beneath the steel. Ruthven made a fine show, horse and man tossing identical black plumes, but no armor, no finery, could hide the boy's lack of skill. I'll grant you bravery, Sidney thought, facing me today, but I'll not hold my hand. His left hand tightened in the manifer, and there was within him a feeling of savage joy as would normally have frightened him into moderation—but not today. Ruthven challenged him on ground on which he was undisputed master. He cherished these exercises and what they represented, the chivalry that still lived, and honor still existent in men. Here was the game in its older form, more immediate, death or dishonor still real possibilities—far more so than in pageant-bound Whitehall—and the recognition of this touched him like a sensual pleasure. Not since Holland, this strange joy.

He edged his horse into the lane and accepted his lance. At the other end, Ruthven's actions mirrored his own. The crowd grew very still, all eyes intent on this, the unacknowledged climax of the day. Ruthven's grip on his lance was tight, but not entirely certain, Sidney saw, and smiled again behind his beaver. The trumpet sounded, and both men spurred forward. And then there was an unholy radiance about Ruthven, surrounding him and his armor, the air wavering around him. Marlowe bit back a curse, seeing his vision sprung to nightmare life: a knight of air, and there was power in that casque of air, power to kill where it touched. The rest of the crowd saw it, too, and cried out in protest. In the royal box, James was on his feet, shouting to the heralds, crying for them to stop the match, but it was too late. Too late for both of you, Marlowe thought, greyly. Fool boy, what did Bothwell offer you, to be his pawn? You're as doomed as he, Icarus flying into the lightning, or Semele in truth, consumed by a power that had always before protected and caressed . . . Oh, God, Sir Philip, don't you see?

In her place beside the queen, Frances Sidney sat rigidly still, only her eyes moving, too frightened now even to pray. There was only a vague blasphemy in her mind: whatever happened now was in Philip's hands, not God's; God watched as intently as the rest of them, and could do nothing else. Raleigh burst half unarmed from his pavilion at the crowd's first cry, to stand in horrified understanding at the edge of the yard. Dear God, was anything ever written to divert this, in any almagest? he wondered, and wiped the thought away in prayer. Greville saw the change in Ruthven's armor, saw, too, the fractional shift of Sidney's hand, and read both danger and response from the tiny movement. The neatest blow of all, lance-tip against lance-tip, coronel to coronel—the most difficult in the canon, and the one that showed most clearly contempt for one's opponenent . . . But is that wise, here, and now, with a third man in the lists? Greville wondered blindly, almost afraid to see. *Sweet Jesus, he rides in Your cause, protect him now.*

Sidney saw the first flicker of the spell, and smiled again, recognizing in a heartbeat the nature of that uncanny armor. It seethed like compact fire, awaiting only their clash to be released, to consume them both. Sidney was to be both fuse and trigger. Or so you think, Sidney whispered fiercely, silently, and shifted his grip on the lance. Bothwell had made certain assumptions, both as to Sidney's pride and his power, and Sidney laughed behind his visor. He'd not taken into account just how great Sidney's pride could be.

The two horses bore down on each other, Ruthven's black mare sweating, shying at the demonic forces surrounding it, Sidney's piebald responding willingly to its master's demands. Sidney adjusted his lance again, settling his target. No time, now, for everything he had spent his youth learning; it was only the base for what he had built since. There were times a man had to act, and quickly, or lose all, and this was the greatest of those. And he could, only because of what he had taught himself. For a brief instant, he felt an obscure pity for Ruthven, less than a pawn, a mere tool, a mechanism through which Bothwell worked, but then that was drowned in a new sense of triumph. He took a breath and drew on the power that shone from his own armor, wrapped his thoughts and will around that power. There was Marlowe's sigil, too; he seized on it as well, and drew it into his new-made spell.

The lances met, tip to tip as Sidney had intended, with a crack like lightning striking. The twinned spells dissipated in the same instant, Bothwell's attack turned aside by Sidney's countermagic. Ruthven lurched backward in his saddle, only the high back keeping him in place, his shattered lance smoking in his hand. Sidney did not turn, but drove the stub of his own lance into the soft ground beside the lists. The crowd shouted, in relief, in fear, even in utter denial of what they had just seen, and the other knights and heralds came running into the yard. Sidney pulled his piebald to a stop—the gelding was sweating now, ears laid back in fear—and lifted his visor, grinning now at the men who rushed to surround him.

At the far end of the lists, the Master of Ruthven wrestled his horse around, sawing ruthlessly at its mouth until he had the animal firmly under control again, and threw away the broken lance. The Englishman was a witch indeed—nothing should have withstood that attack, or so he had been promised. . . . Damn all witches, he thought, and drew the sword he should not have been wearing. With a harsh cry, he set spurs to his horse, and charged down the tilt again.

"Philip!" That was Raleigh, first to see the movement, and others took up the disordered cry. Sidney wheeled, the gelding dancing under him, and saw Ruthven bearing down on him. Someone thrust a sword to him; he snatched at it even as the others scattered before the Scot's mad assault. There was no time for subtlety, or even technique. Sidney took Ruthven's blow on his heavy shoulder-piece, the horses jostling against each other, and smashed the borrowed sword hilt-first into the plates protecting the back of Ruthven's neck. The armor kept him from doing any serious damage, but Ruthven sagged in his saddle, briefly stunned, and Cassilis, leaping forward, pulled him down. One of the other Scots caught the black mare. Sidney gentled his own horse, whispering meaningless words in its laid-back ears. His shoulder ached where Ruthven had hit him, but he put that pain aside. The master lay where he had fallen, held as much by the grim stares of his fellows as by the weight of his armor. One mystery solved, Sidney thought grimly, and glanced in spite of himself toward the stands. But I can't think it will be a welcome solution.

He dismounted slowly, van der Droeghe pushing through the crowd to take the horse's bridle. Sidney lifted off his helmet, and saw with some surprise that his hands were trembling. Frances was suddenly at his side, the bows that held her overskirt open across the brocade petticoat torn loose and dangling.

"Philip—?"

Sidney forced a smile. "I'm all right, love," he said, and wondered afterward where he had found that word. His eyes strayed then to Ruthven, who had pushed himself to his knees and was slowly unlacing his own helmet. The Scots who had been of Sidney's party were watching him closely, and Cassilis had gone so far as to draw the thin dagger he had carried—also against custom—at his waist. Behind him, Raleigh sneered openly at the favorite's discomfiture, but he leaned on drawn sword nonetheless. Sidney's smile soured. "Fulke," he said, and instantly Greville was at his side. "See to Frances, please."

"Of course," Greville answered, and took the woman's shoulders, edging her gently away from the downed man. For a moment she resisted, but then allowed him to draw her a little aside.

"Well, my lord," Sidney began, still staring down at Ruthven, and heard a terrible weariness in his own voice.

"Well, indeed." That was the king, the crowd parting before him. "Or very ill." He stood straddle-legged, hands on hips, glaring at his erstwhile favorite, his face white with fury. Ruthven looked up at him, great eyes pleading, then bowed his head. "You've broken faith with your fellows, with your king, and with God, by this day's work. How dare you, whom I so favored, so betray my trust, ally with my enemies, attack my greatest friend? By God, I wish I'd never seen you—and I intend to see you have no chance to harm any other ever again." He lifted his hand, beckoning to the soldiers who'd followed him from the stands. "Take him to the Tollbooth—and I don't care where you lodge him."

"Sire!" Ruthven cried, and Sidney bit back sudden anger. Dear Lord, could James do nothing moderately?

"Your Majesty," he said, "a moment—a favor, please, if you'd grant it for me."

James turned instantly to him. "For you, Sir Philip, anything—but nothing for this traitor."

"There are some questions I would like to hear him answer," Sidney said. "With your Majesty's permission, of course."

"He will answer anything you ask," James answered. "And if not now, there are those will make him speak."

"I trust that won't be necessary, your Majesty," Sidney said. He looked down at Ruthven again. "My lord—"

"Sire, Sir Philip, I beg you, mercy." There were tears in Ruthven's eyes, and his voice and body shook as though with a palsy. His face seemed somehow to have softened, like bruised fruit, and for an instant Sidney thought he glimpsed something beneath the pallor, something so homely and plain that a part of him wanted to weep. Then the vision was gone, and Ruthven spoke again, weeping openly. "I confess my treason, sire, I was mad to do it. But it was love of you that prompted me—"

"I'll hear no more," James growled, but did not turn away.

"Sire, I beg you," Ruthven cried, frantically. "I feared I'd lose you, had already lost you, Sire, and then the demon came to me. He said it was his doing—" He jerked his head at Sidney, who listened silently, his face impassive. "—that if I could be rid of him, I would have your love again. He said I need but wear his token, speak one word, and he would do the rest. And, God forgive me, I believed him." He lowered his head again, and groped for something beneath his shirt. After a moment, he drew out a leaden seal that dangled from a black ribbon. Sidney held out his hand, and the young man gave it to him.

"And now I've failed him, too. God, God, he'll kill me now."

"If I don't do it first," James snapped.

Sidney ignored them both, studying the medal. It seemed deceptively simple, to provide so marvellous an effect, but it had probably served primarily to call and then to channel the demonic forces. He recognized some of the signs— the sign of the prince of the powers of the air, and the symbol called the mark of Cain—and guessed that Marlowe would know more. Thomas Watson's tutelage was likely to be more thorough in such matters than was Dee's, he thought, and glanced around. The poet was nowhere in sight.

"With your permission, your Majesty," he said aloud, "I'd like to keep this."

James shuddered visibly, but nodded. "I trust you, Sir Philip."

"Sir Philip!" Ruthven cried. "I beg you—please, will you protect me?"

Why should I? Sidney thought, with sudden anger. You've just done your level best to kill me, allied yourself with demons when you knew you couldn't touch me yourself— He put the anger aside with an effort. Charity,

Philip, he told himself. That the boy was tempted I can well believe, and that he fell is perfectly obvious. My God, I can't abandon anyone to Bothwell's mercies, no matter how much I might like to do it. He looked again at James, and saw anger already warring with a shamefaced pity in the king's eyes. "Your Majesty," he said aloud, "for all his crimes, I can't think it's right to throw him back to Bothwell. Rather than sending him back to Edinburgh, can't he be confined within the palace, where both he—and your Majesty—can be protected?"

James hesitated, the anger still evident in his face, and Sidney braced himself to remind the king of his earlier promise. Then, slowly, James relaxed a little. "If you think it's best, Sir Philip, God knows you're the master in such matters. It shall be as you wish." He gestured sharply to the soldiers. "Take him back to the palace and hold him in his rooms. No one is to see him or to speak to him without my personal warrant. Assign one of your men to see to his personal needs, captain—but no one is to see him without my permission."

The soldier bowed smartly. "As your Majesty commands." At his nod, two of his men hauled the Master of Ruthven to his feet and hustled him away, the rest of the troop closing in around the prisoner. James turned again to Sidney.

"Once again, Sir Philip, I'm in your debt. I trust, someday, you'll let me reward you as you've deserved."

With that, the king turned and walked away, the others bowing deeply as he passed. "Let's hope he doesn't come to regret that favor," a familiar voice murmured at Sidney's side.

"Marlowe." Sidney allowed himself a wry smile. "What do you think?"

"Of what?" The poet gave him a rather sour glance. "Your performance, sir, was masterful."

"Of Ruthven's tale," Sidney said, with some impatience. "Good God, you know this sort of power better than I. Is it likely to be true, and can he be trusted if it is?"

Only 'til Bothwell whistles or the devil smiles, Marlowe thought blackly. "The tale sounds plausible enough," he said aloud. "As for the other—am I God, to read men's hearts? Until he does turn again to his black master, he might at least be useful."

"You're a comfort," Sidney murmured, and looked at the knights still surrounding him. "Gentlemen, with your permission—I would like to unarm."

There was a general outcry at that, half apology, half offers of assistance, and Sidney allowed himself to be drawn off toward his pavilion. Frances followed, and Greville did not try to stop her. Perhaps half the company remained behind, and Marlowe stayed with them, the fear-sweat still cold beneath his doublet. Christ, he thought, that was a near thing.

"So that's Sidney," a voice said at his side, and Marlowe started. He had almost forgotten Fletcher's presence, certainly had not expected to meet him here on the field. He turned to the man, and saw the look of frank admiration in his eyes.

"Oh, Christ's balls," he muttered, and said aloud and sweetly, "Why, it's Saint Michael, sir, haven't you seen an archangel before?"

Fletcher smiled. "It must be maddening, dealing with such imperfection from day to day. I commend you for your patience and your charity, Master Marlowe."

"I'm glad someone recognizes it," Marlowe answered, bitterly aware of the weakness of the retort, but Fletcher had already vanished, following the crowd that still headed toward Sidney's tent.

"You really were worried, Kit," Raleigh said, and laughed. "You're never so prickly as when you've been sweating."

"He's the most reliable and least demanding patron I've ever had," Marlowe began, and Raleigh grinned.

"Certainly the most patient."

"And I don't want to lose that," the poet continued, as though the other had not spoken.

"I see," Raleigh answered. "Kind Kit, as ever. What do you make of all this?"

Marlowe paused, considering. "I'm grateful he came through it in one piece. And, now that it's happened, I can't say I'm surprised at Ruthven. We should've watched him more closely." There was such a note of anger in his voice—an inward-pointed anger—that Raleigh looked

sharply at him. The poet shrugged. "Well, it's too late now
for that. Shall we within?"

By evening, Sidney's bruises were stiffening, and he
was glad to accept the ministrations of Ewen Pette, the
king's personal physician. The man murmured learnedly
over the darkening bruises, and prescribed a cordial—
prepared with his own hands—to be drunk before the
Englishman retired for the night. Frances intercepted it
deftly, proffering her own thanks, and set it carefully
aside.

"It smells of poppies," she said, after the doctor had
left. "Not a bad thought, I suspect. I doubt you'd get
much sleep, else."

Sidney managed a wincing smile. "I fear you're right.
But I've some business first. I know Fulke's without. I
want Marlowe and the Pleiadian, too."

"Also waiting," Frances answered, and went to the door
that led to the antechamber. She opened it, spoke quietly
to Nate, and a moment later the three men Sidney had
named filed into the bedchamber. "Shall I leave you,
Philip?"

Sidney hesitated, then smiled almost shyly. "Only if you
wish. But I'd rather you stayed."

"As my lord wishes," Frances answered demurely, and
settled herself on a stool just outside the circle of candlelight. Sidney glanced up sharply, afraid he'd once again
offended without intent, but there was something in her
smile that reassured him.

"First things first, I suppose," he said aloud. "Marlowe,
what happened in Holland? Van der Droeghe said you
were attacked, and mentioned Robin Poley?"

"We were attacked, yes," Marlowe answered. "Not by
Robin—at least, he didn't show up until the fight was well
begun, and then he came to our rescue." He paused, and
added in a bleakly thoughtful voice, "He killed one of our
attackers. A warning, I think."

"And so?" Sidney prompted, when the poet showed no
signs of continuing.

Marlowe shook himself. "Then the watch came, of course,
after the danger was past, and carried us all off to Sir

Robert. Who was most delighted to see Robin. He insisted on Poley's staying there as his guest for some unspecified time—he was still there when we left, and may be there still, for all I know." He glanced quizzically at Sidney, wondering just what Poley had done to him.

Sidney leaned back against his pillows and sipped his wine, trying to hide his pleasure. "Oh, my excellent brother. Cecil will not be pleased—and I'm not sure his displeasure won't be directed at Poley, this time."

Marlowe hesitated, but his curiosity finally overcame him. "You have a grievance against Robin, sir?"

"An old one," Sidney answered, and smiled. "In no way related to Cecil, I might add—for once. Do you remember Babington's plot?"

Marlowe nodded. It had been a nine-days' wonder nine years ago, the final plot to put Mary Stuart on the throne of England—the bungled plot that had finally persuaded Elizabeth to have her cousin executed. "Robin was spying for Walsingham then," he said aloud. "On the conspirators, I'd thought."

Sidney laughed. "Oh, no, my loyalty wasn't doubted even by my father-in-law. It was the conspirators who set Poley to spy on me. I dislike being spied upon—I don't think I'm being unreasonable."

I'm relieved you didn't say you weren't fond of spies, Marlowe thought. *And how typical of Poley.*

"Small wonder Sir Philip has little love for Catholics," Fletcher murmured. "A blessed end it would be if there could be an end to this constant double-dealing." He did not look at Marlowe, who kept his face rigidly neutral, not even the hint of a blush rising to betray him. *I did what I had to do to get what was wanted,* the poet thought. *Any who thinks he could do better in my shoes is a liar or a fool. Or Sir Philip Sidney.*

Sidney was regarding the Catholic with lifted eyebrows. "Indeed, there's fault on both sides," he began, and bit back the rest of the argument. This was not the time for theological debate—and certainly the wrong time to antagonize Fletcher. He reached instead for the seal he had taken from Ruthven. "On more important matters—what do you make of this, Marlowe?"

The poet took the lead token warily, running his thumb over the incised surface. "A nasty piece of work," he said, after a moment. "Rather like its bearer." He shook his head, and shrugged. "I see nothing I didn't know already: Bothwell commands major demons to his service. Burn it, I say."

He handed it to Fletcher, who held it in the circle of candlelight. The scholar crossed himself as he read the symbols. "A man of power, this Bothwell," he said at last. "And damned beyond redemption. I agree, it should—it must—be burned, before it contaminates godly men."

"May I see it?" Greville asked. Fletcher handed it to him, and the older man contemplated it warily. After a moment, he shook his head, and set it back onto the table. "I thought I would be able to feel its origins," he said, almost sheepishly.

"I suppose if it were apparent, it would have frightened his horse," Fletcher said, prosaically. "For God's sake, put it on the fire."

Sidney nodded. "Yes, do that, Kit."

Marlowe took the medal, and went to kneel beside the hearth. It was one of the few times Sidney had addressed him by his Christian name, and the realization made him feel absurdly warm. He shook the emotions away, and began methodically to feed the fire, until a core of flame glowed almost white-hot. He dropped the medal directly into that core, wincing at the heat on face and hands. The black ribbon exploded into a puff of flame and ash that whipped away up the chimney. For a moment the seal remained untouched, the flames curving in strange colors around it, and then, quite suddenly, it wavered and wilted like a flower, the shape shifting in the fierce heat. Marlowe nodded to himself, and stopped feeding the flames. The carved symbols were certainly gone, purged by the fire, the demonic power burned out of it. He sat back on his heels to watch the others.

Sidney smiled at him, then turned to Fletcher. "You've had a more—immediate—impression of what we're fighting than I had wished to give you. But you see why I've sought your help."

Fletcher nodded slowly. "I do indeed. A most difficult

problem: yet I do feel, if what I've seen today was an indication of your abilities, that I will have very little to show you."

"You should have been a courtier, Master Fletcher," Sidney said.

Fletcher smiled. "But, Sir Philip, that is precisely what I am—or what I was, at any rate."

"I confess I hadn't thought of the Pleiade as an academy of courtiers," Sidney murmured. "My mistake, I see."

Fletcher shrugged, an almost Gallic gesture. "And what else could it be? Our ceremonies—our extravagances, if you must—rely on terms, verses that personify great forces for and through our prince. They are necessarily highly flattering: after all, who more fit to act as the personification of any virtue than the reigning monarch?"

"It didn't help Henri III particularly," Marlowe muttered, and was ignored.

"No, I see entirely now," Sidney said, "and I think that will only make you of more help to me. The king is wary of magic—understandably enough, since it threatens him daily."

"As it also preserves life and soul daily," Greville interjected, "one could wish he were more gracious."

"Fulke," Sidney said, with a glance of warning.

Greville sighed. "I beg your pardon."

Fletcher hid a rueful smile. God must have a sense of humor, he thought, to send me here to serve this man in what is clearly a righteous cause. Though the jest isn't on me alone: Marlowe the so-called atheist, burdened with one of England's most godly men for a patron, the witch-wearied king of Scots forced to depend on that same great wizard . . . He realized Sidney was speaking again, and dragged his attention back to the matters at hand.

"I thought I'd made the palace safe," Sidney was saying. "Obviously, I was mistaken, and it will take a much different—much larger, perhaps? I don't know—ritual to make it so." He sighed. "The whole thing begins to resemble a mad tennis match, with myself gaining the first point, then the Catholic faction—I beg your pardon, Master Fletcher. My only consolation is that the Dominies seem utterly incapable of doing anything useful."

"Charity, Sir Philip, I daresay they can pray," Fletcher said.

Marlowe laughed aloud. "You'd better not say that to his majesty, Hal. Melville—one of his more recalcitrant presbyters—did. He made the severe miscalculation of telling his majesty that he should endure like Job, and look to his soul. Well, his majesty was not feeling Job-like that day. He thrust Melville into one of the most hell-ridden places in the palace and bade him see how he liked it." He grinned, savoring the memory. "It was a miraculous conversion."

There was a moment of silence, then Fletcher shook himself away from unChristian contemplation of the preacher's downfall. "I will begin thinking about some appropriate ceremony, Sir Philip, as soon as I may."

"Thank you," Sidney murmured, and Frances rose to her feet.

"It's time you were abed, sir," she said, and darted a quick glance at Greville. "Even Fulke thinks it."

"That's true enough," Greville agreed.

Sidney smiled, but made no protest as Frances brought him the doctor's cordial. "I hope you'll excuse me, gentlemen?"

"Of course, Sir Philip," Marlowe said, and pushed himself to his feet. There were new lines on Sidney's face, he thought—or, rather, the day's labors had exhausted him so that the marks of his age showed clearly. Ruthven is more trouble than he can possibly be worth, the poet thought, more moved than he liked by the sight. I hope I'm there when James finally realizes it—because if any of you think this revulsion will last, you don't knows these affairs at all.

"I hope I may speak with you again tomorrow, Sir Philip," Fletcher said. "With God's help, I may have something prepared by then. His majesty is, you say, wary of magic?"

"Extremely." Sidney smiled. "I think even I frighten him."

"That is not as wonderful as you might think," Greville said.

Fletcher continued as though the older man had not

spoken, "So any ceremony I use would do well to seem as unlike magic and as much like spectacle as possible."

"Master Fletcher, if you can accomplish that, I will be deeply in your debt," Sidney answered.

"Dangerous, Hal," Marlowe said. "The Sidneys are notoriously impecunious."

Fletcher ignored him as well. "I think I can do what you wish," he said. "I wish you and Lady Sidney good night and an undisturbed rest." He bowed deeply, and was gone.

"Wait, Kit," Sidney said. "I still owe you thanks for this." He nodded to the sigil Marlowe had made for him, lying on the table beside the candlestick.

The poet blinked at it for a moment before recognizing his handiwork. The wax had faded from its normal, rather dirty tallow color to an ashy grey, and he could tell at a glance that all the virtue was gone from it. He caught his breath at the thought of the power Sidney had used, to do such a thing, then put the thought aside. "It would be a small matter to make you another, sir, since this one seems to have served its purpose."

"I'd like to keep this, if I may," Sidney answered.

I'm drowning, Marlowe thought. *I'm growing as weak as the rest of them.* "Of course, sir," he said, and kept his voice utterly without expression. "I bid you good night then, you and your lady." He bowed, not extravagantly, and slipped from the bedchamber, closing the door firmly behind him.

Greville shook his head. "Puppy," he said, and bowed to Frances. "I'll bid you both good night myself. It was a lovely day, Philip." With that, he too was gone, leaving husband and wife staring at each other.

"Fulke has a gift for the well-chosen word," Frances said, after a moment.

Sidney grunted. "I feel more like a horse-coper," he said, "he reminds me of a colt I once owned. And why in God's name should I care whether I win him or no?"

Frances ignored the question: he knew the answer as well as she. "Give him time."

"I have given him time," Sidney said irritably, and

sighed. "He's more changeable than any woman I ever met, and less certain of temper."

Frances smiled, and reached for the doctor's cordial, then poured it out into one of the crystal cups. "Thank you for the compliment."

Sidney went on as if he hadn't heard. "Maybe if I could free him from Cecil—though I thought that was finished when your father died, and then again two years ago."

"Robert Cecil doesn't let go of a useful tool that easily," Frances answered, and brought the cup to the bedside. "Solve that when we're home; you've more pressing worries just now."

Sidney grimaced, but accepted the cup and drank off the honey-sweet contents. "I know. So tomorrow we'll see what Master Fletcher can do—I just pray I've not made a mistake seeking his aid.

PART FIVE

PART FIVE

Chapter Twenty-eight

*And if we cannot deny but that God hath given
virtues to springs and fountains, to cold earth,
to plants and stones, minerals, and to the excre-
mental parts of the basest living creatures, why
should we rob the beautiful stars of their working
powers?*
     Sir Walter Raleigh, *History of the World*

"I think it is not unreasonable, your Majesty, to say that
Sir Philip has overstepped his commission." Cecil spoke in
measured tones, wary of provoking another outburst from
the queen, but equally determined to make his point.

Elizabeth lifted a painted eyebrow, knowing the man's
mood, and set aside the letter she had been reading.
Outside the long windows, closed now against the distinctly chilly wind, a pair of pages, briefly free from their
duties, chased a ball across the frost-browned lawn. "Sir
Philip is my good and faithful servant, Sir Robert," the
queen said. "I expect my embassies to overstep their
commissions from time to time—as you well know. It
demonstrates a pleasing initiative."

"I fear this initiative can only be distressing to your
Majesty," Cecil retorted. "To bring a Catholic wizard for
his ally—"

"Sir Robert, I know not whether this be malice or madness," Elizabeth interrupted. She held up the paper he had given her. "The source of this latest titillation?"

"As your Majesty may see, the letter is from King James's ambassador here," Cecil answered. "I need not say how distressed his lordship is by this—at best an inconsistent action. Can a Catholic be expected to help defend a Protestant king? And even if the help is genuinely given, what will be its price?"

"Philip is neither child nor fool, no man less so," Elizabeth said. "Evidently he believes this man will be of service, to him and to James."

"The man is an English Catholic, your Majesty." Cecil leaned back a little on his stool, as though he had added a new dimension to the argument.

As perhaps he had, Elizabeth thought. She slammed her hand down onto the arm of her chair, buying time. "By the mass, Sir Robert, if you accuse Sidney of anything, pray do it in any but that unctuous tone of voice. You'd not regret his fall, would you? I've kept him on too long a lead to suit you, he galls you with his greatness, does he? You are brilliant, sir, no one could deny that, least of all I who have been best served by your talents—but it is a regulated brilliance. It does not shine. It glimmers and gutters, finding phantoms and shadows in corners and making monsters out of human dust. It is not jealousy you feel, I'll grant you that, but it is near kin, and I will not have it."

She paused to draw breath, judging her moment. Cecil was flushed, but he made no overt protest. The queen smiled, spreading her hands across her skirt in a gesture of now unconscious vanity. "Come, Robert, think. No one has a greater disdain—or reason for that distaste, distrust—than Philip has for the Catholics. They are my enemies, they have been his enemies for that cause, and, more than that, they nearly finished him in Holland."

"Yet he has been suspected before this."

Elizabeth laughed harshly. "Of what? I have had cause to curse him, now and again, and wish him at the devil—but *suspect* my Philip? I say again, of what?"

"Sir Philip has many ardent admirers, your Majesty,

William of Nassau and all of Poland among them," Cecil said dryly.

"And it's precisely that ardent admiration that will always keep Philip true," Elizabeth retorted. "He may not be everything that is claimed for him—but he knows by now that he had better try to be. He will remain true to me so long as he remains true to himself—my perfect knight, consecrated to England and to myself at the time when we needed such a one as he." She smiled again, this time with gloriously patent insincerity. "But I thank you, Sir Robert, for your concern. Believe me when I say I do not ignore what you have told me—merely I choose to regard it in a different light."

Cecil bowed and accepted the papers she held out to him. "I will rejoice to be proven wrong, your Majesty."

"Then we shall rejoice together when Sir Philip returns," Elizabeth answered, but she was not displeased with the oblique apology.

Cecil bowed himself out of the queen's presence, wry rather than surprised, certainly not angry. Sidney was a chancy man, too popular with too wide a swath of humanity; it was not to be expected that the queen would be immune to his appeal. He shook his head as he made his way toward his waiting barge, vaguely impatient with himself. It was the matter of Poland that rankled: it was twenty years ago, he thought, and still I can't bring myself to trust a man who can so easily refuse a kingdom. Still . . . The selfless tend to become martyrs, sooner or later. Sooner—at Zutphen, say—might have been more comfortable for England. Selfless as Sidney was, he would risk his life to see James freed from this threat—and by doing so, place all England at risk when the man became king. But it was done. He shook his head as he was handed into his boat, settling himself against the embroidered cushions. He had made his protest, and it had been rejected; the rest was up to Sidney.

Elizabeth sat quite still for a long while after Cecil had left her, ignoring the smothered noises as her ladies crept back into the room. The meeting with Cecil had unsettled her more than she cared to admit: to be Catholic was to be, by very definition, foreign, unEnglish; by papal bull, to be Catholic was also to deny her right to the throne. To ally with a Catholic— She put the thought aside, and turned toward the window. The autumn sunlight filled the room—unflattering to an old face that was, she felt in her darker moments, taking on the distinctly jaded grin of an animate skull. She frowned then, and turned her face away, toward the north. Why a Catholic, Philip? she demanded silently. Aren't there wizards enough among us? Why an English Catholic? There was no answer, except to trust her champion's judgement. And that I will do, she vowed, for the promise I made his wife, and, more than that, for my own honor.

Chapter Twenty-nine

The profession as well of the common, as private Souldier is honorable, which resteth in the maintenance to death, of a good and rightful cause: the condition no less painful than full of peril, the quality clean, diligent, dutiful, delighting rather in brave furniture and glittering armor, than in dainty diet, womanlike wantoness, and vain pleasure.

William Blandy, The Castle

The morning after the tourney, Sidney felt less like a triumphant knight at the lists than a forty-one-year-old man who ought to have more sense than still to be engaging in a young man's sport. His whole torso ached, less from the blow to his shoulder than from the unrelenting tension. *I won, didn't I?* he answered the treacherous thoughts. *Think what Mar must feel. And Ruthven,* an inner voice added. That was a less consoling thought, and Sidney pushed himself up out of his bed, wincing at the too-familiar aches.

Barton tenderly helped his master to dress, and Sidney bit back an impatient reproof. The man was doing his duty; he could do no other. Nate stood by, his eyes downcast, even more silent than usual. Sidney eyed him

437

warily, but remained silent until Barton had fastened the last button of his grey jerkin.

"Thank you, Barton," he said. The valet bowed in grave acknowledgement, and slipped away. "Stay a moment, Nate."

The boy's eyes flashed upwards briefly in surprise, and not a little fear. "Sir?"

Watching him, Sidney chastised himself for not having taken more care with the boy in the past months. I should never have brought him with me, he thought, there was too much chance of his becoming involved in these dangers. But now that I have, it's up to me to do—something. His own Elizabeth was a forward girl; he was always forgetting not to speak to her as he would to another adult. That had done no harm with her, much loved, indulged, and educated, but would it serve for Nate? He hesitated, searching for the right words, and there was a knock at the door. He swore under his breath, and grimaced as Nate's eyes flew upward again. The boy started toward the door, but Sidney lifted his hand.

"Just a moment, Nate, then you can go. I owe you thanks for your service to me, even in the face of your old master. I think you understand as well as—perhaps better than most what's been happening at this court, and I've been pleased with your bravery."

The boy nodded slowly. "Thank you, Sir Philip," he murmured, then looked up sharply, as though gathering his courage. "His grace—his grace can't hold a candle to you, sir, nor he's never been a knight."

Sidney leaned back against the table, trying to keep his amusement from showing. It wasn't fair to laugh—and it wasn't really a laughing matter. Like everyone else, it seemed, the boy trusted him, and he would have to fulfill that trust. . . . "No," he said gravely. "I don't seem to recall facing his grace of Northumberland in the lists. Now you may see to the door."

Nate ducked his head in a bow that would have earned him a blow from Barton or young Madox, but Sidney ignored the impropriety. "Master Fletcher, Sir Philip."

Sidney waved the Pleiade wizard to a seat, but his expression was somewhat abstracted. Fletcher settled himself on the low stool, drawing his long gown up around his knees. It was an old man's gesture, from a man only a few years older than Marlowe, and Sidney repressed a quick smile, but still said nothing.

"Is there anything wrong, Sir Philip?" Fletcher said, after a moment.

"I don't think so," Sidney answered. "I trust not."

"Your page seems a likely lad."

"Oh, very much so." This time, Sidney allowed himself to smile, but he sobered quickly. "Yet I wonder if I've done him any favor by bringing him here."

Fletcher nodded. "I've children of my own, and wouldn't want to see them at this court at this time. It's a frightening place for a child—"

"For this child, yes," Sidney said, more sharply than he had intended. "I beg your pardon, Master Fletcher, I've no cause to turn my anger on you." Fletcher said nothing, and after a moment, Sidney continued, "Nate's seen abuses of power before this. He served the Earl of Northumberland, who bought him from his wretched parents, as a scrying-boy, both for him and for the rest of the School of Night."

"Of which Sir Walter is an adherent," Fletcher said, very mildly.

"Oh, there's no vice in Raleigh," Sidney answered. "His powers are not great and he knows it; he is simply a scholar, fascinated by knowledge." His face hardened. "And if you would confuse the two, Master Fletcher, I'd remind you that Raleigh is here."

Indeed he is, Fletcher thought, but to what purpose? He shook the thought aside: if Sidney chose to trust a man whom he must have known for years, who was a mere scholar to dispute it? He said aloud, "Still, I didn't come to concern myself with your affairs, Sir Philip, and I ask your pardon for seeming to do so."

"No need," Sidney said, and smiled, warmly this time. "I assume, since you're about betimes this morning—no, I hope you've developed some notion of how we can protect the palace and the king?"

Fletcher leaned forward, dismissing the page and the School of Night from his mind completely. "I believe so,

Sir Philip—indeed, I could almost believe the time divinely ordained for my coming into Scotland."

Sidney lifted an eyebrow, but said nothing.

"The Feast of Michaelmas approaches," Fletcher went on. "What better time—what more propitious time—for defending this place against the minions of hell than on the feast day of the great commander of the hosts of heaven, one of the regents of the sun?"

"None, I assume, unless it be resurrection morn," Sidney said, sincerely.

"None at all," Fletcher said, as though he hadn't heard the other's interjection. "And as for making the rite acceptable to his Majesty—well, I suspect that is in truth why you sent for one of us: less for our magic than for the form of it."

"Not at all," Sidney protested, less sincerely this time, and smiled in recognition of that face. "I lack the skill to use your rituals, even if I wished to create one myself. My training has been in another school entirely, a more private way—but you know that. The form is vital here, you're right about that. We must protect the king, and also soothe his not unreasonable fears."

Fletcher stroked his neat beard, visibly pleased with himself. "A pageant of the sun," he said, almost to himself. "Let it be so that his majesty will ride the bounds of Holyrood—a common enough ceremony, too frequently ignored. A holiday outing. Yet we can make it more than that, for he shall stop at the four compass points on his circuit, and at each one a portion of the ceremony shall be completed. His majesty himself will fulfill it—it lies in him, as God's anointed king."

Sidney stood up and walked slowly across the room, pausing by the window to stare out into the crowded courtyard, the servants' liveries bright in the late summer sun. It would suit, he thought, let the spectacle be grand enough, and James will overcome his fears.

Fletcher watched him closely. "All the songs, the rites, I can write. This is a magic I'm well versed in."

Sidney glanced over his shoulder with a pained look, and Fletcher smiled. "I've made some plans already. As you surmised, I was up well into the night—I saw the dawn, in fact. It seemed appropriate." There was a strange serenity in his voice, almost a satisfaction, that made Sidney turn around and look at him. Fletcher held out a sheaf of papers, and the older man took them silently, studying the neat Italic hand.

"Those taking part in the ceremony proper shall accompany the king as the lesser planets follow the sun," Fletcher went on, "and there will be twelve riders for the twelve signs of the zodiac. As many others as wish may accompany the riders, of course, and I trust there will be many, but those are the significant ones."

There were even rough sketches for the costumes—solar livery—to be worn by the principals, Sidney noted, and recalled with some longing the days when there had been so many masques surrounding the queen. There did not seem to be as many, any more. And so many dead, he thought suddenly. Not only Leicester, the greatest giver of masques, but Hatton, Sir Francis Walsingham, and so many others who had been stars in England's firmament when Sidney had been boy and youth. *There is beauty still to rend the soul and offer it a taste of heaven . . .* The thought was too melancholy even for poetry, and he put it firmly aside.

"You've set yourself a pretty problem, determining who shall take these principal parts," he said briskly. Fletcher looked sideways at him, and Sidney would have taken his oath that the Catholic scholar looked sly.

"Oh, but, Sir Philip, you've dealt with that matter already, and neatly, too."

Sidney could not hide his sudden suspicion, and Fletcher looked pleased. "The jousts, sir. The places of honor shall go to those who particularly distinguished themselves in the king's lists. Which gives you pride of place, and the opportunity not merely to oversee the ceremony but to remain close to the king, in case anything should, God forbid, go awry."

He looks inordinately pleased with himself, Sidney thought, but God knows he has a right to be. He glanced at the sketches again, studying the intricate patterns. Gold satin, painted with symbols, gold velvet and laurel leaves . . .

"Will it suit, do you think?" Fletcher asked.

"It's very much to the purpose," Sidney answered. "I offer you my thanks and congratulations, and repeat you should have been a courtier. His majesty, I think, will be pleased." He looked at the neat writing again, piecing out the whole in his mind, and could feel the rightness of it, sensed a pre-echo of the magics it would invoke. The Pleiade's magic was more impressive than he had thought—such pretty innocuous figures, to create such power. The basic rules were those he had learned from Doctor Dee, but they had been heightened, painted over with a shiny glory almost of myth, rendering them invisible, or at least easily overlooked—and as such, it was a suitable power for use about princes who could not afford to risk the accusation of too great a familiarity with wizards. He nodded again, and looked up to meet Fletcher's almost challenging stare. "It will serve."

Fletcher let go of a breath he had not quite known he had been holding. He had known Sidney understood the Pleiade's magic, but after witnessing the display of power on the tiltyard he had started to worry. He didn't know this magic Sidney used, didn't recognize the school or the teaching; he knew only what any wizard would have seen, that this magic was too immediate, too accessible—a temptation, certainly, and possibly a threat. He had half expected that Sidney would have changed his mind, and been ready to dismiss the formal, magnificent magic of the French Academy. He had done the man an injustice—and this same respect, Fletcher thought, demands my respect in return. I cannot condemn it out of hand, but, by God and all his saints, it frightens me. He rose to his feet and bowed.

"If you'll excuse me, then, Sir Philip, I'll continue to work on this."

"Of course," Sidney answered, and grinned. "And I shall bring the proposal to the king."

James was holding court in his privy chamber, surrounded today by the courtiers he counted as his closest friends. Ruthven, pleasantly, was not among them, but Sidney could not help wondering—ungratefully, he knew—just where he was, and who was watching him. A page, this one dark and plump as a pony, bowed deeply and announced, "Sir Philip Sidney."

James rose to his feet as Sidney made his own bow, glancing at his friends. "Gentlemen, give me leave. I wish to have some private discourse with my champion."

I wish he wouldn't do that, Sidney thought, as he bowed again in acknowledgement of the favor. Not only does it give his own people more cause to dislike me, but I can't think her majesty would be pleased to hear him call me his champion. For an instant, he imagined he could hear her tart voice—*Not yet, dear cousin, and never, if I don't make it so!*—and could see the thin eyebrows lift into astonished arches. Then the vision passed, and he said, "Your Majesty honors me beyond my merit." Try as he might, he could not keep an echo of Elizabeth's asperity from his voice, but James did not seem to heed it.

"Nonsense, Sir Philip, and you know it. Come, sir, sit and talk with me."

The nobles had slipped from the room, not without a few backward glances, envious and resentful in equal measure. Sidney sighed, but gave his attention to the king. James seemed oblivious to their feelings—or, more likely, Sidney thought, he had lived so long with it that he could judge it to a nicety.

"I'm glad of the chance to speak with you," James went on, settling himself more comfortably in his chair. He kept his legs tucked under the bulbous rung, but the silk stockings, his favorite shade of pale blue, only emphasized the bowed limbs. "Tell me, who is this person you sent Master Marlowe to fetch? Some friend, a colleague of yours?"

Sidney shook his head. He had been wondering precisely how he would explain Fletcher to the king of Scots, and had been unable to come up with anything but the unvarnished truth. "A colleague of sorts, your Majesty. He was a member of the French Academy, the Pleiade, before it was disbanded, but he's an Englishman, a Catholic, living abroad."

"The Pleiade," James murmured. "The poet wizards." He saw Sidney's brief expression of surprise, and smiled rather grimly. "I have heard of them."

"Indeed, your Majesty."

"And have you less faith in your abilities than your queen—or than I do myself, seeing what I've seen—that you should send for him?"

And him a Catholic. Sidney could almost hear the words echoing in the air between them. Sidney said carefully, "It's not that I lack faith in myself, your Majesty, of that I can assure you. It is, rather, that I know what the Pleiade can do. They excel at the large rituals, and I have never had to work on this scale before."

James smiled, sensing in the older man some other constraint, and with the clarity that sometimes surprised himself, said, "I don't mind that he's a papist, Sir Philip. God's nails, were I to object on those grounds, I'd lose Maxwell, and the Gordons, too—which I will not do for any man."

Sidney bowed his head. "I apologize, your Majesty. But that matter's of some selfish concern to me. It doesn't do me any good, here or in England, to have called on a Roman wizard for help."

"I can see that," James said, with feeling. "And I don't blame you—I cannot. Mind, I shouldn't be sorry to see the presbyters go down. . . ."

"But there must be a middle course between that precisian and popery," Sidney said, without much hope.

"Oh, ay, that there must be," James answered, "but I'm tired of straddling Dame Justice's sword. I've too much to lose."

I do daresay, Sidney thought, working out the implications of the metaphor. "I only hope I can blunt the edges for you, your Majesty."

"It's the point that worries me," James said frankly. "And I don't envy you the chore." He paused then, his expression sobering. "Yesterday—the jousts aside—it cannot have been pleasant for you, facing that assault. . . . Alex—" He stopped abruptly. Sidney said nothing, letting the younger man find his own way, and James sighed. "It needs to be talked of. What ought I to do about him? I can't find it in my heart to call him vile, to think him anything more than a pawn—as any one of us might be, should we fall under Bothwell's spell."

Others have been tempted, Sidney thought, *and have*

withstood the lure, but suppressed the spurt of temper.
Forbes had fallen, and there was no reason to think him
anything but something less than clever—no crime, that.
"The Master of Ruthven was certainly made use of," he
said aloud, "but not without his consent."

"He's young," James said, "he erred once—" He broke
off sighing, and said, more briskly, "More than that, he is
a Ruthven, and I have some need to draw them to my
side. Can he be trusted at all, now that he's repented?"

"So far, no further, or so Marlowe says," Sidney answered, his tone deliberately light. "To be fair, your Majesty? Until Bothwell compels him to service again."

"What singularly useful counsel Master Marlowe gives,"
James said, rather bitterly. "Does he speak from knowledge or envy, I wonder?" He broke off then, and had the
grace to look almost ashamed of himself. "I beg your
pardon, Sir Philip. I've been listening to my—gossips—
again. If you are his patron, and stand for him, no one can
doubt his—virtue."

Sidney laughed softly, well aware of the source of James's
information. Mar, it seemed, had listened well to his
English friends. "Marlowe has his faults, but they are, I
think, the faults of the scholar, your Majesty. He has done
you good service here. And me. I might not have survived
Ruthven's attack—"

"Bothwell's," James interjected, softly, but in a tone
that brooked no argument.

"Forgive me. Bothwell's attack, then, without Marlowe's
aid."

James stared into space for a long moment. When he
spoke, it was in a slow, gentle voice that Sidney had not
heard him use before—almost, Sidney thought, the voice
of a sleepwalker, if such a thing were possible. "I would
have thought them two of the same soul—and yet your
trust remains unshaken." James seemed to recall to whom
he was speaking, and managed a wry grin. "I can count
the men I trust on the fingers of my two hands, Sir Philip,
or thought I could. God numbers sparrows, I number the
honest men in Holyrood—and believe me, I am less edi-
fied than God."

Sidney smiled in return, but said, "You're doing better than God did at Sodom, your Majesty. He found none."

"God is not subject to despair," James murmured, then brightened. "Though one might stretch a point, and call Sodom and Gomorrah a fit of temper, eh? But it's not a day to talk of theology. Have you and your colleague devised a plan to safeguard our palace?"

Sidney accepted the change of subject without demur. James's blasphemies were no more original than Marlowe's, and usually less amusing. "It was that I wished to speak to you about. Master Fletcher and I have spoken, and he craves your Majesty's indulgence and the honor of your participation in a pageant he is creating for Michaelmas. As Michael is God's regent of the sun, and you, as king, are God's regent on Earth, he felt it would be fitting."

"And most flattering, too," James said, but he looked less uneasy than Sidney had feared. "I take it that this is no mere show, Sir Philip."

"No, your Majesty." Sidney bowed his head and waited.

"I would like to know something more of this, before I give my consent."

"As your Majesty wishes." Sidney paused, ordering his thoughts, then quickly outlined the ceremony Fletcher had composed the night before. When he had finished, James smiled.

"I like the sound of it, like it very well—and I don't doubt my lady wife will share my enthusiasm. God's death, I could declare you a danger to my happily wedded state after your performance yesterday. Unlike her, I never thought to see chivalry live again, and so never feared to be supplanted. I never dreamed such things were more than romances: pleasant enough, but believed only by children and fools. And you are neither."

And this, Sidney thought, bowing his head in modest acknowledgement of the royal compliment, was typical of James. The man seemed incapable of loving in moderation— of feeling anything in moderation. His flattery was gratifying, but it sprang from little more than an overabundance of some passing humor, and so could only make the recipient uneasy. Still, if this humor meant that James would accept—and more than accept, participate in—

Fletcher's ceremony, Sidney would accept it, and be grateful.

The courtiers chosen for the Ride were up before dawn, decking themselves in the golden livery that Fletcher had designed for the occasion. Marlowe, fastening the last gilt button, stooped to view his reflection in the little glass, and was dourly pleased. The color did not flatter his rather sallow complexion, but the pale gold doublet, painted and stitched with solar designs in brighter gold, was a magnificent piece of finery. More than that, he hadn't paid for it. He ran his hand down the full sleeve, over the painted suns and crowing cocks and across the stylized heliotrope-and-vine that enclosed the other symbols, wondering if this mummery—he could think of no other word—would have any effect at all. Fletcher swore the Pleiade had practiced this magic for nigh on a decade—but Henri III was murdered nonetheless, Marlowe thought, with a sardonic smile, and you're in exile, Hal. What then?

He shook his doubts away with an effort. If nothing else, the ceremony could do no harm, and would provide further encouragement to a court already buoyed up by Sidney's dramatic showing in the jousts. Besides, he added, with another inward smile, it would please James to see his court so spectacularly arrayed. He glanced down at his own body with some complacence—the knee-length velvet breeches, golden like the rest of the livery, were very fine indeed, and the lace that trimmed both neck and wrist ruffs was of true gold—and picked up the tall hat that lay on the table among his papers. It, too, was gold velvet, trimmed with a cunningly-made wreath of laurel leaves, and a gold pin winked among the dark green leaves. Marlowe frowned—he did not remember adding anything to the carefully designed costume—and then recognized the jewel. Mephistophilis's gift had no place there, among Fletcher's hallowed symbols. Marlowe stared at it for what seemed an eternity. Then, very slowly, he made himself undo the clasp and set the jewel carefully aside. It glittered where it lay, and the poet thought for a moment that he heard mocking laughter.

"I will not aid you," he said aloud, and set the hat firmly

on his head. There was no answer, not even the faint
laughter; Marlowe released the breath he had been holding, and stepped quickly from his room.

The riders were already milling in the courtyard,
peacocking their new clothes and calling conflicting orders
to the long-suffering grooms. They, Sidney saw with some
relief, seemed tolerant enough of their betters' antics—
either they did not suspect the Ride's deeper purpose, or
they were willing to put up with it for the king's sake. He
nodded to the sandy-bearded man who brought his own
horse—the same piebald he favored for the joust—but
said, "Hold him here for me a little. There's still a good
deal to be done."

"Very good, Sir Philip," the groom answered, and backed
the horse away.

Sidney glanced again along the rough line of riders,
making sure that everyone who should be present was
ready, and that none had been offended by the choices. It
had been a stroke of genius on Fletcher's part to make the
favored riders—representing the twelve houses of the
zodiac—the same young men who'd ridden in the joust.
No one, not even the most determined troublemaker,
could quarrel with that, or say that unworthy choices had
been made. Anyone else might, at his own expense, provide himself with the prescribed livery and accompany the
Ride, but the significant positions belonged to the king's
brave knights. There was one exception, of course—the
Master of Ruthven remained behind—but James had picked
the club-footed Lord Campbell of Crinan to replace him.
It had been done with a blasphemous jest—Campbell's
given name was Matthias—but it had given that powerful
family a place it would otherwise have lacked in the
ceremony.

Sidney fingered the medal—Leo's—that hung at his
own breast, smiling slightly. Fletcher's conceit had also
given him, the undisputed victor, the right to oversee this
ceremony. A very clever man, Sidney thought, not for the
first time, and very well versed in the ways of courts.

"Sir Philip." That was Fletcher himself, very neat in a
scholar's gown of golden velvet. "Everything's in readiness."

"Excellent," Sidney answered, and beckoned to the groom.

"The king must leave the courtyard as the sun is rising," Fletcher said, not for the first time, and Sidney smiled.

"I will see to that, Master Fletcher. And everything else?"

"Singers and actors and even her majesty," Fletcher answered. His eyes flicked toward the courtyard door, and he gave a sigh of relief. "And here is his majesty at last."

"It lacks some minutes yet to sunrise," Sidney answered soothingly, and bowed very low as James made his way down the line of riders. The king of Scots was looking very fine, though his costume was no different from the liveries worn by his companions. The golden colors brought out the ruddy lights lurking in his hair and beard, and the tall boots helped disguise the bowed legs, lending new dignity despite the lurching walk. But it's more than that, Sidney thought suddenly, there's something—a freedom, almost, a sense of unexpected security about him that makes him seem, for today, at least, a very king. It bodes well for our venture.

"God go with you, Sir Philip, and St. Michael, too," Fletcher said, and slipped away.

Sidney suppressed a most unChristian curse. How like a papist, he thought, to bring saints into this, but smiled then in spite of himself. Michael, whose day this was, and who was venerated even in the English church as lord general of the heavenly hosts and vanquisher of Satan's black army, was certainly the most appropriate patron for the day's ritual. He allowed the groom to throw him up into the high saddle, gathered the reins with absent ease, and edged the nervous horse forward to join the king.

As always, James was at his best on horseback, freed of the limitations of his own ungainly limbs. He handled his horse—a massive yellow-white brute that even Sidney would have thought twice about mounting—with an off-hand skill as impressive as it was mildly frightening. It's to James's great credit, Sidney thought, that we are all willing to ride so close at hand to that ill-tempered monster.

"Sir Philip, good morning," James cried. "It's a fair day for our Ride."

Sidney bowed low in the saddle. "It is indeed, your Majesty. A good sign."

The sun was rising even as he spoke. He lifted his hand, signaling the riders to take their places, then pointed to the liveried pages waiting by the gate. They threw their weight against the heavy doors, which creaked slowly open. At Sidney's nod, the king rode out into the risen day, and boys' voices broke from the towers to either side of the gate.

"*Great King of Heaven, Regent of the Sun, into our hearts*

"*Pour out Thy mercy, protect us from the slings and darts*

"*Of Thy dread Adversary. This king, Thy earthly emblem, save*

"*And grant long life, and health, and grace, his road to pave.*"

Marlowe, riding at the tail of the procession, winced a little at the doggerel verse. Still, he thought, I suppose if it serves its purpose, I can't complain. And there was no question that it did serve its purpose: as he rode through the wide-opened gate he could feel the powers called by Fletcher's words and the strange, oddly accented music, tingling on his skin. The others around him seemed unaware of it, or at most accepted it as a part of the excitement of the day.

There was a May-day fecklessness among the riders, a lightheartedness that touched even Sidney, and made him set his piebald dancing, mincing through its school-steps at the king's side. James laughed aloud at the sight, freer from fear than Sidney had ever seen him, and did not try to imitate the performance.

The procession made its way along the bounds of the park. As they reached the stand of trees that marked the easternmost point of the palace ground, Sidney reined his horse to a stop, bowing to the king. "If your Majesty will call," he said, "perhaps someone will answer." This was the sort of thing his uncle of Leicester had done for the English queen, though not to any grander purpose than her entertainment; in a strange way, Sidney thought, it's in my blood.

James grinned. "Hello," he called, "who's there?"

There was a moment of silence, and then music, the same odd measured music that had sounded as the palace gates were opened, sounded from the heart of the wood. Children in white and gold, boys and girls recruited from among the noble families still at court, came forward, bowing deeply. They joined hands, and began to dance a solemn figure, moving in a circle before the king. James gentled his horse, which seemed inclined to dislike the music, and watched with open wonder. A boy's voice joined the music then, calling on the angel of the east to protect the king. More doggerel, Marlowe thought, it would be better done in England; but he could feel the power gathering, presences answering the summons. He shivered lightly, and saw several of the other young men glancing oddly at each other, as though they, too, felt something beyond their understanding.

The dance ended then, and the weird sense of watching powers faded. The children made their bows, and the eldest piped a speech of thanks; James made them their expected gift, and the procession continued on its way.

At the northernmost point of the palace grounds, a ragged course of stones that had been the foundation of some vanished house, more dancers answered the king's call. These were young men in earth-brown suits, who moved with grace through the fantastic figures. Professionals, unquestionably, Marlowe thought, and tried to shake off the awareness of greater powers at work. Why can't I enjoy this for a masque, mere display, like all the others? he demanded silently. It isn't fair.

The tension eased as the music and dancing ended, but a shadow of it remained in the air around them. The horses, more sensitive than their riders, shied and fidgeted. James controlled his unhappy mount with an iron hand, and looked to Sidney.

"I trust all is as it should be, Sir Philip?"

Sidney smiled in answer, hiding his own unease. This hovering power, this sense of expectation, should be nothing more than the proper atmosphere of a half-completed ritual; even knowing that, he caught himself glancing more than once over his shoulder, looking for he knew not what.

He could barely bring himself to eat from the banquet laid for the riders in a pleasant glade, though he was glad to see that the rest of the Ride more than made up for his own weakness. It would not do to have the cooks whispering of an uncanny loss of appetite among the lords.

From the banquet, the Ride turned west, riding still along the borders of Holyrood's ground. Twice more they paused to listen to Fletcher's measured music, and to watch the intricate dances he had choreographed. With each performance, the sense of anticipation grew greater still, until even the most unwary among the riders felt it, a pressure like a rising storm, and the seventeen principals, who, as necessary adjuncts to the ceremony itself, had been warned of its full meaning, were hard pressed to control their horses. Sidney glanced warily at the king, half afraid that James would demand an end to the ceremony, but the king's attention was concentrated on his unruly horse, laughing and swearing under his breath at its antics. James was enjoying himself, Sidney realized suddenly; given the chance, he thought again, the man could prove a king.

The horses grew more restless as they approached the stand of trees where the first pageant had waited, until it was all the lead riders could do to control them. Fletcher had warned them of this: not any attack, or active opposition, but the unwillingness of unbounded nature to conform to laws laid down by men. Sidney tightened his grip on the reins, muttering soothing nonsense in the piebald's ear, and knew the others did the same.

Then, quite abruptly, the louring tension vanished: James had reached the place where he had stood to watch the first pageant. Sidney drew a deep breath, and heard young Seton laugh aloud. The mirth was infectious. All along the line of riders, men began to laugh, and two or three of the more reckless urged their horses into sidling trots and school figures. Sidney smiled, though he knew the ceremony was not yet ended, and saw James laugh quietly to himself.

"It's homeward bound we are, Sir Philip," he said, "and all will be well."

"God willing," Sidney murmured, but not even the king's confidence could cast a shadow on them now.

They made their way back to Holyrood in good time, the tired horses scenting their stables, and rode through the gate just as the setting sun touched the tips of the towers. Queen Anne and her ladies, fantastically gowned in blue and silver, with ropes of pearls in their high-dressed hair, were waiting on the steps of the great hall. Music sounded from inside the hall itself; the queen and her ladies curtsied low, and moved into the first figures of their dance. Anne was not a beautiful woman, the body too ripe and promising, the handsome face spoiled by a grandiose nose, but watching her now at the center of her women Sidney was moved almost to tears by the queenly grace. Some of it was the effect of Fletcher's art, he knew, but more was the memory of her face when Fletcher had explained her part in the ceremony. No royal match could be a love match, but there was something more than mere understanding between husband and wife, so seemingly ill-assorted.

"*Escosia fair, our homeland's dame,*" the choir sang, from within.

"*Escosia bows before her king.*
"*Before you now she stoops, and maidens sing*
"*Great King of Scots, to praise your royal name.*

Dear lady, arm'd in virtue, and in light,
"*Whose joy it is, our service to receive,*
"*Grant us now, on this great Michael's eve,*
"*Thy smile, and hand, to shield us from the night.*"

Oh, Christ, more doggerel, Marlowe thought, standing with the rest of the milling riders just inside the gate-house, and papist doggerel, too, unless I miss my guess. I'd lay wager the lady of Hal's second verse is no more Escosia than am I, not when he's clad them all in blue and white. But if it works, I won't quibble with the means.

The dance ended then, with a slow yet joyful strain that brought the queen to a final deep curtsy, rich skirts spreading over the filthy cobbles, almost at the king's feet. There was a moment's silence, and then James shouted for a groom. He sprang from his saddle, leaving the unlucky man to struggle with the white stallion. He bowed as deeply as Anne had curtsied to him, and held out his hands. Anne smiled up at him, and let herself be lifted to her feet. In the moment that their hands touched, Sidney felt the ceremony concluded, and allowed himself a long sigh of relief. *Peace*, Marlowe thought, feeling the last tensions vanish as though they'd never been, *the charm's well ended*, and saw the same thought run like a breeze through the men around him.

"My dearest lady, and my queen," James said, and turned to include his courtiers in his sudden smile. "And you, my lords and gentlemen. Our Ride is ended; now we may go play."

There was a laughing cheer at that, and Sidney smiled rather wryly. Play they would—there was a banquet planned, with a short comedy from the English actors, and there would be dancing to follow. And all I want, he thought, is my bed. But that was churlish, he knew—and besides, Frances would be waiting.

Chapter Thirty

This supernatural soliciting
Cannot be ill; cannot be good. If ill,
Why hath it given me earnest of success,
Commencing in a truth? I am Thane of Cawdor.
If good, why do I yield to that suggestion
Whose horrid image doth unfix my hair
And make my seated heart knock at my ribs
Against the use of nature?
                    William Shakespeare, Macbeth

The banquet was very merry, buoyed up by spirits that had not been so free in many months. The feast was lavish, prodigal with food and wines, so that not a few Scots were under the tables even before the players made their appearance. There was a new prologue for their comedy, spoken by Burbage in his proper person, which flattered James and his queen outrageously. Wise man, Sidney thought, from his own place of honor at the king's right hand. Or, more like, wise William: the comedy was at least partly his own; so probably was the prologue. Outrageous the flattery might be, but Shakespeare had assessed the climate of the Scottish court quite accurately, and written accordingly. Burbage must have wondered if his playwright had lost all discretion, Sidney thought.

How does he do it: find the right words, then know precisely how they'll sound in the right man's mouth?

The play started then, with a flourish from the musicians. It was a slight thing, centered on the ancient division between love and friendship—a good choice, in this court, Sidney thought, and even a daring one. The two heroes were pleasant enough, amusing types, but the two heroines were far more interestingly drawn. With the entrance of the ducal court, the little stage grew crowded, and Sidney was suddenly aware of a familiar face among the play-nobles. I'd half forgotten Massey was with the Chamberlain's Men, he thought, and could not resist a glance toward Marlowe, at the lower table. I wonder what he feels, finding his cruel Ganymede here, and Ganymede no longer, but a man grown? Marlowe's face was impassive at first, but then, as Massey spoke his only line, there crossed his face a glimpse of hell, brief, intense, like sudden lightning. Sidney caught his breath, anticipating thunder. It was not remorse, though God knew Marlowe should be feeling that, for his maliciously brilliant libel— nor even quite regret or loss, but something of all those things, and something more. Not quite natural, Sidney thought, a look of Tantalus, as though some thing beyond his own will or Massey's refusal held him back. . . . The vision faded then, though he kept a wary eye on the poet throughout the course of the play. Marlowe's face betrayed nothing further, and he laughed with the others at the clown's speeches and the dog Crab, so that by the end of the performance Sidney almost doubted that he had seen anything.

When the play was done, and the flattering epilogue spoken by the younger of the apprentices, there was dancing, but Sidney seized the opportunity to slip away. Frances, yawning hugely, submitted helplessly to her women and was led away to be readied for bed. By the time Sidney had changed into nightcap and nightgown, she was already in bed and sound asleep. He stood for a moment, staring at her through the half-opened curtains; then, decisively, closed them again to shut out the candlelight. He loosened the ties of his nightgown, shivering a little in the chill air.

Well done

Sidney's head lifted warily. The voice, all too familiar now after the months in Scotland, seemed to come from everywhere and nowhere, a dry, mocking voice sifting up out of the rushes on the floor.

No, truly, I congratulate you, your work today was not in vain. It is a truly wise man who can shut me out from where I wish to enter.

Sidney let his hand fall to his side, turned slowly. The thing spoke truly: there was no presence in the room. Beyond the walls he could sense the watchfulness summoned by the completed ceremony, and, beyond that, held back by it, he could feel this other, alien spirit. He shook his head, and turned his gaze toward the dying fire.

I have never been so truly confounded, the voice continued. *I misjudged you.*

"Save your praises for one who desires them," Sidney said, but softly, so as not to wake Frances, sleeping soundly now behind the embroidered curtains.

Many desire them. Few deserve them. Have you never faced an enemy whom you respected, but swore still to defeat?

"And I have earned your respect?" Sidney put polite skepticism into his voice.

Commanded it, rather, the voice murmured, as though in Sidney's ear, and it held a rueful note that was purely human. *It was no great desire of mine to find myself so well opposed. I can only wonder if her majesty of England fully appreciates what she possesses in you.*

"I daresay she must," Sidney answered. "She sent me here."

Fear me not, Sir Philip, at least not tonight. I value a worthy opponent as much as any man—perhaps more so, I have so few. I deplore waste, as surely as you do. I can offer you nothing that you cannot win by your own merit. . . . The voice changed then, took on a new, dreaming note. *Coligny, Dee, Languet, Nassau—even Burleigh, all admit your excellence. Some few of them even foresaw the greatness for which you were obviously destined, did you not insist upon hiding your light beneath a bushel. Though it is not too late to seize that greatness.*

"And should I not fear temptation?" Sidney murmured.

Hardly that. I say no more than you yourself have thought. You see the king of Scots, you see the potential in him—if only he had those who could guide him wisely, honestly, without self-interest. If only he would favor those who were worthy of his favor, choosing, with his head and not his fallible heart. Elizabeth of England is old. How many years can she endure? Ten? She has not that many left her, I can tell you that as a favor, no price attached to it. And you know what is promised on her death. Why should England be condemned to such a future, when her own champion has the power to prevent it?

"You offer me, to read your words aright, a choice of damnations," Sidney said. "My own, or England's."

Damnation? The voice held a note of almost human surprise. *All know you seek no rewards for yourself. Call it sacrifice, if you must, for truer words were never spoken than it is fitting that one should give his all so that the whole might not perish.*

"I hold the world but as the world," Sidney answered, with more conviction than he felt. "It is not given to one man to save or damn it, save one alone."

I speak not of the world, that abstraction, but of your world, her majesty's world, the voice urged, *and of a fate she would brave hell itself to avoid. She saw the same greatness in you the others saw, she sought to bridle it and break it to her use, and failed. James needs you; he has seen that himself. The one man capable enough to shut me out—* The voice caught on quiet laughter. *No matter the rites were devised by another, that quibbling's unworthy of you. You know it is your touch that holds it strong against me. You and you alone stand between your Scots king and me. You've seen the excesses of which he is capable, you know the caprice of princes and the danger that lies therein. Sir Philip Sidney is greater than any other that serves the English throne. Why should he be kept down? Elizabeth will not live forever—there's less than a decade left to be told of her life, I told you true before—and then what will become of all she's made? Her advisors, all those she preferred above the great men of her court, all those are dead. James will have the throne of England: a harrowing thought, were it not for the one man who can be to him* what he should by rights have been to the queen of England. You're no boy, no fool—those who've called you so are those who fear you most, and you've triumphed over most of them. You must be at his side, or England goes down.

Sidney shook his head. "And your offer? No, I see that too clearly. What's your price for this advancement? Is it one any man can pay and still remain true?"

True to what? What truth is this? True to himself?

"Hardly the greatest loyalty a man owes," Sidney answered. "To his faith—his soul, if you will, and to his prince and his God. A man loses himself in those services, and finds himself again, as have I."

Not yet, Sir Philip. You have not found yourself yet, that's still to come.

"You drive a clumsy bargain. What price can you expect me to think myself able to pay?"

I know better than to seek what I cannot come near, the voice answered, tinged now with bubbling laughter.

"Then what—" Sidney began, and realized that it was gone, as softly as it had come. His hand was trembling, and he could feel sweat chilling on his back despite the night cold. He took a deep breath, calming himself. Neither Bothwell nor his minion demons could any longer penetrate the palace. Very well, that was to the good, but the battle seemed to have shifted ground without his realizing it. A cunning demon, to touch a man's heart without searing it, echoing too well the words one often tried in one's own mind, and banished before the desire to speak them, to admit to them, became too great to control.

Sidney closed his eyes. *May God help me, when I find myself echoing the thoughts the devil himself has winnowed from my innermost heart. I do not wish these things—no, that's not quite true, but I do not want to wish them. Dear God, lead me from these snares Thy adversary lays before me, which are partly of my own devising, and therefore seem the more enticing. Forgive my pride, that never saw that I could be so drawn in by the influence You've seen fit to let me wield.*

Hubris, Philip, the voice whispered as if from a great

distance, but Sidney shook his head. No, he answered silently. Merely truth, and in denying it, I do myself no favors. If I know the best of me, I also know the worst. A sudden, cool anger washed through him. And I will know your name, demon, and banish you, and destroy your master Bothwell. But no more than my commission will I fulfill. Tell him so!

I must obey, said the distant voice, and was gone. Sidney felt its departure this time, a rushing of air like that which banished the demon Rabdos. He bowed his head. The battle was finished; what lay ahead was war.

After that conversation came an ominous silence. The demonic voice seemed to have spoken unexpected truth: the palace was proof against any further attacks. Once or twice, Sidney felt Bothwell's minions sniffing about the perimeters of the defense, whispering past its barriers like wind deflected around shutters and good stone walls. Then even that ended, while the days grew shorter and the ground stiffened with an early frost. Sidney waited warily, unable to act until Bothwell did, not daring to risk breaching his own barriers for any seeking ritual until he knew more certainly where the wizard was hiding himself. Not yet, at any rate, some inner voice murmured; not yet, while the year is on the wane, and the night of all souls fast approaching. Those were papist thoughts—worse, pagan thoughts, but they held power. Sidney waited, and king and court waited with him, even their faction quarrels suspended, almost as though they were holding their breaths until the siege were ended. No, Sidney thought, it was not a siege—there was more life to war, more movement and false gaiety. This was more like a hunt, a blind hunt under the ground: the ferret was loosed already, down the hole and seeking in the crawling dark, while the rest of the hunt could do nothing but stand and wait, until their creature flushed the rabbit. I only wish, Sidney thought, I knew which of us was hare and which the hunter.

To no one's great surprise, the Master of Ruthven was soon restored to the freedom of the court. The king's forgiveness was as immoderate as his anger, but, truly, Marlowe thought, Ruthven's frantic speeches, repentance and a desperate plea for protection and forgiveness, could have melted stonier hearts than James's. On the other hand, is it too much to ask that a king show some constancy? Or have the wit to hold even a little aloof from a self-convicted traitor? Occasionally, as Ruthven sat demurely at the king's feet to watch some new play—new to Scotland, at least—the poet found himself watching Sidney for some sign of the famous temper, but Sidney remained impassive, and made no public comment on the favorite's reascension. Nor did he make any private comment, and that was even more surprising. Like all the rest of the court, he seemed caught and held in some mysterious spell, as chilling as the unseasonable frost.

At least Ruthven was bearing himself very humbly now, Marlowe thought. There was some satisfaction to be gained from that . . . but not enough. His own demon, his own Mephistophilis, had not vanished with the other apparitions, though the soft voice and mocking laughter seemed to reach no other ears. It was the pin, the satyr brooch he had been given in Flushing, he knew in more rational moments, but he still could not bring himself to be rid of the pretty jewel. It was too rich to destroy, he would tell himself one day, or too beautiful; the next, he would tell himself it would be better to sell the thing, and make some profit from an otherwise unprofitable toy. In the meantime, he did nothing, and the brooch appeared and reappeared mysteriously—not mysteriously enough, the poet thought, not mysteriously at all—pinned to hat or jerkin. He removed it each time he found it, but could not seem to do more.

The king rode constantly. Hunting, he called the daily expedition, though he never crossed Holyrood's protected bounds, or expected to find much game on the barren ground. It was an excuse to be out of the palace, to seem, at least, to be doing something, and, finally, it was one of several ways to ensure he slept at night. If he rode himself—though never his horses—into tremble-legged exhaustion, how could Fletcher's herbal brews fail to do their work and lull the king to sleep?

Inclement weather did not stop the royal departure, though once a heavy downpour drove him and his party back to cover before the day's end. Waking to thick fog and a stinging chill in the air, Sidney did not even bother to hope James would choose not to ride. Frances stirred beside him, murmuring a hopeful and incoherent question, but Sidney shook his head, drawing the heavy coverlet back up over her shoulders.

"No hope of it, I fear," he said softly, so as not to wake her fully if he could help it. "We'll ride, I make no doubt."

He dressed without haste, pulling on thick woollen stockings and heavily padded hose and buttoning his heaviest doublet over a stout shirt. It was no day for a ruff: the damp air would have spoiled the starch within minutes of his setting foot outside. Instead he fastened the ties of his falling collar, and chose the warmest of his long cloaks from the assortment Barton presented for his inspection.

"A raw day, Sir Philip," the valet ventured, and there was a knock at the door.

Sidney sighed. "But not too raw for his majesty," he answered, and nodded to Nate. "Very well, see to that."

The boy scurried away, to return a moment later with Greville and a page in royal livery.

"So-ho, Philip," Greville said, before he could be announced. "We ride in spite of all."

Sidney cast him a reproving glance, and said, "Did you expect anything else?" He nodded to the Scottish page. "You may tell his majesty we would be happy to accompany him."

"Thank you, Sir Philip. His majesty wishes to leave within the hour," the boy answered.

"We'll be there," Greville said, grimly, and Sidney nodded.

"You may go."

The page bowed, and vanished. The two Englishmen exchanged glances, and then Greville said, "Courage, Philip. Who knows, we may find game, today." Sidney gave him a sour look and did not answer.

The horses were saddled and waiting by the time they reached the courtyard, and most of James's favored courtiers were assembled. Even the elderly treasurer was mounted, very brave in a long-skirted, murrey-colored jerkin over heavily padded slops. Perhaps, Marlowe thought, watching from an upper window, the man hoped to persuade James to attend to some of his neglected business, in between jumps. The Master of Ruthven was there, too, very noticeable in a black suit whose unadorned sobriety was not at all relieved by white lawn collar and cuffs. He still seemed somewhat chastened, hanging back as inconspicuously as possible among the junior members of the court, but James looked for him, and waved him forward to the royal side. Marlowe leaned forward, then, but could not make out Sidney's expression, hidden beneath his wide-brimmed hat.

There was even less pretense of a hunt than usual: the master of hounds was not even present, and no one among the royal party carried more than his sword. Marlowe shook his head, watching the group—two dozen men in all, perhaps, counting the stolid grooms—spur from the courtyard, then made his way down the narrow stairway to the stables. The king of Scots and his hunt could go hang; he had business of his own to manage. His hand closed convulsively around his purse, feeling the outline of Mephistophilis's gift through the soft leather. I cannot go on like this, he thought. I must see him, reject him or— He slew the thought half-formed. I must see him and reject him: there's no more than that.

It didn't take long to persuade one of the grooms to loan him a suitable hack; Sidney's instructions on that score had been explicit. Sighing, the poet swung himself up into the saddle, settled his pistols into their case at the saddlebow, then gathered the reins. The hack, chosen for its steady temper and easy gait, twitched its ears backward at him, then condescended to obey his urging heel.

The fog thickened as he rode away from Holyrood, pooling thigh-deep in the dank valleys, swirling up after him to catch at the horse's fetlocks as they ascended the next rise. Marlowe reined in, absently patting the horse's neck, and glanced unhappily over his shoulder. Holyrood's towers had vanished in the fog; the road before him led down another easy slope and into deeper fog. He hesitated then, wondering if he shouldn't turn back, and heard faint laughter.

Oh, come, my Christopher. Surely a little weather doesn't daunt you.

There was a challenge in that mocking voice that Marlowe could not let lie. If he could see no path before him—well, he possessed that which would lead him to his goal. Setting his teeth, he unknotted the strings of his purse, and pulled out the gleaming brooch. Even in the milky fog-light the gold was bright, unnaturally so.

"Showy," he said, and heard his voice flattened by the heavy air. "If you wish me to find you, you will have to show the way."

Look again, my Christopher, the voice whispered. The hack laid its ears flat against its head, took two shuddering steps backward. Marlowe controlled it with an effort, and looked down at the pin. The dark stone was glowing, a point of red like a rat's eye or a drop of blood shining behind the carved satyr. He held it out at arm's length ahead of him, and the light remained unchanged. He swung his arm to the side, and the light faded.

"Very simple," he said aloud. "I—felicitate you."

As well you should, the voice answered. *I will be waiting.* The presence faded then, and Marlowe sat for a moment, shivering. A wise man would turn back now, he knew, not venture any further into weather as unnatural—as demonic? he wondered suddenly—as his only guide.

"So I'm a fool," he said aloud, and urged the hack forward again. It shied and sidled, but he persuaded it at last. Slowly it picked its way unwillingly down the fog-slick hillside, following the red guide in the poet's hand.

The fog swirled thick around the royal party, too, tangling the riders until the once-compact company had broken into several groups and a handful of solitary stragglers. Sidney pulled up inside a particularly foggy copse, and lifted his hand for silence. The other riders obliged, but there was nothing to be heard but the soft noises of their own horses.

"Damn the man," a Scots voice muttered, unidentifiable in the thick air, and no one disagreed.

Sidney sighed. "Did anyone see which way his majesty went?"

"I thought, this way," the Earl of Cassilis said, in a discouraged voice. "Sir Philip, I am sorry—"

"So did we all think, this way," the treasurer interrupted, not unkindly. "Sir Philip, do you think this is wise?"

"I do not," Sidney answered frankly, "though I understand what drives his majesty. We've been cooped up long enough—but let's find him first, and then we can suggest he return to the palace." He glanced around the knot of men, wondering who had been left with the king. Greville was here, of course, and the treasurer, and perhaps half a dozen others, including van der Droeghe, returned to his duties as head groom. Ruthven is with the king, then, he thought, in sudden panic, and tried to thrust the fear aside. There was no need for it: the boy had been remarkably humbled by his experience at the tourney—as well he should be, a part of Sidney's mind said tartly—and in any case, there was no reason to think that the Master of Ruthven had not gotten himself separated from the others as well. He was riding well back in the crowd, the last time I saw him. . . . The thought brought no comfort.

"We have to find the king," he said aloud, and there was a new note of urgency in his voice that brought the others up short.

"Sir Philip?" Montrose said.

Sidney shook his head, angry at his own whims, and frightened by them. "A feeling, nothing more, a—" He broke off, glancing around at the trees and rocks. They were familiar—familiar from the Ride. "Where are we?"

"I don't know," Montrose began, with an apologetic shake of his head, and Sidney beckoned to the nearest groom.

"Do you know, Andrew?"

"Not for certain, Sir Philip." The groom spoke English well enough, but the thick accent distorted his words. "Near the bounds, I think."

"Your Majesty!" Sidney shouted, and gestured at the others. "Call, all of you, now."

They shouted obediently, though some of the younger riders looked completely bemused by the order. Cassilis, at least, would have questioned him, but Sidney held up

his hand for silence. The echo of their call was smothered
by the fog; he waited, stretching every sense, for a dozen
heartbeats. Nothing stirred beyond the muffling blanket.

"What is it?" Cassilis demanded. "What's wrong?"

"We're close to the boundaries here," Sidney answered.
"In this fog—" He bit back the words as ill-omened, but
Greville finished the thought for him.

"You think the king may have strayed across."

"Pray he hasn't," Sidney said, grimly, and set spurs to
his horse. "Keep calling, all of you."

Marlowe paused at the top of a low ridge, staring at the
strengthening light at the heart of the brooch, so bright
now that it almost obscured the dancing satyr. The hack
sidled and fought the bit, struggling to turn back toward
Holyrood and safety. It took all the poet's horsemanship to
control it, and he dismounted, looping the hack's reins
around the nearest sturdy tree. Mephistophilis could not
be far away now—the sense of his presence hung in the
fog, teasingly faint, like a hint of musk or damask. Better
to walk, than to risk losing the horse. After a moment's
thought, he pulled one of the pistols from its case and
slipped it through the belt of his jerkin. It would do no
good against demons, of course; but, as he had once told
Sidney, such creatures often had human agents.

The light in the brooch stayed steady as he picked his
way down the far side of the ridge, clutching at the brush
to keep his footing on the fog-slicked ground. The damp
air worked its way through the judas-color wool of his
doublet, and the rough bark stung his numbed fingers. He
paused perhaps halfway down the hill—it was impossible
to judge distances in the uncertain swirls of mist—to rub
his hands together, blowing on the chilled fingers in a vain
attempt to stop their aching. As he stood there, shivering,
a wind rose from nowhere, wrapping the fog more thickly
around him for a moment. Then the milky curtain was
shredded away, and he saw a slim figure, all in black,
walking away across the hollow. A horse whinnied softly at
its approach, and then the wind shifted, driving the fog
back between them. Ruthven, the poet thought, I'd know
that mincing walk anywhere—

"Well, my Christopher. We meet at last."

Marlowe turned slowly, the brooch hot in his hand. Mephistophilis stood leaning against a scrub pine, his pose a parody of every courtly lover's portrait. He smiled, and Marlowe felt his heart turn over in his breast. *Oh, God, that he, a creature of such power, should want me . . .* Against his better judgment he smiled back, and saw the slanted eyes flicker slightly.

"The time's come for you to choose," Mephistophilis said, still smiling. "You know what I have to offer you, all the kingdoms of the world I can give you, and what can he offer in return? Nothing, for who is he?"

Sir Philip Sidney, Marlowe thought, and spoke the name aloud. The words conjured a brief image, a human image, a slender man of medium stature, with a twisted leg and spreading lines at the corners of his eyes, a man equally capable of gentle humor and blinding rage.

Mephistophilis's eyebrow arched. "You grow as besotted as the rest."

The hinted sneer banished the brief vision. Marlowe's head lifted. "No. But I'm no more besotted with you."

The demon laughed, a soft, intimate sound that offered more than words. "I don't want that. I want your considered love, your free-will gift—and one small thing to prove it."

"And what is that?" Marlowe asked warily.

Mephistophilis smiled again. "To go from here, and meet Sir Philip Sidney, and lead him, not to the place where he will wish to go, but somewhere else."

"I won't be party to his death," Marlowe said.

"Did I ask that?" Mephistophilis shook his head. "My Christopher, he's not worthy of you. He will come to no harm, I swear to you by Lucifer himself. I merely wish to be certain he does not—interfere."

"With what?" Marlowe asked.

"With my plan," Mephistophilis answered. "You know well what it is I seek—what I am bound to do."

Ruthven, Marlowe thought. Ruthven was here, and—presumably, but I think it's a safe presumption—spoke with Mephistophilis—was given orders by him? "You intend to kill the king," he said aloud.

"Do you care?" the demon answered. "I want your answer, Kit. And now."

"You want me to delay Sir Philip," Marlowe said, "keep him out of the way while you—or Bothwell's other minions—kill the king."

"I want your answer."

Marlowe looked away, into the curtaining fog. To give up Mephistophilis, and not merely the proffered gifts but the magnificent damnation himself, an angel, fallen, but still angelic—and for Sidney? What could the man, what could any mere man offer, to equal Mephistophilis? Sidney saved my life, he thought, slowly, and only because he disliked the waste—there's a gesture to match anything any demon can offer. And if I damn myself, if I have already damned myself, let it be for other sins, *knowledge* in all its senses, but not by this betrayal. "I cannot," he said aloud, and, as the demon's eyebrows rose in open skepticism, added hastily, "I pay my debts—"

"You've never paid anything you owe," Mephistophilis said, with slow contempt. "Not you. But rest assured, you will pay your debt to me in full. I will be waiting for you, Christopher, behind each door and in each alley, at the head of every stair; I will lie with you at night, and you will get no pleasure in my company. And when you die, I will be waiting then, and you will spend eternity in hell, my least of slaves, you who could have been my boon companion. That, my Christopher, is knowledge, and damnation."

He lifted his hand, and Marlowe felt the brooch writhe suddenly in his hand, as though he'd unwarily clutched a spider. He cried out, flung it away from himself, but the pin clung wriggling until he shook it free. The fog boiled up around him, hiding Mephistophilis's fading figure; the poet turned in panic, struggling back up the hill toward his horse. The hack was gone, the broken leathers dangling from the tree. From the fog behind him came laughter, and a harsh animal snuffling. Marlowe's nerve broke completely, and he ran, beating the branches aside as he fled.

Sidney reined in for the dozenth time, lifting his hand

for silence. After a moment, Greville shook his head, and shouted hoarsely, "Your Majesty! Seton!"

This time, there was a faint response. Someone—one of the grooms, Sidney thought—gave a choked cry of relief, and Cassilis called, "Who's there?"

"Seton. Is that you, Patrick?"

"Ay."

The fog thinned suddenly, capriciously as it had moved all day, and Sidney spurred forward to meet the newcomers. Seton rode alone save for his grooms, and the feeling of relief vanished.

"Sir Philip, thank God I've found you."

"Where's the king?" Sidney demanded and Seton shook his head.

"At Gowrie House by now, I fear me."

"Gowrie House?" Greville snapped.

"Yes," Seton said. "Sir Philip, I couldn't stop him—how could I, he's the king?"

"Stop now," Sidney said, controlling his temper with an effort. "Stop, and tell us from the beginning. What has happened?"

Seton swallowed hard, visibly ordering himself. "I'm sorry," he said, after a heartbeat's pause. "When the fog came up so thick, and we were separated—well, first we lost your party, Sir Philip, and then some others. The king said then we should try to make our way back to the palace, but no one, not even the grooms, could find the way. Then we heard someone calling, and Ruthven rode up, and said we'd strayed out of the park, toward his brother's house, and would we go there, to keep the king safe. Sir Philip, I didn't like it, and said so, and so did others, but the king was hesitating between the one and the other. And in the end he said, we couldn't be sure to find our way back to that protection, so we'd best take what stone and steel could offer. But he sent me back to look for you, and bade me ask you to follow as quickly as you might."

"Damn the man for a fool," Sidney exploded, then bit down hard on his lower lip until the pain had sobered him. It was not so bad a plan—if only the Master of

Ruthven could be trusted. "Quickly, indeed, my lord," he said aloud. "Where is this—Gowrie House?"

Seton's eyes dropped. "Back—there, Sir Philip. I lost my path in the fog."

Sidney bit back another oath. "Then we will have to find it for you, my lord. Which way did you come?"

"Through the brake, Sir Philip," Seton answered, numbly, and pointed. "The path's just beyond, I think."

Sidney did not bother to answer, but spurred forward, the others at his heels. Seton fell in behind them, urging his tired mount to match the pace set by the Englishman.

Marlowe braced his back against a sturdy tree, his breath coming in harsh gasps. He had outrun his pursuit, if ever there had been any; the fog was silent around him, empty even of the small usual life of the parkland. He shivered, feeling the damp in his very bones. He had torn his hands and sleeves in his headlong rush, and one bootstrap had broken, the soft boot sagging below his knee. The stocking on that leg was torn, too, his thigh bleeding from some fall or a slapping branch he did not remember. He pulled the torn cloth together mechanically, listening again, terrified that Mephistophilis's curse was already acting, that the demon was indeed waiting, somewhere in the soft and shadowless mist. For a long moment he heard nothing, and then, faintly at first, then strengthening, he heard the sound of horses moving on a hard-trodden path. He hesitated only for an instant before calling to them: any human company was better than the demon's.

"Hello, who's there?"

Sidney reined in, recognizing the voice. "Marlowe? Over here."

Marlowe floundered through a last stand of frost-killed brush as stiff as wires, and stumbled abruptly onto a broad path. At least I've found my road, he thought, inanely, and stared up at Sidney in unspeakable relief. "Thank God it's you," he said aloud. "There's a plot, Ruthven and Bothwell together—"

"Sweet Jesus," Greville said, and Cassilis crossed himself.

"We know a part of it," Sidney said grimly. "Get up behind, you can tell the rest as we go." He kicked one foot free of the stirrup as he spoke and held out his hand.

Marlowe took it and swung himself up onto the piebald's back behind Sidney, wrapping both arms around the older man's waist to keep his seat. Pressed close as he was, he could feel Sidney's warmth through the good wool cloak, could smell the homey scent of him, horse and musk and sweat, and nearly wept at the comfort of it all.

"Well?" Sidney demanded, and set spurs to his horse.

The poet shook himself, leaned back a little as though that would give him space to explain. "Ruthven—if he wasn't always Bothwell's, he is wholly now. He's been sent to lure the king—to his death, I think—but I don't know where." He stopped, painfully aware of how little he really knew of Mephistophilis's plans.

"I do," Sidney said. "I won't ask how you know this, Marlowe."

Thank you for that small mercy, Marlowe thought, and found himself on the verge of tears. *I have given up Mephistophilis—and for what?*

Gowrie House was a small place, little more than an oversized farmhouse, recently rebuilt to more grandiose tastes. A brick wall, new-built but already crumbling in the damp, surrounded what had once been the farmyard, and Sidney rode straight for the wooden gate. To everyone's surprise, a greying retainer appeared at once to unbar the massive door, and another, younger man came scurrying from the house to welcome them.

"My lord the earl will be happy to greet you, sirs," he said. "Have you gone astray in this dreadful fog?"

The Scots exchanged wary glances. "Gowrie here, himself?" Seton murmured, and Sidney said firmly, "We seek the king."

"The king?" The steward shook his head. "I don't understand—"

"He was—lost in the fog," Sidney said, more cautiously now. "He told his people he would come here, we were to meet him here."

"The king isn't here." That was a new voice. The Earl of Gowrie himself stepped out into the courtyard, a long, fur-trimmed gown thrown in haste over shirt and hose. "If he intended to come here—my God, he must be lost in good truth, gentlemen. If you'll come within, rest yourselves a little, take wine, I'll send my people to look for him."

Sidney glanced at Greville, seeing his own uncertainty mirrored in his friend's face. If Gowrie were telling the truth—and surely he would not invite them into the house if he were lying—then Ruthven's plan had been something different, and they would have to retrace their steps, with no clues to follow. . . . Then a scream tore the air, a cry of fear and anger from within the house.

"The king!" Seton cried, and Gowrie swore and drew the sword he'd worn beneath his gown.

Greville flung himself from his horse, reaching for his own rapier, but Marlowe moved first. He drew his pistol, praying the damp had not yet reached the powder, cocked it, and fired. Miraculously, the powder caught. The pistol fired with a roar, and Gowrie staggered backward. Cassilis flung himself on him, dagger drawn to lay against the man's throat. Gowrie started to raise himself on his good elbow, then froze, his eyes fixed on Cassilis' stony face. The others rushed past him into the house.

"Through there," Marlowe called, and pointed to a painted door leading off the main corridor. The others could feel it, too, and smell it, a louring, over-sweet carrion taint in the air that seemed to ooze from under the closed door. The Scots hesitated, and then Seton and Greville set their shoulders to the painted panels. The frail lock burst, and they stumbled into the room.

The king stood frozen at its center, trapped within a circle of smoke and flame. The Master of Ruthven stood at his side, dagger held to the king's breast. Something—someone?—else was moving in the fire itself, a hellish shape that wavered between the human and the utterly unknown.

"Back, all of you," Sidney said quietly. "Don't risk yourselves."

Reluctantly the Scots retreated to the doorway, urged there by Greville, but they went no further. Marlowe did not seem to hear the older man's words, staring instead into the flames. So this was what Mephistophilis had planned, this was what Ruthven had ridden away to manage. . . .

"Come away from there, Ruthven," Sidney said, though the flatness of his voice betrayed his certainty that he would not be heeded. "You may yet live."

The Master of Ruthven shook his head, a smile curving his perfect lips, his eyes not moving from the dagger's point that rested against the king's chest.

"So be it," Sidney said, and lifted his head, focussing on the almost-shape lurking in the flames. "I have countered your demons, Bothwell, Francis Hepburn. For every one you invoke, I can invoke the corresponding power. But this goes beyond minions, now. Are you indeed master of power, or merely of those who actually possess the power you yearn for? Face me as whatever you yet are, with whatever you still possess."

The swirling flames shifted and rose, shaped themselves into the form of a man. Fire curled itself into ragged hair, twined into the shape of an untidy beard, swirled into crude parodies of limbs. If that is Bothwell as he truly is, Marlowe thought, God help us all. Sidney smiled deliberately, and the ephemeral shape seemed to tear itself into shreds of flame. Those tattered bits flew upward, like embers born in some unnatural wind, and swirled down toward the Englishman. Sidney lifted his hand, spoke quickly. The flames shrank, and disappeared. He took a deep breath, staring for a moment at the flames, and spoke again. The words were Latin, this time, short, clipped phrases, without the papists' slurring. The air seemed to shift about them, taking on the icy tang of winter. The hellfire ring faded briefly, sinking, then returned to its earlier brilliance. A single gout of flame leaped upward, but fell back as though it had struck some invisible barrier.

Sidney swore silently, and damned himself again for succumbing to his anger. He could not touch Bothwell— the knowledge made him frantic with rage and fear. He could not touch the earl even as the earl could not touch him, and that stalemate was almost worse than naked defeat. The form Bothwell had chosen to adopt, this shape of pure power, incorporeal, had no true strength even as it had no true existence here: the challenge he himself had issued was worse than meaningless. But if I cannot touch him, neither can he touch me, Sidney thought. That can yet be turned to my advantage, and save the king.

James stood frozen in the center of the circle, his eyes flickering from Ruthven to the knife-point to the Englishman and the rest of the hunting party behind him in the broken doorway. He was afraid, certainly—what man would not be, held so?—his face deathly pale, but he had himself under iron control. I can help him now, Sidney thought, and spoke aloud.

For a moment nothing happened, and then, quite slowly, the flames in front of the king bent away to either side. The movement opened a narrow path, a break in the circle. James saw, and took a half step forward, but was stopped by Ruthven's dagger.

"Ruthven," Sidney said. "Think what you do."

The young man did not move, but then James said something in a voice too low for the others to hear, a strange, sad half-smile lighting his pale face. Ruthven's grip faltered, the dagger drooping, and in that instant the king sprang clear. Marlowe leaped forward to catch him, to pull him further away from the flames, and put his own body between the king and Bothwell. Ruthven cried out, and the flames soared back, almost hiding him in their encircling embrace. Sidney spoke again, but shook his head, feeling the spell slide off the lack of substance. Then the flames faded, and something else took its place, a weird shape, a dark mirroring of light. Then it slid apart with a sound like silk on silk, and Ruthven screamed again, a deep-throated, bloody noise. There was blood on his mouth, and dripping from his chin, but he ignored it then, and straightened.

Sidney caught his breath, aware of his own miscalculation and its cost. It was Bothwell now, for the first time in the flesh, though the flesh was not his own. Poor Ruthven, he thought. Whatever Bothwell offered him could not have paid him for this usage. He shook himself then, angrily. Ruthven was dead already, it was useless to waste pity on him.

Ruthven—*Bothwell*, Sidney thought—lifted his hands, the only flaw in his dark beauty, words tumbling from his bloody mouth. Sidney felt the power rising around him, leaching up out of the ground like some infernal spring, and spoke himself, a counterstroke drawn from Virgil's book. The two spells collided with a force that shook the house, as though a mine had been exploded beneath its walls. Ruthven screamed in desperate agony—riven indeed, Sidney thought, with despairing pity, seeing the slim body momentarily transfixed, pierced like Sebastian by arrows of hellish flame.

And then the vision was gone. Ruthven collapsed bonelessly, dead before his body struck the floor. "Ye swords and angels," Sidney cried, groping for words that would stay Bothwell's fleeing shape, insubstantial though it was. "Ye hosts of the lord of power, aid me and serve me, lend me your arms against this enemy of the right." The spell took shape around him, coalesced and formed, but slid like smoke from Bothwell's presence. The form was wrong, Sidney thought, despairing, there's no relation between my power and his, and I cannot touch him. Oh, God, don't let me fail so completely, where so many have placed their trust in me—

There was a sound that must have been what the rending of the temple veil had sounded like, and Bothwell was gone. Sidney bowed his head, tasting defeat. Dee's fears were right, and I should have listened—worse still, I've failed both James and the queen, and in my failure caused Ruthven's death as surely as if I'd put my sword through him. God forgive me, what has my pride brought me to?

"Oh, Alex," James said quietly, and the sound brought Sidney to himself a little. He turned, to see James staring at the crumpled body. The king saw the movement, and lifted his head warily.

"I did what I thought best, coming here," he said. "I was wrong. Once again, I owe you my life, Sir Philip."

Sidney sighed, and shook his head. "I've failed you, your Majesty," he said. "I did not mean to kill, not him, and I could not reach Bothwell." *I was no better than Ruthven*, he added silently, *groping after power whose implications I couldn't understand, and couldn't truly master, rejecting the tested intricacies of Doctor Dee—of all the greatest thinkers—for something too simple, too pragmatic to be effective. . . .* He broke off with a gasp, aware that James had been speaking to him, but unable to reconstruct the words.

"See to him, Sir Fulke," James said gently, "take him home to his lady wife."

"And you, Sire?" Seton asked.

James's face hardened, and for an instant he looked almost terrifyingly like a king. "I have business with my lord of Gowrie," he said, and stalked from the room.

Gently, Greville touched Sidney's shoulder. Sidney smiled, a mechanical response, but let himself be led away. Left behind, Marlowe went to kneel beside the body, cautiously lifting the nearest shoulder until he could see the slack face. The muddy features held no remains of the uncanny beauty, were commonplace, flecked here and there with the scars of childhood smallpox—a face finally in keeping with the common hands. So that was the price, the poet thought, that extraordinary beauty. I wonder, did he desire beauty first, or the king? It was not a question that would be answered now, unless Gowrie knew and chose to reveal his knowledge, and it was hardly important. Marlowe let the body fall again and pushed himself to his feet, trailing after the others into the chill courtyard.

Chapter Thirty-one

For of the soule the body forme doth take:
For soule is forme, and doth the bodie make.
    Edmund Spenser, *"An Hymne in Honor of Beautie"*

The attack—not precisely unexpected, but not expected in that form—cast something of a pall over the court. The Earl of Gowrie was remanded to the Tollbooth to await James's pleasure, despite his protest that he had known nothing of his younger brother's intentions. James was not inclined to show mercy, and, even had he been, there was the fact that Gowrie had lied about his presence in the house to dissuade him. Most of the court rejoiced in Ruthven's death, while shuddering at the manner of it, and the presbyters preached stern thanksgiving for the king's safety. James thanked them publicly, but privately was heard to exclaim that had any of them had a hand in saving either life or soul, they would be welcome to take the credit.

"God's ass," he exclaimed at last, in the privacy of his own bedchamber, "they've even denied that anything but God's personal regard could make this palace safe. I may not be looking far enough, Sir Philip, but it seems I see the main worker of these miracles here before me—and you'll forgive me if I'm not quite sure he's God. Quite."

Sidney's mouth twisted into a wry smile. "Hardly that, your Majesty," he said, and in the same instant a familiar voice whispered in his ear.

He's yours. All you need do is hold out your hand.

Sidney ignored the intrusion as he had tried to ignore the others. "I can do no other. I am—and I will remain, so long as I am at your court on her majesty's service—your humble servant. My abilities are given over to your service."

James smiled rather sadly. "Ay, I understand that well enough. Men have called our cousin of England a witch; certain it is she has some power over men's hearts. But still, I know where to direct my thanks for this same service."

"To God, certainly, your Majesty," Sidney answered, and heard a whispering laugh.

Yours. Want him or no, you can do nothing. Even when you try your hardest you win him, and I win by it.

"Of course, Sir Philip," James said.

Sidney made his excuses then, and fled the royal chambers. He stalked through Holyrood's corridors toward his own chambers, biting his lip in frustration and anger. It was an anger that had been growing in him since the moment of Ruthven's death. Many said it was no loss, his influence over the king having been so great and so malign, but Bothwell's cold-blooded use—rape—of body and soul alike was sickening. And still he could not act. First, he could not act in anger; anger was too dangerous now, could only force him to make mistakes. Second, and more important, he did not know yet how to act. He swore under his breath, and returned to his room to brood on the problem.

The players, huddled together in the lower hall, saw him pass, and read the anger in his face. They were as aware as any of recent events, and Burbage sighed. It had been a profitable stay here at the Scottish court, but he recognized the signs. When the people were frightened, they turned to repentance, and repentance usually meant being rid of the players. He leaned close to Shakespeare. "We should think of taking our leave soon, I do believe. If Sir Philip looks stormy, what hope for the rest of us?"

"It's a bad time for traveling," Phillips objected, though

he had not been addressed. "Hell of a time to go south now."

"I think we should wait," Shakespeare said quietly. "This isn't England. Let's lie quiet, see what happens—I for one would dearly love to see the end."

Burbage's face twisted. Phillips was right, they'd left it very late to travel south—and Will's right, too, he admitted. I'd like to see the end of this myself, if only to know all will be well with the world again. "I think you're mad," he said aloud.

"His majesty favors us still, and the queen, and Sir Philip Sidney still offers us his protection," Shakespeare said, and smiled.

Burbage scowled. "Oh, I know all that. All right, we'll stay. At least we're not losing money on the venture."

"It was a stroke of good fortune that we encountered Lady Sidney that day, wasn't it?" Shakespeare agreed.

"And damned well only right, given the stroke of unutterably vile fortune that loosened Essex's purse and Jonson's so-called wit," Burbage said bitterly. Even now, months after the closing of the playhouses, he could not think of it with any equanimity. Shakespeare grinned, and glanced across the hall to where Marlowe sat close beside but not a part of, a group of Scots.

"If it had been Marlowe, now," he began, and Phillips snorted.

"There would be no more playhouses in England. Count yourselves lucky, my fellows."

Marlowe was well aware of their stares, but gave no sign of it, glancing instead down the hall toward the Earl of Mar. He was more concerned with that gentleman than with his fellow poets—especially since he himself owed Cecil a report, and more than one. And worrying over politics helped fill the strange emptiness in his life: so far from keeping to his threat, Mephistophilis had vanished utterly. Marlowe looked for him as promised, half afraid, half perversely hopeful, and found nothing there. He shook the thought away, concentrating on Cecil. He had not written to the secretary since some weeks before he left for Holland. . . . I wonder if I could win Mar over? he thought. God knows, he could afford to defy Cecil, an he wanted to—there's precious little Cecil could do to punish a Scottish earl. One look at Mar's pale eyes killed that hope. Damn Cecil anyway, Marlowe thought. He'll get the news from half a dozen other sources, if I know him at all—and right now, Sir Robert, Sir Secretary Robert, we are all too busy trying to stay alive to bother with your codes and ciphers.

He smiled slowly. He no longer really cared what Cecil's orders were: if Sidney succeeded as he'd always intended, there would be little Cecil could say or do about it —especially since James's gratitude was likely to be very public. Of course, under the cover of all the noise, it would be an easy matter to try to remove a mere poet. . . . But he'd tried that before, with a conspicuous lack of success. A second such attempt could well prove embarrassing. Let us win, Marlowe thought fiercely, let us free James, and Cecil will be bound. James will be a king in his own right, with no need to fawn to any ministers, his own or others'—and when the time comes and he's king in England, too, Cecil will have to serve him, and not hold any debt of gratitude. He may never be a great king, James may not, but there's a sharp streak in him, canny as her majesty. Put that sharpness on the throne, and surely we'll avoid disaster. Marlowe shoved the thought away as unprofitable. Let's work toward Sidney's victory, and then perhaps we'll survive to see what happens. Else we might as well not care.

Sidney dismissed his servants as soon as he returned to his rooms, and settled himself in front of the bedroom fire. Frances, sensing his mood, withdrew almost at once to the rooms she shared with her maidservants, leaving him to sit and brood in rare privacy. Sidney managed to give her a smile of thanks as she left, but soon returned to staring at the flames, so unlike the hellfires that had surrounded Ruthven. God, God, why won't you show me the way to defeat Bothwell? For defeat him we must, and very soon. He shook his head. The ceremony that had been accomplished at Michaelmas would not last forever, and the waning year was against it. And besides, he added silently, I'll no longer stand for remedies that disguise the symptoms and do nothing for the disease.

He sighed, and took another swallow of his wine. There was a bleak wisdom about Bothwell, which had confounded them from the start. With a power so great that it could strike from seemingly impossible distances, one would have expected some hubris, some failure of pride, and yet the man had an infernal sense that made him hold his hand time and time again, and always to best effect. Certainly his methods were demonic, the black obverse of Doctor Dee's teaching—and that, Sidney thought, and set the Venetian glass goblet carefully away from him so that he did not shatter it in his anger, that was the greatest problem. Bothwell's technique was simply not related to the magic he himself used, and if there was no point of contact, there could be no engagement. And if there were no engagement, Sidney could never destroy his enemy. A humbling lesson, Sidney thought, bitterly. *I wish to God Doctor Dee were here.*

He shook himself then, and pushed himself up out of his chair, turning away from the fire. There had to be a way to use the best of both systems, his own private synthesis of Virgil's magic and Dee's Christian cabala, against Bothwell, some way to command his presence and then to destroy him.

Without really intending it, he began to pace the length of the room, letting his mind roam free. Patterns took shape and shifted in his mind, patterns of power he had learned from Dee, the logic he had learned from Languet and Ramus, the new magic he had learned from Virgil's book, tumbling over each other. *God forgive my pride,* he thought, *I never meant it as a slur on Dee or on his teachings, to look at other systems.* The obvious answer is to forgo what I've learned from Virgil—and yet that angelic magic is not my strength. *It is Bothwell's. I cannot win on those terms, certainly—and I cannot on my own. What then? What other talents do I have?* he demanded silently. *There's the soldier*—and he smiled to himself. There are no city walls to scale here, or convoys to disrupt. The courtier's rapier tongue may have its uses, but I cannot see it in this case. *Dear God, I give myself up to your help. I can no more.* Despite the pious words, how-

ever, he kept walking, pacing slowly up and down the
length of the room.

He did not know how long he had been walking when,
unbidden, a scrap of an old ritual whispered in his mind,
and the entire pattern shifted, falling like a child's toy into
sudden shape. It was a conjuration he had learned long
ago, from Dee; it had been like a key for which he possessed no lock, a curiosity memorable only for its oddity.
It had seemed like a bastard version of a sword-conjuration,
not quite like anything else Dee had ever taught him. As
it whispered and re-echoed within him, he tested it, and
found it reminded him of phrases more current, ones he
had read in the Virgil, which defied augury and conjurations. *Man is enough to act. Let him know his cause, let
him know it for justice and let him be just, and man is
enough to act*—that was the Latin text. No time—or so he
understood it now—no time and no need to protect one-
self by reciting rituals and drawing circles. Let the just
man act, and let the justice and purity of his actions armor
him, and it will be enough.

"*Te Gladi, Vos Gladias*," Sidney whispered, remembering the key for which he'd found no lock, "*Estote meum
castellumque praesidium contra omnium hostes conspicu-
usque et nonconspicuus in quisque magiceum opum . . .
primoque ultimo, sapientia, vita, vitro. . . .*" *O Sword of
Swords, be my fortress and defense against all enemies,
visible and invisible, in every work of magic, by the First
and Last, by Knowledge, Life and Virtue. . . .* It was too
close, too similar to the sword-conjuration, to the magics
Bothwell himself used, and he could have wept with
frustration.

And still hast thou not known me, Philip?

" 'Almighty God, give us grace that we may cast away
the works of darkness, and put upon us the armor of light,
now in the time of this mortal life,' " he whispered, certain now. It was the collect for the first Sunday in Advent—
and it, or rather, what it represented, what it suggested,
was the door to which he had held that key for so many
years. If these powers he held were God-given, so were
the other talents he possessed. Sidney smiled in joyous
self-rebuke. Mary was right. Holland had both freed and

determined the form of his power, Dee had given him the tools to work it, but it was the poet who must now give it shape.

He threw open the door to the antechamber, tried to speak calmly despite the raging joy within him. "Nate, fetch Marlowe for me, and Master Fletcher. Now, quick as you can."

Nate was a good boy, and a perceptive one. He returned in an almost impossibly brief time with both men, Marlowe still fully clad but reeking of beer and stale tobacco, Fletcher in a gown thrown hastily over shirt and hose. Sidney did not bother to apologize, but beckoned them in, and closed the door behind them with his own hands.

"I have it," he said. "I know the form we need."

Marlowe looked warily at him, but Fletcher's impassive face did not change. "Indeed Sir Philip?"

"Oh, yes," Sidney said. "We will have a masque, gentlemen, a masque at which we will include a rite to build the king an armor of light that will protect him from his enemy. And in that ritual will be a challenge, which Bothwell cannot but answer, and on my terms. Then I'll have him."

Marlowe tilted his head to one side. "A masque?"

Sidney nodded. "A way to formalize power—like your methods, Master Fletcher, like the Tilts, only less diffuse, more concentrated, shaped to this one active end. You saw what happened at Gowrie House, Kit—and I daresay more men than I have told you every detail, Master Fletcher! —and I think you both understand what happened then. I need a form for my power, some frame to contain both him and me and to allow us to meet on even ground—an, I pray, hallowed union of Dee's magic and my own. If we can meet so, God willing, I can destroy him."

"A trap," Marlowe said, with a slow smile. "An entire play—no, thank God, a mere masque, to snare a felon wizard." He shook his head. "Did I believe in such things, I might say it was fated."

Sidney nodded. "It has all come together, hasn't it? Frances, God bless her, had the wit to heed Dee's sigil, and fetched the players with her, and I have you and

Master Fletcher, too. I'm a poet, but no dramatist—no maker of masques. I know what must be said, and the necessary words for that one crucial part. But I need you to give this conjuration an innocent shape, one that will lull Bothwell into ignoring it until he has no choice but to answer the challenge."

And you did write one masque before, Marlowe thought, I know it for truth you did. Was it so bad—or is Sir Philip Sidney vain enough, human enough, to fear embarrassment before professionals? The thought was vaguely comforting, even while he cringed at the idea of writing a masque. There was nothing there save idle words, neither plot nor character to catch the heart, stop the breath in your throat—except that this one time the words were far from idle. *I will weave a true web of words, not merely to catch the imagination and win silence from the mob, but to lure a soul. My words call—and Bothwell comes compelled to his doom. Oh, that's a sorcery poor Watson never dreamed of, that Ned would shy away from, muttering about profits and losses, a sorcery the London preachers guess at, dimly, when they try to close the playhouses. A power to make the soul sing, and I will have it.* "We can do it," he said aloud, trying to keep the exaltation from his voice. "Yes, we can do it, Will and I and Hal."

Sidney nodded, and glanced at Fletcher. The Catholic wizard was frowning slightly, but he nodded.

"What were you thinking of, for the larger plot, Sir Philip?"

Sidney felt himself flush. "I confess, I hadn't got so far in my planning," he began.

"Then may I make a suggestion?" Fletcher smiled. "Unlike Master Marlowe, I do believe in Providence. I have read a paper recently, which might be of use to us—I think it might be ordained for it, Sir Philip, and it is dedicated to you. It was written by a man called Bruno, and it deals with a trial in heaven, in which Jove casts out maleficent stars in order to benefit mankind. Let Vulcan forge an armor of light against those evil stars, as he forged great armor for Achilles: I think that is the frame we need."

Sidney caught his breath, excited almost to tears. "Yes," he said slowly. "Yes. With your help, both of you—and God's—we have him."

Chapter Thirty-two

*Almighty God, give us grace that we may cast
away the works of darkness and put upon us the
armour of light, now in the time of this mortal
life....*
        Collect for the first Sunday in Advent

The candles were lit in the great hall. The court entered
laughing from the banquet, and the actors, hidden from
them only by the thin curtain, heard the air grow suddenly murmurous. Augustine Phillips, death-pale as always before a performance, groaned aloud, and pushed his
mask up onto his sweating forehead.

"God in heaven, listen to them, they're drunk already.
Why in the devil's name did we ever say we'd play a
masque?"

John Lowin, already grotesquely padded for his part of
Misrule, the wild-man beard dangling on its strings around
his neck, crossed himself unashamedly. "Mind your tongue,
man, think what's to happen tonight."

"I am thinking," Phillips retorted, and shuddered. "We're
mad to do it, John." He started as a giggling boy, his robe
of silver-tissue hiked almost to his waist and chaplet of
stars askew, pushed past to join the rest of the chorus of
stars, then stared after them with loathing. "And they're
no better than amateurs."

485

"They'll be all right," Lowin said, but his tone was less certain than his words. Most of the singers and the dancers for the masques and antimasques had been recruited from the colleges at St. Andrews and among the more adventuresome of the young nobles; they had performed well enough in rehearsal—the masque made no demands beyond the common ability to dance and follow music—but there was no promise that they would maintain their composure before an audience. At least the principals—the speaking parts—were taken by the London players.

Phillips shuddered again. "I just hope the stage holds together. Scottish carpenters . . ." He sat down heavily on the property anvil, and put his head in his hands.

"So do I." That was Burbage, already costumed as Jupiter, oversleeves tied back in preparation for his entrance by way of the wooden eagle that would be winched down from the heavens. He laid a consoling hand on Phillips' shoulder, smiled benignly at Lowin. "We look very fine, my masters."

Lowin returned the smile a little crookedly. "You certainly do, Dickon, very fine indeed." He was less certain about his own costume—great belly and swollen legs, broad baldric sewn with bells and scarlet sleeves that hung in tatters almost to his ankles, and a wreath of feathers for his head above the shaggy wig and beard—but refrained from further complaint.

Burbage, who knew that the white and gold brocade of his antique suit flattered his dark color, could not keep a certain complacency from his expression. That vanished as he glanced behind him. "Where's that damned boy?"

"I'm here, Master Burbage." Robert Goughe, the oldest of the apprentices, came scrambling up, Jupiter's cloak tucked under one arm while he struggled with the points fastening his brief hose. The tunic of crimson figured satin scattered with pearl pins in the shape of stars and eagles—he was playing Ganymede—left his arms and legs bare, and he shivered in the cool air.

"Stay with me, how many times do I have to tell you that?" Burbage growled. "Miss your entrance, and you'll get such a beating—"

"Mind the fabric," Phillips exclaimed, and dragged the

boy bodily to him. He knotted Goughe's points, muttering to himself, while the boy obediently shook out the magnificent cape. It was carved velvet, royal purple, but so encrusted with embroidered figures that it was almost impossible to determine the original color.

"They've spared no expense, I'll say that for them," Lowin muttered, then turned away, mentally rehearsing his opening lines.

Sidney heard the raised voices, and glanced toward them; seeing only Burbage, he turned back to his much-interlined copy of the script, studying the third masque for the final time. Fletcher, peering over his shoulder, murmured something that sounded very like a prayer. The man was the color of new paper, and Sidney forced an easy smile that he did not entirely feel.

"Courage, Master Fletcher. It's not long."

Fletcher's answering smile was very weak. "Too long, and not nearly long enough, Sir Philip. I wish it were over."

Sidney touched his arm gently, not knowing quite what to say. He himself had taken part in several of the masques written for Elizabeth; his own nervousness was overlain by anticipation, and by the knowledge that the masque itself contained nothing he had not already experienced, and knew he could master. He smiled rather wryly to himself. The Tilts had taught him the value of a good entrance, and he had demanded one here, costume and effects perfectly matched to assure he would command the stage from the moment he stepped into view. After that—his smile became a tight grin. After that, it was even more like the Tilts, a challenge made, and a battle to follow. And, God willing, God grant it of His grace, a victory at last. He became aware again of Fletcher's wondering stare, and shook away the excitement.

"Tell me, Master Fletcher, did you never take part in the entertainments you created in France?"

Fletcher shook his head miserably. "No, Sir Philip, we had actors for that, and singers."

"You've done very well," Sidney said. Fletcher had the unenviable but necessary task of closing the Solomon's circle already carved into the stage floor before the challenge was issued. He alone would be the focus of the courtiers' eyes for some interminable moments, and he had never been on stage before—it was no wonder, Sidney thought, he looked a little ill. He smiled again. "Truth, Hal—and there's no one else I can trust with it."

Fletcher murmured something in a self-deprecating tone of voice, but managed a weakly grateful smile.

Marlowe, peering out the slit in the watchet-blue curtain, the prompt-copy ready to hand, watched as the noble audience settled itself on the long benches, their finery glittering in the candlelight. The flow of arrivals had slowed to a trickle, and he glanced over his shoulder, making sure the musicians were in their places. They were ready, the peppery little consort-master scowling at the middle trumpet, and Marlowe turned his attention back to the audience. How I let myself be talked into holding book, he thought, and tensed as the hall's rear door opened again. A red-clad page stood there, a taper in his hand. That was the signal for the king's entrance, and the poet lifted his hand.

"Places, masters, the king approaches." He pointed to the musicians. "Now, Master Baillie."

The consort-master nodded to his men, and lifted his own trumpet. He sounded the first notes of Fletcher's royal fanfare, and the other trumpets picked up and echoed the complex theme until the long hall rang with harmony. James entered that music flanked by torchbearers, his queen at his side, and his court bowed down before him.

Very pretty, Marlowe thought, but could not summon his usual cynicism. The strange music, the *musique mesuree* of the Pleiade, compelled worship, banished detachment. And that, he thought, is a truly dangerous power. I wish we had Ned Alleyn here, and his safe music. He glanced over his shoulder again, and met his Ganymede's curious look. My Ganymede, and no other's, he thought, and not even that any more. Massey, costumed for the speaking part of a Beneficent Star, grinned nervously at him, then turned back to his fellows.

Two thrones had been set up directly before the stage. James seated himself, Anne at his right hand, and the torchbearers whirled their torches overhead, then crushed the embers out against the ground. Marlowe held up his closed fist, and the consort ended the fanfare with an extended flourish. In the center of the stage, Mercury—George Bryan, resplendent in the traditional costume—closed his eyes and recited a hasty prayer. Marlowe took a deep breath, and nudged the man who worked the curtain. The Scot grinned back at him, and hauled on the rope. The thin blue cloth rose, pulleys creaking, and the consort struck up the first interlude.

There was a patter of polite applause as the scene was revealed, and Mercury came forward to recite the opening verses. They were broad flattery, and Marlowe could not repress a sardonic grin, even as he nodded to the man who worked the winch. The trumpets sounded at the same moment, masking the noise of pulleys and rope, and Jupiter descended from the heavens astride his gilded eagle. There was more applause, and murmuring; Burbage waited for it to end, then bowed low to the king. In the wings, the masque of gods and goddesses came to attention, the young men from St. Andrews nudging each other in an ecstasy of excitement.

"Damn them all," Shakespeare muttered, and Marlowe grinned at him.

"Do they spoil your words, Will?"

"It's all very well for you," Shakespeare answered sourly, "but you're not on with them."

"I thank God for that daily," Marlowe said, but the actor had already moved away again, to rejoin the other actors from the second masque.

Onstage, Jupiter proclaimed his intention to rid the heavens of ill-intentioned and vicious stars, so that his favored kingdom of Scotland, and the munificent king of Scots, might enjoy only happy celestial influences. With grandiloquent gestures he summoned his gods and goddesses to sit in judgment on the stars of heaven. That was the consort's cue; music sounded, quick but stately, and the first masquers danced into view. They were magnificently costumed, each divinity badged with his proper attributes and accompanied by twin attendants, and there was another appreciative murmur from the court. The dance ended with the masquers curtsying to the king, and

Ganymede draped the royal cloak around Jupiter's broad shoulders. Mercury came forward again, lifting his staff in invocation.

That was the cue for the candles to be screened. Marlowe pointed, but the boys—the Lord Chamberlain's apprentices, the only ones the players had been willing to trust with the effect—were already moving forward, to push black-painted screens in front of all but three of the candelabra. The light dimmed perceptibly, and there was a rustle of anticipation from the audience. Mercury's invocation ended, and Marlowe pointed again, this time to the man who worked the curtain of the inner stage. Celestial music sounded—the consort had changed their instruments again, from viols to lute and recorder, and a boy's choir joined with them, the high sweet voices almost unearthly in their beauty—and the masque of stars was revealed. They stood poised for a moment in the discovery space, framed by the bunched curtains, and then the first dancers made their way out onto the stage itself. At Marlowe's signal, the apprentices slid the screens away again, so that the stage grew slowly brighter.

John Lowin watched, grumbling to himself, and glanced warily at the four stout youths from St. Andrews assigned to be his attendants. They looked as warily back at him, and Lowin sighed. Phillips was already on, and Shakespeare, both playing Disreputable Stars—even Massey, who, if he wasn't one of the company, was at least a professional, was onstage, even now responding to Jupiter's catechism. Lowin managed a fleeting smile, listening to the clear young voice—the man was an actor, whatever else he might be—but sobered again as he looked at the costumed students. He missed the company of his fellows, to make the waiting bearable.

"I hope to hell you haven't been drinking," he muttered, under cover of the first antimasque's music, and the oldest student looked affronted.

"Never, not tonight."

Lowin made a face, and looked away. On stage, the antimasque had ended, and the first Disreputable Star answered Jupiter's demands. Shakespeare used his rather prominent eyes to good effect; there were chuckles from the audience, and someone cheered when the Star was firmly banished. As the first notes of the antimasque sounded, Lowin sighed. "Right, lads," he said, "let's be about it."

The students nodded, and one lifted off the lid of the property barrel that stood beside them, lashed firmly to two poles. Lowin eyed it unhappily, hoping that the trick pin would hold the contraption together long enough to get him onstage and then that it would collapse as promised, then took a deep breath, and stepped inside. It was a tight fit, with all the padding; he squirmed uncomfortably for a moment, then nodded to himself.

"All right, lads," he said aloud. "I'm settled."

"Very good, Master Lowin," a student said, and spoiled the effect by giggling.

You'll get a boot up your ass if you fail me, Lowin promised silently, and braced himself to await his cue, one hand resting on the pin. Sidney, watching the struggle from the property rocks that would conceal his own entrance, shook his head. That is the difference that makes an actor, he thought. I would never submit to such a thing, no matter what the effect might be. Lowin—nor any of them—never counts the cost to his own dignity.

The third antimasque ended, but Jupiter shook his head in weighty rejection. The Disreputable Stars were banished from the heavens. The Stars dropped to their knees, Shakespeare facing James, Phillips Jupiter, and cried their appeal: was there no one, Shakespeare cried, willing to speak on their behalf?

That was Lowin's cue. The consort struck up a lively tune, and under its cover, the actor said, "Let's go, boys."

The students hoisted the barrel, staggering until they got their shoulders under the poles. Lowin swore, and heard the patter of footsteps as Misrule's antimasque danced past him. It was a quick, capering dance, full of trills, and there was a murmur of pleasure from the audience. Marlowe, watching from the prompter's place at the side of the stage, saw that James was smiling.

The dance ended on a high note, and Lowin pulled the pin, kicking hard at the same moment. The barrel split apart, and he leaped out, bowing first to James and then to

Jupiter. There was applause, and he bowed again to the king before launching into his speech. Listening, Sidney smiled, and almost forgot his approaching entrance. It was Marlowe's speech, and the poet had felt those words in his very soul, that much was clear. But he is right, Sidney thought; even I have to admit it, puritan though I may be. If one does not have Misrule, how can one know the Rule?

He shook himself, and made himself turn away from the stage. He was too close to his own entrance to spend time worrying about metaphysics. Heminges, who would handle the effect, gave him an encouraging smile.

"It's very fine, Sir Philip," he said, and Sidney shrugged, not daring to tempt fate. "We'll go now."

Sidney took a deep breath, suddenly overtaken by a fear as paralyzing as any he had felt in Holland. He shook himself, telling himself that he stood in no danger, and the panic eased a little. Heminges nodded to him again, his smile a little strained.

"We have to go, Sir Philip."

The actor's obvious concern steadied Sidney even further. "Of course," he said, and beckoned to Fletcher. "We're ready."

Fletcher swallowed hard, and nodded.

"Through here," Heminges said, and pointed to the open trap at his feet. Sidney scrambled down the ladder, moving as quietly and carefully as he dared, and took the lighted candle that the actor lowered to him. Heminges climbed down next, and then Fletcher, his face very white, and someone closed the trap over them. Heminges led them under the raised stage to the central trap, ducking under the heavy beams, and busied himself with the smudgepots. Overhead, the dancers' feet beat against the boards, almost drowning the music. Heminges tilted his head to one side, and nodded. "Almost there," he whispered. "Almost there."

The music ended, the final antimasque freezing in a tableau of appeal that should, Sidney thought, leave four strong men at the corners of the trap. Jupiter spoke, the words only a little muffled, accepting the argument, but refusing to keep the Disreputable Stars in heaven, for fear that they might harm the king of Scots. That was the cue.

As the dirge sounded, Heminges set the candle to the wick of the first smudgepot, then lit the other, fanning the smoke upward. The smoke spread rapidly, rising with the music; under its cover, the dancers slid the trap away. Heminges braced the ladder and Sidney scrambled up, easing himself onto the stage behind the curtaining smoke. Fletcher followed, and the dancers slid the trap back into position, but not before Sidney had seen Heminges slide the metal covers onto the pots. He took a deep breath and stood up, aware that all eyes were on him.

At the side of the stage, Marlowe repressed a chuckle. Notably modest the man might be, but he certainly knew how to make the most of an entrance. God's blood, Ned would be ashamed to make any more of that opportunity. Fletcher had chosen to costume Vulcan as a scholar, but a scholar in gold and black brocade, with a jeweled collar spread across his shoulders—Faustus, Marlowe thought, with sudden dread, and shook the ill-omened image away. Sidney was no Faustus. I am certain of nothing else in this world, he thought, but that I know. Faintly, then, he thought he heard someone sigh, and darted a quick look over his shoulder. There was no one there but the Scotsman waiting by the curtain-rope, and he turned back to the stage. This was the end, the climax of everything they'd tried to do. His hands closed painfully tight, almost crushing the promptscript; he loosened them with an effort, wishing he dared pray.

Vulcan bowed to the king, and then to Jupiter, and began his first speech. Sidney's voice was not an actor's, but it carried well enough, so that the sense of the words reached every corner of the hall. This was in rhyme, formal and without significance, Vulcan offering his solution to Jupiter's problem: the Disreputable Stars need not be banished, if the king of Scots can be armored against their influence. He, Vulcan, will make for him the armor of light, finer even than the armor made for Achilles.

That was another cue. Marlowe swore to himself, and pointed to the musicians. The martial theme sounded, and the masque of the Myrmidons entered. Six of them carried the property forge, and set it in place in front of Sidney before taking their place in the dance.

"He knows how to wait," Heminges said softly, and Marlowe jumped. "He might have made an actor."

"Oh, yes," Marlowe answered, "along with all his other accomplishments. Christ, is there anything the man can't do?"

Heminges turned a level stare on the poet. "I hope we don't find that out tonight," he said, and Marlowe shivered. The masque ended before he could think of a response.

"Your Majesties," Sidney said. The pasteboard armor Burbage had so lovingly gilded lay at the base of the property anvil, and he lifted it into sight. "I have offered you the armor of light, to protect the king of Scots against his enemies. This petty shell will become that, by the grace of God."

There was a stirring in the audience at this shift from poetry to prose, and Sidney smiled. "A song, now, while we set the stage."

The consort struck up again, and a single boy's voice rose in gentle appeal. Fletcher bit his lip, and traced the last of the symbols in the carven circle. His hand was shaking so badly that he could barely write. He frowned, and steadied himself, ducking his head to keep from seeing the onlookers. When he had finished, he bowed, and stepped outside the circle, then bowed again to the king, and scuttled from the stage. To his intense relief, no one laughed.

Sidney lifted his hands, aware as never before of eyes watching him, of a focussed attention too intent to be merely human. He allowed himself a taut smile, knowing now that he had calculated correctly, and spoke. "Heavenly Father, very God of very God, I stand here for the king of Scots, to beg Your protection for him as you granted protection to your champions of old. I pray you, by the grace granted in times past to Joshua, to David, and to the sons of Mattathias, allow Thy angels to pour out their grace and power onto this the visible symbol of Thy protection." His voice strengthened. "And I challenge under Thy hand the enemy of the king of Scots, who sends demons against him. By Thy names, which I am unworthy to utter, I bid him appear, or be forever banished by the virtue of this symbol."

His incantation had gathered and focussed the powers latent in the masque; he could feel the web of words grow taut and strong in the air around him. He laid a hand on the armor, and heard as if from a great distance the consort begin the last of Fletcher's measured pieces. The Myrmidons were dancing again, forming a ring around the anvil, the moving bodies hiding precisely what happened there. Sidney saw them only vaguely. The air thickened, and he heard a faint familiar laughter.

A voice—not the mocker's voice, Sidney thought—said, "So you summon me at last, Englishman."

"I summon you," Sidney agreed. A shape writhed in the air before him, its unstable form briefly manlike, then wavering into something less recognizable, but certainly inhuman. The voice spoke from its center, the same hissing voice that had spoken in the royal chapel.

"A grievous error."

"I think not," Sidney said, and lifted his hand again, tracing the first of his prepared signs. "I bid you come here, Bothwell, and you will obey."

The changeable shape wavered, and Sidney felt it pull away briefly. Then, quite suddenly, the tension vanished, and Bothwell—or something that had once been Bothwell—stood laughing. He was a tall man, gloriously clad in crimson and gold, but the brocade of his doublet was tattered, as though he had not changed it in some months, and his skin was filthy, hair and beard unkempt and matted. There was a carrion scent about him, and the circling dancers faltered briefly in their steps.

"I'm here, Englishman," Bothwell said, "but not at your bidding."

Sidney smiled, and felt the other's rage like a banked fire.

"I will have your heart in my hand, Englishman," Bothwell said softly, and his hand closed over empty air.

Sidney lifted his own hand, gestured, felt the attack deflected into nothing. Bothwell snarled, and struck again, pulling fire from the air to rain down on the other man. Sidney spoke, and the flames melted, became like the petals of some exotic flower, before they vanished into nothing. At his feet, hell gaped; he closed it with a word. Bothwell glared, breathing a little hard, and swore.

"I'll have you," he said again. "I'll pull you down to hell with me. Rabdos, Belial, veniri!"

"They cannot," Sidney said, and felt a sudden stabbing pity. The form of the masque, the careful classical ritual, had closed Bothwell off from his demons; when he had entered the circle—and he had done so willingly—he had left their powers behind. He was a man again, a filthy, unkempt man whose talents had devoured him, and left him a shell for the wind to whistle through. There's nothing to be done but make an end, Sidney thought, and lifted his hands.

"No!" Bothwell cried, and raised both arms in appeal. "Air, bear me, make me of your form, by the prince of your power, carry me hence!"

His shape seemed to fade, became translucent, wavering like a fish seen at the bottom of a shallow pool. Sidney frowned and reached for him, but his power slipped away from this demonic talent as it had slipped at Gowrie House. He tried again, drawing on every reserve of strength and will, but his attack slipped past, finding nothing on which it could fasten. Oh, God, he thought, God, he can't escape again. Don't let this all have been in vain. He spoke, throwing a net of words across the circle, but already Bothwell was dissolving, his power washing through the meshes as though he'd never been.

At the edge of the stage, Marlowe saw Bothwell's shape appear, and then, as its attacks failed, begin to fade again. That can't happen, he thought, and in the same moment felt the demonic presence hovering close. A tall figure moved among the dancers, dark face smiling—one too many on the stage again, Marlowe thought hysterically, don't you ever get tired of your effects? Bothwell was fading, mad laughter distorting his features, and Marlowe threw back his head.

Mephistophilis!

He never knew if he had spoken aloud, but the tall dancer slowed, spun aside, dark face no longer laughing.

Mephistophilis, I name you. I abjure you, in the name

*of the Father, and of the Son, and of the Holy Ghost, and
bid you be gone—*

There are laws that bind even hell, my Christopher, a
demon-voice whispered. *It shall be so.*

Inside the circle, Bothwell shrieked aloud, his body
suddenly his own again. He tore at his own body in
disbelief, nails like talons rending cloth and flesh alike.
Sidney winced, and drew himself together.

"This must end," he said, and again heard the strange
pity in his voice. "Father Almighty, let it end." He gathered his power, shaped it to an arrow as bright as the sun,
and let it fly. Bothwell shrieked again, and fell, the arrow
flaming in his chest. As Sidney watched, the flames spread,
preternaturally strong, until body and bones alike were
consumed, and crumbled into dust. On the anvil, the
pasteboard armor glowed with a light more vivid than the
sun.

"Oh, Father," Sidney said, swept suddenly with weariness and fear, "Lord Jesus, let this have been well done."
He laid a trembling hand against the gleaming armor, and
the kingdoms of the world were opened before him. In
Whitehall, the queen of England danced, an old woman,
frail and glorious, and a world danced with her: the kings
of Europe seemed to bow to her, each one in his court,
dancing at last to her tune. And in Scotland, the king of
Scots bowed his head in prayer and rueful laughter, the
tears running unashamedly down his face.

The light faded from the armor, and Sidney slowly
raised his head, blinking back tears of his own. The music
stopped—somehow, Marlowe had managed to give that
cue—and the dancers made their shaky obeisance to the
throne. Sidney lifted the armor, and in the sudden silence
carried it down from the stage and laid it at the king's feet.

"Your enemy is no more, Sire," he said, and did not
care who heard or did not hear. "I give you this in token of
the victory."

James laid a trembling hand on the older man's head. "I
have no words to thank you, sir." He took a deep breath.
"Should the masque continue?"

Sidney nodded, still kneeling. It must continue, he
wanted to say, all of this must be channeled and finally

released, but he was too tired, too drained to find the
words. James looked down at him with a crooked smile.

"I think it must," he said softly. "Sit you here, Sir
Philip." He gestured to the actors, still standing frozen on
the stage. "Play on, my masters, it must be so."

It was as though none of them had seen the halls of
Holyrood before, like awakening from a murky dream.
Even the torches seemed to burn brighter than before; the
musicians played more skillfully, and the dancers—nobles
now, and gentlefolk, celebrating with the players the end
of danger—trod more nimbly. A new aura seemed to
surround James, a new and palpable majesty, and, seeing
it, Sidney sighed, longing to see England, and England's
queen in the flesh, so transfigured.

"England," Fletcher murmured at his side. "You cannot
know, Sir Philip, how I long to return."

"You see it, too?" Sidney asked, and Fletcher nodded.
Sidney winced, seized with a sudden pity: how crushed,
how tormented would he himself feel, in Fletcher's place?
But it was impossible for Fletcher to return to England, at
least now. Perhaps later, if this new vision lasted—if when
Elizabeth died, as die she must, James could continue to
balance Catholic and Protestant one against the other—
perhaps then Fletcher could return, and know he himself
had helped to make possible that homecoming. It was too
cruel a hope; he did not dare voice it, though he could feel
the possibility strong as magic in his bones.

"Well, I'm pleased enough in Flushing," Fletcher said,
with suspicious brightness, the voice of a man speaking to
convince himself. "I am happy there." The false pleasure
faded from his voice then, and he turned to face the older
man. "And did we do well?"

Sidney frowned, confused. "Do well?"

Fletcher stared through him, seeing something else, his
lips twisted into a frown. "No, I know. You did what you
were sent to do, and there's no denying you rid the world
of a very dark menace. But at what price?"

The note of anguish touched Sidney on the raw. Must
you bring all that—all my earliest, worst fears—to haunt
me now, when it's done, and I was free of them, and at
peace with myself, my power, and my God? Somehow, he

kept his tone light, and said, "Whatever I did, was done with your help. And Marlowe's."

"A not completely reassuring combination, Sir Philip," Fletcher answered, with a ghost of his earlier quiet humor. "What has happened, sir, is entirely your doing. I cannot feel—yet—that it is a good thing. I may be wrong, I pray I am, but I am troubled."

"Be plain, please," Sidney said, and only just kept himself from snapping.

"I mean to be," Fletcher said, and spread his hands helplessly. "Sir Philip, I know how much you respect the Pleiade's magics, the reverence you have for Doctor Dee's, and the good use to which you've put his teachings. But those magics are circumscribed, held in by elaborate rules, rituals, shrouded in mystery, if you like. . . ."

"Not unlike the Mass," Sidney interjected drily, but his eyes were still fixed on the scholar.

Fletcher bowed his head, acknowledging the point. "Precisely because power is common—but the ability to use power properly is less common. Witness some of the things we have seen here."

"I have seen Bothwell, who possessed and was possessed by powers and demons not of the common run," Sidney agreed. His voice sharpened. "But I have also seen a woman hounded almost to her death by those without power, merely because she possesses the same skills you and I possess, and lacks the learning to make it palatable. And she, in gratitude—in justice, perhaps—warned me against an attack." He stopped then, and gestured his apology. "Say on, I interrupt you."

"Power is still a dangerous thing. Yet now . . ." Fletcher lifted his eyes to the ceiling, as though he would find constellations in its shadowed heights. "Magic is loose in the world, Sir Philip, and never again will we be able to circumscribe its use. Mistakes will be made, people will still damn themselves, and it is all so easy now. . . ." His voice trailed off, and Sidney smiled gently.

"I think, fewer than might have." He shook his head. "The powers were always there, Master Fletcher. It's arrogance and selfishness and fear that causes scholars—like ourselves—to bind them up for themselves in their elaborate rituals. It's not that the rituals have lost their meanings, their importance—I could not have defeated Bothwell without them, or without God's favor—but they are not all magic, or the only method. Evil men can master your methods as well as mine, as we have seen, Master Fletcher. Evil men will always find a way to work their wills, and yes, they will take and use this unbound magic we feel about us now—but they would in any case. Only now, perhaps more of us will have a defense against it. More people may find it in themselves, and need not fear it—we should be in agreement over this, Master Fletcher, for magics and wizardry have long had a place in your faith."

"But well restricted," Fletcher demurred, "guarded as all things so dangerous should—must—be."

"Of course it's danger," Sidney said, impatient now. "Life is fraught with peril, we know it and God knows it, and we do what we can with what we're given. But there's no use in regrets. What's set free cannot be called back again—nor do I think I would, even if I could."

After a pause, Fletcher said, almost sadly, "No, Sir Philip. I don't believe you would."

He turned almost blindly, seeking refuge in the crowd, but Sidney caught his arm. "Answer me one thing, Master Fletcher. Would you?"

For a moment the scholar kept his face averted, but then, when he finally turned to look at Sidney, he was smiling, though there were tears in his eyes. "God in heaven, I cannot say. But I miss England." Then he pulled away, and Sidney let him go, sighing. He could just imagine the reaction if he were to plead the Catholic cause to Elizabeth now, even for Fletcher, whom she as well as James owed so much. No, he thought, I've learned that much discretion. I know she can do nothing, not without denying her own sovereignty, and, God help me, that would be a grievous sin. James, now . . .

"He can taste it in the air, and fears it like the reformed drunkard fears wine," said a voice at Sidney's shoulder.

The older man smiled a little sadly, and turned to face his protege. "I think so. And I also think he, of all men, has little reason for fear."

The new air, the new light that filled the room seemed to have touched even Marlowe's dark soul. His smile was warmer than it had been, and held even a touch of sympathy, of understanding, for Fletcher's plight. But there was still a shadow about his eyes, a hint of loss: in winning this great new freedom, Marlowe had rejected—what? "Mephistophilis," Sidney said quietly, and saw the younger man shy away as though from a touch. He winced himself, recognizing an almost physical pain. The wound was healing, certainly, the greater part of the bullet wrenched away from flesh and bone, but there were fragments still to trouble him, and a scar. "He was so much your own creation," he began, and stopped, trembling on the verge of heresy. Perhaps it isn't heresy, blasphemy, though, not now—perhaps in this new world, devils truly are only as powerful as we make them. . . . He put the thought aside, for later, wiser consideration, and touched the poet lightly on the shoulder, wishing he could offer more.

"He was beautiful," Marlowe murmured, almost unaware of Sidney.

"Possibly," Sidney said, and hardened his voice. "You are a poet, a brilliant one. You of all men know beauty, and how to mourn its loss. And how to find it again. Life is not ashes, Kit, we've come through."

Marlowe's eyes strayed almost involuntarily to a knot of players, and Sidney realized that Stephen Massey was among them. If it will wean you from demons, Kit, he thought, surely that's the lesser sin.

"Do you really like my poetry?" Marlowe asked abruptly.

Sidney looked at him, startled. "Yes, very much."

"And you seem to have more than a nodding acquaintance with my plays, for all you've been my patron for two years only."

"I spend a lot of time in London. I could hardly not be familiar with them." Sidney frowned. "You're a fine writer, Kit, and you've always known it. Where does all this lead?"

"It's more than the magic, Sir Philip," the poet went on, unheeding. "There's the plays, mine, and Kyd's, and William's, and all the rest of the inferior lot—we've remade the form, broken all the unities—as you yourself were once so kind as to point out."

Sidney raised an eyebrow. "Did you never say anything in your youth you wished to retract in age?"

Marlowe blushed faintly, and hurried on. "And there's Raleigh, and Drake and Hakluyt—and Dee, for that matter, with his books on navigation. And God knows how many others that I don't know, all remaking their various arts and sciences. And now you. My God, what times we live in."

A world remade. Sidney shied away from the idea, even as he tasted the truth of it. Magic was loose, with everything else. . . .

"What times," Marlowe said again, and there was a strange, fierce joy in his voice.

Oh, trust you to take such pleasure in them, Sidney thought, but could not deny his own, more cautious excitement. *What times, indeed. Dear God, I thank you for this blessing, this new-found, other world. Help us to use it wisely.*

"Philip." Frances stood before him then, her hands folded demurely against her skirts as she made her deepest reverence. There was a new light about her, too, a new ease and comfort, and Sidney caught her in his arms. She returned the embrace willingly, crumpling her skirts, before putting him aside.

"I came to ask you to dance," she said, and gave a breathless laugh.

"Gladly," Sidney answered, and offered her his arm. Yes, he thought, we should dance, tread out the simple pattern so we may learn to tread a greater, and all in joy—humility, and joy, and love. He smiled then, lifting her hands, and they moved together into the dance.

AUTHORS' NOTE

The events of this story are true; they just never happened.

Sir Philip Sidney died in October, 1586, of wounds received a month earlier at the battle of Zutphen. He had been serving with the English armies sent to support the Protestant Dutch in their rebellion against their Spanish Catholic overlords. The Dutch offered to bury him in Holland at the States' expense, a signal honor, but the English refused. Sidney was buried in St. Paul's Cathedral, London, with an outpouring of public mourning unlike anything seen in England before. He had been tutored in his youth by Queen Elizabeth's astronomer, John Dee, and by the greatest scholars of Europe; he had been offered (at least according to reports current after his death) both the crown of Poland and marriage to Europe's greatest heiress, Marie of Nassau. His death, or so his contemporaries unanimously believed, deprived England of one of its greatest soldiers, poets, and courtiers.

Christopher Marlowe was murdered in June, 1593, by Ingrim Frizer, a steward in the household of Marlowe's patron Thomas Walsingham, officially in a quarrel over who would pay the bill for the day's drinking. The story was corroborated by the other two diners: Robert Poley, a known government agent, and Nicholas Skeres, a compatriot of the others later arrested for fraud. The story told at the inquest and in the pardon for the murderer is not

entirely clear, and a sizeable minority of scholars hold that
Marlowe, who had himself been a government agent, was
murdered in order to prevent him from betraying government secrets. Certainly Marlowe was being questioned by
the Privy Council at the time of his death, in regard to his
blasphemous and therefore potentially seditious utterances.

In 1595, James VI of Scotland (who, eight years later,
would become James I of England as well) faced the last in
a series of conspiracies formed by Francis, Earl of Bothwell,
also known as the Wizard Earl. Like all the others, this
conspiracy combined witchcraft (directed against the king's
person) with armed attack; it failed, and Bothwell fled
Scotland never to return. We have taken the liberty of
moving the so-called Gowrie Conspiracy, which took place
in August, 1600, to the autumn of 1595, and of making the
Master of Ruthven (born in 1580) somewhat older than his
actual years, though there is no real evidence that Ruthven
was one of James's many minions. James's fondness for, and
amazingly bad taste in, his male favorites is well documented;
his contemporaries agreed that enough was done in public
to raise grave doubts as to the king's private behavior.

A final note on the Elizabethan attitude toward magic is
perhaps in order. While some educated persons might
question the existence and efficacy of popular magic (though
the majority believed firmly in its reality, and in the witches
who manipulated it), no one would have doubted that some
form of the supernatural did exist and could act in the
natural world. A belief in a supernatural of some kind was
an essential part of their understanding of the universe, as
crucial to contemporary science as our own understanding
of atomic theory is crucial to our perception of the world.
In fact, the majority of Elizabethans probably viewed magic
much as the majority of our own contemporaries view
atomic science: they were exposed to a version of the
theory at some point in their lives, but never encountered—
and hoped never to encounter—any of the more spectacu-
lar manifestations of its reality. Still, a belief in magic was
the underpinning of a quite sophisticated understanding of
the universe, and no Elizabethan would have been particularly surprised to see it demonstrated before his eyes.

Terminat hora diem; terminant authores opus.